IN THE CITY OF
SHY HUNTERS

To Brian —
Oh! The Humanity!
all my best —
♡
Tom Spanbauer
6/21/01

Also by the author

The Man Who Fell in Love with the Moon

Faraway Places

IN THE CITY OF
SHY HUNTERS

A NOVEL

TOM SPANBAUER

Grove Press
New York

Published simultaneously in Canada
Printed in the United States of America

FIRST EDITION

Library of Congress Cataloging-in-Publication Data
Spanbauer, Tom.
    In the city of shy hunters : a novel / Tom Spanbauer.
      p. cm.
    ISBN 0-8021-1691-4
     1. East Village (New York, N.Y.)—Fiction.   2. AIDS (Disease)—Patients—Fiction.
  3. African American gays—Fiction.   4. Transvestites—Fiction.   5. Gay youth—Fiction.
  6. Riots—Fiction. I. Title.
PS3569.P339 I5 2001
813'.54—dc21   00-069926

Design by Laura Hammond Hough

Grove Press
841 Broadway
New York, NY 10003

01 02 03 04   10 9 8 7 6 5 4 3 2 1

This book is dedicated in loving memory to Eric Ashworth.

And to his family: Richard Ashworth, his father; Amy Ashworth, his mother;

and to his brothers, Tucker and Everard.

ACKNOWLEDGMENTS

And in loving memory of those who have passed through the Door of the Dead: Bruce Bradley, Ira Chelnik (Chef Ivan), Anthony Badalucco, Silvio Zignazo, Christopher Coe, Sam McNabb, Carl Tallberg, Arnie Zane, Carlos Curos, Michael Fackenthall, Will Docherty, Emma Dan, Tom Maxwell, Susan Bitney, Debbie Lawson Tate, Russell, all the boys in Key West, all the boys in New York. In loving memory of Candida Donadio.

And, of course, the lovely and talented Ethyl Eichelberger.

My heartfelt thanks to Neil Olson of Donadio and Olson Literary Agents.

My thanks to Morgan Entrekin and my editor, Andrew Miller.

Thank you Carolyn Altman. Your touch gave me, gave the book, a shape to be in the world.

Thank you Grey Wolfe, a true friend and a great therapist.

My love to Julietta Lionetti for the pitadas, the copetines, the tartulias.

Thank you Bengt Oldenbourg elephants all the way down.

My love to the one-eyed fat man, Peter Christopher.

How old Mendy Graves.

My love to Ellie Covan.

Thanks to the parjener, Steve Taylor.

Thank you Alex Cadell.

Bless you Thomasina.

You too Mr. Poopy Head.

Thank you Joanna Rose.

Thank you Carol Ferris for the star stories.

Thank you Maria Kosmetatos for the loving health care.

*   *   *

Thank you Chuck Palahniuk, Stevan Allred, Gregg Kleiner, Laura Zigman, Ken Foster, Jennifer Lauck, Rodger Larsen, JT LeRoy, Brian Pera.

I'd also like to thank Running With Scissors, Tim Hendrickson, Ann Boyd, and the cast and crew of the play: *The Man Who Fell in Love With the Moon*. Zefiro's, The Brazen Bean, the Arvon Foundation, Steve Deardon, Kathy Hanson, Luigi Flammia, Federico Oldenbourg, Charles Lawrence, Clyde Hall *un son baisch*. David Frieierman, Ivan Johnson, David Zakon, David Dubin, Tom Fought, Richard Llense, David Oates, Horatio Law, Lynn Kellor, Erin Leonard, Alan Minskoff, Jim Edmondson of The Oregon Shakespearean Theater, the Penn Foundation, the Oregon Health Plan, and my special thanks to the Visiting Authors Program of the Institut de les Lletres Catalanes in Barcelona. My thanks to the Dangerous Writers.

Darin Eugene Beasely, bless your goddamn heart. And you Zuna Johnson, Ragine, Sophie, Mick Newham, Susan Anderson Newham, and Evelyn Newham. Blessings to you Mel Green, my hero.

My thanks to Common Ground, Outside-In, Bikram's Yoga College of India, Poekoelan Tai Chi, and Dr. Shirley Robbe.

Cole Coshow you forgot my head.

I miss you Chris, Jennifer, Rose, Pete, and Julie.

And you Mikey, *sitakusahao mzee*.

PROLOGUE

Things start where you don't know and end up where you know. When you know is when you ask, How did this start?

Wolf Swamp. That's how this story started. When I crossed over the East River into the mystery, this city, the fuck-you city.

Wolf Swamp. Or, as you probably know it, Manhattan.

Quite a story, this story, how the fog settles and Manhattan shape-shifts into Wolf Swamp.

Like all stories it's a mystery. At the beginning you don't know and then at the end you know. But this mystery isn't the Agatha Christie kind where there's covering up all along and a big revelation at the end.

In this mystery, everything is out there from the first but you don't realize it.

The revelation is when you're going this way and then shit happens and then you're going that way, and for some reason this time you stop, you notice what was there all along, and because you notice, everything gets perfectly clear.

Even myself, at the end of this story, my bare feet on horseflesh galloping up Avenue A, I am the mystery: the Mystery of the Will of Heaven.

There's a couple suicides, a couple sacrifices, a betrayal. An ethical act. A famous movie star. An ancient Indian legend. A journey into the underworld to find a lost lover. There's a greedy king and his evil queen. Vicious Totalitarian Assholes. A virus—an epidemic—thousands of dead.

A hero on a white stallion.

It's a tale lip-synced by a drag queen.

So the ending is happy, sort of.

Torch songs forever.

It's all drag.

*   *   *

AUGUST 8, 1988. This was the headline in *The New York Times*: TOMPKINS SQUARE PARK RIOT. THOUSANDS OF HOMELESS. BARRICADE.

But it's not the truth. The headline wasn't that big. And Tompkins Square Park was no riot. It was war, the Dog Shit Park War.

My tasks were simple: Kill the monster, save the maiden.

Fatum.

The fates lead those who will, who won't they drag.

For me, it was all drag.

My first task was plain as day. I knew this was the monster, and I had to kill him, and I did.

The moment that after, you're different. Didn't know my first task, not really, until the moment I pulled the trigger.

Same way with my second task: didn't know.

All at once, there I was, the hero on the white stallion, rescuing the maiden.

But it's not the truth.

My tasks were not to kill the monster and save the maiden. The truth is, my task was to wake up, to notice.

It's like Rose told me: The life I am trying to grasp is the me who is trying to grasp it. My task was to not abandon myself, to not confuse the confusion with myself, to not turn into salt, into dust, charcoal, into purple bumps of Karposi's sarcoma like the rest.

No one can tell this story the way I know it but me. The characters—Rose, Fiona, True Shot, Ruby Prestigiacomo, Charlie 2Moons, Bobbie, Harry O'Connor, Fred, Mother, Father—are memories of myself.

Except for True Shot and Ruby, the closest any one of them got to each other was me.

In the twilight of what I remember of the day, I am lying, cheating, stealing, but not to mislead you.

I am lip-syncing here, so sometimes the words don't go with my mouth.

Language is my second language.

I'm just making it up where I don't know.

Ergo: The story does not follow a consecutive horizontal plot line.

Ergo: Time gets lost.

Plus also, some of this story, not much, is *en Français*, so there's some places you might get confused.

It all comes around at the end, though. I promise.

What else?

I just got to say it: I can tell I'm already in love with you. Which means I'm going to hurt you.

*   *   *

ON AVENUE C with Ruby Prestigiacomo one evening, one twilight, Ruby stopped, hiked his pants up over his skinny ass, and pointed his finger. My eyes followed Ruby's pointing arm, down from his red polyester shirt rolled up to the elbow, down his forearm, the yellow hair, over the tracks and purple bumps, to his finger pointing the way man points to the Sistine Chapel God.

In the space in between Ruby's finger and God was the hierarchy of humiliations, plus the telephone booth. On the corner, the telephone booth, inside and outside painted all over with words. The cyclone fence behind it, the empty lot, bits of broken glass shiny from the streetlamp light, tiny illuminations in the dust, sandy dirt, rocks, and dead grass. Beat to hell, the telephone booth, receiver hanging down.

Like your limp dick, Ruby said.

Ruby smiled his famous smile.

When all else fails, Ruby said, When there's no place left to go, when you're up Shit Creek. You can come here to talk. A special kind of phone booth: Saint Jude phone booth. Direct line to God, Ruby said. Hopeless cases.

Last call.

THAT TELEPHONE BOOTH got stuck in my head. The telephone booth was more like a Catholic statue, a shrine you could kneel down in front of and pray, a broken shrine to all things broken, a shrine you could lift the receiver off, put your ear against, your lips against, and speak into, and you wouldn't be alone.

It's like what Rose said once: We don't live on things, we live on the meaning of things.

That telephone booth, the thing. The meaning of it.

Not to be alone.

ALL OF US together in Fish Bar.

Fish Bar was the same as ever with the string of fish lights hanging across the back, the light a burnt red on the green and amber bottles, the jukebox with the black-girl songs, songs each one of us knew by heart.

But everything was different. Different and bright. Everything about the world was brighter, clearer, like the kind of painting that, when you first look at the painting you think it's a photograph the photographer took when the light made the edges of things hard and more real, or maybe the photographer took acid and took a photograph of how he was seeing, but then you step closer and you see the brush strokes, you see how the guy painted a painting to look like a photograph that looks just like the world, only brighter.

That night in Fish Bar. At the same round table in the corner by the window with the red lantern-glass candle. When we looked around the table at each other, we didn't know, none of us knew how we'd got so lost, how all at once the world had changed on us.

We were sitting closer together than usual, and we were holding hands. Most always, sitting there, we touched each other, even Rose, but this last night we were hand in hand, a circle of hands holding each other around the round table. My right hand palm to palm with Rose's Sahara Desert palm, my left hand palm to palm with Fiona's bleached sand dollar, my knees touching True Shot's knees.

True Shot, Rose, Fiona, and myself, Ruby and Harry and Fred in spirit, holding hands.

We were just talking talking, playing at talking, and then for some reason we were talking about the one moment.

The moment that after you're different.

Jackson Holeewood, Wyoming, I said, May 13, 1983.

Myself, even myself with my Heineken same as ever, my black zip-to-the neck turtle, my black knit stretch pants, my shiny Shinola black combat boots, my black baseball cap backwards—all that black avant-garde shit covering up my Coors flannel plaid white-trash roots.

Of all the stories I could have told that night, of all the moments, I chose the one about Crummy Dog.

I was waiting tables at Café Libre and living in a room above the Big O Tire Center.

Café Libre was the only place in town with a decent wine list and real coffee.

It was Sunday. I was off. I was sitting with my coffee on the deck of Café Libre, studying French from the Maison de Français book *Première Année*.

Maison de Français: proof I wasn't local.

It wasn't a car, it was a pickup, a blue Silverado, with a gun in the gun rack in the back window, a four-wheeler, and the guy didn't stop.

Sunday morning.

Pauvre petit chien.

Crummy was his name, Crummy Dog, terrier mix. Arrogant little mutt. Crummy ran out, wild fool that he was, kamikaze under the big wheel. There was the sound, the unmistakable sound, and my body did all those things people describe when they know shit has just happened, and I looked. Crummy went under the front wheel, then the back wheel. Sunday morning, in front of Café Libre, after my coffee, the sun shining, *Première Année*.

The hardest part was Crummy running back to me, his back legs dragging, Crummy dragging his back legs back to me.

Frozen moments in time. If we could unfreeze them.

I knelt right there on the pavement, laid *Première Année* down, and that little golden dog, so uncomplicated and real and full of life, the one who loved me, looked up at me with all the understanding, sorrow, and bewilderment that goes with being aware of being alive.

I always said Crummy wasn't really a dog, he was a magic being who could do everything but talk, and right then, at that moment, Crummy talked. He said, This is death, Will, *au revoir*. Then Crummy's eyes rolled back up into his head, and he laid his head on *Première Année*'s open page, and a big gush of blood came out of his mouth and nose, blood on French, and Crummy wasn't looking at me anymore.

WHEN I ASKED Rose about the one moment, I expected Rose's moment to be one of his Elizabeth Taylor stories or one of his *theah-tah* stories—how he dined with Sir Lawrence Olivier and Danny Kaye, cocktails with Cary Grant and Randolph Scott by the pool, or Carmen Miranda without any underwear dancing with Cesar Romero. One of those. But it wasn't.

Rose in his Saint Francis Is A Sissy look, his Marrakesh earrings and his new pedal pushers and the silver lamé top Mrs. Alvarez, Rose's personal tailor, made for him. His shiny oiled head smelling of rosemary and eucalyptus, and his black black skin and the gold loops in his queer ear, his jewels sparkly sparkly.

Drop-dead freshly fucked gorgeous.

Rose put out the cigarette I'd rolled for him and lit a Gauloise, crossed his legs, shook his head so his earrings picked up the green and amber light, lifted his arms up like a symphony conductor, bracelets clack-clack.

The moment that after you're different.

Rose raised his shoulders, lowered his chin, and looked his black eyes straight into my eyes.

Houston 1955, Rose said.

It was hard to look at Rose when he made his eyes so open. Rose hardly ever showed the world his eyes so open that way—a Shy Hunter wasn't supposed to do that—but that night he did. Rose opened his eyes and showed me vasty deep, his fire inside I would stand too close to. Roosevelt Washington King.

I was eleven years old, Rose said. A Saturday night, Rose said. And like most other Saturday nights, my father was slow driving us through the neighborhood on our way to Wooten's Ice Cream Parlor. My two brothers and I, Calvin and L'Irah, and my two sisters, Magnolia and Elnora. We were sitting all five of us, quietly, behaved, me the oldest by the window on my pa's side. My brothers' and my sisters' legs eight sticks across the seat stuck out in front of us, sitting on the old red blanket Mama put over the seat for Saturday nights because kids and ice cream and Texas heat together in the same place always meant trouble.

Ice cream the beginning of sacred, Rose said, Ice cream and riding around in the Buick Saturday night was always how Sunday began, Sunday and church and Sunday clothes and singing and preaching all day at the John the Baptist Church on Dowling, up from the corner of Dowling and Magown and the taxi stand and the Golden Arrow Bar where uncle Elasha King—my father Elijah King's twin brother—drove a taxi and drank and hung out with fancy women. My mother, Montserrat, called them fancy women.

The Buick was washed and waxed shiny with Turtle Wax by my father's big hands. Every Saturday morning, I sat on the curb and watched those hands scrub the whitewalls white with Old Dutch Cleanser. And every Saturday night, the whitewalls and the chrome Buick hubcaps rolling along residential streets, Elijah and Montserrat, waving at the neighbors, Elijah now and then giving the horn a honk at folks sitting on the gary of their skinny wood shotgun houses fanning themselves, heat lightning flashing across the purple sky, the streetlamps on the light poles a mess of mosquitoes, moths, and flying bugs. In the yards, barefoot children running after fireflies. The fireflies, now and then the flash of a TV, the lightning, the lights on the light poles, the headlights of the Buick—solitary illuminations in the night.

Wooten's Ice Cream Parlor, bright windows on Dowling.

My father's big hands, a nickel to each one of us, his children, placed in the our palms. I herded Calvin, L'Irah, Elnora, and Magnolia inside the bright and sat us down at the counter on the high red stools that turned. Each one of us each clutching our nickel, elbows on the counter, plastic-covered menus next to the napkin holders, one napkin each.

In the car, driving down Dowling, licking chocolate, licking pineapple, strawberry—no one ever got vanilla; I always chose chocolate—my father, Elijah King, driving his Buick Special home toward Sunday.

The red flashing light pulling us over, another illumination.

My father steered us to the curb just in front of the Golden Arrow Bar, in front of the neon Lone Star Beer sign. My father looked over to Mama first. Mama looked back. Then my father opened the door, pulled up his weight, stepped out of the Buick saying, What's the problem, officer, sir? Was I traveling over the speed?

Two white cops, the one of them threw my father up against the Buick, frisked him, calling my father, calling Elijah King nigger, over and over again: nigger-nigger-nigger. I was looking out the open back window of the '49 Buick Special at my father's face, his eyes right into my eyes.

Close the window, son, my father said.

So I rolled up the window slow, eyes right into my father's eyes.

There was the split concrete of the sidewalk, the Lone Star Beer sign, Uncle Elasha in his black-and-white cab, the door to the cab open, Elasha smoking, spread-legged, fancy women standing around watching.

Eleven years old, Rose said. Roosevelt Washington King, Rose said, Rolled up the window all the way into the felt slot, my father's face pushing against the window. One cop took his gun and hit Elijah King upside the head, then my pa down and the cops kicking him.

Not a sound, only the blows to my father, the cops' nigger-nigger-nigger, and the breath going out of my father.

Inside the car, from Mama not a sound, not a word, only the horrific whisper, the admonition to us her children in the backseat of the '49 Buick Special to hush, eat your ice cream, don't make one peep, keep your eyes on the floor, keep your mouths closed no matter what.

I never said a word, Rose said, But I did not look at the floor. I looked out the window, watched my father, Elijah King, watched Elijah King's face while the cops broke his ribs and busted his nose.

It was the blood on the whitewall, Rose said, Father's blood on the whitewall tire and the chrome Buick hubcap. The bloodstain on the whitewall when we got home that never scrubbed off for good. The blood there on the whitewall was the moment, Rose said, The moment that after, life and living was different.

* * *

SARAH VAUGHAN WAS singing "Slow Boat to China." After Sarah Vaughan, the jukebox would go through Etta James, "At Last," Chuck Mangione´s "Children of the Sanchez," and Aretha singing "Drinking Again."

Fish Bar sounded like dogs barking. That night at Fish Bar when Rose stopped talking, all around us, dogs barking.

Rose went to pee; we ordered more drinks around. When Rose got back, I rolled cigarettes with one hand like I can, lit each cigarette. Fiona sat back, put her leg over my leg. Rose wiped the sweat off his shiny head with the Fish Bar cocktail napkin from under True Shot's soda and lime.

True Shot. Extra lovely urban Injun, Spirit Schlepper, AA. True Shot at the table, drinking his soda and lime same as ever. A silver ring on every finger, even his thumbs, the red bandanna around his head, his hair tied back in a bun, the way I like it. The blue-beaded horizontal and the intersecting beaded-red vertical buckskin bag hanging on the strand of buckskin around his neck. Designer mirror sunglasses.

True Shot put his index with the silver ring onto the bridge of his mirrors. All his rings catching the green and amber light. The light of the flame in the red candleholder. Then True Shot moved his hand down to his neck, put his palm against the buckskin bag.

The moment that after you're different.

It is this way, True Shot said, Let me tell you a story.

It never failed. Whenever True Shot started out with It is this way, the drums and the rattles always started going in my mind. Like he'd brought his own sound track with him.

You may tell of power, True Shot said, And how power is received only when you are on the battlefield, only when approaching the enemy ready to fight for life, only then are things told—what power has been given, what power you must use. It is at such a time that power, previously hidden, enters you.

It is this way, True Shot said. It was a time of fasting. I call it fasting, True Shot said, But really I was out of frog hides. Flat broke.

One morning I woke up, True Shot said, Put my clothes on, walked out my apartment door, and just started walking. At Washington Square, I started walking up Fifth Avenue, walked up Fifth Avenue, past Fourteenth, through midtown, the Plaza, walked along the park until the park ended, walked across town on 110th Street to Broadway, kept on walking up, through Harlem, kept walking until the city was behind me, the riches to rags behind me, and I was on the palisades of the Hudson River. There was the river and the sun on the river, big brown smooth lava rock, and trees everywhere. I found me a rock under a tree and I sat. The little people—the lizards and salamanders—were laying out in the sun, dashing under rocks, playing hide-and-seek.

Something about the rock, the rock and the little people, made me sit on the rock for three days and nights. I didn't even know I was on the rock for that long until after.

I'd lost three days and nights before, True Shot said, But never sober.

But we've all been captured by the little people, True Shot said, At one time or another; we just always forget.

When I came to, when the rock and the little people let me go, it was dark. My heart felt good, my head was clear, and my belly was empty.

At Dyckman Street, I jumped the stile and got on the A downtown. The clock on the platform said two-eighteen. There were only three people besides myself in the subway car, a middle-aged African American woman in a nurse's uniform, a young Puerto Rican man in a shiny suit, and a drunk, a white man, laying across the seat, a stack of *The New York Times* for a pillow. At 190th Street, a white man in a gray trench coat and a Yankees ball cap got on. His black horn-rimmed glasses were taped together in the middle. Two more stops went by. Nobody got on or off.

At 168th, the train stopped. There was no one on the platform and no one got on the train. When the doors closed, the man in the trench coat and ball cap pulled out a gun. He started yelling something about foreigners, waving the gun around, pointing the gun every which way.

The man turned his ball cap around, and all at once, in the light, his skin was white like milk and his eyes were huge and blue through the magnified glasses. The white man told the people on the train to sit next to each other, to where the white man pointed with his gun, told them to sit next to the drunk man.

Nobody looked at anybody else. Nobody moved.

The white man screamed, high-pitched and crazy, shot the gun, the bullet going out an open window. The nurse and the Puerto Rican man got up, moved next to the drunk. I got up and sat down with them.

At 163rd Street, the train stopped, the doors opened. Nobody moved. There was no one on the platform and no one got on the train. The doors closed.

The white man went to the woman first. He held on to a pole, sliding down as he knelt in front of the woman, the white man with the blue eyes a smiling mask, the gun always pointed at her. Made the woman hike up her white dress so you could see her through the panty hose. The white man with the huge blue eyes put the gun onto the woman's crotch.

At 155th Street, the train stopped, the doors opened. Nobody moved. The white man kept the gun on the woman down between her legs. There was no one on the platform and no one got on the train. The doors closed.

The white man went to the Puerto Rican man next, holding the gun straight-armed, pointed at the man's face. Just then the drunk rolled over, shouting something from his dream. The white man hit the drunk man hard in the face with the gun. Blood gushed out his nose and the drunk man went limp.

Then: Suck this, Pedro! the white man yelled and he put the gun into the Puerto Rican man's mouth.

At 145th Street the train stopped, the doors opened. The white man kept the gun in the man's mouth, pulling the man's head back by the hair, the white man's huge blue eyes not a blink in the neon. There was no one on the platform and no one got on the train. The doors closed.

When the white man got to me, True Shot said, The nurse was crying and the Puerto Rican man was sobbing. The white man told me to take my pants off. My intention, True Shot said, Was to stand up and do that very thing, but something got into my arm and my arm reached out and slapped the white man's face, knocked the glasses off his face— his poor squinty blue eyes—then slapped him again. Then my arm reached out and grabbed the gun and then I shot the white man, where the tape had been on his glasses, shot him between the eyes.

At 135th street, the train stopped. There was no one on the platform and no one got on the train. Everyone got off. I carried the drunk man out over my shoulder, laid him down on the platform.

When the train pulled out, I looked back, True Shot said. What power had been given: A rattlesnake was curled up on the seat where I'd been sitting.

Imagine that, True Shot said, A rattlesnake right here in New York City. On the A train no less, True Shot said.

OUTSIDE FISH BAR's window, the early sun made the smog burnt peach and the buildings on East Fifth maroon and navy shadows. My hand, my arm, fingers, my cigarette were shadows on the table.

Fiona made a joke that she had no shadow, that she was a vampire. Fiona was sitting so her shadow wasn't on the table, and when Fiona said she was a vampire, I looked at her close, her white skin almost blue, kohl around her eyes like two smashed grapes, and for a moment I believed her.

Dogs barking. Coyotes, wolves maybe. Billy Strayhorn and Duke Ellington and "Lush Life."

Rose crossed his legs, his foot against my calf. He reached for his Brandy Alexander, his bracelets clack-clack. True Shot slurped the bottom of his soda water, rattled the ice cubes in his glass, put the green swizzle stick in his mouth. His knees were against my knee.

We all looked at Fiona.

Fiona, beautiful according to Fellini. Beautiful the way New York is beautiful: something monstrous, wrong, dark, corrupt, bigger than you, important, too much attitude, always compelling. High cheekbones. Skin all milk and blueberries. Roman nose. Her right upper lip crooked up to the nostril, even with the three operations. Her voice Tallulah Bankhead from years of practice before she had a roof in her mouth. Too many cigarettes already.

Fiona's black snakes with red-rubber-band tails stuck out from under her backwards baseball cap. She was wearing all black as usual, lips so red against her pale white skin they had a life all their own.

She and Rose—and now that I think of it, Ruby and True Shot and me too—ultimate drag queens. It was our appearance of being real.

Fiona's black leotard leg was draped over my legs, her elbow brushing my crotch.

Cool. I can fuck you blind and keep it simple.

Try me.

At our table in the corner by the window, huddled around a flame in a red glass, all of us, body to body to body to body. The touch that proves you're not alone, that someone else is there.

Fiona ordered just one more Southern Comfort, and Peter the bartender-owner walked through the blue smoke of the bar with the bottle and poured her glass half full. It was way after four and the bar was closed. Fiona took out her compact and looked at herself in the mirror, powdered across her forehead, down her cheeks, her chin, down her nose.

Then the lipstick.

Fiona's long fingers stroked the red from the left top lip down, to the corner of the mouth. Then one red swipe across the bottom lip. Then up to the scar, the vertical scar from under the nostril through the lip, just left of center. Lip line and skin not a line there. Fiona's long fingers with the lip liner made the line.

Cool, Fiona said, puckered her lips.

You could understand so much by just how Fiona said cool.

Fiona snapped her compact closed.

I see that I am playing at being beautiful, Fiona said. She took a breath and pressed her red lipstick lips together.

I see, I said, That you are enjoying playing at being beautiful.

Fiona looked around the table, into Rose's eyes. True Shot's mirrors looked into my eyes.

I'm twice her size, just as drunk.

The fates lead her who will, Fiona said, Who won't they drag.

And just like that, we are laughing. Fiona and Rose and True Shot and I embraced, holding on to our drinks, our cigarettes, holding on for dear life, laughing so hard our gums showed, so hard that man and woman, white and Indian and black, gay and straight, all went away between us and there we were just four people laughing.

The moment that after you're different.

The night Harry died, Fiona said. AIDS. I was on the couch. I woke up and Harry was sitting up in bed. Harry had a tube running up his arm that ran to his heart, and there was a pump that made a whirring sound that pumped medicine into Harry's heart. Harry's cat, Madonna, was sitting by the pump. The only light in the room was the amber night-light, the Christmas-tree-light kind you plug in the socket.

Fiona's lips were rubber around the words. Harry told me, Fiona said, I'm the luckiest man. Life is absolutely, mysteriously beautiful. Life has always been here all around me, in me, of me, has always been this fascinating mystery, but it wasn't until now that I have been present, been aware enough, to witness. I am here now in this room in this light with the sound of the pump and Madonna watching the pump and listening to the pump, and just now, Fiona, you were snoring and I realized I was alive and I was aware. When you're thirsty, Harry said, Water is so beautiful.

I got up, Fiona said, Poured a glass of water, took the glass of water to Harry. I sat on the bed and helped Harry hold his head up. I put the glass to Harry's lips. Harry took a sip. Harry said, Beautiful, just beautiful. And then all at once, Harry was staring at me; his eyes rolled up and Harry wasn't present, wasn't there with me anymore.

LENA HORNE's "Where or When." Snot on Fiona's broken lip. She wiped her nose, smeared the red. Her bird hand perched on my big farm hand, my bitten cuticles. Dogs barking. Then Fiona's ear was at my chest, and Fiona's heartbeat and my heartbeat were one heartbeat.

In all the world, our heartbeat the only thing.

THAT NIGHT IN Fish Bar, not one of us knew what we were really talking about. We were all just talking talking, playing at talking, and then we were talking about the one moment. The one moment that before it we were going this way and after it we were going that way.

Didn't know.

Personne.

True Shot, Rose, Fiona, me. None of us knew that when we started talking about the one moment, what we were talking about was death.

BUT IT'S NOT the truth. We were never all of us in Fish Bar together.

The way this all happened together was only in me.

BOOK ONE

CHAPTER
ONE

The airplane landed at La Guardia, August 3, 1983. My first time ever in New York City, and in all the world, I was leaning up against a cement wall, an unrelenting fluorescent light above me, the bill of my red ball cap the only shade for miles. Exhaust fumes. I was minding my business, just outside the doors where you claim your baggage, waiting for the express bus to the city. My wallet was in my inside jacket pocket. Inside my chest, no room for breath. Sweat rolling from my pits. My duffel bag was against the wall next to me. On top of my duffel bag, my suitcase with the travel stickers on it, and on top of the suitcase, my backpack. I was rolling a cigarette with one hand like I can when I saw the van. A 1970 maroon Dodge van with hippie calligraphy DOOR OF THE DEAD on the side.

Door of the Dead was a game my sister Bobbie and Charlie 2Moons and I used to play.

I took it as a sign.

Blue smoke was coming out the back of the van and people were climbing inside, through the side door, white people all in black. Black leotards, black luggage, black hats, black shoes.

Then, just like that, Ruby Prestigiacomo's face was smiling right in front of me.

Don't let the van spook you, Ruby said. We just bought it from the band, Ruby said, smiling, The Door of the Dead band.

There's room for one more, Ruby said. You'll be all night here waiting for a cab. I can give you a ride for fifteen dollars. Cab'll cost you twenty-five.

Inside my chest, near the sore place where I smoke, so easy, I felt Ruby's smile.

I wished I could be so easy, wished I could smile like that.

My wallet was still in my inside jacket pocket. Ruby just kept there, kept standing in the unrelenting fluorescence, smiling, too close, his blue eyes the way crazy people look at you, moving in on you, like when you go to kiss somebody. Blue eyes and thick red-blond hair, blond hair on his forearms. Beautiful. The kind of skin that freckles and tans gold. His red polyester shirt—buttons open so far down I had to avert my eyes. Hair pulled back in a ponytail. A silver ankh dangling from his queer ear, soul-patch triangle of red-blond hair just under his bottom lip.

Ruby Prestigiacomo, what am I going to do with you?

All death did was make Ruby smile all the more.

YOU'RE GOING TO wait all night here for a cab, Ruby said. Fifteen dollars, Ruby said, Anywhere in Wolf Swamp.

Wolf Swamp? I said.

Manhattan, Ruby said.

Ruby reached into his inside coat pocket and pulled out an old blue Velcro wallet, pulled the wallet open, and from the wad of papers pulled out a business card. Ruby's fingers were long and thin and there was grease under his thumbnail. Thumb print of grease on the business card.

ROMEOMOVERS SPIRIT SCHLEPPERS were the words on the card, WOLF SWAMP. Under SPIRIT SCHLEPPERS was DOG SHIT PARK, then under DOG SHIT PARK was RUBY PRESTIGIACOMO, under RUBY PRESTIGIACOMO a phone number, then under the phone number was CLYDE TRUE SHOT EXPERIENCED DRIVER.

Shit on a business card.

What's Dog Shit Park? I said.

Lower East Side, Ruby said. It's a park. Tompkins Square, but everybody I know calls it Dog Shit Park.

Where you going? Ruby said.

Two-oh-five East Fifth Street, I said.

Between Second and Third, Ruby said.

Ruby grabbed my duffel bag and my old suitcase with the travel stickers on it. I picked up my backpack and followed Ruby past the line of people waiting for taxis. My wallet was in the inside pocket of my jacket.

The four white people all in black were sitting on their luggage in the back of the van, all of them with big red lips, even the man. Big hoops in their ears, all of them smoking cigarettes.

They're from France, Ruby said, *Vogue* magazine. They only speak French except for *fuck you*. You got the fifteen dollars?

My wallet from my inside jacket pocket, when I opened it, my money was suddenly public domain opened up like that on the street.

I gave Ruby a ten and a five, stuck my wallet back in my inside jacket pocket.

Bonsoir, I said in French.

The French Vogues all looked like mannequins. They all said quick French things back. Twice as hot inside the van. I sat down where I was standing, started doing what I always do when I don't know what to do, rolled a cigarette with one hand like I can, French Vogue mannequins all around watching me. When I got the cigarette rolled, I offered the cigarette to the man French Vogue first. He looked away, poked his left shoulder up, pointed his hand and took the cigarette, silver loop dangle side to side, the fuck-you smile on his red lips, red lips pursing, French grunt.

Then it was a cigarette for each of the others, each accepting with a choreography of stance, silver loop, hair tossing.

Sophistication.

Savoir faire.

Postured disregard.

Sexy totale.

Shit from Parisian Shinola.

I'll have one of those too, Ruby said. Then: Where'd you learn to roll a cigarette like that?

A friend of mine, I said. Charlie 2Moons, I said, Taught me, I said, A long time ago.

I have my mother's nerves, so sometimes I stutter.

Language my second language.

CLYDE TRUE SHOT Experienced Driver was big, everything about him big, extra lovely as Rose would say—chest, belly, thighs, shoulders, arms, hands. His big hands on the steering wheel, on both hands on every finger, even the thumbs, the same silver ring. From the side I was on, True Shot's nose was a hook that poked out of two high cheekbones. His hair was black and thick and long and tied back in a bun with a red paisley bandanna tied around his head. From his neck, a beaded buckskin bag. The horizontal line was blue trader beads and the intersecting vertical line, red beads. The buckskin bag hung from a buckskin necklace.

No doubt about it, I was staring. Same way as when you stare at a big snake. And big snakes always look back. On a lava rock ledge in full sun, the big snake doesn't want to even move, but the snake turns, and his eyes end on you.

On me. True Shot put his eyes on me. I mean, his mirrors.

True Shot's mirrors. An accessory True Shot never went without, his mirrored Armani sunglasses.

When True Shot put his mirrors on me, I could see myself in there on the surface, a circus freak, distorted at the state fair, my big circus nose and mustache and bug eyes.

I saw him first! Ruby said. He's mine!

Clyde True Shot? I said.

Drop the Clyde, Ruby said. He's just True Shot.

True Shot, I said. Would you like, I said, A cigarette?

No, thank you, Ruby said. He don't smoke socially.

There was a hand on my shoulder, and it was the French Vogue man handing me one of his cigarettes, rolled fat.

Merci, I said, lit the cigarette, inhaled. Marijuana? I said.

Fucking hashish, French Vogue said.

In the rearview mirror, True Shot's mirrors were on me. Smoke big, True Shot said. His voice was soft, resonant, like a child singing a lullaby in a culvert.

TRUE SHOT AT the wheel, Ruby riding shotgun, French Vogues, me; we are inside, in our smoke cut through with high-beam headlights. Outside, all about us, out the windshield in front, out the windows in back: stars, speeding light, red and amber, huge white flying saucers, eyes.

I was rolling another cigarette, rolling six more cigarettes around. I was not speaking French or any words of any language. My butt was burning on the van floor, so I sat on the old suitcase with the travel stickers on it. Drops of sweat all around me.

True Shot hit the brakes and under us was a screeching. We swerved. One French Vogue banged her head on the side of the van. We slid to a stop. From out Ruby's window, I could see a wall of concrete. A backhoe. An electric sign pointed repeating yellow arrows at Ruby's head. There was water flowing onto the right lane of the roadway, and mud. I thought it was mud. The electric yellow made the water look like thin buttermilk. There were cans and things floating. From the embankment, the thin buttermilk was a waterfall onto the roadway over a truck tire and the back seat of a car. Then the turds. I smelled and I knew: The milk was a river of sewage. True Shot started honking.

Fuck! Ruby said. We should have taken the fucking tunnel.

Fuck! the French Vogues all said. Fuck!

Then: Watch for cops! True Shot said.

True Shot shifted into first and turned the steering wheel to the right.
Watch for cops! Ruby yelled back at us.

Then Ruby watched the right side and True Shot the left side, and
True Shot guided the van through the narrow space in between the
backhoe and the electric yellow arrow sign. Milk-shit river lapped at
the bottom of the side door. There was a bump and the front right tire
went up on the curb, then another bump for the back right tire. True
Shot hugged the wheel, leaned forward, and aimed the van in between
the line of traffic on the left and a wall of concrete on the right.

Clyde True Shot, race-car driver, hit the gas.

WE ARE AN arrow, Door of the Dead arrow, howling through, tilted,
banking, racing down where you're not supposed to go, right wheels on
the curb, left wheels in the gutter, guard-rail concrete wall only inches
from us to the right. To the left, Day-Glo traffic cones, and the Volkswagen Chevrolet Ford Toyota line of cars, pickups, semis, and limou-
sines traffic jam. Where we're heading hellbent is in between, space
enough or not.

Ruby's forehead is shiny with lights on the sweat. Ruby's bones poking through, his smile skeleton big. He's staring straight ahead, like all
of us, at the trajectory, our thrust, but he's watching True Shot too. Ruby
loves True Shot and he's watching True Shot, race-car driver, the two
of them two guys, rodeo yee-haws, Friday-night homeboys, going fast,
right-flanking one mile, two miles, three miles of traffic jam and
counting.

French Vogues lit French cigarettes. Fuck. Merde. Fuck. Fuck. Fuck.

Toll booth! True Shot yelled, like this was Nintendo and toll booth
was the dragon. The right front wheel bumped off the curb back onto
the road, then the right rear wheel. True Shot shifted down to second.

Watch for cops! True Shot yelled.

Watch for cops! Ruby yelled.

One of the French Vogues, a woman, reached down, opened the sliding side door. Blast of hot air, city lights, guard rail right there speeding
by, air. I held my hand against my heart, my wallet in my inside jacket
pocket, pulled my cap off, knelt forward, head out the side door. Wind
blowing in my hair.

There it was right in front of us: the yellow-and-black-striped toll
booth STOP arm coming down. True Shot shifted into second.

Geronimo! True Shot yelled. Geronimo! Ruby yelled.

I closed my eyes.

The yellow-and-black-striped toll booth STOP arm karate-chopped into the roof of the Door of the Dead van.

But it's not the truth.

I knelt back, opened my eyes. Through the back windows, the yellow-and-black-striped toll booth STOP arm was locked in place behind us.

Out the windshield, out the back windows, out the side door, there were no cops.

True Shot yelled, Welcome to Wolf Swamp! And we cheered, all of us, me and the French Vogues, these people I didn't know—we cheered. I rolled more cigarettes, lit six all around, and we smoked and smoked, and it wasn't long before: Waldorf Hysteria! Ruby yelled.

True Shot pulled up to the bright curb. The doorman opened the van's side door. He wore a powder-blue military uniform. He was speaking French, snapping his fingers. Young brown men in matching outfits rushed to the van.

One by one, the French Vogues stepped out. The doorman took each French Vogue by the hand. One by one, the bellhops slid the monogrammed alligator luggage out of Door of the Dead van.

Alligators, True Shot said.

Dangerous cargo, Ruby said.

Faux alligators, True Shot said.

Worst kind, Ruby said.

The only good faux alligator, Ruby said, Is a dead faux alligator.

Every extra lovely muscle in True Shot was laughing. Ruby too, but Ruby had to put his fist over his mouth. A deep cough was coming up, rattling Ruby's bones. Ruby's arm held his side.

I stuck my head out the van's side door, looked left, right, then all around, then up. Waldorf Astoria.

Lunch at the Waldorf was a game my mother and I used to play.

Hysteria. The lights of Waldorf Hysteria were bright bright, unrelenting. The light was inside me, moving through me. On the street was the swirl and flash of lights, a high off-pitch ringing, and something else: a sound, like in monster movies. The footfall of a huge monster.

ALL DODGES SOUND the same when you start them up.

Ruby reached behind True Shot and, from out of a heap, pulled a five-gallon bucket, turned the bucket over, brushed the bottom off, patted it, and said, Here, come up and sit on this bucket, up here between us.

My wallet was in my inside jacket pocket.

Can get stuffy back there, Ruby said. Then: Here, this'll help, he said, and pulled a can of Budweiser out from its plastic ring and handed me the beer, put the joint to his Ruby lips, inhaled, and passed the joint to me.

This'll help too, Ruby said, holding his breath and sucking in the words like you do.

It'll take the edge off, Ruby said. Ruby was smiling.

Seemed like a good idea at the time.

I offered the joint to True Shot.

He don't smoke socially, Ruby said.

I handed the joint back to Ruby. Opened the can of beer.

Driving more like floating.

Punch in that Sioux tape! Ruby said.

True Shot punched in his Sioux tape and both he and Ruby, all at once, started singing, howling, and crying singing, Indian songs like in Fort Hall when Bobbie and Charlie 2Moons and I lived on the rez.

Where are we? I said.

When my words came out, they did not stutter.

True Shot and Ruby looked at me, looked at each other.

Broadway, Ruby said.

You ain't from here, are you? Ruby said.

Broadway? I said.

Earth, Ruby said. His famous smile.

New York, Ruby said. Here, he said, putting both his hands on my shoulders and pushing down. Here.

Now here, Ruby said, Or nowhere, Ruby said. Depends on the space in between.

Outside the windows of Door of the Dead van, neon vegetable stands passed, windows, concrete columns, lampposts, traffic, parked cars, wires, and lights: green, amber, red, go, wait, stop.

The wind was blowing Ruby's gold-red hair.

You know, Ruby said, sucking on the joint, I've been trying to figure out who you look like. He handed the joint to me.

And I think I've figured it out, Ruby said. What do you think, True Shot? Handsome Einstein or intelligent Tom Selleck?

True Shot's bandanna. His mirrors. The silver ring on every finger, even his thumbs. The buckskin bag with the blue horizontal and the red vertical hanging on the buckskin necklace. True Shot's lips, under his mirrors, moved.

Handsome Einstein, True Shot said.

His voice, the child out of the culvert, hollering into the wind.

You sure? Ruby said.

Selleck can't look intelligent, True Shot said.

Then: What's your name? Ruby asked.

William, I said. William Parker.

Friends call you Bill?

Will, I said.

I'll call you Will then, Ruby said. Ruby's smile.

This here's True Shot and I'm Ruby Prestigiacomo.

Glad to meet, I said, You guys, I said.

I shook Ruby's hand, went to shake True Shot's, but thought, He don't shake hands socially, so I just looked at him.

I didn't expect, I said, New York folks to be so friendly.

Ruby ate the roach.

When you're in the Spirit Schlepping business like ours, Ruby said, Friendly's just part of the program. Besides, that's bullshit. New Yorkers can be the friendliest people you ever met.

Not what I've heard, I said. Back west, I said, Where I'm from, folks think New Yorkers are rich Jews, I said, Mafia Italians, and black guys in gangs who play basketball and kill white people.

Ain't too far off, Ruby said.

Then: Where back west?

A bunch of places, I said. Jackson Hole, I said. Most of my time in northern Idaho, but I was born in Pocatello.

Ruby turned his head around quick, put his hands to his cheeks, and screamed: In a trunk in the Princess Theater!

Then Ruby was laughing the way you do on good dope. I started laughing too, though I didn't know why.

You know, Ruby said. The song, *A Star Is Born*, Ruby said. Judy Garland!

I was born in a trunk in the Princess Theater in Pocatello, Idaho, Ruby sang.

Never heard it, I said.

Then: Brooklyn, Ruby said. I was born in Brooklyn. Bensonhurst.

I waited for True Shot to say where he was born, but he didn't.

Staying here long? Ruby asked.

Living here, I said, Now. Got an apartment: Two-oh-five East Fifth Street.

Got a job? Ruby asked.

Restaurants, I said.

Hard time to get a restaurant job, Ruby said. August. You might try Life Café, Tenth and B, on the northeast corner of Dog Shit Park. You could tell them Ruby Prestigiacomo sent you, but it won't do any good.

Dog Shit Park, I said.

Yeah, Ruby said. You remember—Tompkins Square, not far from you.

Why'd you move here of all places? Ruby said.

Shit happens, I said.

Seemed like a good idea at the time, I said.

If I can make it here I'll make it anywhere, I said.

But it's not the truth.

Of all the things I could've said right then, practiced things I didn't stutter, I said this: Because I was afraid to, I said. And also, I said, Because I'm looking for someone.

True Shot's mirrors were on me from the left, and from the right Ruby's too close with his breath.

Ruby crossed his hazel eyes. Crossed over, huh? Ruby said.

Crossed over? I said.

That's when you stop being one way and start being another, Ruby said. Not something many people can do, or want to do. In fact, Ruby said, The only people who cross over, cross over because they're on some kind of Mission Impossible.

I could no longer live and stay the way I was, I said.

But it's not the truth.

I didn't say anything.

Then: Two-oh-five East Fifth Street! Ruby yelled, the same way as *Waldorf Hysteria!*

We were stopped on a street, in front of a building, double-parked. True Shot turned the engine off.

Between Second and Third, Ruby said, On the street where you live. *I have often walked down this street before,* Ruby sang.

THE SIOUX TAPE'S drums was the way my heart was beating. Sweat rolling down from my pits, my head still floating. I was way stoned, sitting on a bucket between a guy named True Shot and a guy named Ruby Prestigiacomo, and there I was in all the world, double-parked in front of 205 East Fifth Street, between Second and Third.

From Door of the Dead van, the light above the steps of 205 East Fifth Street was right behind Ruby's head. The mercury-vapor streetlamp light the color of dust storms, ocher through the windows, hard edges, New York angles.

I knew it, Ruby said, Soon as I saw you.

What? I said.

True Shot's going to tell you a story, Ruby said.

What story? I said.

Who can tell? Ruby said. Maybe the Secret of Wolf Swamp.

My suitcase with the travel stickers on it, my duffel bag, and my back-pack were all lined up. I went to open the side door when Ruby put his hand on my knee, grabbing my knee the way you do when you're trying to keep something still.

My butt was on the bucket.

Just then outside big thunder and a flash of light.

But it's not the truth. The thunder wasn't outside. The thunder was inside me, the flash inside.

True Shot raised his head up and looked at the roof of the van. From under the chin, True Shot didn't look Indian at all, or any one way. He just looked like a kid on a summer night looking up at the stars.

So Will Parker . . . True Shot said.

Handsome Einstein . . . Ruby said.

In True Shot's mirrors, I was a red ball cap with crooked bottom teeth.

Only silence inside Door of the Dead van. True Shot cleared his throat, spit out the window. He put his fingers up to the buckskin bag with the beaded blue horizontal and the red vertical hanging from the buckskin necklace, turned around, and put his mirrors onto me.

Just like that, True Shot took my hand, open palm to open palm, and put his fingers in with mine, his silver rings against my fingers.

It is this way, True Shot said, You will find your friend.

I will? I said, How do you know?

True Shot just knows, Ruby said.

Meanwhile, True Shot said, Have some fun while you wait for the will of heaven.

The porch light in True Shots' mirrors made it look like I had a halo around my head.

I didn't know what to say, so I said something like thanks or Okay see ya, and pulled my hand away.

RUBY GOT OUT of the van and opened the side door, and I stepped out. Smoke out onto the street. For a moment, I thought the smoke was my body smoking. My feet were standing in a rectangle of earth, the rectangle of earth where I'd plant the cherry tree—cement sidewalk everywhere else but where I was standing. My wallet was in my inside jacket pocket.

Ruby and I were about the same: six foot two. I had twenty pounds on him. Something about the way Ruby looked right then—his jaw, the skin of his face below his sideburn—so beautiful. When I stood full up, I was face-to-face with Ruby's smile.

Ruby poked his finger in my chest. The will of heaven, Ruby said, Is in your heart.

Then: New York, new place, Ruby said.

His hands pressed down the lapel of my corduroy coat.

Handsome Einstein new self-concept, Ruby said.

New concept new name, Ruby said.

New name? I said.

When you cross over, Ruby said, You need a new name.

Will of Heaven! Ruby said, his arm in the air; his hand cupped, fingers and thumb together like Italians do, five points of a star: his grand easy smile.

From inside the van, True Shot yelled, William of Heaven! Ho!

Ruby pulled the hair tie from around his ponytail and shook his head. His red-blond hair was shiny all the way to his shoulders.

You got our business card? Ruby said. You're sure?

Sure, I said, and pulled the card from my side pocket. ROMEOMOVERS. SPIRIT SCHLEPPERS. DOG SHIT PARK.

Where's the keys to the apartment? Ruby said.

I took my wallet out of my inside jacket pocket, and out of the side pocket of my wallet I pulled three big keys, one little key.

One for the outside door, two for the inside, Ruby said. The little one's for the mailbox. Get a duplicate made. Give a set to somebody you trust. You can trust me, Ruby said, his smile. Keep the other set. Always remember, New Yorkers love only those who love themselves. Always put yourself first. Dress down for the subway. Get an answering machine. And remember, New Yorkers take pride in always knowing where they are. Buy a map. Always know where you are. If you don't, act like you do.

Then: LA is the *me* city, Ruby said, and New York is the *you* city. In LA it's fuck *me*. In New York it's fuck *you*. Adopt the attitude. It's all in the face. Mostly in the eyes.

Like this, Ruby said.

Ruby's eyes were looking right at me, but they were more like looking through me: no smile, his lip curled up, his nostrils in and out.

New York drop-dead fuck-you, Ruby said. The attitude. Now you try it.

I made like I thought Ruby wanted me to look.

Pull your ball cap down, Ruby said. Look at me but don't see me. No no no! Ruby said, and tapped each shoulder. No chip on your shoulder—somebody will try and knock it off. It's passive, Ruby said. It's like you're already dead and you wish everybody else was dead too.

New York drop-dead fuck-you, Ruby said.

It takes practice, Ruby said.

Ruby picked up my duffel bag, slung it over his shoulder.

Want me to spend the night with you? Ruby said. First night of your crossover and all. I could help if there's a problem. Ain't easy fixing a center, Ruby said. Ruby's smile.

No, I said. No, thanks. I'll be fine.

Don't get me wrong, Ruby said. It ain't usual—Ruby pulled the brim of my ball cap back up—that I feel this way about a person, one that I just met.

Then: If it's the gay cancer you're worried about, Ruby said, We can just hold each other.

Inside Door of the Dead van, I bent and turned my head into True Shot's mirrors. His shiny silver rings. The beaded blue horizontal and red vertical on the buckskin bag hanging on the buckskin strand, his red bandanna.

Ruby said, True Shot doesn't have sex socially. It would be just me.

No, I said. Thanks.

Then: I can carry the duffel bag, I said.

Ruby let my duffel bag drop.

I don't mean to freak you out, man, Ruby said, And I'm not irresponsible. Just lonely. And Einstein's the sexiest man ever, next to Martin Luther King, Jr. And when I saw you at the airport, standing alone in the fluorescence, checking for your wallet, I don't know what the fuck happened to me.

It was just so human how you were, Ruby said. Ruby's smile.

I was wounded by a blow of love, Ruby said.

My heartbeat at my ears was a siren.

Then my lips were flying lips against Ruby's. Ruby's lips were soft, his breath was cigarettes and beer and the sweet smell of his soul. We kissed big, a deep kiss like in the movies, my hands in his hair, down his back, and onto his ass.

But it's not the truth.

Thanks, I said, For the ride. For everything.

ALL DODGES SOUND the same when you start them up.

Vaya con Dios, True Shot said.

Happy Trails! Ruby said. Until we meet again!

Keep smiling until then was the song in my head as I put the key in the door of 205 East Fifth Street. Down the street, Door of the Dead van turned right on Third Avenue. True Shot shifted into second, and just like that the Dodge van was gone. I turned the key and pushed the steel door and I was inside, under the unrelenting fluorescent halo in the hallway.

APARTMENT 1-A WAS on my right. It took me awhile in the bright to find the right key. Just as I turned the key in the top lock, the door behind me, 1-C, opened up as far as the chain allowed. A cat tried to jump out the door, but a foot in a dirty fluffy pink slipper kicked it. The cat yowled and ducked back in. The woman stuck the cat she was holding in her hand out the door first, before she stuck her own self out. This cat was a long-haired yellow and looked at me with the New York drop-dead fuck-you.

What I first saw about the woman was her blue shower hat and the Kleenex under the elastic part of the shower hat. Then her eyebrows: two red swoops exactly the way in my mother's penmanship how she crossed her T's: too fancy. Then it was Scotch I smelled, and cigarettes. Scotch and cigarettes and cat shit and kitty litter.

Mrs. Lupino came together all at once as herself when she spoke. You knew all about her with that voice, deep as a lava flow, soft as mud.

You Ellen's cowboy? Mrs. Lupino said. The one that's moving in?

Ellen? I said. How do you know about Ellen?

She told me about you, Mrs. Lupino said. *Everything.*

The one from potato country? Mrs. Lupino asked.

From Idaho, I said. Yes.

Mrs. Lupino's hand on the yellow cat was liver spots and pink Lee Press-On nails.

Then do it! Mrs. Lupino said.

Do it? I said.

What you do with the cigarettes, she said.

I put down my duffel bag and my suitcase. Rolled a cigarette with one hand like I can, handed the cigarette through the opening in the door. Mrs. Lupino took the cigarette, pink Lee Press-On nails, liver spots, put the cigarette in between her lips, wrinkles all around her lips, no lipstick. I lit Mrs. Lupino's cigarette.

Watch for my babies because I'm opening the door, she said, and closed the door, undid the chain, and opened the door again. Cats everywhere.

Upstairs, another door opened, and at the top of the stairs stood a person and then a little dog, a terrier, who started yapping, then a bigger dog, then an old dog, limping, with spots. There was no light on the second-story landing, and I couldn't see who was standing at the top of the stairs. The person was big and wearing a long robe, that's all I could tell, except I knew this person was black.

Things start where you don't know.

That person was Rose, Rose and his dogs, Mona, Mary, and Jack Flash. Bracelets, lots of bracelets, the clack-clack of them.

Rose upstairs, Ruby just gone around the corner. The closest those two ever got. Except for in me.

It's all right, Rose! Mrs. Lupino called sing-songy up the stairs. This is Ellen's cowboy. You remember Ellen telling us about her cowboy?

The voice from the second landing was a real deep James Earl Jones.

Which one? Rose said. There were so many.

Oh, Rose! Mrs. Lupino laughed. The *cowboy*—you know the one. The one from potato country.

The grilled salmon and the Pinot Gris and the limp dick? Rose said.

Mrs. Lupino inhaled on the cigarette. Wrinkles around her lips, all smiles at me.

Yes, Mrs. Lupino said, That's the one!

The pain starts in my forearms, then goes up my arms, then splashes down through my heart, a cattle prod straight to my cock.

Nice cats, I said.

Cats! What cats? Mrs. Lupino said, eyebrows into Kleenex. There's no cats.

From the deep voice on the second landing: Mrs. Lupino got rid of all her cats.

Every one of them, Mrs. Lupino said. All around her lips, wrinkles, wrinkles.

Every single cat, she said. Not one fucking iota of a single fucking cat left.

There were three cats in the hall. Mrs. Lupino was holding the yellow fuck-you drop-dead cat, and there were cats at Mrs. Lupino's feet, cats running behind her inside her apartment.

No cats, I said.

No cats already! Mrs. Lupino said, and made a click with her tongue. Just like that, the cats in the hallway all ran back into the apartment. Mrs. Lupino closed her door.

My eyes counted up thirteen blue linoleum steps to the second floor.

This *is*, I said loud, The right apartment? I said pointing to 1-A.

Ellen Zigman's apartment, I said. Right?

My mother's nerves.

Clavelle, the deep voice said. She got married. Her name is now Ellen Clavelle.

Right, I said, Clavelle. This is her apartment? Ellen Clavelle's apartment?

You've got it wrong, the deep voice said. Mrs. Lupino is in Ellen's old apartment, 1-C. It's hers now. The landlord, Ellen's uncle, gave her Ellen's apartment when Mrs. Lupino got rid of her cats. Your apartment is Mrs. Lupino's old apartment—1-A—and it's the door to your right.

We're neighbors, Mrs. Lupino said through her closed door. Then: 'Night, Rose, she called out, sing-songy.

Good night, Mrs. Lupino, the deep voice up the stairs said—bracelets, lots of bracelets, clack-clack—and then Rose at the top of the stairs was gone, and the dogs, and I heard the door close, and then each of the three locks were locked, just as Mrs. Lupino locked her three locks, then the chains.

In all the world, in a narrow blue hallway, there I was standing alone, squinting in the unrelenting fluorescence.

ONE-A. THE OTHER key unlocked the bottom lock. The last turn of the key on the bottom you had to push the door. The steel door opened into dark.

Cat shit. Cat piss. Cat spray. Cat hair. Cat food. Cat litter.

To the wall on the right, I reached my hand into the dark. Turned the light on.

A bright box. More fluorescent halos. Unrelenting, the light from above.

Home.

THAT'S WHEN IT happened: the worst possible thing. My wallet was not in my inside jacket pocket. Not in my side pockets, my back pockets, not in the front pockets of my Levi's. Not in the suitcase with the travel stickers on it, not in my backpack, not in the duffel bag. No wallet.

Not in the narrow blue hallway on the floor.

Not on any of the eleven cast-iron steps of the stoop, not on the sidewalk, not in the gutter, not in the street.

Door of the Dead van pulled up. True Shot shifted into second, put on the brakes. Ruby's ponytail, his arm out the window.

Lose something? Ruby hollered.

My wallet! I hollered back. I've lost my wallet!

The red-yellow hair on Ruby's arm. Inside the van True Shot's mirrors, his shiny silver rings. I put my head in close, my body not so close.

My wallet's gone, I said.

That's because I stole it, Ruby said. Ruby's smile.

Ruby handed me my wallet.

In all the world, in New York City on East Fifth Street, standing in the rectangle of earth where I'd plant the cherry tree, I stood looking at my wallet in my hands.

You stole my wallet? I said. Why did you steal my wallet?

Dumb question, Ruby said. For the five hundred and ninety-three dollars, for the traveler's checks, for the cashier's check.

In my wallet: five hundred-dollar bills, the other bills, the traveler's checks, the cashier's check.

It is this way, True Shot said. Ruby stole your wallet because you asked him to.

But that's the last thing, I said, I wanted!

Ruby's eyes were looking right at me, but they were more like looking through me. No smile, his lip curled up, and his nostrils went in and out.

New York drop-dead fuck-you.

Ruby winked.

When you don't want something as much as you didn't want your wallet to get stole that means only one thing, Ruby said.

Your worst fears, True Shot said.

That's what's important about Wolf Swamp and why you've come here, Ruby said. You can't want anything or not want anything that much.

Now that you're in Wolf Swamp, True Shot said, Now that you've come because you were afraid to come—

You're in a whole new ball game, Ruby said. Crossed over. You got to be careful in a whole 'nother way of what you want and what you don't want. What you fear.

Before, you were afraid of your fears happening and you spent all your time making sure they didn't happen, True Shot said. Now that you've crossed over, you're spending all your time making sure they do.

Hell of a fix, Ruby said.

Up Shit Creek, True Shot said.

In a world of hurt, Ruby said.

If you go around checking your wallet every goddamn minute like a goddamn fool, Ruby said, Then you, William of Heaven, are destined for New York Fucking City fucking roadkill.

Then: Did you lock yourself out? Ruby asked.

My hands went quick all over all my pockets, and my keys were in my right side pocket. I held my keys up and showed them to Ruby and True Shot.

I'll bet you left your apartment door open, Ruby said. Never leave your apartment door open!

All Dodges sound the same when you start them up. Blue smoke everywhere. True Shot shifted into first.

Adios, amigo! Ruby said. Don't let the motherfuckers get you down!

It's the Puritan undertow, Ruby said, What we got to look out for.

The van took off, True Shot shifting into second.

Ruby was singing, True Shot was singing:

> *Fools rush in where wise men never go,*
> *But wise men never fall in love,*
> *So how are they to know?*

When we met I felt my life begin was what I was singing this time, standing on East Fifth Street, somewhere between Second and Third—in the rectangle of dirt where I'd plant the cherry tree, my wallet in my hands, holding on to my wallet.

* * *

ELLEN WAS A New Yorker and a Jew, a counselor with Outward Bound who came to Jackson Holeewood with kids who'd never been out of the city. I walked into Cowboy Bar and there was Ellen straddling a saddle at the bar. Big bush of black hair with combs and scarves and chopsticks in it. Her heart-shaped butt in designer jeans snug in the saddle.

As soon as Ellen saw my dog, she fell in love. More women fell in love with Crummy Dog than I can tell you. So it wasn't long before Ellen and I were bellied up to the bar, sitting on the saddles, Crummy Dog on the saddle in between, Ellen and I doing what she called Boilermakers and what I called In the Ditch, which was shots of Crown Royal backed by Heineken for her, Coors for me, Coors not for her politically, she said.

Somewhere in there, I took the Bull Durham from my shirt pocket and, with one hand like I can, started rolling a cigarette. Ellen asked me to roll her a cigarette too, so I rolled her a cigarette, then lit the cigarette for her. Ellen inhaled, then spit tobacco.

I suppose if I asked you to wrestle down a steer for me, you could do that too, Ellen said.

Fuckin' A, I said.

What is this shit? Ellen said. I mean, where does this western shit stop?

Ellen's mouth was moving extra for the amount of her words, and a big hank of hair with a chopstick in it was hanging down over her ear.

It all seems so movie, so stereo . . . typical, Ellen said. So fake.

Tourist Town, I said. Robert Goulet right down the road.

Oh, God, I'm in Camelot! Ellen said. Cowboy Camelot!

Jackson Holeewood, I said.

I can't tell you how funny Ellen and I were just then, so funny that man and woman went away between us, and there we were in all the world, just two people laughing.

THAT SEPTEMBER, 1982, Ellen stayed on an extra week. We went backpacking in the Tetons. Fresh salmon on the grill, Pinot Gris in the wineglasses, her nipples through her halter top, Ellen said love on Jenny's Lake. I said no to sex.

All hat and no cowboy.

My belt buckle the tombstone for my dead dick.

At the Jackson Hole airport, Ellen and I parted friends. Then my dog got run over by a car. I wrote Ellen a letter, told her about Crummy Dog, and proposed a Christmas visit to New York City, thinking as I wrote her, Maybe I should say Chanukah visit. Thinking as I wrote down her address on the envelope—205 East Fifth Street—that I didn't know East Fifth from West Fifth, didn't know the five boroughs from the seven wonders of the world, shit from Shinola. Didn't know what was important, what wasn't.

Chanukah, for Ellen, however, was Monsieur Maurice Clavelle, wedding bells, the Arc de Triomphe, the Tour Eiffel, and Paris, France. Maurice Clavelle was a man she could fuck marry.

Back in Jackson Holeewood, I enrolled in French class and a correspondence course in fine wines called Vin et Vous.

That spring, Ellen wrote a letter back, offering her everlasting friendship, and something else.

Her Manhattan apartment—$650 a month. Ellen's uncle owned the building.

You need to come east, Ellen wrote, To the center of things. Start a new life. Get some sophistication. What are you so fucking afraid of?

IN 205 EAST Fifth Street, 1-A, I turned off the unrelenting fluorescence from above and closed and locked the door behind me. My strange footsteps in my damp, wall-stained, cat-spray home. I opened the kitchen window, stripped down to my T-shirt and shorts, rolled a cigarette, leaned out into the hot August Wolf Swamp night.

Outside was a courtyard. Four brick walls went up five and six stories, the brick walls at the top, where there's more weather, faced with a layer of mortar. Below the line of mortar, the bricks made a dull red grid, chinked, sagging, settled. The windows were barred, were broken, were cacti and suffocating philodendron-pressed, plastic-flowered, window-fanned, were open, closed, filthy, were clean red-and-white checkered curtains. The fire escapes rusted zigzags, cat perches, meat-frying Hibachi stands, catchalls. A patch of city light a diagonal down the side of a building.

In the kitchen, I slid my fingers through a drawer of leftover stuff. A thumbtack tacked itself to my thumb. The kitchen light was an unrelenting halo of fluorescence when I turned it on. I stood right under the bright halo, put the thumbtack between my teeth, opened my blue Velcro wallet, found the folded newspaper clipping.

My fingers unfolded the newspaper clipping, the sound, and then the newspaper clipping was in my hand, against my open palm.

On the wall, on the tobacco-yellow kitchen wall, next to the window, I pushed Charlie 2Moons's photo onto the plaster with the thumbtack, blew the plaster powder off with my breath. My fingers smoothing smoothing the newsprint, the photo out flat.

A photograph. No bigger than the palm of my hand.

Things and the meaning of things.

Charlie 2Moons's head is turned a bit to the side. His hair is in a ponytail, white shirt and tie, black leather jacket, gap-toothed, smiling big, standing on the stairway to an airplane, waving. An Idaho State flag in his hand, a bundle of ocelot skin under his arm.

September 17, 1978. Five years ago.

LOCAL MAN RECEIVES SCHOLARSHIP was the headline in the *Idaho State Journal*. COLUMBIA UNIVERSITY WRITING PROGRAM. NEW YORK CITY. POETRY.

My forearms, the pain always starts in my forearms, up to my shoulders, splashes down through my heart, cattle prod to cock.

Against the tobacco-yellow wall, the photo of Charlie was gray. My index touched the liar's space in between his two front teeth, moved the line down the back of his head, touched the Idaho flag, the bundled ocelot skin. My index led my eyes off the photo, down to the windowframe, to the open window.

Out on the fire escape, my bare feet against iron rods, my bare skin felt the breeze. I rolled a cigarette, lit the cigarette. Tiny orange illumination in the dark. To the horizon was tarred roofs and TV antennae and wooden water towers. The top of the Con Ed building poked up blue and white.

My hands, white knuckles around the fire-escape railing, I leaned onto the railing. Below, through my feet, grids of iron, empty space all the way down.

My breath in. My breath out.

You could call this a prayer.

Into the big smoggy dark loud Manhattan, I yelled, Charlie! Charlie 2Moons! I'm here! In New York City! I've come to find you! Just like we promised!

There was a slight stirring of the wind. Below, between my feet, through the grids of iron, a paper cup rolled across the cement.

Then a voice out of the dark yelled, Shut the *fuck up*!

A big drag on the cigarette. In the night my shorts and T-shirt, my pink skin, glowing like Catholic statues.

My next words I didn't yell. I spoke them clearly, out loud but not loud, pointing their intent to the blue and white top of Con Ed.

Please Charlie, I said, Forgive me. You got to forgive me. I didn't have a fucking clue what to do.

CHAPTER
TWO

August 8, 1961, the day I met Charlie 2Moons, was the day after we moved from Hope, Idaho, to Fort Hall, Idaho—to the reservation.

The reason we moved to the reservation, into the Residency, was because Mother lost a baby, a girl, and when she got home from the hospital, all she did was sit at the kitchen table, her hair sticking up all over, in her yellow terry-cloth bathrobe, staring at the red tulips on the tablecloth and drinking coffee and smoking Herbert Tareytons.

Then one day, just like that, Mother wasn't in the kitchen, wasn't in her bedroom, wasn't anywhere. None of her clothes or shoes were gone and we didn't have a car. I thought the Door of the Dead had opened up for sure.

Bobbie said I got all sweaty and feverish and she had to sit on Mother's bed with me and hold a cold washrag to my forehead.

That night, Father got home late, with his bottle of Crown Royal. Bobbie told him Mother was gone, and Father slammed his fist down on the table.

That woman's gone looking for her baby girl. She's going to break! Father said.

Father didn't go looking for Mother until morning. Then he saddled up his horse and rode out. He found mother, barefoot, in her yellow terry-cloth bathrobe out in the straw field.

After that, it was a regular thing. Mother kept running out into the field. So Father figured we needed a change, that we'd better move, but Mother said we didn't have any money, we'd never have any money to move to a respectable brick home with a fireplace and picture window, and she was right because all my father did was work on the rodeo circuit—bronc riding mostly, steer wrestling, rodeo clown.

Father made a deal to be the caretaker for the red-brick building with the fireplace and the picture windows with this one tribal council guy,

Lou Racing, who Father drank with. Father caretaking and fifty bucks a month in rent got us the brick house.

The house was brick but there were no picture windows, and the windows that were there had bars on them.

The house had been empty since the war. Nobody wanted to live there. No white people wanted to live in the Residency because it was on the reservation and too far to town and any grocery store. No Indians wanted to live there because of all the Indian kids who had gone to the school and been taught to forget their language and forget they were Indians.

The missionaries had built the red-brick house for the Sisters of the Holy Cross to live in next to the red-brick school. There was nothing left of the school, Saint Anthony's Academy; it burnt down in 1953. All that was left was a big empty graveled yard where Father turned his matching swimming-pool-blue pickup and trailer and horse trailer around.

Out back of the house was a red-brick barn with a gabled roof. At one end of the hayloft were bales of straw—most of them broke open on the floor. Yellow sunlight through the gable doors and sunlight through the cracks in the slates of the roof onto the yellow straw made it a soft place. Even just thinking about it made you want to lie down.

The rusted old swing set and teeter-totter were between the house and the barn on the cement playground. Three swings on chains hanging down, each with a 2-by-6 for a seat. Charlie and Bobbie and I used to almost go all the way over on those swings, and there was many a long afternoon when two of the three of us tried to hit balance on the teeter-totter. Charlie was the biggest, then Bobbie, even though she was oldest, and then me. Charlie and I could hit balance—our feet off the ground, me leaning way out over the edge on my end of the teeter-totter, holding on to the handle, Charlie toward the center on his end. Bobbie and I could hit balance too.

Charlie and Bobbie, though, no matter how long they slid their butts center to end, never did hit balance. Bobbie would start ordering Charlie around, lean-forward lean-back scoot-up scoot-back, and in no time at all those two would be going at it.

The good thing about the Residency was the trees: one half mile, each side of the road, one right after another—silver-leafed, silver-tongued cottonwoods.

Big chandelabra tree limbs touching chandelabra tree limbs across the road. One half mile of whispery shade, the only shade like that in

Idaho. And when the cottonwoods got to the Residency, they made a wide arch, taking in about five acres, circled around, and came back into themselves.

Flying over in an airplane, if you looked down you'd see the cottonwoods in the shape of a keyhole, the kind where the bottom's not flared.

Also there was a big cottonwood right next to the house, branching up high, cottonwood leaves poking into my window in the attic where my room was.

All told, there were one hundred and seventy-six trees. Bobbie counted them.

WE MOVED INTO the Residency, into Mother's brick home with a fireplace, on one of those big bright windy Idaho days. Took up residency in the Residency.

The day we moved, Bobbie and I got to ride in the back of Father's old Dodge pickup all the way from Hope, lying next to each other, holding hands so I wouldn't fall off, on Mother's blue Montgomery Ward mattress and box spring, hanging our feet over the edge of the mattress so we wouldn't get the mattress dirty, the wind all around us, people in their cars on the highway looking at us.

That day, lying on Mother's mattress in the back of the pickup, the wind going by outside us blowing against our bodies, through our hair, in our ears, whipping our clothes like sheets on a line, Bobbie told me one of her secrets.

There never was a person with so many secrets as Bobbie.

Bobbie had her secrets; Charlie, his books; Charlie and Bobbie were what I had.

We were between Chubbuck and Tyhee. Bobbie turned her face to me and rolled over closer on the mattress.

The golden flecks in Bobbie's eyes, her brown rusty hair cut short like a boy's. Bobbie wanted to cut her hair so short it looked like brain surgery, but Father wouldn't allow it.

I am the happiest, Bobbie said, With the wind going around me. Wind makes things cool and dry, she said, And you always feel like someone else is there with the wind, touching you and blowing your hair and blowing in your ears.

My father's Dodge pickup the color of swimming pools turned off Highway 30, went over the railroad tracks, and crossed over the cattle guard; then, just like that, hanging over us like guardian angels were the chandelabra branching arms and silver leaves. It was like diving shallow into Spring Creek, the shadows and light and the coolness all around you.

Bobbie and I lay on the blue mattress, hand in hand, me with Bobbie, Bobbie with her secrets, one full half mile of cottonwoods on both sides of us going by going by.

The branching arms of the trees and the sunlight through the leaves was the most beauty and wonder I had known so far.

MOTHER'S ROOM WAS on the same side of the house as Bobbie's, but on the main floor, just off the big green dining hall, the same green as the whole inside of the house, no light at all coming in her windows, the green shades pulled down. We set the bed down and Father put it together, set the vanity next to the bed in the middle of the room. The dresser, night table, and lamp—set them down every which way, not up against the walls, more like five pieces tossed into the room. That bedroom set never moved the whole time we lived there.

Mother didn't even unpack the picture of Saint Cecilía, or the Sacred Heart of Jesus, or the Immaculate Heart of Mary, or the framed holy card of the Baby Jesus. No more rosaries hanging on the bedpost either. No more giving up things for Lent. No more Easter Sunday outfits. No more Midnight Mass. No cocoa and cinnamon toast in the afternoons, no Lunch at the Waldorf. Just green dark in Mother's room with the green shades pulled down, the same green dark in Spring Creek when you dived deep and opened your eyes underwater.

When Mother lost her baby girl, we all lost Mother.

BIG ENOUGH TO feed an army, Father said, when he and Mother walked through the dark wood swinging doors into the dining hall. Father said it too loud, the way he said things when they were his, too loud in the place where everything was too loud, too bright, too big, too green, in the summer too hot—relieved only by the fan Mother bought when she was carrying the baby girl—and in the winter too cold. Never been so cold.

Mother smiled a little, the way she smiled at him, not a real smile. She wore her red housedress that day, and white ankle socks, and her Keds. I remember I told her she looked nice, and she said, I'm doing the best I can.

Bobbie got to choose her room before me because she was older and got things first. Bobbie chose the second floor for her room—even though she liked the sloping ceiling of the attic—because a bathroom was next to her room, and because she said she was tired of being always cheek to jowl with me, and also Bobbie wanted that side of the Residency because there was no Highway 30 on that side, no railroad tracks, only the red-brick barn, the arch of cottonwoods, and the foothills sloping up to hills and then to blue mountains and trees and snow in winter.

Bobbie's room was on the other side of the hallway and one floor down from me. Around the bottom of the room and around the doors, and the doors too, the same dark wood like in my room, like in the whole house. Bobbie's room was green and completely square, Bobbie said, and she knew because she measured it.

First thing Bobbie did after she chose which one was her room was get out her tape measure.

Bobbie tied the carpenter's apron around her waist, unscrewed the cap on the plastic bottle where she kept her finish nails, stuck her hammer in the hammer loop. The gold flecks in Bobbie's eyes shined, and her cropped hair was sticking up all over. Bobbie was wearing her red plaid shirt cut cowboy style with pearl buttons on the pockets. She'd cut the sleeves off and rolled them up so you could see her muscles. Then there was her Levi's and her Red Wing boots.

On the east wall of her room—I held the end of the tape—Bobbie made a mark with her carpenter's pencil and put the head of the dark wood single bed exactly half and half on each side of the pencil mark. Then the green rug exactly in the middle, same distance front and back from the ends of the bed.

The last thing we had to do—and this took damn near the whole day—was find the exact middle point side to side and up and down of the west wall of her room so Bobbie could thumbtack her map of the Known Universe with four red thumbtacks exactly in the middle of the wall.

When we finally got the map of the Known Universe exactly right, Bobbie and I made up her bed with the sheets and the two brown army blankets folded down like in the army the way she liked. Bobbie took her leather apron off, put the apron in her tool box, and lay down on the bed exactly straight, her arms along her sides and her legs out straight and Red Wing boots together and Bobbie looked down her body to the map of the Known Universe.

Perfect, Bobbie said.

Bobbie had such a good look on her face that I wanted to do it too—lie down exactly straight—and so she let me.

Perfect, I said.

The map of the Known Universe was the most beautiful thing Bobbie or I had. The map was the only thing allowed on the walls that wasn't Catholic.

Mostly I loved the map of the Known Universe because of the colors—deep blue background—and then red Mars and orange and red Jupiter and the white white moon and Earth's brown and green and blue, and purple Pluto and swimming-pool-blue Neptune, rose-colored Venus, red-and-yellow Saturn with orange around, and all the rest of them, planets and stars and moons, all in all colors.

The sun a still point in the turning universe.

The problem in both our bedrooms, the biggest problem with the whole house, Bobbie said, was the lights were bright fluorescent tubes from above, unrelenting, and while Bobbie liked how they were exactly in the center of the ceiling, Bobbie never turned those lights on, never.

Unrelenting, Bobbie said, Light from above, Bobbie said, Suicide light.

Good thing she had saved up her S&H Green Stamps for her white glass lamp, set on a wood fruit box spray-painted red.

The stereo hi-fi—which came on a chrome stand with rollers and a place for albums—Bobbie set exactly in the northeast corner at a forty-five-degree angle. In the chrome stand, placed so you could see both album covers, Bobbie's two albums, *Hits from the Movies* and Johnny Mathis, *Heavenly*.

Father bought Bobbie her stereo hi-fi. One day Father just rolled in the yard, after he'd been gone for God knows how long, with a stereo hi-fi for Bobbie but nothing for Mother or me.

The final touch was Bobbie tied one of Mother's scarves around her lamp. The scarf was the color of Marilyn Monroe's fuchsia dress when Marilyn sang "Diamonds Are a Girl's Best Friend" in *Gentlemen Prefer Blondes*, and it was a secret because Bobbie didn't tell Mother she pulled the scarf out of the trash the day Mother threw all her scarves away.

That night—after Father said, too loud, Make us some dinner, Ma!—Mother fixed us Swanson's Fish Sticks and canned peas and mixed ketchup and mayonnaise together for the sauce.

We ate dinner in the dining hall, our forks hard sounds onto the green walls when the forks hit the plates.

After Father excused us, Bobbie and I ran up to her room and turned on the lamp. Bobbie lay down on the bed exactly straight, her arms along her sides and her legs straight out and feet together.

The Marilyn Monroe scarf made a beautiful light in the room that made the planets of the map of the Known Universe glow.

Perfect, Bobbie, said, Just perfect.

Just perfect, I said.

MY ROOM WAS big with a shiny hardwood floor and around the bottom of the walls and around the door and the closet door was the dark brown wood. The walls were sloping green. Outside my window, thick branches, the sigh and scratch of cottonwood leaves. Past the cottonwood south to the railroad tracks and Highway 30 and, across the highway, was Viv's Double Wide House of Beauty.

Nothing else in the room, just the bed and the window. A green rug right along the side of the bed on the hardwood floor to put your feet on when you got up. No pictures on the walls, nothing Catholic.

In the room with the fireplace, we put the couch and the chair and the three-way floor lamp and the end table with the doily, and in front of the fireplace on the hardwood floor the flowered carpet, and the wagon-wheel coffee table on the carpet. We called the room the living room and it looked like dollhouse furniture in there, the green walls way far, the green ceiling way high.

The first winter, above the fireplace, fingers of black reached out of the fireplace and up the green wall, spreading soot like some hand from inside grasping onto the wall.

Chimney needs work! Father said, too loud, I'll take care of it! he said. But Father never took care.

The best place was the kitchen. Not the whole kitchen, because the whole kitchen was big enough to cook for an army, just the alcove part where the table was by the window. The big stove was right there, and we opened the oven door and turned the oven on full blast, and all the burners, and in the mornings before school we sat—Bobbie with Rice Krispies, me with Cheerios, Charlie 2Moons a disgusting mix of Cheerios and Rice Krispies, each of us with our cups of Nestlé Quik hot chocolate—on dark wood chairs in front of the stove with our feet up toasty on the open oven door, with all our clothes on, even our winter coats, and the army blanket over us.

I liked to be the one who got up first, so I could turn the oven on and all the burners and have the milk hot, not scalded—when we had milk; just hot water if we didn't—for the hot chocolate, and have the cereal out and the army blanket ready.

If Father wasn't home, Charlie was always there with us. Mother never said anything about Charlie, one way or the other, except one time when she got drunk. Charlie was like a stick of furniture to Mother. But then, so were Bobbie and I. Mother mostly stayed in her room with the dark green shades pulled down and only came out for coffee and Herbert Tareytons late in the morning and sometimes not at all.

At least she'd stopped running out into the field.

In the summer, you could open the window in the kitchen alcove and right outside was the cottonwood tree, and in the morning the sun came in the window, making a square of gold on the table, and you could sit in the square with the window open and hear the cottonwood and the wind and smell the smells in the wind, of grass—especially after the grass was mowed—and the smell of the cottonwood, and the geraniums Charlie got from Viv.

Viv was Charlie's mother, and Viv's Double Wide House of Beauty always had lots of customers, mostly Indian women. Some white women went to Viv too because Viv was so good with hair, but Mother never did because Mother never left the house. Besides, even if Mother did want her hair done by Viv, Father would never have allowed it.

Father hated Indians.

Ne'er-do-wells.

Especially Charlie.

THAT FIRST NIGHT in the Residency, Father slept on the screened-in porch. Then, later in the night, I heard him down in Bobbie's room, in Bobbie's Marilyn Monroe light with Bobbie.

Before sunrise, out my window, I watched his matching swimming-pool-blue Dodge pickup and trailer and horse trailer drive down the lane in between the cottonwoods to Highway 30 and turn left toward Pocatello. I watched Father's pickup until I couldn't see it anymore.

The next morning, our second day at the Residency, Charlie 2Moons came riding up on his horse, ayaHuaska.

I was out back behind the barn, when up the lane, the cottonwoods touching chandelabras across, I saw a boy on a horse.

The boy's hair was long and thick and almost to his shoulders; his skin was cinnamon brown. When he got close enough for me to see his eyes, that was it.

I was wounded by a blow of love.

Charlie pulled on the reins and ayaHuaska rared up a little. Charlie was big, an Indian; his long black hair was wavy. He was riding bareback and on the bridle was beadwork.

Charlie got off his horse.

Step over the fence! Charlie said. Come meet me! he said.

I knew because Bobbie'd told me that the fence was an electric fence, so I didn't step over, didn't say anything.

What's the matter, Charlie said, Cat got your tongue?

Even back then, the cat got my tongue.

So then Charlie 2Moons called me a fucking queer and threw a handful of gravel at me, and a piece of gravel got me hard next to my eye and I ran crying to Bobbie.

By the time Bobbie and I got back to behind the barn, Charlie 2Moons had disappeared. But Bobbie said, Just wait, he'll be back. So Bobbie and I waited and she was right, and pretty soon Charlie came galloping up the lane, and when he got to us, he pulled on the reins and his horse rared up a little.

Step over the fence! Charlie said. Come meet me! he said.

Eat shit and die, Geronimo, Bobbie said, and flipped Charlie the bird.

Charlie got off his horse and started dancing around making war whoops. He called Bobbie and me fucking *tybos,* called us fucking ugly greedy pink pig people, told us to get off Indian land, and then yelled at us that the place was haunted, the whole area was haunted because of all the Indian children who had died there, and we'd better get our old roses out of there quick or *Tsoavich* Big Foot would murder us and eat us alive, starting with the toes and fingers.

Come over here and say that to my face! Bobbie yelled. Come over here and I'll tell you a thing or two! So Charlie came over because Charlie was bigger than both Bobbie and me, and Charlie thought since Bobbie was a girl this would be a piece of cake. Charlie jumped over the electric fence, an antelope leaping, and came right at us.

Bobbie socked Charlie once hard in the face and then kicked him in the balls, and all at once Charlie was kneeling on the ground, holding himself and crying.

Bobbie took Charlie's long wavy black hair in a grip and pulled his head back. Charlie looking up, head twisted that way, made me all of a sudden sad, his dark eyes rolled back, tears making tracks down his dusty face. Bobbie open-handed Charlie a slap across his face and then again, Bobbie spit in his face—not a lunger, just a spray—and while she held his head back, Bobbie told Charlie 2Moons never to fuck with her or fuck with her little brother ever again and made Charlie promise.

Say it! Bobbie said.

I promise I won't fuck with you or fuck with your little brother ever again, Charlie said.

Then Bobbie said, I ought to make you pee on that electric fence, you goddamn bully.

But Bobbie didn't make Charlie pee on the electric fence, and after that day Bobbie and Charlie and I were best friends. Even though my father hated Charlie, Charlie and Bobbie and I were still the best friends that could ever be.

But it's not the truth.

Bobbie and I were brother and sister.

Charlie and I were the best friends that could ever be.

CHAPTER
THREE

The gods know what's important, what's wrong about you. They know everything. If you go out searching for the Holy Grail, they won't let you find it. So that's why, when I went out into Manhattan, what I did was not-search for Charlie. I'd crossed over the river of shit and I was in a world of hurt, and I was in Manhattan, in Wolf Swamp, and I just let the fuck-you city fuck me.

It's like the killdeer bird Charlie's Grandfather Alessandro pointed out. The killdeer plays a broken-wing trick on you, so you'll follow her as she moves away from her nest. She leads you away from what you really want. Then, after she's betrayed you, the killdeer bird leaves you alone in the middle of the desert in the twilight, she abandons you to what you've been looking for all your life. Yourself.

But there's no fooling the gods. The whole time the gods knew. My only intent, the only thing on my mind, the only reason I moved to New York City, was to find Charlie 2Moons. I looked in every face I came across for the liar's space between his teeth, Charlie's deep-set eyes, his wavy black hair, the scar. In the subways, in elevators, on the bus, on the bar stool next to me, at the café counter, in the toilets, I smelled for him.

Then at the end, when the shit was hitting the fan, after I hadn't eaten or slept for days and everybody in Wolf Swamp was either in the hospital or the loony bin or dead, there was a moment, just before the Dog Shit Park War, there was a moment I ended up forgetting about Charlie 2Moons.

It was only then, just like True Shot said, that I found him. Not the way I thought I'd find him, but I found him.

I mean, he found me.

* * *

NO ONE CAN tell this story the way I know it but me. It's the responsibility of the survivor to tell the story.

The first thing I did at 205 East Fifth Street, 1-A, was to open all the windows and turn the oscillating fan on high. I was down to boxer shorts and crotch rash, praying for a breeze. Alone and counting every penny.

I was creating a center with sweat equity: my home, the ex-cat palace. Cat-shit carpet, cat-sprayed walls, cat-litter bathroom, piss kitchen. Elbow grease, a new broom and mop, roach motels, Pine-Sol, and a box of Brillo. I was on my hands and knees.

Ruby was right: August and September in New York, everybody but the criminals are in Connecticut.

August and September, the way things go when you get home from a job interview with your suit pants stuck up your ass.

I was two hours standing in line at Con Ed. No Charlie 2Moons. Two hours standing in line at NYT&T. No Charlie 2Moons. One-hundred-dollar deposit for a red touch-tone phone. I was digging deep down in my pockets and my pockets weren't deep.

Sabrett sausages with sauerkraut and onions and mustard and ketchup. I stole cans of tuna fish from the A&P.

My résumé of northwest restaurants I'd worked in made me look like I knew what I was doing.

But it's not the truth.

I was from from Idaho and I was New York City fucking roadkill.

The Wine Bar was my first try. I chose the Wine Bar because of Vin et Vous, the correspondence course on fine wines I took in Jackson Hole.

I wore my gray sharkskin suit, a thin black tie, and a white shirt with a tab collar you snap under the tie. Polished my high-top grandpa shoes. Slicked my hair back—went through three whole tubes of mousse before I finally got a job—dumped my socks and underwear out of the old suitcase with the travel stickers on it, and put the red plastic see-through folder with my résumé of restaurants in the suitcase. On the corner of Second Avenue and St. Mark's Place, I bought a New York City map at Gem Spa, a store that sold a drink called Egg Cream that had nothing to do with eggs or cream.

SoHo. *South of Houston.*

The Wine Bar was busy. The maître d'hôtel, a beautiful man with black hair and olive skin, wearing a coke-bottle-green silk shirt, pleated black pants, and shoes with leather the color of Kraft caramels, asked me how many in my party.

I'm lunching alone, I said, and wondered if lunching was a word.

The beautiful maître d'hôtel looked down at my suitcase with the travel stickers on it and sat me in the corner.

No Charlie 2Moons, but I wasn't looking.

The busboy brought the French bread and I cleared my palate with the French bread. Ordered a glass of Zinfandel because the Zinfandel was fifty cents cheaper than the Merlot, went through the Vin et Vous ritual of swirling and gurgling the wine. Ordered a glass of Côtes-du Rhône, cleared my palate with the French bread, went through the Vin et Vous ritual of swirling and gurgling the wine. Ordered a glass of the Merlot—at that point the $6.50 wasn't that bad. Cleared my palate with the French bread, went through the ritual of swirling and gurgling.

Then the Beaujolais and the Oregon Pinot Noir, each time, the palate clearing, the swirling, the gurgling.

And the drinking.

Never did get it up to ask for a job.

The only thing on the Wine Bar menu in English was THE WINE BAR RESERVES THE RIGHT TO REFUSE SERVICE TO ANYONE.

My spray-starched tabbed white shirt was red polka dot with thousands of tiny spills of red wine on it.

Overexuberance with the swirling and the gurgling.

Vin et Moi.

L'addition: Thirty-eight dollars and fifty-six cents.

Mon Dieu.

Twenty percent tip, twice the tax, too drunk to figure.

I left the whole fifty-dollar bill, left the Wine Bar. Me and my suitcase with the travel stickers on it postured our disregard right out of there. Didn't knock anything important over, just an empty glass.

On my way home, no Charlie 2Moons. I looked at everybody as if they were already dead and I was dead too.

A ROLLS-ROYCE with the license plate DR LNDLRD was double-parked outside Ellen's Uncle David's office on Seventh Street betweeen First and Avenue A. There was a small waiting room with bad paneling and orange chairs and a vase on an end table with plastic red roses in it. Bullet-proof Plexiglas between me and a woman. When I asked to see Ellen Zigman Clavelle's Uncle David, the woman—bright red frizzy hair, a lime-green skirt and blouse, and half-glasses that hung around her neck by a strand of pearls—started at my feet and looked up, looked back down again, both times stopping her eyes just below my middle.

Speak up, honey, she said. Can't hear you.

Ellen Zigman Clavelle's Uncle David! I yelled through the Plexiglas. I'm subletting her apartment!

You got some ID? the woman asked.

I pulled out my wallet, took out my driver's license, and handed it to her. The woman took the driver's license and put it under the light on her desk. Lime-green espadrilles. She put her glasses on the end of her nose.

Idaho! she yelled, and threw her head back. Her glasses fell off her nose.

What is this license, she said, To ride a horse?

The woman had to sit down, she was laughing so hard.

Can I see him? I asked. Ellen said he's expecting me.

Who? the woman said.

Ellen's Uncle David, I said.

No, the woman said, You can't see him.

Isn't that his car outside? I said.

What car? the woman said.

The Rolls-Royce, I said. DOCTOR LANDLORD.

Dear Landlord, the woman said. You know the *song*, Bob Dylan. Yes, that's Mr. Zigman's car. But he's not here.

When can I see him? I asked.

Mr. Zigman is a busy man. I can take care of your business, she said, her eyes going up and down on me again.

She put her glasses back on her nose and pushed an envelope through the slot under the Plexiglas.

Sign where there's X's, she said.

I thought I was going to get Ellen's apartment, I said.

Speak louder, the woman said. Spit it out!

My mother's nerves.

I didn't get Ellen's apartment, I yelled. I got twenty years of cat hair.

Ellen didn't have any cats, the woman said.

Mrs. Lupino does, I said, And I got Mrs. Lupino's apartment 1-A. Not Ellen's 1-C.

The woman went back to her desk, adjusted the glasses on her nose, and looked through another envelope with papers.

Not according to my files, she said.

But Mrs. Lupino said—

Who? the woman said. Speak up!

Mrs. Lupino! I yelled.

Who's she? the woman asked.

The person in Ellen's apartment, I said.

Ellen's apartment is empty, the woman said.

I mean the person in 1-C, I said, Mrs. Lupino.

Oh, her? the woman said. The woman that had all the cats. Don't listen to her. She's *verüchte*. Thinks there're devil worshipers in the empty storefront below her.

Then: First and last month comes to thirteen hundred dollars, she said. I don't take cash.

The apartment was covered with cat hair, I said.

Ellen didn't have cats, the woman said. No pets allowed in any apartment.

The refrigerator is filthy, I said. Only one burner works on the stove.

Cupboards are new, the woman said. Kitchen sink is new. New linoleum put down just last year. Sign where there's X's.

I signed where there's X's. Signed the cashier's check.

Rent's due by the fifth of the month, the woman said.

Then: Hey, cowboy? Can you do that roll-up thing with the cigarette?

I don't smoke in the morning, I said.

Her eyes started at my feet and looked up, looked back down again, stopping her eyes just below my belt buckle.

And what else don't you do? the woman said.

Bulletproof. The Plexiglas was bulletproof.

A TALL WOMAN in a white silk dress with long auburn hair got in the passenger side of the DR LNDLRD Rolls-Royce, and the Rolls-Royce started driving off. I ran up to the Rolls, jogged alongside. All I could see was me running and smiling and waving in the window.

The window rolled down. Uncle David Dear Landlord was a man about my age, maybe a few years older. White shirt, paisley tie.

With a small silver revolver. Pointed right at me.

He was already dead. I was dead too.

THE APARTMENT BUZZER sounded like locusts. Took me awhile to get my pants on. Took me awhile with the buzzer. Took me awhile to unlock all the locks on the door.

Package for William of Heaven, UPS guy said. You William of Heaven?
Huh? I said and then: Yeah, that's me.
Nice name, man, UPS guy said, and handed me his clipboard with
the paper to sign.
Mrs. Lupino's door opened a crack.
When I was writing the *of Heaven* part, the UPS guy—who was dark
and chest high to me—said, Nice nips, man.
The gasp was not mine, it was from across the hall. Mrs. Lupino closed
her door.

THE UPS DELIVERY was an answering machine. A red answering machine.
The note:

> *Your telephone is lonely, so am I. NYT&T's got you by the calls.
> You got me by the balls.*
>
> Love, Ruby.

Ruby Prestigiacomo, how'd you know my phone was red?
Ruby Prestigiacomo, what am I going to do with you?
When I plugged the red telephone into the red answering machine,
and the red answering machine into the wall socket, the speaker message clicked on. It was Ruby.
*It is this way: To admit ignorance is the highest knowledge. It is the neces-
sary condition for all learning. Leave a message at the tone. Beep.*

IN 205 EAST Fifth Street, 1-A, breathing wasn't possible so I ripped up
the beige carpet and the foam pad. Felt like my hands had been var-
nished in cat piss. The cat-hair air between me and the light coming in
the windows was shiny like scratches on Plexiglas.
I cut the carpet and the foam pads into sections. One time, I had to
stop and sneeze, and got to sneezing so hard and so much I had to go
outside. I stood in the rectangle of earth where I'd plant the cherry tree.
Finally I just said to hell with it and started throwing the carpet sections and padding out the window, the sections landing in the part lower
than the sidewalk with the iron fence around it next to the cast-iron steps.
Carpet and foam pads hung over the cast-iron fence all across the
sidewalk. I stacked them into two big piles next to the garbage cans, so
there was enough space to walk.

That's when Mrs. Lupino opened her window.

You can't do that, Mrs. Lupino said.

Do what? I said.

Put household articles out in bulk like that, she said.

What am I, I said, Supposed to do with it?

Ask Ricardo, she said.

Who's Ricardo? I said.

The super, she said.

Super? I said. What's that?

What's a *super*? Mrs. Lupino said.

Shit from New York Shinola.

The custodian, she said. You know, the superintendent. The guy who takes care of the building.

Where is he? I asked.

Who knows? she said.

How can I get hold of him? I asked.

You can't, Mrs. Lupino said, Unless you catch him in the building for some reason. But he's never in the building.

But, I said, He takes care of the building.

You got that right, she said.

Then: There's a kid who sets the garbage cans back on Mondays, Wednesdays, Fridays, and Saturdays, Mrs. Lupino said. Ricardo's kid, I guess. But it won't do you any good talking to the kid, unless you speak Spanish. Even if you do, it won't help.

So what do I do, I said, With this carpet?

There's a day for bulk pickup and a number to call, but I don't know them, she said. If you just leave this shit out here, Ricardo will get a citation and he'll have your ass. If Ricardo don't kill you right out, he'll put a voodoo curse on your fucking ass so you wish you were dead, and don't say I didn't warn you.

But I can't live with this cat-shit smell, I said. And the cat hair. How many cats did you have in there?

I don't know what you're talking about, Mrs. Lupino said, And I don't care, she said. So go fuck yourself.

Mrs. Lupino slammed her window down and stood at the window and kept on yelling at me, cats crawling all over her.

I looked both ways on the street for Ricardo, the super, the voodoo custodian who was going to put a voodoo curse on my fucking ass.

As I looked, there was a sound, a huge roar down the street. An orange Dumpster crashed down off a truck onto the asphalt.

The way I did it was I rolled up sections of carpet and sections of foam pad. I walked like I knew what I was doing, walking causually around with carpet and foam pads under my arm. When I got to the Dumpster, I kept walking, didn't break my stride, just tossed the sections of carpet and foam pad into the Dumpster and walked on like I had never seen a stained beige cat-piss saturated carpet and crusty foam pad in all my life. Did that eleven times, then bought a cup of coffee at Café 103. The jukebox was playing my favorite Blondie song about the monster that ate everything. No Charlie 2Moons. I finished the coffee and returned to the scene of my crime.

Two guys were standing in the Dumpster, and the back gate of the Dumpster was open. One of the two guys, the one who was probably Ricardo the voodoo custodian, said he was going to fucking kill the motherfucker who'd dumped that motherfucking shit in there.

Didn't stop, didn't look, just kept walking.

New York drop-dead fuck-you was easier than I thought.

THE REFRIGERATOR LOOKED like an old '53 DeSoto. I moved it out from the wall, and cockroaches and mice went every which way. Had to stop and roll a cigarette. Hundreds of crusty scurryings back into vasty dark. Same with under the sink. Under the sink it was alive. Fuck roach motels, I needed a roach grenade.

I unplugged the DeSoto and filled the garbage can with four jumbo kosher pickle jars, mostly juice, a crusted jar of Grey Poupon, a box of Jiffy mix, six cans of opened cat food, and whatever else was in the refrigerator. I carried the garbage out and dumped it in the cans out front. Then I carried out what was in the freezer—didn't check to see what was inside the four foil-wrapped bundles—just pried the bundles from the glacier in the freezer, carried them out, and dumped them, ice and all, into a garbage can.

When I got back from the hardware store, there was an old man sitting on the sidewalk. He had taken all the jars from the garbage can and set them around him. He was dipping a pickle into the Grey Poupon and he ate the pickle. The four frozen bundles were stacked next to him: unwrapped frozen cats, thawing puddles onto the sidewalk.

Hardwood floor was under the beige cat-piss carpet. Brillo scrub and Murphy Oil Soap made it shine but didn't take away the stink.

* * *

ONE NIGHT, I think it was the night after I scrubbed my beige fake-tile linoleum kitchen floor, I heard somebody singing. All the windows open, sitting on the toilet reading *New Yorker* cartoons. The apartment was the color of the sunset. I crawled on my hands and knees through the apartment on my shiny hardwood floor to the corner by the window, peeked out.

Ruby was standing in the rectangle of earth where I'd plant the cherry tree. He was playing a guitar and his hair was wet, slicked down, looking like he'd just showered.

Come down, come down from your Ivory Tower, Ruby sang. *It's cold, so cold, in your Ivory Tower, and warm, so warm in my heart.*

On the hardwood floor, leaning up against the wall, I was rolling a cigarette. Ruby couldn't see me. My mother's nerves.

I was hiding.

The tracks on Ruby's arms, the purple bumps. His breath when he was close, something sweet like flavored mouthwash or fresh gum. There was something else about the sweet.

The truth was, Ruby was a heroin-addicted hippie with skin problems. Ruby was a ne'er-do-well.

I couldn't have sex with a ne'er-do-well, or anybody. Male, female, dildo, vibrator, dog, cat, goat. *Personne.* No sex for me, none.

Not since Charlie.

Jamais.

My rolled cigarette was in the palm of my hand. I didn't light it. Outside, Ruby sang something Italian. Mario Lanza wavy opera voice loud on East Fifth Street. When Ruby stopped singing, somebody clapped.

Silence from Ruby for a long time. Then—not for me to hear—just like he was talking to himself, Ruby said, William of Heaven, what am I going to do with you?

THE BATHROOM WAS just big enough to turn around in, a big sag in the floor at the base of the toilet, one corner of the shower unit duct-taped, a beige plastic curtain, scum-brown toilet bowl, one narrow opaque window. Cat hair in the shower, in the sink, a cat-hair rug around the toilet. Behind the bathroom door, the full-length mirror screwed to the door whanged my body out in bulges, the light from the fluorescent halo on the ceiling unrelenting from above, light you should never look at yourself in the mirror in.

The shower curtain was held together by mildew. When I pulled it back, a cockroach went up my pant leg. I yelled like a murder victim, and just like that I was naked from the waist down, shaking out my pants, checking my butt crack and balls.

That called for another cigarette.

I fixed the toilet so it would flush, swept the kitty litter and cat shit out of the shower and from behind the toilet. No way that bowl would ever not be brown. Under the toilet the beige fake-tile linoleum curled up; under the linoleum, dry rot. Sprayed the dry rot with Raid.

The on-sale paint was red, real red, the red like lipstick. I had to buy a ladder, too. I started with the ceilings first. Then the walls in the front part. The red paint onto the yellow tobacco-stained walls, the line where the red paint stopped and the tobacco yellow began, made me want to throw up.

About halfway, I started running out of red paint, so I bought two gallons of cheap white and mixed the white in with the red. The color of your cock after choking the chicken. The red-pink paint on the tobacco-yellow walls was even worse.

The worst was the pink in the bathroom. The bathroom was the last room and the bottom of the paint can, so there were streaks of white and streaks of red.

THE DAY I painted the bathroom, my red answering machine clicked on.

It is this way. To admit ignorance is the highest knowledge, Ruby's voice said, *It is the necessary condition for all learning. Leave a message. Beep.*

It was Ruby.

Autumn Sonata, Ruby said.

There was a siren going by on Ruby's end, and the traffic was loud.

I went to pick up, then didn't pick up.

It's this movie, Ruby said, About a mother, Ingrid Bergman, and her daughter, Liv Ullmann, and Liv is pissed at Ingrid because Ingrid was such a shitty mother.

Sounded like Ruby struck a kitchen match against the telephone speaker and deep-inhaled.

That's when Ingrid Bergman says this great thing to Liv Ullman, Ruby said. Ingrid says she's forgotten her life. Her life just passed her by somehow and the reason, she said, was because she didn't have a Talent for Reality.

What a Talent for Reality is, my dear William of Heaven, Ruby said, Is acknowledging that you're here and remembering it. And those two things—being present in your moments and then remembering your moments—is the only way you can make it in Wolf Swamp.

I'm a lot like Ingrid, Ruby said.

But there's still hope for you, Ruby said.

It's a Bergman film—Ingmar Bergman, not Ingrid, Ruby said. Ingrid's just in it. Every once in a while you can catch it over at the Film Forum.

Autumn Sonata, Ruby said. Let's you and me go see it sometime, OK?

Ruby, beloved, beloved Ruby.

You were already dead. I was still dead.

A talent for reality, I had not.

THE CHEAPEST PLACE for futons was on Sixth Avenue. The guy who sold me the futon was a Sikh and had his head wrapped in a turban. Eighty-nine dollars. The futon was covered with plastic. I set the futon on the sidewalk bent like a horseshoe; then I crawled into the bend, stood up, adjusted the futon on my head, and walked home carrying the futon on my head, only able to see a couple of feet in front of me. Three blocks and five avenues. One hundred degrees that day. The worst was the plastic rubbing against my head and neck. I should never have taken Eighth Street, with its narrow sidewalks.

Got called a stupid motherfucker at least a hundred times.

Fuck you, I said back a hundred times, but I don't think anybody heard me.

PLAIN WHITE SHEETS on the futon and a white pillowcase on the feather pillow. The army blanket folded down the way Bobbie liked it. Next to the futon, my ashtray—an old green plate I found on the street. Next to the green plate, on a chipped white plate, a cone of incense burning, Mountain Pine. Mountain Pine still no match for City Cat. Next to the white plate, the oscillating fan. Next to the oscillating fan the red telephone. Next to the red telephone, the red answering machine.

The table in the front window. I used the ladder for a chair. I found the table next to the garbage cans in the middle of the block on East Fifth between First and Second, next to the Ninth Precinct—a chrome *Father Knows Best* table plain as day, out on the sidewalk.

Interesting juxtaposition, architecturally, I thought—the table and the ladder in front of the window.

Out the back window, across the courtyard, was a smaller building, three floors. One night when I looked out, the lights were all on on the bottom floor, soft rose-colored light. A man sat reading a magazine in a wingback armchair, under a lamp, by a table. He wore a starched white shirt with the sleeves rolled up, and a striped tie loosened at the neck. His hair was black and slicked back like he'd just showered. He wasn't wearing pants. Through the opening of his shirt at the bottom, the white of his underwear. The black hair on his legs was the same as the black hair on his arms. He wore shoes, shiny black dress shoes, and argyle socks, and garters around the calves of his legs. Newspapers spread out all around him on the floor.

Just like that, like he knew I was watching, he pulled his white jockey shorts down to his knees, opened his knees wide, stretching the white shorts, and started jerking off. The magazine fell to the floor. The man stopped, pumped again, and then quick grabbed for the telephone, cradled the receiver in his neck, dialed a number with his free hand.

My red telephone rang.

E.T., phone home.

But it's not the truth.

The man talked into the phone, arching his body up and up, his shiny black dress shoes on the newspaper, pointing his cock down, splashing onto the newspaper.

Then he hung up and just sat there and stared at the floor. I could see his heart beating in his chest and belly, he was that close. Then the man pulled up his legs under him, curled himself into the chair, reached for the light, and turned the light out.

TO THE LEFT of the eleven cast-iron steps at 205 East Fifth Street, three cement steps go down to the ground-floor entrance. There's a glass door there with a poster, a picture of the Sacred Heart of Jesus. Jesus points to his bloody heart that's on fire, his heart clutched by a crown of thorns more like barbed wire. What the poster says in swirly letters just opposite the Sacred Heart of Jesus is STRANDED BEINGS SEARCH-ING FOR GOD.

When you get up closer to the poster, you can read about the revival meeting for Charismatic Catholics that was held in October of 1978.

Then there's the three Polaroids across the bottom.

Under the first Polaroid it says: Woman Being Possessed by the Devil. The woman's black hair is sticking up and she's not wearing makeup and her eyes are rolling up into the top of her head and she's wearing a gunnysack.

Under the second Polaroid it says: Woman Being Healed by the Word of the Lord. A priest is holding his hands over the woman's head and her eyes are still rolled up, but her hands are folded the way when you pray.

Under the third Polaroid it says: Woman Healed by the Word of the Lord, Alleluia! The woman is smiling and she's looking right at you and there's a pink bow in her hair and her hair is a pageboy and she's wearing a pink dress.

MRS. LUPINO OPENED her door when I opened my door on my way to the Laundromat.

I know what they're doing downstairs, Mrs. Lupino said and raised her swoops of eyebrow pencil.

The devil is gathering forces, Mrs. Lupino said.

No Charlie 2Moons at the Laundromat. The heat inside was worse because of the dryers and the smell of detergent and that fresh-smell stuff you throw in the dryer with your clothes. The robin's-egg-blue walls and beige linoleum, the tubes of fluorescent light, unrelenting from the acoustic-tile ceiling.

The line of chairs down the middle of the room was orange and curvy plastic. Everyone was smoking. The washing machines all going, the dryers. Three or four big black flies bouncing inside the windows.

All the washing machines were full except for three that were broken. The bulletin board next to the change machine had signs about a lost cat, Tai Chi classes, and an apartment sale; free Drake College Take Control of Your Life brochures; photographs of missing children.

I changed my five-dollar bill into dollars and my dollars into quarters, and on the last dollar the change machine ripped me off for seventy-five cents.

It was noisy in the Laundromat, plus the woman attendant didn't speak English, so I was shit out of luck.

A couple of times, when a washing machine went into the last cycle, I grabbed my duffel bag and started toward the machine, but—twice this happened—just as I got there somebody stepped in front of me.

Finally I got to a machine in time. I turned around, leaned against the washing machine, held my arms out in front of it.

In all the world, I am standing in front of a beige washing machine in a robin's-egg-blue room that's too hot, unrelenting fluorescence from above, sun through the dirty front windows squint-bright, Tide, Era, Downy Fabric Softener, cigarette smoke, sweaty bodies, orange curvy plastic chairs, flies buzzing.

Two men and two women—four people—just trying to get their wash done like me, were standing right there, ready to pounce on the washing machine I held my hands in front of. Four people staring at me, white people, nice, probably good educations—a philosophy major, maybe, physical therapist, movie extra, office temp—staring at my washing machine, ready with their laundry bags and detergents and fabric softeners, waiting for me to make my move.

The problem was, at the washing machine next to the one I was guarding, the guy was taking his wash out—so now there were *two* washing machines available that I was putting my body in front of, stretching my arms out over.

The problem was, I was pressed against the washing machines and my duffel bag was over on the orange curvy plastic chair, too far away to stretch to.

Hell of a fix. Up Shit Creek. In a world of hurt.

These are *my* beige washing machines and you can't have them, I said.

It's been over an hour, I said.

It was no use. I was the baby rabbit. They were the wolves.

My voice was loud and each word that came out of my mouth was a complete word, an uttered word, not stuttered.

You better watch your asses, I said, I'm a Crossover, I said, And whatever happens to me, happens because I'm afraid of it happening.

Then: To admit ignorance is the highest form of knowledge, I said. It is the necessary condition for all learning.

Then: Tony Orlando and Dawn, I said.

The two men went down first, back to their orange curvy plastic chairs. The women didn't advance but they didn't retreat either. The one woman looked over to the other woman.

Fools rush in where wise men never go, I said.

My mother never loved any of her children, I said.

Then: Famous potatoes, I said.

The two women went back to their orange plastic curvy chairs, sat down.

New York drop-dead fuck-you.

One step, two steps, three steps over to my duffel bag, dragged my duffel bag over to my washing machines.

No Charlie 2Moons in the Laundromat, but Rose was there. I hadn't met him yet. But I remember his black hole in the fluorescence. Rose was sitting at the end of the line of plastic curvy chairs, staring at me over his rhinestoned cat's-eyes reading spectacles. His hair was a blond shag. Baggy colorful Bermudas. Long huge black feet, perfect toenails. Thongs. He was smoking a cigarette, fatter than American cigarettes, no filter. French. His one leg crossed over the other, the leg bouncing. He was reading a magazine, The Atlantic, his T-shirt swimming-pool blue with red letters. The T-shirt said FUCK APARTHEID.

LIFE CAFÉ IS called Life Café because all the walls are covered with Life magazine covers: Dwight Eisenhower, Vivien Leigh, Susan Hayward, Dag Hammarskjöld, Adlai Stevenson, Elizabeth Taylor, the Atom Bomb.

The people at Life Café—hair the way I had mine in the sixties. All of them in black, every once in a while a flannel checkered shirt. Vegans: beans and rice, carrot juice, bottled water.

No Charlie 2Moons in Life Café.

Ruby wouldn't stop calling, so I figured if I went out, had lunch with Ruby, talked sense to him, that Ruby would leave me alone.

If wishes were horses then beggars would ride.

Ruby and I sat at the table in the alcove that was the smoking section of the restaurant. Right above Ruby's head was Lana Turner the way she looked in Imitation of Life. Lana Turner was staring at me. Ruby ordered coffee and a cinnamon roll and I ordered a carrot muffin and cappuccino.

Ruby was dressed the same as last time—all in red, shiny red second-hand polyester, a shirt collar airplane wings flying out from under his chin. Red polyester pants with lumpy knees, brown boots with a gold ring on the side, worn-down heels. In daylight, Ruby looked older and even more beat up. But underneath the beat-up, ever-beautiful, according to Duke Ellington. It was like Ruby was an actor playing a role, street and drugs makeup put on him so he looked tired and gray, but really he was Paul Newman or Matt Dillon or somebody healthy and handsome like that.

How's your buddy True Shot? I said. Doesn't he have lunch socially?

Ruby leaned closer, put his hand on my wrist.

Sweet mouthwash, fresh gum.

Something you got to know about Life Café, man, Ruby said. It's a café all right, and it's actually physically here on Tenth and B, but really what Life Café is is an attitude. Life Café is a way of looking at the world. It's a lifestyle. Life Café lifestyle—so Eighties, you know, so predictable according to Noam Chomsky: Disco is out and Café Society is in, Ruby said.

Yeah, Ruby said, It's like when you travel you put yourself in travel mode, right? You just go with what's going to happen next—the rental car, the next restaurant, where you'll stop to pee—you just let things come as they come. So why wait for travel to go into travel mode? Why not just live your life in travel mode? Life happens that way anyway, man. *You* might as well.

Travel mode is the key, Ruby said.

Ruby had white frosting on his soul patch under his chin. His Duke Ellington smile.

Do you think True Shot would ever tell me the secret of Wolf Swamp? I said.

So when people want me to make plans, Ruby said, Want me to make cosmos out of chaos, when people ask me if or when we should meet or where, I just say, See you at Life Café, man. And you know, it always works out.

Then Ruby, just like that, got up off his chair, then stepped up onto his chair and started dancing like he was à go go.

Party at Life Café, Ruby said. So Noam Chomsky, Ruby said. Don't these people know that disco is back in?

The waitress with green hair and ears full of earrings brought us the check. Back behind the cash register and the counter, men who worked in the kitchen, brown men in white, big brown men in white, were at attention, wiping their hands on their aprons, staring at me and Ruby.

I put a twenty down on the check, and the waitress with green hair picked up the twenty and walked quick to the cash register.

Ruby stopped dancing and put his arms up in the air: Evita.

Everybody in the restaurant acting like they were already dead and wished Ruby was dead too.

In Wolf Swamp, Ruby said loud, You'll find a concentration of two types of people: pharisees and fools, Ruby said.

Hey, Ruby, I said, Travel mode is the key, I said, Let's travel on out of here.

Ruby looked down at me from his lofty height on the chair.

Pharisees, he said, Are directed by laws, rites, and ceremonies, are logical and consistent, are focused on values and in love with the power of adding zeros to existing values—are moral, sexually defined, are breast- beaters, squares, promote conformation and exchange, and, if you ask them how they're feeling, will tell you what they're thinking.

The waitress kept her body far away from Ruby when she brought back the change.

Twice the tax, about two dollars.

Let's go, Ruby, I said. Come on, let's go.

But Ruby wouldn't budge.

Fools are directed by spirit and original impulses of the heart, Ruby said, Are illogical and inconsistent, are focused on zero and in love with the power of fixing a center in nothing—are amoral, sexually ambivalent, are tail-eaters, run around in circles, promote transformation and change, and are, if you ask them how they're feeling, scared and lonely.

I grabbed Ruby by the arm and pulled him down off the chair and Ruby walked alongside me, but he wasn't really alongside, he was somewhere else. Not on the premises. The whole time I walked out with Ruby, through the tables and the *Life* magazines, Ruby talking talking.

Fools create, Ruby said, Pharisees assess.

You find pharisees in a center like New York because getting rich, getting laid, and getting success is what the pharisee is about—and commerce, religion, sex, and power are the very nature of the center.

An old guy with a long gray beard, barefoot, just with a pair of pants tied on with string, walked by. I smelled him before I saw him. He and his seven big black Labradors that followed him.

Now, don't get me wrong, Ruby said. Even fools want to get rich, get laid, and get success, but that's not what the fool is about. The main reason you find so many fools in a center like New York is because it's the perfect place to hide.

All fools are fools because they weren't invited to the party, Ruby said. The fool moves to New York because New York is the party. The fool takes up residence in the party so he won't ever have to feel he isn't invited.

Ruby, I said, Is that Dog Shit Park?

That's when I saw Ruby's arms, I mean really saw them. Bright sunlight on the deep blue tracks and purple berries on Ruby's beautiful forearms.

Now Harlequin is a fool with consciousness, Ruby said, A fool who puts on a costume. The difference between a fool and Harlequin is Harlequin knows he is hiding.

Ruby took me by the shoulders and shook my shoulders.

Deep blue tracks, purple berries, on Ruby's beautiful forearms.

Harlequin *knows* he's hiding, Ruby said.

That's the crossover, Ruby said. If you understand that Harlequin is a costume—that the costume is the fool's concept of zero, and that the difference between the fool and Harlequin is Harlequin knows he's hiding—then you will know what's important about New York, about why you've come to New York.

I took Ruby's hands off my shoulders. I wasn't gentle.

Ruby's smile.

So, my dear William of Heaven, Ruby said, Why don't you roll me up one of your cigarettes?

I rolled a cigarette for Ruby and one for me and lit them both.

Ruby inhaled.

A fool can't go around looking like a fool, Ruby said, Or he'll end up New York fucking roadkill.

So put your costume on, honey! Ruby said. Set Harlequin free! That party monster of yours is screaming to come out. Let the monster out!

Ruby, I said, What's that shit on your arms?

What makes a monster scary, Ruby said, Is that he knows everything about you. What makes a monster scary is his gift.

Manhattan is a monster, Ruby said. A dragon. And the thing about Manhattan Dragon is he knows everything about you—what's important, what's wrong, why you stay the way you are. And the secret the Dragon reveals, Ruby said, Is the truth you'd rather run from, rather fall apart than face.

On Tenth and B, in front of the Life Café, the bright sun through the leaves of the English elms, the English elms of Dog Shit Park talking to me.

That afternoon on the northwest corner is where I left Ruby Prestigiacomo.

Ruby yelling at me: William of Heaven! William of Heaven! I love you! I love you! William of Heaven, what am I going to do with you?

I BOUGHT A LAMP the shape of a wagon wheel with cowboys and Indians riding on horses on the lampshade.

I bought a Sony Walkman and a tape with the sounds of a babbling brook on it and wind in the trees.

I bought a boom box.

Ruby kept calling calling.

I went to pick up but didn't pick up.

After a while, Ruby's messages changed. He didn't speak. He left long messages of street noise. Sometimes of Ruby coughing.

On one message, a car alarm went off.

Car alarm—every time you hear a car alarm, Ruby said, Another New Yorker has gone to hell.

TAKE THE R uptown to 42nd Street, then switch to the number 1 uptown and get off at a 116th Street.

It sounds easy enough, but the first time in New York City's subways, crowded into an underground boxcar, clutching the subway map in one hand, a chrome pole in the other, your breath in and out, in and out, trying to look like you know what you're doing, going from the R to the number 1, wandering around beneath Times Square, following the signs—half the time there ain't no signs—the loud metal screech and wail, wall-to-wall people looking like they're dead and wishing you were dead too, everybody in such a hurry, makes you wish for a bareback horse and for riding free through a clear Idaho day, the June grass fancy with wind, the wind lips at your ear, the wind in the leaves of the cottonwoods' sigh and scratch.

Dodge Hall is just on your left as you go through the gates from Broadway. Second story, turn right at the end of the hallway: the Columbia Writing Program. Young men and women, all collegiate-looking New England types, like they just got off the *Mayflower*, all of them, each one looking like they knew what they were doing, savoir faire.

The secretary's name was Janet and she had short dark-red hair, freckles on her skin. She wore a purple-blue dress. I sat down in a big wood chair, smiled big, and told her the name.

Charlie? Janet said. I remember Charlie. He dropped out of the program after Sebastian Cooke went on sabbatical. Last winter, Janet said.

Can you tell me where Charlie lives? I said.

Janet had that business smile that's polite when you've gone too far.

I'm sorry, Janet said, I can't do that.

Behind Janet were big windows, the old kind of big windows like in Saint Joseph's School that were dark wood and you need a long stick

with a hook on the end to open the top part. The top part of the windows were open. It was already a hot day.

My face was still smiling.

I've come a long way, I said, To find Charlie 2Moons, I said, It's very
very important, I said. I must give him a message.

Janet just kept smiling like you do when you don't know what else
to do.

On my way out, when I was at the door, Janet said, I do hope he's all
right!

Was he sick? I said.

No, Janet said, quick, It's just that I worry about him.

The gay cancer? I said.

Janet quick pulled a tissue from a tissue box and swiveled her chair
around to face the big wood windows.

The sun was shining on the green leaves of the trees. No wind. Just
bright sun on leaves.

Janet blew her nose, and when Janet turned around again, she looked
like she knew what she was doing. She thought. I could see the tears.

Charlie 2Moons is a very gifted young man, Janet said. And a dreamboat, Janet said. A real charmer.

Janet's smile wasn't a business smile anymore, just a smile.

I think the whole place was in love with him, Janet said. When he left
the program, Charlie was living in Columbia housing, but now that he
has left, I don't know where he's moved and he left no forwarding address.

Janet reached for another tissue, dabbed at her eyes, blew her nose.

What about this Sebastian Cooke? I said. Can you tell me how to
get in touch with him?

Sebastian Cooke is in Paris, Janet said. Have you read his book on
Andy Warhol?

Charlie's? I said.

Sebastian's, Janet said.

No, I said.

It's fantastic, Janet said.

Where in Paris? I said.

Janet's breath in, her breath out. Janet leaned her head onto her hand.
I went to touch her arm, but didn't.

Why are you crying? I said. What's the matter with Charlie?

Janet looked up at me, tears down her cheeks. Her nose was red. She
made a gesture with her hand, the tissue in her hand, waving, not at
me, but waving things to the side, out of the way.

Give me your phone number, Janet said, And I'll be in touch with you.

On a piece of scrap paper, I wrote down my name and phone number.

Here's my card, Janet said. We'll be in touch.

In my wallet, next to the Romeo Movers card, I put Janet's business card.

In all the world, my cowboy boots walking down the marble steps of Dodge Hall, with each step my lips moved with the syllables of his name.

Char-

lie

2

Moons.

Se-

bas-

tian

Cooke.

Char-

lie

2

Moons.

CHAPTER
FOUR

Café Bistro on 46th Street was where I finally got a job.

My first day at work, as soon as I walked in the front door, Daniel, the boss's brother, lifted his wrist up, shirtsleeve rolled to the elbow, hairy arm, Rolex.

Thought your horse mighta threw ya, Daniel said. Or were you planting your potato over at Show World?

Show World?

Don't ever fucking be late again! Daniel said.

Daniel's face was a mask over his face, handsome underneath like Ruby, but while Ruby was turning into a skeleton, Daniel's face was something still alive floating in old water.

Find Muffy, Daniel said. Muffy's the one training you.

Through the swinging red doors was a room, like a parlor, shelves from floor to ceiling, two espresso machines, a long counter. A person sat behind another counter and a cash register. To the right was an arch and the dish room—stacks of glass racks, old-food smell, the dishwasher loud, steam and spray.

My mother's nerves.

Through the arch in front of me, two stories high, was the kitchen. Red-brick walls, shiny cement floor painted gray, stainless-steel shelves and racks and countertops, steam rising, smoke, the air full of hanging pots and pans. Frying grease. Convection oven air blasting. A side of beef lying on a butcher block. Lamb hanging from a hook. Unrelenting fluorescence from above.

Pots and pans slamming together. Little Asian men, all in white, white caps, yelling.

Muffy? I said. My voice a tiny thing in the bright loud room.

A man on the other side of a stainless-steel counter was chopping lettuce.

Muffy? I said to him, smiled.

The man yelled some kind of kung fu, slammed the knife down on the cutting board—lettuce every which way—then waved it in the air between me and him; he slashed the knife back and forth, brought the knife back behind his head, threw the knife past my ear into a cardboard box of Idaho potatoes behind me.

Hell of a fix. Up Shit Creek. In a world of hurt.

Everyone in the kitchen laughing, Asian men all looking at me, laughing.

Then: Eat! Eat! Kung Fu lettuce guy yelled.

Another man from behind the steam table yelled, Plate! Plate!—pointing at a pile of plates—Eat! Eat!

Rice and a thick stew with meat that was gray.

Kung Fu lettuce guy threw a plate of lettuce onto the stainless-steel counter. Salad! Salad! he yelled. Eat! Eat!

In the dining room, back out through the swinging red doors, a round table of brown men all staring at me. I walked past the table with the plate of thick stew with meat that was gray, the plate of salad. Brown men in white bus coats and white shirts, laughing.

Then: two men and a woman sitting at a table. Waiters. White people.

My name's Will, I said. I'm the new waiter. May I join you?

The men didn't look up; finally the woman did, right at me.

No, the woman said, looking back to her crossword puzzle. That place is saved for Mack.

Mack? I said.

Mack Dickson, she said.

The two men looked at me, looked me up and down. What's important. What's wrong. Went back to eating deli sandwiches.

My deep breath. The exhale brought my eyes to the ceiling. Painted up there, the Sistine Chapel God extended his finger and Man reached out for it, the way we'll always reach.

Other places on the ceiling were clouds and cherubs and pastoral settings. The walls were mirrors. Two columns, Corinthian, divided the room. A wall made to look like a crumbling wall connected the two columns just high enough for privacy on the banquettes. The bar carved maple; a mirror in the bar back; the bar top, zinc.

All the tables were covered with linen and over the linen pieces of butcher paper. On each table a small jar filled with crayons.

On the table where I sat down alone, from the jar, I picked a red Crayola, and with the red Crayola I drew one big red circle on the butcher paper.

* * *

YOU'RE GOING THIS way and then shit happens and then you're going that way.

The moment that after you're different.

Welcome to Café Cauchemar, she said.

The chandelier behind her. I looked for her shadow on the table. Curly black hair poked up under a Yankee cap, a T-shirt, nipples through the pink Day-Glo T-shirt, ninety-eight pounds, black bicycle pants, the book she was holding, Joseph Campbell's *Myths to Live By*.

Fiona. I looked up from the red circle and there was Fiona. I put both feet parallel on the floor, my back straight up against the chair, rested my arms around my middle, chin out, shoulders square, new-shoe stiff, big smile.

When the woman is beautiful, before I know it, my body is at attention.

What's important. What's wrong.

Deep blue eyes, white white skin. Something wild about her mouth.

I had to take another breath.

Her upper lip a life all its own.

When she smiled, the scar.

Cauchemar? I said. Isn't this Café Bistro?

Nightmare Café, Fiona said. It's French. I'm the one who's training you.

You're Muffy?

No, Fiona said, her lip New York drop-dead fuck-you. My name is not Muffy. My name is Susan, Fiona said, Susan Strong.

Oh, I said. Daniel said that Muffy was the one.

Susan! Susan *Strong*, Fiona said.

Fiona pointed her index straight at my nose.

Listen up, she said. This is important, she said. Not Muffy! I'm not Muffy anymore. I'm Susan Strong. Understand?

Things start where you don't know.

When I met her, she was Muffy MacIlvane trying to be Susan Strong. She wasn't Fiona yet. Not yet. It was only at the end, after Ruby named her, that she became Fiona.

FROM UNDER THE chandelier, we went to the three waiters' stations, then to the bar. Then through the swinging red doors to the parlor, through the archway into the kitchen, Fiona talking talking.

Café Bistro, Café Cauchemar, Fiona said, A bistro owned by a Jew, its authentic French cuisine cooked by Thais, tables cleaned and bused, your cappuccino delivered by Puerto Rican busboys when you can find them, dishes washed by Mexicans, served by the generally white, almost young, not quite beautiful *l'Amérique Profond* survivor smiling the drop-dead smile—the actor, singer, dancer, the presenter of the finest medley of fresh vegetables, the musaline sabayon sauce at your table, the ironed white shirt, the black bow tie, the spotted black pants, black sensible shoes, the clean white apron, hair pulled back, fresh-lipsticked unisex clean-shaven slave to attitude, the faggot, the Broadway baby, the hopeful fool this city feeds on, at your table, at your service: the waiters.

The waiters are Davey Dearest and Walter, and Joanie and Mack, Fiona said, Besides me and Harry. Joanie's the worst, one of those fashion disasters who gets all her hair cut off and wears too much lipstick and four earrings in each ear. Be different if she was a lesbian, would give meaning to such heavy accessorization and a reason for being such a bitch.

Then there's *Homo perfectus*, Mack Dickson—Mack Son of Dick. Whatever you do, you don't want to incur the wrath of Mack Dickson. *Thee . . . perfect . . . gay . . . man*. A Mack Attack is hard to survive. Mr. Poopy Pants himself, Big Baby Torpor right there in front of your eyes. Total Caravaggio—did you see the movie? *Caravaggio?* Fiona asked. Harry and I decided that movie should have been subtitled: *or How I Lost My Mind to Have a Perfect Body*. Derek Jarman needs to get a life.

A real Nazi with a tortured gym body—Mack Dickson, Fiona said, Voted for Ronald Reagan and proud of it. Coordinates his socks and underwear. Just check it out in the locker room. Today's Wednesday, so that means his shorts and his socks are red. That's what Harry says. Wednesday it's red. When Mack grows up he wants to be a shallow ugly woman with an attitude and bad fashion sense—namely, Joanie.

Davey Dearest and Walter are actors, nothing more to say, Fiona said. Usually what they're doing when they're talking to you is trying out a human emotion to see if they can make you believe they're feeling it. Life vérité. Walter's the ectomorph with bad toxins in his fat cells so his overriding human emotion is depression and existential facticity. Actually, Walter just drinks too much coffee. Davey Dearest looks like Richard Gere, so Davey's overriding emotion is whatever Richard Gere's is. Watch out for falling gerbils. Davey just became a Buddhist. Any questions?

There are six sections in the dining room, Fiona said, Section One through Section Six. Sections Four, Five, and Six, Fiona said, Are the sections you want to get assigned to because that's where Andy Warhol—excuse me while I throw up—and Whoopi Goldberg and Bette Midler and Faye Dunaway and Ellen Burstyn and Douglas Fairbanks Jr. and Mariel Hemingway and Mary Travis and Leonard Bernstein and David Byrne and Isabella Rossellini and Patti LuPone and James Taylor and Francis Ford Coppola and Judd Hirsch and Harvey Keitel and Robert De Niro and the doctors and lawyers and Wall Street yuppies who order lavishly and tip double the tax are always seated.

Waiters are always started out in Sections One and Two and then theoretically, Fiona said, Are moved to Section Three, then even Four and Five, and—Yahweh be praised—Six.

Sections One and Two are by the bar, where Daniel, the boss's brother, eats his dinner and drinks his wine spritzers and you have to grind fresh pepper onto his soft-shell crabs or his steak *frites* or his couscous that he never eats because his only diet is cocaine, and where the heavy-lidded, jaw-grinding Eurotrash trust funders sit and sit and sit and smoke and order bottled water *con gaz* and refills of espresso or cappuccino or iced decaf cappuccino and then at best leave change, never quarters, under the saucer.

Theoretically you move from Sections One and Two to Sections Three, Four, Five, and Six, Fiona said, But actually you can't get there from here. There: Three, Four, Five, and Six, Fiona said. Here: One and Two. In order to get to Three, Four, Five, and Six you have to sell the specials and your bar check has to be high and you have to sell desserts. Every morning the owner, Daniel's brother, goes through your checks and writes down the number of specials you sold and tallies your bar-check dollars per customer spent on booze and what percentage of your customers ate desserts. The waiter with the highest sales gets Sections Three, Four, Five, or Six.

Here's the problem, Fiona said. Only the customers who order specials and cocktails and bottles of Veuve Clicquot and crème caramel and *tarte tartin* and profiteroles are seated in Sections Four, Five, and Six—when it's busy they're seated in Section Three, too—but never, never are these customers seated in Sections One and Two.

It's the same story with the bar, Fiona said. Every week Daniel's brother, the boss, tallies the bartenders' pour. The better the pour the better the shift. Any questions?

I've been at Café Cauchemar for over a year, Fiona said, And Harry's been here two, and neither one of us has ever had Section Three, Section Four, Section Five, or Section Six.

The reason isn't because Harry and I aren't good waiters, it's just we've never had the chance to prove ourselves.

This is the espresso machine, Fiona said. You first pound out the old coffee into the bucket, hold this handle thing under the coffee dispenser, flip this switch—usually twice—which is the amount of coffee for a good espresso, press the coffee down firmly with this butt plug thing, and then hook this part into the machine and press the button.

The espresso cups and the little saucers and the little spoons are all under the counter, Fiona said, And the sugar packets and sugar substitute packets are on the shelf next to the reach-in behind Georgette. The milk and the *con gaz* water are in the reach-in. Any questions?

You've met the cashier, Georgette? Fiona asked. Then: Georgette, Will. Will, Georgette. Give Georgette the American Express cards when it's busy and she'll do them for you if she can. Georgette's a dyke; her girlfriend is a famous model. Cool.

You could learn so much by just how Fiona said cool.

Don't you just love Georgette's mustache? Fiona said. Cool. White American women need to start dealing with body hair; nothing better than hair on a woman's body. I prefer my women black and lithe.

Number each of your dinner checks, Fiona said. Put your name at the top and date the check, and what day it is, and the table number. Just do what I do, serve drinks from the right, food from the left, always clear from the right, Fiona said—she said, That don't mean I'm a lesbian. I like women, all kinds. I really like women, sexually black and lithe for me. Not into tits, I like little-girl breasts, nubbins. I don't talk about it much because then you got to come out and it's political, and when you're political what do you do when you want to fuck some dumb football guy? All of a sudden you're hiding from your sisters, sneaking around, just to bump some guy who thinks his cock is some kind of big present for you—which it is, but I like Big Macs too, but only on Thanksgiving and Christmas. Do you have a crumber? Fiona said. I'll get you one. It helps your tips if you crumb the table.

It's the difference between individuality and identity, I think, don't you? Fiona said. Identity is your role in life, the part you play. Individuality is who you are, and who you are is revealed to you if you can get to complete presence. We are all, each one of us, huge spirits in our bodies,

Fiona said, And the more our spirit reveals to our bodies the spirit that we are, the more we become who we are. Like the Japanese. They have this aristocratic play language they call *asobase kotoba*, she said, So instead of saying *I see that you have come to Café Cauchemar*, they say *I see that you are playing at being at Café Cauchemar*. The idea being that you are in such control of your life and your powers that everything is a game. One is always literally in play. Nietzsche had a similar concept with his *amor fati*—I call it Fatty Love, Fiona said—love of one's fate. The fates lead her who will; who won't they drag.

Have you seen *Tony and Tina's Wedding*? You're invited to this wedding, see—Tony and Tina's—but it's a play. Tony and Tina are actors, and the mothers and fathers of the bride and groom are actors, everybody involved in the actual wedding is an actor. As a member of the audience you go to the wedding and eat wedding cake and dance to a bad combo band in matching blue outfits and participate in everything as if it were a wedding, Fiona said. I went to *Tony and Tina's Wedding*. Way cool. I think that's how we should all look at our lives, don't you? As if they were real.

Buy yourself the kind of ballpoint pen that you can flip at the top— goes quicker in the rush, Fiona said. It's hell to stop and take the cap off and then put the cap on the other end of the pen. Pretty soon you just say fuck it and keep the cap of the pen off and then you start marking up your white shirt and you can't get that kind of ink out with even Clorox. But we Americans are such orphan bastards and what's left of our European traditions is so meaningless and absurd, Fiona said. My opinion is Europe has no frontier, so they take no risks. Just walk down Paseo de Gracia in Barcelona and what you got is upper-middle-class women in fur coats and high heels and big hair shopping. You get that in New York, too, but the women in New York in their fur coats and Gucci heels are stepping over a homeless person to get into their apartment building. At least, in New York, these women are being confronted with their tiny lives. In Barcelona, they have no fucking idea they're in Connecticut. Any questions?

Of course, if you are an artist, Fiona said, You must have a frontier, so you must break tradition, but when you break tradition you lose your identity, and most human beings can't live without that kind of structure. There is nothing more lonely than a true artist.

You got the bar glasses right? Fiona said. The up glass, the rocks glass, the juice glass, the cocktail glass, the snifter, the old-fashioned. They're all at the bar station. Serve your drinks with a napkin and a straw. You know what fruits to use for the different drinks? Fiona said, So us poor orphan American bastards struggle for some kind of belonging—gay, black, feminists, Native Americans. But don't get me wrong. I love both my two brothers Hunter and Gus and they're both fags—I call them the Hyannisport Homos, Fiona said, she said, And I sleep with women now and then—so how can I not be for gay rights? And women's rights— I mean I'm a woman, right? How could you be a woman and be against women's rights? And black rights and red rights and brown rights and yellow rights—shit, people only get what they get because they fight for it, Fiona said. Keep your mustache trimmed. No earrings. You don't wear an earring do you? Nothing more beautiful on a man. Remember that Joni Mitchell song, *You stuck out like a ruby in a black man's ear?* Joni Mitchell is so underrated. She and Leonard Cohen. Mick Fucking Jagger is still on MTV, but Joni—no!

Ever read *Marat/Sade* or seen the play? The movie? What a great piece of work. A play put on by the inmates of an insane asylum during the French Revolution. Cool. I think great art is always insane, or makes you feel insane. And insane is good, don't you think? I mean, everything is so fucking insane anyway, so when an artist points out the insanity or invites you in to her peculiar brand of crazy, that's what we as artists must do, don't you think? Actually, though, Fiona said, What I said about Europe doesn't apply to Paris. Paris is different. Paris is cool.

You see the woman over on table forty—the woman with the mink draped over the chair? Fiona said, Have you seen those anti-fur commercials, the one with the woman wearing a mink and lying in a New York gutter gnawing off her arm so she can get out of the trap she's caught in? Cool. I think it's way gross to wear fur, don't you? I mean I'd wear old furs, where the animal's already dead, but to go buy a coat that is made up of twenty little dead hairy animals is fucking sick. Ever seen a mink farm? It's totally glamorous—relatives to the weasel—I mean minks are mean motherfuckers, kill a cat or a dog in nothing flat—all living in wire boxes living and eating in the same pen where they shit, growling and hissing and going at it with each other. And minks are carnivorous! Believe me, honey, it ain't manure you're smelling when you're smelling mink shit. You ever smelled an animal's shit that eats other animals—I mean besides your own dump after a big slice of rare prime rib? What becomes a legend most—Jesus! you can smell a mink farm ten miles away.

I'm totally into leather, Fiona said, In all senses of the word. I love smooth leather on my body, love whips and chains. Whenever I get some free time I volunteer at the animal shelter. Animals are always completely present. All animals are Buddha, especially dogs. And I prefer to keep company with higher beings.

Polo, Fiona said. These days every gay man in Manhattan is just pouring that Polo shit on.

What I said about being a good waiter—I'm not a good waiter. My problem is I really don't give a shit. It's all Tony and Tina to me. But in this business, you have to give a shit. The only reason I don't get fired is because I have a nice ass, an unusual face, and the fuck-you attitude. With Harry it's singing Happy Birthday.

When you put in your order, Fiona said, You write down your salad order on the yellow chit first and lay the chit on the shelf above the salad pickup. Make sure it has your name, the date, the day, and the table number on it, same as your dinner check. Call out your order clearly and then get out of the kitchen, Never talk, Never point. Never laugh in the kitchen or Chef Som Chai will have your ass in a sling. You're lucky he's on vacation. Last week, Chef Som Chai had Harry kneeling down and barking like a dog before he would take Harry's order.

When you pick up your salad order—it takes only seconds for a salad to come up, but you still can't act like you're waiting—spindle the yellow salad chit and then immediately put the yellow dinner chit onto the shelf above the dinner pickup. If your chits don't line up with your dinner check, you're fucked, Fiona said. You have to pay the difference for whatever item doesn't tally. It's against the law, but what ain't.

Be careful with Chef Som Chai. I can get on with him because I'm a sexual object. I've got him wound around my left nipple and he's never even come *close* to that nipple, you understand, but with men, with you, with waiters, it's different. He's got the typical—what we Americans call the *third world*—male mentality that women are second class to his first class. Like Yoko Ono said, Women are the niggers of the world, Fiona said. Plus the chef's got that Napoleon shit going on—you know, short-man short-dick bigger-than-thou mentality. Have you seen *M. Butterfly?* My God, what an insight into race and sexuality. There's a part in the play where M. Butterfly says that white heterosexual males— that is, western European culture—see Asian culture as feminine, even the men as feminine, as opposed to the African, which white heterosexual males—that is, western European culture—see as masculine. God, what a way to look at the world! They've defined everything about this culture, about the whole fucking world, really. Fuck white men with thin lips! Fiona said.

Chef Som Chai says all American men are pussy-whipped. What does that mean? He *abhors* gay men, so he really hates waiters, yet he is absolutely fascinated with the waiters' cocks. Men like Chef Som Chai think *everyone* who works for him—not just women—is something he owns. He owns the kitchen. Every one of those men in there are related to him somehow. They all got to America and got a job here at Cauchemar because of Chef Som Chai. And they all live together in houses he owns in Queens. He drives a new black Mercedes-Benz—I mean, someone drives it for him. Scary, huh? At least when *we* leave here we can leave Chef Petty Tyrant behind, but not those guys back in the kitchen. The big boss, Daniel's brother—an educated Jew—lets him get away with it. The dish, if you want to know, is big boss smokes too much dope. He's smoked so much dope he's growing tits and can't get it hard anymore. Can you imagine?

If you use a damp cloth napkin on the wineglasses you'll wipe off the streaks off. Wineglasses are stocked below each one of the three bus stations: next to the window, at the stairs down to the rest rooms, and over by the bar. Be careful. Just know the chef's got an agenda. It's nothing personal, OK? Just put it in your mind: *This is nothing personal.* One waiter, after his first day here, went home and overdosed on insulin—wasn't even diabetic. Offed himself. Harry says he—Harry—even enjoys the abuse now. Says he's going to get Chef Som Chai in bed if it kills him. Cool. It probably will. If anything, sex is going to kill Harry O'Connor.

Desserts are the same trip. You write out a yellow chit, with all that same information on it, and you hand it in to the dessert person, who's the guy next to the salad person. Call out your order clearly. Leave—don't ever wait or look impatient or they'll have your balls—come back immediately, serve the dessert. You can get your busboy to get your coffee if it's busy. But good luck. A busboy never lasts more than two weeks around here. Brush up on your Spanish.

Whether you get a staff cocktail, depends on if John the Bartender likes you or not. Don't take it personal if all he lets you have at first is draft beer. I'm up to Southern Comfort, two, sometimes three. Harry gets whatever he wants but that's because John's an opera queen and Harry is a tenor. Harry sometimes sings in the chorus at the Met. You can't believe this guy's voice. One Saturday night when I first started working here, right in the middle of busy, Harry came out of the kitchen with the candles burning on a *gâteau au chocolat* and started in on Happy Birthday, so hard these postmodern chandeliers shook.

When Harry was done this café was quiet so fast like only New York can get. Then Harry got a standing ovation. John the Bartender was weeping into a bar towel. A standing fucking ovation. I watched Harry's face flush Irish pink while he sang, watched his face as the crowd stood and applauded. Cool. Only in New York. That could happen nowhere else in the world.

I live for stand-up in-the-moment performance art like that. My favorite performance artist is a guy named Argwings Khodek. Ever heard of him? He does this thing with *Hamlet*. He plays *Hamlet* on his accordion, playing all the parts—Hamlet, Claudius, the ghost, Gertrude, Ophelia, Laertes, and Rosencrantz and Guildenstern—in forty-five minutes. On the accordion. He's a master of complete presence. He's my AUI, Fiona said, My Absolute Ultimate Idol. Even more than Leonard Cohen! If I could ever meet Argwings Khodek, Lord! I understand his next performance is *Antigone*. Cool, Fiona said. Can you imagine Argwings Khodek doing *Antigone* on the accordion?

The bar is the same, Fiona said: The chit, the info, call out your order, but stand in line there—don't let anybody get in fucking line ahead of you at the bar or you'll lose your drinks for sure.

Do you know Leonard Cohen? Isn't he the coolest motherfucker in the world? I mean, next to Argwings Khodek. I love his *Songs from a Room*. He came in here twice—*Leonard Cohen* came in here twice—and both times I was shit-spray. Whenever I get around great talent I go shit-spray—the bottom falls out of me and I'm on the toilet sometimes for hours. Of course, now I'm totally freaked because Harry and I have this theory that if you see a person in New York three times, and those three times are somehow meaningful to you, then you have to fuck that person. Can you imagine fucking Leonard Cohen? I'm already wet, Fiona said.

I'll make a tape for you. I just bought the album. "Famous Blue Raincoat" is on it, Fiona said, and "Joan of Arc," and Oh! My! God! Have you heard "Song of Bernadette"? I'm going to have "Song of Bernadette" sung at my funeral. "Song of Bernadette" is so way fucking cool. Harry should sing it for you sometime. Or maybe I will.

I can't imagine what would happen if Argwings Khodek walked in here. Holy Mother of God! Fiona said, What a shit-spray scene that would be!

What makes this place difficult is the place is divided. The owner wants it divided. The bartenders hate the waiters, the busboys hate the waiters, and of course, the kitchen hates the waiters, the dishwashers hate the waiters. The waiters hate everybody, including other waiters, Fiona said. It's the same way all around. The bartenders hate the busboys. The kitchen hates the dishwashers, et cetera et cetera. That way, see, Fiona said, Nobody trusts anybody, so no one gets friendly and scams the boss. Divided, Fiona said, Conquered.

And something else. You see, you got to understand, what makes all this even harder is that Café Bistro is a theater restaurant. At six o'clock this place is going to start filling up, but by eight o'clock this fucking place is empty. And it stays empty pretty much until ten-fifteen or so, and then fills up again until midnight, sometimes one o'clock. The hardest part is getting all your people out of here by showtime.

Any questions?

Fiona's fists were resting on her hips, *Myths to Live By* in one hand. Pit stains on the Day-Glo pink T-shirt.

My mother's nerves. Language my second language.

My breath in. My breath out.

Yes! I said. Do you, I said, Like the book?

Fiona raised *Myths to Live By* up, looked at it.

My hands were folded in front of my crotch, so I moved my hands, put them on my hips, then hung them down next to me.

Synchronicity, Fiona said. I'm reading about synchronicity.

My arms were two wild monkeys hanging onto my body.

Synchronicity! I said. Well then, I said, Have you ever, I said, Met a man named Charlie 2Moons?

Fiona hid the scar of her top lip under her bottom lip, made a smacking sound.

Nevah hoid a him, Fiona said.

THAT'S WHEN HARRY walked into Café Cauchemar. Harry was the pinkest man I ever saw. Green eyes, freckles, short red hair parted on the right side. A blue polo shirt with an alligator, khaki walking shorts, white socks and Nikes. A Polaroid camera hung around his neck.

I thought he was a tourist.

Harry had a long piece of cardboard under each arm.

Fiona put her arm around Harry's shoulders. This is Harry, Fiona said. Mr. Happy Birthday. New York's only Irish Catholic homosexual.

Harry, Will, Fiona said; Will, Harry.

Harry put his arm over Fiona's shoulders.

And this is Susan Strong, Harry said, Living proof that James Joyce's idiot savant daughter fucked a truck driver.

Then: Photo op with the president and the first lady? Harry said.

Harry pulled a tab out at the bottom of each piece of cardboard and turned the cardboards around, and then Harry was standing between a life-sized photo poster of Ronald Reagan and a life-sized photo poster of Nancy Reagan. The Polaroid camera was hanging from Harry's neck and his arms were draped over Ron and Nancy's shoulders and Harry was saying cheese.

Have your picture taken with President and Mrs. Reagan, Fiona said. It's a project we're working on, a performance piece.

Actually, we just say it's a performance piece, Harry said. Really what we're doing is making some extra cash.

Everything is a performance piece, Fiona said. Extra cash is a performance piece. Waiting tables is a performance piece. Ronald Reagan and Nancy are a performance piece. How we get up in the morning is a performance piece. What we're *really doing* is a fucking performance piece.

Joseph Campbell, Harry said, moving his lips so he was talking out the side of his mouth to me, *Myths to Live By*, page one hundred and thirty-seven.

So is *Tony and Tina's Wedding*, Fiona said.

Life is an art and art is a game, Harry said. *Asobase kotoba.*

Even death is an illusion, Fiona said. Death is only a door.

Five dollars a pop in Times Square, Harry said. Bridge and Tunnel people just love Ron and Nancy.

Bridge and Tunnel? I said.

Harry stepped out from in between Ronald Reagan and Nancy, came over to me, and took me by the arm. I was tall and thin next to Harry. Harry stood me in between Ronald Reagan and Nancy.

Just do whatever comes to you, whatever's natural, Fiona said, And Harry will take the photograph.

I don't ever, I said, Do things that come natural.

Cool, Fiona said. Then do what comes unnatural.

Ask your Higher Knowing, Fiona said.

My face smiled.

I don't know, I said, My Higher Knowing.

Polaroid flash.

Five bucks, Fiona said. Goes to a good cause.

Art, Harry said. Performance art.

I took my wallet out from my back pocket, looked at the lone five-dollar bill.

Cool, Fiona said. For you, it's three. Keep two bucks for the subway.

I sat down at a table, took the tobacco from my shirt pocket, and the papers, and started rolling with one hand like I can.

Fiona's blue eyes had violet flecks.

Roll me one of those too, would you? Fiona said.

Then: Me too, Harry said.

Harry moved Ron and Nancy up to the table so they were standing close, then placed a dinner napkin over Ronald's shoulder and a dinner napkin over Nancy's shoulder.

Where did you learn to roll like that? Fiona asked. That's beautiful. I hate smoking these fucking Jesse Helms Marlboros.

Father, I said, Was a rodeo clown, knew all kinds of tricks, I said. My father taught my sister, Bobbie, and Bobbie taught my friend Charlie 2Moons, and Charlie taught me.

Harry, Fiona said, Do you know a guy named Charlie Two Tunes?

Moons, I said, Charlie 2*Moons*.

Two Moons! Harry said. What kind of name is that?

Shoshone, I said.

Nevah hoid a him, Harry said.

Will, Fiona said, It's so cool how you talk. Do you always stutter?

Not when I'm singing, I said.

Fiona's smile almost as good as Ruby's.

You really are beautiful, Fiona said, When you're rolling a cigarette. Your whole aura changes.

Playing at rolling, I said. Art, I said. Performance, I said, Art.

Fiona really laughed out loud. Threw her head back, lots of teeth. Her gums showed. Same way Ellen laughed when I said Jackson Holeewood.

Where you from, cowboy? Harry said.

Harry smelled like Polo.

Idaho, I said.

My brothers went to school in Columbus, Fiona said.

Idaho, I said. Not Ohio, I said. In the Pacific Northwest.

Cool, Fiona said.

Idaho! Harry said, and put his hands on his cheeks. So you're the one!

What one? I said.

Daniel's new slave interest, Harry said. Has he asked you to stay after work yet?

Slave interest? I said.

You were Daniel's slave interest for a while, weren't you, Harry? Fiona said, as she took her cigarette and took Harry's too. He don't smoke, Fiona said.

I lit Fiona's cigarette.

Gentiles, Harry said. Daniel loves them. I needed the job, I'm out, I'm liberated. It's 1983. Jews have super cocks, and Daniel's no exception—got a can of Budweiser hanging down there. So I sucked off Daniel's big beer-can dick. Any red-blooded American boy would have done the same thing, don't you think?

Fiona and Harry looking at me.

Are you a red-blooded American boy?

Harry looked at Fiona. Fiona looked at Harry. Both of them looked at me.

So you like boys? Fiona said.

No, I said, too quickly, then: Well, I mean. . . .

Hell, you ain't one of them bi-sekshuls, are you? Harry said, and hooked his thumbs in his belt loops.

You're going to piss everybody off, Fiona said.

I'm already pissed off, Harry said.

Bisexuals aren't any good if they're a man, Fiona said. Only decent bisexual's a woman. A man just don't have it in him to be good at bisexuality, do you think, Harry? It's too complex. Most bisexual men, I've found, are straight men who like to get fucked in the ass.

You like getting fucked in the ass? Harry asked.

Best man to fuck with is a man who's been fucked in the ass, Fiona said. Makes a man more attentive.

I've never . . . I said. I mean, it's different . . . with me, I said.

Never been fucked in the ass? Harry said.

No, I said. I mean, not for . . . a long time, I said.

Oh, I know what you mean! Harry said.

No, I said, I mean. . . .

Shit happens, I said.

Seemed like a good idea at the time, I said.

But it's not the truth.

Then I just said it. I usually can't, I said.

Harry looked at Fiona. Fiona looked at Harry. They both looked up at the Sistine Chapel God.

Slow-uttered stage whispers: You usually can't *what?*

Usually can't, I said. You know, fuck.

Nightmare Café.

Harry and Fiona threw up their arms.

Wounded in Vietnam! Harry said.

Oh! . . . my! . . . God! Fiona said. *The Sun Also Rises*, Fiona said. You poor man!

Hell of a fix. Up Shit Creek. In a world of hurt.

Not Vietnam, I said. Not anything. Just me.

Harry pointed the Polaroid at me.

Flash. Auras.

Handed the Polaroid to Fiona.

Cool! Harry said, looking over Fiona's shoulder at the Polaroid.

Make it aware, Fiona said. Make art out of it.

Way cool, Fiona said.

I reached for my wallet.

No problem, Fiona said. This Polaroid's on us, Fiona said. She dropped the Polaroid into her huge red leather purse.

That was when Daniel, the boss's brother, big beer-can-dick Daniel, slave-interest Daniel, flashed his Rolex, clapped his hands, and yelled, Three-thirty-six! Come on, you motherfuckers! Let's get this fucking show on the road!

THE NEXT TEN days that I trained with Fiona, Chef Som Chai was on vacation.

Thank my lucky fucking stars.

The espresso machine, steaming the milk, ordering salads, ordering dinners, ordering desserts. Setups for the bar. Learned how to say things French: *profiteroles, poulet florentine, steak frites, salade Méditerranéenne, tarte tartin, couscous.*

Charlie 2Moons nowhere to be found.

Fiona's busboy was what I was. I helped Harry out too.

One night I got coffees for Mack Dickson's table. After the first rush, in the parlor by the espresso machine, next to the garbage can where you can smoke, I was smoking. Mack Dickson walked through the swinging red doors, a wave of Polo, beautiful according to *GQ*. Mack Dickson yelled across the room, Hey, Spud! If I want help with a table I'll fucking ask for it!

After that, I didn't help Mack or Joanie, Davey Dearest, and Walter either. They were on Mack Dickson's side.

That's one thing you had to learn quick that I learned quick: the Dining Room War.

Even the waiters hated the waiters.

Us and Them.

Us: Fiona, Harry, and me.

Them: Mack Dickson, Joanie, Davey Dearest, and Walter.

All of us already dead.

ONE THURSDAY EVENING, after the first rush, I was rolling a cigarette and Fiona said, Roll me one of those, would you? So I rolled Fiona a cigarette. Just as I put the match to Fiona's cigarette, all at once, just like that, I said it. You guys, I said, Must think I'm weird.

Fiona's blue eyes on me, violet flecks.

How so? Fiona said.

The light was unrelenting fluorescence from above.

What I said, I said. You know—the other day.

Harry walked in through the swinging red doors.

What did you say? Harry said.

I looked over at Georgette at her desk.

You know, I said. What I said about fucking.

Oh, you mean your limp dick, Harry said.

Fiona poked my chest with her finger, not hard, on my heartbeat, her lip a life all its own, something wild and red and crooked.

What the fuck, Fiona said. An idiot savant truck driver's daughter and New York's only Irish Catholic homosexual think you're weird? Listen up, Fiona said. This here ain't America anymore where you are. This is a whole new place. Weird here is something we aspire to, something we perfect, get degrees in, get awards for. Don't flatter yourself about weird. This middle-class self-reflection and comparison-to-the-norm is bullshit, is small-town, is petty cash. If you want to spend your life worrying about what a bunch of assholes think, go back to Poontang, Idaho. I could give a fuck about your tiny life. This is New York City. Here, you take what's wrong with you, you make it aware, and you make art out of it. And you take it to the extreme. Hot or cold, anything else you spit out!

The other day, Fiona said, When you were rolling that cigarette, when you told us you can't fuck, you were beautiful, real, and completely present. And I have a Polaroid of it. And now you come up with this shit. Look around you, man, there's a lot to complain about. You're a tall, slim, beautiful white American male. Give me a fucking break. So your dick don't get hard. Fix it or forget it, but be present with it. Besides, it ain't your dick that's broken, it's your heart. So what's new. I don't even have a dick and I'm doing fine. The rest is Connecticut, middle-class cowardice, quiet desperation, something I have no room for in my life.

Fiona put the cigarette out in some mashed potatoes in the garbage can, and walked big steps—lots of shoulders and hips—out the swinging red doors.

Walking Spanish, Harry said. I love it when she walks Spanish.

MRS. LUPINO OPENED her door as I was unlocking my door. A black cat with yellow eyes ran into the hallway.

My red answering machine was blinking.

Ruby.

Ruby sounded like when you dream and you need to say something in your dream and you can't say it because the words are so far away from your mouth.

Ruby Prestigiacomo, what am I going to do with you?

No message from Janet at Columbia University.

Across the courtyard, newspaper spread out in front of him, the E.T.-phone-home guy was phoning home. Again.

There were five of them: mannequins. Standing up in a green Dumpster on the east side of Cooper Square. Two females and three males. All of them, arms and legs and heads intact. No nipples. The males had lumps for dicks and one guy had a beard—not hair, just molded beard. No hair on the others. Took me a couple of trips, but I got them all and scrubbed them up good.

The bearded guy I put in my Jimmy Stewart outfit, another guy in the sharkskin suit, the third my Osh Kosh overalls. The one woman in my big white shirt and my baseball cap backwards. The other in my Japanese kimono and red paisley silk scarf.

Stood them around between my bed and the front windows. They looked like a cocktail party.

Their names changed as often as their outfits.

Make it aware. Make art out of it, Fiona had said.

My Art Family. I called them my Art Family.

CHEF'S BACK, FIONA said. Keep your ass low.

Downstairs in the locker room, I hung up my waiter uniform, sat down on the wooden bench, took my high-top tennis shoes off, took my Levi's off. I pulled my T-shirt off and when my T-shirt was off, I was standing there just in my Fruit of the Looms and white socks. All at once, Kung Fu salad guy walked in the locker room with another Asian man: a short guy, stocky, wearing a chef's hat.

Chef Som Chai.

You're going this way and then shit happens and then you're going that way.

Kung Fu salad guy made like he was throwing a knife, then made a scared face, pointed at me. Chef Som Chai laughed, they both laughed, and I stood there in my underwear.

Show me the dick! the chef yelled.

The chef's voice, Pavarotti in the low-ceiling room.

Hell of a fix.

The dick? I said.

Up Shit Creek.

Show me the dick! the chef yelled, and just like that the chef was standing right there on the other side of the wooden bench.

The dick! The dick! the chef yelled. Show me the dick!

In a world of hurt.

My hand pulled down the front of my shorts and put the elastic under my balls. I didn't look down, I looked up, at the ceiling, just my eyes, at the fluorescence.

Like a horse, Chef Som Chai said to the Kung Fu salad guy. He hung like horse.

Chef Som Chai walked around the wood bench to me, put his index fingers under the elastic of my shorts at my hips, pulled the elastic so it pulled my cock up, then pulled the elastic out in the back, looked in on my ass, then let the elastic snap back. The chef smiled. Kung Fu salad guy smiled. Then the chef poked his finger onto each of my nipples.

Big nipples, the chef said.

The chef made a smile like mine, then said something in his language to Kung Fu salad guy, and they laughed.

Like horse, the chef said.

I took it to mean he liked me.

Ignorance. The necessary condition for all learning.

About an hour later, I was standing next to Fiona in the kitchen, picking up a salade *niçoise*. Chef Som Chai yelled across the kitchen, Muffy! Get Horse Dick out of kitchen!

Fiona looked at me and I looked at Fiona.

Chef? Fiona said.

You heard me! the chef said. I hate him! Mother Teresa always smiling! Get him out of fucking kitchen!

In no time, Fiona and I were outside the swinging red doors, standing next to Harry.

You're smiling, Fiona said.

I see you've met the chef, Harry said.

Horse Dick? Fiona said. It was a question.

Harry was waiting.

A New York minute.

Really, I said, It just looks big.

A shower not a grower, huh? Harry said.

I guess, I said.

Helmet Head? Harry said, Or Anteater?

What? I said.

Circumcised? Harry said.

Me? I said.

You, Harry said.

Yes, I said.

Helmet Head, Harry said.

Cool, Fiona said.

The whole rest of the night, I was my mother's nerves, following Fiona around. I kept asking her, asking Harry, what I was going to do, how was I going to work in a restaurant if I couldn't go into the kitchen?

Maybe I should just confront, I said, The chef, I said, Maybe I should talk to Daniel.

Relax, Fiona said. Don't take it personal. Get a glass of water for table one. See if table three wants another martini.

He'll make you kneel, Harry said. Make you bark like a dog.

This too shall pass, Fiona said. Ask your Higher Knowing.

I don't know, I said, My Higher Knowing.

Start kneeling now, Harry said. Don't growl when you bark. Treat it like a performance piece.

DANIEL WAS SITTING at the table he always had his dinner at by the bar. It was just after his fourth trip downstairs to the bathroom with the cocaine. I served Daniel his soft-shell crabs, ground pepper on them. Fiona freshened up his spritzer.

My breath in. My breath out. I was out of breath.

Chef Som Chai, I said, Hates me.

It is really that big? Daniel said.

What? I said.

Your horse dick, Daniel said.

Hell of a fix.

Can you talk to him? I said.

Daniel's restaurant smile. I've talked to a couple horse dicks in my time, Daniel said.

I mean, I said, The Chef.

Daniel put two fingers to his lips, made a sucking sound.

Roll me one of those, Daniel said.

There was a cigarette already rolled in my shirt pocket. I handed the cigarette to Daniel.

Daniel's face was moldy bread.

No, Daniel said. Roll it.

So I rolled Daniel a cigarette.

The match under Daniel's face. Green-gray under his eyes.

What you doing after work tonight? Daniel said.

I'm, I said, Busy.

How busy's that? Daniel said.

Then—abracadabra!—just like that, Fiona was pouring Daniel more water.

Tickets for P.S. 122, Fiona said. John Kelly. Sold-out late show.

Daniel blew out smoke.

Muffy MacIlvane, Daniel said, Who is talking to you?

Susan, Fiona said. Susan Strong.

Can't you talk to the chef? I said.

Sorry, pal, Daniel said. No schmoozee, no talkee.

Harry was waiting for me at the waiters' station by the swinging red doors.

No schmoozee no talkee? Harry said.

No schmoozee no talkee, I said.

Then bark like a dog, Harry said.

THE CLOCK ABOVE the swinging red doors said eleven-thirty. After-theater rush: the restaurant was full, loud, café society. I hadn't been back to the kitchen. John the Bartender gave me the Beefeater martini up mistake he put an olive in instead of a twist and I one-gulped the martini. Then a Salty Dog mistake: one-gulped that one too.

A woman in a deep blue velvet dress dropped her fork; her long blond hair hung down as she bent and picked it up. You could see down her dress, breasts rife with pink right there next to me.

Surrounded all around, famous people eating *pâté campagne*, steak *frites, mousse au chocolate*—white linen napkins stretched across laps, foodstained, red-wine-splashed, lipstick-smeared. Heavy white plates scrape against white plates, hands touching hands, thighs to thighs, men, women, after-theater fashion-beautiful, cool tall wineglasses to lips, cigarettes to lips, cocktails, all around talking, talking the beautiful, the lovely, the important conversation.

Then, out of the blue, taking off his long coat at the door was Charlie 2Moons. Long wavy raven hair. His deep-set eyes, the gap between his teeth, the scar. All around me, the beautiful conversation was dogs barking. A ringing in my right ear. The pain in my forearms up to my shoulders. Splash down through my heart, cattle prod to cock. My feet, sensible black shoes striding under me. Toward Charlie, beloved Charlie. When he turned and his sad eyes looked into mine, I saw his great love for me.

But it's not the truth.

The guy wasn't Charlie.

Eleven-fifty. Two more martini-up-with-olive mistakes. Even I was beautiful, funny. New Yorkers were looking at me, at my large body moving through the dining room the way I move when I'm alone with the blinds drawn. I was carrying a drink tray with three Stoli Gibsons up to table ten; I was serving the drinks from the right like Fiona trained me. I still hadn't gone through the swinging red doors, back into the kitchen, not once.

You're going this way and then shit happens and then you're going that way.

Oh . . . my . . . God! Fiona said.

Then, from behind me at the bar: Oh, my God! Harry said.

The little scream that gives it all away.

I looked at where Fiona was staring, then looked up at the ceiling. Sistine Chapel God, his finger.

What's wrong? I said.

Argwings Khodek! Harry said.

Fiona ran toward me and Harry.

Oh . . . my . . . God! Fiona said again.

That's the moment, in all the world, right there on that spot in Café Cauchemar, on the white tiled floor with the black grout, at the waiters' station by the bar, under the Sistine Chapel God, the hand of man reaching, almost midnight, everybody beautiful, and there he was.

Rose.

All six and half feet of him, all two hundred and sixty pounds, his black black skin in the bright Café Cauchemar light darker than his skin really was, Rose's black skin so much darker than the pink-white of the skins of the rest of the after-theater fashion-beautiful crowd.

Rose's head was shaved, his beard partially gray. The earrings were rhinestones and holograms and big gold loops. Bracelets up both arms, gold, copper, brass, Bakelite, costume jewels. Capris, I guess you'd call the pants. Avocado Capris, mid-calf, tight, big basket, big butt. The largest red Converse tennis shoes I'd ever seen. A leather bag from the shoulder. A T-shirt with something written on the T-shirt, the neck scooped out, cut to expose Buddha belly and two ropes of muscles up his back. Two strands of pearls, matinee length.

That's Argwings Khodek? I said.

In the flesh, Fiona said.

But it's not the truth.

It was Rose. I just didn't know it yet.

Daniel, the boss's brother, the maître d'hôtel, was guiding Rose through the crowd toward Fiona's section, toward me, on Daniel's face the smile that was the restaurant smile but, with Rose that night, something underneath.

At table thirty-six, a Wall Street–type in a business suit, and just as Daniel passed by the table with Rose, the suit leaned over and whispered to a woman in a suit just like his. The suits laughed.

Rose stopped walking, took a deep breath, tucked his chin, raised his shoulders, and turned toward the table, bracelets clack-clack.

Colorful nigger, ain't he? Rose said to the suits, loud enough for the whole town.

Quiet that only New York can get that fast.

You don't think it's too much, do you? Rose said to the suits.

Rose's hand moved dramatically up and down his body.

No, the suit said. His smile something underneath too.

The suits acted as if they were already dead and wished Rose were dead too.

Then: Why were you staring at me? Rose said.

Nothing from either suit, only the smile.

Excuse me! Rose said. I'm asking you a question. Just *what* do you and your friend find so funny? I'd like to know.

Nothing.

Your table is right this way, sir, Daniel said.

Daniel's arm sweeping to the empty table, the table right next to me.

Ex-*cuse* me? Rose said, eyes narrowed at Daniel. Head thrown back, chin tucked even more, shoulders higher and higher, bracelets clack-clack. I am talking to this rude man here, Rose said, And when I am finished, and when I am ready, and only then, will I sit down at your lovely table.

My AUI! Fiona said.

Her Absolute Ultimate Idol! Harry said.

Rose stared at Daniel for several dramatic moments, then turned back to the suits.

I would suggest, Rose said to the suits, That from now on, if you have something to say about me or my outfit, that you say it to my face, rather than snigger it to your little friend here. Of course, Rose said, If you *were* to have the balls to address me directly, I'm sure I'd respond that if I were interested in your tiny opinion I would ask for it.

Rose lifted his arms, bracelets down his arms, clack-clack.

Consistency is the hobgoblin of little minds, Rose said. Good evening. Enjoy your lovely profiteroles.

Daniel seated Rose at the deuce, table ten, the table I was standing next to.

Just like that, in the dining room, it was dogs barking and people talking again.

That's when Fiona said to me, It's the perfect time for your first New York customer.

What? I said.

I couldn't possibly wait on him, Fiona said. I'm going shit-spray! Fiona handed me the dinner check.

Shit-spray?

Susan Strong always goes shit-spray when she's around genius, Harry said. And this is genius, Harry said. This is AUI Argwings Khodek!

Then you, I said to Harry, Wait on him.

Can't, Harry said.

Can't?

Vomit-spray, Harry said. Susan Strong goes shit and I go vomit-spray.

But, I said, The kitchen! I can't go in the kitchen!

I'm shitting my pants! Fiona said, took off her apron, and started running down the stairs.

You just don't understand, Will, Harry said. That's Arwings Khodek! The first person to take performance art into the realm of complete presence!

Harry took off his apron and started running down the stairs.

Harry! I said. Get back here!

Don't wait for the chef to ask you, Harry said. Just kneel. Then bark. Three times. Loud. Don't growl.

WHEN I FINALLY stood myself at Rose's table, my ballpoint pen was ready. The dinner check was on the drink tray in my hand. I was smiling, so I stopped smiling.

Good evening, I said.

Negroni, Rose said.

My mother's nerves.

Excuse me? I said.

Ex-*cuse* me? Rose said. The chin, he started to tuck the chin.

I didn't hear, I said.

Negro, Rose said. You know *Negro*, don't you? Rose said.

Yes, I said. Negro, I said.

Very good! Rose said. Now it's Negroni, Rose said.

Negroni? I said.

Rose threw up his arms, bracelets clack-clack.

Rose yelled, Go ask the fucking bartender. And get me a Mediterranean salad.

Harry was back at the bar. He looked kind of green and he was spraying Binaca into his mouth.

Negroni, I said to Harry.

Tall glass lime setup, Harry said. Three-fifty.

Negroni, I said to John the Bartender, writing down *Negroni* on the bar chit, the bar chit with my name, the date, the day, the table, the tall glass iced, garnished with lime, and the straw, the cocktail napkin.

When I delivered the Negroni, I read what it said on Rose's T-shirt.

CURE AIDS: FUCK THE CENTERS FOR DISEASE CONTROL.

Just like that—I didn't mean to—I laughed out loud.

Rose's chin tucked, moving only his black eyes straight into my eyes at an angle just above his rhinestone reading glasses.

Ex-*cuse* me? Rose said.

I was just laughing at what your T-shirt says, I said.

Do you know what AIDS is? Rose said.

No, I said.

Maybe you know it as GRIDS, Rose said. The gay cancer—gay-related, you know. Gay and Haitian, that is. At least that's the White Paranoid Patriarchy's fucking scapegoat propaganda.

Gay cancer, I said. Yes, I've heard of it.

Then why are you laughing? AIDS is a *terrible* disease, Rose said. And not something at all to laugh about. Do you think just because it's black people and queers who are dying it's something to laugh about?

No, I said.

Well, then, Rose said, I suggest you stop your little comic outburst and just go do it.

I said, Do it?

Yes, yes, go do it! Rose said. Just do it! Go fuck the Centers for Disease Control!

At the bar for the second Negroni, my hands shook as I did my setup.

Don't let it get to you, John said. She's a local Diva—come in here before. Some kind of Shakespearean ac-*tor*, specializing in *Othello*, John said.

Othello? I said.

She's black, ain't she? John said. Got one of those new ethnic names. Armadilla Kowabunga or something.

Argwings Khodek, Fiona said.

Fiona was beside me. Fiona's circumcised lip.

John said, Performance Art, right? That Lower East Side shit. Those kind are all the same, black or white or blue. Underneath the attitude all you got is another Norma Desmond queen.

Harry whispered in my ear. There it goes. The lip, Harry said. Susan Strong's lip is getting large. Performance Art, Joni Mitchell, Leonard Cohen, or Argwings Kodek, never fuck with any one of them around Susan Strong.

I watched Fiona's lip, and sure enough, Harry was right.

Sometimes it grows so fast it peels her lipstick back, Harry said. Remarkable phenomenon. Only other thing I've ever seen grow like that's a hard-on.

Fiona was kneeling on top of the bar. Her face poked into John the Bartender's face.

When you make something more of your life, *bartender*, Fiona said, Besides blowing the boss's married brother, and meeting the boss's pour in your little playpen back here, I'll listen. Until then, dickhead, Fiona said, Pour the fucking drinks I tell you to pour and shut the fuck up with your expert attitude.

John closed his mouth. His eyes clouded over. His face started melting.

This is where the large lip becomes lazer lip, Harry said. Lazer lip: Why she'll never see Sections Four or Five, Harry said, Let alone Section Six.

You're going this way and then shit happens and then you're going that way.

I can't believe what I do next.

Just like that, I am marching through the swinging red doors, past Georgette, past the reach-in, into the kitchen. I am writing down the date, the day, the table, my name, and *Med Sal* on the yellow chit. I am just about to call out the order in my clearest, strongest voice, when I see this: Crummy Dog. My Crummy Dog is sitting on the gray-painted cement floor in front of the dinner station, smiling the way he always did, tail flipping, tongue hanging out. Barking like a dog.

Just at that moment Chef Som Chai slips and, trying to get his balance, reaches out for the deep fryer, misses, and sticks his hand into the boiling grease.

Fatum. I look over just as Chef Som Chai's hand goes into the grease. I see nothing else.

Everyone is just standing around, so I start hollering and pointing and reach over and grab Kung Fu's plastic salad tub, dump the lettuce out, run to the ice machine, fill the tub with ice, run behind the service line to Chef Som Chai, grab him, spin him around, stick his hand and arm into the ice up to his elbow, walk with him, my arm across his shoulder, guiding the chef out of the kitchen, past Georgette, yell at Georgette to call 911, walk through the swinging red doors, Crummy running ahead of us, the chef walking along with me, getting pale, looking at me like I am the Big Guy above us on the ceiling. We walk through the dining room—me holding the chef's arm in the tub of ice, Crummy leading the way through the crowd—the chef getting paler with every step, past Fiona going shit-spray, past Argwings Khodek Rose, bracelets clack-clack, past his Negroni, past Harry standing with a piece of *gâteau au chocolat,* the candle melting, Harry just about ready to belt out Happy Birthday, past Daniel, the boss's beer-can-dicked-married-getting-blown-by-John-the-Bartender brother, and then out the front door.

There was no ambulance, but two cops in a car drove by. I yelled to the cops, *Burn victim! Stop!* But the cops kept going.

Then, just like that, all at once, Kung Fu salad guy pulled up in a black Mercedes, got out, opened the passenger door, and helped the chef inside. The chef was not pale anymore. He was green.

Mercedes better than ambulance, Kung Fu salad guy said. Then: Thank you, he said, I manage from here.

The black Mercedes drove off, east, evens east, shit from New York Shinola. I stood on the street, Manhattan wrapped all around me. Steam rolled out of the manhole in the street, the Mercedes driving deeper into the form, into the function, into the dark.

Beyond the pile of black plastic garbage bags, through the steam, people inside Café Cauchemar gathered at the window. The street, ahead of me, behind me, not a dog in sight.

My grandpa shoes on asphalt skin. I looked up my body, my black pants, white apron, looked up the buildings, across to just the tip of the Chrysler Building, up to the moon rising over 46th.

Then I heard it: Happy Birthday. Harry's singing Happy Birthday.

Wounded by a blow of love.

The sensation was a finger drawing a circle around my heart. A tenderness not since Charlie 2Moons. I was sure it was God, the word of God, God's voice, The Great Mystery, Sistine Chapel Big Guy extending his hand.

But it's not the truth.

It was just Harry, New York's only Irish Catholic homosexual, holding a chocolate cake and singing Happy Birthday in a bar.

It was not God.

It was only Manhattan.

And I knew, right then. In all the world. Finally.

Hey, Charlie! I yelled. It's me, Will! I'm home!

BOOK TWO

CHAPTER
FIVE

One time it wasn't Ruby on the phone. It was True Shot. What do you say we go get a doughnut? True Shot said.

In the unrelenting Dunkin Donuts fluorescence, True Shot looked green and my skin looked beige.

No Charlie 2Moons in Dunkin Donuts.

True Shot sat down at the counter, his shoulders hunched over. I asked him what was wrong and True Shot told me he was feeling poorly because Ruby'd ripped off the petty cash for Spirit Schleppers.

Spent the whole day, True Shot said, Trying to find that damn guy.

Fucking junkie! I said.

True Shot's mirrors were snake eyes on me. On his mirrors, my nose was big and my mustache was a hairy arch of brown hair. Bug eyes.

Be careful with your words, True Shot said. Words are real things. Ruby is our brother.

In the fluorescence, my baseball cap was the only shade for miles.

My mother's nerves.

But Ruby, I said, Calls me all the time. I said, And he don't speak. Every night, I said. My answering machine is street noise and Ruby coughing.

True Shot drums left-hand silver rings against the Formica counter-top. In his right hand at his neck, the buckskin bag with the blue-beaded horizontal and the red-beaded vertical.

In this world, True Shot said, There is no one like Ruby Prestigiacomo, and he needs our help. Besides, True Shot said, I promised a friend of mine I'd take care of Ruby.

I went to say *What friend?* but just then, down the Dunkin Donuts counter from us, the cop tipped his cup up and drank, set the cup down on the saucer, did something with his gun on the side of him, stood up, threw a quarter down on the counter, and walked toward us, his one eye on me, the other on True Shot. A big guy, red hair, drank green beer on Saint Patrick's Day, his roll of fat I thought a bullet-proof something around him. Still, True Shot made two of him.

The cop tilted his cap back, said, You, Brave Arrow, mind taking those Foster Grants off for me?

True Shot said, Yes, sir, Officer, and took his mirrors off, and looked right into the eyes of the cop. Cop looked back. The staredown.

That's the first time I noticed True Shot's eyes. They were the color of jade. And something else. True Shot's eyeballs did not hold still. Back and forth, back and forth, up and down too. Saint Vitus Dance eyes.

Driver's license, please, the cop said.

When True Shot put his hand in his extra-lovely black leather jacket pocket, the cop put his hand on his gun.

The cop took True Shot's driver's license, looked at it close. Then the cop took the rain slick he had draped over a chair, put on his rain slick, said to True Shot, After you.

The cop followed True Shot out the door into the rain. I went to follow them out and the cop said, You stay inside. Have a cup of java, the cop said. On me.

So I stayed inside while True Shot and the cop walked out to the van, looking at myself in the window looking out at True Shot talking to the cop, showing the cop the registration, then going through the brake lights, the turn signals, low beams and high beams.

True Shot stood in the rain while the cop was in the patrol car, talking on the radio, the static radio sound coming all the way inside Dunkin Donuts.

When the cop took off, I took True Shot's Maple Bar and coffee out to the van. True Shot was sitting, rain on the roof, staring straight ahead, Dunkin Donuts' fluorescence on the surface of his mirrors.

True Shot took a bite out of the Maple Bar and started the van.

All Dodges sound the same when you start them up.

I punched in the Sioux tape.

At the Interborough Parkway, True Shot doubled back onto Broadway, the ticket the cop gave True Shot stuck under the plastic Virgin Mary on the dashboard next to the photo of Brigitte Bardot in the green-sequined frame.

Obstructed view.

True Shot's designer mirrors were obstructing the view.

Back over the Brooklyn Bridge, the steel grating under the tires, the vibration up through Door of the Dead van was like an airplane landing on top of the van—so loud I couldn't hear myself think.

Do cops give you so much shit because you're Indian? I asked.

The dashlights were amber and green on True Shot's mirrors.

What cops smell when they see me, True Shot said, Is their own asshole. Only thing that keeps a cop from being an outlaw is his badge. Cops see me and their dirty shorts just start stinking.

You weren't doing anything, I said. You were just sitting there.

That cop wasn't as bad as some, True Shot said. A classic case. White kid, football player—probably time in Vietnam—now carrying twenty extra pounds from dunking his donut and driving around, wondering what his wife's doing while she's home alone. Red-blooded American boy who believes that without him, without the law, mankind would turn into the savage beasts they truly are.

And this young Donut Dunker, True Shot said, Knows a lot about savage beasts, because what his life has come down to is him sitting in his patrol car at four in the morning.

The cop has looked, True Shot said, And what he found was a beast inside his tiny Catholic heart too savage to name.

Inside Door of the Dead van: rain and windshield wipers, *too savage to name*, the hole in the floorboard, the plastic Virgin Mary, the green-sequin-framed photo of Brigitte Bardot, the ticket for obstructed view, the amber and green in True Shot's mirrors.

Why do your eyes do that? I said.

Astigmatism, True Shot said. That's what the white doctor said.

What the Injun doctor said is different, True Shot said. A Hopi medicine man told me my eyes don't stop moving because I'm looking for the space in between, and someday I'm going to find that space in between, and when I do I'll be able to disappear into it.

We drove along silent for some miles, just the Sioux tape. Then, all at once, True Shot pulled Door of the Dead van over and we stopped. He shut the engine off, leaned back against the seat, and put the last of the Maple Bar in his mouth. It wasn't raining. It got real silent in the van with the Sioux tape off.

Outside my window was a big old stone building with pillars and grand steps: Brooklyn Academy of Music. Not a person in sight, *personne*, no Charlie.

It is this way, True Shot said. Let me tell you a story.

The drums and the rattles started going. Like he'd brought his own sound track with him.

I was in for something important, so I rolled a cigarette.

A long time ago, when the white man bought Manhattan from the

Indians, True Shot said, The white man bought Manhattan for twenty-four dollars' worth of coins and beads. The white man thought he'd really put one over on the Indians and made jokes about how dumb the Indians were to sell the island of Manhattan so cheap.

It is this way, True Shot said. The joke was on the white man.

True Shot said, The secret name the Indians called Manhattan was Wolf Swamp, and Wolf Swamp, from ancient times, was a sacred place. A family of wolves lived on the island, and their home was at the heart of the forested island near the mouth of a beautiful spring.

What you couldn't see, though, True Shot said, What was obstructed from your view, hidden in the rocks of the beautiful spring, was the entrance to a deep cave. The cave was full of intricate passageways and blind alleys. In the heart of the cave lived a monster whose name was never spoken aloud.

It is this way, True Shot said. The wolves of Wolf Swamp were a special family whose task it was to guard the cave, to keep the monster inside and keep everything, everybody else, outside.

Once a year, True Shot said, Every year in the dog days of summer, the monster began to roar and beat the walls of the cave. His roar was earthquake or thunder. And when the family of wolves heard the monster earthquake thunder, the wolves began to howl.

Across the river, True Shot said, When the native people heard the howl of the wolves of Wolf Swamp, they knew. The monster was trying to escape the island and kill the people.

At this time, True Shot said, The native people chose a young woman and a young man to make the journey to Wolf Swamp. As was the custom, the women of the tribe took the young woman and taught her the secret steps into and out of the cave. As was the custom, the men took the young man and taught him the secret way to hurl the rock that repels the monster. As was the custom, the women of the tribe counseled the young woman never to look into the eyes of the young man until their task had ended and they were safe outside. As was the custom, the men of the tribe counseled the young man in the same way.

It is this way, True Shot said. Only the young woman knew the steps through the cave. Only the young man could send the monster back into the cave, and only by hurling a rock.

On the night of the full moon of the dog days, True Shot said, Riding on a white stallion, the stallion's mane and tail combed and soft—the stallion prancing, stepping high, ears up, tail up, a magic horse like a piece of the magic moon—the young woman and the young man crossed the river, rode to the spring, and offered the customary gifts of tobacco and herbs to the family of wolves, and after smoking pipe they feasted. After feasting, and before the woman and the man entered the cave, as was the custom, together the young woman and the young man blind-folded the white stallion. The young man mounted the horse and the young woman led the horse into the cave. When they came upon the monster, the young man hurled a rock and the monster turned back. Then the young woman, remembering the steps, led the young man and the white stallion out of the cave.

And so it went on for many years, True Shot said, Until there came a year that something happened.

Different people tell the story different, True Shot said. Some say it was the young woman, some say the young man. In any case, one of the two of them looked the other in the eyes.

These things happened next, True Shot said. Immediately the monster came after them. Immediately, the young woman forgot the steps, and they were lost.

The young woman knew her only choice was to offer herself as a sacrifice to the monster, and she knelt down and begged the young man to sacrifice her. The young man refused and, in his panic, tore the blind-fold from the white stallion and rode off to fight the monster alone.

When the monster came upon the young man on the white stallion, True Shot said, The young man hurled the rock, but just before he hurled the rock, the white stallion saw the monster, reared, and the rock missed. The young man fell off, the white stallion ran away, and the monster devoured the young man.

When the young woman heard the young man's screams, True Shot said, She lay down in the cave and closed her eyes. She tried so hard to remember the steps. She could hear the monster coming closer and closer. With each step of the monster, instead of remembering, though, the young woman forgot even more. She forgot even what it was she was trying to remember.

The monster came so close the young woman could smell the decay and feel its cold breath in her ear, True Shot said. Just then, the family of wolves arrived, and the wolves surrounded the young woman.

It is this way, True Shot said. The wolves made the young woman one of them. The wolves gave the young woman the shape of Wolf.

It is this way, True Shot said. With all gifts there is a sacrifice. When the wolves shape-shifted the young woman into wolf to confuse the creature, in exchange, as a sacrifice, the wolves lost their memories.

The sound wolf makes is *wolf*, True Shot said. *Wolf wolf* the wolf says, *wolf wolf*, because the wolves have forgotten who they are, where they came from, what their purpose was. The family of wolves have forgotten everything but their name, which must be continually repeated or they will forget the name too.

The only one who can help is the white stallion, True Shot said. The white stallion has not forgotten. It is this way, True Shot said. The special powers of the white stallion are his strength, his speed, and his memory. The white stallion remembers where the gate is, remembers the steps through the cave, remembers how to hurl the rock, but the white stallion was so terrified by the sight of the creature that he is now only blind fear, running running.

Wolf's howl is a cry to the white stallion for help, True Shot said. Even though Wolf does not know it, Wolf's howl is trying to soothe the white stallion, trying to calm him, so that the white stallion can hear where the young woman is, can hear that the young woman has been shape-shifted into Wolf.

If the white stallion would only stop and listen, True Shot said, He would recognize the cries of Wolf as the young woman's, and he would go to her, acknowledge her, and she would change back into herself.

And so it is this way, True Shot said, Wolf Swamp became a marsh lost in fog where the Wolves of Amnesia roam, where the white stallion never stops running, and the monster, set free of his boundaries, rules in chaos, unchecked.

The story goes, True Shot said, That Wolf Swamp became a prison camp. The island of banishment from the tribe. The worst punishment, even worse than torture and death, was being sent to Wolf Swamp, because the banished one knew he was condemned to keep himself alive. The only way he could keep himself alive was by repeating his name. If he stopped repeating his name, he would die. It is said some people grew so weary of repeating their name they chose to stop. But just as they stopped, at that moment, they started again because what opened up before them was too much to bear.

Some say the island itself ceased to exist, True Shot said, That the island was only the fog, the sound of the white stallion running, and the howl of the wolves.

And so it was this way, True Shot said, For many years. That is, he said, Until the white man came along.

The legend goes that one night, True Shot said, Sitting around the fire, somebody told the white man about Wolf Swamp. They got the white man drunk and told him about Wolf Swamp, told a real good story about Wolf Swamp so the white man wanted to go there. Nobody would take the white man to Wolf Swamp, but they did tell the white man they would sell it to him, that he could buy it.

And so this fucking dumb drunk white man bought Wolf Swamp, True Shot said. Twenty-four dollars for a place of torture, banishment, terror, and amnesia, complete with a monster set loose upon the land.

But then something quite remarkable happened, True Shot said. As soon as the white man bought the island, the island reappeared again, as if it were real.

As if, True Shot said, As if to appear.

It is this way, True Shot said. The white man acts as if he has a heart. But he has no heart. He has a paparazzi advertisement for a heart. As it is inside, so it is out, True Shot said. So as soon as the white man bought Wolf Swamp, he created Wolf Swamp.

God may have created the world, True Shot said, But the white man made Manhattan. It is a match made in hell.

Take away the architecture, True Shot said, Take away the fashion, the photography; take away the grid, the profiteering, the exchange, the stocks and bonds, the money, the fools and the pharisees, the careers, and all that's left is a foggy swamp, a family of forgetful wolves, a scared stallion, and a monster.

New York is structure, True Shot said. You'll find it's nothing else. Form, function, no content. Manhattan is point zero, the place where nothing occupies space and holds power that becomes something only because you have entered it. Like that.

This island exists, True Shot said, Only because we name it, buy it, sell it, trade it, build it, tear it down, dress it up, undress it, fuck it, fight it, forget it, get it high.

We the residents of Wolf Swamp, True Shot said, Exist only because we say we exist, because we can prove we exist because we got it memorized, can repeat it like a wolf, where I'm coming from, how much I'm worth, what my purpose is, how much you need me, what I can do for you, what's in, what ain't, where to go, what to wear, what not to wear, what to buy, where to buy it, what to build, how high, what to tear down. Look at me! This is me! This is how important I am, right here in Manhattan is where I am, and this is who you are, and this is where you are, and if you don't know exactly who you are, if you don't know exactly where you are, then where you should go is go back to Idaho or go fuck yourself.

Through the van window, the Brooklyn Academy of Music was ancient Greece in the red-dirt dust-storm mercury-vapor light. Its grand stone steps, the columns, the big wood door was the Alexandria Library, was Rome burning, was the Oracle of Delphi.

I rolled cigarettes, one for me, one for True Shot.

When I poured the tobacco into the bright square of white, I looked at my forearms, where the fear always starts. I looked at the fear going up my forearms to my shoulders.

I lit True Shot's cigarette, lit mine.

Jesus, True Shot, I said. My God, is that story true?

SHOPPING FOR AN *Honest Man* is what Fiona and Harry called their performance piece. Fiona scored the gig for Halloween night at Dixon Place, a performance space on East First Street.

At Café Cauchemar, two weeks before the performance, all Fiona and Harry did was say *Shopping for an Honest Man* dialogue back and forth, serving cocktails, in the kitchen, busing tables, after work with the staff cocktail, in front of Ronald and Nancy—even one night sharing a cab downtown—back and forth, those two.

One night walking home after work, the week before *Shopping for an Honest Man*, I must have passed ten posters of Fiona and Harry—an enlarged Polaroid of Fiona and Harry, draped in white sheets, wreaths in their hair like Greeks, holding up lanterns.

No Charlie 2Moons on 46th or Second Avenue, no Charlie on East Fifth. But there was somebody else. Halfway to my apartment on East Fifth I stopped in my tracks.

There he was: Argwings Khodek, sitting on my stoop with the three dogs from upstairs.

Upstairs.

Ever since I moved in, only sounds; the tin flip of the mailbox door in the hallway, two hundred and sixty pounds up thirteen steps, the locks on his door. One night, I barely caught the unrelenting fluorescence on his bald head, his big hand running along the second-floor banister.

Argwings Khodek, Rose.

In all the world, on *my* stoop.

Rose was wearing long johns, red, unbuttoned to below the navel just above where there's hair, long johns cut off at the knees, and no shoes, just thongs—Rose hated all men's shoes except for combat boots, every once in a while, and thongs. Women's shoes—Rose hated most of them too, made his arches hurt, but he had a closet full of women's shoes: heels, mules, fuck-me stilettos, studio flats—because Rose was an ac-*tor*.

When I got to the stoop, Rose's dogs were on leashes, leashes every which way, and the dogs were all at once wild with smelling the turkey thigh I'd bought at Schacht's.

I didn't look at Rose, but I still saw the big chest of him, the big arms and legs, the deep black of his chest and arms and legs. Didn't dare look at the crotch. Instead I looked off to my left at the poster of the Sacred Heart of Jesus and Stranded Beings Searching for God and the three Polaroids. I said a little prayer to the Sacred Heart of Jesus when I took the step, policing my body, new-shoe stiff, and sure enough, what I did was step on Mary—my grandpa shoe right onto her poodle paw—and Mary yelped and I bent down to comfort her and the little shit bit my hand.

I was smiling when I looked at Rose and then stopped smiling. Kept walking. Rose was holding Mary in his big black hands, Sahara Desert palms, and Mary was yelping yelping.

Sorry, I said.

On the back of Rose's long underwear, the black letters said FUCK THE POPE.

I was unlocking the front door when I remembered I had a free pass to Fiona and Harry's *Shopping for an Honest Man*.

Seemed like a good idea at the time, so I took the free pass out of my wallet, then the free pass was in my hand, and I held my hand palm out to Rose.

My friend, I said, Susan Strong. You're her idol. Her AUI, I said. Absolute Ultimate Idol, I said. Please come to the show.

When Rose took the free pass, my hand didn't touch Rose's hand, Rose didn't look at the free pass, didn't look at me, bracelets clack-clack.

When the front door closed behind me, Mrs. Lupino opened her door—just her eyeball and her eyebrow swoop under the chain.

They're gathering forces, Mrs. Lupino said.

Mrs. Lupino, I said, Does he live here?

Lucifer? Mrs. Lupino said.

Argwings Khodek, I said. The guy out on the stoop.

Mrs. Lupino opened the door more, raised her hand, caught the air with her fingers, brought her hand back down.

You mean Rose? Mrs. Lupino said. You should be proud to have a famous person living just up the stairs from you!

Susan Strong, I said, Is going to go shit-spray!

Gathering forces, Mrs. Lupino said. Lucifer and his disciples. Don't think I don't know.

My Art Family were all in the kitchen, peeping toms at the E.T.-phone-home guy. I walked over to the window to see what they were staring at: the E.T.-phone-home guy was sticking the phone receiver—the ear part—up his ass.

Two messages on my red answering machine, both from Ruby. Street noise, Ruby breathing breathing, clearing his throat and breathing until the answering machine clicked off.

No message from Janet at Columbia University.

I threw my grandpa shoe at my red answering machine. Knocked it and the red telephone onto the floor.

HALLOWEEN NIGHT. DIXON Place was two steps down into a long narrow room. People dressed in black were sitting everywhere, on chairs, on tables, on the floor. There wasn't room to walk, so you had to step over people. Somebody laughed as I was stepping over people. It was my outfit, my sharkskin suit and beatnik tie outfit, my Beatle boots, and I almost turned around, but I didn't, because it was as far back out as it was in.

Susan Strong was right. Who cares what a bunch of assholes think?

I sat down next to a big guy with one of those drape things Jews or Arabs wear on their heads, sat in the last chair left to sit in, looked around the room. No Charlie 2Moons.

Then, in all the world, the big guy with the drape thing I was sitting beside was Argwings Khodek.

I was sitting right next to Rose.

Rose was extra lovely in black leather—pants, coat, combat boots. His T-shirt was black, too, with white words: FUCK THE WHITE PARA-NOID PATRIARCHY.

I didn't say a word to Rose, not one damn word.

But it's not the truth.

I didn't move any part of my body, just turned my head.

The first time I saw you, I said, At the Laundromat, I said, When I was protecting my beige washing machines, I said, On your T-shirt was FUCK APARTHEID.

The second time I saw you, I said, In Café Cauchemar, I said, I was your waiter and you ordered Negroni and a Mediterranean Salad, and on your T-shirt it was FUCK THE CENTERS FOR DISEASE CONTROL.

I smiled, stopped smiling, and pointed at Rose's chest.

The third time, I said, On the stoop of 205 East Fifth Street with your dogs, it was the Pope, I said, FUCK THE POPE. On your red long johns.

But actually, I said, The first time I saw you, I said, I didn't know it *was* you, I said, You were just a dark figure at the top of the stairs with three dogs—remember? I said. The first time I set foot in 205 East Fifth Street. That night with Mrs. Lupino and her no-cats. I couldn't see what you were wearing that night so I couldn't tell who you wanted to fuck.

Now tonight it's white paranoid patriarchy, I said. That you want to, I said, Fuck.

Rose turned his head at me. His eyes were beautiful too, deep black eyes. When he spoke, Rose raised one eyebrow and moved his head a little closer. He didn't smell like Polo.

Deep black eyes on me, not at me, through me.

Rose smiled but it wasn't really a smile, it was just an expression he put on his face.

And the next time I want to fuck something, Rose said, What I'm going to fuck is you.

Rose never blinked.

Bracelets clack-clack.

Cattle prod to my cock.

Cool, I said.

THE HOUSE LIGHTS went down and the stage lights went up, and I was sitting in the dark.

If we could freeze moments in time.

I felt I belonged there in my seat. Things had meaning and purpose. Fiona and Harry were my friends and they were up there on the stage and the audience was waiting—you could feel the anticipation, the hope of theater to lay bare the human heart. And I was there, I wasn't in Jackson Holeewood, or Boise, I was avant-garde in Manhattan in a basement theater on the Lower East Side.

Harry was on the stage, lying on a bed in only his shorts reading a magazine. Harry O'Connor in front of fifty people in his underwear.

The magazine was *Screw*. Above the bed, on the wall, was a portrait of Andy Warhol and a painting of his of a woman's nose, before her nose job and after her nose job: BEFORE AND AFTER. A full-length mirror stage right. A TV set was on, a porn film—all sorts of people fucking all sorts of ways—groans and moans and little screams. There was a knock on his apartment door.

Harry said, Who is it?

The voice on the other side of the door was old and gravelly and sounded Jewish.

Open the door, let me in, the voice said. I have a gift for you.

What is it? Harry said.

Turn that porn tape off! the voice said.

Why? Harry said.

So you can hear me! the voice said.

This is New York City, Harry said. It's the eighties. I can watch porn if I want to.

Virtual hard-on! the voice said.

Virtual what? Harry said.

When's the last time you got it up? the voice said.

Harry got up off the bed and faced the audience.

If you're trying to make me feel ashamed of my impotency, Harry said, It won't work. My dietician has taken me off meat, my doctor has prescribed medication for depression, my therapist says I'm no longer in denial, and I've joined a support group for impotent males. We meet at the gym every Thursday night and pump iron. We call ourselves Wounded Warriors.

Why meat? the voice said.

It's impure, Harry said.

So's a hard-on! the voice said. Look, open the door, will ya? the voice said. I've come a long way. I'm tired. This is all wrong, you got it all wrong. There's something dead wrong at the core of your life. You have disregarded your peculiar essential nature, the voice said. And think of yourself as a thing, a commodity.

Then: I'm lonely, the voice said. Open the door.

That's it! Harry said. I'm calling the police!

I am lonely because I am pure, the voice said. And I am original.

Harry walked to the phone on the nightstand and picked up the receiver. That's it! Harry said. Nine-one-one!

It ain't your dick that's broken! the voice said, It's your heart. Now open this fucking door. I've got a gift for you.

Harry hung up the phone.

Who are you? Harry said.

The guy with the lamp, the voice said.

Are you searching for an honest man? Harry asked.

I'm searching for a hard dick, asshole, the voice said. Open the fucking door!

Then: Just tell me one thing, the voice said. You ever met Andy Warhol?

Andy Warhol? Harry said brightly. Why, yes, of course, I've met Andy. I used to hang out at the Factory once in a while.

Oh, God, the voice said, Here it comes! I just knew it!

Great parties! Harry said.

Don't tell me! the voice said. Andy Warhol didn't—he didn't ask you if he could draw your genitals, did he?

Yes, Harry said proudly, looking down at his crotch. Andy Warhol drew my genitals.

Oh, misery! the voice said. He's captured your erection!

No, Harry said, I wasn't erect.

He's captured your passion, the voice said.

My passion? Harry said. No, it was just my cock, and my cock wasn't really erect—just half mast—and Andy Warhol didn't capture it, he just drew it.

Appearance is all there is, the voice said. These days it's the image of the thing that's important—at least for fifteen minutes. The thing itself can be discarded once you have the image of it. No use for a cock once it's sucked dry, the voice said.

He didn't suck it dry, Harry says. He didn't even touch it. He just drew it.

Same difference, the voice said.

The meaning of things is they have no meaning, the voice said. The appearance of the thing is what's important. If you take a photo, if you draw it, if you capture the image, you capture the thing.

Don't you see, by drawing your balls, the voice said, Andy Warhol got your balls?

How can somebody do that? Harry said incredulously. How can somebody get your balls? That's impossible.

Harry cupped his balls in his hand.

Look, they're right here, Harry said. My balls are right here!

A lot of good they're doing you, the voice said. We are the hollow men, the voice said. Codpieces stuffed with straw.

What? Harry said.

It's a joke, the voice said.

What's a joke? Harry said.

What you're holding in your hand! the voice said. Nothing is original anymore. Nothing is pure. What's left is the world of appearances;
ergo, your endless repetition of pop images, your bottomless narcissis-
tic desire for attention, your need of acknowledgment from privileged
insiders, your limp dick.

Huh? Harry said.

The author is dead! the voice said. Your dick is dead! the voice said.
Andy Warhol took your cock and balls with him when he left.

But how could he do that? Harry said.

He's Andy Warhol, the voice said. This is New York City. It's the
eighties. Just look at the hidden meaning of his name: War Hole.

All he did was draw it, Harry said.

Postmodern totemism! the voice said. Open the door! the voice said.
There isn't much time left! I have an antidote for you.

Antidote? Harry said.

Art, the voice said.

Harry unlocked the chain and opened the door.

THE LIGHTS ON the stage dimmed. The TV went off. Through the door,
the lights went up on the back wall. In the background, you could hear
Fiona on the accordion singing "Ah, Sweet Mystery of Life." There was
a painting like the woman's nose in BEFORE AND AFTER—only the *before* was a flaccid cock and the *after* was a hard cock. Between the flaccid cock and the hard cock was a section of empty canvas. In the section
of empty canvas hung a small lantern on a hook.

Harry picked up the lantern and held it out to the audience.

Anybody out there seen my erection? Harry said.

Anybody out there seen a drawing of my erection? Harry said.

Anybody out there know where Andy Warhol is tonight? Harry said.

Anybody named Charlie 2Moons out there? Harry said.

A loud gasp from the audience. It was me.

Charlie 2Moons?

The pain in my forearms, up to my shoulders, splash down through
heart, cattle prod to cock.

Harry walked to the mirror, held the lantern up to the mirror, looked
at himself.

Anybody *in* there? Harry said.

* * *

THE LIGHTS WENT up, and everybody clapped. Rose wasn't clapping, though. Neither was I. Rose and I weren't clapping because I was holding tight onto Rose's hand.

My mother's nerves.

Rose put his bottom lip over his top lip. The color of the inside of his lips, I wondered what other parts on his body were that color.

So you know this Charlie 2Moons, Rose said.

I know him, I said.

Then: Crossed over, my mouth said. What you used to run away from happens to you here. Go to a performance in somebody's basement and there's your cock up on the stage!

Rose's bracelets clack-clack.

So *Tony and Tina's Wedding*! Rose said.

Susan Strong said that, I said.

I said it first, Rose said.

Rose put his extra-lovely hand on top of my hand that was holding his hand.

The play's the thing, Rose said, To catch the conscience of the king.

All hat and no cowboy, I said.

The grilled salmon, Rose said. The Pinot Gris, the limp dick.

Fuck! I said, First Ellen broadcasts it all over the neighborhood, then Susan Strong makes performance art out of it!

Ah, fame! Rose said. Your cock is becoming a household word. Then: Make it aware, make art out of it! Rose said.

Susan Strong said that, I said.

Rose's lips went together and he pushed them out. He took his hand away from my hand. Rose lifted his hand up between me and him, stuck his index finger up, moved it side to side, back and forth, back and forth.

No no Yoko Ono, Rose said.

I said it first, Rose said. I'm her AUI remember? Her Absolute Ultimate Idol.

Rose pulled the drape of the Jew or Arab hat from his face, bracelets clack-clack. I was back to clutching Rose's leather coat.

That was the moment, the first time Rose didn't use his eyes as a weapon. Rose really looked at me.

First rule, Rose said. Never touch me.

I let go of Rose's leather jacket, put my fists in my armpits, folded my arms in front of me.

Rose pushed his chair back, stood up, leather sounds from his pants and jacket and combat boots.

You know, Rose said, You're not the first man in history who thinks his cock is the path to wisdom. You're not the first man to make his hard-on into the Holy Grail.

That's different, I said.

What's different? Rose said.

Searching for something to get you hard, I said, Is different from searching for your hard-on.

What's different? Rose said.

What gets you hard, I said, Is out there. Getting hard, I said, Is in here. I was pointing at my chest.

Rose's leather crotch was inches from my face. I not-looked at his crotch while I looked up at Rose's face. His lips opened into a big smile, but it wasn't a smile. Just something he put on his face.

So this Charlie 2Moons guy has your hard-on? Rose said.

No, I said, He's got my heart.

Rose was looking at me again, really looking.

The Greeks, Rose said, Believed the hero is allowed to struggle against the superior power of destiny. The lucid compulsion to act, Rose said, To act polemically, Rose said, Determines the substance of the self.

Polema-*what*? I said.

Polemically, Rose said.

By resisting the gods, Rose said, The hero substantiates himself.

Rose turned his crotch around and there was his butt. He wasn't wearing black leather pants. He was wearing black leather chaps, and his bare black butt was staring me in the face.

Wounded by the aroma of love. Definitely not Polo.

Rose kept talking as he walked away. It's to ourselves, Rose said, That we are strangers. *La lutte*, Rose said—Rose raised his fist—The struggle, Rose said, Reveals to us who we are. The hindrance to our task is our task.

Rose had to duck his head to get through the Dixon Place door. His slick shiny big black butt, his leather legs, his combat boots, walked up the stairs.

Then, all at once, Rose turned, crouched down.

I'm curious, Rose said, Did Andy draw your cock?

Andy Warhol? I said, No way!

You're lucky, Rose said, Because if it was Andy Warhol stole your erection, you'd never get it back.

Why's that? I said.

Andy Warhol could be the Ultimate Shy Hunter, Rose said, But he's too afraid.

Rose was across the street at the telephone booth by the service station when I caught up to him.

What's that? I said. A Shy Hunter?

The black leather shine of Rose in the unrelenting service station light. The shine on his shaved head. Rose's eyes at me were two bits of hard coal. The shine of coal.

Family secret, Rose said.

Rose took off walking again, and it was the rub of leather chaps tight around hard muscle. Rose's ass. The unrelenting fluorescence on the hairs of Rose's ass. Two combat-boot steps and, just like that, the shine was gone and Rose walked into the night.

So what's he afraid of? I said loud, Andy Warhol? What's he so afraid of?

In the unrelenting fluorescence, I put my hand above my eyes. My skin was beige, dull green. No shine.

The shadow of Rose in the Manhattan night kept walking up Second Avenue, didn't look back.

Your genitals, Rose yelled, He draws your genitals. Not your eyes, your lips, not the slope of your neck.

My hand went down from above my eyes and touched my neck.

And so what if Andy Warhol did draw my cock?

Now I was yelling too.

How would I get it back? I said, Do I have to be a Shy Hunter?

Then smooth, just like that, one long dark leap and Rose was out of darkness, back in the service station light, right there in my face, Rose's face. His smile. The gap between his two front teeth.

Second rule, Rose said. You got to be one to get one.

CHAPTER
SIX

The liar's space.

That's what Bobbie called the gap between Charlie 2Moons's two front teeth.

Don't know which came first, Bobbie said, The liar's space or the lying.

But Charlie didn't *lie*. Charlie liked to tell stories, tall tales. Probably because of all those books he read. Like *Robinson Crusoe*, *A Tale of Two Cities*, *Huckleberry Finn*. As soon as Charlie opened his mouth to tell you about something that happened to him, or to his mother, Viv, or to his grandfather, Alessandro, or to his horse, ayaHuaska, you could bet your life there was some truth in what Charlie was telling you.

Bobbie said Charlie was a born bullshit artist.

Maybe it's the truth. But I think it was Charlie's nature to tell a good story, which means he expanded on some of the details.

Mostly Charlie's stories were about his father, his famous fancy-riding, trick-riding father, who was a full-blood descendant of Geronimo, who worked as a movie extra in Hollywood and hung out with Gene Autry and Roy Rogers and Tom Mix and Gary Cooper and Randolph Scott and Cary Grant and John Wayne.

Charlie's father discovered Clint Eastwood. Charlie said his father one day was buying himself a new saddle in a saddle shop in Beverly Hills and the guy waiting on Charlie's father was Clint Eastwood, and Charlie said his father took one look at Clint and saw Spaghetti Western written all over Clint's face.

Another story Charlie always told was that his father had supernatural powers that he inherited from the spirit of Geronimo, and one of these powers was that his father could change into different animals any time he wanted.

Mostly, though, Charlie said, What my father turned into was Wolf.

One day lying around in Bobbie's bedroom, listening to Johnny Mathis, *Heavenly*, Charlie told Bobbie and me that his mother, Viv, of

Viv's Double Wide Beauty Salon, wasn't a hairdresser at all, she was an alien being who had come to earth to gather information about the effects of despair on the cosmos. Charlie said the task of his alien mother on this earth—being an Indian and woman and all—was to study despair by feeling it.

Then there was one night when Charlie and Bobbie and I were up in the barn, in the back, where the bales of straw and the straw on the floor were. We were sitting on the old white-trash couch, the black-and-white wedding diamond quilt over us, a kerosene lamp for light, the floor swept clean of straw around where the lamp sat. It was nice up there in the barn, listening to the big old Zenith radio.

The only station we could get was KSEI. On Saturday nights KSEI played the top ten hits, and every Saturday night for sure—if Father wasn't home—you could find Bobbie and Charlie and me up in the barn, sliding a two-step on the straw on the barn floor, slow dancing, jitterbugging, listening to Patti Page singing "The Tennessee Waltz" and Tennessee Ernie Ford singing "Sixteen Tons," and then, of course, "Love Me Tender" and "Hound Dog."

Father had taught Bobbie how to roll cigarettes with one hand, and Bobbie was teaching Charlie. Bobbie was showing Charlie how to undo the Bull Durham pouch with your teeth, how to hold the paper, how to lick the paper.

Neither one of them would let me learn how to roll because I was too young. I told them that I was already a sub-teen and sub-teen meant it was high time you started smoking, but both Bobbie and Charlie shook their heads.

The only thing Bobbie and Charlie ever agreed on was me. What was best for me.

Ray Charles was singing "I've Got a Woman," and Bobbie was singing along, her eyes closed, chin up, rolling her head back and forth like you do when you're alone in your room, her brown hair long enough to fall back.

Charlie's hair was long, pulled back wavy and braided into one big braid. He finished rolling his cigarette, put the cigarette in his mouth, lit the cigarette, and inhaled, and when he exhaled Charlie said, You know this here barn we're sitting in is haunted.

It was summer because we were all barefoot. Bobbie was rolling a cigarette too.

Charlie 2Moons, Bobbie said, You told us that shit the first time we ever met you.

Charlie leaned in closer to the flame, the flame in Charlie's eyes.

I'm serious! Charlie said. This barn is haunted, Charlie said. And it's not only haunted, Charlie said, It's *sexually* haunted.

Bobbie didn't move her head. She wiped her wrist across her brown bangs and just kept looking at the hand rolling the cigarette.

What do you mean *sexually*? I said.

Charlie 2Moons, Bobbie said, Every goddamn time you open your mouth that space between your teeth gets wider and wider.

It's the truth! Charlie said. I've experienced it myself.

Bobbie raised her head up, just her head, gold flecks in her eyes. She lifted up her butt cheek, farted.

The Green Door was playing on the Zenith.

You experienced *what* yourself? Bobbie said.

Charlie raised his head up too, looked right into Bobbie's brown eyes, didn't blink. Being sexually haunted, Charlie said.

What the fuck does that mean? Bobbie said.

Charlie poked his chest up, his chin out. His hands started flying all over in the air.

You're a girl, Charlie said. You wouldn't understand.

Bobbie moved her face closer to Charlie's. She took a match out of the matchbox, struck the match on her thigh, lit her cigarette. Blew smoke into Charlie's face. Tossed the stick match onto the broken green dish we had for an ashtray.

What's *girl* got to do with it? Bobbie said.

I'm not a girl, I said. I don't understand.

Shut up, Will, Bobbie said.

My forearms.

Charlie struck a match with his thumbnail, lit his cigarette, blew smoke into Bobbie's face, tossed the stick match onto the broken-green-dish ashtray.

Girls don't have cocks, Charlie said, Now do they?

Bobbie sucked on her cigarette, wiped back her bangs.

You need a cock to be sexually haunted? Bobbie said.

Helps, Charlie said.

What's it help? Bobbie said.

Helps you get a hard-on, Charlie said.

A what? Bobbie said.

A hard-on, Charlie said, smiling his gap-tooth smile.

Bobbie smiled too, a little bigger but not really a smile.

Bobbie Parker! Charlie said. You of all people can't tell me you don't know what a hard-on is.

Bobbie quick-looked up from the kerosene lamp, over at Charlie. The gold flecks in her eyes were fire.

What's a hard-on? I said.

Shut up, Will, Bobbie said.

You'll find out soon enough, Charlie said.

Bobbie leaned back on the couch, pulled her leg up, leaned her head on her elbow, flicked the ashes off her cigarette into the broken-greendish ashtray.

Bobbie's face was real red, not Indian red but blotchy red, the way she got.

You dumb son of a bitch! Bobbie said. You fucking men don't have a clue.

When I looked over at Charlie, Charlie was biting his thumbnail, and I knew it was the truth. Charlie was a fucking man without a clue.

Just like that, Bobbie got up and walked down the length of the barn, walked down the stairs, her footsteps inside every board on the floor of the brick barn.

The Everly Brothers were singing "Cathy's Clown." I poured some tobacco into my hand and started rolling it up.

Charlie looked like an Indian James Dean with the cigarette hanging out of his mouth, his eyes squinting, the cigarette going up and down, up and down, as Charlie spoke.

You'd better not let your sister catch you doing that! Charlie said.

I don't do everything, I said, Bobbie tells me to do.

Yes, you do, Charlie said.

After a while, we heard Bobbie at the stairs and I quick put the tobacco back in the Bull Durham pouch.

Charlie just looked at me. Charlie never made fun of me, or put me down, or made me feel small in any way ever. He just looked at me.

Bobbie walked up to us and threw some magazines down on the straw on the floor in the kerosene lamplight.

Charlie's eyes got real wide and he leaned back like the magazines were some kind of black magic or other scary thing that you like to be scared of.

One of the magazines was *Playboy,* and there were two other magazines, I don't remember the names, with half-naked women in them. I'd read the magazines before lots of times. Bobbie kept them in the secret place in her closet, along with *Lady Chatterley's Lover, The Song of the Red Ruby*, and *Peyton Place*. I read all those books too, but I never told Bobbie.

Charlie 2Moons, Bobbie said, her hands on her hips, Here's some education for you. Read these and then get back to me about just what a hard-on is, OK?

Charlie didn't say anything, just picked up the *Playboy* and opened up to the centerfold. Charlie was breathing hard and sweat was coming out his forehead. I thought he was going to pass out.

A woman's got a vagina, see, Bobbie said and pointed to in between the *Playboy* bunny's crossed legs.

Some call it a vagina, Bobbie said, Some call it a pussy. I like to call it and everything around it my Deep Flower, but when I'm feeling especially horny, I call it my poon.

When a woman gets hot, Bobbie said, Her poon gets wet, and inside her poon is the most wonderful place on a woman's body, and that place is called the clitoris.

Clit, Bobbie said. Clit's inside the poon. And the clit gets hard when it's right for a woman, Bobbie said. If it ain't right, forget it, but when it's right the clit gets hard and stands up like a man in a little boat.

Granted, Bobbie said, The clit don't get as big as a cock, but to a woman size doesn't much matter, and even though the clit don't get as big as what you call a hard-on, the clit's got it all over the hard-on, hands down. Hard-on shoots its cum out in one big load, while clit just keeps on purring and purring and purring and cumming and cumming.

With a hard-on, Bobbie said, It's usually a one-shot deal. If you're lucky, maybe two.

But with a clit, Bobbie said, And a nice wet poon, you can come for days.

Charlie threw the *Playboy* down, jumped up off his butt, and, just like that, ran off into the dark. Charlie in the dark groaning groaning. Then silence.

When Charlie came back into the light, Bobbie was rolling another cigarette, her head bent, her eyes looking down at her hand.

Bobbie's splotches were fading back into skin.

Roll me one of those, would you? Charlie said.

Bobbie laughed. One laugh, chest up and down. She flashed the gold flecks of her eyes up to Charlie.

Need a steady hand to roll a smoke, Bobbie said, Now don't you?

Yup, Charlie said.

This time Bobbie's laugh wasn't hard and loud.

Bobbie licked her tongue across the glued end of the cigarette paper.

But I know what you mean, Bobbie said.

About what? Charlie said.

This barn being sexually haunted, Bobbie said. Every time I come up here alone I start pulling back the petals, digging deep into Deep Flower, just pumping poon.

Me too, Charlie said. Sometimes two or three times a day.

You whack off three times a day? Bobbie said.

Sometimes more, Charlie said. Got to tame the savage beast.

What's whacking off? I said.

I've never done it more than twice a day, Bobbie said. At least so far.

Charlie opened the *Playboy* to the centerfold. Laid the centerfold out in the kerosene light. Charlie traced his finger along the woman's naked back.

Bobbie? Charlie said.

Yeah? Bobbie said.

This is a big stack of magazines, Charlie said. Full of half-naked women. You a lesbian?

Bobbie sucked long on her cigarette, let the smoke come out her nose.

I never saw Bobbie look that way, not once, except for that night. She hacked and spit and I was thinking all hell would break loose, but instead Bobbie's face got soft, her eyes got big. Bobbie's lips lost their cuss, just like that, and out of the blue, Bobbie was showing Charlie and me the only part of herself she could keep safe from Father.

Bobbie knelt down next to the kerosene lamp, laid her forearm right up next to the fire.

You know Charlie 2Moons, Bobbie said, Your skin is almost as white as mine.

And those waves in your hair, Bobbie said. Injuns got straight hair. Where did you get them waves?

LATER ON, WHEN Bobbie and her magazines had gone back to the house, Charlie and I stayed in the barn. Charlie came over to me and lay down next to me on the straw. My head in the crook of Charlie's arm, my ear on his heart.

That sister of yours is something, Charlie said.

She's a lesbian, I said.

Then: What's a lesbian? I said, and moved in closer.

A lesbian is a woman, Charlie said. But she really ain't a woman. What she is is a man with the power to suck his cock and balls up inside himself and push his chest out into titties.

Did you make that up? I said.

No, Charlie said. It's the truth.

Mice in the straw, a gust of wind in the slates on the roof of the barn.

Does it work the other way around too? I said.

Which other way? Charlie said.

Can a woman, I said, Have the power to push out her clit into a cock and suck in her titties?

Of course! Charlie said.

Then, I said, With that power, I said, Bobbie could actually be a boy.

She could, Charlie said.

Charlie cupped his hand over the lantern, blew out the flame. Charlie's skin in the broken bits of moon was the same color as mine. The wind was warm, stirring up the straw, shaking the barn, rattling slates. I pulled myself in closer to Charlie.

Charlie? I said. Maybe I'm really a girl who can push her clitoris out and suck her titties in?

Not a chance! Charlie said. I mean, you'd know, wouldn't you?

It's always me, I said, Who screams like a girl, I said. When we play Door of the Dead, I said, No matter how hard I try not to.

That's when Charlie kissed me. The first time Charlie ever kissed me. On the mouth, just a little, just before we went to sleep.

A blow of love. Wounded. Absolute. Ultimate.

CHAPTER
SEVEN

Fiona was pissed at me for bringing Argwings Khodek to her performance piece without telling her.

In Café Cauchemar, standing under the Sistine Chapel God, staring at Fiona's cruel lip, a life all its own, I made my face go New York drop-dead fuck-you, took a deep breath, and spoke.

My mother's nerves.

Susan Strong, I said, You are a conniving bitch.

And: How dare you. I said, Take my private life, I said, And put it up on the stage.

The curl of Fiona's lip, Fiona's hands on her hips, her black hair flying up every which way. Fiona said, If the shoe fits, wear it.

I almost slapped her face.

Instead I said, You didn't have to, I said, Bring Charlie 2Moons into it.

Fiona said, I didn't. Harry improvised!

So, I yelled at Harry. What the fuck you doing with my private life? It was bad enough, I yelled, having my cock up there on the stage, let alone you drag Charlie's name through the fucking mud.

Harry's pink face went fuchsia. The mud? The mud? Harry said. You call our performance piece mud? Get a grip, Mary! Charlie's name just came out of my mouth. I knew you were looking for him, and onstage at that moment it seemed appropriate so I said it: *Anybody out there seen Charlie 2Moons?* You should fucking thank me for helping you to find your old fuck buddy. Fuck you, asshole.

No, fuck you, Harry! I said.

And I didn't *bring* Argwings Khodek, I said, I gave him a free ticket. It was synchronistic that I sat down next to him.

Fuck your synchronicity, Fiona said.

Fuck you, Susan Strong! I said. If you want to tell the truth so much, put *your* poon up there on the stage. Leave my cock out of it.

Poon? Fiona said. Is that what they call it in Ohio, poon?

Fuck you! I said. It's Idaho.
My, my! Fiona said. Mild-mannered Clark Kent isn't stuttering now!
Fuck you! I said.
Go fuck yourself! Harry said.
Fuck you! I said.

FOR ME, THE whole fiasco was over after the first night. But not for Fiona and Harry. Neither one of them spoke to me until the day Chef Som Chai came back to work.

It's tough—working alongside of people, standing together at the bar, the dessert station, at the espresso machine, smoking at the garbage can—not looking at them, not speaking to them. Especially Fiona. I really missed talking to Fiona, looking at her. Missed not being talked to, looked at by her blue eyes.

The chef came back on a Thursday. I was polishing silverware in Section Two. Fiona walked in the door.

Just like that: Howdy, pardner! Fiona said, breezing by, red lips a life all their own, *sexy totale*, her huge red leather purse over her shoulder.

Chef's back! she said.

IN THE LOCKER room of Café Cauchemar, I was just reaching for my shorts when Kung Fu salad guy walked into the dressing room, followed by Chef Som Chai.

The chef's hand was a big white boxing glove of gauze, and the chef made like a boxer when he came up to me, like he was going to punch me, but he didn't. The chef put his good hand on my shoulder, just long enough to let me know he'd touched me, then extended his good hand, palm open, toward me. I took his hand, still not smiling, and we stood that way, looking at each other, the chef standing too close, my one hand shaking the chef's hand, the chef holding his boxing-glove hand in the air above his heart, my other hand holding up my shorts in front of me.

How's your hand? I asked.

My boys tell me you good waiter, the chef said. You different from other waiters.

The chef turned and said something in his language to Kung Fu salad guy. Kung Fu salad guy said something back to him.

Respect, Chef Som Chai said. They say you have respect.

Most Americans don't know respect, the chef said. You think you know everything. So we do our best to teach you. Sometimes this very hard.

The chef looked at Kung Fu salad guy, and Kung Fu salad guy barked like a dog. I thought they'd never stop laughing.

Then: Ocean is big, Chef Som Chai said, Because ocean is lower than rivers. But one thing you must always remember. This here New York City, and you need to speak up when you put order in. You speak too soft and not fast.

Yes, sir, I said.

Chef! the chef said. I am Chef.

Chef Som Chai took his good fist and banged it against his chest.

Yes, Chef! I said.

What your section tonight? the chef asked.

One, I said. Section One.

Well then, the chef said, I change schedule. This week you have Section Three and maybe Four and Five, maybe Section Six.

You're going this way and then shit happens and then you're going that way.

Thank you, I said. Chef.

I was still shaking his hand.

How much money you make this week? the chef asked.

Some, I said. Hundred and ninety-five dollars, I said. Seven shifts.

Now you make twice as much in half of time, the chef said.

He let go of my hand and rolled just his eyes up to the unrelenting fluorescence.

But now, the chef said, smiling big, Now you have many enemies.

Chef took my hand that was holding my shorts in front of me and raised it the same way his bandaged hand was raised.

In all the world, naked, standing with two guys from Thailand in a locker room of a New York restaurant, both the chef and I, our left hands wrapped, his in gauze, mine in Fruit of the Loom, left hands in the air.

You are hung like Asian man, the chef said.

Chef looked down at my cock.

Shows wisdom, he said.

Wisdom? I said.

You and your body not identical, the chef said. American men with big cocks don't know that, the chef said, But you been blessed. Your spirit is great, your body is big, and your dick is little.

I was smiling. Stopped smiling. The chef had to sit down, he was laughing so hard. Kung Fu salad guy too.

But when our cocks get hard, the chef said, They get *really* hard, no? Stainless steel! the chef said, making a fist with his good hand.

Then, all at once, my mouth said, Then why you calling me Horse Dick?

Chef Som Chai walked to the door, opened the door, Kung Fu salad guy behind him. I was still standing with my left hand and my shorts in the air.

You in big trouble now, the chef said. Next week you Section Six, and Mack Dickson think your cock bigger than his.

I covered myself with my Fruit of the Looms.

Kung Fu salad guy closed the door behind them: laughing; the two of them laughed all the way up the stairs.

FIONA WAS STANDING at the espresso machine, looking up at the schedule.

Oh . . . my . . . God! Fiona said. They've moved Mack Dickson into Section One.

Then: Fuck, Will! You're in Section Five!

Walter, the ectomorph who drank too much coffee, Walter the actor with the new haircut, boy's regular, just like Davey Dearest's haircut which was just like Richard Gere's, walked over to the schedule, made the sound of inhaling air, said something ferocious, and ran out through the swinging red doors.

Life vérité, Fiona said.

Fiona walked over to the schedule. Put her index under my name.

Then: Will! Fiona said, and looked right at me.

Fiona's blue eyes holding me in them again.

You sly son of a bitch! Fiona said. Way fucking cool!

Over by the garbage can where you can smoke, I was filling out my checks with my name and the date.

What did Walter say? I said.

Something about sucking yellow dick, Fiona said.

Fiona looked through the window on the red swinging doors.

Look! Fiona said. Walter's talking to Daniel! Cool. Now Joanie's getting in on it, and there's Davey Dearest. *Oh . . . my . . . God!* Mack Dickson's walking over to them now. Look at 'em all together, like flies on shit.

He's coming our way, Fiona said. Mack, Son of Dick! Thee perfect gay man!

Then, cupping her hands around her mouth, she hollered, Prepare for Mack Attack! Prepare for Mack Attack!

I looked around for somewhere to run, to leave the premises, but the only way out was through the swinging red doors. I kept writing my name down and the date. Name and date. Name and date. I was practicing what to say, but I couldn't remember, not one word in English. Language is my second language. There was no time to roll a cigarette; besides, I was already smoking a cigarette.

Fuck! Fiona said. Wish Harry was here!

The swinging red doors burst open, and Mack Dickson was standing there all of a sudden like in vampire movies.

Frozen moments in time.

I acted like I was already dead and wished he was dead too.

Davey Dearest was behind Mack Dickson, then Walter, then Joanie. They were all standing with their hands on their hips, as if they'd practiced at home. If they were cowboys they'd draw six-guns and OK Corral the place.

Then Mack Dickson, Mack Son of Dick, Mack-Attack Dickson, Perfect Gay Man, Republican, tortured gym body, matching underwear and socks, possessor of perfect Caravaggio body, walked to the schedule, followed his finger along the line, came to the place where my name was and his name used to be, turned, and walked the way American men with big cocks walk, right up to me.

Everything about him was beautiful. Even his nose hairs were beautiful.

Horse Dick, Mack Dickson said, I'm going to get you for this!

My arms folded in front of me, I leaned back on my heels and looked Max Dickson straight in the eye.

So I'm a yellow-dick-sucking asshole, I said. What the fuck you going to do about it?

But it's not the truth.

My mouth was moving but nothing was coming out.

That's when Harry walked in through the swinging red doors with Ronald Reagan and Nancy under his arm. Harry set Ron and Nancy up against the counter. Mack Dickson, Walter, Davey Dearest, Joanie, Georgette, Fiona, and I—we all looked at Harry and Ronald Reagan and Nancy.

What is this, Harry said, A convention?

Then Chef Som Chai walked in from the kitchen and stood right in the center of us waiters, his chef's hat just high enough for me to see over.

Quiet only New York can get that fast.

Hello, Chef, Mack Dickson said.

Hello, Chef, Joanie said.

Hello, Chef, Davey Dearest said.

Hello, Chef, Walter said.

The chef looked at Fiona, then me, then Harry.

How's it going, Chef? Fiona said.

Hello, Chef, I said.

Harry barked like a dog three times, loud. Didn't growl.

Then Daniel, the boss's brother, walked in through the swinging red doors.

Hey, Spud, Daniel said to me. Can you stay after work tonight? I need to have a talk with you.

Everybody—Mack, Walter, Joanie, Davey, Fiona, Harry, Georgette, even Chef Som Chai—laughed out loud all at once, then tried not to laugh, and quick they left the room, yawning, covering their mouths, coughing, all of them, even Georgette, into the kitchen, into the dishwashing room, through the swinging red doors, into the dining room, away, and then it was just me and Daniel standing there. I wasn't laughing.

What's wrong? Daniel said. What the fuck's so funny? What'd I say?

Through the swinging red doors, I was out of there. In the dining room in nothing flat.

SNOW ON CHRISTMAS Eve. Big flakes coming down in the mercury-vapor light. On the R downtown, slick parkas and the smell of wet wool. My first Christmas in New York.

No Charlie 2Moons.

I was just some guy in a ball cap and a pea coat sitting in an orange plastic chair, in the unrelenting fluorescence, roar all around, speeding through massive rock tunnels under massive Manhattan buildings, some guy, me, Merry fucking Christmas, already dead, everybody around me on the train already dead too. Some guy in a white beard and red cap walking through the subway car shaking his can for change. The floor of the train New York gray slush.

Snow on the cast-iron steps. I unlocked the door to 205 East Fifth Street, stamped my feet on the wet gray rug. In the hallway, in the long narrow hallway painted blue, under the fluorescent halo, I walked to my mailbox and there, beyond the mailboxes, just under the stairs, leaning against the door to the basement: the dead man, on the floor, wavy raven hair, the needle still stuck in his arm. Blood all down his arm

that was thick and in the light looked black running down onto his
pants, down onto the floor, down between his legs, down to a dark pool.
Looked like the needle in his arm had poked a hole and let out a black
snake in him that had kept him alive.

The dead guy's face, free of blood, stone smooth, his eyes, just his
eyes rolled up.

Charlie 2Moons.

I sat down right there on the floor next to the black snake. Laid my
face into the pool of blood. Sucked up the blood. Charlie's blood. Blood
that I didn't want to live without. My own blood.

Out of my mouth, the unmistakable sound.

But it's not the truth.

The dead guy wasn't Charlie.

The next thing I knew, what was coming down the stairs was the
kind of Moroccan shoes that point up at the toe, yellow, huge. The huge
yellow Moroccan shoes were connected to black ankles and thick black
calves and then African cloth tied around Rose's middle, bare chest.

Argwings Khodek, I said.

In the unrelenting fluorescence, Rose was black as the snake.

The dead guy's eyes weren't looking up at me anymore. They were
looking up at Rose. At Rose's beautiful gold loop in his queer ear.

Jump through the gold loop.

Rose took one look at the dead guy on the floor, raised just his eyes
up to the unrelenting fluorescence, closed his eyes and took a deep
breath, then walked over to me, put his arm across my shoulder, turned
me around.

Rose put my right hand in his, his big hand open on mine, his Sahara
Desert palm against my sweaty palm, bracelets clack-clack.

Never touch me.

Rose gave me a hand up.

My friends all call me Rose, he said.

My face was smiling. I stopped smiling.

Hello, Rose, I said. My friends, I said, All call me Will.

Rose looked over to the dead guy lying in the narrow blue hallway,
his wavy raven hair, the needle stuck in his arm, the black snake running
out of him; then Rose looked up again at the halo of bright fluorescence
from above.

Even myself, Rose said, I am just here, isn't it?

I stared at Rose. At Rose's mouth, the inside color of his lips.

I don't understand, I said, What you just said, I said.

Even myself I am just here, isn't it?—is what I said, Rose said.

Rose smiled, and when he smiled, my eyes went straight to the gap between his two front teeth.

I just got back from a tour of East Africa, Rose said, bracelets clack-clack. And in East Africa, especially on the island of Lamu where they speak the purest Kiswahili—the word is not *Swahili,* that's incorrect; the correct word is *Kiswahili*—I'd be standing there in the street or in a bar or wherever and a native man—*Mwanainchi*—would walk up to me and that's how he'd introduce himself. He'd say, Even myself I am just here, isn't it?

Fluorescence the sound of insects.

What *you* need is a cocktail, Rose said.

Rose took me by the arm, the way a man takes a woman by the arm when he escorts her. Rose held me up on the one side, the banister held me up on the other, all the way, Rose and me, that way up the stairs, Rose talking talking about Africa, to his apartment door, dogs barking on the other side, me against the wall while Rose unlocked his door, opened his door, then dogs every which way, and then Rose's arm was in mine again, and all at once my legs weren't under me anymore, and I was in Rose's never-touch-me big black arms, bracelets clack-clack. Rose carried me, talking talking, over the threshold, and all around under me was dogs, barking barking dogs.

I'm a big man and big men don't get carried and there I was being carried, my whole body touching Rose. Rose took off my ball cap, unbuttoned my pea coat.

Rose's bathroom was pink—sink, bathtub, toilet, tile on the walls, floor tile, shower curtain—everything pink except for the gold frame around the mirror and the gold lights in the shape of flowers on either side of the mirror and the gold frame around the photograph of Elizabeth Taylor sitting on the sink.

Pink? Rose said. White people are pink, Rose said. *Fuchsia,* Rose said. The correct name of the color in my toilet—Rose used the French pronunciation, *twalette*—is *fuchsia.*

Fuchsia twalette.

My head was in Rose's fuchsia twalette, fountain mouth. Barfing like Bobbie used to, lid up, holding on to the twalette's sides.

When I flushed and rinsed and could stand without holding on to the sink, when I didn't need Rose's gold-framed mirror anymore, I walked back out of Rose's bathroom, through his dark bedroom, everything draped in velvet with just his lava lamp on. On his bedstand, next to the Joey Heatherton bed, incense going next to a Buddha as big as half the bed, and an oil painting of Elizabeth Taylor in her white swimsuit in *Suddenly Last Summer* as big as the Buddha.

The apartment was Tallulah Bankhead Went to Africa. Red velvet curtains hanging from Rose's windows. An Italian crystal chandelabra from the ceiling. Faux leopard-skin throws, faux zebra-covered pillows, texture, texture, texture.

On the carved wood African coffee table with a brass top was a bouquet of long-stemmed red roses in a brass vase, a tin lunch box with a cowboy on it, a bunch of long stick matches, a paperback book, *Antigone*, Rose's pack of Gauloise no-filters, an ashtray that was Dwight D. Eisenhower smiling, a two-gallon jug filled with an amber liquid, and two glasses—Baccarat crystal glasses—and a bottle of Courvoisier VSOP.

Sitar music.

Rose was sitting in his purple-velvet overstuffed chair, his legs crossed. Rose had put a top on—another African-looking thing all white and soft with lace around the neck. His head was shaved. I learned later on, Rose's head was always shaved and the different hair he had was all wigs.

My body had stopped shaking, my throat was raw and nasty. I sat on Rose's fainting couch, the blonde, fainting. I was policing my body, new-shoe stiff.

I thought the dead guy was Charlie, I said, 2Moons.

Rose poured a glass of VSOP for me and a glass for himself and offered me a Gauloise. I took the Gauloise and Rose lit it for me with one of the long stick matches and then lit his.

No, Rose said, That was not your lovely Charlie 2Moons, that was Ricardo, the super.

Ricardo the voodoo super? I said.

Le même, Rose said.

The cowboy on the tin lunch box was Randolph Scott. Out of the lunch box, Rose took a pipe the shape of a penis—not a huge penis like you see in the magazines, but just a penis, an erect penis attached to a set of balls.

Now *this* is *pink*, Rose said.

Then Rose took something wrapped in cellophane out of the lunch box.

Chocolate, Rose said but he said it the French way, *Sho-ko-lat*.

The Sho-ko-lat looked like a big rabbit turd to me. Rose put the rabbit-turd Sho-ko-lat in the pipe at the base of the penis and lit the rabbit turd and held the pipe by the balls and sucked on the erect pink penis head and then passed the thing to me.

In my hand, I held an erect pink penis by the balls.

Third rule, Rose said. It's all metaphor, Rose said. It's all drag.

So I went ahead and sucked on the metaphor.

Just out the door and down the stairs, in the long narrow blue hallway, the unrelenting fluorescence, the fluorescent insect sound was the black snake run out of the dead guy's arm, thick black down his arm, down onto his pants down onto the floor into the hole where the linoleum buckled and was a low linoleum valley, the thick black lake.

My mother's nerves.

I took another toke on the erect pink penis.

Rose's dogs were all lined up on the Persian carpet, sitting on Rose's feet.

Mary, Rose said: part Alaskan wolfhound, part Tuesday Weld.

Mona, Rose said: part poodle, part overweight Italian girl.

And Jack Flash, Rose said: part terrier, part dictator, part bundle of love.

All dogs are Buddha, Rose said.

Rose held the erect pink penis by the balls in his extra-lovely hand, his Sahara Desert palm, then handed the erect pink penis to me.

It's yours, Rose said.

The pink penis in my hands looked exactly like mine. Lifesize.

I set the pipe in my open palm, right hand.

It looks familiar, I said.

I *mean*, Rose said, It's my *gift* to you. Your erection, Rose said.

My face was smiling. I stopped smiling. Sat and held the erect pink penis in my hand, not the way you'd hold a pipe but the way you'd hold your erect pink penis.

Second rule, Rose said. You've got to be one to get one. Now you got one.

The Jews have their mezuzahs, Rose said, The Catholics their crucifixes, Native Americans their eagle feathers. It's a totem, Rose said, Something outside you to remind you that you have what it takes.

Rule number four, Rose said. Law of the jungle, Rose said. You have to have an object so you can treat your struggle as if it were outside.

Then: *Ceci n'est pas une pipe*, Rose said.

That French? I said.

It is, Rose said. Magritte, to be exact. Magritte stunned the art world by a simple painting of a pipe, on which, Rose said, were the words: *Ceci n'est pas une pipe*.

This is not a pipe, Rose said.

Rose's long black index pointed at the erect pink penis in my hands.

But in this case, *Ceci n'est pas un penis, c'est une pipe*, Rose said.

I set down the erect pink penis that wasn't a penis on the brass table.

Where did you get it? I said.

Randolph Scott had it, Rose said. In a lunch box.

All the while I'd been sitting there, every once in a while Rose's eyes went off and stared at something behind me. At first I thought maybe Rose had the kind of eyes that don't focus, so when they're looking at you they're not looking at you, but then I turned around to see what it was behind me and it was a painting of Elizabeth Taylor as Cleopatra.

Just above Rose's armchair, on the south wall, was a photograph of Elizabeth Taylor the way she looked in the wedding gown in *Father of the Bride*.

All around the room, everywhere you looked, photos and paintings of Elizabeth Taylor.

So, Rose? I said. You're really into Liz.

Rose rolled just his eyes up to heaven. His shoulders went up and his chin went down, bracelets clack-clack.

Rule number five, Rose said. Never call Elizabeth Taylor Liz.

That's when Rose, sitting in his purple-velvet overstuffed armchair, his huge yellow Moroccan shoes crossed, feet up on the brass table; Rose's red, black, and green African skirt gathered at his knees, the black skin of his ankles, calves, knees, the bottom part of his huge black thighs, exposed; the dozen red roses, the paperback *Antigone*, the two-gallon jug with the amber liquid, the Dwight D. Eisenhower ashtray, the Randolph Scott lunch box; Rose a Gauloise in one hand and his VSOP Baccarat crystal glass in the other—that's when Rose said this impor-tant, this beautiful, this incredible thing:

I am very shy, Rose said.

And so is Elizabeth, Rose said. In fact, Elizabeth Taylor is the only person in the world shyer than I.

Most people misconstrue this for standoffishness, Rose said, But it is not. It is *social terror*, Rose said. The Shy Hunter is terrified that others will destroy the truth within his heart, Rose said, And so the Shy Hunter armors himself.

No one surprises a Shy Hunter, Rose said. Not even death, because the Shy Hunter has covered his ass and, thus armored, he watches and waits and studies meticulously, hunting the world for prey.

Then all at once, just like that, Rose squared his shoulders to mine and leaned forward over the brass tabletop. He put his open palm on his chest.

Prey not in the sense of devouring or murder, Rose said, But prey in the sense of hunting for the sore truths within another human heart. Prey for truth, Rose said.

The serpent in Rose's eyes.

The sore truth which is in *your* heart, Rose said. So that *I* may uncover mine.

The blonde fainting on the blonde-fainting couch, I leaned back, crossed my legs, clutched a batik emerald-green satin pillow, and laid the pillow in my lap.

It is the best of combinations, Rose said. The Shy and the Hunter.

Elizabeth Taylor, Rose said, Is impeccably shy and an impeccable hunter. She is quintessential. When Elizabeth finds someone true, it is simply divine to watch her move. Have you ever watched Elizabeth move?

She is a better dancer than Rita Hayworth, Rose said, And a better singer than Marilyn Monroe. They made Rita Hayworth dance, made Marilyn sing, but Elizabeth Taylor, you notice, never had to do such silly things as sing and dance. From the very beginning, all Elizabeth had to do was be Elizabeth.

Rose put a rabbit turd of Sho-ko-lat into the erect pink penis, lit the rabbit turd, sucked in, sucked in again, and then handed the erect pink penis to me and I sucked in the hashish smoke, so much sweeter than marijuana, started coughing right off, and handed the erect pink penis back to Rose. Rose took two hits—Never more than two, Rose said— and then he took two more. Rose sucked the smoke into his lungs and then talked like you do when you're holding smoke in your lungs. Rose said he never did more than two hits because Sho-ko-lat always made him think too damn much and he couldn't sleep, or else he'd get just too too too wild and he would have to put his heels on and go out and generally make a goddamned fool of himself.

After about his seventh hit on the smoke was when Rose told me that not only was Elizabeth Taylor the most beautiful woman in the world but the kindest too. Rose said he didn't like to talk about it too too too much because people always thought he was trying to put on airs. Rose said he could give a fuck about what people thought, but he still felt a little funny talking about her, Elizabeth Taylor.

When I went to take the pipe from Rose, Rose held on. I had the balls, Rose had the head.

The black serpent in Rose, in his eyes, ready to spit.

My eyes wanted to look somewhere else, but I couldn't. I was the rabbit in the headlights.

I think, Rose said, I can trust you.

Rose's fingers came up the lovely erect pink penis. The Sahara Desert on the inside of his index and third fingers touched my fingers.

Which has been blowing my mind away, Rose said, Because I have never trusted anyone as fast or as much as I have come to trust you—except for her.

Rose let go of the lovely erect pink penis head, sat back in his purple-velvet overstuffed chair, and crossed his legs.

The lovely erect pink penis was still where Rose had left it, in my hand, by the balls.

So, Rose said, I have decided I am going to go ahead and just be who I am with you.

I stuck the lovely erect pink penis in my mouth and sucked.

And something, Rose said, That has very much to do with who I am is that I am best friends with Elizabeth Taylor.

AFTER THAT, ROSE quit talking for a while. Actually, I don't know if that's really the truth. I don't know if Rose quit talking or not, because with the Sho-ko-lat you just go away somewhere and watch how you are—not on the premises, nowhere, not here—well, that's what I was doing when I was thinking that Rose had quit talking. Maybe he hadn't, I don't know, but when I came back I was looking at Rose and thinking about the dead guy's face in the hallway, thinking about the peace in the dead guy's face, and the no-peace in Rose's face—the black serpent still in Rose, coiled and ready to spit.

Then Rose bit his lip. The breath in him came out in a cough. With his Sahara Desert palm, Rose wiped the sweat off his forehead.

How it is, Rose said. You never know when it's going to hit you. One day you're walking around and talking and eating and tying your shoes and paying your phone bill, and the next day you're in a coma with tubes in your nose and mouth and up your ass. In most cases, they can usually bring you around after a month or so in the hospital. You look around your room, and your room is full of flowers and cards and chocolates if you're one of the lucky ones, and if you're not, people bring you flowers and chocolates from the overflow of the lucky ones. And when you get out of the hospital, you have all the hope in the world. You think you're the one who's going to beat this shit. Your immunity level goes up to twenty-six percent and you start going back to work a couple days a week. There's all the hope, and then you're flat again, out-of-control fever and shitting your pants. Things start growing on your tongue and throat and you begin to wonder if it is really true that God is punishing you for being how you are. And the fear. Then your bone marrow goes, or something else. They might be able to whip you back into shape for round three. Meanwhile, your hospital bill is pushing a hundred thousand dollars.

That's just how it is, Rose said. I tell you, I'm not going to do it. I got my jar of Valium or something dramatic—I'm going out with a bang, a big fucking bang, no whimpers here.

I'm not saying I'm going to get it, Rose said, But if I do, honey, I'm not going out like that sorry stupid fuck down in the hallway.

I am going out in style.

YOU KNOW HOW it is when you're loaded. Well, that's what I was doing sitting on the blonde-fainting couch across from Rose. I was watching Rose. Watching me watch Rose.

When I squinted my eyes, all there was was the low chandelabra light on the orange and gold, burnt red and purple.

With that light around Rose, I knew, I just *knew* in my heart, that Rose was going to be OK.

I didn't have to worry because Rose was going to be OK.

IN THE NARROW hallway painted blue were two cops in blue uniforms and two ambulance guys in white coats. The thick black lake was still in the blue linoleum valley, but Ricardo the voodoo super was zipped up in a gray bag.

In the unrelenting fluorescence, one of the policemen was talking to Mrs. Lupino. Mrs. Lupino was wearing sweatpants and a sweatshirt with MERRY CHRISTMAS and a Christmas tree on it. She was holding the yellow drop-dead fuck-you cat.

Satan worshipers, Mrs. Lupino was saying. Below us. Lucifer himself. They sacrifice live animals. Every day one of my babies is missing.

Then Mrs. Lupino screamed and raised her hand at me, caught the air with her fingers, brought her hand back down.

There he is! she screamed. Lucifer! He's the one who has murdered our poor Ricardo!

The yellow New York drop-dead fuck-you cat hissed.

The two cops stopped and looked at me; the ambulance guys stopped and looked: me, on the bottom step, Lucifer himself.

I cupped the pink penis and put the pink penis in my front pocket.

The officer who came up to me was handsome, a young Mel Gibson, already too many doughnuts. He wore a black slicker over his hat and uniform. At first I didn't know if I could speak to the Mel Gibson officer—talking to a cop was hard enough, let alone a handsome cop, plus I was way not-on-the-premises stoned and there was a hashish pipe the shape of a penis in my pocket.

But when I looked into the cop's eyes—his eyes were dark brown—youth mostly what was in his eyes, a cop who wouldn't hate True Shot. Mennen aftershave, and a place on his chin where he'd shaved too close.

The cop and I went and stood in the rectangle of earth where I'd plant the cherry tree, but you couldn't see the rectangle of earth for the snow. Even the streetlights had globs of snow on them, and the tree branches were thick with white.

Mercury vapor from the streetlamp light, and red flashes on the snow, around and around, from the ambulance and the cop car, red flashes on the snow on the street, on the sidewalk, on the finger-bone branches, red flashes on the officer and me.

The cop pulled out a yellow pad and pencil and asked me my name and phone number and if I had been the one who called it in and what time it was when I saw the body.

My mother's nerves.

It's OK, the cop said, You're going to be all right. I remember the first stiff I saw.

The officer's hand was shaking, and the yellow pad and pencil.

It's not like in the movies, he said. So just take a breath, the officer said. This is tough stuff.

My breath in. My breath out.

I came in, I said. After work. He was lying there. On the floor. In the hallway. Needle stuck in his arm. Blood on the floor.

Was he already dead?

He was dead, I said.

How do you know? the officer said. You touch him?

Red flashes all around on the snow.

No, I said.

Then: You ever run into a guy, I said, An Indian guy, I said, Named Charlie 2Moons?

The officer didn't have time to answer because right then, all at once, out of the blue, was the muffled sound of horses' hooves on packed snow, and from the east, St. Nicholas came riding up, through the snow on a white horse, Jolly old Saint Nick.

But it's not the truth.

It was a cop.

A cop on a white horse, SGT. RICHARD WHITE on his name tag.

You're going this way and then shit happens and then you're going that way.

The horse was the most beautiful horse I'd ever seen. When I first set my eyes on that horse, I thought I was dreaming: Wolf Swamp and the family of wolves and the monster in the cave and the scared white stallion running wild across foggy meadows.

Sergeant, sir! the officer said.

The door to 205 East Fifth Street was open and the ambulance guys were pushing the stretcher out the door, down the stoop.

The sergeant started hollering at everybody, shouting orders every which way, the white horse stamping and turning, and everybody was saying yes, Sergeant . . . yes, Sergeant . . . yes, sir!

The sergeant yelled at the officer, Help with the body!

Yes, sir, Sergeant!

Radio sounds: Ten-four and other cop numbers like that in static.

The white horse was a stallion, and he sized me up in a New York minute. I liked him and he liked me, we both knew it. He smelled I was once truly loved by a horse and loved the horse back. Probably could smell Charlie's ayaHuaska too.

All horses are Buddha.

The sergeant's eyes looked down at me through big square thick plastic glasses. No doubt about it: I was the deer in the headlights, he was the Mack truck.

Name?

Will Parker, I said, Apartment One-A.

The sergeant's foot in the stirrup was right across from my crotch.

Cat got your tongue? the sergeant said.

There was something quick with the sergeant's arm, like his arm had a life of its own. The sergeant's big smile, red flashes on his big smile, pointy teeth. He was wearing a heavy wool coat. All around his belt there were heavy things hanging on him: bullets, a gun in its holster, a radio, the place for his stick.

You a faggot? the sergeant said.

Round face, pinker than Harry O'Connor, thin blondish-red hair.

Then: Relax, he said, and pushed his hat up off his forehead. I understand how it is with you guys, the sergeant said. Cigarette?

I took the Marlboro, lit the Marlboro, lit his.

Scared of cops? the sergeant said.

I guess, I said.

You always stutter?

When I'm not singing, I said.

Big smile. Red flashes on the sergeant's big pointy-teeth smile.

Ever had sex with him? the sergeant said.

On the street, voices sounded deep, the way things sound covered with snow.

Who? I said.

Ricardo Aguirre, the sergeant said.

Red-light flashes on the white stallion's flesh. I touched the white stallion on the neck, looked up. I was already dead and Sergeant Richard White was already dead too.

No way, I said. I've never seen him, I said. Before.

Ricardo Aguirre would do anything for cash, the sergeant said. Even turn fag for cash.

The sergeant's arm quick moving all around.

He had a big one, the sergeant said. Puerto Rican. 'Course, you know all about Puerto Ricans. And Italians. And blacks.

The sergeant pulled the reins and the white stallion stepped back a step, jumped his front legs up a little. The sergeant choked the reins and the stallion reared up like Hopalong Cassidy. The Lone Ranger. Randolph Scott.

It's just routine, the sergeant said. We know this guy. Hundred times we've booked this guy. Surprised he lived as long as he did. A blessing to society he's dead.

Then: You Italian? the sergeant said.

Language my second language.

I'm black, I said—just like that—I'm black.

Big smile, pointy teeth, red flashes on Sergeant Richard White. He kicked the white stallion in the flanks, and the stallion reared up again, showing me his smooth white underbelly, his cock, his stallion balls.

Sergeant Richard White slapped the stallion on the hip with his riding crop. The stallion jumped, made a deep sound. His eyes looked back, trying to see the bastard on his back. The sergeant snapped the reins, hit the stallion on the bridle just under his beautiful white ear. Fear in the stallion's eyes, only fear.

Rest easy tonight, Will Parker, the sergeant said, Because law and order prevail.

The sergeant reined the stallion around so the stallion's ass was right in my face. The stallion made little jumps with his front legs. Then the sergeant backed the stallion up.

I took one step, two steps back, but stallion ass kept approaching. I put my hands, one on each side of his tail, pushed back.

Hey, I said, I'm walking here!

Between horseflesh and parked car, all that was left was asphalt.

But I didn't have to drop to the asphalt.

As the horse stepped away, he gave my face a brush with his tail.

No doubt about it, the white stallion could smell my horse Chub all over me.

CHAPTER
EIGHT

or the most part, I'd say if you crossed a cat with a smart dog, made him a matriarchal vegetarian, gave him sleek beauty, a mass of muscle, and the desire to run, then what you'd have is a horse.

Chub was a gelding, half Morgan, half quarter horse, and old by the time Bobbie and I got him. Chub was black and if you didn't keep him brushed he had a reddish tint and, just before he died, silver. Chub was like an old grandfather who loves his grandkids. Big brown eyes that really loved you. He'd do just about anything for you if you fed and watered him regular.

Chub liked me better than Bobbie, because every chance I got I fed Chub a carrot in front of ayaHuaska, just to get ayaHuaska's goat.

AyaHuaska was an Appaloosa and loved Charlie 2Moons.

AyaHuaska was only four years old, a gelding too but lots of macho spirit. Knew he was one beautiful creature, so I didn't trust him for one minute. AyaHuaska was real possessive of Charlie 2Moons. AyaHuaska would make his lips go like Mister Ed cussing you out and look right at you with his ears back and stand between you and Charlie, wouldn't let you near Charlie, would stick his spotted gray butt right in your face and make like he was going to kick you. Charlie'd yell at ayaHuaska when he did that, and ayaHuaska would stop, but underneath Charlie liked that ayaHuaska was jealous and so protective of him.

I still got a scar where one time that damn horse took a bite out of my backside.

Another weird thing about ayaHuaska was when you fed him a bucket of grain he wouldn't let you watch him eat it. AyaHuaska would start kicking the stanchion or whatever was behind him and putting his big horse's ass in your face and kicking at you if you tried to watch him.

After ayaHusaka bit me, every once in a while, I'd go over to the corral where Charlie kept ayaHuaska behind his grandmother's house behind Viv's double-wide trailer, and when Charlie wasn't around, I'd get the bucket and put grain in the bucket and sneak through the corral poles and put the bucket of grain just far enough into the corral, then run back out and wait and watch. Drove that horse nuts with the bucket there, him wanting to eat the grain, and me leaning up against the corral poles watching him.

Charlie could always tell when I'd teased ayaHuaska that way with the grain. It was in the spots.

AyaHuaska's mane and tail were silver and his butt was covered with spots of gray. Charlie said he could tell the future by the gray spots on ayaHuaska's butt. Charlie said ayaHuaska's spots changed every day and, like tea leaves, you could read them.

It's going to be a good day today, Charlie would say.

Or: Your father's coming home early next week.

Or: The barn spirits have invited me up to jerk off with them today.

Or: Weather's gonna turn bad Thursday.

Or: Grandfather wants us to come haul him some water.

One time it was: The nuclear power plant in Arco is blowing a fuse. All on ayaHuaska's butt.

The liar's space between Charlie's two front teeth. Charlie and his stories.

The thing was, though, Charlie was usually right.

Father's horse, Star, never got along with ayaHuaska. Star was a big roan, Arabian and quarter horse, a rodeo performer, used to an audience, liked the spotlight. It was important for Star to win. Both of them, ayaHuaska and Star, drama queens. Mack Dicksons of the horse world. Pretty boys, used to all the attention.

ONE DAY, OUR first summer at the Residency, out back of the barn, Bobbie and I were sitting in the sun with our backs against the wall. Charlie was lying in the grass. We each had a stem of grass in our mouth, sucking on the juice, the good kind of grass to suck on that Charlie showed us.

Charlie rolled over, squinted his eyes in the sun, chewed a couple times on his stem of grass, and started talking about his famous trick-riding father, the fancy rider, who traveled all over Europe and even had a show in Madison's Square Garden in New York City.

Usually Bobbie would've said, Charlie 2Moons, you're so full of horse shit. But Bobbie didn't say anything. Maybe it was the sun shining on us, or the grass juice, or the ladybug that flew on Bobbie's arm, or because Bobbie wasn't grown up yet.

Maybe in the sun behind the barn that day Bobbie was tired of nothing to believe in and just needed something, a story, some hope, so when Charlie told us about his fancy-rider father, Bobbie's eyes didn't flash gold flecks and Bobbie didn't say, Charlie 2Moons, your father sounds like a damn drunk rodeo fool same as mine.

Instead Bobbie said, Madison's Square Garden, huh? How about that, a fancy rider in Madison's Square Garden in New York City!

Why is Madison's Garden, I said, Square?

Charlie and Bobbie just looked at each other, didn't say anything.

THE THREE OF us decided to get an act together, a trick-riding trio. We'd practice and travel all over, even to Europe, and finally to Madison's Square Garden in New York City too.

First we had to find a name for our trio. Charlie wanted to call us the Madison's Square Garden Trio. Bobbie hated that name. Bobbie wanted to call us the Badland Boys, even though she was a girl. I wanted to call us the Fancy Frees, and both Bobbie and Charlie hated that, so we drew straws, or stems of grass, and Bobbie won. Bobbie always won, because she was the one holding the stems of grass.

Charlie bought the book, *The Complete Book of Trick and Fancy Riding*, by Frank E. Dean. It was a big orange book with photographs of trick riders trick riding and drawings showing you how to do the different tricks and, in the beginning of the book, how to get started.

That's all we did that summer, Charlie and Bobbie and me, was read *The Complete Book of Trick and Fancy Riding* and practice on ayaHuaska and Chub in the side corral of the barn.

Of course, before we could start, Bobbie had to measure the side corral, get the one hundred feet from station to station—one side of the corral to the other—exactly perfect. We had to take the whole south end of the fence down and move it in eight feet. Had to redig the post holes, reset the posts, and nail the corral poles back on the posts. Then we had to pull the weeds around the fence, rake the weeds into a pile, and burn the weeds. Then Bobbie found a few places where the corral poles were sagging and we had to repair them.

Charlie and Bobbie were at each other the whole time we worked on the corral.

We're trick riders, Charlie said, Not cheap labor.

It has to be a certain way, Bobbie said, Before we can start. You can't play unless you know the rules.

The rules, Charlie said, Is to have some fun on your horse.

The rules, Bobbie said, Is to have some rules.

Back and forth, those two.

Some days Charlie didn't even show up to help us.

When it was all done, the side corral looked real square and new, and clean because of no weeds.

Perfect, Bobbie said.

Just perfect, I said.

IT TOOK US a good two weeks to get the basics of trick and fancy riding down—getting ayaHuaska and Chub used to us doing weird things on them, getting ayaHuaska and Chub to do their boring job of just walking and then galloping back and forth, back and forth, station to station.

The first trick we all learned is the simplest and it's called the Two-Hand Horn Spin, where you get galloping from station to station. As you're galloping, you put both hands around the saddle horn. Then you lift yourself up with your arms and put your right leg over to the left and you're straddling the horn with both your legs to the left, then you lift yourself up with your arms and you bring your left leg over and you sit facing backward, straddling the saddle horn, then your right leg over to the left and you sit sidesaddle that way, then your left leg back and you're back in the saddle where you started.

Bobbie did the Two-Hand Horn Spin first. Then Charlie. Then me.

Next was the One-Hand Horn Spin, and then the No-Hands Horn Spin.

We had the Two-Hand Horn Spin and the One-Hand Horn Spin and the No-Hands Horn Spin down in two days.

Next was the Hippodrome Stand, which was real hard even though it sounds easy. The Hippodrome Stand is just you, standing up on the saddle and sticking out your arms, while the horse keeps galloping.

The first time I did the Hippodrome Stand was after both Bobbie and Charlie had done it. For two days they had been galloping and Hippodrome standing, and I had tried and tried but I just couldn't make myself stand up in the air and stick my arms out. There was nothing holding us down except for the loop of rope Charlie'd fashioned across the saddle that we stuck our boots under.

On my third day at this, I still couldn't make my legs just stand up and put me up into the flying air. It was late morning and we were all hungry, and I remember there wasn't anything in the kitchen except for carrots and Cheerios and Rice Crispies, no milk and no sugar, and we never went over to bother Viv, Charlie's mother, while she was banging hair, and the sun was getting hot, so once again I got Chub galloping, once again I got my one foot up and then my other foot up and both feet stuck under the Hippodrome strap that wasn't really a strap, just a piece of rope, and once again I went to stand up and once again my legs just wouldn't do it.

That's when Bobbie called me a spineless ass. Bobbie was sitting on the fence, and she cupped her hands around her mouth and said, For chrissakes, Will! You're nothing but a spineless ass!

Charlie was sitting right next to Bobbie when Bobbie cupped her hands over her mouth and yelled out *spineless ass* at me, and just like that, all at once, Charlie backhanded Bobbie square in the face and Bobbie went off the fence ass over teakettle.

All the while, Chub is galloping back and forth, back and forth, galloping galloping, station to station, and my feet are under the Hippodrome strap.

Bobbie hits the ground in a cloud of dust and it ain't two seconds and Bobbie is back up and has Charlie by the belt and then Charlie's flying off the fence.

Galloping galloping, back and forth, back and forth.

All I can see of Charlie and Bobbie is flying arms and legs and dust, them screaming and yelling at each other, just going at each other like mad dogs.

I talk to Chub first—Chub, I'm standing up now, just hang in there with me, please—and then I'm standing up, in the air, the wind and the sun all around me, and I put my arms out and the way I feel is the way I'd always wanted to feel and never knew it. It's the way the ocean feels, I figure, rolling rolling, or why birds like to fly so much. I let out a big whoop! and look over at Charlie and Bobbie, and their faces are all snot and blood and dirt and they're smiling big smiles and they start clapping like they're the audience and I am doing the Hippodrome Stand and this is New York City and this is Madison's Square Garden.

THE NEXT TRICK was Double Vaulting, but Bobbie never got to Double Vaulting. Bobbie didn't get past the Hippodrome Stand. Late that summer, after Father got home, Bobbie got sick and stayed sick and pretty much stayed in her room except when she barfed in the bathroom.

Bobbie told me not to worry. She said she was fourteen now and grown up and had to put aside the ways of a child. I took it to mean Bobbie was no longer on the premises and that she couldn't ride with Charlie and me because she had breasts and her period.

So that was it for the Badland Boys. It was just Charlie and me after that.

One morning in the corral, Charlie doing the Hippodrome Stand on the back of ayaHuaska, he yelled over at me, Fuck the rules, Will! Why do we have to stay in the corral?

Going Slack is what Charlie and I called it, the game we played.

Out the barn door, tying the reins together and letting them go slack, ayaHuaska and Chub racing flat-out to the bottoms, through miles of sun on tall waving grass, ayaHuaska and Chub taking us to Spring Creek, to the river, to old Fort Hall, to the cemetery, Ferry Butte, to the cliffs, to the mystery, to where we ought to go.

Charlie and me doing the tricks: Double Vaulting, Going Under the Neck, One Foot Slick Stand Over the Hips, Back Roll to a Crupper Jump, through the yellow and the blue and the green, fancy riding, riding free.

One night by the campfire, owl hooting in a cottonwood, coyote singing at the moon, Charlie 2Moons told me his grandfather told him once about a beautiful warrior on a stallion who lives in our dreams. The warrior is strong and gets his strength from riding the stallion without reining the horse. If you ride fast enough, letting the reins go slack, if you shut your eyes and dream hard enough, you can make the warrior's stallion your own and live forever that way, riding free.

And something else. Something else I'll tell you.

But I never told Bobbie this.

That summer, before Father got home and before Bobbie got sick and stayed in her room, one night lying up in my bed, I heard something and looked over at my window and there's Charlie 2Moons in my window with his big liar's smile, with the moon and the stars behind Charlie, the moon and the stars solitary illuminations, plus the crickets and the frogs and the whole noisy night.

Charlie stayed up in my room with me and slept in my bed with me. In the middle of the night, Charlie's arm around me, holding on to me, all night long.

CHAPTER NINE

My first spring in New York.

On 77th Street, across from the Museum of Natural History, we found a parking place right after True Shot said his prayer to Saint Carlotta. True Shot shifted and backed into the parking space.

For a moment, True Shot and I sat in Door of the Dead van. Shadows of sycamore and sunlight, like the bark of sycamores, camouflage spots, moving moving on the windshield, on the dash, on the plastic Virgin Mary, on the green-sequin-framed photo of Brigitte Bardot, on our legs and arms, on the seat, our crotches, on our hands, True Shot's silver rings; sycamore shadows and light on the surface of True Shot's mirrors, on the beaded blue horizontal and red vertical buckskin bag hanging on the buckskin necklace around his neck.

No Charlie 2Moons in the crowd of Polo Calvin Klein white people. No Ruby Prestigiacomo either.

Ruby was supposed to meet us on the steps.

On the wrought-iron fence was a sign that said THEODORE ROOSEVELT PARK. The trees on the other side of the fence were mostly sycamores and looked like some flowering trees too.

The Museum of Unnatural History, True Shot said.

The Museum of Unnatural History had big brown stones and turrets, an architectural style I didn't know. When I asked True Shot what style the building was, True Shot said, Neo-White Male.

At the corner of Central Park West was a guy selling hot dogs, Sabrett. I saw True Shot's face when he smelled the hot dogs, and I knew underneath True Shot's mirrors, his eyes were quivering like light through sycamores for a hot dog, so I stood in line, and when I got to the Sabrett guy I asked True Shot if he wanted one or two. True Shot said two and so I ordered four—sausages, not hot dogs; hot dogs were the skinny ones, sausages the fat ones that were spicy hot—with everything, mustard, relish, sauerkraut, and onions, and a Seven-Up for me and a Perrier with lime for True Shot and a fistful of napkins.

We sat under the statue of Theodore Roosevelt, in the sun, on the steps of the Museum of Unnatural History, everybody in the world walking by.

Japanese tourists from a bus that said BIG APPLE TOURS kept themselves all herded together taking pictures of everything. One Japanese guy, in a green shirt with an alligator on it, really pressed slacks, perfectly shined shoes, and a floppy tourist hat, came over to True Shot and me and put his camera up to his eyeball and pointed his camera at us. True Shot gave the Japanese guy a big open-mouth smile with Sabrett sausage in his open mouth, and the Japanese guy just took the picture as if we were a statue of two guys eating Sabrett sausages.

When the Japanese guy walked away, all at once his camera fell onto the sidewalk, just like that, camera crash and camera parts all over on the sidewalk.

My big nose and mustache, my crooked bottom teeth on the surface of True Shot's mirrors.

My Japanese brother broke his camera! True Shot said.

I didn't say anything right off, just looked at myself trying to look through True Shot's mirrors underneath to his eyes.

It is this way, I said.

That made True Shot laugh.

I was finished with my two sausages in no time at all and I rolled a cigarette, lit it, and gulped the last of the Seven-Up. True Shot looked like he could eat two more, and I said to True Shot, I've got enough money for two more. But True Shot didn't say anything, just his mirrors and the sun in his mirrors.

No Ruby Prestigiacomo.

No Charlie.

Then: You're sitting under it, True Shot said.

Under what? I said.

True Shot had a sycamore branch in his hand with a bunch of leaves on it. One by one, True Shot broke the leaves off the branch and left the leaves in a pile on the hot cement. When the branch was just a skinny stick, True Shot pointed the stick.

Notice that the stallion is bridled, True Shot said, And Teddy has the reins. He's choking the stallion back so hard the stallion's mouth is open.

True Shot stood up, brushed his butt off, and flip-flopped around the front of the statue. I followed him around.

The sun in True Shot's mirrors looked like True Shot's eyes were two big suns staring at me.

True Shot pointed the stick.

Teddy's got a handgun in his holster, True Shot said. I wonder if he's got a permit? And what about that belt of bullets around his waist?

Just then a Japanese tourist took a photo of True Shot, pushing the stick against the thigh of the statue of the man walking next to Theodore Roosevelt.

This here's my African brother, True Shot said. Notice that he is naked except for a drape of cloth, and mark that his crotch is just over from Teddy's boot.

True Shot pointed the stick at the man's head.

Notice that my African brother's head is just high enough so Teddy can lean over and speak softly, or, if Teddy wants to, he can use his big stick.

True Shot flip-flopped around the back of the horse.

When we were back around the other side again, True Shot touched the stick to the thigh of the statue of the man walking next to Theodore Roosevelt on that side.

True Shot's mirrors, two bright suns.

This here's my Native American brother, True Shot said. Notice that he's naked except for a blanket and that his crotch is just over from Teddy's boot.

True Shot pointed the stick at the man's head.

Notice that my Native American brother's head is just high enough so Teddy can lean over and speak softly, or, if Teddy wants to, he can use his big stick.

That's when, in broad daylight, True Shot reached his hand up and took his mirrors off.

I always, when True Shot took off his mirrors, looked at True Shot in the eyes, to see those eyes, back and forth, back and forth, Saint Vitus' dance in his head, searching for the space in between.

True Shot squinted up at Theodore Roosevelt.

Look like anybody familiar? True Shot asked.

I put my hand above my eyes.

Perhaps you detect a certain resemblance to our nation's *current* leader? True Shot said.

Who, Reagan?

No, True Shot said. Nancy.

True Shot and I got to laughing then. True Shot was laughing so hard he sat down on his haunches, sitting in the way I never could for long. He was laughing and flipping the stick back and forth, back and forth.

He put his mirrors back on.

Belly jumping, shoulders rolling, I thought me and True Shot were in for a good laugh.

But it's not the truth.

Under True Shot's mirrors, tears coming down his cheeks, snot out his nose.

Then just like that, True Shot jumped up and went flip-flop up the steps and I was following.

What about Ruby? I said.

Ruby couldn't make it, True Shot said.

Charlie couldn't make it either.

True Shot and I walked into a big hall with dinosaurs, and I wanted to stop and look but True Shot knew where he was going, so I just kept up with him. On the left on the wall were all sorts of things Teddy had said about life, and I only had time to read the one that said *All daring and courage, all iron endurance of misfortune, make for a finer, nobler type of manhood.*

True Shot walked right by where you had to pay, and I walked by too, but the woman stopped me and I had to go back in line and pay a suggested donation of five dollars. So I paid five dollars and got the clip you clip on your shirt collar that I clipped on the bottom of my shorts.

True Shot was waiting in the Eastern Woodlands and Plains, standing next to an exhibit of a pack of wolves. Taxidermy wolves. Art wolves. I followed True Shot through the Eastern Woodlands and Plains, through the Asian Peoples, and at the end of Asian Peoples we turned left and True Shot flip-flopped up the stairs and I followed to the third floor to Asian Mammals, where there were two elephants, and then we walked through a bunch of mannequins my Art Family would love to know. A sign said MECCA UPSTAIRS, but we didn't go to Mecca. We went into Primates of the Eastern Woodlands and then, all at once, right there in front of us was the tipi.

But it's not the truth.

Ceci n'est pas un tipi.

BEHIND THE THICK glass was a tipi scene. Mannequins. Native American Art Family. Two women on the left and two men on the right. In the middle was a phony fire. One man was standing, holding a pipe and a pipe bag. The women were sitting by a game of sticks on the floor and one woman was braiding the other's hair. The Native American Art Family all were wearing buckskin, beadwork on their buckskins. In the background were reed chairs on the ground you could lean back on.

Indian drum music from speakers.

On the left side of the glass were some words on a piece of paper. True Shot walked up and read the words out loud: In this scene an 1850s Blackfeet family relaxes in a tipi. The two women play a game of dice, a popular women's pastime. The man standing at the rear of the tipi wears an outfit of tanned deerskin decorated with porcupine quills, horsehair, beads, and white weasel tails. He holds a pipe with a wooden stem and a stone bowl and a beaded pipe bag. Smoking was an important part of ceremonies, but both men and women also smoked for pleasure.

True Shot had his head in his hands, in his hands his red bandanna. Just as I looked, True Shot's chest went up and down, up and down, and a big crying sob came out of him.

Then: a woman in a white blazer and skirt pulled her child away from the glass and said, Don't touch, honey. The little girl was wearing a sunbonnet and fluffy dress, and the little girl said, Where's their bathroom, Mommy?

True Shot's big tears were coming down under his mirrors, and pretty soon True Shot was sobbing way loud and his chin moved funny and he was weeping weeping and you could hear him all over inside the halls of the Museum of Unnatural History. The woman in a white blazer and skirt picked up her daughter and took long steps away—the daughter, under her sunbonnet, watching True Shot the whole time.

Why is the man crying, Mommy?

That kind of crying is like puking. Someone else doing it always makes you do it too. I put my arm around True Shot's extra-lovely shoulders and there we were, the two of us, crying our eyes out.

Then True Shot sniffed up and wiped under his mirrors with his fingers.

They're going to do this to the whole world before they're done, True Shot said. Make it into a picture and put it in a frame.

Then True Shot was off weeping again, his whole big extra-lovely belly bouncing and his chest up and down, up and down.

It is this way, True Shot said in between sobs, when he could. I came, I saw, I conquered, I put it in a museum, True Shot said.

Then True Shot made his extra-lovely hands into fists and said, Someday I'm walking in here, and when I walk out I'm walking out with that medicine bundle.

With what? I said.

With the medicine, True Shot said, pointing at the Native American Art Family guy holding the pipe and the pipe stone.

To my people, True Shot said, That pipe is their life, their medicine.

It is this way, True Shot said, raising his extra-lovely fists into the air. Someday I'm walking out of here with that pipe.

Ceci n'est pas une pipe.

You're going this way and then shit happens and then you're going that way.

In all the world, this distracted globe, just then, right then, when I looked over at the Native American Art Family relaxing in their tipi—and I swear this is the truth—the guy in the tanned deerskin and beads and porcupine quills and white weasel tails, holding the pipe with a wooden stem and the stone bowl, smiled at me. Winked.

The sensation was a finger drawing a circle around my heart.

I went to tell True Shot an inanimate object had just smiled at me and winked, but True Shot was busy with something else.

True Shot said, Cover me.

I said, Cover you? Cover what?

It is this way, True Shot said. If you want something, you got to piss on it.

True Shot rolled his eyes up to heaven.

I'm marking this place, True Shot said.

He pulled down the elastic of his red cotton shorts and the elastic of his underwear and pulled out his extra-lovely anteater cock. In the middle of all the people walking by in the Museum of Unnatural History on a Sunday on the Upper West Side, True Shot pulled his cock out.

True Shot was standing right next to the door into the wall on the right side of the glass the Blackfeet Art Family were relaxing in, when he started peeing. I looked around. People everywhere. No Charlie 2Moons.

True Shot was peeing, really loud, walking along the glass, more like he was dancing, singing, not holding on to his cock, his arms out wide: True Shot singing, dancing, his cock and his pee all up and down, back and forth, on the glass and on the floor.

I put my arms out wide too. How else do you cover somebody?

True Shot was just about at the door into the wall on the left of the glass case the Blackfeet Art Family were relaxing in, when a guard, a white guy, came around the corner. I stepped up to the guard, right in his face, and said, Excuse me?

And the guy said, Yes?

Language my second language.

I said, Can you tell me, I said, Where the bathroom is?

And the white guard said, Down Primates, past North American Birds at the stairs.

I said, Thank you, and I was still standing right in front of this guard, so the guard went to step by and I stepped that way so he couldn't go, and he stepped the other way and I stepped that way too, and then the guard got this look on his face, so I stepped away and looked over to True Shot and True Shot was still peeing under where the words on the left are.

All at once I said right to the guard, clearly, not one stutter: All daring and courage, all iron endurance of misfortune, make for a finer, nobler type of manhood.

The white guard just looked at me, checked for my little clip, saw my little clip on the bottom of my shorts, and went to step around me.

Then: C'est un penis, I said.

Fuck you, the guard said. He stepped around me. I looked over to the Blackfeet Art Family relaxing at home. My eyes went right to the place on the words to the left where it said both men and women smoked for pleasure, and all at once, that's all I wanted to do, roll a cigarette and smoke it for pleasure. The place smelled like a toilet and True Shot was standing there all put back in; under his mirrors his eyes were smiling. True Shot nodded to the guard, and then when the guard turned the corner, True Shot had an extra-lovely smile for me.

You want something, True Shot said, You got to piss on it.

A FEW WEEKS later, I was lying on the futon in my shorts listening to Power 95 on the boom box and reading jokes in The New Yorker. The red-pink walls of my apartment, my Art Family, the E.T.-phone-home guy, the empty '53 DeSoto, the oscillating fan. The humid sooty air.

At four-thirty, I called Janet at Columbia University. The message machine again. I left the same message again: Where is Charlie? Where is Sebastian Cooke? Please call me back.

Mrs. Lupino's cats across the hall yelling and scratching—it all got to be too much, and when the phone rang and it was Ruby breathing

breathing in the phone again. I climbed the stairs to Rose's apartment door and knocked. Dogs barking but no Rose.

I sat on the stoop, rolled a cigarette.

Charlie 2Moons nowhere.

Garbage all over the sidewalk and under the stairs. The hot summer night made the garbage worse, the flies and the stink. People walking by on the sidewalk had to step around cardboard boxes, black plastic bags, holes in the bags, every kind of trash flowing out of the holes. Somebody'd thrown away a bunch of photographs, so all over the sidewalk and into the curb, little squares of smiling people holding beers looked up at me. Two garbage cans were turned over, one can in the street. Books, papers, old food, a brassiere, dog shit, beer bottles and cans, an empty bottle of Yukon Jack, a plastic gallon of Clorox. Blue and white paper coffee cups, a wadded-up slice of pepperoni pizza.

I started walking, just walking wherever my feet wanted me to walk. In St. Marks Books, I opened a big book by Robert Mapplethorpe that said DISPLAY COPY on it. One of the photographs was of a guy who looks like a Catholic saint, beatific smile, eyes rolled up to heaven.

The guy was jerking off.

Charlie 2Moons. I'd seen Charlie 2Moons look like that.

At Hebrew National I bought two hot dogs. They're the good kind of hot dogs, so I bought a third. I sat in the air-conditioned window and ate the hot dog, the paper napkin wadded up tight, red and yellow-orange in my left hand. People walking by on the street.

THAT EVENING WAS probably the last twilight walk I ever walked when the monster and its heavy footfalls was still a secret deep inside Manhattan's heart. All around me, behind the million windows, in their apartments, young men stood in front of mirrors and looked into their eyes, trying to understand the strange new sense of everything falling away.

Bad diet, too much coffee, too many drugs last weekend.

Slow down, that's all.

My God, this rash. What's this in my throat?

It's only a cold, the flu. This bump, this purple bump. I've never had a bump on my body like this.

At the gym, the young men stood on the scales and moved the weight across the scale, and then stared at the seven pounds that used to be on their arms and chests and butts and legs.

Behind the million windows, sleepless, the heavy fall of the monster's footsteps shaking the glass of water on the nightstand, shaking the nightstand, shaking the whole building.

Only the week before, the *Post* reported that a couple on East 70th Street had thrown a big party—champagne and the works. After the party, when their friends were gone, the two young men joined hands, stepped to the window ledge, and jumped out of their penthouse apartment.

THE FOLLOWING WINTER, one night after Cauchemar closed, it was just Daniel, the boss's brother, and John the Bartender and me sitting in the long angled shadows, the windows fogged, the doors locked. Big flakes of snow falling in the mercury-vapor light. Latin beauty Sade on the music system, "Smooth Operator."

Slave interest.

Got a straw? Daniel yelled over to John.

Then: And John, Daniel yelled, On your way over here, bring me a fresh Hennessy—make that two.

Daniel tapped his gold American Express card against the butcher paper, ran his thumb and finger down the edge of the card, made a face that was like a smile, and then rubbed his thumb and finger on his gums above the capped teeth.

John set the two snifters of Hennessy down on the table, one by me, one by Daniel. Daniel said, straw? and John walked back to the bar, singing "Smooth Operator," moving his body to "Smooth Operator," a nice way with his shoulders and butt.

John was shiny bald on the top of his head, a fifty-dollar haircut on the sides, and in back a ponytail just to the collar. A barrel chest, big black mustache, those black garters on his arms over the white shirt, black bow tie.

John came back with a straw, cut in half, and laid the straw on the table on Daniel's side. John winked at me. The halogen light was right on John's bald head, and the moment when he winked at me around his head was illuminated.

You want some of this? Daniel said, and handed John the straw.

John sat down on the banquette too close next to Daniel. Daniel put his arm on John's back and John leaned the straw into the cocaine, pushed the straw into the line of white, put a finger to his nose, pushed the nostril closed, and sniffed up the line. John sat back up straight, wiped his nostrils and his mustache, snorted, and cleared his throat, Daniel's arm draped over his shoulder.

Hell! Let's have a party! Daniel said. Just bring that Hennessy bottle over here!

When John got up to get the bottle, Daniel handed me the straw and started singing Bob Dylan, *Bring that bottle over here*, and I took it but Daniel kept holding on to it until he finished singing, *I'll be your baby tonight*.

I had to stand up to get to the line of cocaine on Daniel's side. Either that or I had to go sit next to Daniel the way John had, so I stood up and leaned over the table.

On the end of the white line on the white butcher paper, I put the straw. I cussed my hand for my mother's nerves, made a fist with my other hand behind me, released the fist, then quick switched the straw to my steadied hand, held the straw to my nose, my other hand's index finger against my nostril, and pushed the straw toward Daniel's third shirt button, inhaling the cocaine, then stood up straight and breathed in deep through my nose.

That one's yours too, Daniel said, and pointed at the table.

I changed nostrils, leaned down, pulled the cocaine in, tapped the straw onto the table.

Done this before, Spud? Daniel asked.

Daniel was smiling his restaurant smile.

Didn't know if you'd have blow in Idaho, Daniel said. He laughed, said: Didn't know. Blow. Idaho.

Daniel dumped the rest of the cocaine from the bottle onto the butcher paper and, with the straw, scraped out the cocaine that was stuck on the glass inside. Daniel looked up at me then and kept looking right at me as he leaned back against the banquette and pushed up so I could see the crotch of his suit pants, and he reached into the pocket of his pants and moved his hand around in there and pulled out a shiny square of red paper.

Daniel leaned his elbows onto the butcher paper, pushed his shirt buttons up against the table, unfolded the shiny red square slow, then held the red paper between his thumb and index and tapped the cocaine in the square onto a pile on the table next to the pile of cocaine from the bottle.

Daniel scraped the square of paper with his long pinkie fingernail, fanning the rest of his fingers out. His fingers were thick and there was black hair on the backs, black hair smashed down under his diamond ring, third finger, left hand.

Daniel made eight lines, longer than his gold American Express card and thicker this time.

Yes, I said, I have.

Really? Daniel said. Where'd you do cocaine?

Just about everywhere, I said. Jackson Hole, Boise, Missoula, Ketchum, Coeur d'Alene, Hope.

Hope? Daniel said.

He inhaled four lines, fast, nothing left of the lines, not one particle of cocaine, when Daniel was finished. Daniel held his nostrils for a moment with his thumb and finger, then handed me the straw.

That's a place? Daniel said. Hope? Hope, Montana?

Hope, Idaho, I said.

You lived there? Daniel said.

For a while, I said.

Then: Not in Hope, I said, just outside. Beyond Hope, we called it.

Daniel's smile was not his restaurant smile, not polite, not sophisticated, just a big smile on Daniel's face.

Hey, John! Daniel yelled over. Did you hear that? Spud here used to live in a place called Beyond Hope!

John called over: What do you hope for in Idaho?

I did two more lines, my hand steady, not shaking at all. John brought the Hennessy bottle over, and a snifter for himself, put the bottle on the table, and sat down on the banquette too close to Daniel. Daniel handed John the straw.

For cocaine, I said. You hope for cocaine.

I thought Daniel was having a heart attack, but he was laughing. John had to stop snorting the line of cocaine because he was laughing too. I was surprised I was so funny. But when I did the next two lines, my hand was totally steady, and Daniel and John were still laughing and I was laughing, and I knew why I was so funny and I was laughing.

Hope no more, Spud! Daniel finally was able to say. You've come to the right place, Daniel said. In New York you don't have to hope. There's nothing to hope for. It's all right here. Fuck hope, Daniel said. You never have to stop and hope, all you have to do is reach out and take what you want.

Fuck hope! John said, and raised his Hennessy snifter.

Daniel raised his snifter. Fuck hope! Daniel said.

I raised my Hennessy snifter.

Fuck hope! we all toasted.

* * *

FUCK HOPE AND all the tiny little towns, one-horse towns, the one-stoplight towns, three-bars country-music jukebox-magic parquet-towns, pressure-cooker pot-roast frozen-peas bad-coffee married-heterosexual towns, crying-kids-in-the-Oldsmobile beat-your- kid-in the-Thriftway-aisles towns, one-bank one-service-station Greyhound-Bus-stop-at-the-Pepsi-Café towns, two-television towns, Miracle Mile towns, Viv's Double Wide Beauty Salon towns, schizophrenic-mother towns, buy-yourself-a-handgun towns, sister-suicide towns, only- good-Injun's-a-dead-Injun towns, Catholic-Protestant-Mormon-Baptist religious-right five-churches Republican-trickle-down-to-poverty family-values sexual-abuse pro-life creation-theory NRA towns, nervous-mother rodeo-clown-father those little-town-blues towns.

Daniel laid out three more lines and did his line first, then John, then me.

Fuck 'em.

Matching pickup and horse-trailer towns, superbowl Sunday towns, America-Love-It-or-Leave-It Ronald Reagan towns, the heartland, *l'Amérique profond* apple-pie mashed-potatoes-and-gravy towns, grain silos-by-the-train-tracks towns, county-sheriff-black-and-white-Chevy towns, Vietnam-vet-Native-Americans-buying-beer-in-the-open-24-hour-neon-by-the-freeway towns, Paul Harvey good-day towns.

John poured more Hennessy. I rolled cigarettes all around. Three more lines, one line each.

Fuck 'em.

All you local yokels. Four-wheel-drive Silverado fucking dog murderers. From the fuck-you town: Fuck you!

Fuck hope, Daniel and John and I all toasted.

And the horse you rode in on, I toasted. Fuck the scared stallion hope rides in on! I said.

Daniel took a quick look at John. John's smile made Daniel smile.

And the horse you rode in on! Daniel and John said.

Fuck it.

We toasted.

A DARK RESTAURANT all around. Halogen light down onto the smooth butcher paper on the round table. Café Cauchemar, Sade singing. The clock above the swinging red doors says 2:10 A.M. if you squint. I've drawn an orange tree next to the cornflower-blue Fuck Hope. The butcher paper is the moon, reflected light, and the moon is my table.

With the pink red, I draw a moon on the paper, an image of the moon on the moon, two moons.

Oh, hell, Charlie.

Daniel and John are just beyond the moonlight, beyond hope, fucking New Yorkers in each other's faces talking talking, loud, fast, smoking the cigarettes I've rolled. I can't roll cigarettes fast enough, we're smoking so much, so we're smoking Marlboro Lights too. The Marlboro Lights are in the moonlight shadow of the Hennessy bottle, the line of Hennessy in the bottle low. With Harvest Yellow I trace the arch of Hennessy, then outline the shadow of the bottle.

High enough to think I am New York.

There's the moon, my arms and hands in the light of the moon, the Crayolas, the ashtrays overflowing, the Marlboro Lights, my bow tie, my corkscrew, my pens, the rolling papers, the tobacco. Then there's another bottle of Hennessy, and for John seltzer, and for me a can of Heineken, then John lights a joint and there's more smoke on the moon, clouds, and then I'm rolling cigarettes again.

The Sistine Chapel God is out there in the dark up on the ceiling, pointing. Out there, again again, is Sade's stuck loop "Smooth Operator."

On the table, on the moon, into the light, I place my hand, fingers spread, and trace around my hand, cornflower blue, and my hand is on the moon.

How I love, how I cherish this moment, this tiny moment of redemption from the ordinary, my fifteen minutes of super-cool *sexy totale*. My long reach to the hand of God.

But it's not the truth.

It's not God, only cocaine, and this moment in between I am so present in, a moment so full of meaning and understanding, is a moment I will forget.

Daniel took his long-nailed pinkie finger to the next square of red paper. You hope for cocaine! Daniel said, and laughed again, so hard he had to stop with the red square and put it down. John was laughing too. John was leaning up against Daniel, laughing, Daniel's hand inside John's white shirt, under John's third button, moving his hand around under the shirt, up and down, side to side.

Champagne! Daniel screamed a little scream and threw his arms up like Rose, Rolex flash in the light, diamond ring flash-flash. John's shirt was unbuttoned to below where I could see. Daniel took his hand from John's nipple ring and John got up and danced out of the light into the dark, where there was the bar if you squinted. John put the flower bottle on the butcher paper next to the Hennessy bottle and three chilled tulip glasses, popped the cork with his thumb, and screamed the little scream the way the guy in *La Cage aux Folles* screams when the champagne cork startles him, and John and Daniel laughed and started in on *La Cage aux Folles* and the time when the guy screams and gives the homosexuality away.

The little scream that gives it all away.

John lit a joint; we passed the joint around. I rolled cigarettes, John poured the champagne. We toasted. The old joke.

Fuck hope.

Beyond all hope, Daniel said.

Abandon hope, John said.

Reach out and take what you want, I said.

Daniel and John gulped down the champagne, threw the champagne glasses over their shoulders into the dark, tiny shatterings. Daniel first, then John, held their hands out, fingers spread out all the way, reaching out to take me. They were laughing. I laughed too.

John walked into the dark to the bar. I rolled cigarettes. John came back with two more tulip glasses. When John sat down I saw his eyes were blue. In the light, John's chest was white, not white like the moon but harvest yellow, and his skin, in the light, not like the table but soft. Nice kind of hair on his chest.

THE CLOCK SQUINT showed 3:30 A.M.

Across the table, just beyond the light, John's head was back against the banquette and his eyes were rolled up a little, Saint Theresa Gone to Heaven.

Daniel scraped the flakes of white from the red square onto the reflected surface of the moon. From the surface of the moon, from the third button of his pin-striped shirt, Daniel was looking at me. Under the surface of the moon, from the third button of his pin-striped shirt down, Daniel moved his hand slow up and down.

John's eyes were half closed like Mapplethorpe's guy, coming, not praying. His shirt was open and the way the hairs on his chest were looked beautiful.

I got up and walked thick arms and thick legs around the table. I sat on the other side of John. John's pants were open and John's cock was hard. Daniel reached over and made a fist around John's cock. Daniel made a sound and his mouth said the word *lovely* at me soft and slow. I laid my head down, my ear on John's chest, on the nice hair, against his heart.

John smelled like Polo.

Then: Horse dick! Daniel said. Just what the fuck is going on here? Get over here, Daniel said. I'm going to show you something.

Daniel pushed the table away from the banquette with his feet. The scrape against the black-and-white tile was loud, glasses and bottles clinking up together. I jumped out of the light into the darkness.

Daniel unbuttoned his shirt, kicked his shoes with the tassels off, King Lear Gypsy Rose Lee; Daniel unzipped his pants, pulled down his Calvin Kleins. Daniel bent over, pulled his one black sock off, lost his balance, went down on one knee, got up, pulled off his other black sock.

Daniel stood in his spotlight for life poking out his hard beer-can dick, his Rolex, his diamond ring left hand third finger, waving his dick back and forth, back and forth, pumping on it.

In the halogen light, Daniel's soliloquy he'd never remember:

Come take a look at this, goddammit, Daniel said. Do you work for me or not?

All daring and courage, all iron endurance of misfortune, make for a finer, nobler type of manhood.

Sit down, Daniel, I said.

Next to John, Saint Teresa Gone to Heaven, Daniel sat down.

On the floor, on the black-and-white tiles of the floor, I knelt down. I was so close I could smell his balls. The halogen light on his pubic hair. Polo.

Nice one, huh? Daniel said. Big, Daniel said. Do you like it?

Beer-can dick, I said.

Monster cock, Daniel said. Faggots love it.

Daniel put his third finger left hand, the diamond wedding ring finger, onto his piss slit.

You want to suck it? Daniel said.

All of us silent, even Sade, all of us all one thing.

How do you get your mouth open that wide?

Then: I want, I said, To draw a picture of it.

Language my second language.

Daniel's breath in, his breath out.

What? Daniel said.

For posterity, I said. Postmodern totemism. Pretend I'm Andy Warhol, I said.

On the table, I found the cornflower blue, grabbed a Heineken beer can, and I tore off a piece of the butcher paper. I put the butcher paper on the black-and-white tiles of the floor.

Daniel leaned back and spread his legs, his cock pointing straight up.

I handed Daniel the Heineken can.

Hold the beer can, I said, next to your beer-can dick, I said. That way the drawing will have a proportion.

Daniel smiled and put the Heineken can next to his beer-can dick. Daniel's cock was as big around at the bottom as the beer can, but not as big around at the head as the beer can, and Daniel's cock was longer than the beer can.

In the circle of light, Daniel's milky white bare feet, his yellow toenails, his hairy legs, bony knees, Daniel's beer-can dick and big sagging ball sack hanging down over his dark crack.

Pas sexy totale.

On the butcher paper on the black-and-white tiles of the floor, I drew the outline of Daniel's cock first and, when I got the shape and dimensions right, I colored in between the lines, using the red pink. I used a lime green for the Heineken can. The grid of the black-and-white tiles on the floor poked through.

When I was finished, I showed the drawing to Daniel, his big pink and blue beer-can dick, his ball sack hanging down, the dark crack, juxtaposed with the lime-green beer can.

Daniel took the drawing, pulled the drawing close to his eyes, squinted.

Monster cock, Daniel said. Nice one, huh?

Beer-can dick, I said.

Only blacks got bigger cocks than Jews, Daniel said.

What about Italians? I said.

Now it's your turn, Daniel said. Let's see this big horse dick of yours.

I stood up. Just like that, all at once, Daniel grabbed me around my waist and pulled my white shirt from out of my waiter pants.

Just like that, I twisted out of Daniel's grasp and was out of the circle of unrelenting brightness, outside in the darkness, looking in.

Daniel tried to stand up, couldn't, farted instead.

Rule one, I said. Never touch me.

Fuck you, Daniel said.

Daniel took the straw and put the straw onto a line on the butcher paper and the line was one of my Crayola cornflower blue lines, and Daniel snorted up the cornflower blue and didn't know the difference.

Daniel took the cigarette I rolled him. Lit it.

Daniel sat down next to John, pulled the table back into him, loud scrape, glass clink, pulled John's head down into his crotch. Across the surface of the moon, on the red banquette, John was doing the impossible, swallowing Daniel's cock. Vasty deep. Daniel's restaurant smile.

Table for three? Daniel said.

John's head up and down.

This is what faggots live for, Daniel said. Faggots are so good at this. This faggot will do this for you too, Spud. Make your horse dick feel real good.

Then: Come on, Spud, reach out and take what you want.

That's when John puked Hennessy, flower bottle champagne, cocaine, seltzer, cum, a red-pink splash all over Daniel's cock, down his legs, onto the red banquette, onto the black-and-white tiles of the floor. I grabbed my bow tie, my corkscrew, my pens, the drawing of Daniel's beer-can dick.

Outside on 46th Street, drifting snow.

My arm was in the air and a blast of cold wind blew up my white shirttails.

Two-oh-five East Fifth Street, I told the cabbie. Between Second and Third.

It was the kind of cab with greasy Plexiglas in between. Outside my window, speeding light, darkness, speeding light.

I'm already dead, Charlie, I said, And you're dead too.

Where the fuck are you, Charlie 2Moons?

Fuck hope, Charlie.

Fuck fucking hope.

CHAPTER
TEN

AyaHuaska and Chub were chomping at the bit, raring to go, neck and neck. We backed their butts up against the barn door, the way we always started. Charlie took his red T-shirt off and tied it to the saddle strings, then tied his two reins together in a knot at the end, making the two reins one rein, then placed the knot in his crotch between him and the saddle horn. I did the same thing with my T-shirt, tied my reins together the same way. Then, as close as we could to the same time, we let the reins go slack, gave the horses a kick in the flanks, threw our heads back, and raised our arms into the air.

Flying manes, tails up, Charlie and ayaHuaska, me and Chub, galloping through the shadow tunnel of cottonwood leaves and branches, kicking up dust and horse farts, then over the railroad tracks, across Highway 30 to the sagebrush plains, the low flatland and the tall grass, into the tules, down into gullies, to the bottoms.

I did an Arabesque, which is where you get behind the saddle and balance on one knee, then raise the other leg in the air and point your toe and arch your back, face up, and look up at the sky.

Charlie did a Suicide Drag, where you start out sidesaddle, then you put your left foot through the strap loop that's tied to the horn, and then you arch your back, and your whole body hangs head down over the saddle with your free leg in the air, toes pointing at the sky.

THE WAY THE sun was, Charlie's Grandfather Alessandro and his house seemed to be sitting in a pool of water. Alessandro was sitting out on his porch in his rocking chair, in the only shade for miles. Back and forth, the rocking chair on the old wood, the whole house a drum of Charlie's grandfather, back and forth in his rocking chair.

Hello! Hello! Alessandro called.

It's me, Charlie! Charlie yelled. And Will!

I know who you are! his grandfather yelled. I'm old but I'm not blind!

Charlie grabbed the reins and pulled ayaHuaska to a stop just at the two cedar posts and the old iron gate in front of the house. Charlie was tying up ayaHuaska to one of the cedar posts when Chub and I got there.

Before walking through the old iron gate, Charlie put his red T-shirt on. I tied Chub to the other cedar post, pulled on my T-shirt, and when I walked through the iron gate, Charlie was on the porch, bending down and hugging his grandfather.

Grandfather Alessandro looked like any old cowboy. Dusty cowboy boots sticking out the bottom of his Levi's, his Levi's hanging down over his skinny butt, a leather belt that had 2Moons tooled into the leather, a red Bannock Rose beaded belt buckle. An old blue shirt, sleeves rolled up to above the elbow, wrinkled elbows, rough skin, like rubbing your hand over a wall of wet weathered cedar shingles—same color too. An old straw hat totally molded to his head. Between his hat and his shirt collar, big wrinkles on the back of his neck that made diamonds on his skin.

You boys been jerking off in the sagebrush? Grandfather Alessandro said.

Charlie laughed. No jerking off today, Grandfather! We've been playing our game, Going Slack.

Going Slack, Alessandro said. I know that game, he said. That's a good game. Boys should play games, instead of keeping their nose in a book all day.

Charlie smiled gap-tooth at his grandfather.

Grandfather, Charlie said, You know I love books.

Books are in the mind, Grandfather Alessandro said. Too many books and you forget your body is in the world.

Then: I see you brought your buddy Hey-Soos, Grandfather said.

He always called me Hey-Soos, Spanish for Jesus. Grandfather Alessandro talked funny. Half of what he said you could get, but mostly it was like Shakespeare—English, but another language at the same time. I don't think Alessandro liked me much. Because I was white, I guess, or maybe because of my father.

I walked up to the porch, and, like I always did with Grandfather Alessandro, I didn't look at him, just looked down at my feet and stood where I stood until Grandfather Alessandro put his hand out and I took it.

You boys must need some water! Grandfather Alessandro said.

Charlie walked in the door of the square one-room house, painted white once, with only half a window. The shiny wet milk can with the water in it was right by the door. When Charlie pulled off the lid, there was a metal echo sound.

Charlie lifted the red tin cup off the nail where the cup always hung, dipped the cup into the milk can, lifted the cup out, dripping, and handed it me. The red tin lip against my lip, I swallowed big. When Charlie drank, two drops of water fell on his red T-shirt.

You want water, Grandfather?

Charlie held the red tin cup out in the air between me and Grandfather Alessandro.

No water for me, Grandfather Alessandro said. But you better get your horses some from the trough in the back.

Then: I'm going to the Sun Dance, Alessandro said. They're dancing over at Buffalo Lodge. You coming along?

The metal echo sound. Charlie pushed down on the lid of the milk can with both hands, then sat his butt down on it. Hung the red tin cup back on the nail.

We were there yesterday, Grandpa, Charlie said. Don't you remember?

Grandfather rocked back and forth, back and forth, the whole house a drum.

Sundance takes three days and three nights, Grandfather Alessandro said. Today's the last day. Why don't you come along?

I kept my eyes on the old gray wood of the porch floor. Grandfather's eyes were really looking at me.

If Einstein was an Indian and somebody took a chisel to his face and then fed him sagebrush for a year, Einstein might look like Grandfather Alessandro.

You always took a chance looking into them eyes.

Let me tell you something, Grandfather Alessandro said. So you'll know.

Sundance is sacred, Grandfather said. The power of the dance is to dance with God. It's our religion. And the sweat lodge. Don't let no book tell you different.

Then: Bring your friend Hey-Soos, Grandfather Alessandro said. He might learn something.

Charlie twisted his index finger into his red shirttail and looked down at the porch floor. Squashed an earwig next to the milk can with his black tennie.

I promised Will we'd go to Spring Creek, Charlie said. Besides, Sundance ain't no place for *tybos*.

Tybo being me. White man, Cotton Parker's boy.

Grandfather Alessandro's eyes, the way they were like a child's. Nothing in between you and him. Just then his eyes got as big as my heart inside me. Two long tears down his old face. About the time the tears hit his chin, Grandfather Alessandro slapped his knee just like that and let out a big whooping laugh. His whole face laughing, his whole body, Charlie laughing too. With the rocking back and forth, I thought the house was going to fall in.

OK, Grandfather Alessandro said. OK. You boys go to Spring Creek. Have some fun. But Charlie, I want you to remember what I told you.

Grandfather sat up in his chair, put his boots down firm on the gray wood. The rocking chair quit rocking. No sound at all, just the wind in the sagebrush. Grandfather tilted his cowboy hat back. With his hat off, his head was like some people's feet that's been in boots so long they should just always stay in them boots.

You remember what I told you, now, he said. Don't you forget.

CHARLIE ON AYAHUASKA, me on Chub, galloping through the sagebrush and dust. I tried the Acrobatic Back Bend, which is where you stand up in the saddle facing back and you bend backwards and hold on to the saddle horn, and I was doing it just fine when Chub dodged a big sagebrush and I didn't dodge. I kept holding on to the saddle horn, did a flip, turned, and when my feet hit the ground I used the momentum to throw myself back into the saddle.

Charlie didn't do a trick for a while, just kept free-standing. I guess I'd surprised him—I had surprised my own self.

At Spring Creek, on one side it's all willows, willows almost as tall as you on a horse. When we got to the willows, Charlie and ayaHuaska ran into the stand of willows, into the path we'd made through the willows, then me and Chub. We ran curving through the path, willows stinging our arms and faces, until we got to our willow tree, which really wasn't a tree, just a section of willows that were taller, and there was one willow with bark on it as big around as a horse's leg and the willow branches leaned over onto the water. The meadow there was real green grass and in places soggy with mud.

Charlie 2Moons slid off ayaHuaska. Shirt up over his head, his arms in the air, the black hair of his armpits, one armpit on each side of the dividing line down his middle, from his Adam's apple down, one nipple on each side, all the way down one side of Charlie meeting the other in the middle, at his belly button, the hair at the top of his Levi's.

Charlie kicked his black tennies off. Sometimes Charlie wore socks and he'd have to pull off his socks, and he'd go back and forth, back and forth, one arm out, dancing on one leg, then back and forth, other arm out, dancing on the other leg, but that day Charlie didn't wear socks. His one foot was on a patch of really green grass and his other foot was in the mud, toes sunk in the mud.

Charlie sucked in his belly, his hands at the top button, and just by pulling the Levi's at the top he gets all five buttons. That day the sound of the buttons five thumps in my chest. Charlie stepped out of his pants one leg at a time, then with a kick his Levi's went sprawling and hung on a willow, Charlie never wearing undershorts, and—*ta-da*—there was Charlie, the sun-and-willow shadows on his skin, all of his skin from his widow's peak down his nose to his shoulders down the long dividing line to his flat belly, to his belly button, the hair, the surprising bounce, the weight of him down there.

So different that day for some reason how real his body was. Was like I'd never even seen Charlie's body before.

Charlie whooped, running to the bank into Spring Creek, the jump into the air, the gasp of breath, raven wavy hair flying back, Charlie's big butt between earth and water, the top point of a jackknife. Then I was in the air too. My body, Charlie's, one long arched uninterrupted muscle, each. Charlie dived into his reflection, I dived into mine. One long breath through clear water, one long hot dusty day, one long sunset shadow.

CHARLIE WAS LYING naked on his back in the sun on the grassy part. I was sitting, crossed-legged, chewing on a piece of grass.

Charlie sat up and walked his butt along the grass so he was sitting, knees touching my knees.

I'm going to tell you something, Charlie said, So you'll know. But before I tell you, Charlie said, We got to promise.

Promise what? I said.

Never to tell, Charlie said.

Tell what? I said.

Charlie had his red Swiss army knife in his hand, and Charlie opened the knife and handed me the knife and said, Cut me right here on the wrist.

With his index, Charlie made a line onto his wrist.

Charlie? I said.

We'll be blood brothers, Charlie said. We'll have the same blood, and everything I know you'll know and everything you know I'll know.

Cut your wrist? I said.

I've got something I want to tell you, Will, Charlie said, And the only way I can tell you is if we're brothers.

What if I hit a vein or something? I said.

You won't, Charlie said, If you cut right here.

Charlie's index across his wrist, just below the wrinkle of his palm.

You go first, I said.

Let me see your hand, Charlie said.

I unfolded my right hand from my other hand.

Charlie held my hand in his hands. The vein in my wrist was pumping blue.

We got to do this fast, Charlie said. I'll cut you first and then give you the knife and you cut me, and we'll hold our wrists together and we'll promise.

What do we promise? I asked.

To be brothers, Charlie said. To always respect and love each other and always tell each other the truth and to keep each other's secrets and to never forget.

I don't think I can do this, I said.

You don't want to be brothers? Charlie said.

Oh, I do! I said.

Charlie sliced the knife across my wrist, and blood was up in a thin line, then blood up higher than my skin and then blood down my arm, to my elbow, dripping off my elbow, onto the hair inside my hip, down.

OK, now you, Charlie said.

I took Charlie's knife and cut, but I didn't even break the skin.

Do it again, Charlie said. It's all right, Charlie said. Lay the blade on my wrist, press, and pull the blade across.

I laid the blade on Charlie's wrist. I pressed. My breath in. My breath out. Top teeth to bottom teeth grinding. I closed my eyes. I pulled the blade across.

That's it! Charlie said.

I opened my eyes and there was Charlie's blood, more blood than mine, blood all over down his arm, dripping off his arm, down.

Charlie laid his wrist on mine, wound to wound, blood to blood. Charlie bent near, his brown eyes into my eyes.

Lips at my ear.

My little brother, Charlie said, I promise to always tell the truth to you. I promise that your secrets are always safe with me. I promise always to respect and love you. I will never betray you. I promise I will never forget you.

Now you go, Charlie said.

I put my forehead against Charlie's forehead.

My brother, I said, Charlie, I promise too. I'll always tell the truth. I'll always keep your secrets. I will always respect and love you. I will never betray you. I promise I will never forget you.

Then Charlie put his hand that wasn't bleeding behind my neck and we sat, forehead to forehead, both of us looking down at Charlie's wrist crossed over my wrist, looking down at the line of blood into Charlie's belly button, the line of blood along my hip. Blood on my cock, on Charlie's cock. Charlie and I forehead to forehead looking down at my hard cock, at Charlie's hard cock. The line of blood dripping down onto the green of the marsh grass.

My legs behind Charlie's back, I pulled Charlie up to me, pushed myself up against him, opened my mouth, kissed Charlie on the mouth, put my tongue into the liar's space, in between his two front teeth.

Love. Wounded by the blow.

I promise, Charlie said.

I promise, I said.

Then Charlie and I were rolling all over, and there was a feeling all around me, on my skin, a finger drawing a circle around my heart.

Charlie's back and Charlie's arms and his hands, Charlie's butt, his legs, his smooth cool skin, his hard cock beside mine sliding up and down, and then Charlie was shooting strands of cum all over onto my belly. I was hanging on to willows, one in each hand, and then I was cumming too, and we were yelling and kissing and rolling around. Charlie and I were not on the premises, no rules, the space in between us went away, and we went in, both of us, and everything, the whole known universe, was silent and all one thing, perfect, just perfect, and in my mouth was mud and grass and sweat and blood and cum.

CHARLIE ROLLED OVER on his back. The wind through the willows was a voice whispering. Charlie poked me with his elbow and I looked over and Charlie was pointing up. In the big willow was a redtail hawk.

Grandfather said, Charlie said, That we are all of us our brother's keeper. But me especially I am my brother's keeper.

Charlie's chest jumped up with a laugh, but he wasn't laughing.

Just then the redtail hawk sang out a screech and flew off west into the yellow-gold sun. Charlie eyes followed the hawk, the sun coming up gold on his chin.

Then, when he spoke, Charlie put his face right into my face. His black eyes deep as a new bruise, his smooth cinnamon skin, his lips that had kissed me, sucked me, his tongue so pink behind his white teeth.

Grandfather Alessandro said, Charlie said, That I am your brother.

Brother? I said. What does he mean?

Charlie raised his shoulders up, let them drop.

Charlie's smile. The liar's space between Charlie's two front teeth. His hair wet and shiny slick, just starting to curl.

Hell if I know! Charlie said. I just thought we should make it official, Charlie said.

Charlie touched his hand on my shoulder, brought his hand down my arm, to my hand, off my hand to my thigh, then onto my cock, cupped my balls. Charlie's bruised black eyes got darker.

Something else, too, Charlie said. Grandfather told me that you and I must go into a sweat lodge together and smoke the pipe.

What's a sweat lodge? I said.

Charlie let his hand slide up my belly, up between my nipples. Then he took my hand, put my hand inside his, open palm to open palm. The blood.

My grandfather loves me, Charlie said, Like nobody else. And he wants me to be happy. He's seen me, Will, and you, and Grandfather wants to bless it. Bless us.

Will you do it, Will? Charlie said. For me?

What about Father? I said. He hates anything Indian.

Fuck your father, Charlie said. Jeez!

Charlie leaned up on his elbow. His full soft lips against my lips.

My breath in. My breath out.

Sure, I said, I'll do it.

Promise?

I promise, I said.

Between us and the sun, ayaHuaska and Chub were horse shadows, the gold sky behind them getting fancy with pink.

Then just like that, Charlie sat up quick, threw his leg over me. His hands grabbed my wrists and pushed my hands out above my head. Charlie slow-sat his cock and balls down onto my belly.

When the fuck didya learn the Single Vault? Charlie said.

The what? I said.

Riding down here today, Charlie said, You went from the Acrobatic Back Bend to the Single Vault off the horse, feet on the ground, then jumped back on.

Learned it just now, I said.

Never could lie to Charlie.

That was real pretty, Will, Charlie said. I'm going to have to try that.

Where'd you learn the Acrobatic Back Bend? Charlie asked.

It was in the book, I said.

You been practicing without me? he asked.

Wanted to surprise you, I said.

It was a surprise all right, Charlie said. I didn't know you could bend that far back.

Double-jointed, I said.

Charlie's breath in. His breath out. Charlie licked his lips before he spoke.

If you can bend that far backwards, Charlie said, Can you bend that far frontwards?

I can, I said.

Then that means . . . Charlie said.

That I can give myself a blow job, I said.

A blow job? Charlie said. You don't even know what that is.

I knew what the Acrobatic Back Bend was, I said, Now didn't I?

Charlie's head jerked back quick to make sure he could see all of me.

Will Parker, Charlie said, You son of a bitch. You been practicing without me.

Charlie let go my arms, sat up straight.

My eyes were so happy. All they could see was Charlie, his hair sticking up all around his face, the sun gold and pink through the black waves.

The liar's space between Charlie's two front teeth.

Can I watch? Charlie said.

KNEES AND ELBOWS, I was shits and giggles, taking off my pants, standing naked outside in the sun, Charlie naked too. Alessandro's big old cock with gray hairs all around it.

Alessandro went into the sweat lodge first. Then me. When I stepped in, when I crossed over into the darkness, what I remember is trying not to laugh at Alessandro's butt crack. Then inside, sitting cross-legged, knee to knee around a fire pit in a dark hut with two men, I tried to cover myself. I thought it was my cock hanging out I was trying to cover, but it was another nakedness.

Grandfather Alessandro reached behind him and in his hands was a bundle, two red strings around a piece of spotted fur.

That bobcat skin? Charlie asked.

Ocelot, Alessandro said.

In all the world, there I was, inside a hut made from bent willows, the hut covered with animal hides, old blankets, canvas, plastic, Alessandro cross-legged on the other side of the fire pit from Charlie and me.

Alessandro undid the red strings and unrolled the piece of ocelot fur out in front of him. The medicine pipe was in two pieces, The pipe stone and the stem. Alessandro's crooked hands picked up the stem, picked up the pipe stone, put the stem against the hole of the pipe stone, twisted the stem inside.

Regard the male and the female, Alessandro said. How they come together and make a whole.

Alessandro picked up the pipe and held the pipe with both hands.

The bowl of the pipe is red stone, Alessandro said, It is the female, it is earth. The buffalo carved into the stone represents the four-leggeds. The stem of the pipe is the male, it is wood and represents all that grows upon the earth. The twelve feathers that hang here are from eagle, and they represent all the wingeds of the air. The shells and the beads that hang from the stem represent the one-leggeds, the fish that swim in the rivers and the sea.

When you pray with this pipe, you pray for and with everything, Grandfather Alessandro said. With this pipe you will be bound to all your relatives, those living and dead, your grandfather and father, your grandmother and your mother, your brothers and sisters.

Alessandro lifted the pipe above his head, looked up, said something in Indian, held the pipe that way, then laid the pipe down inside the circle of our knees.

Regard the medicine pipe, Alessandro said. When you are with this pipe, when you hold the pipe in your hands, you must speak only truth.

Alessandro started singing high, yelling, magpies and crows.

Out of a buckskin bag, Alessandro pulled a pouch of Bull Durham tobacco and some paper sacks. He took a pinch of Bull Durham and held the tobacco between his crooked thumb and long fingers, next to the dirt. He lifted the tobacco above his head, then moved the tobacco in a circle around him, stopping four times.

Alessandro put the tobacco on a square piece of polished wood, into a circle of brass tacks on the polished wood.

Out of one sack, a pinch of sage. Alessandro held the sage, same way as the tobacco, singing high, his voice flying around my ears. He held the sage to the earth, to the sky, to the four points of the circle around him, then put the sage with the tobacco into the circle of brass tacks on the polished wood.

There were other herbs, cedar and red willow, I think, and some I didn't know. Each time, with each pinch, Alessandro sang, held the herb down, up, and around, and put the herb into the circle of brass tacks.

Alessandro mixed the herbs together, grinding and sifting them between his crooked thumb and long fingers.

My arms were behind me, my hands on the dirt, and I was leaning back on my hands. I couldn't take my eyes off the pipe. I just kept staring and staring at the different parts of the pipe put together—the dark blue beads, the feathers, the pipe bowl, the carved buffalo, the stem.

My breath in. My breath out.

In my forearms, it started.

What scared me was that the pipe was alive.

ALESSANDRO HELD UP his hand, his wide palm another face. He folded down his fingers into his palm except for two.

I'll tell you something, Grandfather Alessandro said, So you'll know.

There are two roads, Alessandro said.

The red road is the vertical road. It runs north and south and is the good or the straight way. North is for purity and south is the source of life.

Then there is the blue or black road, which is the horizontal road. It runs east and west and is the road of error and destruction. He who travels on this path is one who is lost, distracted, ruled by his senses, sees only what is in front of his eyes, and lives for himself rather than his people.

All that there is, is represented by the offerings to the powers of the four directions, Grandfather Alessandro said. And all things—represented by the pipe mixture—all come together in this single point, to the bowl or heart of the pipe.

The pipe, Grandfather Alessandro said, Is the universe. The pipe is also us, and the person who fills the pipe becomes one with the pipe.

So the pipe is not only the center of the universe but also my own center, Alessandro said, and I expand and the six directions of space are brought within myself. It is by this expansion that the person stops being apart and becomes whole or holy, and is no longer here, and the world is out there, and the illusion of separateness is shattered.

As you take this pipe and smoke it, as you take this universe in your hands and put it to your mouth, you too stop being apart; you become one, you become whole, with the holy and the sacred.

Alessandro picked up one of the dark red embers with his bare fingers and put the ember into the pipe bowl. When he smoked, he blew the smoke down to his crotch, then above him, then four times around in a circle. The song he was singing sounded more like crying to me—when you really cry and can't stop.

Alessandro handed the pipe to Charlie, and Charlie sucked on the pipe and blew the smoke out the same way as Alessandro. Then Charlie handed the pipe to me. When I put my lips on the pipe, I thought I'd feel one with the universe, but I coughed on the first puff and kept coughing through all six directions.

GRANDFATHER ALESSANDRO'S HAND reached across through the light of the door and pulled the door flap down.

The only way out is in, he said.

The black inside the sweat lodge was the black inside my soul, the black inside my head. Black breath came up fast from my lungs. My hands fighting the black air nothing. Never been no breath so much. The water onto the rocks hissed up against my ears. Burning steam on my shoulders.

Charlie's hand came out of the black and grabbed hard onto my hand, palm to palm. We went down quick. Faces, lips against the earth, sucking up what air was left on the ground. The black inside was outside, was a solid mass of dark fire.

Everything was only hot and dark and the fear I knew but hadn't met yet. *Steam fear dark* came up hard through my kidneys, burnt open my stomach, scorched out my lungs.

I was screaming. Charlie was screaming.

Alessandro was singing, high and broken off, far away deep inside. Only Charlie's hand.

There was nothing else.

* * *

SUNLIGHT WAS A hole.

Grandfather Alessandro's hand reached across through the darkness and opened the sweat-lodge door.

Grandfather Alessandro's eyes were too big, too scary to look into, but I looked into them.

Hear me, young Charlie and Hey-Soos, Alessandro said. When a promise is broken, we are lost. To leave the red road is to lose your soul. Always remember! The only way to get on the red road is to get yourself back to the place of beginning. This is extremely hard, because you cannot see through your own confusion. The only way to get back to the point of beginning and begin is to get back to the bowl and heart of this pipe, the pipe that is the center of the universe, which is also your own center, and you expand and the four directions of space are brought within yourself and the illusion of being separate is shattered.

Take heart, my Charlie and Hey-Soos, Alessandro said. Your love is great and good. Trust it. Never doubt it.

Just remember, Grandfather Alessandro said, And I'll tell you so you'll know. When you're lost on the blue road, when you're in the west and cannot see, remember that the bright light coming toward you at first appears to be a charging iron horse, a locomotive train that will run over you, that will crush you.

But that bright light, Alessandro said, Only appears to be an iron horse. What it really is is the light at the end of the tunnel.

STEAM ALL OVER the windows. Grandfather Alessandro and Charlie and I were sitting aound the Formica table in Viv's double-wide kitchenette. Viv had cooked us up a big feast of beef stew, fry bread, and chokecherry pudding.

Charlie and I were on our second bowls of beef stew. Grandfather Alessandro was on his second bowl of chokecherry pudding.

Grandfather Alessandro put down his spoon, stuck his crooked index finger into his white bowl, and scraped up the sides for more chokecherry.

I'll tell you something, Grandfather Alessandro said, So you'll know.

There's this Jewish story, Alessandro said.

Viv was at the stove stirring something in a pot. When Alessandro said *Jewish story*, Viv turned around, wiped her mouth on her sleeve, and smiled her gap-toothed smile.

In Russia, Alessandro said, There was a famous rabbi. Whenever he saw misfortune threatening his people, this rabbi would go to a place in the forest and meditate. Then he would light a fire, say a special prayer, and the miracle would happen and the rabbi's people would be safe. Things went on and on like that and the rabbi died, and later, his disciple, another rabbi, whenever there was a misfortune threatening his people, this rabbi would go to the same place in the forest and say to the Great Mystery: I'm sorry but I do not know how to light the fire, but I still know the prayer, and here's the prayer. And this rabbi would say the prayer, and the miracle would happen. Then that rabbi died, and another rabbi, his disciple, whenever a misfortune threatened his people, he would go to the place in the forest and say, I do not know how to light the fire, and I do not know the prayer, but I know the place and this must be sufficient. And the miracle would happen. When that rabbi died, his disciple, a fourth rabbi, whenever a misfortune threatened his people, would sit in his chair at home with his head in his hands and say to the Great Mystery, I don't know how to light the fire, I don't know the prayer, and I don't know the place in the forest, or even which forest. All I can do is tell you about it, and this must be sufficient. And the miracle would happen.

God made man because he loves to hear stories, Alessandro said. That's a good story, huh?

CHAPTER
ELEVEN

The cabdriver was the blackest man. His ID above the meter said Samueli and then an African name. When I looked in his eyes, his smile was quick and bright.

The bullet-proof Plexiglas in the Checker cab had been hit by grease, which somebody tried to rub off. Around the tray in the window where you pay, deep scratches on the Plexiglas.

On a warm spring night, streaking light into darkness, the windows all open, underneath the Checker cab's wheels Manhattan monster lifted the three of us up on its back for a ride. Huge river, wide avenues, our cab a yellow tub setting sail, wind around our ears and hair, white-water bump and roll, changing lanes, swirling eddies through traffic. Harry's arm was across the top of the seat above my shoulders. Harry's white shirt the deepest white and also yellow, green, blue, red—every color of every light we passed through. Harry's Polo smell and his three staff Heinekens, after-restaurant sweat, and ironed white cotton-polyester mix from under his arm. Harry's other arm out the window, white sleeve rolled up, the red hairs on his arm past the Triple-X-Rated, past neon vegetable stands, coffee shops, past Macy's Art Family windows, darkness, figures standing in darkness, speeding light, darkness, speeding light.

No Charlie 2Moons.

Ronald Reagan and Nancy lay across our laps. My left hip was touching Fiona's hip; the wind through the window blew her white shirt collar. She'd loosened her hair and it was all over, sometimes just floating around her face. She sat back into the seat, now and then with her hand pulling her hair from her eyes, out of the corners of her red mouth. Her smell was Southern Comfort mixed with herself. She was smiling, really smiling, in the yellow-tub Checker cab.

High enough to think we were New York.

Fiona set her huge red leather purse onto Nancy's face, fumbled through papers, makeup, Polaroids.

Cool, she said, and pulled out a joint.

I had to push my crotch up so I could get into my pants pocket for matches. Ronald Reagan slid down and Nancy slid down. Fiona looked at my crotch and Harry looked. Fiona lit the joint, cupping her hand over the flame, inhaling, inhaling again, then tapped on the hologram Plexiglas, holding up the joint so the blackest-man cabdriver could see. The cabdriver smiled again. Fiona handed the joint out the window to him; little sparks flew from the joint out into Manhattan. The cabdriver toked, toked again, and for a moment I fell through, in between continents, cultures, color, Plexiglas. A merge.

All it takes is getting shit-faced. All it takes is a joint.

The cabdriver handed the joint back out the window, more sparks. Fiona took the joint, toked again, handed the joint to me.

A kiss. Fiona called toking on the joint a kiss.

Kiss? she said, holding the inhale as she passed the joint to me. Kiss?

Kiss? I said, and passed the joint to Harry.

The marijuana smelled like inside a hay silo. My shoulders were against the Checker cab backseat, Harry's red arm hairs touching my neck. Ronnie's dark crotch and Nancy's dark crotch under the cigarettes as I rolled them. Then it's the part I love most, falling into the big hole in between, and all I want to do is smoke cigarettes and smoke cigarettes.

At about 14th Street, Fiona told us about her friend Jesse's new cat. The cat's name was Green Date, and the reason the cat was named Green Date was because the cat had a special green towel he masturbated on.

Two weeks with that cat in Jesse's house, Fiona said, And all her other animals are humping the green towel too. Two dogs and two other cats all going at it. Even the cockatoo humping the goddamn green towel.

The laughter came from deep inside me, and the more I laughed, the more it made Harry and Fiona laugh. Fiona lost all her eye makeup.

The blackest-man cabdriver, Oh Captain Our Captain of the speeding yellow tub, was laughing too. He turned the music up way loud, music not from anywhere I know, Nairobi, Mombasa, the island of Lamu—drums, deep rivers, wolves, a rhythm low in my body just before my butt crack, a little place down there in me where all at once people from Nairobi and Mombasa and the island of Lamu are dancing and singing Kiswahili.

Harry passed the joint to me.

The one in the middle always gets the highest.

Powerful shit, Harry said, This dope.

I took a kiss, handed the joint to Fiona.

Cool, Fiona said.

Ronald Reagan and Nancy were a hit in Fish Bar. Five bucks a shot; just about everybody in the bar had to have a photo op with the president. But this was the Lower East Side. It wasn't like in Times Square, Fiona said. In Times Square it was tourists and Republicans standing new-shoe stiff next to Ronald Reagan and Nancy, smiling, maybe putting their arms around them.

Not so in Fish Bar. One guy pulled his pants down and mooned Ronald Reagan and Nancy while Harry took the photograph. Two lesbian women felt up Nancy while Harry took the photograph. Three union guys all stood flipping Ronnie and Nancy the bird. Another guy took Harry and Ronnie in the bathroom and pulled his cock out and made like Ronald Reagan was sucking his cock, then made like he was cornholing Ronald Reagan.

Twenty exposures, one hundred dollars.

Performance Art, Fiona said. Cool.

Harry went home about two-thirty. He said he was tired. Said he had a date. A Green Date.

But Harry was more than tired.

The monster's heavy footfall, a ripple in Fiona's Southern Comfort, my Crown Royal, what was left of Harry's Heineken.

Fiona and I wanted to keep going, so we kissed Harry good night and walked to Third and Avenue C, to a secret after-hours club Fiona heard about called Network.

Fiona's long white arms and white legs were poking out of a little black dress. The moon was almost full and I remember the moonlight on Fiona's arms. The sky wasn't a dark sky with stars. The sky was navy blue with a white jet stream heading uptown.

In all the world, three o'clock in the morning, Fiona, the moonlight on Fiona, and me standing in the middle of Third Street at Avenue C. Third Street same as all the other streets down here—just a street and a bunch of doorways to six-story walk-ups. Not an after-hours club in sight.

New York is cold, Fiona sang, *But I like where I'm living. The music on Clinton Street all through the evening.*

What's that? I said.

That's a line from "Famous Blue Raincoat," Fiona said.

Leonard Cohen? I said.

Then: Now's a good time, I said.

For what? Fiona said.

Leonard Cohen, I said. The song. You said you would sing me the song.

"Famous Blue Raincoat"? Fiona said.

No, I said. The other one you told me about.

"Song of Bernadette"? Fiona said.

That one, I said.

Cool! Fiona said.

Fiona in her spotlight for life, under the streetlamp light, the solitary illumination in the night, in her little black dress, three in the morning. Fiona stood straight, her white marble-statue arms at her sides, feet square beneath her on the pavement. Just over her shoulder, the moon.

Fiona cleared her throat, started singing, was off-key, tried again, stopped.

Quiet as only New York can get that fast.

This is making me nervous, Fiona said.

Why? I said. You have a captive audience.

I don't know, Fiona said.

Are you playing at being nervous? I said. Or *being* nervous? It's all so *Tony and Tina's Wedding*, I said. Can't you be synchronistic?

Go fuck yourself, Will, Fiona said.

Then, in all the world, the hope of theater to lay bare the human heart, the scar on Fiona's red lip a life all its own.

Beautiful according to Fellini.

Fiona sang Leonard Cohen's song how her heart was inside her, the way my heart was inside me too, on fire the way the night was, longing for things that probably weren't going to come, and sad because I knew they probably weren't, but still foolish enough to wish, but most of all clear and smooth and beautiful.

> *There was a child named Bernadette.*
> *I heard the story long ago.*
> *She saw the Queen of Heaven once*
> *And kept the vision in her soul.*
> *No one believed what she had seen,*
> *No one believed what she heard.*
> *That there were sorrows to be healed*
> *And mercy mercy in this world.*

We've been around, we've fought, we've lied.
We mostly fall, we mostly run.
And every now and then we try
to mend the damage that we've done.
Tonight, tonight, I just can't rest.
I've got this joy inside my breast.
To think that I did not forget
That song, that child named Bernadette.

On the corner of Third and Avenue C, the darkness outside the circle of light was the dark side of the moon. Inside the spotlight Fiona's marble-white arms up Patti LuPone Evita.

I just want to hold you.
Won't you let me hold you
Like Bernadette would do?

I just want to hold you.
Come on let me hold you
Like Bernadette would do.

Muffy MacIlvane, Susan Strong, Fiona Yet.
Wounded by a blow of love.
I walked to the curb, stood behind a car.
Where you going? Fiona said. Wasn't I great?
You were great, I said. I got to pee.
It was a lie.
Pee? Fiona yelled, Not on Third Street! This is the Hell's Angels' block. They catch you pissing here and you're in deep shit.
Can I pee on Avenue C? I said.
Cool, Fiona said. Just go up a ways and point it toward Fourteenth.
My cock pointed toward 14th Street, I didn't pee. Chin quivering, silent, pointed toward 14th Street, my back to Fiona. *Won't you let me hold you?* Instead of peeing, I started crying.
When I got back to Third Street, Fiona was skinny white arms and legs, up one stoop, then down, then up another.
Where the fuck is this fucking place? Fiona yelled.
Two guys in white T-shirts and Levi's and earrings and a woman with a bald head in a faux leopardskin jumpsuit came out of doorway. They were smoking and laughing and stumbling into each other. One guy

messed the other guy's hair, and the guy said, Watch the hair, man!
And the other guy said, Fuck you *and* your hair! Then they looked at
the bald woman and said it to her—Fuck you *and* your hair!—and all
three of them laughed.

Fiona and I walked up the stoop where the three fuck-you-and-your-
hairs had come from. Fiona knocked on the door. The Most Beautiful
Asian Man in the World, with bleached-white hair, opened the door.

What you here for? the Most Beautiful Asian Man said.

We're here to party, Fiona said.

The door opened, and Fiona and I stepped into a vestibule where
other people were standing. The door closed behind us. Fiona gave the
Most Beautiful Asian Man in the World twenty dollars. I gave him
twenty dollars.

There were maybe seven people in the vestibule. No Charlie 2Moons.
One guy had a flask and he took a drink, then passed the flask to Fiona.
Fiona said cool and took a drink and handed the flask to me. Somebody made a joke about *Candid Camera.* I looked up and there was a
camera in the corner of the vestibule on the ceiling.

Looking for UFOs, one woman said. Uninvited Fuck-Offs.

Underdeveloped Foreign Organizers.

Ultra-Feminine Onanists.

Ultimate Fellatio Orgasm.

We were all laughing when the door in front of us opened.

There was a long bar on the right and just enough space to walk
between the wall and the stools at the bar. Beyond the bar was a room
that looked like somebody's kitchen in the fifties. Square black-and-
white tiles on the floor, chrome *Father Knows Best* tables and chairs.
The light in the room like the light on a kitchen stove or in a telephone
booth. Mostly dark, tiny bright fluorescences, big film-noir shadows.

Charlie 2Moons was everywhere, in every face, in every beat of the
music.

Marvin Gaye was singing "Give It Up." Fiona checked her purse and
we walked into the dark shadows of people dancing.

There was a table for two under the window. Venetian blinds on the
window—the old big white horizontal kind. Southern Comfort two
rocks for Fiona, In the Ditch for me. The table next to us was black
men and women dressed to the nines, passing a joint. Fiona smiled when
she saw me staring at the joint.

It ain't Omaha, Fiona said.

Idaho, I said.

Fuck Idaho.

I rolled a cigarette. Fiona rolled a joint.

Kiss?

The DJ was standing in a box like a pulpit at the top of some stairs. All he had was a stereo hi-fi, a lot like Bobbie's only bigger speakers, and when the song was over you had to stand and wait for the next song or go sit down.

In the Ditch the second round, and Fiona asked me to dance. I stood right up, even though I only dance alone in my apartment, lights off, Sony Walkman on. My big long body doesn't move the way a man's big long body's supposed to. At least not in Pocatello, Idaho, or Boulder, Colorado, or Bozeman, Montana, or Hope, Beyond Hope.

Fuck 'em. Those little-town blues.

Who cares what a bunch of assholes think? Take what's wrong with you and make art out of it. Martha Graham meets Joe Cocker.

So when Fiona asked me to dance I stood right up because of all the things I just told you, and because it was Fiona who asked me, and because the last time I'd danced, not counting naked alone in my room, was when I danced that night with Charlie 2Moons in the barn.

It was a slow one. "Love and Affection," Joan Armatrading.

Fiona leaned her body against my body, her bushel of hair under my chin, her head against my chest, the long firm muscles of her arms, her shoulders, so white.

Standing with Fiona, I was the boy when we danced, my hand on her hip, my other hand holding up her hand, our feet on the black-and-white checkered tiles, the venetian blinds pulled, the kitchen stove light, the smell of her body and something secret, waiting for the record to drop.

The needle on the record, that sound, our invitation to faraway, Fiona and I dancing in somebody's after-hours kitchen, smiling, somewhere else.

Only your body can know another body.

Because you see it, you think you know it. Your eyes think they know. Seeing Fiona's body for so long, I thought I knew her body.

I'll tell you something, so you'll know: It's not the truth. Only your body can know another body.

My hand on her back, my hand in her hand, her toes up against my toes, Fiona's body wasn't sections of a body my eyes had pieced together. In my arms was one long uninterrupted muscle, a body breathing life, strong and real.

And the strangest thing, this wonder woman Susan Strong my eyes had known was the girl when we danced, following me. Where I moved, she moved.

Fiona let go my hand and put both her arms around my waist. She leaned back and looked up at me. Her eyes clear, open. Her broken lip fuck-you.

You smell good, I said.

I see that you are playing at being a great dancer, Fiona said.

To know the power of the dance, I said, Is to dance with God.

Fiona made her face like a vampire's and put her hands around my throat. Just who the fuck *are* you? Fiona said.

Fiona's eyes, a Spanish dancer who's trained to use her eyes.

First you're some cowboy from Ohio rolling cigarettes with one hand, Fiona said.

Idaho, I said.

Then you tell me you can't fuck, Fiona said, And that day—remember that day in Cauchemar?—just as you told me that, when I looked at you there was a beautiful light all around you, and I thought: Cool. This guy is being very genuine.

Then later on you're whining like every other sorry mother's son, Fiona said.

Then you're walking out the door with Chef Som Chai under your arm, Fiona said. Then you're Daniel's slave interest.

Then, at *Shopping for an Honest Man*, at *my* performance piece, I look out into the audience through the hole in the curtain and there you are male-bonding with Argwings Khodek, my Absolute Ultimate Idol.

And now you're Section Six, Fiona said, And I'm still fucking the dog in Sections One and Two. I ought to kick your fucking ass.

Fiona grabbed my ass.

And I got two brothers, Fiona said, So don't think I can't.

The song stopped about then, there was a scratch at the end, then silence. Dogs barking and big shadows and smoke and sweat and kitchen-stove light. My feet on the black-and-white kitchen tile were twice the size of Fiona's.

Surrounded by a room full of Charlie 2Moons.

Who am I?

Where are your brothers? I said.

Greenwich, Connecticut, Fiona said. Twins, both tax lawyers, both queer.

Both? I said.

The Hyannisport Homos, Fiona said. YUFAs, Fiona said. Young Urban Faggot Attorneys.

Fiona hit her fists against my chest once, hard.

Come on, Will, Fiona said, Cop to it! I asked you a question.

I AM A white male six-foot-two one hundred and ninety pounds, thirty-one years old, brown to blond hair, hazel eyes, big butt, big legs, big nipples, should be bigger in the chest and arms. Big spirit, big body, big nose, crooked bottom teeth, little dick. Crossed-over scared stallion.

Five people I know: Ruby, True Shot, Rose, Susan Strong, Harry. One's a junkie, one's a spirit schlepper, one's a Shakespearean drag queen, one's idiot-savant mother fucked a truck driver, one is New York's only Irish Catholic homosexual. Two I count as friends, Rose and True Shot. One is just a voice on my answering machine, Ruby. One is attached to the other one, Harry. I cry too much. Think about Bobbie too much. I am on a journey. I have a task: Find Charlie 2Moons and ask his forgiveness.

Nobody really knows who they are, I said. Even God don't know.

Cut the crap, Will! Fiona said.

Then: Why should I tell you, I said, Who I am?

Because I'm your friend, Fiona said.

Fiona put her hand on my cheek, on my forehead. I took the chance and looked her straight in the eye.

You said everything's a performance piece, I said. Life is an art and art is a game, I said. This is all an illusion, I said. *Asobase kotoba.* So why not continue playing? I said, I see that you are playing at being a great Susan Strong, I said, And I'm playing at being a great Will Parker, I said. If that's all there is, why not keep it that way, I said, And just keep dancing?

Fiona took her hands off my body, lifted her hair off her neck, twisted her hair around, and tied her hair up in a knot. Her armpits weren't shaved, the smell from her pits.

I love it when you talk, Fiona said.

Fiona put her open palms, one on my waist, the other on my open palm.

That's not all there is! Fiona said.

All her face was smiling but her lip.

Look, I'm just like everybody else, Fiona said. I have a belief and I am working myself into that belief. This *is* all illusion, this *is* all folly, and my choice is to live my life as aware of that folly as I possibly can. But that doesn't mean it's *only* folly.

My spirit, Fiona said, Has gone to Susan Strong for an extended vacation. Your spirit has gone to Will Parker for an extended vacation. This birth. This incarnation. What's important is the lesson. What's important is this moment—here together now, looking at each other.

Fiona's eyes were special blue in the kitchen-stove telephone-booth light. She leaned back a little, her hips into my hips, so she could see me better, her hands looping her arms around my neck, her lip a life all its own.

We need to look into every situation, Fiona said, And examine it, so we won't be fooling ourselves. I want to make a personal discovery of reality, Fiona said, Through my own intelligence and ability.

It's a sense of trust, Fiona said, That when you look into a situation, you know that you will get a response, a message. Trust, Fiona said, Is knowing there will be a message.

Fuck trust.

Fiona undid my white waiter shirt, one, two buttons, slid her open palm against my heart.

Your heart is beating, Fiona said. My heart is beating. What is it that is beating our hearts?

Shit happens.

Everything is an illusion, Fiona said. Everything. Even death is an illusion. So we must listen to our Higher Knowing, Fiona said, And be present, because this is our life. When the vacation's over, We go home.

You're sure about that? I said, Absolutely?

Absolutely, Fiona said, If you trust hard enough, you will get a definite response, and what you know is a tiny bit bigger, and what you don't know is a tiny bit smaller.

Underneath it, Will, beyond the illusion, this all means something, Fiona said.

Believe that it hath been given, Fiona said, And it shall be given unto you.

Did Argwings Khodek say that? I said.

No, Fiona said, It was Tarkovsky.

Is Tarkovsky another one of your AUIs? I said.

There's only three, Fiona said. Argwings Khodek, Leonard Cohen, and Tarkovsky.

And Joni Mitchell? I said.

And Joni Mitchell, Fiona said. And John Kelly doing Joni Mitchell.

Fiona put her hands, palms open, onto my shoulders, shook my shoulders.

There is a deeper meaning, Fiona said. Otherwise we'd all turn into Andy Warhol and live in the world of appearance.

Fiona's hands smooth across my shoulders, to my neck. One finger touched my throat.

It was *Adam's* apple, Fiona said, Not Eve's.

Then: Come on, Will, Fiona said, We're on vacation. Let's have some fun!

Fiona's smile, her broken lip trying to smile. Fiona's lips at my ear.

Show me your underneath, Fiona said, And I'll show you mine.

The needle on the record: Stevie Wonder. Fiona put her long fingers on my eyes.

I'm a man of many wishes, I hope my premonition misses.

This won't end up a performance piece somewhere? I said.

You are so fucking beautiful! Fiona said. I love your bottom teeth.

Most people misconstrue this for standoffishness.

My breath in. My breath out.

Then: My friends call me William of Heaven, I said.

JUST BEFORE SUNRISE, the both of us pissing on Avenue C pointing up-town. The sky above us and beyond midnight blue, lighted doorways of six-story walk-ups, streetlamps on the avenues, garbage cans overturned, black plastic bags ripped open. Fiona and I walked, following Third Street across Avenue B, Avenue A, First Avenue, to Second Avenue, talking talking, past Angel's Pizza, Dress Suits to Hire. Past the Greek restaurant on Second and Fifth Street, past Fish Bar.

Fiona got my whole long sorry story.

But it's not the truth.

I didn't know the whole story, hadn't remembered the whole thing yet.

Not yet.

On the stoop of 205 East Fifth Street just across from the rectangle of earth where I'd plant the cherry tree my arm over Fiona's shoulders and her arm around my waist, just like that, at the same time, Fiona and I looked up.

Morning wind in the trees. The dust-storm light of the streetlamps on the green leaves, the shadows of the green leaves on the sidewalk, curb, on the street.

A color from another incarnation, Fiona said.

Fiona leaned against me, her head on my shoulder, her hand on my knee. We smoked the cigarette, present with the night, with the morning wind in the trees, with the color from another incarnation, enjoying, and enjoying that we were enjoying.

Then: He lives here? Fiona said.

Who? I said.

Argwings Khodek, Fiona said.

Apartment Two-A, I said.

Can I come in? Fiona said.

You want to see Rose? I said.

No, Fiona said. I want to see you.

BEFORE I GOT the lights on, Fiona went right to the bathroom. When she flushed, I listened to the sound of someone else in my apartment flushing.

My Art Family were all gathered around the ladder in the kitchen, looking out the window at sunrise on the city. One of them, the man with the bumps of mannequin beard on his face, was sitting on top of the ladder.

When Fiona came out, I walked to the ladder, stood among them. This is my Art Family, I said.

Art Family? Fiona said.

Make it aware, make art out of it, I said.

So this is you and Bobbie and Charlie and your mother and father? Fiona asked.

Sometimes, I said.

Fiona stood herself next to me by the ladder. I introduced them. Their names that day were Massimo, Grazia, Parjaner, Sophia, and Marlon. Fiona touched each one, their hands, their faces, arms, their backs, shoulders.

Out the window, below, the pit bull, dark shadows. The E.T. guy had already phoned home.

Kiss? Fiona said.

Fiona's mouth on my mouth. Not a big tongue kiss. Just lips to lips. The red onto my lips, the smell of the red.

Fiona's scar against my lips.

Nearly two years in New York City and no one had been on the premises in my apartment besides me, and just like that, out of the blue—abracadabra!—there she was, Susan Strong at my kitchen window, within my Art Family, the light, a color from another incarnation coming in on her white marble skin.

Susan Strong kissing me. I was kissing back.

Shit-faced. That's all it takes.

Car alarm in my ear. Another New Yorker gone to hell.

In my forearms first, the fear, then up my arms, through my heart, splash down into stomach, cattle prod to cock. New-shoe stiff.

But it's not the truth.

It wasn't stiff.

The muscles in my back jumping.

And something else.

Something clear and smooth and beautiful. The feeling of a finger drawing a circle around my heart.

Fiona took my shirt off. I kicked my shoes off, pulled off my socks. Fiona pulled my pants and shorts down together.

My body all smelly dance sweat and restaurant leftover.

Black bra and black panties under Fiona's black dress. I pulled the bra straps down, unclasped the back of the bra. The full sway of her breasts.

Fiona kicked off her shoes, pulled her panties down.

Vagina, pussy, Deep Flower, poon.

The unmistakable smell.

How big I was next to her. My skin so pink-brown and brown-blond hairy. Fiona's skin white marble. Black hair in her armpits, in her crotch.

Fiona and I stood so still, just like my Art Family. Fiona put her finger on each of my nipples.

Nice nips, Fiona said, And I love the hair on your forearms. Nice chest hair.

Fiona rubbed her hand across the hair of my chest.

You give great clavicle, Fiona said.

My hands were cold my feet were cold my cock was freezing. Frozen moments in time. I was smiling. Stopped smiling.

Beautiful skin, I said. I love this part. Under your breasts.

Which part?

Where it curves up, I said. It's so soft.

My nipples are ugly, Fiona said.

No! I said. They're fantastic.

Diamond nips, Fiona said. I'm in need of areola fulfillment.

My arms should be bigger, I said.

No, Fiona said. Look here, she said.

Fiona drew a line with her finger from my elbow, along my bicep, up to my shoulder.

Perfect, she said. The arc is just perfect. And look how nicely it moves to the chest.

Fiona's finger up my arm down across my chest.

I wish I were taller, Fiona said, With shoulders like yours.

I shouldn't be so tall, I said, So clumsy big. I love your size. I said, I'm so surprised by your strength.

You're shaking, Fiona said.

My whole body like True Shot's eyes.

Fiona's breath in deep, then exhale out her nose.

Will, we don't have to do anything—be any way, Fiona said. I just want to hold you, be held by you. I promise I won't hurt you.

Like Bernadette, I said.

Like Bernadette, Fiona said. I promise.

My hand, my index on Fiona's lip, the scar, the map of the Known Universe.

Tell me about your scar, I said.

Fiona's blue eyes got dark blue. The breath in her raised her diamond nips against my chest. Her tongue stuck out and licked the scar, licked my finger.

Lletre ferit, Fiona said. Two words put together, formed by Fiona's red lips.

What? I said.

It's Spanish, Fiona said—Catalan, that is, not Castilian.

Catalan? I said.

Go to Barcelona, Fiona said. Stop anybody on the street and ask them about the bastard son of King Ferdinand.

Believe me, Fiona said, They'll tell you.

What's it mean? I said.

Lletre ferit, Fiona said, Means *the word that hurts*.

Fiona's index pressed on the scar.

You have touched me, Fiona said, Where I hurt.

My arms on Fiona's shoulders, my hands on her neck, under her hair. Fiona pushed her hips against my hips. Pubic hair to pubic hair.

It's all drag, I said.

Fiona's fuck-you smile that was never a smile.

I was born with a cleft palate, Fiona said. I've had three operations. The first they put a roof in my mouth and then did two plastic surgeries on my lip.

Does it look weird? Fiona asked.

I love it, I said.

And what about your scar? Fiona said. Where'd you get yours?

I stepped back, turned around, and showed Fiona the scar; a half moon on my left cheek.

AyaHuaska, I said, Charlie's horse, bit me.

The scar on my ass you could read like tea leaves.

Really? Fiona said. Cool.

Fiona put her hand on the scar.

Nice ass, Fiona said. Just enough hair on it. I like men with hair on their ass.

Fiona brushed the hair on my ass back and forth, back and forth.

But I didn't mean *that* scar, Fiona said.

What scar? I said.

Fiona's lips at my ear. You know, Fiona said, The one on your spirit. How'd you get your heart so broken?

Fiona's open palm on my heart.

Oh, that one, I said. If I told you that, I said, I'd have to tell you everything.

THE SHEETS COULD'VE been cleaner. Glad I had two pillows. I turned off the lamp the shape of a wagon wheel with cowboys and Indians riding horses on the lampshade. Fiona lay down, her bushel of black hair on the pillow, the white of her skin the same white of the sheets, if the sheets had had a heart and veins that were blue.

I lay down next to her. My forearms when she folded herself into me. My arm under her neck, my hand in her hair. Her head on my chest. Her hair in my mouth.

The hair of her crotch against my leg.

My heart, the broken pieces scraping up against my chest.

My breath. There was no air.

I sat up quick, grabbed my tobacco, the papers, rolled a cigarette, one for Fiona, one for me, lit hers, mine.

Only silence.

Fiona pulled her legs into her, wrapped her arms around her legs. Her foot tapped against my hip. Her white white fingers pulled tobacco from her teeth.

Men got it rough, Fiona said. All that macho stuff they got to live up to. Prowess, achievement, all that I-came-I-saw-I-conquered shit. Plus, you don't get to talk about it.

Men in the eighties are like women in the fifties, Fiona said, Isolated, unaware of the social construct keeping them isolated. Each man thinking his problems are only his.

Fiona's big toe slow between the futon and my ass, into the crack of my ass.

Plus, Fiona said, A man's life source—the nipple, his food, his sustenance and source of ecstasy—has been dependent on a woman. On his mother most of his life. Then one day—no rite of passage, no help from his family or his culture—all at once he's got to go out and be this stud.

Way uncool, Fiona said.

And this size thing . . .

Fiona's whole foot between my ass cheeks, her toes up and down, up and down, on the back of my balls.

. . . I really think it's a guy thing. I mean, Fiona said, Just imagine yourself a woman being chased by some big ape with this huge hard reptilian schlong he wants to shove up inside your body.

Not tonight, motherfucker! Fiona said.

In the broken-green-dish ashtray, I stubbed out my cigarette. Fiona stubbed out hers. I pulled the sheet over us. We curled into a ball, my back to Fiona. Fiona's hands on my back, on my shoulders, on my ass.

Lips at my ear.

Nothing's as sexy as vulnerability, Fiona said, Men or women. I can understand why people get into children. I mean I'd never do that, Fiona said, Too blatant a power trip. But openness and innocence is definitely a turn-on.

The light had changed. The light was just gray. New York gray. I uncurled, rolled over, looked into Fiona's blue eyes. Her roman nose. Her scar.

And you? I said. Do you like feeling vulnerable?

Hate it, Fiona said.

Fiona sat up and pulled the sheet off. She reached down and put her hand around my cock, cupping my balls.

Fiona was looking at my cock, saying things to it, the way you talk to children or animals. Behind her, on the wall, the drawing of Daniel's beer-can dick and the lime-green Heineken can.

Will, darling, Fiona said, What's wrong with you? This here's no little cock. This here's the cutest hunk of man meat I ever saw.

Fiona flipped my cock side to side.

Too much bigger and you can't do anything with it, Fiona said.

Shower not a grower, I said.

Believe me, Fiona said, I've handled some cocks in my time, and this cock is just the right size. It's just fine.

Look, Fiona said, The crown is spectacular.

Fiona leaned down and kissed the tip of my cock.

Perfect, Fiona said, Just perfect.

SOME CALL IT a vagina, Bobbie said, Some call it a pussy, I like to call it my Deep Flower, Bobbie said, But when I'm feeling especially horny, I call it my poon.

When a woman gets hot, Bobbie said, Her poon gets wet, and inside her poon is the most wonderful place on a woman's body, and that place is called the clitoris.

I am behind. My arms drape over her shoulders, my hands curl under her forearms and pull them back. My long legs drape over her legs, her ass crack pushed up against my cock, my feet curled under her calves, with my legs I pull her legs back.

All of us all one thing.

My hands down the front of her, her breasts, I look down over her shoulder like they are my breasts; my hand on her stomach, my stomach; my hand on her hair, my hair; into her hair to Deep Flower, my flower.

Deep Flower petals folded back, my fingers warm and wet on either side of her clit, pressing my fingers, crushing the bloom, my bloom, my reach into hair and flesh to the bone. Soft. She stretched her neck back, let her hair hang down my back, my right ear against her left ear, my face marble next to Fiona's white marble, chipped lip, Michelangelo's David and Venus de Milo, I can fuck you blind and keep it simple.

My Art Family our voyeurs.

Her nipples are hard, my nipples, sweat on her neck; I am making her make strange sounds and rock the boat and push her hips up to the sky. My tongue into her ear, perfect, just perfect, slow the way my hand moves slow, deep inside Fiona, inside me, Deep Flower the way Bobbie liked it.

Long deep breaths, her diamond nips could cut glass, a little scream in her throat, the little scream that gives it all away, Fiona pushes her nice wet poon against my hand, my fingers up and down, up and down, my hand grasping at and pulling the flower like a cow's tit, I take my tongue from her ear, lower my head down, kiss Fiona's long long neck.

Fiona's scar is lifting, her smile never a smile.

When she comes it looks like pain, sounds like pain.

Fiona falls from me like old skin, curls on the futon into a ball, her forehead on her knees, her arms around herself.

Outside, the city is just waking up. The light through the windows, Edward Hopper windows. Gray light onto Fiona, blue-black hair, blue-white skin, Sleeping Beauty, breath deep and slow. I roll a cigarette, light it. Sit and listen to Fiona breathe. In the kitchen, my Art Family a frozen moment, huddled, five little shadows onto the floor.

After who knows how long, I get up out of bed, walk over into my Art Family, touch them the way Fiona did. A salty taste on my tongue before I cry. For some time, who knows how long, I stand with them all around me, and I smoke.

Then, out of the blue, Fiona's talking.

There's this film, Fiona said, A Bergman film called *Autumn Sonata*. Ingrid Bergman's the mother and Liv Ullmann is the daughter. There is this other daughter that Liv Ullmann is taking care of who is some kind of metaphor about crippling and the lack of love in a person's life. One day, Liv Ullmann gets totally pissed off and tells Ingrid Bergman what a shit mother she's been. Then Ingrid Bergman says this wonderful thing. A talent for reality, she says. Ingrid Bergman says she lacks a talent for reality. And what a talent for reality is, is being present in the moments of your life and remembering them.

Ingmar Bergman? I said.

Ingrid's the mother, Fiona said.

Mothers always catch it, Fiona said, It's always Mom's fault. Dad's always gone and it's always Mom's fault.

Fiona stretched and turned over on her side.

The blue of her eyes all the way across the room.

Do you ever get hard? Fiona said. I mean, maybe you could see a doctor.

Just like that I had to take a wicked leak. I walked naked into the bathroom. I pissed, then stood for a while and looked at my whanged-out body in the mirror.

You are the mess, I said to the mirror. I am the mess, I said.

When I walked back into the room, my hands kept trying to cover up my crotch.

Strong piss flow, Fiona said. Shows good muscle tone.

What? I said.

I heard you pissing all the way in here, she said. Could you bring me a glass of water?

I walked back into the kitchen, filled a glass with water. When I walked back to the futon, I was holding the glass in front of my cock.

It gets easier, Fiona said. If you do it enough times you get used to it.

What? I said.

Being naked in front of someone, Fiona said.

Fiona drank the water one big gulp.

I knelt down, Japanese style, pulled my balls up, my cock.

I get hard, I said. Just don't get hard with anyone.

Shy, Fiona said.

Social terror, I said.

You're obviously not a virgin, Fiona said. Right?

I'm not a virgin, I said.

Both women and men? Fiona said.

Both, I said.

When you're on a Green Date, Fiona said, Do you think about both? Or do you think about men? Or do you think about women?

Charlie, I said. I think about Charlie 2Moons.

JUST BEFORE WE fell asleep, Fiona's back to my back, Fifth Street was a loud garbage truck. I was staring at the cracked white dish.

Then: White-trash tartar sauce, Fiona said. The color of the walls. Ketchup mixed with mayonnaise.

More ketchup in the front room, Fiona said, Less and less ketchup as you go into the kitchen. In the bathroom streaks of ketchup and streaks of mayonnaise.

Bottom of the paint bucket, I said.

Then: William of Heaven?

Yeah?

You know you got to find him, Fiona said. This Charlie 2Moons guy. He's your soul brother. You got to find him.

Everything I know, you'll know.

Everything you know, I'll know.

I know, I said.

THE NEXT MORNING—I mean afternoon—Mrs. Lupino opened her door just as Fiona kissed me good-bye in the hallway.

With my fuck-you finger, I scratched my eye.

I stood barefoot on the stoop. The sun was bright and I covered my eyes. Fiona's butt down the stairs. I put my fingers to my nose. The unmistakable smell.

Fiona put her hand on the newel post and swung herself down onto the sidewalk, and then she stopped dead in her tracks.

You're going this way and then shit happens and then you're going that way.

Will! Fiona screamed. Come down here!

Two leaps and I was down the stairs.

What?

Fiona was standing two steps down, leaning her arms against the door with the poster STRANDED BEINGS SEARCHING FOR GOD.

The first Polaroid: Woman Being Possessed by the Devil.

The second Polaroid: Woman Being Healed by the Word of the Lord.

The third Polaroid: Woman Healed by the Word of the Lord! Alleluia Alleluia!

The big red FOR LEASE sign in the window.

Fiona said, What's your landlord's name?

Zigman, I said. David Zigman Realty.

Three days later Fiona had the space rented. The storefront half under me and half under Mrs. Lupino: Fiona's own performance space.

STRANDED BEINGS SEARCHING FOR GOD.

Cool name, Fiona said.

ROSE UPSTAIRS.

Fiona down.

* * *

RUBY'S VOICE ON my red answering machine was a raw, swollen throat. They gave me one call, Ruby said, So I called you. Dear William of Heaven, what am I going to do with you? How *is* my old friend, anyway? It's been a long time, buddy. You on the planet yet?

On the tape, the sound of people walking in a hallway, talking, a door opened and closed.

So, Ruby said, Looks like I'm going to do this treatment, maybe this time it'll work. Turn me into a Republican and I can vote for Ronbo.

I'll be out in three months, Ruby said, And you and I and True Shot can go to Sardi's and look at our pitchas on the walls.

On the tape, around and around, Ruby coughing coughing.

Then: You know, *MacNeil/Lehrer* isn't the news, Ruby said, It's AT&T's presentation of the news.

All we are is who we think we are, Ruby said, And most of us think we are who we are because somebody like AT&T told us. Noam Chomsky is not talking about ABC, CBS, NBC, or CNN, Ruby said, He's talking about U and I. He's talking about G-O-D. He's talking about who it is we're listening to, and how we'll listen to most any goddamn thing we're told because we're so afraid. Afraid to tell our own version, Ruby said.

When Ruby spoke again, his voice was so quiet I could barely hear.

I'm afraid, Ruby said, and sucked in smoke.

Around and around, on the tape, people walking, the door opened, someone hollered something, the door closed.

Then: Because we each have the eyes we have, Ruby said, The world looks the way it looks.

I could hear Ruby smile.

See ya when I get outta here in three months, buddy, Ruby said. Don't let the fucking pharisees get you down.

SUMMER 1985, THREE months later, and True Shot and I were driving in Door of the Dead van, not-looking for Charlie 2Moons, not-looking for Ruby Prestigiacomo.

True Shot shifted into second.

So Ruby got out today, I said.

Yesterday, True Shot said. He said he'd meet us here tonight, eleven o'clock.

In the meat-packing district? I said. Why?

Ruby likes it, True Shot said. He had an old friend he used to hang out with down here.

How we going to find him? I said.

Life Café, True Shot said. Travel mode's the key.

Outside my window, sun-baked night wind off the sidewalks and streets, the buildings. The van's always-on heater frying my feet.

True Shot was wearing his hair in pigtails. The beaded necklace around his neck, the buckskin bag. Big pits on his chambray shirt.

True Shot, beautiful according to Chief Joseph.

Door of the Dead van drove around the block again. At the corner, just like that, True Shot banged the palm of his hand against the steering wheel.

I swear! True Shot said. Ruby looked so *good* when I picked him up yesterday. He's gained weight, and there's color back in his face, plus he's shaved his head! He's a fucking skinhead!

True Shot looked his mirrors over at me. On the surface of his mirrors, I was a sweat-drowned rat, big circus nose, hair on my lip, a yellow-stained T-shirt.

And check this out, True Shot said. Ruby Prestigiacomo has got him a full-moon tattoo above each fucking eyebrow! I told him, Ruby, I said, You ain't gonna get no Madison Avenue job with them moon tattoos, and Ruby just smiled. You know how Ruby can smile. God, it was great to see Ruby smile again.

I gave him his old room back, True Shot said. And we bought groceries. Last night we watched *Jeopardy!* and he went to bed at ten o'clock.

Ruby's gonna be fine, True Shot said. If anyone can make it, Ruby Prestigiacomo will.

What about the purple bumps? I said. Does he still have the purple bumps?

True Shot's mirrors were straight ahead. He reached and turned the Sioux tape on, shifted down into second.

Little West Twelfth, Gansevoort, Horatio, Jane, Bethune. Narrow streets, cement loading docks, shed overhangs. At night, sometimes half a block between lightbulbs. The city is old here, before the grid. No stoops, no front doors to six-story walk-ups. No doormen, no shiny steel and glass to the sky. Cobblestone streets made for horses, streets going every which way.

During the day, the meat was beef, pork, lamb, chicken. During the night, human.

The cement of the sidewalks and curbs, the cobblestones, the asphalt, blood-soaked in a century of meat death.

A black Mercedes, a yellow convertible Saab, a bronze Cadillac, two Chevy Novas gray and red, a white Cadillac, and a Dodge van, Door of the Dead van, circling circling, Gansevoort, Horatio, Greenwich, Jane, West Twelfth, Bank, to Hudson, headlights pushing the night into shadows up against warehouse walls. Now and then, on the loading docks, on the corners, under a shed roof, bits of light—sequins, rhinestones, cut-glass beads, rings, bracelets, necklaces, silky gowns, tiaras, high heels, glitter eyelids, belts, bracelets, fingernail polish—anything that shines, adorns the body, anything that shimmers, catches light.

The moon, reflected light.

Then: Where do you think that Wolf Swamp spring is, I said, Where the family of wolves guards the mouth of the cave?

True Shot's silver rings on every finger tapped a beat on the steering wheel. His mirrors. True Shot raised his hand, touched the buckskin bag hanging from the beaded necklace.

Where do you suppose? True Shot said.

Spring Street? I said. It's right next to *Prince*.

Under True Shot's mirrors his eyes were smiling. How about *Maiden Lane*? True Shot said.

Is *Maiden Lane* close to Spring and Prince? I said.

Nah, True Shot said. World Trade Center.

Cultures always build their monuments on top of an older culture's monument, True Shot said. What better place for the entrance to the underworld than under the World Trade Center?

My arm in the window, the sun-baked night air blew against my arm and neck.

What about here, though? I said. There's something here, don't you think?

You mean the meat district? True Shot said.

The smell, I said.

Meat and blood, True Shot said. Like that.

West Fourteenth Street, right on Hudson; True Shot shifted down from third to second, double-clutched to first, put on the brakes.

You see that basement door there? True Shot said.

It's an S&M Club, True Shot said. Used to be called Hell, now they call it the Phoenix.

The building was a triangular brick building. It was painted white-trash tartar sauce.

In the mercury-vapor light, above the basement door, the word
PHOENIX.

The entrance to Hell.

Centuries of meat death.

On the south corner of the pink triangular building, a woman in a
tight red dress and black stiletto heels, seams in her nylons, stepped
out into the van's headlights. She pulled her dress up, and her black
lace codpiece was not a woman's, and the guy who was not a woman
bent over and showed us his smooth ass. The guy pulled the black butt
floss over and stuck his index up his ass and wiggled it around and
then stood up and turned, struck a pose, put his index in his mouth,
and sucked it.

The women, I mean the men, with the guy who stuck his index up
his ass, all laughed loud and hard and made chirping noises at us with
their lips.

The guy in the red dress, his glitter eyes stared right at us, not a blink.
Out of a history book, his face. Craggy, high cheekbones, big full lips.
Chin pushed out; even from inside the van you could see each one of
his bottom teeth, framed within the red red lips.

Devouring. Devoured.

That Charlie? True Shot said.

No, I said. Charlie was long and thin, but that guy don't look like
Charlie at all.

He's from the plains, True Shot said.

He pulled over to the curb. Just like that, the guy was right next to
my window. I moved my arm and the guy leaned in the window, his
long black shiny hair falling soft around his face. Halston. The guy was
wearing Halston.

Name's Crystal, she said. What's yours?

I'm Will, I said. This here's True Shot.

Nice van, Crystal said. Room for three in the back.

I didn't say anything. True Shot said, We're looking for somebody.

Two somebodies, I said.

Aren't we all? Crystal said.

You studlies are two somebodies, Crystal said, and put his glitter eyes
on me and his big-lips smile. Crystal pulled his hair behind his ear. An
earring, shells, and mother-of-pearl.

One's an Indian guy, True Shot said. Name is 2Moons, Charlie
2Moons.

And the other guy's got a shaved head, I said, And a full moon on his forehead tattooed above each eyebrow. His name's Ruby, I said, Ruby Prestigiacomo.

Crystal's voice all at once got lower.

You guys cops? Crystal said.

No, I said. We're just, I said, Looking for old friends.

Are they dragons? Crystal said, and drew her hand, her long fingers, red Lee Press-On nails, slow across the skin of her neck.

Dragons? I said.

You know! *Dragons*, darling! Crystal said. Life's a drag if only you know it. Like me, Crystal said.

Crystal's red Lee Press-On nails went from below her clavicle to over her shoulder to the dragons on the street corner behind her. The dragons were mostly young, mostly thin, mostly dark-skinned, all strapped into tight hot pants and miniskirts. In the light from the streetlamp, their faces glowed, faces painted on faces. They all looked at me through the faces on them. Patti LuPone, Diana Ross, Patti LaBelle, Donna Summer.

The dragons all clucked their tongues and pushed their hips out and raised their arms, oo-la-la, shaven armpits, Evita, "Don't Cry for Me."

Like them! Crystal said.

My face was smiling. I stopped smiling.

Where's this Charlie Two Spoons from?

Moons, I said. He's from Fort Hall, Idaho.

And Ruby? Crystal said.

From Mars, True Shot said.

It'll cost you, Crystal said.

How much? True Shot said.

Twenty, Crystal said.

True Shot and I both went to our wallets. True Shot had a couple fives, I had a ten. I went to give the guy our twenty dollars but True Shot grabbed my hand.

That's when True Shot said something to Crystal in another language.

Crystal's eyes were the deer in the headlights. Set in her jaw, the Mack truck.

Look, Crystal said and flipped her hair, Halston, seashell, and mother-of-pearl earring flash. I don't know these fucking guys, Crystal said. Just because I'm Injun don't mean I know some Injun. And just because I'm on the street don't mean I know a guy with two moons tattooed on his forehead.

Two moons.

My breath in. My breath out.

The first time I'd heard the two words, two moons, put together that meant Ruby.

Splash down through my heart into my stomach.

Crystal had four long bottom teeth. The better to eat you with.

South Dakota is a long ways away, Crystal said, and squatted down the way Charlie and his grandfather always squatted down.

Crystal put her hand in between her legs, pulled the black lace codpiece aside, and there was her cock and her cock started pissing. The stream down between the black stilettos onto the curb into the street.

Dragon piss.

It's a place I'll never see again or want to, Crystal said.

Then Crystal started singing. Baritone:

It isn't very pretty what a rez without pity can do.

Crystal shook her cock, put back the lace codpiece, stood up.

White people, Crystal said, got no special privilege to those little-town blues.

Crystal put her Lee Press-On nail under my chin.

What town without pity you from, honey?

Pocatello, I said, Mostly.

Fuck Pocatello.

Crystal's Lee Press-On nail was a sharp blade.

People like me, Crystal said, Don't fit anywhere but here. This *island* where we land.

Headlights from behind Door of the Dead van went past, slow radials on the cobblestones. Crystal's eyes followed the headlights, big snake little snake, prey.

There's hundreds of corners on this island, Crystal said, And there are thousands of us. Exiles from the heartland without a heart. Out of the old country, a brand-new tribe, dancing to new tunes around a bucket of fire in a vacant lot.

We all know each other's stuff, Crystal said, But that don't mean we know each other.

True Shot took off his mirrors and looked right at Crystal. I looked at True Shot, into his eyes, Saint-Vitus'-dance jade. True Shot said something in the language, something really beautiful and soft. He let go my hand with the money.

I took the yellow Post-it with my phone number and Charlie's info and Ruby's info on it along with the twenty dollars and handed them out the window.

Please, I said. Here's my phone number.

A car behind us blinked his headlights, bright to dim, bright to dim.

How do I look? Crystal said.

Perfect, I said. Just perfect.

Crystal dabbed her eyes with the pad of an index finger, the red Lee Press-On nail sticking straight up. She sighed deeply, lots of shoulder, put the yellow Post-it and the twenty dollars down her dress, turned her back on the blinking headlights, pulled the back of her dress up, poked her smooth brown cayenne ass at the blinking headlights, looked into the headlights, her spotlight for life, moved her dragon lips, the bottom four teeth.

Got to go, honey, Crystal said, and looked in at me, right at me, put her palm against my cheek, Lee Press-On nails on my ear.

If I find him, Crystal said, I'll call. Right now, I've got to go.

Love ya, mean it.

Mr. Right, Crystal said, Is waiting.

TRUE SHOT AND I in Door of the Dead van on Gansevoort in our Saint Carlotta parking place. Meat trucks were parked all along the narrow streets. No Charlie 2Moons. No Ruby. Across Greenwich, on the other side of a Premium Meats truck, a woman—I was pretty sure she was a woman—on her knees on the sidewalk, sucking off some guy. All you could see of the guy was his potbelly and a cigar in his hand.

Why don't you get yourself one of those? I said to True Shot. I can go for a walk.

A cigar? True Shot said.

A blow job, I said.

True Shot's mirrors.

It is this way, True Shot said. When the Little People told me to quit drinking, quit smoking, quit picking pockets, and quit with the drugs, they also told me to quit whoring. It's not good for the spirit, True Shot said. And especially these days.

Then out of the blue: True Shot, I said, Those purple bumps on Ruby, I said, Could be AIDS.

True Shot turned his mirrors back to the windshield, put the clutch in, shifted down into first.

All Dodges sound the same when you start them up.

* * *

AT 205 EAST Fifth Street, True Shot stopped the van. I put my hand on the door handle, then pulled my hand away. I started rolling a cigarette.

True Shot, I said, You know so much about me, I said, I'm the one who's always talking. What about you? I don't even know where you live.

True Shot's mirrors straight ahead out the windshield.

Bedford, True shot said, First stop on the L train after the river. Eighty-five North Third, corner of Wythe and North Third.

What's it like over there? I said.

Over there, True Shot said, There's a motorcycle shop on the corner, the guy who runs it's called New York Slicker and the place is crawling with Rottweilers. An old aluminum diner across the street vacant since I've been there.

What apartment? I said.

You can't really call it an apartment, True Shot said, Let's just say I live in a shed on the roof.

Where do you park the van, I said.

Across the street, on the fourth floor in the southwest corner of the parking garage.

Then: So what do you do? I said.

I live there, True Shot said.

I mean sexually, I said.

True Shot's breath in, his breath out. Mirrors straight ahead out the windshield.

Do you Green Date? I said. Masturbate?

Like that, True Shot said. And I have two friends.

The E.T.-phone-home guy, I said, Sticks the phone receiver up his ass. You ever stick things up your ass?

As far as my ass is concerned, True Shot said, No things go in, things only come out.

How do you like it best? I said.

True Shot turned the key off. His hand, all the silver rings, playing with the turn signal.

Sex is best for me, True Shot said, With me on top, on a bed or on a couch so my back doesn't get kinked. I like my feet up against something solid, like a wall, and I like her with her legs spread wide and me just fucking the shit out of her.

So your two friends are your girlfriends? I said.

Like that, True Shot said.

Do you fuck them a lot? I said.

I fuck one of them about once a week, True Shot said.

Only girls? I said.

Only girls, True Shot said.

Yeah, I said, That's what Ruby said.

True Shot's mirrors over at me.

What did Ruby say? True Shot said.

That the only dick, I said, You'd ever have in your hand would be your own, I said. And in your mouth, the only dick would be your own dick, but you're too fat to get to it.

Yeah, well, True Shot said, Ruby's lucky to even *find* his dick these days.

Then: What did you say to Crystal the Dragon? I said.

Just some things, True Shot said.

What language was that?

Sioux.

Where did you learn Sioux? I said.

Wounded Knee, True Shot said.

Wounded Knee? I said. Charlie was at Wounded Knee!

You never told me that, True Shot said.

Not yet, I said.

Maybe you knew Charlie 2Moons? I said.

I didn't know him, True Shot said.

Do you know Leonard Peltier? I said.

It is this way, True Shot said. It's best I don't talk about Wounded Knee.

Are you wanted by the FBI?

True Shot's mirrors. On the surface, the color from another incarnation.

It was a sacred time for me, True Shot said, And I made a promise not to talk about it.

I could tell True Shot wasn't going any further with Wounded Knee, but I tried one more time.

I said, True Shot, I tell you everything. Just about everything.

I promised, True Shot said.

Inside the van only silence. For the first time, there was a space between us. Outside, the moon came out, a little bit of a slipper of a moon.

True Shot, I said, there's something wrong. I can feel it. There's something wrong.

With his right hand, True Shot swiped the dashboard and killed the Virgin Mary. Ripped the green-sequined photo of Brigitte Bardot off the ashtray. True Shot threw his mirrors out the window. Then, just like that, he let out a long coyote howl, his chest up and down, up and down.

You stupid asshole, True Shot screamed, You gullible stupid fucking Idaho spud motherfucker! Can't you see I'm a total fucking fraud? I've been lying to you all along.

True Shot's spit all over my face.

But it's not the truth.

True Shot hadn't moved. He just sat there and stared out the windshield.

True Shot, I said, Did you tell Ruby Prestigiacomo about Charlie 2Moons?

No, True Shot said, I didn't.

What about Ruby's full-moon tattoos? I said. Two of them, I said. Two moons.

Not a word, True Shot said.

Promise? I said.

Honest Injun, True Shot said.

All Dodges sound the same when you start them up.

Then: Charlie's got a scar, I said. A big scar. Goes from his forehead through his left eye and down his cheek.

True Shot shut off the van and took off his mirrors, pushed his face right into mine. My God, the color of those eyes, the way they moved.

You never told me that! True Shot said.

My eyes started blinking blinking.

Not yet, I said.

My father, I said, After Bobbie died, I said, Took his bullwhip to Charlie.

True Shot leaned back quick into his seat, put his mirrors back on. He reached up and touched the buckskin bag, held it in the palm of his hand.

I rolled a cigarette, lit the cigarette.

Lots of silence.

True Shot? I said. Are you sure you're OK?

The horrific whisper: Fine, True Shot said. Just fine.

CHAPTER
TWELVE

Jupiter walked into the Residency yard one day, a little black dog with long hair and tail and floppy ears. Bobbie didn't ask Mother or anything, she just scooped the dog up and named it and made the dog hers. Bobbie tied a red bow around Jupiter's neck and an old rhinestone bracelet of Mother's, and the red bow and the shiny bracelet against Jupiter's black hair made him look real pretty, and at night Jupiter running around in the moonlight looked like pictures you saw of fireflies.

Jupiter and Bobbie were always together up in her room, her hair up in rollers, listening to the hi-fi stereo. Jupiter even slept on her bed with her.

The trouble with Jupiter was Father. He didn't allow us any cats or dogs. Said they would interfere with his animals, and his animals was how he made a living, so we never had cats or dogs, let alone a dog in the house, let alone sleeping on the bed.

But it was summer and we never saw Father in the summer, sometimes not till November.

It was a scorcher, and the sun was unrelenting light through my bedroom window. Charlie and I were lying on the bed. Charlie was reading My Ántonia, and I was playing Chinese checkers with myself.

The unmistakable sound. I ran to the window. It was hard to see anything with the cottonwood right there, but Charlie and I were scouts and we knew how to look through the leaves down into the shade of the cottonwood lane, and sure enough, from in between the branches and the leaves, there was Father's atom-bomb swimming-pool-blue pickup and matching camper and matching horse trailer, coming up the lane. In August.

There were two things fast we had to do. We had to get to Bobbie so we could figure what to do with the dog, and we had to get Charlie out of the house. The two things were in that order, because Charlie and I figured Charlie could go out the window and climb down the cottonwood without being seen, no problem, once Father was inside the house.

Charlie stayed in my room and I beat it down to Bobbie's room. When I knocked on Bobbie's door, Jupiter started barking.

I just went ahead and opened the door and Bobbie was painting her toenails coral and listening to "Chances Are" and she was about to lay into me with *What the fuck?* when I said, Father's here. He's pulling in the yard.

Bobbie jumped up fast, which made Jupiter bark all the more.

Oh, shit! Bobbie said.

I said, Give me the dog!

Give you the dog? Bobbie said.

I'll put him in my room, I said.

He can stay in my fucking room, Bobbie said.

No, my room, I said.

Why your room? Bobbie said.

Father doesn't ever come in *my* room, I said.

Bobbie with her shades drawn in the Marilyn Monroe light, and the map of the Known Universe, standing by her perfectly made bed with her coral toenail polish brush in her hand, "Chances Are," Jupiter running around barking—Bobbie looked at me, and everything that had ever gone on that we never talked about was right there in the room between us.

OK, Bobbie said. Take the dog.

Charlie and I waited till we heard Father, too loud, in the hallway, calling his family to him.

Charlie jumped out the window and scaled down the tree, Jupiter under one arm. I watched Charlie and Jupiter all the way until they crossed Highway 30.

FOR DINNER, MOTHER got a roast out of the freezer, and we had roast and potatoes and canned beans. She even made a pie. Peach. Mother hadn't made a pie since before the baby girl in her had died. We sat in the dining room, at one of the long tables. Mother at the foot of the table, in her violet dress with the sequined orchid all the way down the front, her hair done up, Orange Exotica lipstick, her nylons with the swooping seams, her high heels with no toes; Bobbie on one side of the table, in her sundress with the yellow daisies on it and her white

Keds, her hair all bouffant. She wasn't tanned at all, from being in her room. I was on the other side of the table, in clean Levi's, boots, my white shirt; Father at the head of the table, behind his Crown Royal and Coke, needing a shave. His Levi's shirt was open a few buttons. He smelled like the inside of his pickup.

Just before we started eating, Father proposed a toast.

To the Pendleton Roundup! Father said, and Bobbie and I raised our milk glasses and mother her iced tea.

Assholes fired me! Father said. Artistic differences.

After dinner, Father did some of his tricks. He pulled a quarter out of Bobbie's ear, made his Crown Royal and Coke disappear, pulled the ace of hearts from the front of Mother's dress. Did his imitation of Al Jolson imitating a black man singing "Mammy." He was asleep on the green couch in front of the fireplace by eight-thirty.

MOTHER DID PRETTY well for about a week, fixing her hair and wearing dresses and cooking dinner. Dinners the first week were things like mashed potatoes and gravy and steak, pork chops and french fries, baked trout and potatoes au gratin. The first week, Mother was pretty and she smiled at Father, and when Father said things—like I'll show 'em! I'll take my show to Madison's Square Garden! What the hell does Pendleton, Oregon, know about putting on a show?—Mother would smile and say, Oh, Cotton!

Or Father said, Mother, you're the prettiest girl in Bingham County next to your daughter!

Mother lit a Herbert Tareyton and sucked in hard, the smoke out her nose when she smiled.

Oh, Cotton!

THE SECOND WEEK it was back to frozen fish sticks and white-trash tartar sauce, and Mother went back to wearing her old yellow terry-cloth bathrobe.

Father said he felt too cooped up in Mother's room and started sleeping out on the porch.

Most nights, Charlie, late, crawled up the cottonwood and came in my window. When Charlie slept over, I always made sure to lock my door. One night, Charlie and I lying next to each other, we heard Father down in Bobbie's room.

We ought to kill that motherfucker, Charlie said.

You can't kill your father, I said.

FATHER PUT HIS horse Star out in the corral with Chub. That whole month, poor old Chub stood in the corner of the corral. Star wouldn't let Chub eat or drink, so at night I had to sneak out and feed Chub some hay and haul a bucket of water over for him.

Father's German shepherd he called Heap Big Chief was tied to Grandmother Cottonwood in front of the barn. At night, I had to feed Heap Big Chief first, so he wouldn't bark while I was tending to Chub—which wasn't an easy chore because that dog was a mean dog and didn't take to nobody but Father. Even with a piece of steak or roast, sometimes I was sure Heap Big Chief was going to tear my arm off.

The monkey Father named Ricky and the mean goose he named Sea Bass stayed in the horse trailer, and the horse trailer was parked in the backyard, on the smooth concrete, out in the full sun. The monkey was tied up, but the goose was loose in the horse trailer. I never had to go in there to feed the monkey or the goose, thank God, because Father said his animals was his and they had to remember they was his, so he was the one to tend to them. Still, days and days went by sometimes without Father going near the horse trailer. The monkey would start screeching and the goose honking, and still Father didn't feed them. When it got too bad, I'd throw alfalfa in there and sometimes scraps from the table and set a tin can of water through the swimming-pool-blue rungs of the back gate. One night all hell broke loose, the monkey and the goose fighting over the tin can of water. Scared me to death watching those cooped-up animals—a white goose and a dark-brown skinny monkey—animals so different from each other—honking and hissing and screeching and going at each other, feathers and monkey blood flying. Then Heap Big Chief started barking. Such a racket I thought was going to wake the dead. Wake up Father. But Father didn't wake up. That August, with his Crown Royal and Cokes, an earthquake or a house fire wouldn't wake Father.

BOBBIE TOOK ME in her room and closed the door. Father had bought her two more albums, something by Mitch Miller and one by Pat Boone. Bobbie hated the Mitch Miller, but she was listening to *Love Letters in the Sand*.

Bobbie sat down on her bed. I sat down on her bed too, careful not to mess the covers. Bobbie was wearing her lime-green pedal pushers and Keds and a white blouse. Her hair in her blue curlers. It was a bright summer day and Bobbie had her blinds down and we were sitting in the dark, in the Marilyn Monroe light.

Bobbie didn't say anything for a while. I didn't either. We just sat on her bed listening to Pat Boone.

How's Jupiter? Bobbie asked.

Fine, I said. Charlie made him a muzzle.

Bobbie twisted around quick. The points of the little swords stuck through the blue curlers pushed into the skin of her forehead.

Something about Bobbie so mean and raw when she looked at me that way, something I never did understand.

A muzzle? Bobbie said.

So he can't bark, I said.

Bobbie's hands were spread out wide. The coral fingernail polish on her fingers was drying.

I just have to see Jupiter! Bobbie said.

Bobbie touched me just a little on my knee, careful with the coral polish, then left her hand on my knee.

I put my hand next to Bobbie's hand on my knee.

We can sneak over to Viv's double-wide tonight, I said.

Under the sword points poking into her forehead, Bobbie's bangs were taped down with Scotch tape.

I can't, Bobbie said.

What? I said.

I can't leave, Bobbie said. He'll know.

We'll wait till he's drunk and passed out, I said. Then we'll go over to Viv's.

Bobbie got up, pulled the record arm off *Love Letters in the Sand*, and started the song over again.

Can't, Bobbie said. He'll know.

THAT NIGHT, CHARLIE brought Jupiter over with him. Charlie and I were lying in bed with Jupiter in between us when the doorknob turned and somebody pushed up against the door. Charlie grabbed his pants and shirt and crawled out the window and sat on the roof beside the dormer. I unlocked the door and opened it. It was Bobbie. She was wearing a black dress with spaghetti straps and black high heels and black nylons with no seams.

When Jupiter saw Bobbie he started whining and groaning. Bobbie came in, and I closed the door fast.

Where'd you get that dress? I said.

Bobbie had Jupiter in her arms and he was licking her as much as the muzzle would let him and Bobbie was going, There there my little puppy dog, Jupiter baby doll don't cry don't cry, and then she undid the muzzle and Jupiter was licking and licking her and barking.

Bobbie! I said. Father's going to hear!

He's too drunk to hear shit, Bobbie said, and when she spoke, I could smell it on her breath: Crown Royal and Coke.

Bobbie, I said, What, are you drinking with him now too?

Too? Bobbie said.

In the gold flecks in Bobbie's eyes, I saw hate.

Then: Come on, little Jupiter baby, Bobbie said, Let's go downstairs.

Bobbie walked down the stairs to her room, walking the way you do in high heels, the way you do when you've had too much to drink, Jupiter cradled under her arm, his tail wagging.

A couple times that night Charlie and I could hear Jupiter barking.

IN THE MORNING, at breakfast, I'd set out the cereal boxes and the milk carton and the sugar on the table in the breakfast nook. Bobbie made Father's coffee, and Father was sitting just in his boxer shorts and T-shirt, staring at the table drinking his coffee. No magic tricks in the morning with Father.

Bobbie was eating her Rice Krispies, and I was eating my Corn Flakes, when Mother walked into the kitchen in the black dress Bobbie had been wearing the night before and the high heels, but mother's nylons had seams. Swoops in the seams. Mother was too big around the waist for the black dress and the zipper up the back wasn't zipped up all the way and you could see her brassiere strap. Mother had her face painted on and her hair done up.

Mother walked the way you do in high heels right to the drawer where she hid her Herbert Tareytons, tapped a Herbert Tareyton out of the pack, lit it, got the 30 Club ashtray out of the cupboard, then walked right over to the table and sat down and crossed her legs.

Only silence. In all the world, only silence.

Then Bobbie said: Mother!

Bobbie smiled just with her mouth.

That dress you're wearing! Bobbie said.

Oh, this old thing? Mother said, and swirled her cigarette around like Bette Davis. I found it out on the porch on your father's bed. It's two sizes too small, Mother said, but hell, nothing's perfect.

Mother's Orange Exotica lipstick was on the end of her Herbert Tareyton.

A jealous woman, Mother said, Would think the dress was a gift for some other woman. But that's not the case, Mother said. Is it, Cotton?

In my forearms first, the fear, up to my shoulders, splashed down through my heart, into my stomach.

Mother leaned her elbow on the table, inhaled on the cigarette, and blew smoke across the table right into Father's face.

Father's face didn't need clown makeup. His mouth was open and he was staring at Mother. So was Bobbie. So was I.

The wind in the cottonwood made the leaves shake, the sigh and scratch, into the kitchen. The shadows of the leaves on the table, on us, our family at the table, the shadows moving quick over the bowls and cups and cereal boxes, over our hands, on Father's head, Bobbie's face, the smoke of Mother's Herbert Tareyton, made it look like the shadows were still and the world was shaking.

Mother pushed her chair back, stood up quick.

Cotton Parker, Mother said, Now you listen up! We ain't afraid of you no more. We ain't following your rules no more. We're tired of being bullied by a damned old drunk sonofabitch!

Mother puffed and puffed on her cigarette, smoke all around her head.

So I'm smoking in the house, Mother said. And Bobbie's got a dog in her room. And your son Will's got an Injun in his.

So there it is, Mother said. Like it or lump it!

That's not all Bobbie's got in her room, I said.

But it's not the truth. I didn't open my mouth.

Father reached across the table and grabbed Mother by the hair. The table knocked over and dishes and cereal and cereal boxes and milk and coffee went flying. Father was dragging Mother back into her room. He slammed the door, and behind the door it sounded like the mean goose and the monkey were going at it, like all hell was breaking loose.

Bobbie wasn't anywhere around.

Behind the door, Mother screamed out and then a low sound against the floor. I ran up the stairs to my room and there was no sign of Charlie anywhere. I looked in Bobbie's room and Jupiter was on her bed, whining through the muzzle.

When I got back to the kitchen, I couldn't believe what was waiting for me.

The bedroom door was open and Father was holding Mother by the neck. Bobbie was standing in front of the bedroom door with Father's double-barreled shotgun pointed at Father's middle.

Bobbie's hair was every which way. Bobbie's body was skinny straight up and down, her pink seashell top, her poodle skirt, high heels spread wide apart, the shotgun right-angle to her body. Bobbie had her finger on both triggers.

Mother and Father didn't move. Father in his boxer shorts and T-shirt and Mother in a black dress that didn't fit; Mother and Father stared down the barrels of the shotgun. No doubt about it, they were the deers and Bobbie was the Mack truck.

Then: Well, now, Father said. My dear sweet little Bobbie girl, Father said. The light of my life! You sure do look mighty pretty today.

Shut up! Bobbie said.

You'll shoot your mother too at this range, Father said.

She wants to go too, Bobbie said. Don't you, Mother?

Mother smiled, smoothed the black dress across her hips, stepped closer. Father's hand fell off her.

Careful, Mother! Bobbie said. Don't block him.

Mother stepped aside a little so she didn't block the line of fire.

Listen up, Mr. Rodeo Fucking Clown, Bobbie said. Don't you ever, fucking ever, lay a hand on Mama again.

Bobbie, Father said. His hands were open, palms up. Come on, baby, Father said. This is your daddy.

Shoot! Mother said. Don't think about it, just shoot!

We've had enough! Bobbie said. All of us! Bobbie said. Isn't that right, Will?

Mother's Herbert Tareyton was burning on the linoleum. I stepped on it.

He knows about Charlie, Bobbie said. He knows about my dog. We got to kill him.

Just shoot! Mother cried, and fell down on her knees. Dear God, just shoot!

Bobbie swung the shotgun to the left and pulled the trigger. Shotgun blast real loud and a hole in the plaster wall bigger around than Father was wide. Mother screamed, or Father screamed. Maybe it was me.

Then quiet after something so loud. Plaster dust, buckshot bouncing on the floor.

Then a little black ball of fur and red bow and something shiny ran through the kitchen: Jupiter. He ran to the back door and jumped up through the screen door, but the screen stopped him.

He made it through the screen the second time, and he was running, but his leash got caught between the floorboards of the porch, and he damn near choked himself to death.

Jupiter started screaming dog screams. Dog diarrhea.

Jupiter! Bobbie yelled.

Jupiter! I yelled.

Bobbie kicked off her high heels and was out the kitchen door first, still with the shotgun, then me. She bent down quick and pulled the leash from between the floorboards, let go of the leash, then knelt down to pick the dog up.

But Jupiter was off.

Jupiter! Jupiter! Bobbie yelled.

Bobbie! Bobbie! I yelled.

But Jupiter didn't stop. Muzzled, in his red bow and his rhinestone collar, Jupiter ran and ran around the house, around father's atom-bomb swimming-pool-blue pickup and trailer, around the horse trailer, around the rusted old swing set and teeter-totter, ran to Father's big German shepherd, ran right for him.

Like on TV when you see the lion break the gazelle's neck.

Just like that, Jupiter was a high-pitched muzzled dog scream, a black and red dishrag flopping around in Heap Big Chief's mouth.

On the smooth cement, Bobbie stopped.

Bobbie raised the shotgun, aimed at Heap Big Chief, cocked the shotgun.

I caught up to Bobbie just before Father did.

Father had his arms out and was about to grab Bobbie from behind when I stepped between Father and Bobbie and crouched down. Father went flying over me.

Bobbie shot. Fur flying, brains, bone, pieces of dog muzzle. Heap Big Chief was lying on the ground, his legs twitching, one whole side of his head gone. Jupiter a bloody rag still clenched in Heap Big Chief's mouth.

Bobbie's flying hair, her pink seashell top, her poodle skirt, bare feet firm on the smooth cement. Father on his back right on the cement, white hairy legs, white hairy arms, piss stains and duck butter on his shorts.

Dog blood a red pool from the dog pile.

Bobbie dropped the shotgun right there.

The black dress on Mother in the unrelenting sun was a dark hole in the morning. Bobbie walked to Mother, put her head on Mother's breast, and Mother was holding Bobbie and Bobbie was crying crying. They walked that way, those females, holding on together, back into the house.

Father got up off the smooth cement, cussed, brushed his butt off. He walked toward me like he was going to hit me, but things were different. I squared off and put my fists up. But Father just walked past, not even looking at me. Then from behind, he hit me in the ear, then my other ear. I fell facedown on the smooth cement. The blood on the cement was from me.

Father unhitched the trailers, got in his pickup, started the motor. All Dodges sound the same.

Father left rubber on the smooth cement, threw rocks when he got to the gravel. The pickup sound down the lane through the cottonwoods got farther and farther away.

But he wasn't going far without his pants.

CHARLIE WAS BEHIND Viv's double-wide, sitting on the wood step. He took one look at me, went in the double-wide, and came out with Viv, and Viv had a warm washcloth.

Viv held my head against her cantaloupe breasts, wiped the blood from my ears. She smelled like permanents and fry bread. Her shoulder was so soft.

Viv cried the whole time she held me, wiped the blood. When she wasn't cussing Father, she was talking something beautiful in Indian.

When Viv got up, her knees cracked. Viv went inside, and in no time at all, came out with two bologna sandwiches and two RC Colas and two paper napkins. At our house, we always tore the napkins in half, but Viv gave Charlie and me whole napkins.

On the wood steps of Viv's double-wide, Charlie came over and sat down next to me. Charlie put his arms across my shoulders. Only then did I start to cry.

I told Charlie about the shotgun and the dead dogs and everything. I told him Father knew Charlie was coming over to the house.

Charlie said, Don't pay it no mind, Will. He can't stop me from coming over.

* * *

CHARLIE AND I buried the dogs in the corral behind the barn. We had to dig a big hole for Heap Big Chief.

Charlie said, Heap Big Chief heap big hole. And that got us to laughing. Jupiter's hole was just a little hole. We put some rocks around Jupiter's grave and Charlie painted the rocks white with a can of spray paint from Viv's garage.

Later on, Charlie and I went up in the sexually haunted barn and lay down on the straw and looked up at the sunlight coming through the holes in the roof. Charlie took hold of my hand. I pulled my hand away.

It's probably best you don't come over tonight, I said.

What if he comes home all drunk? Charlie said.

All the more reason for you to stay out of here, I said.

ABOUT MIDNIGHT, I heard Bobbie in the bathroom. Out the window, Father's pickup wasn't in the yard. I ran down the dark wood steps and down the hardwood floor of the hallway to the bathroom and the crack of light under the bathroom door. I knocked on the door and said, Bobbie?—but Bobbie didn't hear me so I just walked in the bathroom, and Bobbie told me to get the fuck out of there, but I didn't.

Bobbie was all sweaty and her hair was wet and the big red T-shirt she wore to bed was soaked all the way through and bunched around the middle of her and you could see Bobbie's pink panties and the hair of her poon under her pink panties. Bobbie was kneeling on the green linoleum, really fountain-mouth, barfing, barfing, her head way into the toilet, her body jerking every time she barfed, her one hand a pillow on the rim of the toilet and her other hand holding tight to the green shower curtain. I didn't know what to do.

Bobbie yelled at me, Stop your fucking crying! which made me cry all the more.

I got the blue washrag from the closet in the hallway and went to the sink and turned on the enamel knob that said cold in black letters on it and let the cold water run on the washrag and left the water running, and then went and knelt down on the green linoleum by Bobbie, touched her on the back first, then put the washrag on her face and wiped her face. Her barf smelled awful. Peanut butter and grape jelly sandwiches and Nestlé Quik and milk. But I stayed holding the washrag to her face.

When she was done barfing for a little bit, I asked Bobbie if she wanted me to turn off the ceiling light and Bobbie said, Yes, thank you. And I turned off the unrelenting fluorescence.

Who knows how long Bobbie and I sat on the bathroom floor in the dark with just the cold water running into the sink.

Bobbie and I are still sitting there.

Then, all at once, the unrelenting fluorescence went back on and Mother was standing at the door. She had her same yellow terry-cloth bathrobe on, same slippers, her hair was the same too, everything the same, but something about Mother that night was beautiful.

She went right to Bobbie, and at first Bobbie waved her arm and tried to keep her away but Mother just took Bobbie's arm and helped Bobbie up and then held Bobbie close to her with Bobbie's head on the yellow terry cloth.

I couldn't look at Mother holding Bobbie, so I looked in the mirror at them. I expected Bobbie any minute to say fuck you or something, but Bobbie didn't. Bobbie just put her head against Mother's yellow terry cloth and kept her eyes closed, tight, like if she opened her eyes Mother would go away.

Then they walked out together, Mother saying, There, there, it'll be all right, Bobbie. And Mother and Bobbie went down the dark wood stairs, and down the hardwood floor of the hall, past the living room, through the dark wood swinging doors to the dining room, then into Mother's bedroom with the bright ceiling light on, the fan on the vanity on, but no windows open, green shades drawn. It smelled like Herbert Tareytons in there, it smelled like her.

Both of them lay down in Mother's bed, and Mother pulled her white chenille bedspread over them and told me to close the door and turn the light off because Bobbie never has liked a lot of light.

I shut off the light, closed Mother's door, and went back upstairs into Bobbie's bathroom and shut the cold water off and flushed the toilet again and folded up the blue washrag on the side of the bathtub and turned off the light.

I sat in the cool bathtub in the dark for a while, until the mosquitoes found me, so then I walked on the hardwood floor into Bobbie's room, into the Marilyn Monroe color of her room, and lay down in Bobbie's bed, exactly straight, feet together, and there was all the colors of the map of the Known Universe just to the left of my toes. I turned off the lamp. I pulled the sheet over me. Even in the dark I could see the colors.

In my dream, Bobbie and I were on Chub and Charlie was on aya-Huaska, and Jupiter was running alongside, and all of us running fast across the bottoms.

When I woke up, I didn't know where I was, then I knew I was in the Residency, then I knew I was in Bobbie's bed, and then I knew there was somebody in the room with me. I could hear somebody taking off their clothes. A belt buckle, boots. Then there was a big body on the bed, pushing that side of the bed down and a hand on my leg under the sheet.

In my forearms, up to my shoulders, splash down through heart, cattle prod to cock.

SOMETHING SO BIG as your life is hard to tell.

My father's hand and my father's breath, Crown Royal and Pall Malls, and my father's naked arms. His hand up my leg, up my thigh. Father made deep sounds in his throat and stopped with his hand and then pulled off the white of his boxer shorts. Father sat himself across my chest. His cock was right there sticking up, pointing right at me, at my mouth, and his hands were behind him back down on me and Father was saying, Oh, my dear sweet little Bobbie girl.

When Father reached my shorts, he pulled them down and found me there.

Father yelled and jumped out of bed and turned on the unrelenting fluorescents—and there we were, in all the world, father and son, in Bobbie's room, cocks poking up.

You're going this way and then shit happens and then you're going that way.

Father laughed, just one laugh that jumped up in his chest and made his cock bounce.

Well now, Father said. This is my son.

Father pointed at me, at my cock. He laughed just one laugh, chest up and down.

Father reached over and flipped my cock with his finger.

You didn't even get *that* from me, he said. Everything from her, Father said. Even got your dick from your mother.

My heart, the broken pieces scratching up against my chest.

From me on the bed, up, my father was the hair on his balls and his cock poking out, then the hair of his chest and his big nipples, the unrelenting fluorescence around his head.

Guess it's time for a little father-to-son talk, Father said.

He sat down on the bed. He pulled up the sheet, covered me. He wiped my hair back from out of my eyes and moved his big hand down the side of my face.

Listen up, son, Father said, This is important. Someday you'll remember these words of mine I'm saying and you'll thank me.

Then Father was between me and the unrelenting light, Father a shadow onto my eyes. His beard against my face, his breath, his body sweat, his lips at my ear.

It's a horse race, Father whispered. Out there, it's a horse race. You got a good horse, you got a chance a winning. You don't and you got a snowball's chance in hell. The way I figure, most people don't know it's a horse race, so if you know, even though your horse ain't worth a damn, even though you ain't got a snowball's chance in hell, you got the edge.

And I'm here to tell you, son, Father whispered, You ain't got a snowball's chance in hell.

But now you know, Father whispered, So you got the edge.

Father got up off the bed, picked up his Levi's and Levi's shirt and his boots and socks and his underwear. His hairy butt walked to the door.

Before he left, Father shut off the light.

Just remember, Father said. Winning and losing, they need each other.

Like you and that Injun. And Will? The horrific whisper: Tonight you lost, Father said.

CHAPTER THIRTEEN

April or May 1985. The photograph was lying on the sidewalk in front of Café Cauchemar. It was a photo-booth photo, and I picked it up. The guy was thin and had thick glasses and his face looked smashed in on one side. He wore a hat with a small brim, the brim cocked up all dandy with a little peacock feather in the hatband. You couldn't tell if the guy was smiling or just had gas pains, his eyes big dark gray behind his thick glasses, looking up through his smashed face right at you. I stuck the photo in my white shirt pocket and forgot about it.

FIONA ALL IN red, Medusa hair, her broken red lip, wearing big black wraparound sunglasses, walked into Café Cauchemar. Then Harry: green Lacoste shirt, khakis, and Nikes. A serial killer and a golf pro.

Harry leaned Ronald Reagan on one part of the banquette, Nancy on another.

Fiona kissed me on the forehead and sat down at the table with her ginger ale and her peanut butter and jelly and banana sandwich.

Fiona, beautiful according to Fellini.

Harry's pink freckled skin looked as green as his shirt.

Harry, I said, you OK?

He's fine, Fiona said. A touch of the stomach flu.

Must have been something I ate, Harry said.

Fiona dug through her huge red leather purse and pulled out two round white pills.

Tylenol with codeine, Fiona said. Take two of these.

I reached into my white shirt pocket to get my tobacco and papers and put my hand on the photo-booth photo, pulled it out, and looked at it, and Harry said, What's that?

I slid Harry the photo across the butcher paper.

He kind of looks like Truman Capote, Harry said.

Fiona leaned over and looked at the photo. His eyes look like smashed grapes, Fiona said.

Fresh grapes in a fruit compote, Harry said.

Fresh Fruit Truman Compotee, Fiona said.

That's how the game started. What happened was I didn't want the photo back, and Harry didn't want the photo, and Fiona didn't want the photo, and we started pushing it at each other, Harry going *eeuuw!* and Fiona going *eeuuw!* and then me going *eeuuw!* Like the photo was the plague or something.

AFTER THE FIRST rush, when Cauchemar was empty, Fiona and Harry, Davey Dearest and Walter and Joanie and Mack Dickson, and John the Bartender and I stood around Georgette's desk and drew up the rules to Fresh Fruit Truman Compotee.

The rules to the game were there were no rules. Except one. The person who had the photo, the Fresh Fruit Truman Compotee, on him or her or on or around the body, at twelve o'clock midnight that night was the loser.

What do I have to do if I lose? Joanie said. Something like give everybody a blow job?

Joanie smiled her cute smile.

No, Fiona said. It should be something unusual.

Moon the kitchen? Davey Dearest said.

Midnight, Harry said. The kitchen's empty.

Eat food out of the garbage? Walter said.

Garbage is out on the street by then, Fiona said.

John the Bartender stepped through us, with a bus tub of glasses. His white shirt was soaked through.

Make it a performance piece, John the Bartender said. Some Lower East Side Shit. You know, Armadilla Kowabunga or something like that.

Fiona spit into the garbage can.

It's Argwings Khodek, asshole, Fiona said. And performance piece it is.

Interpretive dance? Harry said.

Merce Cunningham! Walter said.

Twyla Tharp! Joanie said.

Martha Graham! Davey Dearest said.

Pina Bausch! Walter said.

Bill T. Jones and Arnie Zane! Davey Dearest said.

A strip! Mack Dickson said.

When Mack Dickson spoke, everybody looked at him: his thin lips, the extreme beauty of his bone structure.

The loser, Mack Dickson said, Has to do a striptease.

All the way, Mack Dickson said, his eyes on me, too cruel to be beautiful.

All the fucking way, he said, In the employees' dressing room, after closing.

A little sparkle of light shone off his capped teeth.

What do you say, Horse Dick? Mack Dickson said. A striptease OK with you?

Language my second language.

Fine, I said, With me.

Let's shake on it then, Harry said, and Davey Dearest and Walter and Joanie and Mack Dickson and John the Bartender and Fiona and Harry and me—we all touched our hands together in the middle of our circle.

May the true loser lose, Mack Dickson said.

May the true loser lose, everybody else said.

Then: May the true loser, I said, Lose.

DURING THE BUSIEST part of the first rush, I was next to Harry in the waiter station. Both Harry and I were in the weeds. I was punching away on the adding machine; Harry was pulling an American Express card through the credit card machine.

That's when Harry opened his ticket book.

Inside was the photo-booth photo, the dark gray eyes, the thick glasses, the thin smashed-in face.

Seven-forty-five: Harry screamed.

JOANIE HAD A deuce on table two, and as she was presenting the Domaine Chandon, Harry brought the ice bucket over, set the bucket down on the stand, and draped the white cloth napkin over it. Joanie went to put the bottle in the ice bucket.

Eight-thirty: Joanie screamed.

JOHN THE BARTENDER picked up the intercom phone, said OK, hung up the intercom phone, and told Davey Dearest that Walter had a phone call on the pay phone downstairs. Davey Dearest told Walter and Walter ran down the stairs. Walter picked up the ringing pay phone.

Eight-fifty-two: Walter's scream came up the stairs.

DAVEY DEAREST WAS standing next to the garbage can. He'd just made himself an espresso and lit a cigarette.

Davey Dearest said, I know that fucking Walter is going for me!

Then Davey Dearest reached into where the sugar packets are, pulled two sugar packets out, shook the packets, and went to rip them open.

Nine-seventeen: Davey Dearest screamed.

I WAS SERVING the single guy on table twenty. I delivered his couscous, set the terra-cotta bowl and cover on the table, took the terra-cotta cover off and—*ta-da!*—there was the couscous. I reached for the serving spoon.

Nine-twenty-seven: I screamed.

JUST BEFORE THE second rush, nine-forty-five, Daniel, the boss's brother, came up from downstairs and stood at front door, greeting dinner guests, menus in hand, with the look on his face he always gets just after doing cocaine: Good evening, welcome to Nightmare Café, I am the Maître d'Hôtel who was hit by lightning.

Then it was cocaine for everybody else. First, John the Bartender went downstairs, then Joanie, then Davey Dearest and Walter, then Mack Dickson. Running back up the stairs, each one of them looking like there'd been an alien being in the bathroom and they couldn't wait to tell you about it.

Cocaine was a beauty drug for Mack Dickson. When Mack Dickson walked up the stairs, his smile was sleepy, his hair was neatly tousled, and he had that perfect one-day-beard look. His eyes were bluer, his skin olive, his forearms, the silky black hair, perfect.

Too fucking perfect.

WHEN DAVEY DEAREST and Walter walked through the swinging red doors and went downstairs, I saw that Davey Dearest didn't have his ticket book with him, so I went in by the espresso machine and looked all over, on the shelves and under things, but I couldn't look like I was looking all over, on the shelves and under things, because Joanie had her mesomorph self planted in the middle of everything.

I looked over, and Georgette was moving her eyes real weird, and she was screwing her lips over to one side. Then Georgette pointed her pen in the direction of the dishwashing room. I walked to the dishwashing room and just as I was about to go into the dishwashing room, Georgette said, Will, would you please get me one of my Diet Uncolas from the *reach-in*.

I went to the reach-in, slid open the door, looked all over, but all I could see was the gallon of milk, the half and half, some butter plates, but no Diet Uncola.

On the fucking top, for chrissakes! Georgette yelled. Look on the top!

I put my hand on top of the reach-in and there was Davey Dearest's ticket book.

Joanie gave Georgette a New York drop-dead fuck-you and walked out the swinging red doors.

NINE-FIFTY-TWO: Chef Som Chai was standing right next to Davey Dearest when Davey Dearest opened his ticket book and screamed.

TEN O'CLOCK. THE restaurant was full. Harry had his double-fudge brownie prepared with the funny candle that won't blow out. He lit the candle and cupped his hands over the flame as he pushed his butt up against the swinging red door. Fiona was heading for the bar and ran into Harry from the back. Harry spun around and yelled, Get that fucking thing away from me! Don't you touch me!

Harry! Fiona said, and opened up her hands. I haven't got it! Fiona said.

Lying bitch! Harry said. You're lying! You just gave it to me, didn't you?

No, Fiona said. Will just gave it to Davey Dearest.

HARRY WAS AT the birthday table. He set the cake in front of the beautiful silver-haired Coco Chanel two-piece and burst into a huge Happy Birthday. The chandelier jingled. Quiet as only New York can get that fast. Just as Harry was getting to the big Dear Da-da-da that shatters crystal, Davey Dearest walked up to Harry and put Fresh Fruit Truman Compotee in Harry's shirt pocket.

Harry didn't sing the Dear Da-da-da part at all, just stopped. Turned so white all his freckles stuck out.

Ten-thirty-five: Fucking son-of-a mother bitch! Harry said.

SECTION ONE, ALL Fiona's tables, know about Fresh Fruit Truman Compotee. Section Two, all Harry's tables, know about Fresh Fruit Truman Compotee. Section One and Section Two were watching as Mack Dickson pulled his ticket book out from the back of his pants, expanded his chest, flexed his biceps, flashed his winning capped-teeth smile, and opened the ticket book to give the check to the customer.

Ten-fifty-seven: Mack Dickson screamed.

Uproarious laughter in Section One and Section Two.

Daniel, the boss's brother, looked around, gave the whole restaurant his big restaurant smile, then looked at me like: What the fuck?

Eleven-oh-two: In the dining room, a scream from on the other side of the swinging red doors. Fiona and Harry and Joanie and Davey Dearest and I ran to the swinging red doors and looked through the windows. Mack Dickson was chasing Walter around the room.

THE MAN WITH the check on table nineteen motioned to me. I went over to him and he said, What credit cards do you take? And I said, Any one of them. And he said, In that case take this.

I reached out and took the check and the credit card on the check tray.

Eleven-seventeen: I screamed.

OF COURSE, THEN all at once I had everything to do. I had to do the check for the six-top. I had two deuce orders up, and the chef was yelling. There was a bottle of Sancerre I had to serve, and I still had the order for my four-top to put in.

I picked up three of the four plates and lined them up my arm, and the fourth plate I held in my other hand, and delivered the dinners, poured each deuce more wine, ground fresh pepper, said Bon appétit, rushed to the bar, got the Sancerre, served the Sancerre, smiled as I presented the bottle.

In the kitchen, as I was writing out the chit, I took Fresh Fruit Truman Compotee out of my pocket and looked around. No one was within twenty feet of me. I ran up to the dinner station, called out my orders in a clear voice, and put the chit on the stainless steel.

Eleven-twenty-eight: The chef screamed.

THE ENTIRE WAITING staff, John the Bartender, and most of the customers in Café Cauchemar knew the chef was *it*.

The waiters were pacing.

John the Bartender was standing in the middle of the bar.

The chef burst out the swinging red doors.

Fiona and Harry and I ran to the waiter station in front of the dining room.

Joanie and Walter were on their knees in the waiters' station, their hands on their heads, kissing their asses good-bye.

Davey Dearest was at the front door, putting a customer's overcoat on himself.

Daniel was at the end of the bar, staring into a gin rickey.

Mack Dickson was in Section Six, at a four-top, his bubble butt to the swinging red doors and the approaching chef.

The restaurant got quiet as only New York can get that fast.

Mack Dickson swung around.

Chef Som Chai was right behind him.

Mack Dickson let out the high homosexual scream that gives it all away and ran around to the other side of the table. The chef chased Mack around to that side, and Mack ran to the other side.

It was a standoff. Mack and the chef, the four-top between them, the four people looking at Mack, looking at the chef, back and forth back and forth.

The chef screamed, Stop moving!

Chandeliers swayed. Flowers withered. Ice cream melted.

The chef screamed: Take this!

Mack took it.

Now keep Flesh Fluit Tluman Compotee out of kitchen! Chef screamed.

JOHN THE BARTENDER asked José the busboy to get him some ice from the ice chest in the kitchen, and when José returned with the

ice, José said, A message from Daniel, and handed John a pink envelope. John quick took the envelope, walked to the middle of the bar,
and opened it.

Eleven-thirty-eight: John the Bartender fell against the back bar,
grabbed for the draft beer spigot. Beer all over the place.

John's head up, facing the Sistine Chapel God.

The scream: Fuck!

FIONA HAD A rush of Eurotrash in section One: twelve cappuccinos,
twelve grappas neat, two *tarte tartins*, twelve forks. Fiona put the grappa
order in to John the Bartender, set up the neat glasses on a tray, ran
into the kitchen, and started on the cappuccinos. I had some time, so I
got twelve saucers while Fiona got twelve cups and twelve spoons, and
I started with the espressos—two clicks of espresso into the Portafilter,
smash down the espresso in the Portafilter, screw the Portafilter onto
the machine, push the switch, wait for all the espresso to pour into the
cup. Fiona did the jet plane steam milk part. I unscrewed the Portafilter,
banged it out into the shit can, and started over—twelve times—Fiona
roaring away on the foam all the while.

Fiona got a big tray, and we set the twelve cappuccinos on the tray.
I told Fiona I'd carry it if she set the tray jack up by the table. Fiona
said, The tray jack's already there. I'll get the grappas.

Took you long enough, John the Bartender said to Fiona.

Fiona picked up the tray of grappas and said, I was making twelve
fucking cappuccinos, asshole.

And John said, Spindle your fucking ticket, asshole.

John handed Fiona her drink ticket, but it wasn't the drink ticket.

Eleven-fifty-six: Fiona does not scream.

THE TRAY JACK was nowhere around the table, and I was standing there
with twelve cappuccinos on a tray on my shoulder, watching Daniel
fill up my section. Fiona cussed and grabbed a tray jack, and I put the
tray of cappuccinos down. Fiona said, Spindle this, would you? and I
took the piece of paper Fiona handed me.

Eleven-fifty-nine.

Love ya. Mean it. Every woman for herself, Fiona said. Cool.

Ten . . . nine . . . eight . . . seven . . . six . . . five . . . four . . . three
. . . two . . . one.

Ask your Higher Knowing, Fiona said. Obstacles are opportunities. Everything is an illusion, even death. Besides, you need the practice walking naked, Fiona said.

YOU'RE GOING THIS way and then shit happens and then you're going that way.

Mack Dickson and Joanie pushed the benches up against the lockers, so there was a runway down the middle. The chef had Joanie put a RESERVED card on each end of the section of benches. Davey Dearest and Walter lined up the ice buckets for the champagne. On a white cloth-covered card table at the end of the runway was the boom box from the kitchen and the photo-booth photo of Fresh Fruit Truman Compotee.

The front door was locked.

One-ten: My triple Long Island Ice Tea was on the back of the toilet, along with the toilet paper roll and two lines of cocaine.

A knock on the door.

Miss LaRue! Harry singsonged. Five minutes!

The fluorescent light from above the mirror made a shadow on my eyes. The toilet was running water into the brown bowl. There were water splashes all over on the sink, a bar of cracked dirty-white soap, pieces of lettuce, pubic hair. The faucet was rusty chrome and the faucet dripped.

The fluorescent light sounded like insects.

The paper towel dispenser was empty, but it was always empty.

Under the sink, a box of Brillo pads, a black plastic garbage pail full of wads of paper, overflowing onto the cement floor, which was painted gray.

Underarm deodorant, somebody'd just shit in there, old piss.

On the other side of the door, Kool and The Gang were singing "Celebration!" *Let's all celebrate and have a good time!*

Miss LaRue, Harry singsonged, Five minutes!

Then, lower, in a voice just for him and me, Harry said, Everybody's waiting, Will. Are you all right? Open the door. Susan Strong's got something for you.

What is it, I said, A razor blade?

No, Harry said.

A used car? I said. A Ford Pinto—the ones that blow up when you get hit from behind?

Will, Harry said.

An Uzi? I said.

Will, Harry said.

Fuck *her*, I said.

I opened the door and Harry handed in a brown paper bag. Harry closed the door.

Inside the bag was a black strap-on dildo.

What? I said. Did she have this in her *purse*?

Through the door: You never know, Harry said. Susan Strong is always prepared.

A yellow Post-it stuck to the big black dildo: *The fates lead him who will; who won't they drag.*

Fuck *her*.

I FINISHED THE Long Island Ice Tea. I finished the joint. I snorted the lines of cocaine. I looked in the mirror.

On the other side of the door: Horse Dick! Mack Dickson yelled, Where's Horse Dick?

A knock on the door.

Go away, Harry! I said.

It's John, John said. I've got another cocktail.

The natives are restless, John said, and stepped into the bathroom. I could smell all of John this close: booze, grease, sweat, Polo. He put a triple Long Island Ice Tea between the empty one and the toilet paper on the back of the toilet.

John looked in the mirror, said, Oh, Christ! and covered his face with his long hands.

Fuckin' hell! John said. I look like shit!

I never look in this mirror, John said. Everything imperfect is exaggerated in this mirror.

Do I look yellow? John said. Or green?

It's the light, I said.

John took out his bottle with the black spoon, put the spoon to his nose above his mustache, snorted up the powder, then did the other side.

This is a dangerous place to spend any time alone, John said. If I were you, I'd get my booty out of here fast.

The black strap-on dildo was on the sink. John picked the dildo up and turned it around in his hands.

What's this? John said.

Performance art, I said. A little help from my friends.

You don't need this kind of help, John said.

John sat down on his haunches, leaned against the door. Just like that John unzipped my black waiter pants and pulled my Fruit of the Looms down.

John? I said.

Shut up! John said.

I just turned my eyes up to the fluorescents.

Oo-eee! John said. You need to take this thing out of the barn more often. Give it some air! Take it for a walk around the block!

In the mirror, what's imperfect is exaggerated.

Sure ain't, I said, No horse dick.

No, John said. Ain't no horse dick.

Then John had my cock in his mouth warm and wet, and there was John's bald head and ponytail down there where my cock used to be. Then John took both my balls and put my balls in his mouth.

John, I said.

Breath in, breath out. Can you get AIDS this way?

John stood up, didn't look at me. His lips were cracked, bloody at the corners.

Just wanted to fluff it up for you, John said. You see? It looks a lot better now. Now, what you do, John said, Is you comb back the hair at the top so you can see all the way to the root. Makes it look bigger.

John went to the faucet, turned on the faucet, waited for the water to get warm, then got some water on his hand and took the warm water and brushed the hair up from around the top of my cock.

John laughed. I can see you *like* that.

I looked down.

Just keep it like that, John said. Half mast. That way people think half mast is flaccid, and if that's flaccid, honey, there's still a long way to go.

Shower not a grower, I said.

Nice helmet head, John said. Then: Gotta go now! You look fabulous, darling!

When John opened the door, the crowd was yelling, *Horse Dick! Horse Dick! Horse Dick!*

The show must go on, John said. When you walk, John said, When all your clothes are off and you're walking back home down the runway, pull your balls up—you got a big set of balls on you—let your balls ride in front of you, so your dick is resting on your balls.

John kissed me a little on the forehead.

Then: If it helps at all, John said, I think you're very sexy. And one of the sweetest men I've ever met.

John closed the door.

I sloshed down the triple Long Island Ice Tea, stepped into Fiona's dildo one leg at a time, strapped the dildo onto the outside of my black waiter pants.

Dildo against the door, I stared at the door.

All daring and courage, I said, all iron endurance of misfortune, makes for a finer, nobler type of manhood.

I unlocked the door, put my hand on the doorknob, and opened the bathroom door and—*ta-da!*—went out and did a Gypsy Rose Fucking Lee that left my audience shocked and breathless.

But it's not the truth.

The Brillo box. I grabbed the Brillo box from under the sink and held the box in my arms the way you hold a bouquet of flowers or a baby.

Dildo against the door, I stared at the door.

I unlocked the door, put my hand on the doorknob.

A ROOM FULL of eyes and about twenty people are screaming, clapping, whistling.

The hope of theater to lay bare the human heart.

Chef Som Chai, the Kung Fu salad guy, the other Thai men of the kitchen, Walter, Davey Dearest, Joanie, José and the other new Puerto Rican busboy, Georgette, John the Bartender, Fiona and Harry, Mack Dickson.

I know everything about them—where each person is standing, how they are standing, how their faces look, what they are thinking, who they are deep down inside.

Slow motion, I put my arms out, and the way I feel is the way I've always wanted to feel and never knew it. It's the way the ocean feels, rolling rolling, and why birds like to fly so much.

I let out a big whoop! And I walk on the wild side, I walk shake-it-don't-break-it, push my hips out, the black dildo boinging boinging back and forth, side to side, into the bright fluorescence.

Walk the walk down the runway, do a Rump Spin at the card table with Fresh Fruit Truman Compotee in a champagne glass with rose petals on it, sashay back.

The roar of the crowd.

To know the power of the dance is to dance with God.

I set the Brillo box down next to Fresh Fruit Truman Compotee for the juxtaposition. I unclip my black clip-on waiter tie, put the tie in my black waiter pants pocket, pull the white shirttails out. I undo the top button of my white waiter shirt, then the rest of the buttons.

Fiona's at the boom box. She pushes the button.

Aretha: *Respect. . . .*

In the fluorescence, unrelenting, dildo boinging up and down, back and forth, side to side.

The white waiter shirt, off one shoulder, then off the other shoulder, stretch the shirt across my chest, just above my nipples, lift my bare shoulders *Gentlemen Prefer Blondes* décolletage. Drop the shirt, catch the shirt, twirl the shirt above my head, let the shirt drop next to the Brillo box.

Raise my arms, Patti LuPone Evita. Underarm ass crack testosterone stink.

Don't cry for me.

Re-re-re-re-re-re-re-re-spect.

Dildo boinging up and down, back and forth, side to side.

MY FIRST PROBLEM is shoes and socks.

I lie down on my side on the runway and pull one leg up to me, dildo boinging and poking up, unlace the black sensible waiter shoe, pull the shoe off, pull the black sock off over the heel. But the sweaty sock sticks to my skin. I roll over on my back—butt in the air, legs in the Air Bicycle, dildo boinging boinging in my face, the one sock dangling—reach up and pull the sock off, twirl the sock around in the air, give the sock a toss. Then pull the other foot down and unlace the black sensible waiter shoe but the fucking lace knots, so I just kick off the shoe and pull the black sock off.

Then I do an Arabesque and flip up onto my feet from on my back, do a spin, two revolutions around, jump up, dildo boinging boinging, and come down, Crupper Split to a Hip Roll—a fancy maneuver all right and it sends the crowd into ecstasies, but my problem is the dildo boings under me and my nuts land on the dildo and for a while I think I'm going to die.

From the Crupper Split, I push myself up and lift my body by straightening my arms, bring my one leg through and around, do a back flip to a full standing Stick Ride position, dildo boinging back and forth, up and down, side to side, a life all its own.

Sock it to me sock it to me sock it to me sock it to me.

My next problem is to take off my pants and my Fruit of the Looms without taking off the strap-on dildo.

There's no solution to this problem, even for Houdini.

I shake my ass around, strut up and down the runway, bump and grind, boing the dildo, but there's no getting away from it.

I got to take the dildo off.

Beyond, out there, John the Bartender starts in first, singing along with Aretha. Then Harry, then Georgette, then Chef Som Chai.

I pull the straps of the dildo down, slow, hips back and forth, the way you would a girdle or a jockstrap.

Everybody out there is singing and clapping. I twirl the dildo by the strap around my head the way you throw a lariat, and I throw the dildo, and the dildo hits Mack Dickson in the head.

Then I dance, really dance, not no closing-time locals-kicking-up: Joe Cocker meets Martha Graham and Gypsy Rose Lee.

I undo the top button of my black waiter pants.

A gasp from the crowd. Cheers.

I unzip my zipper.

Do a Rump Turn, three revolutions this time, step out of my black waiter pants one leg at a time, lay my black waiter pants over my shoulder, the Hooker Arm Drag, I shake it don't break it, walk on the wild side, walk the walk, strut my stuff down the runway and back to Fresh Fruit Truman Compotee and the Brillo box. Drop my pants, my Fruit of the Loom ass to the crowd.

I do a Shoulder Stand, then back-flip and land on my feet, pull my Fruit of the Looms down over one cheek, then the other, pull my Fruit of the Looms down to my ankles, then Go Under the Belly, head down, butt up, to unrelenting fluorescence.

Pull my big balls aside, stick my head down there like I can, put my chin between my butt cheeks, look out at my audience, hands on my butt cheeks—spread my butt cheeks wide, cross my eyes, give 'em a big smile, stick my tongue out.

Who cares what a bunch of assholes think.

Screams and screams. The crowd is going wild.

I reach over, pick up the Brillo box, take my chin out of my ass, raise up, turn my body around, quick put the Brillo box in front of my cock and balls.

Postured disregard, savoir faire, I can fuck you blind and keep it simple, *sexy totale*. I walk on the wild side, walk the walk, bump and grind, strut my stuff down the runway, sashay, do the Rump Spin, reach in the Brillo box, pick out a Brillo pad, and throw the Brillo pad in the air.

Up and down the runway, tossing Brillo pads.

At the end of the runway, when I run out of Brillo pads, I throw the Brillo box.

Brillo box hits Fiona in the head.

Then—*ta-da!*—all daring and courage, I turn around, face the music, face the eyes.

I pull my balls up like John the Bartender told me, walk balls out, cock lying on top, half mast, on the wild side, sashay, strut, it ain't the meat it's the motion, back to the Brillo box.

Nobody even looks at my cock.

IN ALL THE world, I'm the Leonardo da Vinci guy spread-eagle on a stage. I'm completely present, buck naked, original, pure, red-blooded American boy, high enough to think I am New York, out there in the spotlight, my spotlight for life.

Nowhere.

Now here.

Something from nothing.

Beyond, out there, all around the runway, a semicircle of arms around each other. Chef Som Chai's got his shirt open, his arm over Kung Fu salad guy's shoulder, while Kung Fu salad guy does the bump with the Mexican dishwasher. The sous chef, Walter, and José are leaning on each other, barbershop quartet, singing *Respect*. Harry and Joanie are showing the three other Thai guys in the kitchen how to twist. Davey Dearest and the new Puerto Rican busboy, Georgette, John the Bartender, even Mack Dickson, shaking and rubbing up against each other.

All of us all one thing.

Dancing with God.

Fiona is holding the Andy Warhol Brillo box. She just stands there and stares at me, smiling her broken-lip smile.

* * *

ABOUT 2 A.M., Joanie stumbled a bump and grind down the runway. Off with her white shirt, off with her pants.

Harry yelled, Put it back on! Put it back on!

Fuck you! Joanie yelled.

No fuck you!

Then, just like that, Joanie walked over to the card table, picked up the champagne glass, poured the rose petals out, and with her index and thumb pulled out Fresh Fruit Truman Compotee.

The tape was over, the champagne gone. No more cocaine.

Joanie stood like a cellulite Statue of Liberty in a pink bra and pink bikini underwear, hairy armpit, holding Fresh Fruit Truman Compotee up to the sky.

Joanie started laughing, really laughing, so hard she had to bend over and couldn't talk.

Who knows how long Joanie stood bent over laughing.

How long we stood watching.

When Joanie stood up straight, she held the photo out in front of her, pointed the photo around the room, pointed Fresh Fruit Truman Compotee at each one of us.

Each one of us waiting for the joke.

Then: AIDS! Joanie shouted.

Truman Compotee looks like he has AIDS!

HARRY'S FACE WAS SO white it was green. The deep breath he took, pushed his shoulders up, his head. His chin rolled back and his eyes were staring up.

Both Fiona and I looked up at where Harry was staring at the ceiling.

Harry, in the basement below the dining room, sat just about right under table twenty-eight, which was just about right under the Sistine Chapel God.

Table twenty-eight just about right under the space between man reaching and God's finger.

The hierarchy of humiliations.

Harry let his head roll. Fiona just like that was next to him, her open palms on his neck, her open palms on his head. Harry leaned into her, put his face against her white waitron shirt, put his head on Bernadette's breast.

Fiona's red lips, a life all their own, kissed Harry's head.

Mack Dickson and Davey Dearest and Walter, Chef Som Chai and the Thai kitchen crew, the Puerto Rican busboys, the Mexican dishwasher, had turned into Art Family.

John the Bartender held his hand over his mouth and ran into the toilet. Only cocaine and champagne in his stomach, John's fountain-mouth was one loud long scream and splash, scream and splash.

Joanie had not moved. She still held the photo-booth photo up with one hand, her other hand over her mouth.

Joanie's eyes had the red puffy stare of one who has spoken unspeakable truth.

Mack Dickson stepped out from the crowd, walked slow up to Joanie. His olive-skinned hand made a swipe. Ripped Fresh Fruit Truman Compotee out of Joanie's hand.

Snot out of Joanie's nose; she tried to wipe it.

John the Bartender barfing. Harry weeping. Joanie making little hiccup sounds. Her hands open, palm up.

My God! Joanie said. My God!

Mack Dickson slapped her hard, one cheek, then the other.

Fiona closed her eyes, pulled Harry in closer.

Mack Dickson hit the EXIT door, slammed the door open. Then it was Davey Dearest, then Walter.

The Thai kitchen staff left behind them.

Then the Puerto Rican busboys.

The Mexican dishwasher.

In all the world—abracadabra!—in the unrelenting bright fluorescence, all that was left was John the Bartender barfing in the toilet like Bobbie.

All that was left was Harry kneeling on the floor between Fiona's long legs, shoulder-rolling big sobs into Fiona's lap.

Fiona. Her lipstick a big red scar. Her hair every which way. Black mascara puddles under her eyes. Her porcelain arms a loop around Harry.

All that was left was Joanie standing in her spotlight for life in her pink bra and pink bikini underwear. Sobs so big they'd break a rib.

All that was left was a Brillo box.

All that was left was a tiny photo-booth photo next to my foot on the floor.

All that was left was my naked self.

Even myself.

CHAPTER FOURTEEN

harlie's back was to the door. I was sitting on the bed, and Charlie was kneeling on the floor sucking my cock.

Just like that, Bobbie walked in. The doorknob turned, the door opened, and Bobbie walked in.

Bobbie had her hair done up in a French twist, and she was wearing a new dress Father bought her, shiny pink. Bobbie standing in her new shiny-pink dress she wanted to show me, staring. I tried to get Charlie to stop, tried to push Charlie's head off, but he wouldn't stop, not till I said, Charlie, I didn't lock the door. Not till I said, Charlie, Bobbie's right behind you.

Charlie kept kneeling, turned his head around.

Hi, Princess! Charlie said.

Bobbie's hands on her hips.

What the fuck are you *doing*? Bobbie said.

Giving your brother a blow job, Charlie said.

He's just a child, Bobbie said.

He's thirteen, Charlie said.

He's twelve, Bobbie said.

Almost thirteen, I said.

Then: Did Daddy buy Princess a new dress? Charlie said.

Bobbie jumped at Charlie and Charlie got up quick, turned his whole body around, and faced her. Charlie stood in place, his hands fists, his cock still hard enough to bounce, his face smiling but not his eyes.

Bobbie's arms were out in front of her like she was Superman and going to fly.

That's disgusting! Bobbie said.

Disgusting? Charlie said.

You two! Bobbie said.

Not as disgusting as you fucking your father, Charlie said.

Like she was holding a planet of the known universe, Bobbie bent forward more, spread her arms more. You could see she'd shaved under her armpits.

If you can fuck your father, Charlie said, I sure as hell can suck your brother's cock.

Bobbie's fingers spread out; her fingernails were painted the same pink as her dress.

We're not so different, Charlie said. I like Parker dick as much as you.

Bobbie stepped forward quick, swung hard with her open hand, and slapped Charlie across the face. The slap was loud and stayed in the room. Charlie didn't move.

Then Charlie swung hard with his open hand and slapped Bobbie across the face. The slap was loud and stayed in the room. Bobbie didn't move.

Then Bobbie slapped Charlie.

Then Charlie slapped Bobbie.

Those two would've kept on forever until the both of them were bloody stumps, I knew, so I covered myself with a pillow and pushed them apart at the hips, stuck my head up in between them, pushed myself up through.

I was shorter, looking up.

Charlie and Bobbie chin to chin, eye to eye.

Charlie didn't look down at me, didn't blink, kept staring right at Bobbie.

Then: Will, Charlie said, take that fucking pillow off your cock. You got nothing to be ashamed of.

I looked over at Bobbie.

Bobbie didn't blink, didn't look down, kept staring right at Charlie.

You heard him, Will, Bobbie said, You got nothing to be ashamed of!

So I dropped the pillow, my feather pillow I always slept with.

All of us silent, all of us all one thing.

My heart, the broken pieces scratching up against my chest.

The pillow on my green rug, Charlie's cinnamon-brown feet, my pink feet, Bobbie's feet in nylons in her shiny black patent-leather shoes.

Of course I started crying. Big sobs, snot running out my nose, my chest up and down.

Then pretty soon Bobbie was crying and then Charlie was crying too. Two of us naked, one of us in a shiny pink dress, all of us a forearm apart, crying. Then Bobbie leaned over to me and hugged me and said, I'm sorry, Will honey, and Charlie leaned over to me and hugged me and said, I'm sorry too. And then we were all hugging each other and we were crying so hard, big loud sobs and body jerks, crying our guts out.

Stayed standing, holding each other up that way, most of the afternoon.

Charlie and Bobbie and I are still standing there.

THE SECRET PACT was Bobbie's idea.

Bobbie and I were sitting on the two-by-six boards of the swings on the old swing set, not swinging up high, just letting our bodies roll around in the swings, our hands on the rusted chains, dragging our feet on the smooth concrete. Bobbie and I chewing on stems of the good kind of grass, the sun low, just starting to set, making the sky fancy with colors. The wind through the cottonwood trees sounded like God whispering. Charlie'd just ridden ayaHuaska home to Viv's double-wide, and Bobbie and I were sitting in the swings, rolling rolling.

Then: You and Charlie been sexifying for quite a while now? Bobbie said.

Bobbie had changed into her plaid pedal pushers and white top. Bobbie was looking at her thumb, scraping pink off her thumbnail.

Beginning of the summer, I said.

You do anything else? Bobbie said.

What else? I said.

Besides blow jobs? Bobbie said.

We jerk off, I said. And rub up against each other, I said. Then one time we cut each other's wrists, and became blood brothers, I said, And promised.

Bobbie pushed her feet against the ground and swung back. Forward and back, forward and back, faster and faster, Bobbie pumped herself up in the air higher and higher. Bobbie's body was dark and the sky was orange and apricot and the swing made the back-and-forth squeak, the squeak pitched higher and higher as the swing got higher. Bobbie's hair was flying all around her head: off her face when the swing went forward, into her face when the swing went back, and sometimes just all over the place because of the wind. Bobbie got the swing so high she almost went all the way over.

Then Bobbie quit pumping, just let her legs dangle, and the back-and-forth, back-and-forth of the swing got slower and slower, and the swing sound not so high-pitched, and pretty soon Bobbie in the swing was sitting still next to me.

Bobbie's pink thumbnail was bleeding.

Just the wind and the way things sound at sunset.

The horrific whisper: Promised?

What did you promise? Bobbie said.

My breath in. My breath out.

To always tell the truth to each other, I said. That our secrets are always safe with each other, I said. We promised to always respect each other and never forget each other.

Bobbie's big brown eyes. She reached her hand across from her swing to my swing, put her hand palm up against my open palm.

Just then was perfect, the exact moment in between dog and wolf. *Entre chien et loup.* The world went from day to night, the wind stopped, the cottonwood trees stood perfectly still, and, in the whole world, Bobbie's whisper was the only thing you could hear.

Bobbie's whisper: Charlie and me. We got to do that.

THE WAY BOBBIE figured it, she and I were the same in blood and Charlie and I were the same in blood, so she and Charlie had to be the same in blood too.

So the next day we saddled up ayaHuaska and Chub, and Charlie rode ayaHuaska and Bobbie and I doubled on Chub. The spots on ayaHuaska's butt said: wind.

Big wind, Charlie said.

Horse farts, Bobbie said.

We tied the reins together and let the reins go and we played Going Slack. Charlie and ayaHuaska in the lead, Bobbie and me on Chub, just behind. Just like old times, the three of us riding free, the wind in our hair, the long yellow grass fancy-waving, the blue sky coming down all the way around us.

Charlie did the Hooker Arm Drag and the Saddle Spin.

Bobbie wasn't going to be outdone so Bobbie and I worked it out, and Bobbie and I stood up on Chub, and Bobbie and I did a Duet, our arms sticking out, and Bobbie and I felt the way we'd always wanted to feel. The way the ocean feels, rolling rolling, or why birds like to fly so much.

Double Hippodrome Stand.

Through the paths in the willows to Spring Creek, galloping, willow leaves and branches stinging our face and arms, Charlie ahead on ayaHuaska, Bobbie and me on Chub, we rode until we got to our willow tree.

Who can get their clothes off first?

Bobbie was the first, way ahead of Charlie. Charlie was still on his Levi's buttons when Bobbie dived off the bank, the smooth round white arc of her in the blue sky, big splash into the blue-green water.

Charlie's body, then mine, one arched uninterrupted muscle each, one long breath through clear water, one long hot dusty day; our youth.

Whooping and hollering, water in our ears and nose, our breath in and out, in and out, the mud under our feet sticky and deep.

THEN LATER, LYING on the grass in the sun, naked on our towels. Bobbie's towel a cornflower-blue rectangle. My towel a white rectangle. Charlie's swimming-pool blue. Bobbie lined up the three towels, just so, facing north and south, Bobbie in the middle, each one of us chewing on a stem of the good kind of grass, swatting deerflies, frogs and crickets going, a blue jay yakking in the willows, dragonflies, a water snake through the soggy grass. The sun heading west, the sky yellow bright.

Bobbie got up, walked to Charlie's Levi's and picked them up, took Charlie's red Swiss army knife out of the pocket. I turned my eyes away when Bobbie walked back. The hair of her down there, I never did get used to.

Bobbie knelt on her cornflower-blue towel and sat down on her calves, her back to the sun. Bobbie took Charlie by the wrist. Charlie sat up.

Bobbie's first slice across Charlie's wrist drew blood.

Charlie looked at the blood coming out of his wrist, then up at Bobbie, over to me.

We got to be equal in all of this, Bobbie said.

Charlie's hair was wet and hanging down his back. So black and wavy in the sun. For a while, Charlie didn't know what to do with his face. His black eyes under his broad brow were two dark holes. Then Charlie smiled. The gap between his two front teeth was another dark hole.

Bobbie handed the knife to Charlie and held out her wrist. Charlie laid the knife blade on Bobbie's wrist, but he didn't cut.

You son of bitch! Bobbie said. Cut me or I'll cut your fucking balls off.

Charlie pushed the knife and sliced. You could hear the slice.

Blood coming up out of Bobbie's wrist, rolling down her forearm. Blood coming up out of Charlie's wrist, rolling down his forearm.

Charlie pressed his wrist to Bobbie's wrist and with his other hand grabbed Bobbie's forearm. Bobbie put her hand around Charlie's forearm. Charlie leaned his forehead against Bobbie's forehead.

Magpies in the willows, blue jays yakking, frogs, crickets. The sun on the down side. All at once, everything loud and bright and full.

My sister, Charlie said, I promise to always tell the truth to you. I promise that your secrets are always safe with me. I promise to always respect you and love you and never forget you.

A drop of blood fell on Bobbie's cornflower-blue rectangle.

Now you go, Charlie said.

Bobbie reached behind Charlie's neck and pulled Charlie to her, forehead to forehead.

My brother, Bobbie said, I promise to always tell the truth to you. I promise that your secrets are always safe with me. I promise to always respect you and love you and never forget you.

I promise, Bobbie said.

I promise, Charlie said.

CHARLIE AND BOBBIE slid down the bank to the water and washed the blood off. It took awhile for the bleeding to stop. We tore my T-shirt in half and wrapped one half around Bobbie's wrist, the other half around Charlie's.

We were lying on our towels again, Charlie on his swimming-pool-blue rectangle, Bobbie in the middle on her cornflower-blue rectangle, me on my rectangle of white. Chub and ayaHuaska were snorting, tail-swatting deerflies, munching on the green grass.

Charlie was up on his elbows, looking over at Bobbie's breasts. Charlie's cock was getting hard.

Charlie getting hard started getting me hard.

I tried to think of something else. Starving Korean children. President Kennedy getting shot. The Mormon church taking over the world.

Bobbie pulled herself up and leaned back on her elbows.

Bobbie's hair was wet and pulled back off her face. Her cheeks were rosy from the sun. Her neck was long and her breasts curved down to her nipples, the slope under her breasts. Her belly was flat and in the sun the light blond hair on her white skin. Then, farther down, the dark hair of her crotch.

Never did get used to that hair.

THAT WAS WHEN you two first made love, Bobbie said, Wasn't it?

When? Charlie and I said together.

When you became blood brothers, Bobbie said.

Charlie slapped a mosquito on his back. Bobbie slapped a deerfly on her ass cheek.

Well, I said, Not really. Charlie was always jerking off, and sometimes I'd help him out.

But, Bobbie said, That was the first time the two of you *made love*, right?

Made love? I said.

Charlie sat up, crossed his legs, and crossed his arms over his crotch.

That's right, Charlie said. That day was the first time.

We made love, I said.

A big old rainbow trout jumped up out of Spring Creek right then, and Charlie and Bobbie and I all saw the trout, and we went: Ah! Wow! Fuck! Did you see that? That was a rainbow!

All of us sitting up, pointing. All of us all one thing. All that was left of the trout, a circle of water going out.

YOU'RE GOING THIS way and then shit happens and then you're going that way.

Fatum.

Trouble in my forearms, up my arms, down through my heart, splash down into stomach.

So that's what we should do, Bobbie said.

Bobbie didn't look over to Charlie or to me. The sun was straight in her face, the circle of water on her face, sun reflected.

Do? I said.

We should make love. Bobbie said, All of us.

What? I said.

Charlie's eyes two black holes in his face. Underneath his hands, in the shadows, the head of his cock poking through, leaking cum.

You're brother and sister! Charlie said.

And Cotton Parker is my father, Bobbie said.

And you two are both males, Bobbie said. Homos. They throw you in jail for that. So what the fuck?

Bobbie, I said.

Bobbie pulled a piece of grass out of the ground, the good kind, stuck the stem in her mouth, chewed on it, then took the grass out of her mouth, held the stem like a pointer, and shook the pointer in Charlie's face. In my face.

Listen up! Bobbie said. All of us, each one of us here, is fucked up.

Goddamned square pegs in a world of round holes. Ain't one of us fits in anywhere. And we never will. Ain't one of us got a friend in the world. And I doubt we ever will.

Charlie 2Moons, Bobbie said, You're a half-breed oversexed homo.

Will Parker, Bobbie said, You're a crybaby and a homo and don't have the gumption to hurt a fly.

And me, Bobbie said, Me, Barbara Lynn Parker, I'm a sixteen-year-old slut who's fucking her daddy.

Now I might be wrong, Bobbie said, But I don't think so. There ain't a whole lot of hope for us. We ain't got a prayer, Bobbie said. Not one of us.

Bobbie lifted up her shoulder nearest me, leaned her head in to the shoulder.

Unless we win the lottery, Bobbie said. And fucking Idaho don't even *have* a lottery.

Fuck hope.

But we got each other, Bobbie said. And now we got each other's blood, and you two got each other's cum. And I feel left out, Bobbie said. We're all in this together. We've promised to love and respect each other and keep one another's secrets. This will be our secret. The thing that we'll never tell. The thing that will bind us together forever.

Bobbie poked Charlie in the arm.

Charlie 2Moons, Bobbie said, Your fucking dick's hard just thinking about it!

The strips of my T-shirt around Bobbie's wrist, Charlie's wrist, big red splotches of blood.

What about a baby? I said.

The wind in the tules, the willows. Frogs and crickets, deerflies. Mosquitoes. The whole noisy afternoon.

Bobbie turned her head around to me, spit out grass juice. Bobbie's big brown eyes.

Baby? Bobbie said, Baby? What fucking baby? I ain't never going to *have* no fucking baby!

ON HER CORNFLOWER-blue rectangle, Bobbie spread her legs just as wide as her cornflower-blue towel and put her hand in her hair down there. She pushed off her hips. She pulled the folds of her aside down there. The red-pink hole in the dark-brown hair.

With her hand up and down, Bobbie showed us how to make the little man in the boat stand up.

Deep Flower, Bobbie said.

First Charlie put his hand down there and rubbed up and down with two fingers like Bobbie did. Bobbie made a low sound and lay down off her elbows, her hair spread out against cornflower blue, her eyes staring up at the sky.

Then I put my hand down there. I was surprised it wasn't a small hole down there like the hole at the end of my cock. And how gushy Deep Flower was and warm and endless. I pulled my fingers up and down on Bobbie's man in the boat.

The clitoris, Bobbie said, The clit.

It was like a piece of gristle you wanted to bite.

Charlie kissed Bobbie full open kiss on the mouth. I kept pulling my fingers up and down and Bobbie was arching her back and making little cries. Charlie was hard, his cock poking straight up at his belly button like it does. Cum tracks and love strands all over his belly, his leg, Bobbie's leg.

I was hard too and I reached down and put Charlie's cock in my mouth. Bitter in the back of my throat. Charlie pushed his cock in and out, in and out, Charlie humming some tune.

Then I put my mouth into Deep Flower, on the clitoris, bit gristle like I wanted, sucked on it, made a line around the clit back and forth, up and down, with my tongue. Bobbie's pubic hair softer, browner than Charlie's.

Equal in all of this.

Charlie put his cock in her first. His cock up into her all the way. All around me, on my skin, I felt the miracle the way Charlie and Bobbie fit.

Kiss me, Will, Bobbie said.

I put my lips on my sister's lips, just touching. Bobbie whispered, and when she whispered sometimes her lips touched my lips, sometimes not.

It's our secret, Will, Bobbie said.

I closed my eyes tight and pretended she was Charlie and kissed her.

Charlie had Bobbie's legs pushed up high and Charlie was in and out, in and out, faster and faster. His eyes were up to Saint Theresa Gone to Heaven, his back was arched, chin up, Charlie looking back at the sky. Then Charlie started screaming and I put my hand over Charlie's mouth, and Bobbie pulled my hand away from Charlie's mouth.

Let him scream, Will! Bobbie said. It's what we all live for!

Charlie's scream howl yell sob, like Indian music, high, off- key, full with everything.

MY TURN WAS like the first time with the Hippodrome Stand. I just couldn't get my cock to stay hard to do it. Not till Bobbie turned around and knelt down on her hands and knees on the cornflower-blue rectangle, and pushed herself into me. Charlie held my head with his hands, looked at me way down inside me. Then Charlie kissed me, one of his soft kisses that I wanted to last all day.

My lips against Charlie's, Charlie humming some tune.

The silent rising of the phalli.

Warm and wet and tight inside Bobbie. The smooth soft round of her hips. Connected at the hips. A feeling like dragonflies on my tongue, creek mud in my balls. Wind all around my head, rainbow trout jumping, willow leaves for hair.

My cry yelled out into Charlie's mouth, the savage beast, the sweet, sacred secret cry we all live for.

Bobbie's cry at first I thought was me. When my ears heard the cry was hers I knew it in my blood: It was the cry inside Bobbie all her life.

Looks like pain, sounds like pain.

The little scream that gives it all away.

Help.

CHARLIE WAS LYING in the muddy grass. Mud on his knees, his butt, his face. His long wavy hair all undone, in the mud. Bobbie was lying curled up into herself, perfectly inside the cornflower-blue rectangle.

I was on my knees.

To God.

The tune Charlie was humming was "America the Beautiful," the *above the fruited plain* part.

I let myself fall, just let go, splat onto the muddy grass.

No Known Universe. No map. Nowhere. No way out but in.

Bobbie, Charlie, and me lying crooked like after a tornado, arms and legs every which way.

We are all still lying there, in the meadow, on the muddy grass, after the tornado: Bobbie, Charlie, and I.

Roadkill.

CHAPTER FIFTEEN

Sparrows in the trees in Sheridan Square Park, and the streetlamp light made the lime green of the trees look neon.

That's where I saw Rose.

But it's not the truth.

It was Argwings Khodek I saw. On the poster in the theater window for upcoming attractions.

The face that stared back at me from the poster had extreme eyebrows painted on his forehead, and gobs of eye makeup and lipstick, a dark red drape over his head, and a long black wig.

Theater of the Ridiculous presents:
ARGWINGS KHODEK PLAYS ANTIGONE.
ONE-WOMAN SHOW PERFORMED IN ONE ACT
ON THE PIANO, THE ACCORDION, AND THE VIOLIN.
Tickets on sale at the box office.

On my way back home, just down from Saint Luke's Hospital, a young man sat in a doorway. He was wearing penny loafers with no socks, khaki pants, and a blue T-shirt. Short-cropped hair, Armani glasses, Polo. The young man was holding his knees and rocking back and forth, wailing and sobbing.

He was not Charlie 2Moons, but Charlie had wept like that, and even myself I had wept like that too.

I went to go over to sit next to the young man, hold his hands, hold him steady, be the somebody else there for him, but like everybody else in the street I walked on by.

He was already dead and I was dead too.

When I got back to the piles of garbage and the squares of smiling people holding beers looking up at me, I realized I was home.

Sitting on the stoop of 205 East Fifth Street were Rose and Mary and Mona and Jack Flash.

Rose's T-shirt said FUCK BERNHARD GOETZ.

There were two Budweisers in the '53 DeSoto, cold ones. I put the beers each in a brown paper bag and just before I went back out on the stoop, I opened the window, moved my boom box around so the speakers were pointed out the window, and turned the volume up.

Power 95 was playing Michael Jackson's "Beat It." When I got out on the stoop, "Billie Jean" came on.

On the stoop next to Rose, old Mary was panting panting, and Mona was an overweight Italian girl panting, and Jack Flash panted with his head between Rose's butt and the cast-iron step.

I sat down, handed a beer to Rose. Rose tipped his beer up and I tipped my beer up, long drinks. Rose's black thighs were as big around as my waist, the skin shiny, slick with sweat. He was wearing his leather-tooled studio flats. The only other thing on his body was a pair of black Speedos—smuggled grapes under those Speedos.

You been looking for your buddy? Rose said.

Not-looking, I said.

The way Rose looked at me, I knew I had to explain myself, so I told Rose about the killdeer bird and the trick she plays on you, and how when I looked for Charlie 2Moons I didn't look for him.

I rolled cigarettes, one for me, one for Rose. Lit Rose's, lit mine.

Right next to me Rose's arm, his skin, the green Bakelite bracelet, the copper bracelet, the silver Sikh bracelet, the gold bracelet with the lapis, the jade bracelet, clack-clack.

Rose's lips were full and round and black at the line where lip meets face, then inside, that color, not pink, not fuchsia. Rose, sunset rose, the inside color of Rose's lips. Where else on his body was that color?

Then: Say, I said, I saw you on a poster tonight.

Antigone, Rose said.

On the accordion, I said.

And the piano, Rose said. Perhaps the violin.

Antigone, I said, Just who was she? I get so confused. I said, The Greeks and the Romans with the same gods calling them different names.

Rose tipped the Budweiser up. The light from the porch of 205 East Fifth on the wet brown bottle.

It's all drag, Rose said.

On Rose's forehead, there were two horizontal lines, parallel, then from the bottom line, two vertical lines, parallel, down to in between his eyes. The bump in between, like a clitoris.

I came, I saw, I conquered, Rose said. What the Romans conquered they made their own. Same old story.

The more Rose talked, the higher he lifted his chin. Sometimes all he could see was sky.

Rose, beautiful according to Africa. Deep, violent beauty, jungles of heat, sun-baked Sahara, a black snake winding along the rim of a sand dune.

How's the play end? I said.

Everybody dies, Rose said.

THAT'S THE WAY the evening started. It was always that way with Rose. Sit your butt down on the stoop, crack a beer open, break the ice by saying something nice like *I saw your face on a poster*, and before you know it Jack Flash is under the stoop, there's a quick fuss, then Jack Flash comes walking up the steps with a dead rat half his size in his mouth, and you look over at Rose, at the gap between Rose's two front teeth, at Rose's lips, and Rose is talking talking, and you're up to your eyeballs in Theology, Shakespeare, and Greek Mythology.

Wasn't long and the beers were gone and there wasn't any more beer in the '53 DeSoto, so I went to the deli and bought another six-pack. When I got back, on the stoop next to Rose was a bottle of mescal, cut-up fresh limes on a white linen napkin, and a shaker of salt.

Power 95 on my boom box: Madonna, "Like a Virgin."

Rose unscrewed the cap on the mescal, tipped the bottle up, drank, handed the bottle to me.

Forgot I had this, Rose said.

The mescal was the color of piss after B vitamins. A dead worm floated on the bottom.

A big smile on Rose, nostrils flaring. The black pieces of coal that were his eyes direct into my eyes. The gap between his two front teeth. The black snake.

Whoever gets the worm, Rose said, bracelets clack-clack, Gets his wish.

In my forearms first, the fear, then up to my shoulders, splash down through heart, cattle prod to my cock.

Rose. His breath, the sunset color of the inside of his lips, his open mouth, his Sahara Desert open palms, Rose's heartbeat, Rose's black skin. Africa.

And me, just me, my broken language, my broken dick, my broken heart.

The worm in the mescal floated at the bottom of the bottle.

All that mescal between me and the worm.

Then: All daring and courage, I said, All iron endurance of misfortune, I said, Make for a finer, nobler type of manhood.

I took a swig and handed the bottle back to Rose.

You're on, I said.

So Rose and I passed the bottle back and forth, back and forth between us, on the stoop, surrounded by garbage, photographs of people smiling and drinking beer staring up at us, mercury-vapor light, flies, garbage stink, three dogs and a dead rat, traffic, cars and vans and trucks and taxis hitting the pothole, Power 95 "What's Love Got to Do with It" on the boom box.

Rose tipped the bottle up, Rose's chin up up, poured the mescal down his throat, his Adam's apple up and down, up and down.

I'm going to plant a cherry tree right there, Rose said, and pointed to the rectangle of earth where I'd plant the cherry tree.

I tipped the bottle up, took a long drink, sloshed the mescal inside my mouth. Through my heart. Splash down into the stomach.

There should be a cherry tree in front of Two-oh-five East Fifth Street, don't you think? Rose said.

The bottle was between my legs on the cast-iron step.

Surprised they even grow, I said, in this place.

Trees will always grow, Rose said. Trees are kind and enduring.

But look at all this fucking garbage, I said. What a mess this place is.

Rose took the bottle, tipped the bottle up, took a long drink. When he gave the bottle to me, Rose's eyes were black holes in a white firmament.

Out of balance, Rose said. The sun and the moon, light and darkness, male and female. Out of balance.

The Greeks called it the Golden Mean, Rose said, And an excess on either end of the scale causes imbalance. Imbalance disrupts order, Rose said. Destroys context, creates chaos.

Rose set the bottle down on the cast-iron step. I started rolling cigarettes, one for him, one for me; lit his, mine. The way Rose inhaled, the way Rose stared straight ahead at something inside him, the way

Rose exhaled the smoke through his flaring nostrils, I knew I was in for a Rose soliloquy, so I quick took a drink, a long one. No worm.

In the beginning, Rose said, bracelets clack-clack, The world was female, one huge maelstrom of being. The problem was there was no place for the male. But this one day something happened, and an Alpha male stepped outside the maelstrom and said, Wait a fucking minute! This is too confusing. I'm going to *think* about the huge revolving maelstrom instead of constantly rolling around in it. And then the Alpha male sat down like Rodin's sculpture, *Man Thinking*.

Rose on the stoop, on the third step, sitting like Rodin's *Man Thinking*. The porch light across Rose's shoulder made *Man Thinking* a blacker blue.

The male principle, Rose said, Provided a scaffolding, provided order. And pretty soon, everybody was *Man Thinking*—men and women both—and now we're all sitting and thinking about it rather than being it.

Look around us, Will, Rose said, At the imbalance, at the garbage, the monkey chatter, the mind chaos. We are living in a time where meaning has been obliterated by an excess of the male. We take it as given that the world outside us must be approached through thought. We are so busy filling the void, we are filling the world with garbage. We take it as given that the White Paranoid Patriarch—who is the master of domination, achievement, *veni, vidi, vici*—is our voice, our spokesman. We take it as given that Christianity and the belief in Jesus H. Christ as our savior is the only religious truth because some white guy says so. We take it as given that some Polish sausage is the Vicar of Christ on earth. We take it as given that it is not fiscally possible for the ordinary American citizen to have access to health care. We take it as given that more Latinos and African Americans should be in prison than go to university. We take it as given that women do not make as much money as men. We take it as given that Native Americans are a conquered people and should live on those patches of infertile land we let them have. We take it as given that sex is male penetrating female.

We are living in a world of false assumptions, Rose said, bracelets clack- clack. Ergo: that which appears to be is not.

Rose reached up to my ear, pulled a quarter out of it, laid the quarter in my open palm.

Now don't get me wrong, Rose said. Without the male principle we would still be spinning in the eternal maelstrom. We need the male principle to exist. It's the *balance* of the male and the female that's important.

I know plenty of men, Rose said, Who have more female energy than most women. And vice versa.

Rose's chin was way up, Rose staring, so I looked up too and there it was across the street, the moon just above Mother's Sound Stages.

Our society, Rose said, Is based on hatred of everything the Greeks called female. Our society hates everything we can't rationally explain, everything dark.

Everything black, Rose said, bracelets clack-clack.

The dust-storm light from the streetlamp was just under the moon. The two lights together were WALK and DON'T WALK. On East Fifth Street, to the left, to the right, no people walking. No Charlie 2Moons.

I picked up the bottle, missed my mouth, mescal all down the front of my Guinea T-shirt.

It's a mess, I said.

Life is a mess, Rose said. You can fix the mess human beings make, Rose said, But you can't fix the mess being human is.

L'énigme! Rose said. The Golden Mean is sought but never found.

I tipped the bottle up, looked quick to see how far was the worm, couldn't even see the worm, so I just drank and drank and drank.

No worm.

I handed the bottle back to Rose.

Then: You're Catholic, Rose said.

Not anymore, I said.

In recovery, Rose said.

Yeah, I said.

With Catholicism, Rose said, One doesn't recover.

Rose tipped the bottle up, sloshed mescal, swallowed, Adam's apple up and down, up and down.

One has to reupholster, Rose said.

When Rose took a drink this time I saw the worm float up.

It's absurd—life, Rose said. But by acknowledging the absurdity there is a consciousness, a self-reflection that, with refinement, can bring a certain enjoyment. Don't you agree?

I was smiling, stopped smiling. The bottle was on the step between my feet. I took a swig, set the bottle on the stoop between us, and rolled a cigarette—one for Rose, one for me. Lit his, lit mine.

The Top Forty was over and I'd been listening to Rose so hard I missed what number one was, and the music was sounding like CBGB's, so I got up and went in and changed the radio station from Power 95 to Harlem WBLS at the end of the dial.

Rose yelled in the window at me: Bring your lovely erect pink penis back with you!

Rose put a rabbit turd of Sho-ko-lat into the erect pink penis, lit the rabbit turd, sucked in, sucked in again, then handed the erect pink penis to me and I sucked in the hashish smoke so much sweeter than marijuana, started coughing right off, and handed the erect pink penis back to Rose, and Rose took two hits—never more than two, Rose said— and then he took two more.

Rose burped big, lifted his leg, and let go a fart. His arms and hands waving in the air in front of him, bracelets clack-clack.

Don't get me started, Rose said. The whole goddamn Christian story is a load of crap. Christianity never dwells on those awful nasty three days Christ was in darkness. Christianity puts its blinders on like good little sheep and waits for the Hallmark card in the mail on the bright Easter Sunday morning.

Rose handed me the erect pink penis. I handed Rose the bottle. I toked, Rose chugged mescal.

What about our Higher Knowing? I said. Susan Strong says to listen to your Higher Knowing.

The two parallel lines on Rose's forehead dipped down into the two verticals, the clitoris bump between his eyes. Rose set the bottle down hard on the step, bracelets clack-clack.

This fucking New Age shit drives me mad, Rose said. My Higher Knowing, my black ass. New Age, same old fucking story.

Puritanism, Rose said. Pure Unadulterated All-American. White trash contemplating the mysteries of the universe, Rose said. Steven Spielberg filming an Ivory Soap commercial on location with the Nike of Samothrace.

What about my Higher *Unknowing?* Rose said. What about darkness?

Rose handed me the bottle. I handed Rose the erect pink penis. The bottle was half empty, half full.

You mean like in *The Exorcist?* I said.

Rose's bracelets clack-clack.

No, Rose said, Like in the Garden of Eden.

THE DISTANCE ACROSS Rose's Sahara Desert palm was the distance from the top of the mescal to the worm.

Darkness is not something out there that we must make rules against, Rose said. Darkness is not something we must reject from our lives. Darkness is part of us.

Without our mantle of darkness, without pretty Jesus, without the feminine, Rose said, bracelets clack-clack, We should perish in an angry God's light.

The unrelenting fluorescence from above, I said.

Rose's black eyes looked real close at me. He had the pipe and the bottle, one in one hand, the other in the other.

Rose poured salt on the back of his hand, slugged down a shot, bit on a piece of lime.

In a society, Rose said, Where darkness has no place, the society is a fluorescent madhouse.

It's not that there's too much darkness, Rose said, There's too much light. The dark womb protects us from the unrelenting.

These days, chaos is not unrelenting darkness, Rose said. Chaos is unrelenting light.

After the second rabbit turd, after a salt lick, another slosh of mescal, lime, my head was in my hands and I was *Man Thinking* thinking.

The Shy Hunter knows underneath it all there is nothing, no thing, Rose said. The *thing* is a lie, an illusion. The only *thing* there is is your concept of the thing. That's Illumination.

The worm was three inches away.

Rose took the bottle, tipped the bottle up, drank and drank and drank.

Then: He was Catholic too, you know, Rose said.

Who? I said.

Ricardo the voodoo super, Rose said. You saw his eyes—Santa Theresa Gone to Heaven.

We haven't had a super, I said, Since Christmas?

Rose's black eyes into my eyes. Just now you notice? Rose said.

Rose picked the bottle up, held the bottle up close to his eyes, turning the yellow mescal through the porch light. An inch to the worm.

The Greek hero, Rose said, Is *allowed* to struggle against the superior power of fate. Not like this submissive Christian shit that turns everyone into a flock of sheep.

Why would somebody fight against their fate, I said, If they knew they were going to lose?

Because we are fools, Rose said. And because the lucid compulsion to act polemically determines the substance of the self. By going against the gods, you become more and more who you are.

I had the bottle.

You know, Rose said, You forget to stutter when you're drunk.

MY FINGERS WERE way stoned rolling the cigarettes. You know how it is when you're loaded, you just go off somewhere and watch yourself. I had fingers and was sitting with my big pink Idaho legs sticking out of my khaki shorts on a stoop in New York City, but where I was really, I was a naked marble statue wrestling with a big black snake that was the fate I was struggling against.

It was late and quiet, and for the first time in New York City I felt the way I'd always wanted to feel in New York City—hot in my Guinea T-shirt on a dirty street on the Lower East Side late at night with my friend Rose, drinking mescal, each of us a can of Bud, the erect pink penis, rabbit turds, Mary, Mona, and Jack Flash lying around with their tongues hanging out like wet bologna. The taxis were honking on Third Avenue up and Second Avenue down, sirens swirled around us, the air humid and heavy, and everything sounded the way things do when it's hot in the summer. The garbage cans stunk to high heaven and hot flies were landing on us and we'd slap them off. The piss smell came up from under the stoop where the men from the men's shelter on Third Street always pissed. The taxis and the police cars, going by yellow, going by blue, going by all other colors of cars in the mercury-vapor light, and the cars bouncing when they hit the pothole where the city repaired the water lines last winter, mufflers banging against the chassis, heading west because it's evens east and this street's odd. My boom box was cranked up on WBLS, coming through my open window over the sound of my oscillating fan. Rose, my friend, and I on the stoop, listening to the clear smooth kind of saxophone jazz that made you listen because the black man playing the song didn't care if you listened or not, just playing his song how his heart was inside him, the way your heart was inside you too, on fire the way the night was, longing for things that probably weren't going to come, and sad because you knew they probably weren't, but still foolish enough to wish, but most of all clear, and smooth, and beautiful.

High enough to think I was New York.

I drank and swallowed the worm.

Smiling. I was smiling.

I swallowed the worm, I said. I conquered my fate.

Then what's this? Rose said, and lifted the bottle to the mercury-vapor light.

I looked, my eyes up close.

Another worm! I said. Stopped smiling.

The worm, Rose said.

No, I said. I swear, I said, I just swallowed the fucking worm!

There weren't *two* worms, Rose said, There was only *one*.

Rose tipped up the bottle and drank the rest of the mescal and the rest of the worm. Rose set the empty bottle down hard onto the cast-iron step.

L'amour de la bouteille, Rose said. The last drop in the bottle is the love of the bottle.

Rose looked up at the mercury-vapor streetlamp light, put the fingers of both hands together, stetched his arms out, his palms up, and cracked his extra-lovely knuckles.

All right, Rose said, We *both* get wishes. You go first.

No, I said, You go first.

No no Yoko Ono, Rose said. You ate the worm first, Rose said, So you go first.

I WISHED MY dick wasn't broken, wished my heart wasn't broken. Wished Charlie 2Moons would come walking up. I wished I wasn't so afraid. Wished to press my body up against Rose.

But it's not the truth.

I wished Rose wouldn't make the wish I figured he was about to wish.

OK, I said, I made my wish.

What is it? Rose said.

I'm not telling, I said.

You got to tell, Rose said. We're splitting the worm, so you got to tell.

I looked around for something, anything. Little squares of smiling people holding beers looked up at me.

Language my second language.

I wish, I said, I could find Charlie 2Moons, I said, Everything would be all right then, I said, If I found him.

Below the prizefighter bump, Rose's nose came down his face to a point, like the tip of a thumb, and under the point each nostril was big enough to put a thumb in. The nostrils flared out when he talked, a life all their own.

My mouth had a life all its own too.

My mouth would not speak.

Then, finally:

And, I said, What's, I said, *Your* wish? I said.

In Rose's eyes, a Mack truck.

My wish, Rose's lips said, Is to go out to dinner with you, my treat.

My heart beat. My breath. God, I wanted to kiss Rose right then.

Dinner? I said, smiling, then stopped smiling, That's all?

Then: Cool, I said.

Rose stood up crooked. When I stood up, down the stoop, the sidewalk was a lot farther than three steps away.

Rose burped big, put his extra-lovely hand around the cast-iron railing, reached his one foot back into his leather-tooled studio flat, then the next foot.

Rose stepped wrong off the step and just like that Rose was head over heels, his eyes rolled back up, his chin up up, his face turned to the sky—waving his arms in circles, bracelets clack-clack. I reached out to grab him, but Rose was already gone. Ass over teakettle, Rose hit the back of his head on the opposite hand railing; then he rolled down the steps, the sound, the unmistakable sound, a bang, a big fucking bang, the dogs yelping and barking and trying to get out of the way, then Rose was lying spread-eagle on the sidewalk, on all those little squares of smiling people holding beers up.

As soon as he hit the cement, Rose was back up standing, crouched down the way cornered animals move. Rose's eyes were staring ahead at nothing, at everything. Not on the premises.

In nothing flat, I was down the steps and next to Rose. I remember looking over at my hand in the air on the way to Rose's shoulder, the porch light on my hand, and when my hand touched Rose's shoulder, Rose ducked down and swung around kung fu. His extra-lovely foot struck me in the stomach, kicked the breath right out of me.

Never touch me.

When I woke up, *I* was the one spread-eagle on the sidewalk and the squares of little people. My head was in Rose's lap, and Rose's extra-lovely arms were cradled around me. My head was bouncing up and down, Rose was crying so hard. I smiled and then stopped smiling and just let myself lie that way for a while, my eyes closed, my head bouncing up and down, in Rose's arms, in Rose's lap. Jack Flash was licking my arm.

Then: Why you crying, Rose? I said.

Rose didn't smell like Polo. Hard ebony-smooth his eyes. Nostrils a life all their own. His lips, the inside color of his lips. Rose went to speak but his lips wouldn't let him. Rose's breath in. His breath out.

Fuck! Rose said. Only you would ask a question like that.

Are you all right? I said.

Rose put his bottom lip over his top lip, slid his bottom lip down.

I'm fine, Rose said. Just made a goddamned fool of myself.

Rose put his Sahara Desert palm onto my cheek.

And you? Rose said. How bad does it hurt?

There was a rock in my gut, but I was breathing.

First rule, I said: Never touch me.

One big tear came out Rose's eye and rolled down over his eight-ball cheekbone, then down the line to the corner of his mouth.

First rule, Rose said.

Up the stoop, to the left, Mrs. Lupino was looking out her window down at Rose and me. Behind Rose's head, I flipped her the bird.

We lay there like that for for a while, just listening to how quiet New York can get. A gust of wind hit the cherry trees, and the leaves sighed and scratched.

Who knows how long I lay in Rose's arms that way.

I am still lying in Rose's arms.

When shall we have dinner? Rose said.

I'm off Mondays and Wednesdays and sometimes Thursdays, I said.

Next Thursday? Rose said.

Thursday's cool, I said. Then: Could we, I said, Could we go somewhere special? I said, I mean if you can afford it?

Name the place, Rose said.

The Waldorf, I said. And not for dinner. *Lunch*, I said, Lunch at the Waldorf.

Lunch at the Waldorf it is, Rose said.

In the narrow blue hallway, in the unrelenting fluorescence, Rose set the cooler down, handed me the erect pink penis.

Don't forget this, Rose said.

My hand touched Rose's hand when I took the pipe.

Without it I am nothing, I said.

YOU'RE GOING ALONG this way and then shit happens and then you're wounded by a blow of love.

Just like that, Rose put his extra-lovely arms around me.

Mrs. Lupino's door opened a crack.

Rose kissed me on the mouth. Inside lips against mine. A full lips-to-lips kiss. I didn't breathe. Mrs. Lupino closed her door.

Rose's lips at my ear:
Doubt thou the stars are fire;
Doubt that the sun doth move;
Doubt truth to be a liar;
But never doubt I love.

CHAPTER
SIXTEEN

There were two ways Mother and I played Lunch at the Waldorf. One way I was Mother's boyfriend, either Rory Calhoun or Errol Flynn, and I wore my Sunday clothes and shined my shoes, new-shoe stiff, and clipped the clip-on tie to the collar of my white shirt, and wet and parted my hair, and sometimes, when it was Errol Flynn, with her eyebrow pencil we made a mustache on my lip.

The other way I was a girl, Hedy Lamarr or Garbo, and I was her oldest and dearest friend and was visiting her from Hollywood or New York or Paris or Rome or Barcelona.

I remember one Lunch at the Waldorf especially. It was the last time we played. Mother was pregnant and was walking around inside the house, close to the walls. She was crying hard, and I thought for sure she was going to run out into the field.

Instead, in the afternoon Mother took a bath. She stayed in the bathroom a long time, and I could hear her crying in there.

When she got out of the tub, after she set her hair in pin curls, Mother walked in her yellow terry-cloth bathrobe into the front room where I was playing with my Tinkertoys. She sat down on the green couch and put her bare feet together on the flowered carpet.

Lunch at the Waldorf? I said.

Mother's eyes up, Saint Theresa Gone to Heaven, full of tears.

Who am I? I said.

I WAS HEDY Lamarr that day, because Hedy Lamarr wore the green taffeta dress with the big buttons and the white shoes.

Mother put the cloth tablecloth on the table and put coffee into the percolator and plugged the percolator in. She set the table with the coffee cups with matching saucers, the little spoons, the fancy bowl with the sugar cubes, and the fancy creamer. She made toast in elegant shapes and sandwiches with the toast with watercress or dandelion leaves or mint jelly. Mother wore the violet dress with the orchid all the way down the front, and fluffed her hair and put on her eyebrows and the Orange Exotica lipstick, and a touch of Evening in Paris behind each ear from the tiny deep-blue bottle, her high heels with the holes in the toes, her nylons with the seams.

In the kitchen, at the table, we started with Mother saying, Oh, how I love lunch at the Waldorf!

Then I'd say, Oh, how I love lunch at the Waldorf too.

But this day, because she was crying, only I said it. I had to say everything that day, do everything.

I poured the coffee, mixed the cream in, and one cube of sugar the way she liked it, had to get out the Herbert Tareytons she hid from Father in the drawer next to the kitchen sink. I gave her a Herbert Tareyton and lit the kitchen match on the stove and watched her pull the flame into the cigarette. Then I went in her bedroom in the second drawer of her nightstand and got the magenta velvet photograph album with the gold edges, and put the photograph album on the table between us, the way she always did, but this day I did it.

First, I rubbed my hand over the velvet of the book, smoothing each corner. Touching the book that way made it there. When you opened the book you could smell the pictures. The sound the book made when you turned the pages was like it was on fire.

On the first page was the first photograph of her. I told the story the same way, the same words she used, like I was her telling me.

This is when I traveled by train alone to visit my cousins in Saskatchewan, I said. I put my finger at the bottom, careful not to touch the photograph, then pointed around to each corner, to the four black corners that held it in the book.

I said: I was eighteen and that old car was a Model A and it's my Uncle Fritz's. You can't see it, but Uncle Fritz is playing the accordion and I started dancing, lifted up my skirt just a little and started dancing. I always loved that hat.

When I turned the page to the second photograph, during the sound of the page, the smell, I looked sideways over to my mother. She was smoking and wasn't crying.

That's when I worked at Newberry's, I said, pointing my finger the way she always pointed hers, first on the page, then at the four black corners. I said, A dollar five an hour. That was just before I married your father. This photograph was taken my last day at work. The night before, I went to a liquor store and bought a pint of whiskey even though I wasn't twenty-one. I lived in the Dolley Madison Arms, a rooming house for women, and I took the pint of whiskey home in my purse. I had taken some snow and made the snow into ice cubes and set the snow ice cubes on the windowsill outside. I had stolen a glass from Newberry's—you mustn't ever tell that your mother was naughty and stole something—the crystal kind you put whiskey in, and I took the snow ice cubes I had made and put them in the crystal whiskey glass. I had my room just the way I liked it with everything clean and just the one light on. Then I opened the closet door with the mirror so I could see myself, and I put on my favorite dress, this one I'm wearing—the violet one with the orchid all the way down the front—and my nylons with seams in them, and my high heels with holes in the toes. The mother-of-pearl earrings. Then I sat and drank the whiskey, looking in the mirror, watching myself sip, listening to KSEI on my radio, the top ten hits, and I danced, I really danced.

Perfect, I said. Just perfect.

I love to dance, I said.

That's when we'd dance in the front room to Mother's two records, her only records, her favorite ones, "My Buddy" and "Slow Poke." "My Buddy" first because it was slow and easy and got you into the mood, and then "Slow Poke" because it was faster and we could twirl.

The best part was waiting for the record to drop, standing with her in the front room, always the boy when we danced, my hand on her hip, my other hand holding up her hand, our feet on the flowered carpet, the drapes pulled, the light through the drapes, Evening in Paris, waiting for the record to drop.

Both of us silent, both of us all one thing.

The needle on the record, that sound, my first invitation to far away, Mother and me dancing in the front room, smiling, somewhere else, the both of us, somebody else.

But that day, she wouldn't dance.

So I turned the page, the sound of the page, the smell, to the third photograph, looked sideways over to Mother and she still wasn't crying, and I got her the ashtray that said 30 Club on it.

My wedding day! I said, pointing again to the page under the photograph, the frame of the black corners. I sighed, deep, the way she always sighed, and said, On the steps of Saint Veronica's. Look! Your father's big hand is on my shoulder, his other big hand about to scoop me up. What a dreamboat! Took me three weeks to make that dress, white satin, and the veil—I thought I'd never get it right. The bouquet is Baby's Breath and daisies, white daisies. It was snowing.

The fourth photograph was the last one, and when I turned the page, I looked over sideways to Mother and she was smiling. Mother was smiling.

Honeymoon's over! I said, and clapped my hands, and then my mother clapped her hands, the way she always did, and that's when Mother started laughing.

That's the damn Holstein cow my mother gave us as a wedding present, I said, A kicker! And that shack the cow's tethered to, behind us, is where I lay down with him. Never expected that. Didn't know what to expect, bliss I guess, but not sex. *Gott im Himmel.* Sure never expected sex!

That was the end of the photographs. I closed the album. Mother was laughing so hard her gums were showing and she wasn't making a sound, and for a while I thought maybe she was crying and that she'd run out into the field, but she was laughing, her gums were showing, and she was laughing so hard she lost all her eye makeup, and I loved that she was laughing, and I was laughing too and it was so funny that mother and son went away between us and there we were in all the world, two people laughing.

I remember I promised myself I'd always try and make Mother laugh that way.

Then Mother put her arms around me—something I never got used to—and held me real close up to her big belly with my brother in there, the beads of the orchid of her violet dress against my face.

What else.

I made another promise, the promise she asked me to make.

Oh, Willy, she said. Promise me one thing, will you?

Yes, I said, anything.

The horrific whisper.

No matter what happens, even if something bad happens, Mother said, promise that you will always love me. That you won't forget me. That you'll remember me. Promise me you'll never leave me.

Herbert Tareyton breath, green eyes right into my eyes, her hands on my shoulders, Evening in Paris, Orange Exotica lipstick, my mother said this to me: Why else do we live, except to be loved and remembered by those we love?

I promise, I said.

CHAPTER
SEVENTEEN

At Columbia University, in Dodge Hall, the guy with real red hair and black horn-rimmed glasses behind the desk said Sebastian Cooke was still on sabbatical and Janet was on vacation.

I pulled the chair up, straddled the chair, started rolling a cigarette.

Where'd you learn to roll smokes like that? Red Top said.

A friend of me and Janet's, I said.

Cool, Red Top said.

Then: You know Janet?

And Sebastian, I said. Met them through Charlie 2Moons.

Red Top pushed his black horn-rimmed glasses back up his nose.

God, he said, Charlie was so *cute*.

Wasn't he? I said. And a real sweet talker.

Red Top's glasses were tinted yellow. Made it look like his eyes were soaking in piss. He started moving papers around on his desk.

Then: What the hell, who cares what a bunch of assholes think?

I just said: Did you and Charlie ever, I said, Have sex?

Red Top turned beet red all over. Even his fingernails were blushing.

No, Red Top said, I didn't really know him. I was in Sebastian's class with him.

He and Sebastian an item? I said.

Red Top just stayed red. Through his black horn-rimmed glasses, he watched my fingers finish up the cigarette.

Janet said they were in love, I said.

Red Top's eyes were red inside all the yellow.

When will Janet get back from France? I said.

I'm not sure, Red Top said.

How's Sebastian? I said. I hear the French hospitals are good.

Yeast infection in the stomach, Red Top said, Then pneumocystis, now this.

Karposi's? I said.

Janet told you? Red Top said.

Yeah, I said.

Then: I lost Sebastian's address, I said. Can you give it to me?

Sure, Red Top said.

THAT NIGHT, I got out my favorite fountain pen and the bottle of black ink. I filled the pen with the ink, and in my circle of light, at the *Father Knows Best* table, in my best penmanship, my words out of the pen were beautiful onto the yellow page. Just how one word looked next to the other was beautiful.

Dear Sebastian Cooke. I forget all of what I wrote. I told him what my Art Family told me to tell him. Told him everything. I folded the yellow pages into thirds, put the pages into the business-size envelope, licked the flap, stamped it.

ONE NIGHT, RIGHT after I got home from work, my red telephone rang. I didn't pick up.

On the tape, around and around, traffic noise, breathing. Ruby coughing coughing. Then Ruby hung up.

A half hour later another call.

Ruby.

Just like that, I decided to go find Ruby. I quick grabbed my wallet and my keys and I was out the door. At Second Avenue, I hailed a cab.

I didn't know where to go, so I said, Below Houston, south of Alphabet City.

ON THE CORNER of telephone and telephone, Saint Jude phone booth, last call. I didn't know who it was in the phone booth at first.

At first, it was some kind of painting of a skinhead in a bright telephone booth, a cyclone fence, shiny bits of light in the dirt of the vacant lot. In all that dark.

I walked up slow behind the booth, looked in through the glass on the side.

The man was bald and he was wearing a Hawaiian shirt and khakis hanging low, no butt to hold up his pants. Brown boots square toe with the gold ring on the side. Two blue moons tattooed to his forehead. On his forearms, on his neck, purple bumps.

The skeleton poking through Ruby's smile.

Ruby had a quarter in his hand. He was trying to get the quarter into the coin slot. In slow motion—between his thumb and finger, the quarter held up next to his nose—Ruby in slow motion dived his head and his hand and the quarter to the coin slot but missed.

Then, slow motion, Ruby stood up straight, held the coin again next to his nose, and dived his head, his hand, and the quarter slow motion to the coin slot, but Ruby missed again; he missed the telephone altogether and almost fell forward, slow motion, caught himself, stood up straight, held the coin next to his nose, dived his head, his hand, and the quarter slow motion to the coin slot, missed.

Who knows how long I stood there, leaning up against Saint Jude phone booth, so close to Ruby I could smell him. Ruby slow motion high, horse diving at AT&T.

I'm still standing there.

Then, some kind of miracle, Ruby got the quarter in the slot and the quarter dinged.

Then: Six, Ruby said aloud, and slow motion dived his head and his finger to the six, but missed.

Then: Six, Ruby said aloud again and slow motion dived his head and finger to the six, hit the six, pulled the dial to the right.

Then: One, Ruby said aloud, and slow motion dived his head and his finger to the one.

Then: Four, Ruby said loud.

I pressed my forehead against the glass, reached my hand around, touched Ruby Prestigiacomo on the shoulder, but Ruby couldn't feel me.

Seven eight seven zero, I said.

But Ruby couldn't hear me.

THE MONSTER'S HEAVY footfall.

I had to sit down right there on the curb, my head between my knees, my sensible black shoes on New York City pavement.

Big sobs, snot running out my nose, my chest up and down, up and down.

Who knows how long I sat there.

I'm still sitting there.

Then, out of the blue, a black guy in an African hat put his hand palm out to me.

I reached up and took his hand. In his palm was a dollar bill.

Peace, brother, the guy said, and walked on.

Chin quivering, snuffing up, I was staring at the dollar bill in my pink palm. Then—abracadabra!—out of nowhere, an Asian woman, a little girl holding onto her hand, reached in her pocket, pulled out a quarter, and put the quarter on top of the dollar in my hand.

AT HOME, AFTER I showered, I pushed PLAY on the red answering machine.

Around and around on the tape, Ruby's breath in and out, traffic sounds, someone crying.

Even myself, me.

Then a low voice, far away: Peace, brother.

IF YOU UNDERSTAND that the difference between fool and Harlequin is Harlequin knows that behind his costume he is hiding, then you'll know what's important about Rose and yourself, and why you've come to New York.

Lunch at the Waldorf.

I was not Rory Calhoun that day, not Randolph Scott, not Errol Flynn, not Hedy Lamarr or Garbo.

On the corner of Park Avenue and Fiftieth, I was Jimmy Stewart, including the hat, rolling a cigarette, standing in front of the bright doors of the Waldorf Hysteria, just at the place where True Shot had parked Door of the Dead van my first night in Manhattan with the French Vogues. The sky was real blue with sifty clouds pointing at the sun. Warm, big gusts of wind up the avenue.

Two o'clock the third Thursday in October, on the corner of Park Avenue and Fiftieth, a cab pulled up and a guy with a long white beard, no mustache, wearing a black turban and a long blue-black velvet cape got out. Lots of gold. Gold rings, gold bracelets, a gold loop in his queer ear, a thick gold choker. Purple fingernail polish. A gust of wind blew the velvet cape and the cape flew up, the wings of a crow.

It was Rose.

Rose and I embraced and kissed like they do in Europe, both cheeks. The doorman opened the door and I took Rose by the arm, the way a man takes a woman by the arm, and Rose and I walked that way, the Sheik of Araby and Jimmy Stewart, into the Waldorf Hysteria.

The people in the foyer, the Calvin Klein Polo tweeded Ronald

Reagan and Nancy Connecticut blond tourist Republican people, were staring at us. Every eyeball on me and Rose.

Rose smiled theatrically, bowed deep to the crowd.

L'Amérique profonde! Rose said.

My first impulse was to run. I'd never been out in *L'Amérique profonde* with Rose before. But Rose's hand was tight around my arm, and so I stood.

Rose was extra tall in the black turban, extra strong. And Rose's black eyes, two shiny round ebonies steady straight ahead, meeting every gaze with his.

All my life I'd been new-shoe stiff, clean, pressed, polite, driving the speed limit. All my life I'd done all I could not to get noticed, and there I was in all the world in the lobby of the Waldorf Hysteria, every eye in the place on me, arm-in-arm with the Queen of Conspicuous.

Rose and I walked arm-in-arm up the stairs, through the crowd, Rose smiling and waving his hand, elbow elbow, wrist wrist wrist, the Queen of England.

The huge clock in the foyer struck two chimes just as Rose and I stepped into the restaurant. A Brazilian version of Daniel the boss's brother in a tuxedo flashed his Rolex and showed us to a table in the back corner. One business-suit guy looked up and poked his friend, but Rose didn't see.

When I put the match flame onto Rose's cigarette, Rose's eyes were on the match, then Rose closed his eyes, inhaled, and leaned back, and, just like that, Rose was an old photograph of Rose.

BLACK AND WHITE, a shadow across his face, Rose in a black turban and beard leaning against a fringed brocade cushion between a peacock mural on his right and a brass vase of primroses on his left, Rose just opening his eyes, just about to look at me, just starting to smile.

Rose is just about to say, Even myself, I am just here, isn't it?

You put the photograph in a magenta velvet photograph album with gold edges. This is when I lived in New York City, and I had lunch at the Waldorf with my friend, an Arab prince.

WHAT YOU LOOKING at me that way for? Rose said.

I'm taking a photograph, I said.

Paparazzi wherever you go! Rose said.

You ever know a guy named Ruby Prestigiacomo? I said.

The magician, Rose said.

What? I said.

Prestigiacomo means magician in Italian, Rose said, And no, I do not know him.

You're a lot like him, I said.

The magician? Rose said.

Ruby, I said.

We both exaggerate ourselves so we can be noticed? Rose said.

Is that what you do? I said.

No, Rose said.

TURN THE PAGE of the velvet book; the sound of the page turning sounds like fire.

The photograph of me, my elbows on the table, my Jimmy Stewart hat pushed up off my forehead, my tie an old pattern of butterflies and dice, my big face, crooked bottom teeth, intelligent Tom Selleck–handsome Einstein, the look on my face like I'm about to ask a question.

Rose? I said. You're a Shakespearean ac-*tor*, I said. You know all about the Greeks, you're doing a one-man show of Antigone on the accordion and piano and maybe the violin, you're a Shy Hunter, Elizabeth Taylor is your best friend, you're an extra-lovely African American who lives upstairs from me with your three dogs, and you kissed me on the lips.

I think of you as my friend, I said, But I don't know anything about you. Rose, I said, just who *are* you? Where did you come from?

Rose looked down at the Gauloise box, closed the box with his fingers, the purple nails, then looked back up, his ebony eyes hard stones.

Bloomingdale's, Rose said. I had some things to pick up.

The Bloody Marys came right then. The waiter's name tag said RAMON and he was short with black hair and had a little mustache and those big glasses that are light sensitive. He set the Bloody Marys on the white linen tablecloth.

Rose tapped the ash of his Gauloise into the cut glass ashtray, then raised his Bloody Mary. I raised mine and we toasted.

The story, Rose, I said. Tell me your story.

The black turban, the glued-on Sheik of Araby beard. The gold loop in his queer ear.

Rose put both his arms up on the back of the banquette. His right hand under the peacock mural, his left next to the brass vase of primroses. Rose's Adam's apple up and down, just above the gold choker.

You want story, Rose said, Or do you want *history*?

Sixth rule, Rose said. The stories you tell tell more truly who you are.

Jimmy Stewart took a bite of his celery.

So tell me your stories, I said.

Then I'll tell you about Antigone, Rose said.

Antigone?

Rose's eyes were even darker under the black turban, the coiled-up black serpent, ready to spit.

Hers is the story I'm telling these days, Rose said.

For lunch Rose ordered a bottle of the Graves, and the medallions of veal with basil and oven-roasted tomatoes and cappellini. They didn't have a Waldorf salad, so I ordered the chef's salad with fresh grilled artichoke, roasted beets, and spiced green lentils.

When Ramon presented the bottle of Graves, Rose asked me to test the wine, so I did my Vin et Vous gurgling routine and didn't get a drop on me.

Dry, spicy, I said, Just the right touch of fruit.

The primrose color inside Rose's lips. Rose's big Harlequin smile. The liar's space between his two front teeth.

Then: Your story first, Rose said, bracelets clack-clack.

No, I said. I asked you first.

But, Rose said, You are my guest. Guests always go first. Will Parker, Rose said, What on earth is *your* story?

The crystal wineglass was at my lips. Through the bottom of the glass, Rose was distorted like I was on True Shot's mirrors. I put the glass down, wiped the moisture of my fingers against the starched white tablecloth.

William of Heaven, I said.

What? Rose said.

My friends all call me William of Heaven, I said, And I was born in a trunk, I said, In the Princess Theater in Pocatello, Idaho.

Rose smiled big, the gap between Rose's two front teeth. He raised his wineglass.

Well, then, William of Heaven, Rose said, Here's to stories!

Here's to stories! I said and lifted my wineglass. We clinked.

Fuck history, Rose said.

Fuck history, I said.

Fuck hope, I said.

Then: Why Antigone? I said.

Rose lowered his chin, his face up close to my face, his ebony eyes hard stones.

Comment? Rose said.

Why not Electra, why not Ariadne, why not Athena, why not Madonna, why not Elizabeth Taylor?

Rose put both hands to his turban and moved it to the left.

Are you mildly curious, Rose said, Or do you really want to know?

Still a half bottle of Graves, two inches left of Bloody Mary.

I'd like to know, I said.

Maybe there's some things you shouldn't know, Rose said.

I took my Jimmy Stewart hat off, undid my tie.

Maybe there's some things, I said, You're afraid to tell.

I was smiling. Stopped smiling.

Rose's smile got bigger.

That one may smile and smile and smile and be a villain, Rose said.

I'm preying, I said, For truth.

The gap between Rose's front teeth. The inside color of his lips.

Then: You know I'm falling in love with you, Rose said.

My heart beat. My breath.

Rose, I said, Why Antigone?

Rose's chin started going up. He folded his Sahara Desert palms together. One huge black fist. He rolled just his eyes down from the ceiling. A muscle under Rose's right eye, ticking.

Give me one good reason, Rose said, Why I should tell you.

I put my skinny pink hand on Rose's one big black fist. I'm your friend, I said. You can trust me.

Rose folded his Sahara Desert palms around my hand. Trust? Rose said. In Rose's eyes, the deer in the headlights.

Sweet William, Rose said, Dare I trust the truth of my sore heart to you?

Why do we live except to be loved?

Yes, I said. I am a Shy Hunter, I said, Also.

I folded my hands inside Rose's, like when you pray but don't stick your fingers up.

I promise, I said.

La promesse.

Then: Waiter! Rose yelled out. Waiter!

The Peacock Room quiet as only New York can get that fast.

Two dirty Bombay Sapphire martinis up with olive! Rose yelled. Chill the glasses!

ROSE PUT HIS chin in his hand, rubbed his chin.

Antigone, Rose said.

His eyes moved up to the ceiling, down to the floor, then side to side across the whole room.

My hands were tight around the Bloody Mary glass. Maybe what Rose wanted to say, Rose couldn't say yet.

Then just like that, Rose snapped his fingers loud.

Let's say I'm Rupert Murdoch, Rose said.

Rose picked up the largest silver knife next to his plate. He balanced the silver knife on the end of his index, then let the blade end tilt down.

And my power of persuasion, Rose said, Is strong enough to convince you that this knife is in balance, even though both you and I can see plainly that it is not.

Where we get into trouble, Rose said, Is when we are persuaded to see balance where there is no balance, order where there is no order.

Rose tossed the silver knife in the air, and the knife flipped end to end. Rose caught the knife, and then—abracadabra!—the silver knife disappeared into thin air.

The element in excess so dominates, Rose said, That it creates the illusion of order, of reality, and we live in that illusion as if it were true.

When we live in an illusion as if it were true, Rose said, We are actually living in chaos.

Rose put his elbows on the table, leaned closer and closer to me. We are living in chaos, Rose whispered.

I started rolling cigarettes.

Rose held the silver knife blade pointed directly at my heart.

My entire existence is based on a false assumption of reality, Rose said. My existence is not grounded in my body, my heart, or on mother earth, nature, substance, the firmament, but rather in what I *think*.

What is real, Rose said, Is actually a concept of what is real.

Rose's smile. The silver knife pointed at my heart had become a silver spoon.

We are not seeing with our hearts, Rose said.

We are just *Man Thinking*, Rose said.

Rose's Sahara Desert palm clasped my hand around the silver spoon. Rose put his thumb with its purple nail into the valley of the spoon.

The female, Rose said, Is the bringer of life from out of darkness. She brings life, but because she gave us life, now we must face death.

And therein lies the rub, Rose said. Our fear of death has turned us against the female; our fear of darkness has tipped the Golden Mean to allow the male principle to dominate.

The excess of the male principle, Rose said, Has created an illusion of reality we all assume is true.

But what we are really doing, what we are grounded upon, Rose said, bracelets clack-clack, Is a monster, the excess of the male principle.

The way I was staring at Rose made Rose smile big, made the big old liar's space between his teeth show. Made Rose wipe his forehead with his white linen napkin.

Antigone had the same problem, Rose said. The society she lived in feared the female as well, for the same reason every mother's son has ever hated the female: With life comes death.

Antigone's brother Polynices is lying dead outside the walls of the city, exiled, Rose said. According to divine law, the right thing to do is to anoint his body, but Antigone can't because Polynices has been officially declared an enemy of the state. For Antigone, the law of the state is in contradiction to divine law.

L'énigme! Rose said. The holiest act Antigone can perform as a woman has been declared a crime by the government.

Antigone has two choices, Rose said: Obey the manmade law, or break the law and go where her female heart leads her.

The punishment for breaking the law, Rose said, Was to be buried alive. Antigone knew the stakes, yet she chose to tend to her brother, Rose said, bracelets clack-clack. Antigone broke the law. She dared to go beyond the proper place for women, did not give way when everything was against her, defied the status quo, trusted her heart, tempted madness, and went ahead and anointed Polynices.

Her decision, Rose said, And her action upon her decision restored divine order, restored the Golden Mean.

Ergo, Rose said, Antigone is a classic hero.

The lucid compulsion to act polemically, Rose said, Determines the substance of the self.

Run that by me again, I said.

By flipping off the law of the state, Rose said, Antigone tempts fate; ergo, she crystallizes her freedom and comes to the substance of herself.

All daring and courage, I said, All iron endurance of misfortune, make for a finer, nobler type of manhood.

Womanhood, Rose said.

Antigone is a Shy Hunter, I said.

Exactly! Rose said. Because she follows her heart despite her fears.

I was still rolling cigarettes. I handed a cigarette to Rose, but he shook his head no no Yoko Ono, and pulled out a Gauloise.

Rose, I said, You can't fool me.

Rose pulled the match flame into the Gauloise. Smoke filled his mouth. He kept his mouth open, the smoke curling, then just like that, the smoke went up his nostrils, French inhale.

Fool you, Rose said, Why on earth would I want to fool you?

Because, I said, You're a Shy Hunter, I said, You may be talking about Antigone, I said, But what you're really talking about is yourself.

Silent. As soon as I said *yourself*, the Peacock Room, the Waldorf Hysteria, in all the world, only silence. Silence and the breath of air and smoke exhaled from Rose's nose.

Then: My dear William of Heaven, Rose said, bracelets clack-clack.

Well put, Rose said.

ROSE AND I were on cigars and cognacs when Ramon set the check down on the table—exactly in the middle of the white tablecloth. Just like that, Rose's Sahara Desert palm covered the leatherette folder and pulled the folder to his side of the table.

That was it right then.

Just like that, the world got drunk.

Rose's black turban was sliding down in the direction of his right ear, Rose's lips sliding down same way as his turban, the gold loop in his queer ear all tangled up.

Rose's right eye drooped and his left eye got way open.

Rose put his snifter into the same ring of wet on the white tablecloth.

Even myself, I said, The substance of myself, I said, Is quite drunk.

Rose put his bottom lip over his top lip, the inside sunset color of Rose's lips, the black skin just above Rose's false white beard.

I say, William of Heaven, Rose said, bracelets clack-clack, We shouldn't stop now, should we? What we need to do to is dress it up and fluff it up and get it high. What we need is a real cocktail! Rose said, What we need is Sho-ko-lat!

Rose's arms every which way in the air.

I feel a party coming on! Rose said.

Then let's order another drink, I said.

No no Yoko Ono! Rose said, bracelets clack-clack. Not *here*, Rose said. Not in *l'Amérique profonde*. These Yankees are dry sphincters. Let's go to the Monster! Rose said. It's just about cocktail hour.

Rose tipped the snifter up and swallowed all the cognac, his Adam's apple up and down, up and down.

I have just the outfit, Rose said.

Outfit? I said.

But I've got some shopping to do first, Rose said.

Rose lifted the purple velvet sleeve, and among his gold bracelets was a watch that looked like an hourglass.

What do you say you meet me at the Monster in two hours? Rose said. Seven-thirty?

THERE ISN'T MUCH stopping Rose when he gets an idea in his head. So after we kissed like Europeans do in front of the Waldorf Hysteria, Rose took a cab uptown. I took the subway home, turned the shower on, dialed WBLS on the boom box. Luther Vandross was singing My Sensitivity.

I sat down in the shower, let the hot water hit my face. Who knows how long I sat in the shower. New Yorkers don't recycle garbage or worry about water tables, so I just sat and sat, the hot on my drunk forehead, my knees, down my frog-belly-white Idaho legs, through my toes.

Then my doorbell rang. I grabbed for my blue towel and wrapped it around me.

Like on True Shot's mirrors, Rose through the peephole was a black tumble of turban, big smile, the liar's space. I unlocked my three locks, opened the door.

Rose was so big, I didn't know how he fit in the hallway.

The droop of his right eye, the wide open of his left.

I found *exactly* what I wanted, Rose said.

He lifted up a big bag with BARNEY's on it.

The color is perfect, Rose said.

Purple? I said.

Never you mind, Rose said.

Then: Are we still on for seven-thirty? Rose said. You're not giving up on me, are you?

Rose was looking at my big nipples. I folded my arms in front of me. Then the towel started to slip, so I grabbed the towel.

No, seven-thirty's cool, I said. I'll come up.

Rose's index at me back and forth in the air.

No no Yoko Ono, Rose said. I'll meet you *there*. Come ten minutes late. That way, Rose said, You can see me at the dimly lit smoky bar.

Across a crowded room was what Rose was singing as he made his exit up the stairs.

THE MONSTER HAS windows along the sidewalk and you can look right in at the bar. I stopped on the sidewalk and looked where there wasn't steam. Men inside, so many you couldn't see anything but men. The light was not bright but warm and rose-colored, a haze through the steam.

Above the door, the sign was a black reptile.

A short stocky black man with a gray beard and stocking cap gave me the once-over, asked for my ID. All I had was my Idaho driver's license. He looked down at my ID, then looked up at me again.

Jesus Christ! the guy said. It's an Idahomo! Welcome to the Monster! he said and pushed open the door.

Warm rose-colored light, and loud the way that makes you want to turn back. Hundreds of men drinking, talking. The bar was a rectangle with the bartenders inside; you sat around on the outside. Three or four men deep around the bar. The light was from deco sconces on the walls and a crystal chandelabra hanging above the bartenders.

On the other side of hundreds of men talking was a piano and some men singing. *Lullabye of Broadway. Those Little Town Blues.*

Across the crowded room, at the far end of the bar, Rose, a head taller than anybody. He was wearing a navy blue gabardine suit with Joan Crawford shoulder pads, a starched white shirt, and a wide red, white, and blue tie, the stars and stripes of the American flag. The blue was so blue and the white so white, red so red against Rose's skin.

Rose was sipping a martini up with olive, smoking his Gauloise. From across the crowded room, Rose's head was shiny with rosemary oil. He wore a mustache and a Fu Manchu beard.

Rose was surrounded by men, but right around him there was a space. Eight to ten inches of never-touch-me. The space in between that kept Rose himself.

When I got to Rose, I stood behind him. He was at least a yardstick from shoulder to shoulder. I didn't touch him.

First rule.

Rose? I said.

Rose turned around, well-heeled gentleman. His nostrils flared out, a life all their own. Rose's extra-lovely navy blue arm raised the martini to the sunset color of the inside of his lips.

Rose, a black snake winding along the rim of a sand dune, beautiful according to Africa.

On his left arm, between the navy blue sleeve and Rose's palm, over the starched white cuff and rhinestone cuff link, Rose's bracelets, clack-clack.

The gap between Rose's two front teeth.

Rose, I said, You are so handsome. So Gary Cooper, I said.

It's all drag, Rose said.

He stood up from the high stool, did a turn for me, sucked in his gut a little, puffed out his chest, buttoned the top button of the blue gabardine jacket.

How do I look? Rose said.

In the rose-colored light from the crystal chandelabra and the deco sconces, all at once Rose was a twenty-year-old kid, Roosevelt Washington King.

Beautiful, I said. Fucking beautiful.

Bartender! Another martini! Rose said.

Then, to the guy sitting on the stool next to him, Rose said, You got to leave now.

The guy said, What?

Rose raised his chin up, up, looked down his eight-ball cheeks at the guy.

William of Heaven is here, Rose said, And that's his stool, and you got to leave now.

The guy was skinny, bad silver comb-over hair, just a touch of makeup. He crossed his legs, uncrossed them, looked at me, then up at Rose, took his white wine spritzer, and got off the stool.

Even ourselves, Rose said. We are just here, isn't it?

Rose and I, thigh to thigh, bunched up together at the bar. The top of the bar was shiny wood that slopes to the edge in a curve. The room grew louder and louder. The men around the piano in the back of the bar were singing that song from *Phantom of the Opera*. I looked over at the dark black of Rose's neck. The starched white collar against the black.

When Rose and I clinked glasses—*Salud, Na zdarovya, L'chayim,*
Here's Looking at You, *Usife moyo*—when I put the thin rim of martini
glass to my lips, I remember my breath in, my breath out. I remember I
was completely present and the moment I was in forever expanded.

Who knows how long I sipped at the martini.

I am still sipping the martini.

THAT'S HOW THURSDAY night started. With that moment, with Rose
and me doing what we both like best. Sitting on stoops or bar stools,
watching, drinking. A room full of men gathered under a crystal chandelabra, cigarettes, cocktails, arms around each other at the piano, singing. Human beings in a bar.

All of us all one thing. Getting shit-faced.

Rose ordered another round of martinis. I rolled a cigarette for Rose,
one for me. Lit Rose's, mine.

There's two more questions, I said.

When Rose smiled, Rose had a fake gold front tooth just left of the
liar's space.

What did your father do?

And the second? Rose said.

Do you really know Elizabeth Taylor?

Rose crossed one leg over the other. His socks were also red, white,
and blue. He sipped his martini and put his glass down right into the
ring of wet on the wood bar.

Rose's extra-lovely hand, his thumb and third finger up and down
up and down on his Fu Manchu.

Are you mildly curious, Rose said, Or would you really like to know?

I'd like to know, I said.

My father was president of the United Negro College Fund, Rose said.
He lifted the martini to his sunset lips. And Elizabeth Taylor *adores* my
black ass.

Rose, I said, You're *so* full of shit.

Human beings in a bar, Rose and I laughing.

The bartender brought the martinis. He was young and pumped up,
wearing a camouflage T-shirt. Both the bartenders were all style and
performance, throwing the mixer in the air behind their backs, flipping
bottles, pouring drinks into glasses from above their heads.

Do you think the bartenders are sexy? I asked.

Rose lifted the martini glass to the inside color of his lips, sipped, put the glass back down.

There's got to be something wrong, Rose said, Something a little off, before I find a man sexy. Some kind of scar or crack or wandering eye—something broken about him that's been repaired, or he's trying to cover up.

These two bartenders—Rose waved his hand, bracelets clack-clack—well-thought-out bodies. Now I ask you, Rose said, Who'd want to fuck a well-thought-out body?

Not one surprising bone! Rose said.

The whole time they'd be counting the repetitions, Rose said.

TO OUR RIGHT, men were crowding up.

They were standing in line to get in the bathroom. The bathroom was a single toilet where you could lock the door.

Facilitates things, Rose said.

Fascilitates what? I said.

Cocaine, Rose said, You can lock the door and do your cocaine. White death, Rose said.

You don't do cocaine? I said.

That is correct, Rose said.

No shit? I said.

Don't get me started, Rose said, and as soon as Rose said *Don't get me started*, Rose started.

A Republican plot, Rose said, bracelets clack-clack. Opiate the yuppie masses leading lives of quiet desperation, Rose said. It's the White Paranoid Patriarch drug.

Think about it! Rose said. White powder that gives you a sense of potency, importance, and lucidity.

One snort and *voilà!* You act as if you're the primogenitor of Mountbatten.

Snorting cocaine, Rose said, bracelets clack-clack, You always end up in the burbs in somebody's bright kitchen at four in the morning talking about municipal bonds and real estate.

Every line of that white powder you put in your nose or in your veins, Rose said, You are perpetuating the illusion that there is something profound out there and you are privy to its profundity.

Adding insult to injury, Rose said, Every line of that white powder you put in your nose or in your veins, you are putting your good money into the pockets of the White Paranoid Patriarch Vicious Totalitarian Republican Assholes.

Ergo, the enemy, Rose said.

I'd be willing to bet, Rose said, That at this very moment, Noriega and George Bush are dining on Beluga caviar—champagne and dancing boys—on us, Rose said, On the 'Merican people, on all us welfare queens in designer jeans.

Even myself, Rose said, I only take drugs that enhance the folly, the pageantry, the foolishness, the lie, Rose said.

I was rolling cigarettes.

WITH THE TWO martinis, I had to stand for a while up against the wrought-iron fence of Sheridan Square Park. Rose put his navy blue cashmere overcoat on, didn't button it, and for a moment stood next to me and stared up into the trees too. Then he grabbed my arm and Rose and I were walking arm-in-arm along the park fence with the bare trees and the chirping sparrows.

A black guy with long dreads every which way, smelling of old wine, a big rip in his pants and wing-tip shoes, no laces or socks, something on his face—dried blood all over his face—stopped on the sidewalk, held out his hand, palm up, and said, Hey, brother, can you spare some change?

Rose reached into his pocket and pulled out some change and put it in the guy's palm.

Two or three more steps, and from behind us, the guy said, Nigger? Is that all you got? Eighty-five cents?

Just like that, Rose wasn't walking next to me anymore but was back to the guy. The guy didn't move, just stood there with his hand stuck out, palm up. In the streetlamp light, the guy's eyes looked red, just red, and the silver change in his palm was shining. Rose hit him—I mean that's what I thought at first—but the swipe I saw of Rose's arm wasn't a blow. The swipe was Rose snapping up the change from out of the guy's hand.

Hey! Fuck you, man! the guy said. Give me my money back! This guy stole my money! the guy yelled. The motherfucker stole my money!

Rose in the streetlamp light, his coat collar up, patent-leather shoes flash-flash: Rose walked back to me, then was walking next to me, and at Seventh Avenue, Rose threw the eighty-five cents into the gutter.

Fag! the guy yelled. Nigger fag!

People on the street all around us stopped. Quiet as only New York can get that fast.

Rose's hands were in his coat pocket. He was looking down in the gutter at the three quarters and the dime.

That nigger, Rose said, quiet, Better watch his mouth in *this* neighborhood. Old African proverb says, Never insult the crocodile in the middle of the stream.

CHRISTOPHER STREET WAS a merge of yellow cabs, red brake lights, headlights, horns honking. So many people, no place on the sidewalk to walk, people walking in the street. A convention of policemen and drag queens, or some kind of holiday for women on Harleys. The sound of things so different too—there was still the traffic and the trucks and garbage trucks and sirens and the Harleys and the squealing tires, but underneath was a Saturday-night sound and it wasn't Saturday night.

Not far down the street, some wild-ass cowboy, silver-studded boots, John Wayne hat, stepped out of a bar, the open door of the bar so loud the disco beat *Tainted love, oh tainted love,* and the cowboy stood on the stoop, smiling like a goon, half again as tall as the humanity on the street, high enough to think he was New York. He leaned back, took his hat off, let out a big Ya-hoo!

Across Sheridan Square, Rose stepped out onto Seventh Avenue and made a high-pitched whistle by putting his fingers in his mouth the way Bobbie and Charlie used to. One yellow taxi cut across traffic—all honking horns—and drove right over to Rose and me, slowed down to right in front of us, and then sped up again, drove a ways down the street, and stopped.

I've never seen Rose move so fast. Just like that, Rose was down standing by the taxi. When I caught up, he had his hand on the open back door.

Rose hunkered down, put his extra-lovely body into the backseat of the cab, pulled his legs in. I got in after him, closed the door.

It was one of those taxis that doesn't have bullet-proof Plexiglas between the front seat and the back. Rose leaned his body over the front seat, put his one arm over the seat. His face right up next to the driver.

No yelling or screaming or anything.

You're going this way and then shit happens and then you're going that way.

Rose put the barrel of a silver revolver at the driver's temple. Pushed the barrel hard into the driver's skin. The driver kept looking straight out the windshield and Rose's lips were right in his ear, moving slow.

Above the meter, the taxi driver's photo, a rough-skinned big-boned face stared out; above the photo, Andre Something with a bunch of consonants all together and his driver number.

Rose? I said.

Shut up! Rose said.

I did what I always do when I don't know what to do. I pulled the tobacco and the papers out of my pocket, and started rolling a cigarette.

Turn the meter on! Rose said.

The driver slow reached his hand out, not moving any other part of his body, pulled the meter lever down.

The red lights of the meter flashed on $1.75.

Drive! Rose said, and pushed the driver's head over more with the silver revolver barrel. Two-oh-five East Fifth Street, Rose said. Between Second and Third.

The driver took Seventh to Houston, turned left on West Houston, the whole time Rose's silver revolver at the driver's temple. In the mirror I could see Rose's lips moving, speaking into the driver's ear, but all I could hear was a low mumbling, couldn't hear what Rose was saying. Outside the cab, speeding light, darkness, speeding light.

The driver didn't say a word, stared straight ahead.

I lit the cigarette.

The meter was $2.25, $2.50, $2.75, $3.00.

At the stoplight at Houston and First Avenue, the driver turned left. Rose, I said, Put the gun down. Please!

Rose didn't turn around. Didn't move at all. Just kept the revolver pushed up hard.

We're not home yet, Rose said.

At Fifth Street, the driver turned left again, past the A&P, past the Ninth Precinct. On the sidewalk outside the Ninth Precinct there were two cops, sitting on motorcycles, talking to each other. The traffic light on Second Avenue was red: $5.25. $5.50.

Inside the deli, an old woman was picking up garbage out of the garbage can and throwing the garbage at the man behind the counter.

The light went from red to green and we drove across Second Avenue.

Toward the end of the block, Rose said, On the right.

The driver stopped in front of 205 East Fifth Street.

Stop the meter! Rose said.

The driver slow-reached his hand out over to the meter, pushed the lever up.

Let's see now, Rose said. Five-seventy-five plus twenty percent is what?

About seven dollars, I said.

Give him eight, Rose said.

I reached in my wallet. Thank God I had a five and three ones.

I handed the eight dollars over the seat so the driver could see them. The driver's hand was shaking shaking. He curled his fingers around the money.

I opened the door, got out of the taxi, policing my body, new-shoe stiff, walked over to the rectangle of earth where I'd plant the cherry tree, stood in the dirt.

Rose stayed in the cab, the revolver still at the driver's head. I listened for the gun blast and blood all over the windshield. But all I could hear was Rose talking low. Then Rose poked his extra-lovely butt out the door, stood up, slammed the door. Kept his revolver in his hand until the taxi was at the end of the street and turned the corner onto Third.

Rose sat down on the stoop.

I sat down on the stoop. My breath in. My breath out.

Fuck! I said. I thought you were going to shoot him.

A piece of thea-tah, Rose said, slapping his palms together, bracelets clack-clack. Performance art.

But a gun? I said too loud, then quick looked around us.

Across the street, the Doberman in Mother's Sound Stages sat in the window. A blue car drove by. Then a black Cadillac.

When I spoke again my voice was low.

Is it real? I said.

Of course it's real, Rose said, bracelets clack-clack. Of course it's loaded. To the Shy Hunter every battle is a battle of life and death!

But a gun? I said. You had the gun against his head!

The lucid compulsion to act polemically, Rose said, Crystallizes my freedom.

By putting a gun to somebody's head? I said.

By putting a gun to somebody's head, Rose said.

But why didn't you put your gun against the head of that black bum back there who called you a nigger? I said. Seems like you're being awfully selective on whose head you threaten to blow off.

In fact, Rose said, I *am* very selective. That black bum back there was *born* with a gun at his head.

But what's the fucking point? I said. Like your gun up against that taxi guy's head is really going to make him stop his cab for the next black person?

I don't give a fuck if he stops or not, Rose said. The issue here is not better race relations. Race relations died when Octavian burned the library at Alexandria, killed Cleopatra's son, Caesarion, and the Western World scorned Mother Africa.

The white jig is up! Rose said. The dominant culture is already no longer the dominant culture. It's the white guy's last gasp. Right now in New York City, Rose said, It's about sixty–forty nonwhite to white.

Those who would hunt a man, Rose said, Need to remember that a jungle also contains those who hunt the hunters. Malcolm X said that, Rose said.

Christian Fundamentalism, Rose said. Return to family values. Increase in police forces, emphasis on law and order, construction of more prisons—all these are signs of the White Paranoid Patriarch's approaching extinction.

All these white yuppies, Rose said, In their Volvos with zero population growth, and all these black people fucking their brains out—I'd say, by the year 2020, you white folks are overrun and basically fucked.

When you're old and your skinny white ass is sitting in a old folks' home, Rose said, You watch. It's going to be some really pissed-off brown person who'll be wiping your ass and pushing your wheelchair around.

The effect, Rose said, of my silver revolver, against this fucking immigrant Russian's fucking head was not to make the world a better place to live. My sole intention, Rose said, Was to inform this white man— or any white man who dares to personally insult me—that the jig is up. The prey this White Paranoid Patriarch asshole has been preying on for centuries, Rose said, Is now preying on *him*.

IN THE NARROW blue hallway, in the unrelenting fluorescence, my hands were shaking shaking. The key just wouldn't get into the lock.

Rose put his Sahara Desert palm onto my back. I swear it was the voice of Isaac Hayes who asked, William of Heaven. Will. Please come upstairs with me.

Rose put his arm over my shoulder. His aftershave smelled clean and cool. I put my arm around his waist. Never touch me. We walked that way up the stairs. Each step we took, I thought the step would break.

The blonde on the blonde-fainting couch. I was my mother's nerves, rolling cigarettes. Rose took the silver revolver out of his jacket pocket, opened the chamber. In the kitchen drawer, the sounds of bullets hitting pressboard. Rose spun the chamber, closed it, laid the silver revolver in the drawer, closed the drawer.

He pushed some buttons on the stereo.

Rose sat in his purple-velvet overstuffed chair, Mona, Mary, and Jack Flash on the floor around his feet. His tie was undone. On the brass table, two glasses of beer and the erect pink penis full of rabbit turds, pointing my direction. Johnny Hartman and John Coltrane on Rose's stereo. *They say that falling in love is wonderful.*

Wanna dance, stranger? Rose said.

Only a body can know another body. My head fit perfectly under Rose's chin. My hand fit perfectly on the muscle of chest above his heart. Under Rose's Italian chandelabra, Rose's big arms around me, I was completely present and the moment I was in forever expanded.

Who know how long Rose and I danced?

We are still dancing.

ROSE PULLED OFF my Jimmy Stewart jacket, undid my tie with the pattern of butterflies and dice, started unbuttoning my shirt.

Rose, I said, Don't.

My shirt was undone, the cuffs, my shirt was off. Then Rose knelt down and I watched the muscles move under navy blue gabardine as he undid my Jimmy Stewart wing tips, pulled the wing tips off, pulled my socks off.

Rose, I said, I can't do this.

Rose was standing up, his face way too close to my face. Rose's left eye.

Do what? Rose said. Let a friend touch you? When's the last time someone touched you?

Not long, I said.

Bullshit, Rose said. I mean *touched*. Maybe you've had skin next to your skin, but when was the last time you let yourself be *touched*?

Rose's open palm on my forehead, pressing.

Never touch me.

My Jimmy Stewart pants were unzipped, the fly button unbuttoned, the suspenders off, the pants a pool of Jimmy Stewart around my feet.

Please, Rose, I said. Stop it.

Quit worrying about your famous fucking cock, Rose said. You and your cock don't need to do a thing. All you have to do is lie down on the bed. I'll light some incense, put some music on, and I'll take a white hundrd-percent-cotton Bloomingdale's washcloth and I'll rinse it out with cool water and I'll wash your body.

My breath in. My breath out.

One foot, then the other, I stepped out of my pants.

Down below, under my eyes and my chin, I could see my big nipples poking out, my skinny arms, my stretched-out Fruit of the Looms.

Rose put his extra-lovely palms one on each of my shoulders, bit his lower lip, and looked me straight in the eyes. His left eye too wide, his right nearly shut.

Rose ripped his mustache off, his Fu Manchu, undid his tie, unbuttoned the white buttons of his starched white shirt. Rose's skin so close. When Rose lifted the navy blue gabardine jacket off, his armpits mixed with rosemary oil, his aftershave. Then Rose's hand on his belt buckle, the unzip of zipper.

In nothing flat Rose was just Rose, smuggling grapes under French-cut white cotton underpants.

It's OK, Rose said. William of Heaven, You can trust me.

Trust? I said.

Trust, Rose said.

Rose's lips were right at my eyes.

Rose hooked his thumbs each on the sides of my Fruit of the Looms, his thumbnails against my hip bones.

The inside color of Rose's lips.

Rose pulled my shorts down.

Rose pulled his shorts down.

The insides of Rose's apartment, the chandelabra, the purple-velvet overstuffed chair, the faux zebra skin, the brass tabletop, the light, the red velvet curtains, the steam heat from the radiator: everything touched me. In front of the dogs, in front of the photos and paintings of Elizabeth Taylor, everything, everything touched me, air wind breath spirits on my cock and balls.

The surprising weight of me down there.

I stood Art Family, just stood. Rose lit the candles on each side of Buddha. Sitar music on his stereo. The porcelain pan filled with water in front of Buddha.

Four giant steps to Rose's Joey Heatherton bed. I was butt up, flat on my belly. The sound of water dripping into water when he squeezed the cloth.

Rose sat on the bed and my arm touched Rose's thigh. Then his hand, the cool washcloth, against my back, down my sides, down my spine to just above my butt crack.

A drop of water running into my armpit.

Is this, I said, What Antigone did for her brother?

Something like it, Rose said, Yes.

Down my arms, the slow soft cool washcloth down my biceps, on my elbows, my forearms, my hands. Rose held my hand as he washed my hand, the washcloth between each finger.

Mother was crazy, you know, I said. Certifiable. We played a game where I was her boyfriend, Errol Flynn or Rory Calhoun. Or her girl-friend, I said, Hedy Lamarr or Garbo. Hedy Lamarr was the green dress.

The wet cool washcloth down my arm, slow into my armpit.

We called the game Lunch at the Waldorf, I said. That's why I wanted to go there with you, I said. Have lunch at the Waldorf.

Mother killed herself, I said. They say it's inherited, I said.

Wherever Rose had touched me was warm, the rest of my body was hot or freezing, I couldn't tell which.

I knew you were nuts the first time I saw you, Rose said.

The sound of water dripping into water.

Rose lifted up my leg from the knee, touched the pad of my foot, around and around, then up in between each toe.

And Father, I said. In prison for life. He was a rodeo clown and a drunk.

My father wasn't a preacher, Rose said, He was a custodian at the high school. He stayed away from drink, but he could be a crazy old goat.

Rose lifted my other leg up from the knee, the washcloth onto my toes. Rose's other hand, the touch, on my lower back.

And Charlie, I said. I betrayed my best friend, Charlie. And my sis-ter too, I said. Bobbie. Father started fucking her when she was eleven or twelve.

The washcloth across my shoulders, up the back of my head, into my hair.

Then: Rose? I said. I fucked her too.

Rose's hand stopped. The washcloth stopped in my hair. Then Rose wasn't touching me. The sound of water dripping into water. Rose's bracelets clack-clack.

The cool washcloth on my buttocks. When the cool hit, I pulled my ass in tight.

Rose, I said. I fucked my sister!

Around and around on one butt cheek, then the next, the muscles stretching, loosening, opening up the crack. The cool washcloth down my crack.

My breath in.

The sitar music had stopped. Only silence.

Rose's voice was deep. It was always deep, but right then Rose's voice was *deep*.

Most people, Rose said, Remain stuck in *Fatum,* believing they are who they are because of the childhood they had.

The sound of water dripping into water. The washcloth down my one thigh, then the next, smooth and slow and cool.

The Shy Hunter, Rose said, Has emerged into his life as a character in a play. The only way out of his pain is polemical. He has to change the role he is playing.

Instead of Polynices, Rose said, He'll play Antigone. Instead of Anne Frank, he'll play Mother Theresa. Instead of Clark Kent he'll play Superman, Rose said.

My body was part of the bed. My hands, fists in the pillow.

Rose touched my shoulder, put his open palm firm on my curve of arm, pulled steady.

I closed my eyes, rolled over.

Silence. Only silence.

Then: William of Heaven? Rose said, Are you still with us?

Through my eye slits, Rose was an outline of Rose in front of the Italian chandelabra. My legs were spread. Rose was kneeling between my legs, his hands on my calves, holding on.

My mother's nerves.

Yes, I said.

Rose's breath, deep, in and out.

And now my dear William of Heaven, Rose said, You said you are my friend. You said I can trust you.

Rose's hands went down my calves to my ankles, his hands gripped my ankles, pulled.

And I believe you, Rose said. But it's not that easy with me. And so I propose a little test.

Test? I said. What kind of test?

Rose let go my ankles and got off the bed, the bed bouncing. He opened a drawer, pulled something from the drawer. When Rose sat back on the bed, he sat by my thigh. When he spoke he leaned over close.

You must trust me, Rose said.

Rose wrapped the ends of a red silk scarf around his hands, pulled the scarf tight. He placed the red silk scarf on the sheet, a gash of red on the white. Rose picked up my left hand, laid my wrist on the red silk scarf, and tied a bow around my wrist like a Christmas present.

I was smiling. Stopped smiling.

Rose, I said. What the fuck?

A Shy Hunter is a warrior, Rose said. The key to being a warrior is not to be afraid of who you are.

Rose tied the red silk scarf onto the bedpost.

In my forearms, up to my shoulders, then up into my left wrist.

Or who *you* are, I said.

Exactly, Rose said.

When Rose went for my right wrist, I jumped myself up off the bed. My body ran smack into Rose, extra-lovely brick shithouse. Our bellies, our chests, our necks were naked, and we were touching.

Rose's lips at my ear: Lie down, Rose said. How can you have a friendship if you can't trust?

I don't want to trust, I said. I don't want a fucking friendship.

Rose pushed me back, took my right hand, pushed my hand down into the pillow.

Just like that, I pulled my left leg up, put my leg between my chest and Rose's. Then brought my other leg up. My feet were against Rose's hips.

I pushed with everything I had.

Between me and the chandelabra light, Rose was a flying body off the back end of the bed.

Silence. Only silence.

My right hand was busy undoing the bow on my left wrist. I almost had the bow undone, when Rose laid his hand, open palm, on my back.

My elbow into Rose's chest.

Fuck you, Rose, I said. How fucking long do I have to take this Shy Hunter shit? Jesus Christ, I said. Why the fuck should I trust you to tie me up? Fuck trust. Bring out your designer gun, I said. Maybe I can trust you even more if you bring out the designer gun.

The red silk bow fell off my wrist. I turned to jump off the bed, but there he was again, all two hundred and sixty pounds of him. Brick Shithouse Rose.

Naked chest to chest, Rose's lips at my ear.

The hero gains the substance of himself, Rose said, By struggling against his fate.

That's when Rose kissed me. The inside color of his lips, his tongue, the sunset color flowing into my mouth, down my throat, through my heart, splash down into stomach, cattle prod to cock.

THE RED SILK scarf was around my left wrist, the yellow silk scarf around my right wrist. Rose tied the Christmas-present bows, then tied the scarves to the bedposts.

In all the world, there I was, naked and tethered to a bed.

My face turned toward Buddha.

Rose lit a pyramid of incense and turned the sitar music back on.

The scarves got tighter the more I pulled.

The fates lead those who will; who won't, they drag.

Rose's hand touched my chest, the cool wet washcloth across my nipples, down my sides to my hips, over my heart, down my middle.

The Shy Hunter, Rose said, Knows he is not only the prey but, in fact, he's also the vicious totalitarian asshole.

Vicious Totalitarian Assholes 'R' Us, Rose said.

Rose's hand, the washcloth slowly down, down, down to the base of my cock, down the shaft, up the sides of it poking up, around the helmet head, down under along the cord of stretched muscle. The washcloth cool on my ball sack, Rose rolling my balls in his extra-lovely hands.

But, I said.

Nice butt, Rose said.

Rose rubbed his Sahara Desert palm across my butt.

Then: There is nothing, Rose said, There is no thing but you regarding the thing, and there is nothing left to do but regard the thing that is you, as prey.

It's all drag, Rose said.

Stalking yourself gives you something to do, Rose said. An existential project. There is no greater project, Rose said, Than trying to connect with your heart. And then showing the pathetic little thing to someone else.

Rose's hand cupped my balls, the soft white wet washcloth around my cock up, a slow massage, up and down, up and down.

That's when I saw the stars.

All over on Rose's bedroom ceiling were planets and stars. Gold sun, silver moon, red Jupiter, purple Pluto, Saturn with its rings. The whole Milky Way. The light from the candle flickers, tiny illuminations up there in the dark.

The Known Universe.

Just like that, down low, down deep in my loins, the known universe was twisting onto itself, sore and soft, hard and dense.

The scarves were stretched to the max.

I was levitating, I swear, my pointed toes so pretty, my body two feet off the bed, sucked out the window to the Con Ed building.

Good thing I was tied down.

The sensation, a finger drawing a circle around my heart.

Friendship, trust, Rose said. Tenderness in sadness. We must believe in love, Rose said.

Rose knelt on my feet so I wouldn't fly off. My back arched and arched, Rose's firm grip on my cock slow and steady.

Perfect, just perfect.

Just keep dancing, Rose said, And cop an attitude.

Rose pushed my legs up, his smooth head against my inside thighs. Rose's breath right up against my balls. His voice inside my balls.

The known universe, the soft sad hard dense funnel of wind inside me, was blowing out fast.

Some people like to bitch, Rose said. Bitching is OK. But for me, I choose a kind of joy—a lucid compulsion—a polemical kind of fuck-you-motherfucker joy.

We are the mess, Rose said, So we might as well enjoy it.

Enjoy, my lips said. *Enjoy*.

Deep down deep, up hard through ancient pathways, old highways, labyrinths, haylofts, my raw heart, sweat sperm and pigeon shit, the cum in me, cumming not praying, the wad of life burst out of me, slap into the air, a fist, flying flying, a falling star, a meteor, a tiny illumination across the universal sky.

ROSE WAS A smooth black stone on the white sheets. We weren't touching. We were smoking Sho-ko-lat rabbit turds in the lovely erect pink penis. I rolled cigarettes, one for Rose, one for me. Rose got up, pulled back the red velvet curtain, and opened the window, and early morning, *entre loup et chien*, was coming in through the window. Mel Tormé, *Born to Be Blue*, on Rose's stereo.

It was on the second toke that Rose leaned back and put his hands behind his head, the big muscles of his arms flowing down into his armpits. Rose blew out smoke, took another toke, held the smoke in. Blew smoke slow out of his black nostrils.

You, my dear William of Heaven, Rose said, Are very strong.

Did I hurt you? I said.

I deserved it, Rose said. Did I hurt you?

Yes, I said.

How's that? Rose said.

I ain't ever going to be the same, I said.

Rose's fingers touched my fingers when he handed the erect pink penis to me. His fingers went down my arm and wrapped around my bicep.

You know, Will, Rose said, You're in a unique situation.

My situation wasn't as unique as it had been only minutes earlier, tied up to the bedposts, my cock hitched to a star, shooting sperm all over Rose's clean white bedsheets. But I didn't say anything. Rose had taken his fourth toke, and I knew I was in for a story.

The Greeks, Rose said, Believed that when incest was vertical—that is, Rose said, Father with daughter, mother with son—that the child of this union was born a hero.

In my forearms.

Rose toked again, held his breath, and talked the way you do holding smoke in. Hero, Rose said, in the sense that the child's task is to restore order to the universe, since his or her own birth, because it was incestuos, destroyed the Golden Mean and brought chaos into the cosmos.

Rose let out the smoke and handed me the lovely erect pink penis.

Antigone is a good example of a hero, Rose said. She was Oedipus' daughter.

Outside the window, in the street, another New Yorker gone to hell.

On the other hand, Rose said, If the incest was horizontal—that is, brother with sister—the child of this union was born a monster, a creature who could bring about the twilight of the gods.

Up my arms, to my shoulders.

Fucking like *that*, Rose said, Was reserved only for Zeus and Hera. And when they did it, she was a cloud and he was a mountain.

I sat up in bed, put my feet on the floor, my head between my legs. Cum on my inside thighs.

And your situation, my dear William of Heaven, Rose said, Is unique because actually you were your mother's boyfriend—psychically speaking, weren't you? Plus then you fucked your sister.

Through my heart, splash down into stomach.

Vertical *and* horizontal, Rose said.

Ergo, Rose said, You are both the hero and the monster. The hunter and the prey. Vicious Totalitarian Assholes 'R' You.

The monster your hero has to slay, Rose said, Is within you.

That's when Rose reached around me, put his hand on my stomach, rubbed my stomach, then rubbed up to my heart, touching me where it hurts when I smoke.

Then: You know, Rose said, You white people can be fucking spooky.

WE TOOK VALIUMS because we were so jacked on the Sho-ko-lat. Plus the sound in my head. My mother my sister my mother my sister. So Chinatown my mother's nerves in my head.

Warm and dark and soft on Rose's bed.

Then, out of the dark, Rose's deep voice.

Will?

Yeah, I said.

Like Antigone, Rose said, I too must follow my heart.

The way the candlelight hit Buddha, the Buddha was floating.

I'm going to nail these motherfuckers for giving me this disease, Rose said.

I pushed myself up, put my hands on Rose's face, on his ears, on his shaved head.

AIDS? I said.

The word that hurts.

HIV positive, Rose said.

My heart, the broken pieces scratching against my chest. I put my chest against Rose's chest.

You know who gave it to you? I said.

Yes, Rose said, I know.

Who? I said.

The horrific whisper: God, Rose said.

God? I said.

You've got to liberate yourself from your concept of God, Rose said.

Rose's face in his hands, the candlelight on Rose's shaved head.

The God who gave me this disease is the God of Taken as Given, Rose said: Ronald Reagan, and Nancy, Margaret Thatcher, George Bush, the Pentagon, the CIA, the FBI, Oliver North, Bernhard Goetz, Ed Koch, and Cardinal O'Henry, the whole fucking hierarchical gaggle of White Paranoid Patriarchs.

AIDS is the shadow of Christianity, Rose said.

He sat up. His right eye was almost closed, his left eye one hard ebony stone rolled smooth.

I am the hero, Rose said. And I am queer, and I am here to restore natural order. And believe me, Rose said, the jig is up. There is a new order and these honky white heterosexual motherfuckers are going to pay.

Antigone made of herself a sacrifice, Rose said. There must be a sacrifice, Rose said, To restore order.

In all the world, in Rose's apartment, just like that, out of the blue, the huge footfall of the monster, breaking glass, crushing buildings, darkening the sky.

Everywhere dogs barking, wolves.

JUST BEFORE WE slept, my body spooned into Rose. I put my lips to Rose's ear. Rose, I said, Rose, you got to get rid of that gun.

BOOK THREE

CHAPTER
EIGHTEEN

A fter work one night, when I grabbed the newel post of 205 East
Fifth Street and swung myself up the stairs, there in one of the
garbage cans were a couple of two-by-fours and a black plastic
bag filled with plaster, and Fiona was banging away inside Stranded
Beings Searching for God.

I put my face to the glass under the poster of the Sacred Heart of
Jesus and put my hands around my eyes. Fiona was knee deep in rubble.
Her bushel of black hair was tied under a red scarf and she was wearing
cutoffs and a white T-shirt that were covered in the thin black dust that's
everywhere in the city. She was trying to pull a big nail out of a two-
by-four.

Fiona unlocked the door and I said something nice, like, Hi, Susan
Strong, would you like a beer? or something really simple, and just like
that Fiona's arms were around my neck and she was crying. Not just
crying a little bit but an all-out wail.

All I could think about was how was I going to get my white shirt
clean again, but there was no getting away from her. Plus, the last time
anybody held on to me like that was Charlie 2Moons.

So I held Fiona.

After she settled down, I went upstairs and got two beers and brought
them back down. I kicked the Sheetrock and plaster and crosshatch out
of the way, and Fiona and I sat down. My black waiter pants were covered in white dust. I rolled a cigarette for Fiona, one for me.

When I asked, What's wrong? Fiona snuffed up and wiped snotty
black off her nose with her arm.

Everything, Fiona said. Every fucking thing is fucking wrong. My
father and my mother are giving me such shit about Stranded Beings
Searching for God. Mom's trying to convince Dad not to give me anymore money. My mother is such a bitch! I can't find anybody to do the
work, and all my clothes and my computer and everything I own is

covered in this fucking black dust. And how can you have a performance space if you don't have anybody to perform? I can't even pull this fucking nail out of this fucking board, let alone open a performance space!

And then, Fiona said, To top it all off?

Fiona's bottom lip started shaking and her whole face seemed to cave in to the scar under her nose. Fiona grabbed on to me again, her body against mine, the big sobs in her against me.

Fiona's body against mine was jerks back and forth, back and forth, waves of in and out. How much like cumming it was, Fiona crying like that.

My hand on Fiona's scarf on her head. I touched her shoulders, put both arms around her. She was so tiny.

You're going this way and then shit happens and then you're going that way.

My brothers, Fiona said, lips against my ear. My twin little brothers, Fiona said, The Hyannisport Homos, the YUFAs—both of them are in the hospital. Intestinal flu, Fiona said.

Both of them? I said.

They can't stop shitting, Fiona said.

After a couple more beers and more smokes, I got Fiona to come up and take a shower. We called out for Chinese. Fiona came out of the shower wrapped in my big white towel, rubbing her hair with my blue towel, her skin so white against the white towel. Fiona sat down on my futon, I lit a cigarette, put the cigarette in my green-dish ashtray, drank from her can of Budweiser. The Chinese came and I paid for it, and I got some dishes and paper towels and sat down next to Fiona. Fiona Garlic Chicken, me Szechuan Shrimp. Just my wagon-wheel lamp on, WBLS on my boom box, low jazz at the end of the dial, her white legs in the lamplight, the white towel wrapped around her, Fiona cross-legged sitting on the futon eating Chinese, talking talking.

You know, Fiona said, Sometimes I just go shit-spray thinking about it: Argwings Khodek, the essence of performance art, the master of complete presence, just up the stairs from me. If I could get him to perform at Stranded Beings Searching for God, it would be a big help.

I was ripping open the soy sauce with my teeth. Fiona laid down her fork and took a drag on the cigarette.

I've contacted Alien Comic, Fiona said, But he hasn't got back to me. Holly Hughes might be interested, but she's in Minneapolis. And Ethyl, Fiona said. Ethyl Eichelberger! And can you imagine getting John Kelly?

I need a microphone system, an amplifier, a curtain. Where the fuck do you buy a stage curtain, Pottery Barn? And chairs, Fiona said. And I've got to sell beer and something to eat. What do you serve at a performance space? Do you microwave corn dogs or make little sandwiches? I don't have time to make little fucking sandwiches. I hate little fucking sandwiches. Maybe soup?

How much do you think I should charge for a performance? Fiona said. Five dollars? Of course the performer will get a *huge* percentage of the till, but how much do you think? Sixty? Seventy-five?

Ruth Fuglistaller has a great act, Fiona said, This internationale lounge act with the femme fatale Lana Lynx. Cool. Then there's Watchface. Maybe Ellie at Dixon Place would give me some suggestions.

The performers will have to dress in my bedroom, Fiona said, And there's just the one bathroom: for the performers, for the public, and for me. Harry said we should paint the walls black and make it a black box in here, but I want to keep it light. Creamy yellow or off-white, don't you think? What kind of chairs, Conran chairs, or should I go buy old chairs, all different kinds? I think a couch and a standing lamp, Fiona said. Give it a homey feeling. A throw rug and a coffee table.

Reno's good. George Osterman. KimX.

Fiona sighed a big sigh and stuck a forkful of Garlic Chicken in her mouth.

Then: Do you know what New York's true and hidden nature is? Fiona asked.

True and hidden? I said. No.

Charcoal, Fiona said.

Charcoal? I said.

Charcoal, Fiona said. Do you know how to make charcoal?

No, I said.

You take a live substance like a tree limb and burn it in a kiln from which air is excluded.

That's us, Fiona said. That's what's left of us.

We are so compressed here, so pressured, that carbon is all that's left of the human spirit. Charcoal is what's left that still burns after the fire has passed through. All the extra shit is gone. What's left is what burns.

New York is America's charcoal heart. New York burns out all the extra stuff in your life. You have to be able to state what you want and why you want it as precisely and concisely as possible. There's no time for anything else. Life is an art and art is a game, Fiona said. I see that you are playing at enjoying your Szechuan Chicken, Fiona said.

Shrimp, I said. Szechuan Shrimp.

Why do you think cocaine's so popular? Fiona said. Cocaine—charcoal—same shit, different names.

That Mrs. Lupino bitch is a fucking pain in the ass, Fiona said. Any little squeak I make she bangs on my ceiling. I'm going to have to cut her nipples off if she starts up during a performance. Do you think the curtain could be velvet? Like a dark green velvet? I wonder how much a velvet curtain would cost. My fucking dad said he won't give me another dime. 'Course that was with Mother standing right there. If I get him alone he'll be fine. Plus I still have my credit cards.

David Cale is funny, Deborah Hiett, Lisa Kron, Terry Dame, Eva Gasteazoro, Linda Mancini. But no stand-up, Fiona said. I don't do stand-up.

Then: It's performance *heart*, Fiona said. She put her hands on her heart. And that's why I love Argwings Khodek so much.

He's a dervish, Fiona said. His art is a devotional exercise that he delivers with ecstatic abandonment. Argwings Khodek is a man dancing alone in a room, not a man dancing alone in a room in front of people watching, even though there are hundreds of people watching. Argwings Khodek is never *Look, this is me* dancing in a room. He is the wedding itself, Fiona said, not Tony and Tina's wedding. So given, Fiona said. So not-taken-as-given.

So un–Noam Chomsky, I said.

Argwings Khodek, Fiona said, Is so this-very-second.

The breakthrough to wordless knowledge, Fiona said, Really is the climax of our whole existence, don't you think? All being as one's own being.

Laying bare the human heart, I said. All of us all one thing.

I suppose I'll have to rent a Dumpster for all this construction garbage, Fiona said. I hope they take Visa. Do you know anybody who's a carpenter who's handy and needs a job?

I was rolling cigarettes, one for Fiona, one for me.

I can help you, I said. I'm pretty good with a hammer.

Will! Really? Fiona said. Cool! I'll pay you. How's six bucks an hour?

You don't have to pay me, I said.

No, Fiona said, I don't take charity. Let's make it seven.

OK, I said. Seven.

I lit Fiona's cigarette, lit mine. Fiona leaned over and kissed me on the forehead and then put her forehead on mine.

I'm Diogenes, Fiona said, And you're my honest man.

Fiona's hair smelled of my Herbal Essence shampoo. The towel had fallen down from her diamond nips. We finished the Chinese and I turned off the wagon-wheel light and Fiona and I lay on the futon and smoked in the dark. WBLS low jazz on the boom box, car alarms outside, ambulance sirens, fire sirens. The light from another incarnation on East Fifth Street through the window and onto the sheets, onto her body.

Fiona talking talking.

Spalding Gray and Wally Shawn are probably too big to hope for, Fiona said. I think I'll paint the floor in some wild-ass pattern. I'll have to buy curtains for the window and the door.

Finally, Fiona said, Our lives just come down to moments, don't they?

IN ALL THE world, this distracted globe, my arms around Fiona, her hair in my face, in my mouth. Her smooth white back, holding Fiona like Bernadette would do, Fiona holding me.

The still point in the turning world.

Now here.

Fiona's lips at my ear: Harry looks awful, Fiona said. I can't get him to go to the hospital. It can't be AIDS, Fiona said. Harry's just like my brothers—so fussy. Harry and my brothers are so fussy. Everything clean clean. No mess. My God, you should see my brothers' house. Right out of *House Beautiful*. Museum-piece quality. When they get done shitting they fold the last piece of toilet paper over like in hotels.

It can't be AIDS, Fiona said. It just can't be. Not Harry. Not my little brothers.

Then the next moment, just like that, Fiona was sleeping. Deep long breaths of sleep in my ear, her belly up and down, up and down. I pulled my arm out from under her, bent over. I pushed my ear slow into her heart.

I rolled another cigarette. Got up, took a leak. Stood among my Art Family. They were covering their eyes, their mouths, their ears, covering their crotches and breasts.

Outside, the monster's footfall, shaking doors, rattling windows, big cracks in the brick walls.

Another New Yorker gone to hell.

In my forearms, up to my shoulders, down through my heart, splash down into stomach, cattle prod to cock.

Trouble.

None of us, not any one of us, no one knew how much trouble we were in.

JUNE 1986. WHEN I told Rose I'd never been to the Gay Pride march, Rose said, Well, put your tank top on, Mary, you're going this year.

That Gay Pride Saturday morning, though, I woke up with my mother's nerves.

In my forearms first, then up to my shoulders, then some hard thing in my chest that stayed and got bigger, the closer it got to noon.

Half a million homosexuals all together in the same place all at once on a hot day.

I knew Rose wasn't home. I dialed his number, left a message.

Sorry, Rose, I said, But I can't make it to Gay Pride today. I am going to Connecticut to visit an old friend.

On the R uptown, no Charlie 2Moons.

I got off at 57th and walked up to Central Park, Bethesda Fountain. Sat on the edge of the fountain, took my shoes and socks off, rolled my pants up, and stuck my feet in the water.

The day was clear and already hot. The sound of the falling water on my ears made me feel I wasn't alone. Wasn't long before I pulled my T-shirt up over my head. The sun spread his open palm across my back.

People everywhere. A man and a woman, both dressed in khaki shorts and Nikes, she in a lime-green Polo shirt, he in a navy blue, pushed a blue baby carriage. A skateboarder jumped the curb next to a NO SKATE-BOARDING sign. A man with long silver hair, torn pants, and no shirt, asleep on a park bench. A woman in a red jogging bra and a blue hair tie, Nikes, carrying weights, running.

Just over from me on the rim of the fountain was an old man. He was smoking, wearing a Jimmy Stewart hat, an old tie with butterflies and dice on it. His shoes and socks were off too, his suit pants rolled up. The cane he leaned on was stuck in the fountain. He looked down into the water.

The water wasn't just milky green. It was blue too, and gray. The bubbles were white. Under the water, a Pepsi can, a straw, some blue plastic thing.

The sun made wavy illuminations on the water. I squinted my eyes and—abracadabra!—out of nowhere were the willows, the dark earth, the wet meadow grass of Spring Creek, Charlie's naked one long uninterrupted muscle diving through the blue Idaho sky.

Who knows how long I sat on the lip of stone sloshing my feet back and forth in the water.

My breath in. My breath out.

WHAT I CAME up with was this: Since I was a Crossover, and a Crossover is someone who what he's afraid of happens to him, I might as well let it happen.

Let gay, let pride, happen to me.

I loved Charlie, and Charlie was a boy, a boy I had sex with. I couldn't get it up for Fiona. Now Rose.

MY LEGS WADED through gray-green water. When I got to the splashing water, I looked up, raised my arms into the sky, reached.

It's the Gay Pride march today! I said, out loud to Bethesda Fountain. Then I turned around, cupped my hands around my mouth. Gay Pride! I yelled. *Ta-da!*

The old man quick looked at me, poked his Jimmy Stewart hat up.

So, he said. You going?

How about you? I said.

Nah, he said. I'm too old for *mishegoss*. But *you*, he said, You're young. You should go give 'em hell.

All daring and courage, I said, All iron endurance of misfortune, make for a finer, nobler type of manhood.

The old man flipped his cigarette into the fountain, rubbed his nose.

Ah fuck Teddy Roosevelt, the old man said. Just go be who you are. Who you are is what it is, the old man said. And you don't have much time.

ON THE STEPS of the 42nd Street Library, I sat down next to a lion, around one-thirty, just about the time they were releasing six hundred thousand purple balloons into the air.

On the pink Gay Pride pamphlet, I read the marchers would observe one full minute of silence in memory of those who had died of AIDS.

One full minute of silence in Manhattan isn't that silent. The balloons were pretty, though. The whole sky was purple at first, purple shining down on the men and women looking up, but as the balloons floated higher and higher, what we were staring up at was the bright sunny sky, unrelenting.

When the one full minute was over, people cheered, cried, waved flags, held each other.

The show must go on. A band started playing. Disco music from the Monster float.

I followed the parade on the sidewalk, not on the avenue with the marchers. I pretended like it was just another New York day and I was just another New York guy who was walking toward Washington Square Park.

At Washington Square, the parade turned west. The farther west I walked, and the closer to Sheridan Square, people were jammed in so close there wasn't enough air. Marching bands, baton twirlers, guys in tutus on roller skates, franticker and festiver, elaborate floats. Drag queens and muscle men and Dykes on Bikes and black gay men and black lesbians, and Latino gay men and Latino lesbians, Asian men and women—really, I don't think you could find a bunch of people who were so different yet so the same all together in the same place at the same time.

A half million homosexuals, showing off, parading, dancing, running, roller skating, strutting, skateboarding, rickshawing, you name it, through the streets.

Next to me on the sidewalk was a Latino woman in a wheelchair with a rainbow on the back of the chair. Her white silver-haired lover behind her leaned up against the wheelchair. They were laughing their asses off. And then there was these two Asian guys—I don't know if they were Korean or Chinese or Vietnamese or what, but they were scrubbed up and starched white, their thick black hair shiny in the sun, and they were both standing there like schoolboys waving little flags with pink triangles on them.

Then the leather guy drove by on his Harley-Davidson, long hair—looked like ZZ Top with his beard—and there was his big bare white hairy ass arched up out over the seat. The Asian boys, when they saw the Harley guy's ass, covered their mouths, little screams.

In the arch of shade under the Washington Square monument is where I saw them: four policemen on horses. I recognized the white stallion right off.

The cops were just sitting there, watching the parade, smoking and talking to each other. I mean Richard White was talking and the other cops were listening.

The Monster float went by: nearly naked men disco dancing. Sergeant White and the other cops didn't even look up.

What followed the Monster float was a group of people in uniform. Four women, six or seven men. Their purple and pink flag: Gay cops.

The crowd gave out a big cheer.

Even from where I stood, I could see Sergeant White's face get red. He threw his cigarette down, then quick pulled back on the reins. The white stallion reared and the other horses jumped, horse hooves onto cobblestones.

Sergeant White started shouting orders.

Yes, *sir*! Yes, *sir*!

Each cop, each white-guy cop, followed Sergeant White in formation and turned his horse to the right.

More shouts from Sergeant White.

Yes, *sir*! Yes, *sir*!

The cops turned their horses completely around and faced the other direction. Turned their backs on the gay cops. Pointed their four horses' asses at the gay cops.

If I'd had a gun, Rose's silver revolver, I might have shot Sergeant Richard White right then.

I DON'T KNOW how long I stood there, but when I went to move on, a bunch of people had crowded in behind me and from the side. I was in a place no bigger than my body, stuck between a light pole, a garbage can, and a parked car.

From down the street, marching bands, drag queens on stilts, belly dancers, you name it.

The wilder the crowd got, the bigger the hard place inside my chest.

I pushed through the crowd of people, put my head down and just pushed. Then I was running in and out, in and out, through the crowd, heading as fast as I could to 205 East Fifth Street, 1-A. So many people on the sidewalk I had to move into the street to run. Running against the parade.

I heard the drums and whistles a block before I saw them. Around the corner, a huge burst of dust storm, lightning, thunder, wind blowing tumbleweeds and sagebrush: Native American gays.

The song of the men and women dancing sounded like hundreds of waterfalls and wolves. Horses when they fight. Made you want to lie down and cry, or laugh your ass off, or both.

* * *

THE ONLY WAY out is in.

If I barfed I'd feel better, but I didn't barf.

After some time, who knows how long, I raised my head and looked into the sun.

Nothing but heat and dust on my shoulders, June grass in my hair.

The drums, the bells around their ankles, the high *heya-heya-heya* cry to the Great Mystery. The bear claws, the whistles, the porcupine quills, the breechcloths, the smell of buckskin and sweat, the sun shining onto the gold, copper, turquoise, the silver glint.

From out of the dust came a rider on a horse. His hair was long and black and wavy and his horse was ayaHuaska.

Charlie 2Moons was doing the Hippodrome Stand; then he leaned down into a Crupper Jump. I reached my hands up and Charlie grabbed my hands and I was flying in the air; then my butt was on ayaHuaska's fortune-telling butt and my arms were around Charlie's middle, his hair in my face, and I was holding Charlie close to me, holding him safe.

Charlie and I on ayaHuaska galloped up Fifth Avenue, all the way up, through the riches to the rags, through the grid, downtown to uptown to out of town, all the way out to the shadow tunnel of cottonwood leaves and branches, kicking up dust and horse farts, then over the railroad tracks, across Highway 30, to the sagebrush plains, the low flatland and the tall grass, into the tules, down into gullies, to the bottoms.

But it's not the truth.

No Charlie. Nowhere.

RUNNING AGAIN, FASTER and faster, the hard place in my chest a hurt where I didn't even know hurt.

I saw a space in the marchers and quick ran farther out into the street—and smack into the next group of marchers.

People with AIDS. Walking wounded. Thousands.

I sat down right there on the pavement on the corner of Fifth and Washington Square North, put my head between my legs. All around me, above me, the humanity. Several men stopped, asked if they could help. I could only shake my head.

My eyes looked only at the feet.

Who knows how long I sat there, how many pairs of shoes, flip-flops, Nikes, sandals passed over and around me, how many shadows walked by.

Below me, a puddle on the pavement, sweat and tears and snot, a river of mucus run out of me.

I got up, made it to the curb. An old woman in a babushka gave me a drink of water from her Evian bottle.

The sun, it's so hot! Drink!

My breath in, my breath out, I stood up straight, made myself look.

One after another, every way a person can look—old young white black brown red yellow men and women—some in wheelchairs, some on crutches, some of them blind and walking with white canes, some of them just skin and bones, some of them healthy-looking as can be. They were marching, smiling, waving at the crowd, elbow, elbow, wrist wrist wrist.

One guy my eyes went to right off was walking close to an older taller guy. You could tell it was his first time, first time in a gay parade, first time with AIDS. There was nothing special about how this guy looked, just a thirty-year-old white guy in khaki pants and white shirt with the sleeves rolled up, socially shy, terrified, mostly his eyes on the ground or looking into his lover's eyes.

In that moment, my body understood what it was to be brave. I'd always thought that brave people were just brave. Martin Luther King, Jr. was brave. Malcolm X was brave. Harvey Milk was brave. Rosa Parks was brave. Red Cloud was brave. Brave was something in their bones they just did.

But looking at that guy in the khaki pants and white shirt that day—that whipped-dog look some people have, that he had—I knew: Brave meant you were afraid, real afraid, but you went ahead with it anyway. You invited fear in for a Brandy Alexander and kept going on with your life.

WHAT WAS NEXT on the street was causing a commotion. People were cheering and clapping way before you could see what was coming up.

When the crowd parted, what charged up the crowd this time was Rose, beloved Rose.

It's the truth.

The gold vestments, the pointy hat, the miter and staff of a bishop: Rose in drag as the cardinal. Rose was walking like Palm Sunday, *In nomine patris, filii, et spiritus sancti*, blessing the crowd. On Rose's right, a young bare-chested brown man waved the censer, the Catholic incense floating through the crowd. On Rose's left, another brown man, all in white, who was a woman in drag to look like Jesus, carried a crucifix.

Six-foot-four Rose, a bright spot of yellow sun. Rose's face and hands were blacker than ever in the sun and the gold. As he walked, Rose bowed to the left, bowed to the right, always making the vertical and the horizontal with his hand.

As he passed, the crowd fell to their knees and cried, Papa! Papa! Everybody scrambling to get to kiss his ring. One guy from the crowd ran up to Rose, unzipped, and pulled out his cock. Rose didn't even blink; he bowed down and made a cross with his thumb on the man's cock.

Rose was only ten feet away when he passed in front of me. I could see the sweat on his forehead, could smell him.

I stayed behind the lamppost.

ONE LAST THING: A man in a red ball cap, T-shirt, and plaid shorts. Just a gray-haired old guy, maybe sixty, ordinary-looking except he was smiling extra lovely. He wore signs on the front and back of him that said I AM THE PROUD FATHER OF A WONDERFUL GAY SON.

In my forearms, up to my shoulders, down through my arms, splash down onto concrete.

When I got my eyes open, I was surrounded by Catholic nuns.

Some of these nuns had beards and mustaches.

The sister holding my head said, Now just go ahead and have a good cry, honey, we've all been there.

In all the world, on the corner of Fifth Avenue and Washington Square North, snot flinging, crying my fucking eyes out, my head held by Sister Mary Fellatio, I was surrounded by the Sisters of Perpetual Indulgence.

BUT THE DAY wasn't over. That same night, about midnight, the front door opened and my Art Family gasped.

The vestments scratched against the walls of the narrow blue hallway. Rose's step was heavy past my door, past the mailboxes. On the stairs, I heard him fall.

My Art Family froze in position.

Just like that I had my door open.

Up close, Rose's gold vestments in the unrelenting fluorescents looked like cheap jewels.

My hand through the balusters, I reached and put my open palm against Rose's cheek.

Never touch me.

Rose, I said, Are you OK?

Rose's eye opened up, and the way that eye looked at me I stepped back.

Rose, I said, It's me, William of Heaven.

Rose's eye was wet and red. He was staring at something just over my shoulder, something he hated.

Rose, I said, I'm coming around, I said, And I'm going to help you up the stairs. You won't go ghetto on me, will you?

Rose opened his mouth, the inside color of his lips. His lips were cracked and dry.

No, Rose said.

When I put my face down to Rose's, what I got was a blast of Brandy Alexanders and Gauloises. And something else. Rose was able to kneel so I could get my shoulder under his armpit. We made it up the stairs, one step at a time. I kept stepping on his damn cape. Behind Rose's door, the dogs were barking.

Down deep under twenty layers of drag was Rose's pants pocket. I got the keys.

When the door opened, I wished I could carry Rose over the threshold, lay the fainting Rose onto the blonde-fainting couch, But there was no way.

I got Rose to his bed, undid the clasp of the red-velvet-lined golden cape, took the cape off, took his hat off, let the dogs up on the bed to kiss him.

In Rose's gold-framed medicine chest in the bathroom, I found aspirin. It took some doing, getting the pills inside Rose's mouth. I had to hold the glass to his lips, to the inside of his lips. Then I got up on the bed, shooed the dogs off, and lit the candles on each side of Buddha.

From behind, I lifted Rose's shoulders up, then put one leg on each side of him. Rose was sitting on part of the gold chasuble, so I had to pull it out from underneath his butt in order to get the damn thing over his head.

When Rose leaned into me I felt the heat. The cotton robes tied around him were soaking wet.

Rose? I said, Are you drunk or are you sick?

Rose let his head fall back onto my shoulder. He reached out his extra-lovely Sahara palm and laid the palm on my arm.

A multifaceted ambivalent combination of the twain, Rose said.

Let's get these clothes off you, I said.

Yes, please! Rose said. Divest me!

I got off the bed and stood myself in front of Rose. I pulled the scarf thing over his head and was just undoing the white cotton drawstring at his neck, when Rose said, The Vicious Totalitarian Assholes got City Hall.

We got helium, Rose said. We got floating fucking purple condoms.

Rose took a deep breath in, breath out. Rose kept his chin down, raised just his deep black eyes, put them square into mine. I tried to look back but couldn't.

I saw you at the parade, Rose said.

In my forearms.

How could you? I said. I was hiding.

You can't hide from me, Rose said.

The prizefighter bump on Rose's nose, his eight-ball cheeks, the inside color of Rose's lips, not sunset but purple red.

Then: Gay, Rose said. You can say it.

My lips were rubber bands around the word. The word that hurts.

Gay, I said.

And proud, I said.

I smiled.

Sweat all over on Rose's face, his head, rolling down his neck.

Rose smiled too.

We're queer, Rose said, And we're here.

The lucid compulsion, I said.

Cop an attitude, Rose said. A fuck-you-motherfucker kind of joy.

WHEN I FINALLY got all the gowns, the cassocks, the surplices off Rose, the pile of Catholic drag filled up the whole front room. Rose lay down on the white sheets. The not-so-white sheets. I gave him two Valiums. In the bathroom closet, I got a Bloomingdale's white one-hundred-percent-cotton washrag. Turned on the faucet, rinsed the washcloth in cool water.

When I put the washcloth to Rose's head, I could feel the fever.

You going to tie me up, Rose said, And fuck me?

The washcloth across his lips, down his chin, onto his neck.

No, I said.

Quell dommage! Rose said.

I put Maria Callas on Rose's stereo: "Norma." I turned the rheostat down on the chandelabra. Lit the candles on each side of Buddha. Fed Mary and Mona and Jack Flash.

There in the light, under the stars and planets and moons of the Known Universe, I stayed with Rose, wiping his face, his neck, his arms.

When Rose was snoring, I turned off all the lights, blew out the candles.

At the door I whispered: I'm just downstairs, Rose. If you need anything, give me a call.

Then: Will?

From out of darkness, the dry of Rose's mouth made his voice even deeper.

The Left will always lose, Rose said, Because the Left is passive. The Right will always win, Rose said, Because when all the talking's done, when the marching's done and the parade's over, when the purple helium condoms float through the ozone layer, the rednecks will bring out their firepower.

Down the thirteen steps, past the mailboxes, at my door, when I locked my door, brushed my teeth, got into bed—the whole time all I could think of was eleven gay cops.

And four horse's asses.

CHAPTER NINETEEN

O n October 3, 1986, one year and a day after Rock Hudson died and four months after Gay Pride, I dialed 911 for Rose.

It was three-twenty-two in the morning when my red telephone rang. It wasn't Ruby. It was Rose.

The moment that after, you're different.

Fatum.

My waiter's pants and white shirt were closest to the futon so I put them on. My red Converse tennis shoes. Only laced them up halfway.

Upstairs, Rose's door was unlocked. I opened the door and it was dark, and inside the dark something darker. Rose was lying in bed. Next to his bed was the red lava lamp going next to Buddha, and the votive candles, and the oil painting of Elizabeth Taylor in the white swimsuit in *Suddenly Last Summer*. The smell of the rooms was sharp in my nostrils.

Hello, Rose, I said.

William of Heaven! Rose said.

Rose turned the nightstand light on. The dogs were all lying around him. Rose was sweaty and his color was black under charcoal. The two horizontal lines were deep deep in Rose's forehead, and between the two vertical lines down to his nose, Rose's third eye, the clitoris bump, the little man in the boat standing up.

Rose's navy blue sweatpants were on his purple-velvet overstuffed chair. My arm under Rose's head, his neck slick with sweat, never touch me, I helped Rose raise up, moved his legs like in the No Hand Horn Spin—so black, his legs, dangling off the side of the bed—helped Rose put each foot on the floor, onto the red Persian carpet by his bed on the floor. Rose's cock a grower not a shower. One foot at a time into the legs of Rose's navy blue sweatpants. I put my arms under Rose's arms, clasped my hands behind his back, and lifted. Rose helped, and we stood him up. Rose stood alone, held his arms in the air, bracelets clack-clack, and I pulled a burgundy T-shirt on him that said FUCK JERRY FALWELL. His leather-tooled studio flats.

Dialed. Rose's phone, the fancy fuchsia French kind, with a gold dial and a gold earphone and speaker.

Nine.

One.

One.

I have to brush my teeth, Rose said.

Rose's eyes were swollen and he was squinting. His voice a deep Tallulah Bankhead.

Your teeth are OK, Rose, I said. Just sit down.

No no Yoko Ono, Rose said.

In his fuchsia bathroom, his arm over my shoulder, my arm around his waist, I took Rose's fuchsia toothbrush from the medicine cabinet, spread Arm and Hammer toothpaste on the toothbrush, handed the toothbrush to Rose.

Rose's hand shaking shaking.

The brush a slow back and forth, back and forth, against his beautiful white teeth. The color of his inside lips in the gold oval mirror above the fuchsia sink was blue.

Rose bent over and spit out his toothpaste. I had my hand on his back, and just then the muscles of his back started shaking. Then it was Rose's whole body shaking. Rose held on to the sink and I held on to Rose's waist. Mary, Mona, Jack Flash barking barking. Like an earthquake inside Rose, shaking him, shaking the whole room, knocking the gold oval-framed photograph of Elizabeth Taylor into the sink.

I still don't know where I got the strength to hold him up.

When the earthquake stopped in Rose, we looked at each other in the mirror, completely present, staring at each other, at the immensity of what had passed through Rose's body.

What the fuck was that? Rose said.

God, I said. It was God.

But it's not the truth.

I turned on the cold water, took a fuchsia washcloth from the cabinet, held the washcloth under the water, squeezed the water out, laid the washcloth on Rose's head, then slow down his forehead, down onto his eyes, over his eight-ball cheeks, his nostrils, his lips, his chin, his neck.

Come on, I said. Let's go sit down.

On Rose's stereo, I put in the tape—Maria Callas, "Norma"—pushed PLAY.

Rose in his purple-velvet overstuffed chair, me on the arm of the chair, my arm aross Rose's shoulders. Mary in Rose's lap, Mona and Jack Flash on the floor at his feet.

The brocade blonde-fainting couch, the brass coffee table, the Dwight D. Eisenhower ashtray, the gallon bottle full of amber liquid, the Randolph Scott lunch box. The fancy fuchsia telephone with the gold dial and gold earphone and speaker. The Persian rugs. The red velvet drapes pulled. Only the light from the lava lamp. "Norma."

Who knows how long Rose and I sat there.

Sitting in the space in between.

Rose and I are still sitting there.

IT TOOK THE ambulance half an hour.

The buzzer. I got up, walked to the buzzer.

Miss LaRue, five minutes.

Tell them I'll be right down, Rose said.

They can come up here, Rose, I said.

Tell them I'll be right down, Rose said.

Out the door, Rose's arm over my shoulder, my arm around his waist. Rose leaned against me while I locked the door. The dogs barking barking.

The horrific whisper: I'll be back soon, my puppies, Rose said.

Rose grasped the banister. Together Rose and I put our right feet onto the first step, then brought our left feet down. Then the second step, right feet, left feet, third step, right feet, left feet, unrelenting the fluorescence from above, sweat rolling off Rose's brow, his black smooth ebony stone eyes facing the deep inside, Rose's T-shirt soaked through, right foot, left foot, *l'esprit de l'escalier* shaking shaking down and down the thirteen steps, past my door. Mrs. Lupino's door open a crack. A black cat ran out into the narrow blue hallway.

Mrs. Lupino raised her hand, caught the air with her fingers, brought her hand back down.

Rose? Mrs. Lupino said.

It's nothing! Rose said, bracelets clack-clack. Just a touch of the flu, my dear!

The ambulance guys, one brown man, the other blond, were too tired, chewing gum, had the stretcher out, had the red-and-yellow light flashing.

Rose's keep-your-chin-up kind of chin.

Lights! Camera! Action! Rose yelled, waving his one arm, bracelets clack-clack.

The ambulance guys, big smiles, each grabbed a side of the stretcher and started up the stoop.

Rose moved a swift karate chop across the sky.

Get the fuck away from me with that foul thing! Rose yelled. You're ruining my exit!

The ambulance guys stopped in their tracks. The blond said something low.

Ex-*cuse me?* Rose said. If you have something to say to me, at least have the balls to speak it clearly so that I may hear!

Nothing from the ambulance guy. He just stared up like you do in movies when you have to sit in the first three rows.

Rose's arm over my shoulder, my arm around his waist, step by step down the stairs. Not one step at a time, but one foot on the step and then the next foot on the same step. Eleven steps to the sidewalk.

Cool morning air, no traffic on the street, the mercury-vapor dust-storm light from another incarnation on Rose's shiny head, on the chrome of the stretcher, the white sheets, the white ambulance. Across the street, the Doberman in Mother's Sound Stages at the window, slobbering, bared its teeth at us.

On the rectangle of earth where I'd plant the cherry tree, Rose and I stopped.

Rose turned, pointed at the stretcher, his index shaking shaking.

Put the stretcher in the ambulance! Rose said. We'll sit on it.

The ambulance guys looked at each other. The brown guy started to say something, but then he stopped. New York drop-dead fuck-you, they folded the stretcher into the back of the ambulance.

OK, the brown guy said, But *he* has to ride in front.

The ambulance guy was nodding his head at me.

Rose rolled his eyes up, Saint Teresa Gone to Heaven, his shoulders went up and his chin went down, Rose going ghetto, the black snake coiled up in him that kept him alive. The veins in Rose's neck, his nostrils flaring flaring, his hard eyes dark bits of shining light. Arms every which way, then landing on my shoulders.

He, Rose said, Is my companion of many years, Rose said, And my dearest entrusted friend. This man is my brother. And I have *every* right to have him sit next to me wherever we are in the world, including in the back of this fucking little circus you call an ambulance.

Quiet only New York can get that fast.

The ambulance guys stepped way back, looked at each other. They put the stretcher in the ambulance.

Rose put his arm out in front of him, his hand dangling off his wrist. I took Rose's arm, folded his hand into mine, my pink palm against his Sahara, and we walked that way, a queen and her consort, to the back door of the ambulance.

The lucid compulsion.

Rose's leather-tooled studio flat on the back bumper of the ambulance, I put my arms against Rose's back and Rose stepped up into the ambulance. He didn't bump his head. I followed Rose in and sat down alongside him on the stretcher.

Rose put his hands on his knees, took a deep breath.

So even myself, Rose said, I am just here, isn't it?

The brown ambulance guy stepped in, knelt down, looked at Rose for a good while, then said, May I have your wrist?

You may, Rose said.

Rose pointed his wrist to the ambulance guy, bracelets clack-clack.

The ambulance guy put his smooth brown hand onto Rose's black wrist, looked at his watch, and stuck a thermometer in Rose's mouth. The other guy jumped in, strapped a blood-pressure thing around Rose's arm, pumped it up, and watched the heartbeat on the dial beat down. Stethoscope to Rose's chest under his burgundy FUCK JERRY FALWELL.

The brown guy took the thermometer out between Rose's cracked lips.

One hundred and four, he said.

High pulse rate, blood pressure OK, the blond guy said.

Flu, the blond guy said. Take some aspirin, drink plenty of liquids, get some rest.

The brown man looked at Rose, looked at me.

May I touch your neck? he said.

You may, Rose said.

The brown man's brown hand rubbed up and down the ropes of Rose's neck, behind his ears, down his throat.

Gay, he said. He's gay. We'd better take him in.

My breath in. My breath out. Mother's nerves.

I'm gay too, I said.

The brown ambulance guy looked up at me. His face was round, and he had a diamond in his queer ear.

Me too, he said.

* * *

ALL THE WAY to Saint Vincent's, red and yellow lights flashing, siren all around us, speeding light, darkness, speeding light. Rose and I hanging on to each other inside a New York siren.

Another New Yorker.

The earthquake started in Rose again. Rose's arm over my shoulder, my arm around his waist, his wet burgundy T-shirt, FUCK JERRY FALWELL FUCK JERRY FALWELL FUCK JERRY FALWELL. My other arm around in front of him. I held Rose so tight.

Who knows how long the earthquake passed through Rose.

Then for a moment the shaking stopped. Rose sat up, tried to wet his lips with his tongue, but it was no use.

Will? Rose said.

We're almost there, Rose, I said.

Will, Rose said, I'm going to fuck the cardinal.

Just try and lie back, Rose, I said.

And the president too, Rose said. And Nancy, Rose said. And Oliver North.

Rose? I said.

I'm going to fuck them all, Rose said. Infect them all, Rose said. I'm going to kill them.

Rose, I said, Just be quiet, I said, We're almost there.

Then: Rose, I whispered, You're not even allowed to *say* that.

You mean *kill the president?* Rose said. Then he yelled it: Kill the president! I can't even say I'm going to kill the president?

From the ambulance guys up front: Hey! What's going on back there! Just four more blocks! Hang on!

Rose's eyes were red rings around yellow surrounding black, way gone, not on the premises, the sweat coming off him like a faucet.

Suddenly Rose's fist was at my shirt collar in nothing flat and I was spun around, pressed down onto the stretcher. Rose's grip around my neck; there was no breath. My head up and down, up and down, on the mattress.

Fuck you, Rose said. Fuck this whole fucking racist patriarchy. I'm going to fuck God, Rose said. Who we think is God.

Ronald Reagan up his flabby butt, Rose said. I'm going to fuck him.

Nancy the first lady his wife, Rose said. I'm going to fuck her while I got my foot up his ass.

Then on down the hierarchy, Rose said. Congress, Jesse Helms, Orrin Hatch. Not just fuck them. I'm going to split them open and make them scream and beg for more. Then I'll shoot my nasty viral load up their lower intestines.

The House of Representatives, Rose said. Every sphincter split open, fucked deep.

Then on to the leather queens in the Pentagon, Rose said. Bend over, guys, spread 'em!

When I'm done with the politicians and the military, Rose said, I'm starting with religion.

The pope and I, Rose said, Are going to play Hide My Big Black Polish Sausage.

Then on down through the Vatican, Rose said. Bishops, cardinals, monsignors. I'm going to fuck them.

Hasidic Jews—*the chosen people*—what fucking arrogance! Rose yelled. Dilate those assholes so far, they'll use their yarmulkes for butt plugs.

Khomeini and the fundamentalists, Rose said. They're too used to having cock up their butt, so they are going to chant *Praise Allah* as they suck me off.

Then there's the Mormons, Rose said, And the Baptists, and the Jehovah's Witnesses.

Going to fuck them, Rose said, Every fucking thin-lipped dry-skinned tight-assholed honky motherfucker.

Fuck them, Rose said. I'm going to fuck them.

My hands were on Rose's hand that was gathering up my white shirt into a noose.

Rose! I said. Rose! I can't breathe.

When I'm done with this white male Ponzi scheme, Rose said, All that will be left is a huge pile of fucked dead white meat.

My open palm slapped Rose hard in the face. I was about to return with a backswing but Rose grabbed my hand and let go of my throat.

I sat up, palm on my throat, breathing up all the air I could get.

Fuck, Rose! I said. You promised me, I said, I can't breathe.

Rose's eyes opened way up, the breath inside him a rattle. He looked down his arm at his hand, looked up and around, looked at the ceiling, the siren. The charcoal color of Rose's face was the skeleton poking through.

Will, Rose said. My God.

I have AIDS, Rose said.

White all around Rose, white ambulance, white stretcher, white sheets, white white white. Rose ashen black. His eyes with a ring of red, yellow, the black serpent coiled up in there. Rose's beautiful lips, cracked, burnt.

My finger on the inside color of Rose's lips.

Rose, everything's going to be all right, I said. Everything's going to be all right.

But it was not the truth.

THE AMBULANCE STOPPED and the back doors opened. Both the blond guy and the brown guy held out their hands. Rose didn't get up, kept sitting and sitting.

Then: Please! Everyone! Move to the side, Rose said, bracelets clack-clack. I need some room.

I got out first, helped Rose get his leather-tooled studio flats onto the back step, then to the asphalt.

Rose's arm over my shoulder, my arm around his waist, Rose and I walked through the flashing lights. Above the double doors: EMERGENCY ENTRANCE. When the doors closed behind us, just inside, before Rose could get to the wheelchair, the earthquake hit Rose again and I couldn't hold on.

Rose, a mountain tumbling down, a tree in the forest falling, the world crumbling in, a dark heap on the shiny green-and-brown tiled floor, unrelenting white hospital light above us, all around us. The little scream that gives it all away. The fluorescent insect sound. A shit-spray sound and running brown shit on the back of Rose's navy blue sweatpants. Drops of shit spray on the shiny green and brown tile. Nurses and doctors running all over the place, yelling things.

In nothing flat, Rose had an oxygen mask on. It took four men to lift him on a stretcher. A nurse stuck a needle in his arm hooked to an IV, and I stood in the bright shine alone, the urine ammonia medicine smell all around me, as they wheeled Rose down the hallway, down and down and down through the swinging doors.

Rose's shit spray on the shiny tiles.

Frozen moments in time. If we could unfreeze them.

A nurse or an orderly or some kind of hospital guy came up and stood next to me with a clipboard. His left wing tip was right next to Rose's shit spray. He looked like Dr. Kildare.

Insurance? he said.

Four drops of yellow brown, then a smudge.

Do you have a napkin? I said, and pointed.

Dr. Kildare looked down at Rose's yellow-brown shit spray on the shiny green and brown tiles.

Dr. Kildare pulled his wing tip away fast.

Nurse! Dr. Kildare yelled. Nurse!

THE CLOCK ON the wall was round white with black numbers and black hands. Four-twenty-eight. Above a bank of tan leatherette chairs, a painting of a river and a sunrise. Industrial beige carpeting. I sat down in one of the chairs. Put my arms on the chair's wood arms. Foam was coming out along one edge of the cushion. A real fat woman in a stained white blouse was reading *Field and Stream*. A TV showed an infomercial about black people's hair. I thought I'd get up and go out and roll a cigarette, but my butt stayed stuck to the seat, my red tennis shoes did not move on the industrial beige carpet, my fingers stayed holding on to the edge of the wood arms. Not on the premises.

Who knows how long I sat there.

I am still sitting there.

THE WHITE AND black clock said ten after five. My body was still in the chair, my red Converse tennis shoes still on the industrial beige carpeting, in the unrelenting bright in the waiting room.

The crowd on Seventh Avenue was men, smelling just shaved, women coiffed. Power suits, men and women, everybody with eyes looking at the new day. The man on the corner was about the size of Rose. I squinted my eyes, squeezed my hands together palm to palm, tried to make it so that Rose was standing there, extra lovely, bracelets clack-clack, just ordinary, on the street corner.

But I'll tell you something. So you'll know.

It was not the truth.

No Rose.

No Charlie 2Moons.

THE NEXT SEVEN months were for shit.

As an actor, Rose was a member of Screen Actors Guild, so he got to stay in the hospital. Room 335. He had the new kind of pneumonia: Pneumocystis.

On the way to Room 335, you had to pass all the other rooms on Rose's floor, in each room a young man, skeleton poking through, lying on his bed, the bed slowly swallowing him up. Room after room after room, hundreds of young men with green tubes up their noses, IVs in their wrists, wandering through the hallways looking like Auschwitz, an IV bag on a skinny pole trailing behind them. Sometimes there were screams. And the smell. More than the ordinary urine ammonia medicine smell. Another smell.

The first week, I went to see Rose every day .

Usually I just sat in the green Naugahyde chair and Rose lay in bed, either asleep or staring at the ceiling. The ceiling was that kind of ceiling tiles, horizontals and verticals, that made rectangles, and the rectangles had swirly holes in them that you could make figures out of. Faces. Dancers. Horses running. Dogs and cats. Inside two of the rectangles, instead of ceiling tiles with swirly holes there was a piece of plastic covering two fluorescent tubes, the unrelenting light, a muffled insect sound, and then in the corner near the bathroom door was another rectangle that had a screen over it and beneath the screen was a vent of some kind, to let air in or take air out, or something, but whatever the vent was for, it didn't work, because inside Rose's room it was hot and stuffy, and the urine ammonia medicine smell—and the other smell—hung on you.

The shiny floor, the cranked-up bed, the food tray that swung back and forth, the nightstand, the TV hanging from a ceiling tile, dirty New York City light coming through the dirty window.

The way Rose lay sunk in the bed, the bed was quicksand and Rose was going down. Sometimes I wondered if it even was Rose there, lying so still.

One afternoon, the sun came out for a moment, and I went over close to Rose, put my hand on the horizontal lines. Rose's forehead was so hot. Rose smiled a little.

Lips at his ear: Rose? I said. You OK, Rose?

The green tubes up Rose's nose. Sweat on Rose's forehead onto the palm of my hand, sweat dripping down the verticals. Rose's beautiful lips cracks in a sidewalk. Inside his lips, a pale blue.

The horrific whisper: Just a touch of the AIDS, Rose whispered.

Rose laughed a little, but I didn't laugh.

THE SECOND WEEK, Rose was sitting up in his bed, but still Rose didn't say much. The black serpent in him was not coiled up, was not ready to spit, wasn't even there. Sometimes Rose and I watched TV, but one day, the second day of the second week, Rose said, Daytime TV makes you want to slit your wrists.

So I turned the TV off and it was just Rose and me in a hospital room: Rose cranked up in bed, his head back, his eyes staring up at the ceiling tiles, me in the green Naugahyde chair. Rose with AIDS, me not a clue.

How about that Antigone? I said. Then: What was her brother's name again?

Rose just stared ahead, didn't even blink.

Then: This fucking hospital's full of White Paranoid Patriarchs, I said. Did you see all these white doctors?

Rose stared at the ceiling tiles, green tubes up his nose.

Vicious Totalitarian Assholes, I said, Every damn one of them, I said. There better not be, I said, Any fucking Catholic priests walking though that door.

Then I got up, walked to the bed, and sat my butt cheek on the side of the bed. I took hold of his hand, the hand on the arm with the IV in it, turned over his hand, spread out his fingers, and with my index traced the life line on his Sahara palm.

Jesus, Rose! I said. Where's your lucid compulsion to act polemically?

Rose turned his head away, closed his eyes.

The hospital bracelet on his wrist, no clack-clack.

At the dirty window, I looked out at the dirty world, leaned my hands on the sill.

Where the fuck is Liz? I said, When you need her?

Still Rose didn't move.

One day, on the TV hanging from the ceiling tile, Oprah was talking about toilet paper and whether to attach toilet paper to the roller so the paper comes from underneath or the paper comes from above. The audience was divided.

The figures in the ceiling tiles were all running, trying to get away from the swirling werewolf in the ceiling tile above the window.

Ripples through the water in the glass on Rose's bedside tray.

NIGHTS SITTING IN the dark in the green Naugahyde chair, the blue and amber lights of the dials and the bells and whistles by Rose's bed were tiny illuminations in the dark. Above my chair, the floor lamp shined down a circle onto my open palms. When I looked at the window, there was me in the circle of light, and the blue and amber dials and bells and whistles, a hologram on the window, and, beyond, a hologram floating above the lights of Manhattan.

That same week, at night. It was Saturday, and I could hear *Saturday Night Live* on the other televisions on the floor. Rose's TV was off. The lights were off. Rose had taken his trazodone, and he and I were floating in the hologram.

Sometime in there, sometime in the staring at my palms, in the laugh-track *Saturday Night Live* hologram, all at once, the guy they put in the bed next to Rose—just like that, shit happens—the guy sat up. Like he'd been stuck with a cattle prod, this guy sat up. He was young, maybe twenty, but he had no hair and his skin was yellow and covered with purple bumps. He just sat there, his eyes staring straight ahead at the green wall. First, he pulled the tube from his nose, then looked at the tube and threw it to the side. Then he reached around and pulled a tube out of his ass. Pulled the IV from his wrist.

He pulled his stick legs around off the side of the bed. His back was a ladder of bones. When his feet hit the floor, he looked down, then around the room. He was smiling like a child who'd taken his first step.

He walked little steps to the end of Rose's bed, stood there, and stared at us. He was white, crew-cut. Tattoos of snakes on his arms.

Rose stared back at him; I couldn't. What was in the guy's eyes, I couldn't look at, so I put my eyes on Rose. Rose smiled a little bit, just enough to move the cracks in the cement of his lips.

It's the birds, the guy said, The fucking birds in the tree. The fucking chirping fucking birds. I'm sorry, the guy said, I just can't take it anymore. It's just too hard.

The guy pulled something off his pinkie finger, held it out to me. I stuck out my hand. On the palm of my hand, the guy laid a gold ring.

Inside the ring it said: TO ERIC WITH LOVE, TOM.

Then, just like that, out of the blue, the guy picked up the other green Naugahyde chair, turned with the chair in his hands, and threw the chair through the window. The loud crash of breaking glass. Shiny night on the pieces of glass.

As I looked, the green Naugahyde chair, for a moment, was a still point in the black New York sky, and then the chair was gone.

Nowhere.

Quiet only New York can get that fast.

Then the guy ripped off his nightgown. There was a tattoo snake on his penis. His hip bones stuck out, all his ribs, the skeleton of his head poking through.

He turned. Three giant steps, bare feet onto glass, one step, two steps, three, and with one leap, one long uninterrupted muscle, the guy dived through the window.

Just as I looked, the naked guy in the air—his arms Evita don't cry for me, his cock pointing up—for a moment, the guy was a still point in the black New York sky, waving at Rose and me, smiling, and then he was gone.

Nowhere.

Death is only a window.

Rose lifted himself up in his bed, threw the covers back, pulled the IV off his wrist.

That's when I dived, dived onto Rose, a full body press against him, grabbed the bedposts with my fists, tangled my feet in the bedposts at the bottom end of the bed, used every fucking ounce of strength I had to keep Rose down.

Rose went ghetto on me, calling me a motherfucker, a dumb white honky son-of-a-bitch dog, slamming his fists against my kidneys, in the back of my head.

Rose under me was a bucking bull, a bronco, a panther, a black serpent squeezing the life out of me. My face was in his neck, my body pushing down hard onto him, my feet hooked into the bars, my hands pressing his hands down.

Beneath me, just under my shirt and my khakis, the earthquake of Rose, the monster's huge footfall.

My lips at Rose's ear: Rose, no! Please, Rose, no!

After a while, who knows how long, Rose sank down into the quicksand mattress.

My heavy breath in and out was the same as Rose's breath. I raised my head up, looked into Rose's face, into his eyes.

The whole world was in Rose's eyes, every pain and joy, every betrayal, every first date, every jerk-off, every giddy moment, every death, was staring right back at me.

Rose's lips, his cracked sidewalk lips: Let me jump, let me go; please, Will, please, just let me go!

The horrific whisper.

The way I shut Rose up was I laid a big old wet lots-of-tongue-and-heavy-breathing Hollywood kiss onto him.

All daring and courage, all iron endurance of misfortune.

No way was I going to wave at Rose out the window out there, the still point for a moment in the black New York sky.

No fucking way.

*   *   *

THE FOURTH WEEK, things started looking up. They'd moved Rose into a nicer room. He was alone and the room was yellow instead of green, and the window faced west, so there was sometimes a nice color in the room when the sun went down. The inside of Rose's lips wasn't blue, was getting back the sunset color. His skin wasn't so charcoal. No sweat on the horizontal lines of his forehead, no sweat dripping down the verticals.

One day, an old Cary Grant movie was on the TV, the one with him and Randolph Scott, and that day was the first good day. Rose laughed out loud. Cats fucking. Rose's laugh up and down the hallway of Saint Vincent's, like cats fucking.

EVERY DAY I went up to Rose's apartment and fed Mona and Mary and Jack Flash. While they were eating, I walked around touching things. The ghost of Rose on everything: the brass table, the purple-velvet chair, the blonde-fainting couch. Buddha. The red lava lamp. The Joey Heatherton bed. The French fuchsia telephone with the gold earphone and speaker. The fuchsia bathtub and toilet and sink. The photograph of Elizabeth Taylor as *Cleopatra* behind the brocade blonde-fainting couch, the photograph of Elizabeth Taylor in the white swimsuit in *Suddenly Last Summer* by his bed, and all the other paintings and photographs of Elizabeth Taylor. The Dwight D. Eisenhower ashtray. The Randolph Scott lunch pail. The red velvet curtains. The Persian rugs. The Italian chandelabra that needed dusting.

One day I uncorked the lid on the gallon jar that always sat on the brass coffee table. Leaned over and smelled. The amber liquid was gasoline.

THE FIRST TWO weeks, every day, at the deli on Second Avenue and Fifth, I bought a carnation for Rose. White ones. Pink ones. Red ones.

One day in the third week, when I walked into Room 335 with another red carnation, Rose pointed at me, then moved his index up next to him. I followed his finger, put my ear down close to his mouth.

Lips at my ear: Fucking funeral flowers! Rose said. Get those motherfucking carnations out of here!

The next day I brought a calla lily.

And the next day black-eyed Susans.

Forget-me-nots.

Chrysanthemums.

Primroses.

A half dozen long-stemmed red roses.

The Cary Grant day, I brought some kind of big purple flowers.

And then—I couldn't believe it—the next day when I walked in—*ta-da!*—the room was *full* of flowers, not just mine. Vases and vases, roses, lilies, daisies, Canterbury bells, phlox, heather, lavender, you name it—every kind of flower every color you could imagine. Except carnations.

There were vases on top of the nightstand, the tray you swing over where you eat, on the windowsill, on the floor, on top of the television, on the shelf above the sink, huge draping fuchsia flowers standing on great Grecian pedestals on the green-and-tan tiled floor. They even had to put some of the flowers in the bathroom.

I was standing in a fucking flower shop.

Elizabeth sent them, Rose said. Isn't she sweet!

ON THE THIRTY-THIRD day in the hospital, the day he got out, Rose told me what outfit to bring: the black and avocado striped pedal pushers, the red seersucker shirt, his red bikini briefs, the mules, and the hologram earrings.

I brought Rose's mirror and barber clippers like he told me, and in the hospital bathroom, Rose holding the mirror, I clipped Rose's inch of curly black and silver hair down to stubble. Then, Rose's special Kiehl's shaving lotion rubbed in my hands, I applied the shaving lotion open palm to Rose's head.

New razor blades in the razor.

Every pull of the razor against Rose's scalp was a cattle prod to my cock, but I didn't nick him, not once. Then a mixture of rosemary and passion flower oil made Rose's head shine.

The nurses came in, all smiles. Every kind of woman you could imagine, black brown white yellow, short fat thin. Each one of them gave Rose a kiss. They'd made him a card, a drawing of Rose in purple Mae West drag. Under the drawing, the words:

No no no, Yoko Ono!

Rose screamed when he opened the card.

The little scream that gives it all away.

Oh, you shouldn't have! Rose said, bracelets clack-clack.

* * *

FROZEN MOMENTS IN time.

The way Rose walked out of that hospital was something to behold. Ankles, knees, hips, belly, back, shoulders, arms, neck, head, head bone connected to the tail bone, one long graceful black muscle, mules snapping on the shiny hospital green-and-brown tiles with every step.

Rose handed out roses as he walked.

The bright hallway, shiny tiles, Rose's runway.

Every orderly, every doctor, every anesthesiologist, every nurse and aide, every candy striper, every janitor, every lab technician, every patient who was still alive stopped, watched Rose walk.

You could feel the anticipation, the hope of theater to lay bare the human heart.

In all the world, every eye on Rose, on Rose's body, deep from the center of him, from his balls out to his shoulders, his calves, his ass, to the tips of his fingers, the top of his head. Rose thirty pounds slimmer. Rose's size thirteen mules, his pedal pushers stretched over his ass, his big basket, the red seersucker shirt open and tied at the waist, hologram earring dangle, shiny head, catching light, Rose's bracelets—the green Bakelite, the copper, the silver Sikh, the gold with the lapis, the jade—clack-clack.

In full participation with the life flowing through his body. A man dancing alone in a room. Complete lusty presence, his lucid lucid compulsion, Rose extra extra extra lovely.

Keep dancing and cop an attitude.

A polemical kind of fuck-you-motherfucker joy.

MONA AND MARY and Jack Flash were barking barking, their tongues hanging out like wet bologna, jumping up on Rose. Jack Flash was back and forth every which way around Rose's apartment, running like the wind.

WELCOME HOME ROSE was the banner I'd hung from wall to wall, and I'd bought helium balloons, fuchsia helium balloons. I'd found an old photo of Elizabeth Taylor in a secondhand shop on Second Avenue. The photo was in an Egyptian deco frame and Elizabeth was Cleopatra. The photo was sitting on the brass coffee table.

The little scream that gives it all away.

Rose picked up the photo and the frame, his eyes, ebony stones rolled smooth, looked at Elizabeth the same way she looked at Montgomery Clift in A *Place in the Sun.*

Rose laid the photo up against his heart.

Perfect, Rose said. Just perfect.

Then Rose threw his arms around me, bracelets clack-clack, and we kissed like they do in Europe, both cheeks.

ROSE SAT DOWN in his purple-velvet overstuffed chair. I brought him the lovely erect pink penis with a big Sho-ko-lat rabbit turd in it, lit the rabbit turd, and Rose sucked in.

Rose's Sahara palm holding the erect pink penis, Rose's inside sunset color of his lips, Rose's head shiny, his hologram earring, flash flash. Jack Flash was lying in Rose's lap, and Mary and Mona were on the Persian rug at Rose's feet, and the lighting was just so, like Bobbie's Marilyn Monroe light, soft, the red velvet drapes pulled. I put on Maria Callas, "Norma," and I rolled cigarettes, one for Rose and one for me, lit Rose's, lit mine. I got the Baccarat crystal glasses out, poured us both a Courvoisier VSOP, and we toasted: *Salud, L'chayim, Na zdarovya*, Bottoms Up, Here's Looking at You.

For a moment there, I believed everything was going to be all right.

But it wasn't the truth.

Just like that, Rose threw up, all over himself, the purple-velvet overstuffed chair, the brass coffee table, Jack Flash, his red seersucker shirt, and his black and avocado pedal pushers.

CHAPTER TWENTY

The first big winter blizzard that year—whirling big wind like to knock you over—I turned my ball cap back around so the bill could keep the snow off my face, turned the collar of my pea coat up, hunched my shoulders, kept my head down, tried to bury my ears, stuck my hands in my big pea coat pockets, but it was no use.

Show World was warm inside. I stomped off my feet and I could feel my socks wet inside my wet shoes. There was a big black man, not big pumped up, he was just a huge man, like if you took a man my size and stretched everything out a foot longer—this huge man worked at Show World and he's checking me out, so I went right to the magazines in the row of magazines down the center of the room. Unrelenting neon light from above. The magazine I stopped at said *Big Boobs* and there was this blond woman on the cover whose breasts were bigger than her head, twice as big as her head, even with all her big blond hair.

The sign just above on the magazine stand said HOLD MAGAZINE WITH BOTH HANDS. My hands were wet and in the unrelenting fluorescence looked like cooked lobsters.

On down the magazine stand: *Blow Job. Wet Pussy. Licking Lesbians. Back Door Love. French Tickler. Bi-Frenzy. Tits and Ass. Ebony and Ivory. Eight Inch Tongue. Yellow Snow. Piss on Me. Cum Suckers. Cock Crazy.*

Downstairs was the gay part. The men were every kind of man and were not looking at the magazines so much as holding the magazine out with both hands so you can see what it was they liked.

Fuck Buddies. Big Cock. Black Dick. Suck and Fuck. Fuck Frenzy. Big Balls. Up the Ass. Latino Lovers. Top Man. Black Brothers. Master and Slave. Sodomy Man. Cum Crazy. Sweaty Assholes. Asian Glory. Cowboys and Indians.

I picked up *Cowboys and Indians* with both hands and flipped through the pages. A cowboy sees an Indian and a white horse by a stream. The cowboy pulls a gun on the Indian. Ties the Indian's hands behind him.

The Indian has a big bulge under his leather pouch. The cowboy lifts the pouch, sucks off the Indian. The Indian loves it. Then the cowboy's hands are tied behind him. The cowboy's hat is still on, and his boots, and the holster and gun around his waist and his legs are in the air and the Indian is fucking the cowboy in the ass. The cowboy loves it. Some Union Army guys see the white horse and then see the Indian fucking the cowboy. Then the army guys are all fucking each other and sucking each other and the cowboy and the Indian. Three Indians see the white horse, then see the army guys fucking and sucking each other and the cowboy and the Indian. The Indians all start sucking and fucking the army guys and the cowboy and the Indian and each other. The last page, the Indians and the army guys and the cowboy all are riding off into the sunset on their horses and it says on the last page: *How the west was won.*

In the corner under the stairs was another section and a shelf of books. These books were not magazines, they were novels. INCEST LITERATURE the sign said in red letters above the shelf.

Uncle John and Me on the Lake. Out in the Woodshed with Tommy. Kissing Cousins. Sodomy Brothers. Daddy Dearest.

The guy behind the counter in front of the wall of dildos was white, shaved head, Hawaiian shirt. His nails were bitten. I gave the guy behind the counter one dollar.

Inside the booth, I closed the door, pulled the seat down, and sat in the blue light. Token into the slot.

A football team of jock cocks, a classroom of student cocks. A prison cell of inmate cocks. A submarine full of sailor cocks. An army barracks of army cocks. A swimming pool full of swimmer cocks.

Every cock a huge cock.

Fifty-four channels.

In each side wall of the booth, there was a window with a curtain over it. Two buttons next to a red arrow said CURTAIN RIGHT and CURTAIN LEFT.

I pushed both curtain buttons and the curtains on each side of me went up, and just like that, on my right on the other side of the greasy Plexiglas, was a white guy, his pants down around his knees, cock poking up, the guy pumping tokens into the slot, watching a video of a guy sitting in a chair, shitting out one firm dark-brown turd at a time, one at a time.

The guy on my left looked like a Korean guy. He was totally naked sitting like Buddha on the seat with a huge black dildo up his butt. The

Korean guy, all Saint Theresa Gone to Heaven, looked over at me, pinched his nipple, blew me a kiss.

And then on down the line, the same way as when you open a mirror and angle the mirror with another mirror so it looks like you looking at yourself forever and forever.

Frozen moments in time.

On each side of me, forever and ever, men in their booths, every kind of man, each man in his booth, dancing alone in his room with someone watching, with his curtain up, with his savage beast, his tiny Catholic heart, his legs up, his cock out, his cock against the Plexiglas, his butt hole against the Plexiglas, his mouth. Men in the blue light, the images on the videos screaming and fucking and coming and shitting and sucking. The men, each in their booth, jerking off with one hand, pushing tokens into the slot with the other.

The janitor at Show World looked like Grandfather Alessandro. The guy had a mop in his hand, a mop bucket next to him on the floor. I went to step around the guy. I looked down at my feet. I was standing in his mopped-up pool. The pool looked like sticky New York City melting gray snow.

But it's not the truth.

DURING THOSE MONTHS Rose was so sick, I called and called Romeo Movers. I really needed to talk to someone besides Rose, and Fiona was always wound up in her trip with Stranded Beings Searching for God. But True Shot never picked up, or wasn't there, or else had suddenly dropped off the face of the earth. Ever since that night in the meat district when I told True Shot about Charlie 2Moons' scar, there had been no communication, nothing at all.

Ruby kept calling. Same old shit. Breathing, burping, street noise, sirens. One time I picked up.

Ruby, I said, where's True Shot?

Ruby coughed and coughed and coughed, hacked up, spit.

William of Heaven, Ruby said, from underwater.

Ruby, I said, Where's True Shot? Is he all right?

Street noise.

Ruby, I said, Can you stop being so fucking stoned for just a second and tell me where True Shot is?

Fools, Ruby said. Pharisees, he said. Noam Chomsky.

* * *

I'D CALLED THE Columbia Writing Program several times. I'd spoken with a Joe, a Mary, a Harriet, a Mark, a Liz, a Jane, even the head of the department, a Stephen Something-or-other, but no Janet, and not once did anyone ever know anything about Sebastian Cooke.

Sebastian Cooke never returned my letter.

Most of all, nothing, nowhere, nohow, ever, never one single iota of a shred of info about Charlie 2Moons.

Nothing.

No Charlie 2Moons.

Nowhere.

APRIL OR MAY 1987. Outside on East Fifth Street a Conran truck was double-parked. Someone was yelling so I opened my window.

It was Fiona.

You're two fucking hours late! Fiona was screaming. Next time I'm going with Pottery Barn!

The truck driver was a small brown man. He just stood on the back of the truck, staring at the screaming woman in a black leotard, her hair flying up all over the place.

The chairs were in cardboard boxes and Fiona didn't want the cardboard boxes, she only wanted the chairs, and the truck driver said the chairs come with the boxes, and Fiona said, I have no place for the boxes, and the truck driver said, That's your problem, lady, and Fiona said, I'm not a lady, asshole, and why can't you just put the cardboard back in your truck and take it off with you to cardboard heaven? And the truck driver said, It's against company policy, and Fiona said, Fuck company fucking policy, I've got a tiny theater and what the fuck am I going to do with three acres of cardboard? Burn it?

You can shove it up your ass, lady! the truck driver said.

Fuck you! Fiona said.

No, fuck you! the truck driver said.

No, fuck you! Fiona said.

Fiona stomped back into Stranded Beings Searching for God. The truck driver was just about to jump out of the truck.

I yelled out at the truck driver to wait. I ran out of my apartment, out the front door, down the stoop. Stopped running, walked up to him, reached up my hand for a handshake. The truck driver looked at my hand New York drop-dead fuck-you. I took my hand back and put it in my back pocket.

This woman, I said, She's my friend. Her name is Susan and she is a very high-strung person. I said, She's taking high-blood-pressure medication.

The truck driver stayed squatted. The muscles in his legs were tight against his jeans. He was wearing a red T-shirt, rolled-up sleeves, a tattoo of Puerto Rico on his right bicep.

The truck driver said something in Spanish, *puta*, I think.

She's got an even bigger problem, though, I said. In fact, everybody in the building has this big problem.

I stepped closer to the truck, leaned my arm against the truck bed. When I spoke, I kept my voice low.

The building's super is the voodoo super from hell, I said. He's a devil worshiper who casts spells on the tenants if they fuck with his garbage.

The truck driver looked up the street and down the street when I said *voodoo*.

Please, I said. Can't you please take the cardboard?

Then I brought out the twenty-dollar bill.

On the inside of his arm, the truck driver had a red heart tattoo that said *Crisantema* across it.

The truck driver took the twenty.

I helped him take each black steel folding chair out of its box, fold up the carboard, and put the cardboard on the truck.

Fiona said, Cool.

We were just bringing in the last of the chairs when it started to rain. I grabbed two chairs, and Fiona grabbed two chairs. We were just running down into Stranded Beings Searching for God when Rose came walking down the stoop.

First time I'd seen Rose outside his apartment since he went in. His face under a huge red umbrella looked purple. Rose was wearing Lolita sunglasses, a checkered skirt like the Prince of Wales, combat boots, a leather jacket, and a black T-shirt with yellow lettering that said FUCK JESSE HELMS. Mary, Mona, and Jack Flash were on leashes.

When Fiona saw Rose, Fiona dropped the chairs she was carrying and headed quick for the door.

Rose stopped on the stoop, leaned over the railing.

Shit spray, my dear? Rose said.

Fiona stopped.

It was not a heavy rain but a quick splash, just enough to make everything wet.

Argwings Khodek, Fiona said, and looked up Rose's skirt, You're my Absolute Ultimate Idol.

AUI, Rose said, bracelets clack-clack.

In all the world, at the bottom of the stoop, on the sidewalk, in the rectangle of earth where I'd plant the cherry tree, everything wet, the dirt wet, Rose's huge red umbrella scratching the top of my head, is where it happened.

Argwings Khodek, I said, Susan Strong.

Susan Strong, I said, Argwings Khodek.

Fiona's hand was so small and so white inside Rose's.

Fiona knelt down. At first I thought it was supplication, but she was kneeling so she could pet Mary and Mona. Jack Flash started growling.

Then: I understand, Rose said, That you need a headliner to open up your new performance space. I've heard many good things about you, Rose said. I understand you have a fine spirit, so I agree to do it. You can talk to my agent, William of Heaven here, for the details.

Fiona stood up, and it was like when you stand up too fast and you see colors.

Oh, my fucking God Jesus Christ shit! Fiona said.

I assume that means yes, Rose said.

Rose's bracelets clack-clack.

Yes, Fiona said.

Shall we set a date then? Rose said.

Fiona looked around for something, for anything.

June, Fiona said. The first Saturday in June.

Rain again. Harder this time, then hail.

Rose and Fiona and Mary and Mona and Jack Flash and me all trying to stand under Rose's huge red umbrella, big white pieces of hail banging down on cars and on the sidewalk and on the umbrella.

The first Saturday in June it is, Rose said.

Cool, Fiona said. Totally cool.

THE LAST WEEK in May, posters all over the Lower East Side, on every telephone pole and empty wall space you could imagine, all different colors—purple, pink, green, blue, yellow—there it was, the Xerox photograph of Rose in his Antigone drag.

STRANDED BEINGS SEARCHING FOR GOD
OPENING NIGHT, ARGWINGS KHODEK
SATURDAY, JUNE 7, 8 P.M.

On Second Avenue and Fifth Street I tore a poster off a telephone pole and thumbtacked Rose's picture to the wall above my bed next to Daniel's beer-can dick.

SATURDAY AT LAST. My hair was still wet from the shower, and I wore my black cutoffs and my black T-shirt and my white socks with a red stripe at the top and my combat boots and a string of cheap imitation pearls Rose gave me.

I taped RESERVED on four chairs : One chair for the *Village Voice*, one chair for *The New Yorker*, one chair for Dance Theater Workshop, and one chair for *The Times*.

A snowball in hell, Fiona said, *The New Yorker* or *The Times* showing up, Fiona said. Still, it looks cool.

At seven-thirty, when I unlocked the door to Stranded Beings Searching for God and looked outside, already there were a dozen people standing on the steps and on the sidewalk. I took everybody's five dollars at the door.

At seven-fifty, the place was almost full. There was a break in the line of people coming in, so I ran over to Fiona, who was busy behind the counter selling corn dogs and beer.

Is he here yet? Fiona asked.

Who, Harry? I said.

No, Fiona said. Argwings Khodek.

Not yet, I said. He's changing upstairs, I said. Don't worry, he'll show. Where's Harry? I said.

My parents here? Fiona asked. I haven't dared look.

Don't know, I said. What do they look like?

Fiona gave some guy a napkin with his corn dog.

High-maintenance chick, Fiona said. Silver hair, tall, covered in silk.

With three guys? I said. Who look like lawyers? I said.

Oh, fuck! Fiona said. My father and my brothers.

Aren't your brothers sick? I said.

Fiona was looking across the audience. Then all at once Fiona smiled so all her teeth were showing and waved. The high-maintenance silver-haired chick covered in silk waved, and the three lawyers.

Where's Harry? I said.

Throwing up, Fiona said. He's real dizzy. Just opening-night jitters. He just called, Fiona said. Said he'll be here. It's cool.

Who's going to run the lights and sound if he doesn't show? I said.

He'll show, Fiona said. Harry will show.

ROSE CAME THROUGH the door just before eight o'clock with his purple velvet cape draped over him with the hood up. All I could tell was he had a lot of makeup on. Dark glasses. He was carrying the large BARNEY'S bag and went straight to the dressing room.

Eight o'clock, I walked out onto East Fifth Street.

No Harry.

No Charlie 2Moons.

I closed the front door. Fifty-four people. Forty seated, fourteen standing. Only two empty seats, *The New Yorker* and *The Times*.

Harry was nowhere, so I went to the light board and turned up the house lights. On the stage were two Greek pillars with a piece of emerald-green velvet cloth draped between them.

FIONA WAS ALL in black. Zipper-up-the-front top, black tights. On her arms about a million bracelets. Red lips a life all their own. She walked onto the stage and grabbed the mike like she was finally home.

Welcome to Stranded Beings Searching for God, Fiona said. And now, ladies and gentlemen, Argwings Khodek as Antigone!

Whistles, Yee-hahs, people going wild clapping. People were yelling *Vive la Rose!* so loud you couldn't hear yourself think. I was clapping too, so hard was I clapping for Rose.

ROSE WALKED OUT into the unrelenting light of the spotlight. The black wig was fake shiny with marcel waves. He was wearing a white bedsheet, draped like Greeks over just one shoulder. Purple platform high heels you could see when he walked. Rose close to seven feet tall. Huge eyelashes, maybe three inches long, up and down, up and down. Painted-on eyebrows in the middle of his forehead. Rose's red lips twice their size. Glitter everywhere.

A red accordion hung from the crook of his right arm. Rose undid the clasp of the accordion, and the bellows out made a sound, and the audience laughed a little bit, and I laughed too.

On Rose's fingernails, purple Lee Press-On nails.

Rose didn't smile. Didn't look at the audience. His shoulders bent back a little when the accordion settled.

My heart beat. My breath.

There he stood, the fake shiny wig above the red accordion, the three-inch false eyelashes, the red lips, his huge black arms poking out of his sheet, the purple Lee Press-On nails pressed onto his fingernails, his fingers on the black and white keys.

Rose took a breath in and the accordion stretched out. He flexed his arms and went to press down on the keys, but he didn't press.

Sweat on Rose's neck, his arms, beading up on the eyebrows painted on his forehead.

Rose took another breath in and the accordion stretched out. He flexed his arms and went to press down on the keys, but he didn't press.

Who knows how long Rose stood that way.

Quiet in the theater. Quiet only New York can get.

Another breath in. Then Rose looked down like he suddenly realized there was a red accordion hanging off him.

His black hands, his fingers, began moving up and down, Lee Press-On fingernails click-click against the keys. The song came out some polka *oom-pah oom-pah.*

Just as quick as he started, Rose stopped playing.

He bent forward as if the accordion were so much heavier than an accordion. His arms went down, purple Lee Press-On nails pointed to the floor.

Rose stood and stood, his left eye open wide, his right eye almost closed. Beads of sweat tiny illuminations on his painted face.

People coughed, someone giggled. I laughed a little loud so Rose would know.

Then: This is all wrong, Rose said, bracelets clack-clack. All wrong. I'm not doing Antigone tonight. It's too late for Antigone.

Could somebody, Rose yelled, Please get this Greek shit off the stage?

Low murmurs from the audience. I quick jumped up to get the Greek shit off the stage. But then Fiona walked out, stage left.

Shit-spray.

Fiona was shit-spray. Her lip a life all its own. She walked behind Rose, her shoulders low. She pulled the emerald green velvet drape off from between the pillars, picked up one Greek pillar and put it under her arm, grabbed the other Greek pillar.

Rose cupped his hands over his huge painted red lips.

William of Heaven? Rose yelled. Rose looked right out at me. Turn the house lights up! he said.

The house lights was a switch on the top left of the light panel. One flick and the audience all at once wasn't sitting in a theater anymore, just a bright room with chairs in it.

Could you come up here, Rose said, And help get this shit off me?

Low murmurs from the crowd. I tripped over a chair. The step up to the stage was a big one. All over on me, the house lights, unrelenting.

Help me with this goddamn thing, Rose said.

Rose looked right at me and was talking to me like we were just two ordinary guys, not on a stage in front of fifty-four people.

Rose's body was dripping sweat. The white sheet was sticking to his legs. One arm, then the other, Rose pulled himself out of the accordion and then the accordion was in my arms, an accordion breath scream, the bellows pinching a long slice of my chest and belly.

Just put it over there, Rose said.

Over there was stage left, so my feet walked across the stage four steps. I bent over and set the accordion down and it made a sound. My breath was in and out. Then, just as I turned to take my four steps back to Rose, the audience gasped.

Rose was naked. The sheet was off and there he was, Rose standing naked in a bright room with chairs in it and people sitting in the chairs.

Rose's arms, his chest, his Buddha belly, his cock and balls, his thighs and calves and knees, bare naked on the stage.

Under him, his feet stuck into purple platform high heels.

On his fingernails, Lee Press-On nails.

On top of him, the painted face and the wig.

Get my makeup kit out of the Green Room, Rose said. It's the big bag that says BARNEY'S on it.

Even backstage, I was still onstage, like every eye in the fucking world was on me. I turned on the light in the bathroom. Fiona was on the toilet, head in her hands, shit-spray. I grabbed Rose's BARNEY's bag, shut the light back off.

The line, the black hard-edged line between offstage and onstage. From the dark back into the bright, over that hard edge, my mother's nerves, it was four steps, four giant steps, and I was back next to Rose.

The bright on Rose's chest and belly, on his balls and cock, the hairs sticking up off him into the house lights unrelenting, Rose standing in his purple platform high heels, paint on his face, fingernails—Rose was so much more than naked.

I stepped between him and the audience, looked up.

Up that close, in all that bright, all I could see was paint.

Rose, I whispered. Rose, are you all right?

Of course I'm all right, Rose said.

His big eyelashes up and down, up and down.

And you? Rose said. How are you?

Behind me, the audience. Fifty-four pairs of eyes on my back.

Cool, I said.

Fabulous, Rose said.

Rose took the BARNEY's bag. Even his Sahara palms were sweating. A muscle in his naked bicep jumped.

Rose? I said.

That will do for now, Rose said, I'll call you if I need anything else.

It was so hard to tell if this was a performance Rose was doing or if it was just Rose standing on the stage talking to me.

Except that Rose was sweating. Except that his hands were shaking.

Then, just like that, Rose said, just ordinary: Where's Harry?

Didn't show, I said.

Rose's lips a Bronx cheer.

I *love* the theah-*tah*, Rose said, bracelets clack-clack.

Rose's smile, the fake gold tooth. Rose's lips were chapped. Blood in the corner of his mouth.

Well then, Rose said, You'll have to do the light board. Line up the yellow dot on the rheostat with the yellow mark, the amber dot with the amber mark and then turn the fucking house lights off.

Don't worry, Rose said, You'll do fine. When I tell you, Rose said, Turn the spot on. Make sure I'm in it.

Then: Susan Strong! Rose yelled.

The toilet flushed.

I had to laugh, then other people laughed.

Fiona walked onstage, a bright smile an erector set for her broken lip.

Rose touched Fiona on the shoulder. The muscles in her back jumped. Rose leaned his head down, whispered something in Fiona's ear.

THE YELLOW, AMBER, and the red dots were aligned with their marks. I flipped the switch and the fucking house lights went off.

The light on the stage a soft gold color.

The bedsheet a pile of folded gold.

Behind Rose, stage left, stood Ronald Reagan. Stage right stood Nancy.

Rose sat cross-legged on the floor, center stage.

Fiona put a tape in the tape player and just like that music started, just a trombone and a bass, playing music I only knew as Deep South. Slow sorrowful jazz about death.

OK, Will! Rose yelled. Give me the spot.

The spotlight was the second rheostat from the left. I pushed the rheostat up. Onstage, Rose was sitting right in the middle of the light.

C'est parfait! Rose said.

Rose pulled off his wig, threw it out into the audience. The woman from the *Village Voice* caught it. Then his purple platform high heels, one each flying into the air.

Hands spread out in front of his face, palm in, Rose finger-to-thumb flipped Lee Press-On nails, spit ten purple chips out into the light.

Next, the eyelashes. Rose pulled them off from the nose out, let them drop. Spiders falling through the spotlight.

Out of the BARNEY's bag, Rose pulled out a jar of something, unscrewed the lid, wrapped the sheet around his other hand, dipped the sheet into the jar. Rubbed the sheet around and around on his face.

The eyebrows, the eyeliner, the eye shadow, the lipstick, the lip liner, the mascara onto the sheet, glitter red and blue and purple.

The bass and the trombone, *Nobody knows my sorrow.*

Fiona held her stomach with one hand and in the other she carried a blue bucket onstage. The way she leaned the bucket was heavy. She set the bucket down next to the BARNEY's bag. When Rose pulled the bucket upstage, little splashes of water.

Rose knelt up. His knee cracked. Then Rose sat back down on his feet, Japanese style. Pulled his cock and balls up, closed his thighs, let his cock down nice inside his ball sack.

His face down next to the water, Rose stared into what he could see. What I saw was the scar on Rose's head from when he fell on the stoop, the rolling muscles across his back.

Then Rose stood, Atlas, the whole body of him, his arms raised up, armpit hair, the blue bucket in his hands. Rose looked up at the blue bucket as he poured the water down his body. Water caught the light, splashed down onto him. Splashes of water dark spots on the floor making one big dark spot. Some people in the front row pushed their chairs back.

A man standing alone in his room, Rose took the sheet and wiped his face, under his arms, his crotch, his ass.

Then Rose was back down again, sitting cross-legged like Buddha, his arms round down onto his legs. His hands, his Sahara palms, thumb and index a circle on each knee. Rose's inhale brought his chest up and his belly in. With the exhale, Rose smiled his gold gap-tooth smile.

The sheet. Rose took two corners of the sheet and flipped the sheet up. In the soft gold light, the sheet above was a sunset cloud. The cloud settled down over his head, his shoulders, his knees.

In the spotlight, the sheet was white unrelenting.

Except for the eyeholes. Rose's two black eyes, behind, within the eyeholes he'd cut into the sheet.

Nobody knows.

Not a breath in the room.

Who knows how long Rose sat there.

Rose is still sitting there.

THE SHEET. ROSE stood up, pulled the sheet off his head, wrapped the sheet around his waist, pulled a corner up through his crotch, cinched the corner into a loincloth.

From stage left, the wheel rolled in. It was a mounted whitewall tire with a stain of red on the white wall. BUICK on the chrome hubcap rolling through the four directions. Rose put out his hand and stopped the wheel. BUICK a perfect horizontal. Rose's palm open just next to the stain.

Rose spit on his fingers, scratched at the red.

From inside the BARNEY's bag, Rose pulled out two cans of Old Dutch Cleanser.

A can in each hand, Rose looked out at the audience, turned the cans upside down, shook.

White cloud Old Dutch Cleanser, white powder, white floating up, white dust, white, white. Pretty soon white powder on the floor an inch deep.

White powder on Ronald Reagan. On Nancy.

White powder on Rose's legs, arms, shoulders, hands. White powder on Rose's face and head. Sweat through white.

Rose's eyes black holes in the white.

Rose's one knee buckled, then the other, he turned his back to the audience. White powder, sweat, on Rose's back.

Rose reached in the BARNEY's bag, grabbed the scrub brush, laid the brush against the stain on the white-wall tire, leaned his muscle into it. Back and forth, back and forth, the scrub.

Nobody knows the trouble, the sorrow.

Nobody knows.

INSIDE STRANDED BEINGS Searching for God was unrelenting house lights. And chaos.

People were clapping, screaming, yelling. One man ran up to Rose, knelt down, and started kissing Rose's feet.

My mother's nerves.

In nothing flat, I was out the door and up the three steps. My heart beat, my breath. The pain in my forearms. The car parked at the curb was a Buick. The whitewalls, all four of them, no blood. I walked around the Buick again, checked for sure.

My hand in my shirt pocket for my tobacco, I leaned my ass against the Buick, and wouldn't you know it, I set off the car alarm.

Another New Yorker gone to hell.

The fucking alarm blared for ten minutes. All I could do is what I usually do, and that's roll cigarettes, one right after another. All around on the sidewalks, people were standing close, in small groups, lighting cigarettes too, holding on to each other, cussing at the car alarm, talking talking.

Was that blood on the tire?

Do you think BUICK is significant?

Why Old Dutch Cleanser? Why not Ajax?

Above us, the June stars were tiny illuminations in the navy blue sky. The wind was cool and the cool felt good on my sweat.

When I looked down from the stars to the top of 205 East Fifth Street, down and down, my eyes stopped at the first-story window.

Mrs. Lupino was standing in her window. She had a white sheet wrapped around her and something on her head like a Christmas decoration with gold stars and moons on it. In the crook of one arm, she was holding a statue of the Virgin. In her other hand she held a red votive candle. The light from the candle, below her face, made the lines of her face look like a mask. On the windowsill were two cats, the yellow New York drop-dead fuck-you cat and the black cat with the green eyes.

Some people on the sidewalk were staring up at Mrs. Lupino too, but nobody thought it was weird. She looked like the logo for Stranded Beings Searching for God.

That's when I saw Harry.

Harry sat down next to me on the stoop. His bright Hawaiian shirt, green and red and blue, was soaked through. Sweat stains on his khaki pants. Crusty critters in the corners of his eyes. His pink skin not so pink. His hair wasn't carrot-top curls anymore but just a red rug on his head. Harry's hand was hot.

Roll me a cigarette? Harry said.

You don't smoke, I said.

I'm smoking tonight, Harry said.

I pulled one of the cigarettes from my shirt pocket. Lit Harry's, lit mine.

Where *were* you, Harry? I said. You all right?

Opening-night jitters, Harry said.

This always happen to you?

Harry pinched a button on his Hawaiian shirt and pulled the shirt away from his chest. It was Argwings Khodek, Harry said. Vomit spray.

Then: Jesus! Harry said. What's that?

What? I said.

Up there in the window! Harry said.

Oh, I said, That's Mrs. Lupino.

While Harry was looking up at Mrs. Lupino, I was looking at Harry, at his face turned toward the porch light of 205 East Fifth Street. A drop of sweat under his sideburn rolled by his ear down to his jaw.

You feeling all right, Harry? I said.

How was the performance? Harry said. Brilliant?

Complete presence, I said.

Then: Say, Harry said. Let's see if we can ditch Susan Strong's family and the three of us go have a beer somewhere.

We could go to Fish Bar, I said.

Does Argwings Khodek want to join us? Harry said.

Rose? I said. I don't know. Have you seen him?

No, Harry said.

He's probably too tired, I said. Usually on Saturday nights, we watch *Saturday Night Live*.

Harry put both hands on his Hawaiian shirt stomach.

Oh, good, Harry said. I couldn't handle any more vomit spray.

Then: Excuse me, Harry said. I need to talk to Susan Strong.

Cool, I said.

Harry pushed his hand against the stoop and pushed himself up. I stood up too because Harry was weaving. I put my shoulder into him. Harry stepped back quick, reached into his butt pocket, and grabbed a red handkerchief. Right side.

I'm all right, I'm all right! Harry said.

Harry wiped his face, and when he turned he used the newel post. Just when Harry was at the door of Stranded Beings Searching for God, I quick hollered out, Harry! Argwings Khodek might still be in there!

Harry stuck his head slow inside the door, hollered something inside, then something else. Then Harry turned my way and made his lips pronounce the words big: *He showered, then left*, Harry said.

Up the eleven steps of the stoop, up the thirteen steps to Rose's apartment, I knocked loud on Rose's door, three or four times. No dogs barked.

Back down the thirteen steps, on the stoop, left and right, no Rose in the crowd of people on the sidewalk.

Rose was not in Fish Bar.

No Rose in either of the bathrooms.

Then I got to thinking Rose was up on the roof, so back down the block, back up the eleven steps of the stoop, then up the one hundred and two steps to the roof.

No Rose.

No Charlie 2Moons.

Back down on the stoop, Harry was sitting on the bottom step.

Harry, I said, No Argwings Khodek?

God forbid! Harry said.

Harry poked his elbow into my ribs.

There! Harry said. Right over there.

Rose? I said. Where?

Not Rose, Harry said, Her parents—Susan Strong's parents.

Who?

Susan Strong's family, Harry said. Over by the garbage cans.

I handed Harry a cigarette and lit it for him. Harry's hands were shaking.

Susan Strong's parents, Harry said. Dave and Margo.

Harry blew out smoke, coughed, spit tobacco.

And her brothers, Harry said. Gus and Hunter.

Harry held his stomach when he stood up.

All this family shit! Harry said. How can you reinvent your life if the original versions won't leave you alone?

Even if they're dead, I said.

Just a car length away from the stoop, the silver-haired high-maintenance chick and the three lawyers all stood together, close, in some kind of circle. The father and the sons on the outside, the silver-haired chick in the middle.

No matter where they go, Harry said, The MacIlvanes always look like a garden party in Greenwich.

They're so collegiate! I said.

Perfect family, Harry said. Anti-Defamation League. Amnesty International. Dave is a lawyer for Greenpeace. They love their children—their two little queer sons and their headstrong Muffy. Margo is head of Catholic Mothers with Gay Children, CMGC. House on Martha's Vineyard.

God, Harry said. It goes on forever.

Susan Strong, I said, Has a mother.

Insidious! Harry said.

And a father, I said.

Susan Strong and I figure we're aliens, Harry said. We both have Pluto right next to our ascendants.

James Joyce's idiot savant daughter, I said. Fucked a truck driver.

And New York's only Irish Catholic homosexual, I said.

On the rectangle of earth where I'd plant the cherry tree, I put my one hand on Gus's shoulder, one hand on Hunter's, on the seersucker of their sports jackets. Hunter turned and Gus turned. They looked like twin Christopher Reeves when he's Superman, not Clark Kent.

I was just wondering, I said. How did you get so sure, so believable, so beautiful?

Hunter said, Good genes.

Gus said, Good education.

Hunter said, Good connections.

Gus said, Good vacations.

Hunter said, Friends.

Gus said, Family.

Hunter said, Wealth.

Gus said, Privilege.

But it's not the truth. I didn't go over to Fiona's family.

* * *

HARRY HELD THE cigarette between his thumb and index finger. All around him on the stoop were drops of sweat.

You ever seen *Autumn Sonata*? Harry said. It's this film, Harry said, About a mother who is a professional pianist, Ingrid Bergman and her daughter, Liv Ullman.

A talent for reality, I said.

Right, Harry said. A talent for reality. Being present in the moments of your life and remembering them.

Ingrid Bergman? I said.

Ingmar too, Harry said.

Just then, Margo and Dave and Hunter and Gus all laughed. All at once, all the MacIlvanes laughed.

Then, all at once, Fiona was standing on the sidewalk, just up from the steps of Stranded Beings Searching for God.

On one person, in all my life, I'd never seen so much leather, so many chains and studs. Leather bra. Leather body halter. Leather miniskirt. Leather studded belt. Leather studded bracelets. Chains dripping off her ears, her shoulders, her waist. Leather boots. Leather jacket slung over her shoulder. Studs and chains on the jacket. Fiona's hair was piled on top of her head about two feet high, wires and electrical shit and red combs and rhinestones in her hair.

I can fuck you blind and keep it simple. Try me.

All that standing right underneath Mrs. Lupino in her window wearing the white sheet and holding the Virgin and the votive candle with the cats.

Heaven above us, Hell below.

Thank God she left off the dildo, Harry said.

Fiona, walking performance space that she was, leaned against the newel post. She raised her chin, poked her breasts out, and with a smile as large as her lips cried, Mother!

Fiona waved her hand, elbow elbow, wrist wrist wrist.

Father! Wasn't it marvelous?

The MacIlvanes' bodies all pointed at Fiona. The high-maintenance silver-haired chick and the three lawyers were smiling smiling.

Margo MacIlvane was a tall woman, big-boned, thick silver-white hair parted down the middle of her head, white hair curling in line with her chin. Tanned. Blue Fiona eyes. No makeup, maybe some eye makeup and a little peach lipstick. High cheekbones, long narrow nose. She was wearing a white silk blouse, a deep purple paisley scarf, and dark slacks with a belt. Tan ankles, long feet, in soft brown leather shoes, no heel. Her shoes matched her belt and her purse—the purse strap across the front of her. The purse was small, monogrammed, at her hip. She moved the purse from her hip and put it in front of her, folded her hands over it, pushed her hips forward, leaned back.

Dave MacIlvane was smoking a pipe and looked like a Kennedy—dark brown hair longish from the sixties, gray at the temples, tortoiseshell glasses that he poked back onto his nose. Dave was wearing those leather kind of slip-on shoes men from New England wear on boats, khaki pants, belt, a blue button-down oxford shirt, silk paisley tie loose at the collar.

The twins, Hunter and Gus, were not dressed exactly alike, but close. Seersucker suits, white shirts, silk ties undone. Variations of Dave. YUFAs. The Hyannisport Homos were leaning back, same angle as Margo, hands folded in front of them same as Margo.

The MacIlvanes all started to talk at once and then they all stopped.

Then it was Margo. She hadn't moved from her leaned-back angle, and she didn't move while she spoke.

Yes, simply marvelous! Margo said. The smile. We enjoyed it, didn't we, Dave? Margo said. A naked black man is just what we wanted to see tonight.

Hi, honey! Dave said to Fiona. You were great.

Margo MacIlvane walked over to her daughter, long strides toward Fiona, took Fiona by the shoulders, leaned back at an angle, the same angle, her eyes square into Fiona's, Fiona's eyes back, not a blink.

Margo smiled, then kissed Fiona on the cheek.

Fiona was battling with complete presence, you could tell. It was her lip—curling up the way Charlie's horse ayaHuaska always curled his lip before he bit you.

Fiona grabbed me by the hand, stood behind me, and pushed me to her father.

Mr. MacIlvane, I said. Nice to meet you, I said.

Our two hands together, one firm shake up and down.

His hand was small.

Will! he said. Dave.

Fiona pushed me to her mother next.

Mrs. MacIlvane, I said. Nice to meet you, I said.

Margo leaned back, smiled, looked at my pearls, put her hand in my hand for a moment, then leaned forward.

Call me Margo, she said.

Then it was Hunter and Gus. Both of them shook my hand, said, Nice to meet you. Their hands were larger than their father's. Each one of them, my hand to their hands, one firm shake up and down. Neither of them looked at me.

I'd been practicing what to say to Hunter and Gus, but when it came time to say something, I just smiled, looped my index through my strand of pearls, and stopped smiling.

You look great! Margo said to Fiona. Like Carly Simon on that album cover. Dave? Don't you think Muffy looks like Carly Simon?

Mother! Hunter or Gus said.

You look great, honey, Dave said.

Dave knocked the ashes out of his pipe onto his shoe, blew on the pipe, and then walked over to Fiona.

How's my little girl? Dave said, and put his arms around Fiona. Leather sounds.

Margo leaned back, hands around the purse in front of her, smile-gazing at Fiona. Of course, Margo said, You'll have to change.

Dave the Dad stepped back. Way back.

Hunter and Gus stepped back too.

Change? Fiona said, and brought her hands to her throat. Change? I can't imagine. What should I change?

Muffy! Hunter or Gus said.

Well, Margo said, We're going to your father's club, and you know their silly dress code. They won't let you in looking like an album cover.

Mother! Hunter or Gus said.

Fiona's fist on her forehead.

Oh, Mother! Fiona said. How foolish of me! I've made reservations for us at a downtown place, Fiona said. It's called Life Café, and it's just the newest place. They've torn out pages from old *Life* magazines and made art on the walls. I'm sure you'll recognize some of the old covers, Fiona said.

Mother! Hunter or Gus said.

Andy Warhol may be there, Fiona said.

Just then a wind caught Margo's silver hair.

Andy Warhol is dead, Margo said.

Ah, Fiona said. Yes, so he is.

What I meant, Fiona said, Was that Robert Mapplethorpe will probably be there.

Is he the photographer with the bullwhip up his butt? Margo asked.

That's him, Fiona said.

Margo leaned back even farther.

Dave! Margo said, still smile-gazing at Fiona, Let's go to Fiona's place and see Robert Mapplethorpe. It would be fun, don't you think?

Do they take credit cards? Dave asked.

Dad! Hunter or Gus said.

Oh, I just know they do, Fiona said.

It's settled, then! Margo said.

Margo's hands were all of a sudden two large things on the end of her arms she didn't know what to do with.

I do hope Robert's there, Margo said. You know, I saw him once at a fashion show on the West Side. Doris Berkland and I sat two chairs from him—Robert Mapplethorpe. The show was some new designer—crinkly little dresses I wouldn't be caught dead in. The designer, poor man, had to rent one of those discos over there.

Margo's large hand went up and pointed west.

Well, Margo said, The place smelled like *sperm*. The industrial gray carpeting, I swear, must have been saturated. Dottie and I started giggling. Can you imagine? Two chairs from Robert Mapplethorpe, everything smelling of sperm, and we get the giggles?

Are there cabs down here? Dave asked.

Dad! Hunter or Gus said.

We can walk, Fiona said. It's not far.

Walk? Margo said.

Walk? Dave said.

Walk? Hunter or Gus said. Mom, Dad!

Mother! Gus or Hunter said.

Hunter or Gus raised his arms up, then slapped his arms against his thighs. We're walking across the Lower East Side at night?

Margo was between her sons. Her legs were long too, like Fiona's. Margo took a big step east on East Fifth and grabbed Hunter and Gus both by the arm, pulling them to her.

Don't be so serious, you guys! Margo said, This is a free country. And besides, Margo sang, Who's afraid of the big bad wolf?

Margo's laugh, exactly like Fiona's. High, off-key. Something mean in it.

Dave put his arm over Fiona's leather shoulders and Fiona walked with her father, khakis to leather. At the corner of Second Avenue, the WALK/DON'T WALK was DON'T WALK. Dave leaned over, kissed Fiona on the cheek.

Harry and I brought up the rear.

On the corner of Fifth Street and First Avenue, a small woman, dark hair and skin, in Levi's and a Levi's jacket, walked up to us. She was barefoot.

San Simeon? she asked.

Dave reached into his pocket and pulled out some change and put the change in the woman's hand.

Dave! Margo whispered loud. Mayor Koch said not to give these people any money. They'll just buy drugs.

To hell with Ed Koch! Dave said. He's a latent Republican!

And a fag! Fiona said.

Up Avenue A, Harry and I were following the MacIlvane men. Margo and Fiona were arm in arm, in the lead.

Connecticut Matron meets Leather Queen.

On all the street corners, tennis shoes hanging from the telephone wires. Fiona turned around and said, loud enough for the whole street to hear, Third Street is the safest block in the city.

Two black guys in hooded sweatshirts turned around and looked at the group of us following Fiona.

It's the Hell's Angels' block, Fiona said loud, But these days everybody's a Hell's Angel. Still, Fiona said loud, Don't try and piss on their block!

Fiona said loud, There's a mortuary not far from here on First Avenue. Right next to it used to be the Club Baths.

Muffy! Hunter or Gus said.

The dish is, Fiona said loud, There was a door between the Club Baths and the mortuary. Of course, Fiona said, The door existed only for those who were into fucking dead people.

Necrophilia, Margo said, like she'd say *espadrille* or *Jack Russell terrier*. Door of the Dead.

It's closed down now, Fiona said loud.

Because of that disease? Margo said.

Mom! Dad! Hunter, or Gus said.

Then, in all the world, Fiona, Margo, Dave, Hunter, Gus, Harry, and I were at the entrance to Tompkins Square Park. Dog Shit Park.

Hunter or Gus said, We're *not* walking through there, Muffy!

My name is not Muffy, Fiona said.

What *is* your name these days? Margo said.

Susan Strong, Fiona said.

We can't walk through there, Hunter or Gus said. It's ten o'clock at night!

Then Fiona said, It's no different in there from anywhere else down here. Come on! Fiona said. We're homosexuals, we're feminists, we're liberal Democrats. It's cool!

In the lamplight, Harry looked green.

Harry, are you feeling all right? I said.

Fuck you, Muffy! Hunter or Gus said.

Then, all at once, the whole MacIlvane family, Margo and Dave and Hunter and Gus and Muffy, were yelling at one another. All of them all at the same time.

She's always got something to prove! Fucking chip on her shoulder!

Don't say fuck to your sister!

Dad, this is Tompkins Square Park. You can say fuck in Tompkins Square Park!

What's wrong with being a liberal Democrat? Fucking Republicans don't give a shit about poverty!

Don't say fuck in front of the children!

Mom! Dad!

This is Dog Shit Park! You can say fuck in fucking Dog Shit Park!

I'm sure if Muffy thinks it's OK to walk through here, it's OK to walk through here!

My name's not Muffy!

I'm sure if—Susan Strong—thinks it's OK . . .

Don't patronize me!

Who's patronizing? I'm just trying to remember your fucking name!

What are you afraid of? This is a city park!

Goddammit, why do we always go through this?

Because your daughter is an asshole!

Always something to prove!

Don't call your sister an asshole.

Then: But she *is* an asshole.

It was Fiona's mother. It was Margo. Margo wasn't yelling, she just said it, and everybody stopped. Even Fiona.

Muffy was an asshole, Margo said, And *Susan Strong* is an asshole, and whoever she's going to be next will be an asshole too, Margo said.

Dave and Hunter and Gus were all standing together. Fiona wasn't standing with them, she was standing alone. Margo was standing alone too, leaning. Margo's blue eyes on Fiona's blue eyes. Fiona's blue eyes back.

Harry had his hand on his chest.

Harry's lips at my ear: Bitch fight to the death.

And so am *I*, Margo said to Fiona. A liberal rich-bitch Connecticut Democrat asshole.

Mother and daughter's lips large, laser.

First time ever when Fiona had nothing to say.

Margo took one long stride over to Fiona. Fiona didn't move. Margo looped her arm, the same white as Fiona's, inside her daughter's arm.

He lives around here, doesn't he?

Who? Fiona said.

Robert Mapplethorpe, Margo said.

Then mother took daughter's arm. They walked that way, those females, through the wrought-iron arched gate of Dog Shit Park.

Abandon all hope! Margo said, her large hand waving an arc under the wrought-iron arch, TOMPKINS SQUARE PARK, Ye who enter here!

This ain't no walk in the park! Fiona said.

Fiona's head-back laugh, just like her mother's.

Dave and Hunter and Gus and Harry and I followed.

Fuck Hope.

INSIDE DOG SHIT Park, the trees were big shadows hanging in the wind above us. Through the low brush, a couple of small fires. Shadows sitting around the fires. What kept us walking was that Dog Shit Park still looked enough like a city park: winding sidewalks, benches along the side, lampposts from the turn of the century—some of them still working. Dave knew the name of the style of lampposts they were and who designed them. There were wrought-iron fences and gargoyles and lions and fountain stuff made out of concrete that Dave knew the names of too.

Margo's low heels on the winding sidewalk and Fiona's stilettos and leathers and chains were the only sounds beside the wind above us in the trees. Now and then low sounds from one of the small fires we passed by. I suppose we were about halfway through the park when Margo moved in closer to Dave and Fiona walked closer to me and Harry, and Hunter and Gus moved in closer too. None of us were talking, not even our leather tour guide, Fiona.

Then all at once, through the dark trees, out of the navy blue sky, a bright silver moon was above us.

Oh! Margo said, Look at the moon!

A gibbous moon, Dave said.

Right next to me, Harry looked up, the moon on his face, one of those immortal marble-statue expressions on Harry's face.

In all the world, there we were, the MacIlvanes and Harry and me, huddled together in a clearing in Dog Shit Park staring up through the trees, glow-in-the-dark statues in the silver light, staring at the moon.

I looked down, and right next to me, right by my leg in the silver light, on a bench were the faces of two children asleep under a black plastic bag.

Then through the trees and out of nowhere, out of the dark, just like that, all around us, under blankets, coats, clothes, canvas tarps, plastic, people of every color and size you can imagine sitting and lying on the benches, looking up at the moon.

This one woman lying on the bench next to Harry put out her hand, palm up. The moonlight on her palm.

Harry gave her a dollar.

She said, Thank you. She had no teeth.

At the band shell, a sign was stretched across the stage. There was a fire burning in a barrel just under the sign, the red letters, red paint running down.

HOMES FOR THE HOMELESS.

The moon in the navy blue sky, the wind in the trees, the red dripping words HOMES FOR THE HOMELESS floating back and forth, back and forth, above the barrel of fire.

Under the banner, huddled around the fire, people, hundreds of people, lying on the ground.

My God! Dave said. I can't believe this!

Dogs were running all over.

No Charlie 2Moons.

Harry and I took the lead. The winding winding sidewalk. We came to a place where the lamppost was working, shining silver light out, a closer moon, silver light through the leaves, shadows of leaves—a place in a park under a lamppost just like the place in the park in the movie in Manhattan where Fred Astaire and Cyd Charisse dance in the light and the shadows and sing a romantic song.

In the lamppost's silver light was a woman hunched over on a bench. She had no hair. When she looked up, at first I thought it was the shadow, but then I could see, under her eyebrows around her eyes, was painted black. She was wearing nothing, no shoes. The woman's body was white arms and legs and thighs and breasts and shoulders naked. Skin on a body naked and glowing in the light.

A man in a ball cap with a stringy ponytail—he had all his clothes on—a gold ring on the side of his boot, was kneeling in front of the woman. A scarf was tied around her upper arm, a scarf around his upper arm too. He was sticking the needle in the woman's arm, pushing the needle in, slowly up and down, side to side. They were making low heroin sounds.

The man looked up, his eyes scared rabbit in the headlights. Above us, birds flew out of a tree. What we saw in the man's eyes we all looked away from. We on the tour made a wedge, walked closer together, faster, counting every step, past the kneeling man and the naked woman.

When we were in the English elms, Avenue B almost right next to us, almost safe out of the park, we were all breathing easier. Harry O'Connor stood up on a bench. Behind Harry's head from where I was standing were the bright red letters: Life Café.

Harry raised his arms, cleared his throat dramatically. Margo, Fiona, Dave, Hunter, Gus, and I looked up at Harry with all the hope of theater to lay bare the human heart.

Quiet only New York can get that fast.

Harry's Irish tenor booming through the English elms, through the park, out all over Manhattan. Harry sang:

> *I'll be homeless for Christmas,*
> *You can forget about me.*
> *Reagan got my dough,*
> *And I'm so po',*
> *We're peasants throughout the country.*
> *Christmas Eve will find me,*
> *Where food stamps redeem.*
> *I'll be homeless for Christmas—*
> *If only this all was a dream.*

Just like that, applause and cheers from the crowd underneath the juniper bush.

Harry bowed deeply.

I put my arm across Harry's legs to hold him steady.

Margo and Dave and Hunter and Gus and Fiona and I—we all looked at each other in the silver light and laughed at the surprise applause and cheers from the crowd under the juniper bush.

In all the world, two liberal Democrats, two YUFAs, a leather dominatrix, Harry and I and a world of homeless people, everybody clapping clapping.

Standing ovation.

* * *

THINGS START WHERE you don't know.

You're going this way and then shit happens and then you're going that way.

That's when the heroin guy, gold ring on his boot, jumped from nowhere out of the bushes. Out of the navy blue night, just like that, he was a dark figure between us and the mercury-vapor light on Avenue B, his ball cap, his ponytail bouncing.

Harry was still standing on the bench. Dave and Hunter and Gus quick stepped in front of Margo and Fiona—Dave in the middle, Hunter on one side, Gus on the other. The men locked their arms together.

Fuck this shit! Fiona said, and pushed Hunter or Gus aside, stepped out in front, next to Harry on the bench, behind me.

The heroin guy was yelling something. I didn't know what he was yelling. I knew it was English and it was loud and you could see spit come out of his mouth with the light the way it was, and also you could see the bruises and purple bumps on his arms and you could see he was weaving back and forth.

Then: This is my home! the guy was yelling. Fucking yuppies get out of my park!

The wind in the English elms, the mercury-vapor light through the leaves, pieces of light the color from another incarnation moving moving all over the ground, around us.

The guy stepped or tripped forward even closer to me, and the light was plain as day on the knife blade side to side, up and down.

I could smell the guy, he was that close.

First the eyes. His eyes in between, somewhere else. Not on the premises. And then his smile, the light on the knife blade hand to hand, back and forth, up and down under his smile.

His smile, that smile. A finger drawing a circle around my heart. Ruby Prestigiacomo, what am I going to do with you?

Just what the fuck is so fucking funny? Ruby said, looking up at Harry on the bench. What the fuck you singing about, man? Ruby said. These are my people!

Stick 'em! somebody under the juniper yelled. He's going to stick 'em!

Dave stepped out next to me, pushing his tortoiseshell glasses back onto his nose, holding his leather wallet out.

Here, take our money!

Ruby's smile, Ruby's gone eyes. Knife blade, the light, hand to hand, back and forth, up and down.

Fuck you, pharisee! Ruby said, And your fucking money!

Ruby fell to one side, grabbed onto a tree limb, shook his head, talked for a while so you couldn't hear.

Then: Who's the singer? Ruby said.

Knife flash at Harry.

Who's the leather chick? Ruby said.

Knife flash past my arm.

You fuckers! Ruby said. Think you can come here in your yuppie sex leathers and sing and dance?

Harry held his hands out to Ruby, palms up. Hey, I'm sorry, man, Harry said, I was just—

Ruby stomped his foot down on the sidewalk, strands of red-blond hair in his face.

This is my fucking home! Ruby yelled. Dark veins in his forehead and his neck. Don't you understand? This is where I live, man! Ruby yelled. You're in my fucking living room! You're standing on my fucking *couch*!

Harry moved his head, looked down slow.

Drops of sweat on Ruby's couch around Harry's feet.

Dave stopped holding out his wallet.

Ruby, I said.

Ruby was so close.

A siren. Shouts. Somebody screamed. Stick 'em! He's gonna stick 'em!

Ruby, I said.

Under Ruby's smile, the shine of the knife blade hand to hand, back and forth, back and forth.

Just what the fuck is so fucking funny? Ruby said.

Ruby, I said.

Fiona grabbed my shoulder, pulled my shoulder back.

Shut up, Will! Fiona said.

Fiona was standing next to me, moving between Ruby and me.

We meant no harm! Fiona said.

Ruby's smile up Fiona's body, up to her face. His face leaning closer in to her face.

What are you? Slumming? Ruby said. His spray of spit in the light. Want to see how the other half lives? Ruby said.

Shouts and screams and people were running. Stick 'em! He's gonna stick 'em!

Then there were horses. All around us, I could hear horses running.

Ruby! I said. Life Café, man! I said. Travel mode's the key!

Ruby stopped his smile, stopped with the knife, squinted hard in my direction.

Quiet only New York can get that fast.

Hey! I said, my arms open wide. Hey, dude! I said. Ruby Prestigiacomo! I said. Where's True Shot tonight?

Will? Ruby said.

Then: William of Heaven! Fuckin-A, man! Is that you?

All around us, sirens, shouts from inside the park. A woman screamed, more screams. Horses running.

Ruby put the blade back into the knife against his leg, slid the knife into his front pocket, stepped toward me.

I caught Ruby in my arms.

Ruby bones.

Lips at my ear: Hey, I'm fucking sorry man, Ruby said. No offense, huh?

His chin sharp against my upper arm.

Ruby's ribs, I could feel every rib. His clavicle. Ruby's shoulder bones hard in the palms of my hands. His breath against my neck. Puke smell stronger than horse piss.

Ruby put his hands onto my chest, the bones in his hands. Ruby pushed himself back.

Ruby's smile.

William of Heaven, Ruby said, What the fuck are you doing with these people? These people are pharisees, Will.

Then: When're you going to call me back, motherfucker? Is red OK? True Shot said I should buy the *red* answering machine. Said he had a vision, man, that red was the color for you.

Ruby put his open palm on the back of my neck, steadied himself with me, put his forehead onto my black T-shirt, onto my pearls, for a moment. The part in Ruby's hair, a tiny road to nowhere.

Now here.

William of Heaven, man! Ruby said. You got to understand. There's so much you don't know about Wolf Swamp, man! This place'll eat you up! You don't know it but you need me! I was just like you when I got here! I know a lot. I could save you from going through this shit! We need to talk, man!

Both Ruby's hands on the back of my neck. He was shaking me.

There's only two kinds of people in Wolf Swamp, Ruby said, Fools and pharisees, Will. You should call me back on that red fucking phone of yours. Did you get my messages? You should have called me back, Will. Pharisees are why the fools are homeless, man. Why the fuck haven't you called me back?

A woman holding a child in her arms ran past us. Two old men running. Dogs barking. Breaking glass. Shouts. Screams. The red-and-white flash of cop cars.

Then Ruby, still hanging on me, forehead up and down on my black T-shirt, turned his face to Margo and Dave and Hunter and Gus, to Fiona and Harry.

You all, Ruby said, Had better get your bourgeois butts out of this park! Hear that? Ruby said. The Riders are here for their routine head bang. And Riders don't give a fuck if you're Gucci or not. You better get out of here or you'll never look so pretty.

All the MacIlvanes, and Fiona, and Harry, looked at me.

This is Ruby, I said. This is my friend Ruby.

My face was smiling.

Tennis anyone? Ruby said.

Will? Fiona said.

He's OK, he's OK! Ruby yelled at Fiona. William of Heaven's in good hands! Ruby yelled. Now get your posh fucking asses out of here! Run along and play croquet or you're roadkill!

THE WHITE STALLION and the cop on the white stallion jumped out of nowhere through the bushes, and the people under the juniper were yelling and running every which way. Fiona and Margo and Dave and Harry and Hunter and Gus were running too, through the English elms onto Avenue B, across Avenue B.

Margo MacIlvane stopped on the avenue. She was looking up and down the street, waving her big hands in the air for a cab. Fiona yelled, Jesus, Mother! and grabbed her mother and they ran into Life Café.

There were more horses, cops on the horses, cops with clubs beating the bushes. In all the world, so many people yelling and screaming.

Ruby grabbed me by the arm and we were running running through the dark, with other people and dogs, running past trees and bushes and benches, jumping over people lying on the ground, speeding darkness, speeding light.

Between a cement thing and bush, at the base of a big tree, Ruby jumped into a bush and I jumped in after him, landed on top of him, rolled over.

The sweet smell of evergreen, the smell of dirt. Ruby and I breathing breathing.

Secret place, Ruby whispered. Riders don't know about yet. Keep your ass down.

My breath going in and out of me.

Ruby put his hand on my shoulder.

You got your mother's nerves, Ruby said. It's OK. We're safe here.

I could smell dog shit and wondered if I was lying in it. But it was Ruby. I wormed myself around, put my head on my elbows, and looked around. The bush was an arborvitae, the branches draping over us to the ground. There was just room enough to sit up. There were plastic cups and Kentucky Fried Chicken boxes lying around. A cushion from a chair.

Home Sweet Home, Ruby said.

Screams. More gunshots.

A horse ran by so close you could hear horse flanks.

William of Heaven, Ruby said, What am I going to do with you?

Ruby covered his mouth. He was coughing. He jumped toward the chair cushion and held the cushion while he threw up.

My nose went right into my armpit.

Ruby's body was all bones under his khaki pants and Hawaiian shirt and there were dark-brown bumps up and down his foreams, the backs of his arms, on his neck.

Ruby Prestigiacomo, I said, What am I going to do with *you?*

Ruby's smile. Skeleton poking through.

Then: Shh! Ruby whispered, wiped his mouth.

I took a breath and Ruby took a breath.

Ruby pointed his long bony index. Through a hole in the arborvitae branches, in the streetlamp light, next to an English elm, was a cop on a white stallion.

Sergeant Richard White.

You see that fucker there, Ruby whispered, On the white horse? Kind of looks like Porky Pig? Around here, they call him Sergeant White Supremacy. And talk about *short*. His dick is *ugly!* Tiny little pink thing, no bigger than your thumb. Likes to get drunk and come down here. Likes black men with big ones. Gives the brothers a vial or pays 'em— five, four, sometimes only three dollars—to fuck them. I hate the motherfucker. Fucked me one night. I've got one big Mussolini myself so he liked me. Gave me some cocaine, but it was cut with something awful—made me fucking sick. I was throwing up my deepest guts, man, while that fucker White was pounding my ass.

In all the world, Lone Ranger Hiyo Silver Sergeant White sat there on the horse in the park under a tree like a statue of a cop on a horse in a park under a tree.

Ruby brought his body up along mine, shivering. That's all this shit is about, Will, Ruby whispered. Power, Pentagon, politics, governments, money—what it comes down to in Wolf Swamp is one very simple thing: a man and his cock, how a man is with his cock, the stuff of great literature, great art, man, me and it, tragedy or comedy hanging down there between your legs. That's all it comes down to.

Ruby coughed, his whole body coughed. He hacked and spit.

Lips at my ear: Some day soon, Ruby whispered, Mark my words, some day I'm going to kill that cop!

When I looked again through the hole between the arborvitae branches, in the streetlamp light, Sergeant White Supremacy and his white horse were gone.

SUN WAS COMING through the arborvitae branches when I woke up. Tree shadows and sun on Ruby's body. Ruby's head was still on my chest and his open palm was on my cock. I stayed that way, awake, for a while. My leg was asleep and I didn't know if I could move my leg.

I managed to move Ruby off, got the blood back into my leg, zipped up my pants, and moved the cushion and put the cleanest part of the cushion under Ruby's head. For a moment, I thought Ruby was dead he was so stiff and gray-looking, but then he pulled his legs up and put his hands between his legs, and I was glad to know it was only sleep. I brushed myself off, trying to look presentable, then laughed because I was in Dog Shit Park.

Touched him, Ruby, a little on the shoulder before I left to get coffee. His pant legs were up around his knees and his legs were brown and purple sticks into his boots. His ball cap was off. Two moons tattooed on his forehead. Ruby was smiling a little. Even in sleep, Ruby had a smile.

THAT MORNING, WHEN I ducked out from under the branches of the arborvitae, I had no idea it was the morning that after everything was different.

America—the land of the free and the home of the brave, O beautiful for spacious skies—was never the same again.

The fog settled. Outside was inside.

I was at the center of things, face-to-face with the monster in the labyrinth.

This is where I started to notice.

ALL AROUND ME, far as I could see, people were lying on the ground. Looked like the whole world was lying on the ground. Piles of people like in movies of concentration camps or a battlefield after war.

In the night, while Ruby and I were sleeping, the riders had come again and slaughtered the people. Or a bomb was dropped or poisonous gas or *The Andromeda Strain* or *Planet of the Apes*—something science fiction, *On the Beach*—and only Ruby and I, in all the world, left alive.

But it's not the truth.

I walked, and with each step I wondered if the step would reach the ground, or with each step maybe I'd start floating up, over buildings, Manhattan below a grid, just a street map, the street map a state map, the state map a map of North America, North America the world, the round globe hanging in the blue firmament, the globe a postage stamp on a letter, a stone on a gold ring, a flake of bright dust.

I stepped on somebody's hand and the guy called me a stupid son of a bitch, so after that, I walked policing my body, new-shoe stiff, through the bodies, careful where I stepped.

A little girl under a gunnysack waved a fly away from her nose. A man in a dirty yellow sleeping bag scratched his gray beard. A skinny brown dog wagged his tail. A woman lay on top of a man under a green blanket, kissing. A young woman with dirty-blond hair wearing a purple muumuu sat on a bench, her baby sucking at her breast—the woman smiled at me. Her smile was old. A man snored by the boarded-up rest rooms.

No Charlie 2Moons.

I looked again, squinted my eyes over the bodies as far as I could see, and the bodies weren't dead, the bodies were moving with breath.

Kiev was the closest restaurant open, and I bought two cups of coffee and some chocolate doughnuts. Everybody was staring at me in Kiev, and I got to thinking maybe I smelled like dog shit, and then I thought, Who cares what a bunch of assholes think?

The sun was shining full and bright and in Dog Shit Park steam was rolling off of things. People were standing up and stretching, taking their morning pees. A radio played "Born on the Bayou." Farts and groans. I policed my body back through the crowd, postured disregard, savoir faire, acting as if I knew things and belonged there.

Under the arborvitae, where I left Ruby, Ruby was gone.

I sat under the arborvitae, where we'd spent the night, waited for Ruby, drank both coffees, and ate the doughnuts waiting for him, but he didn't show.

I started thinking about Charlie lying out somewhere, just another body on the ground.

Only sleeping. Charlie 2Moons on the ground, not dead, only sleeping.

Things started getting hot and my skin felt greazy. All around me people were talking and moving around, and then two teenage girls sat down on the cement thing and started in with the needle. I had to get out of there. Left a ten-dollar bill under the cushion Ruby had vomited over, crawled under the arborvitae branches, and got out of Dog Shit Park quick, through the bodies, over the bodies, through the gate, over the curb of running shit.

I was walking East Village streets I'd walked so many times. People sat in sidewalk cafés same as ever, reading the *Sunday Times*, coffee, omelets.

Everywhere, all around me, law and order prevailed.

But in my heart, there was no home.

At Stranded Beings Searching for God, I walked down the three steps to the door, and that morning the poster of the Sacred Heart of Jesus and the three Polaroids were different too. As if I'd really never looked at them before.

Ruby possessed by the devil. Ruby being healed by the Word of the Lord. Alleluia Alleluia. Ruby healed. Alleluia Alleluia.

Rose possessed by the devil. Rose being healed by the Word of the Lord. Alleluia Alleluia. Rose healed. Alleluia Alleluia.

Charlie possessed by the devil. Charlie being healed by the Word of the Lord. Alleluia Alleluia. Charlie healed. Alleluia. Alleluia.

In my apartment, the red to pink walls, Rose's poster as Antigone, the drawing of Daniel's beer-can dick, the futon, the *Father Knows Best* table, the ladder, the broken green plate, the boom box, the wagon-wheel lamp with cowboys and Indians on the lampshade.

Hi, honey, I'm home! I said. My Art Family was the cast from *Les Miserables*. They all smiled, whispered quick things to one another.

I took off my black cutoffs, my black T-shirt, the pearls, socks, and combat boots, my underwear. My God, the shower! I was so happy to be in my shower! Even the cockroach in the shower. I opened all the windows.

My bare feet, just a towel wrapped around me, I walked the thirteen steps up to Rose's room. Knocked.

No dogs.

No Rose.

I left a message on Rose's machine.

Vive la Rose! I said, Where are you? Give me a call.

THAT EVENING, THE red light on the red answering machine was blinking.

Ruby.

I stood in front of the red telephone and the red answering machine the whole time, stood among my Art Family, through all the beeps, through the whole long message Ruby left, Ruby's quarters dinging in the pay phone, stood and listened, for the last time ever, to Ruby's voice, to Ruby far away trying to get to his voice.

Do you still respect me? Ruby laughed his low laugh and coughed and started singing, *Just call me angel of the morning.*

Then: You men are all alike, Ruby said. He cleared his throat, spit, coughed. So, Ruby said. I'm calling from a phone booth somewhere in the Midwest, Ruby said. Midwest Manhattan. Actually I'm calling from the special phone booth I pointed out to you one day, the Saint Jude phone booth, in Alphabet City somewhere in the southeast. Last call, Ruby said.

Lletre ferit. The word that hurts

I've got to tell you some things. First off, Ruby said, I loved holding your cock all night. I knew it would be beautiful. Wish I could have seen your legs, your chest. I got close enough to smell, though, and I must say, William of Heaven, you smell like heaven.

Then: Now listen up, William of Heaven, because this is important. Fools and pharisees, Will. When I'm done telling you this here stuff you should know, I'm going to hang up and go kill me a cop, going to find that motherfucker Sergeant White Supremacy and kill him dead.

Today's the day, Ruby said.

Your girlfriend, the one with the white skin that looked like piece of moon—her name has to be Fiona or Phaedra or Persephone or Daphne, or the fair Ophelia, one of those fucking *f*'s—the chick in the leather outfit, she's a damn fool, Ruby said. And last night she was Harlequin, a fool in costume.

It remains to be seen, Ruby said, Whether or not this Fiona knows what the fuck she's doing—whether or not she knows she's a fool. And if she knows she's a fool, does she knows she's hiding? I gave her a hard time, Ruby said, Which she deserved. She's one of those Helen Reddy women with a Lolita problem. They think all they have do do is put some tiny thing on, tits and ass, and the world is theirs. Trouble is, in most cases it's true. More power in a pair of tits than any chariot. But I think your friend Fiona might be all right. Just be careful. Before you fall in love with her, make sure she knows what the fuck she's doing, because falling in love is always trouble, and if she don't know she's a fool, if she ain't Harlequin, you're in for a world of hurt.

Wish I could give the bitch a run for the money, Ruby said, But by the looks of the inside of this telephone booth here, I'm out of the running altogether.

Ruby dropped another quarter in. I heard only street noise for a while and then: The singer's OK too, Ruby said. Got a voice on him, a little too opera pants for me, but a good spirit. You'd be better off falling in love with him. You could help him with the high notes. But the rest of them, Ruby said, The rest of your friends last night—pharisees, Will. Be careful.

Last night, being in between things like I was. There you were, at first just another yuppie fucking-pharisee asshole in my park trying to exploit me, and then all of a sudden it was you, my sweet William of Heaven, and it was *satori*, and my life went by me in one flash, just like they say in the books.

Ruby's voice was higher now, or lower, just different, like you do when you come to the end of something, and you make your voice higher or lower because it's your last chance to make it sound good.

The hope of theater to lay bare the human heart.

Ruby put another quarter in. Sirens. Cars, trucks.

True Shot said he finally told you the secret of Wolf Swamp, Ruby said. That's good. Myself, Ruby said, I think the words themselves, the words of the story of Wolf Swamp have a power, the words transform you, so when you hear them you're never the same.

William of Heaven, Ruby said, You're never going to be the same.

When the veil falls, Ruby said, Manhattan is only a foggy swamp, a pack of wolves, a damn damsel in distress, and a scared stallion.

My money's on True Shot to fall in love with, Ruby said. He's a fat old fart and full of tall tales and spooks and soccer games—all that male stuff; only cock he'll ever hold is his own—but still my money's on True Shot. There's so many ways to love. And when the shit comes down, Will, when the truth comes out, don't be too hard on him. He's a lovely man and only done right by me.

Ruby was coughing so hard. Ruby's cough rattling around and around on the tape of my answering machine, all over the apartment, all of us, me and my Art Family, still completely present, listening.

I feel a song coming on, Ruby said, and then he's singing:

> *Fools rush in where wise men never go,*
> *but wise men never fall in love.*
> *So how are they to know.*
> *When we met I felt my life begin.*
> *So open up your heart and let this fool rush in.*

Life Café, Ruby said, his voice all wavy, Travel mode's the key.

Then: William of Heaven. What am I going to do with you?

Only silence, for a moment, in all the world, all of New York, only silence. Dead silence.

Well, buddy, Ruby said, It's the puritan undertow you got to beware of. I'm tired of these fucking pharisees. Time to kill me a cop.

I could hear Ruby smile.

Liberation from suffering can be found in any moment, Ruby said. Having a wonderful time, Ruby said, Wish you were queer.

Then it was the dial tone. Ruby hung it up and it was the dial tone.

CHAPTER
TWENTY-ONE

A week or two later, True Shot's voice on my red answering
machine.

I found Ruby, True Shot said.

The tape of my answering machine rolling around and around.
All over in the apartment, all of us, me and my Art Family, still, completely present, listening.

He's dead, Will, True Shot said. Murdered.

Sergeant Richard White, I said.

My Art Family gasped, darted, ran for cover.

True Shot's breath in. His breath out.

Will, True Shot said, You're going to have to help me on this one.

TRUE SHOT PICKED me up in Door of the Dead van. The sound of the
van door opening, the smell inside, the seat against my butt and back,
the hole in the floorboard, the heater going full blast.

True Shot's face was hanging on his skull. When he shook my hand,
it was not the square firm handshake I remembered.

True Shot, I said, Where have you been? Why haven't you called?

True Shot's mirrors looked back only to show a contorted circus me
on the surface of his mirrors.

True Shot parked Door of the Dead van on East Eighth Street, not
far from Saint Jude phone booth, just east of Dog Shit Park. There were
all kinds of parking places because there were no cars. True Shot cut
the engine, shut off the headlights.

Next to me, True Shot's mirrors reflected nothing.

Our breath together, in and out, in and out.

The buckskin bag with the beaded blue horizontal beads and the red
vertical beads on the buckskin strand around True Shot's neck. The
silver rings on his fingers, reflecting moon.

True Shot took off his mirrors, folded them up in the leather Armani case, stuck them in his vest pocket, snapped the pocket shut, opened the door, and got out of the van. So did I. He slammed his door and I slammed my door.

Up and down the dark empty street, the only sound was the doors slamming.

True shot had picked up a body bag on one of his Spirit Schleps. The body bag was hanging over True Shot's shoulder next to True Shot's hair, which was hanging down in one long braid. I carried the rope, looped around my shoulder.

He's in there, True Shot said, and pointed at the front door to a condemned building.

The building leaned over us, a slanting rectangle black against the dark burning sky. Big planks were nailed across the door and a NO TRESPASSING sign, and spray-painted words covered the front of the building. You could see where people had been going in and out, through the planks, the wood worn smooth like the poles of the corral behind the barn where Bobbie and I kept the horses.

True Shot hunched his extra-lovely body and pulled himself through the worn place between the planks. I was right behind him.

Inside, in the narrow dark hallway, all around us, cold and dark. The only light we had was True Shot's flashlight, the kind airplane guys use to signal planes. Just one circle of bright with True Shot's cowboy boots and my combat boots on the cracked-open green linoleum floor. One circle of bright down through the dust of the long hallway, on the spines of glass in the window, the exploded stairway, the caved-in ceiling.

A rat ran along the wall. I followed True Shot, my hand on his shoulder and on the plastic body bag, his braid now and then brushing my hand.

Under what used to be the stairway, True Shot shined the flashlight into a doorway. A gray mop, a can of Drano, cockroaches overflowing the toilet.

I jumped away and ran into True Shot's extra-lovely arm he quick stuck out.

Don't move like that, man! True Shot said.

True Shot shined the circle of bright onto a hole in the floor right next to my foot. The hole was the size of a manhole cover. I leaned over True Shot's arm and looked down. Bright circle showed water below.

He's down there, True Shot said.

True Shot squatted by the hole. I held the flashlight and pointed the circle of bright at the water, and just like that, True Shot jumped down off the world into the hole, bright circle all on the splash.

You all right? I yelled down. My voice like talking through a long tube. How deep's the water?

Couple inches, True Shot said.

Then: Tie the rope around the newel post, True Shot said. A slip knot.

One circle of bright on my boots. One step, two steps, three steps to the newel post. I stuck the flashlight in the crook of my arm, and as I lashed the rope the circle went wild on things in the dark—an archway up the stairs, a deco ceiling light, dark wood molding around a door, circle of bright up and down a broken hand rail, up and down the balusters—the strange extreme baluster shadows alive on the gray wall. I tied the slip knot and pulled hard. The newel post didn't budge.

Throw down the rope! True Shot yelled. His voice like in a tank.

I threw the rope down, the circle of bright onto True Shot's face.

You're sure the knot is good? True Shot said.

Yeah, I said.

And the newel post'll hold?

Looks like it, I said.

Now you got to jump down here too! True Shot said.

My mother's nerves.

I hunkered down, gave True Shot the flashlight, handle first, the light in my face, in my eyes.

There's a terrible smell, I said.

Wait till you get down *here*! True Shot said.

All daring and courage, all iron endurance of misfortune, I held my arms close in and jumped.

The only way out is in.

True Shot had his arms around me.

You OK? he said.

The flashlight was between us, its bright circle poking up through our faces. The gap between True Shot's front teeth. The shadow of True Shot's buckskin bag on his throat. Saint-Vitus'-dance eyes.

From around us, there in the dark, the smell.

True Shot pointed the flashlight. All over above us, every which way, a hundred twisted arms of octopus furnace, circle of bright on slimy wet dark things hanging. To our right, a screened-in shelf and green mason jars with yellow lumps in them, a Barbie doll head, a can of Raid.

Water seeping in my boots.

My God, the smell! Putrefaction of the flesh.

True Shot walked slow. My hand on his shoulder and the plastic body bag. His braid brushing up against my hand. The circle of bright on a hole in the cement foundation wall ahead of us. True Shot walked toward the opening.

True Shot shined the light through the opening, into a whole huge dark room on the other side with dark objects standing in the room. He turned, put his face up close to mine, coffee breath and chocolate doughnuts, and grasped my shoulder with his extra-lovely hand.

It is this way, True Shot said. No matter what happens, stay aware of your breath. Keep your mind still and listen to your breathing.

True Shot put his leg in the hole in the cement foundation, pulled himself through. True Shot's hands on the concrete. Then his hands were gone and I heard a splash.

You OK? I said.

Water's deeper in here, True Shot said.

I jumped into the hole, stood on the cement foundation. Looked down. Circle of bright onto True Shot.

I jumped.

True Shot's arms were around me.

From around us, inside the dark, the smell.

My breath in. My breath out.

True Shot took a step ahead and so did I. Water sloshing. Another step. True Shot with the flashlight. My hand on True Shot's shoulder, now and then True Shot's braid against my hand.

A jukebox, an old wood bar back, broken mirrors, old radiators, rolls of linoleum.

Water sometimes so deep it came up mid-calf.

Flies, the high buzz of flies. Green flies and yellow flies and black flies through the circle of bright. Flies landing on my face, sticky on my hands. Flies all around True Shot's head.

My breath in. My breath out.

My stomach ready to barf like Bobbie.

A standing lamp, a coat rack. No water here, but the floor was slick with a dark green slime. I followed True Shot around some huge piece of cement.

True Shot put his hand on the buckskin bag around his neck.

It is this way, True Shot said.

We had to laugh. I can't tell you how funny *it is this way* was just then, so funny that the stink and flies and wet darkness all went away and there we were in all the world, just two people laughing.

Old two-by-fours poked out of rubble like broken arms and legs. A floating folding chair, stacks of cardboard boxes. Just beyond a stack of concrete blocks, True Shot stopped.

A gut sound came out of him.

Circle of bright on two skinny white naked legs, two white feet in the air, silver wire twisted around the ankles, hanging from the floor joists above.

True Shot threw aside a white metal kitchen cabinet, stepped over an overstuffed chair, kicked over a box of books, threw aside a broomstick. Shined the light onto a white body on a soggy mattress.

The smell.

Circle of light onto Ruby Prestigiacomo. The flies on him.

Just a T-shirt and his big Italian cock, legs hanging in the air.

Circle of light to the green Heineken bottle stuck up his ass.

True Shot dropped the flashlight and bent over and yelled a puke out of him that splashed. True Shot's foot kicked the flashlight all over the huge piece of cement, the milky water around our boots. Another puke yell splash and True Shot was crying big sobs.

In all the world, in wet darkness, flies, and the smell of death, I held on tight to my big friend. My other friend, Ruby, circle of bright onto Ruby's skeleton, smile poking through, flies in and out of his nose. Big sobs, snot running down my face, my chest up and down.

After a while, who knows how long, True Shot said, They found him last night.

Sergeant Richard White, I said.

True Shot knelt down on the mattress. Water circled around his knees. True Shot took a deep breath and grabbed the Heineken bottle sticking out of Ruby's ass. His hand pulled but the bottle end didn't budge. Circle of bright onto True Shot's hand rotating the bottle side to side, then another sound, an awful sound, and runny shit onto the mattress, the smell, and the beer bottle was out. Fly swarm.

True Shot threw the beer bottle into the dark. The shattering sound distant.

True Shot took Ruby's one leg and I took the other. I didn't think about it, just put Ruby's leg between my body and my arm and lifted.

True Shot held the light onto Ruby's foot and the silver wire. There were purple bumps on his ankles and feet and a deep gouge and open skin and dried blood around Ruby's ankle. That close, I saw the wire wasn't silver, it was a stretched-out coat hanger, white, the kind you get from dry cleaners.

Got a pair of pliers? I asked.

No pliers, True Shot said.

So I worked the wire, twisted, and after a while, Ruby's foot fell, but I caught Ruby's foot, held on.

True Shot handed me the flashlight to shine on Ruby's other foot while True Shot undid the wire hanger.

Ruby's other foot fell and True Shot caught Ruby's foot in time, and with me on one side of Ruby, True Shot on the other, we laid Ruby out straight. True Shot took the plastic body bag from his shoulder, laid the body bag out on the mattress next to Ruby, and unzipped the bag.

Roadkill, New York City fucking roadkill.

True Shot was holding Ruby's head in his extra-lovely hands. I was holding the circle of bright on Ruby's face. True Shot knelt down, pulled Ruby up onto his lap, wiped the long red strands of hair out of Ruby's face, brushed his hand over Ruby's red poky beard.

True Shot spit on Ruby's eyes, spit on Ruby's forehead, held Ruby's mouth closed, and spit on Ruby's lips.

I waved away the flies.

True Shot put his red handkerchief over his hand and touched the red handkerchief to Ruby's lower lip, pulled the handkerchief across Ruby's smile, slow like when you put lipstick on, and then True Shot touched Ruby's upper lip the same way.

True Shot wiped the mud from Ruby's forehead, but it's not the truth. It wasn't mud. He wiped the deep purple bumps and black-and-blue bruises on Ruby's cheeks, pulled Ruby's red stringy hair back from his face, and washed the spit across Ruby's face.

True Shot held Ruby's head for a moment longer, touched his forehead to Ruby's forehead.

We must give respect back to our friend, True Shot said.

Then: Roll him over on his belly, True Shot said, And roll him on his back onto the body bag. You get his feet.

True Shot put the flashlight in the white metal kitchen cabinet, on one of the shelves, so the circle of bright was on Ruby, right on Ruby's middle, below the T-shirt, on Ruby's cock. True Shot stood at Ruby's head, put his hands on Ruby's shoulders, and turned. I took Ruby by the feet and turned.

Cockroaches, the big water-bug kind, the color of cooked lobsters, hundreds of them all over on the mattress and all over Ruby's back.

My big breath in.

Oh, God! True Shot yelled. Oh, motherfuckers! True Shot grabbed the broom handle and started beating the mattress, screaming and smashing cockroaches, cockroaches flying like locusts through the circle of bright, snot and spit flying out of True Shot's nose and mouth, buzzing green flies and yellow flies and black flies.

I was Art Family, even when the cockroach flew against my neck, even with the flies around my ears. I stayed in my place, stayed tight into myself, my breath in and my breath out, didn't move an inch— huge holes in the water all around me, bloodsucking dark alive water moccasins in the holes.

I squished onto the mattress. The cockroaches were gone, just yellow-black smashes.

Let's roll him over, I said.

True Shot still at Ruby's head, me at the feet, we rolled Ruby onto the body bag. I pulled the plastic up around Ruby's feet and started the zipper. True Shot put Ruby's hands crossed over his heart. Waved flies away. Zipped the body bag shut.

We got Ruby's body onto True Shot's shoulder. I shined the flashlight at the water at True Shot's feet and we walked step by step, water sloshing, through the flies, around the huge piece of concrete, past the white metal kitchen cabinet, the overstuffed chair, the boxes of books, the underwater typewriter. Past the old two-by-fours poking out of rubble like broken arms and legs, past the concrete blocks, past pallets of car tires.

I was in the lead. True Shot followed carrying Ruby. Past the floating folding chair, the plastic garbage can lid, the jukebox. Past the old wood bar back, the broken mirrors, old radiators, rolls of linoleum, back to the hole in the cement foundation we'd jumped through all the way to the manhole in the ceiling.

True Shot took the rope and tied the rope around Ruby's ankles. Then True Shot laid Ruby on my shoulder.

I held the flashlight and True Shot tied the rope around Ruby's middle, looping the rope around.

It ain't going to work this way, True Shot said. We got to open the bag back up.

True Shot unzipped the bag and there was Ruby's skeleton smile poking through. True Shot peeled the plastic down to where the rope was tied around Ruby's middle, then pulled out both Ruby's arms, made one loop around Ruby's body under the arms, a second loop, and then tied a knot.

We leaned Ruby against the screened-in shelf, left him there in the dark alone, and True Shot and I went back and shined the circle of bright up into the manhole we'd jumped down at the beginning.

True Shot put his hand under my butt and lifted, and I grabbed onto a solid-feeling two-by-four and pulled myself up. One leg up, then the other. I stood and stretched my back.

The narrow dusty hallway seemed so cheerful.

True Shot handed the flashlight up, handle first, and the end of the rope that was tied around Ruby. I was about to offer True Shot a hand when, just like that, he leapt up. I had the flashlight on his face, and just like that True Shot's face was right by my face and he was pulling himself up through the hole.

I laid the flashlight at the edge of the hole. True Shot straddled the hole and I straddled the hole and we took the rope in our hands and we pulled; hand over hand we pulled Ruby's skinny body from the screened-in shelf, dragged Ruby through the water, sitting up, standing up. Then Ruby's head came up through the hole, into the circle of light.

OUTSIDE, THE STREET was a dark star, a crater on the moon. True Shot threw Ruby over his shoulder, opened the back door of Door of the Dead van, laid Ruby inside, slammed the back door, walked around, and opened the driver's side door. I opened mine.

Up and down the empty street, the only sound was the van doors slamming.

Rolling a cigarette, I had death all over on my hand.

True Shot unbuttoned his vest pocket, took the Armani case out, took his mirrors out, put his mirrors on.

True Shot's mirrors kept staring at me. Staring and staring, reflecting nothing. True Shot turned on the headlights of Door of the Dead van.

All Dodges sound the same when you start them up.

* * *

AT THE CORNER of Tenth and B, the red traffic light was in True Shot's mirrors. Life Café was just past True Shot's window. There were people still sitting at the outside tables, smoking, talking. Just as I looked, a guy in a green baseball cap let out a big laugh.

Café society. People were alive and laughing and drinking cappuccino. The waitress with green hair, the woman who waited on Ruby and me that one time, was leaning against the bricks on the wall. She had an empty drink tray in her hand. She toked off a joint, leaned her head back, and stared out at the English elms of Dog Shit Park.

True Shot turned the corner and drove halfway up the block, parked under the English elms, close to the arborvitae and the cement thing, close to Ruby's Home Sweet Home.

Just like that, as soon as True Shot cut the engine and shut off the headlights, a crowd of people—looked like Russian immigrants—came out of the dark and gathered around Door of the Dead van.

I quick locked my door.

True Shot said, It's OK, they're family.

True Shot got out and didn't slam the door; he shut the door quiet. I unlocked my door, got out, shut my door quiet. Somebody opened the back door and two people carried Ruby in the body bag into the park into the shadows around back of the big arborvitae. Nobody was talking, just whispering, and everybody was acting like they knew what to do next.

Some old guy in a stevedore's cap smelling of cigarettes and whiskey got in Door of the Dead van and drove off down Avenue B. He didn't turn the headlights on until Seventh Street.

Behind the arborvitae was the woman I'd seen a couple times in Dog Shit Park and one time on Third Street—Black Plastic Woman, I called her—a big black woman covered head to toe with black plastic bags, even her hair. She was standing next to her grocery cart. There were buckets full of water on the ground around her, lamplight reflected on the water. Black Plastic Woman had Ruby unzipped and lying on a patch of grass.

For a moment, Ruby looked like a streak of light from a lamppost or passing car. But it was Ruby, white white, lying on the grass in the dark. Just as I walked up, Black Plastic Woman made some kind of ululation in her throat, and I knew she was a he.

Black Plastic Woman threw a bucket of water onto Ruby.

Ruby jumped up, shook his long skinny white self, and hollered.

But it's not the truth.

A couple guys with gray beards picked Ruby up, one guy at Ruby's head, one guy at Ruby's feet, and turned him over. Another ululation out of Black Plastic Woman, and *whoosh* went another bucket of water.

Black Plastic Woman went to work on Ruby with a bar of Irish Spring, working up a lather on Ruby's back and butt and legs. She was singing low, her black hands in the white lather, the purple bumps on Ruby's back as if those cockroaches had got inside him.

Ululation, *whoosh*, another bucket of water, and the two gray beards turned Ruby back over and Black Plastic Woman soaped up Ruby head to toe, even washing Ruby's genitals.

Most of the time, though, Black Plastic Woman spent on Ruby's head, washing his hair and parting it down the middle, the way he liked.

Out of the dark, True Shot walked up next to me, put his arm over my shoulder.

We're burying Ruby, True Shot said, And having a pipe ceremony.

I looked up at True Shot, and the English elms were curvy black arms above his head and the light made the elm leaves look all on fire.

Elm tree fire in True Shot's mirrors.

Here? I said. In a city park?

Dog Shit Park ain't no city park, True Shot said. It's home.

These people were Ruby's family. If we don't bury him proper, he'll end up in the city dump.

Bury him? I said. Where?

Where he lived, True Shot said. Under his arborvitae. We about got the hole dug.

Then: I didn't know you had a pipe, I said.

Inherited it, True Shot said, From an old friend.

WHEN I CRAWLED through the hole in the arborvitae, next to the cement thing, at the base the elm tree, I couldn't see anything at first, just shadows and the noise of someone digging.

Can I spell you? I said.

Hell, yes, a woman's voice said.

She held up a shiny thing which was a short-handled shovel.

Karolyn, the woman said. With a K.

Hi, I said. My name's Will.

Ain't much farther to go, Will, Karolyn said. Throw your dirt to the south on the piece of plastic.

When her body passed by me in the dark and out the hole in the arborvitae, the smell of her sweat was heavy and sweet.

Wasn't long till my eyes got used to the dark. The hole was maybe four feet deep and probably four feet across, too. I started digging. The dirt was dry and caked hard. You had to use the shovel like a pick and pierce the earth and then scoop out what you'd pierced.

The smell of the earth, and being in the earth, made the time go by fast. Plus I was thinking about Ruby, me and Ruby Prestigiacomo spending the night in that very same place together.

How long ago was that?

Every time I struck the shovel into the earth, it was Sergeant Richard White's body I was striking.

Maybe the Riders would attack Dog Shit Park again tonight.

SEVEN PEOPLE ALTOGETHER, including me and True Shot, made a circle around Ruby's washed body. Ruby shined like a glow-in-the-dark statue. All around us, dark. The wind in the elm trees blew against my ears. There was Black Plastic Woman, tall and lanky Karolyn with a K, the two gray-bearded men who had turned Ruby over, and a young kid, a skinny boy about fourteen or fifteen with a bad complexion, wearing a T-shirt that said CUSTER DIED FOR YOUR SINS.

True Shot stepped up to Ruby, bent down, and lifted Ruby onto his shoulder again—no body bag, just Ruby naked. I crawled in the hole under the arborvitae first and True Shot laid Ruby down and I pulled Ruby through the hole.

Ruby smelled like Irish Spring and something else not so much like spring. True Shot stuck his head in and told me to put Ruby's head pointing east and then to curl his body around clockwise.

I was knocking dirt in the hole because there wasn't a lot of room. Finally I just squatted down.

In a dark tiny space wrestling with a dead body.

Ruby's arms and legs, Ruby's cock, his head—soft, heavy things against me. I got Ruby's head as east as I could and then folded the rest of him around on his side clockwise. Tucked Ruby's right hand under his left armpit, pulled his left arm down so his right hand couldn't move, then put his left hand in his right armpit. That way Ruby had his arms crossed. Pulled his legs up to his chest.

True Shot handed me a lit candle, the votive kind like in church when you put a quarter in a slot and light a candle in front of a saint. I put the candle in the center of Ruby's curl, between Ruby's hands and his head. The light was soft on his face.

I climbed out of Home Sweet Home. The gray-bearded men, Black Plastic Woman, Karolyn, and the kid with the Custer T-shirt stood in line to see Ruby.

On the green bench, I sat down hard, the sigh and scratch of the English elms all around me. The leaves were yellow in the dust-storm mercury-vapor light.

Black Plastic Woman made the high loud ululation in her throat. I heard the others, too.

People in the next room saying their prayers.

The kid wearing the CUSTER DIED FOR YOUR SINS T-shirt came over to where I was sitting and said, OK, man, he said, It's your turn.

The whole time I walked I was thinking, Last call. I was walking up to Ruby Prestigiacomo's grave and this was it.

Inside, under the arborvitae, there was Ruby. Looked like somebody had thrown a pint of blackberries in on his skin. Ruby Prestigiacomo in the light brown dirt hole, Home Sweet Home, curled up around the little votive fire.

Not sleeping.

I said Hail Mary Full of Grace the Lord is with thee and Holy Mary, Mother of God, pray for us sinners—and then I stopped. Somebody else's Catholic words. Pharisee words.

I didn't know any others.

So I just knelt there, looking in, my folded hands pointed down at my friend.

I tried to sing "Fools Rush In." But I couldn't sing.

Ruby Prestigiacomo, what am I going to do with you?

TRUE SHOT KNELT down next to the cement thing, his extra-lovely butt sticking out of the hole in the arborvitae. True Shot took off his mirrors. His shoulders moved up and down, up and down, and the muscles in his back shook.

True Shot's voice was a child's whispering in a culvert.

When he stood up, True Shot brushed the dirt off his Levi's knees, brushed off his butt, put his mirrors on.

True Shot bent over and, from underneath the arborvitae, pulled an old suitcase covered in buckskin with beadwork on the handle around where the locks flapped up.

*   *   *

THE CHANDELABRA ELM tree limbs and leaves were darker above us than the rest of the night. Hard bits of stars. True Shot was sitting west facing east. He had washed himself and put on a clean red shirt. Two small fires on the surface of his mirrors. I sat on True Shot's right. Next to me, the kid with the Custer T-shirt. Next to him, a graybeard, next to the graybeard the other graybeard. Across from me, Black Plastic Woman, and, to the left of True Shot, Karolyn on the drum.

Seven people in a circle around the fire.

Between me and True Shot's boots was one of those Catholic candles with a saint on it—Saint George killing the dragon—a big eagle feather with a piece of red flannel tied to it, and a white bowl full of water. An earthen bowl the size of one of True Shot's hands was directly in front of him.

From out of a buckskin bag, True Shot poured sand through his fingers into the bowl, and out of another buckskin bag, True Shot poured dirt—not the tan-colored hard pan dirt we buried Ruby in, but dark loamy earth I could smell over where I was sitting. True Shot mixed the earth and the sand together with his fingers.

When True Shot told me, I lit a Fish Bar match and put the match to the bottom of the piece of charcoal and the charcoal started fizzing, and I put the charcoal on the mixed earth and sand in the bowl, and the edges of the charcoal started turning white.

All at once, a high wind blasted through the elm trees. For a moment, they sounded like cottonwoods.

True Shot's old suitcase covered in buckskin sat on the grass. The suitcase was open. Inside was animal fur, beaded bags, and little boxes and paper sacks tied with ribbon. On the inside of the suitcase lid, where the cloth pocket with the elastic trim usually is, was the same painting that Charlie 2Moons used to have of an Indian on his horse, tired and beaten, the sun setting in the distance.

True Shot took a square piece of polished wood out of the suitcase. There was a circle of brass tacks on the wood. Then out of the suitcase, he pulled out bags: leather bags, plastic bags, paper bags.

Karolyn was on the drum, heartbeat, heartbeat, heartbeat.

True Shot took off his mirrors, folded them, put his mirrors inside the Armani case. He stuck the case in his shirt pocket. From out of the suitcase, True Shot took a spotted piece of fur. It looked like the collar to an old fur coat, mountain lion or bobcat.

But it's not the truth.

The spotted fur was ocelot.

True Shot unrolled the ocelot skin, and behold, just like that, lying there next to the Saint George and the dragon candle, right in front of me, was the pipe.

The moment that, after, you're different.

The dark blue beads, the feathers, the pipe bowl black around the hole, the carved buffalo, the pipe stem as long as your arm, the male and female of the pipe put together.

The pipe was Grandfather Alessandro's pipe. Charlie's pipe.

Voici la pipe.

What scared me was the pipe was alive.

My hand on the end of my arm reached out, and when I touched the pipe—just like that—I'd touched Charlie 2Moons again.

My eyes turned slow, like a rattlesnake in the sun, its eyes following the horizon, taking everything in, and when my eyes landed they landed on True Shot.

True Shot laid the pipe on the ocelot skin pointing out from him. Then from the buckskin bags, he pinched herbs and sage onto the charcoal, took the pipe, and moved the pipe in a circle through the lick of smoke.

Then he spoke. I couldn't believe my ears.

It is this way, True Shot said. I heard this story once. In Russia there was a famous rabbi. Whenever he saw misfortune threatening his people, this rabbi would go to a special place in the forest and meditate. Then he would light a fire, say a special prayer, and a miracle would happen and the rabbi's people would be safe. Things went on like that and the rabbi died, and later, another rabbi, whenever there was a misfortune threatening his people, this rabbi would go to the same place in the forest and say to the Great Mystery, I'm sorry but I do not know how to light the fire, but I still know the prayer, and here's the prayer, and this rabbi would say the prayer, and the miracle would happen. Then that rabbi died, and another rabbi, his disciple, whenever a misfortune threatened his people, he would go to the place in the forest and say, I do not know how to light the fire, and I do not know the prayer, but I know the place and this must be sufficient, and the miracle would happen. So then that rabbi died, and his disciple, another rabbi, whenever a misfortune threatened his people, would sit in his chair at home with his head in his hands, speak to the Great Mystery, and say, I don't know how to light the fire, I don't know the prayer, and I don't know the place in the forest, or even the forest.

All I can do is tell you about it, and this must be sufficient. And the miracle would happen.

It is this way, True Shot said. The moral of this tale is that God made man because he loves to hear stories.

True Shot? I said.

True Shot blew on the embers in the pipe bowl, the embers in the bowl inside glowing, a thin line of smoke trailing up around True Shot's head. The light from the Catholic saint candle back and forth, side to side in his eyes, on his face, his face like rocks and cliffs.

That's a good one, huh? There's lots of stories, True Shot said. Each one of us has one.

The locomotive, I said. Tell us the one about the locomotive.

Only the drum heartbeat, the wind in the English elms.

True Shot's gap-toothed smile. His hand went up to his throat, his open palm on the beaded blue horizontal and the red vertical of the buckskin bag around his neck.

It is this way, True Shot said. When you're lost on the blue road, when you're in the west and cannot see, remember that the bright light coming toward you first appears to be a charging iron horse, a locomotive train that will run over you, that will crush you.

But that bright light, I said.

But that bright light, True Shot said, Only appears to be an iron horse, we said together. What the light really is, we said, Is the light at the end of the tunnel.

MY HANDS REACHED out for the medicine pipe, past the Saint George candle, and I put my hands under the ocelot skin, around the wooden stem as long as my forearm, put my hands around the pipe bowl. The eagle fluff and the blue trader beads and mother-of-pearl shells. I held the pipe to my heart, to my head, to my belly, to my penis. Held the universe, known and unknown.

Held Charlie.

When I turned my head and looked up at True Shot, his lips had turned to rubber.

True Shot's chin was on his chest, and he had his thumb and index on the bridge of his nose. His extra-lovely shoulders started shaking up and down.

Who knows how long True Shot wept?

True Shot is still weeping.

When True Shot lifted his chin up, what was in his eyes I wanted covered with his mirrors.

Then: My friends, True Shot said, True Shot is not my real name.

THE MOMENT THAT, after, you're different.

The mystery. The true mystery.

Everything is there all along and you just don't realize it.

Then, just like in Agatha Christie, a twig snapped, or wind, the fire popped—something. True Shot's hummingbird eyes stared at something straight ahead. The light from the flame back and forth, back and forth, onto True Shot's face.

My eyes looked where True Shot was looking.

Black Plastic Woman screamed.

We were surrounded by Indians. In all four directions. Indian people stood just outside the light of the fire.

From where I sat, the line of the tops of their heads made the horizon. Rolling dark black shadows. The fire gold on their faces.

The man who stepped out seemed so big standing above us.

We seven on the ground seemed so small, so broken open.

My left hand on the bowl, my right on the stem, I pulled the pipe inside my arms, the ocelot skin smooth against my forearms.

Heartbeat.

The man took off his camouflage cap and shook his head so the long black shiny hair moved from his face. He wore dark aviator glasses and a Levi's jacket with an eagle beaded on the pocket.

True Shot's hummingbird eyes stared at the space in between. It is this way, True Shot said. You have arrived just in time, True Shot said. Welcome!

My name is Peter Morales, True Shot said.

The heartbeat stopped.

Yellow leaves, wind, a campfire in the night. The fire on Beaded Eagle's skin, his aviators, his shiny black hair.

We know, Beaded Eagle said. That's why we're here.

The Indians we were surrounded by all made low sounds, moved their weight from side to side. The line of horizon lifted and fell, waves in a lake or ocean.

Beaded Eagle threw his hair back, lifted his arms, and looped his hair in a knot. He put his camouflage hat back on, pulled down the brim.

We've come for the pipe, Beaded Eagle said. We've been looking for this one for a long time.

Fire in his aviator sunglasses, Beaded Eagle took his sunglasses off, hunkered down, sat the way I never could for long. His Levi's knees were pointed at me, his boots. His whole body was pointed at me.

From over the fire, he reached out his hand, his palm the color of cut cedar, his hand moving out from him like a bird flying. His index went straight for my heart but touched the carved buffalo on the pipe bowl instead.

I looked down. His index wrapped around the pipe stem.

This is Charlie 2Moons's pipe, I said.

Give me the pipe, Beaded Eagle said. We're here to return the pipe to its home.

Then his finger reached up and he touched me on my hair, my forehead.

His eyes were open, clear, like a child's with nothing in between.

I'll tell you something, Beaded Eagle said. So you'll know.

Beaded Eagle's hands, palms up, were open to me.

The fire on his skin, his shiny black hair, he looked so much like Charlie.

It took everything I had. Palms open, I sent my hands across the fire into the night, placing the ocelot skin and the pipe into Beaded Eagle's hands.

Beaded Eagle tapped out the pipe, dumped out the earth and sand from the earthen bowl, folded the ocelot skin over the pipe, placed the pipe in the suitcase that was covered in buckskin. Then, one by one, Beaded Eagle took the square piece of polished wood with the circle of brass tacks, the Saint George candle, the earthen bowl, the white bowl, the eagle feather with a piece of red flannel tied to it, and placed them in the suitcase. He closed the suitcase, pulled each beaded lock down, snapped the suitcase closed.

Beaded Eagle's cowboy boot stepped on the white piece of smoldering charcoal, crushed it.

Beaded Eagle put his aviators back on. Smiled real big.

When I opened my eyes, the horizon was back to the tops of buildings and Lower East Side water towers.

Beaded Eagle and the others had shape-shifted into Wolf Swamp and the night.

TRUE SHOT STILL sat like Buddha—Buddha in a clean red shirt—his Saint-Vitus'-dance eyes moving like the fire. Then he stood up, not stooped like usual. His shoulders were back and his chest was out. He dusted his pants off and looked around him on the ground.

He pulled the Armani glasses case from his shirt pocket, opened the case, unfolded the mirrors, and put the mirrors over his eyes.

Peter Morales, I said, What's the fucking deal?

On the surface of True Shot's mirrors, my face was a solitary illumination.

True Shot stood taller, pulled his shoulders back farther. His red shirt filled up with air.

Where did you get that pipe, I said, Ruby's friend's pipe? Who was Ruby's friend?

Only silence. Just the yellow leaves, the wind, the fire.

Fred, True Shot said. Ruby's friend was Fred.

I went to land a Hollywood punch onto True Shot's hooked nose, but that's when I heard them.

Horses. All at once, all around us, cops on horses.

A white stallion jumped over the fire, hitting True Shot straight on.

I was running through tree limbs, juniper bushes; I was jumping over benches; I was out of there, out of Dog Shit Park, out; I was on First Avenue and Sixth Street; I was far away, running.

Nowhere.

CHAPTER
TWENTY-TWO

For three days I got True Shot's answering machine.

On my next day off I took the L train to Bedford. On the corner of Wythe and North Third, at number 85, there was no buzzer. I banged on the door, kicked the door, hollered.

Nobody on the street, not one person. *Personne.*

Up the flights of stairs in the building across the street. When I got to the fourth floor, my heart was pounding pounding. Around the corner there it was, plain as day, Door of the Dead van.

I got the key from under the wheel well, unlocked the passenger-side door.

True Shot was not dead in the back of the van.

There was nothing in the back of the van except the bucket I sat on between Ruby and True Shot on the ride from the airport and two empty vodka bottles.

All Dodges sound the same when you start them up.

I drove Door of the Dead van for a week, to all the places True Shot and I had gone to look for Charlie. The World Trade center. The parking lot where you could see the Lady with the Paintbrush out in the harbor. The meat district. Over the Verrazano Narrows Bridge. Staten Island. Jackson Heights. To the very tip of the island where Manhattan starts. Even drove to Harlem.

Not-looking for True Shot.

For Charlie.

One day about a week later, sitting on the green bench next to Ruby's Home Sweet Home—abracadabra!— just like that there was the CUSTER DIED FOR YOUR SINS kid.

This time his T-shirt was gray with nothing on it. Pizza face. Just below his hairline was an arch of dirt and sweat.

He looked even more scared in the daylight.

I bought him a veggie burger at Life Café.

Have you seen Black Plastic Woman? I said. Maybe she'd know.

The Custer kid had such a mouthful of veggie burger he couldn't talk.

After he swallowed, after a drink of water, the Custer kid wiped his mouth.

Morales is on a bender, the kid said. You'll never find him.

Morales. Peter Morales.

The yellow English elms were bare.

But there's got to be some way, I said.

Make him come to you, the kid said.

How do I do that? I said.

Just open up that place in you, the kid said.

YOU'RE GOING THIS way and then shit happens and then you're going that way.

The beep on my red answering machine and Fiona's voice was around and around in my rooms.

Will? Are you there, Will? Please pick up if you're there! Will, are you there? Look, I'm at the hospital, Saint Vincent's, Room Three-oh-five. It's Harry. Harry's lying in the bed all blue breathing on a machine. He doesn't even know I'm here, Will! Please come as soon as you can!

I rewound the tape.

Will? Are you there, Will?

WHEN I CALLED work, Daniel, the boss's brother, answered the phone.

Daniel? I said. Why are *you* answering?

John is in the hospital, Daniel said.

John the Bartender? I said. Hospital?

Saint Vincent's, Daniel said.

What room's he in?

You can't see him, Daniel said. Quarantined.

What?

They think it's TB.

Tuberculosis?

You're Section Five tonight, Daniel said.

I'm sick, I said.

Shit! Daniel said. What's going on, Spud?

Flu, I said.

You been to a doctor?

I'm all right, I said. Just the flu.

Vitamin C, Daniel said. Take big doses of Vitamin C. Rest. Walter and Joanie are out with it too.

And Harry, Daniel said.

IN THE CORRIDOR, Saint Vincent's unrelenting light from above. Through the swinging doors, a man in swimming-pool-blue shirt and pants and cap pushed a gurney past me, the IV a snake into the arm of a bald guy. The steel-gray eyes of the bald guy looked up out through his skin and bones at me like I was a vision, Saint Vincent himself, some kind of saint.

Breathing from everywhere you could hear, in and out, in and out, words above my head on the ceiling intercom, somebody coughing. Wax buildup on the floor in the corners and along the walls. Pine Sol, urine, stool samples, blood, recycled air. The flowers I bought for Harry, miniature red and yellow roses. I put them up to my nose.

My eyes on my combat-boot feet. Step. Step. Step. Step.

Policing my body. New-shoe stiff.

My breath in. My breath out.

On my right, on my left, doorway after doorway, under their one dirty window in their room, skinny gray men in beds with tubes and flowers, canned TV laughter, *General Hospital, Days of Our Lives*. The Manhattan sky was the gray shine on them, on their boxes of facial tissues, their bent plastic straws in plastic glasses, their fancy get-well cards from Mom, Manhattan sky the gray shine on the shiny green floor.

Harry was another doorway, his body just lumps in the bed, his mouth open, a blue tube in his mouth, blue tubes in his nose. The tubes made a sucking sound like at the dentist. His eyes were closed tight the way a child pretends to sleep. Coming up from deep, on his face, *cauchemar*.

Fiona was sitting in a tan Naugahyde chair covered with a purple velvet shawl with fringe. Fiona all in black. Her black hair in a French twist under a little hat with a veil.

Leonard Cohen in drag.

The room was full of lilacs. Lilacs on the windowsill, on the nightstand; lilacs in a big vase on the floor. Lilacs on the swingaway tray of the bed. A strip of purple velvet, a valence above the window. A purple lava lamp next to an amethyst crystal the size of her big red leather purse. Brian Eno on the boom box.

Fucking Nurse Rat Shit! Fiona said. The fat bitch who runs this floor is one motherfucker! Told me I was not allowed to redecorate the hospital. Redecorate? I said. Redecorate! Since when is a lava lamp redecoration? Besides, I said, Everybody knows daytime television gives you cancer. And lavender is healing, Fiona said. Lavender is the color of your fifth chakra, and if you could sit in a purple room with amethysts and lilacs and other purple flowers and listen to Brian Eno, you'd be fine, just fine. But Miss Nurse, Miss Grand Chooser 1987, Miss Nancy Fucking Reagan bitch cunt won't have it. She wouldn't know Ruth Draper from a Baby Ruth. So I called my lawyer, right here on this phone right in front of the Nancy bitch, and Father told me I have every right—Harry—has every right in the world to have a purple lava lamp in his room if he wants it.

It's a free fucking country! I yelled at the nurse, Fiona yelled at me. And the bitch yells back, Not on my floor!

Big fucking deal, Fiona said. So what, who cares? Who cares what a bunch of assholes think?

Fiona stood up. Her long black skirt, her black leotard ankles in her black shiny Doc Martens, Fiona walked around the bed, long strides like her mother, between me and Harry, didn't touch me, didn't touch Harry, looked out the dirty window at the dirty gray sky.

How is he? I said.

Who? Fiona said.

Harry, I said.

His fucking mother and father won't come to see him, Fiona said. I called them and his mother wouldn't talk to me, and his father said, My son died years ago, and then hung up.

Can you imagine, Will? Fiona said, His own fucking father!

Harry's skin is all gray, his eyes closed tight, tubes in his nose. An IV in his arm.

New York's only Irish Catholic homosexual, I said.

Just then, a nurse walked in the room and heard me say *homosexual.* She was young, with that Farrah Fawcett hair. The nurse didn't look at Fiona or me. She went straight to the boom box and pulled the plug. Then over to the bed, looked close at Harry, put her hand to his neck.

Then, when the nurse took her hand away—*ta-da!* abracadabra!—Harry's eyes opened. A big smile on Harry's face. Harry pulled the blue tubes out of his nose and mouth, out of his arm, threw the covers back, said, I say, Terence! Let's have a cocktail!

Fiona said, Cool!

And we walked out the door, laughing at Harry's bare pink butt sticking out of his hospital gown.

But it's not the truth.

Harry's eyes stayed tight.

Fiona stared into Manhattan gray.

The nurse said, Here, let me put the flowers in some water for you. The nurse didn't smile. She took the flowers from me like the flowers were sick too.

In the corridor I asked the nurse, What's wrong with him?

Pneumonia, the nurse said.

Your friend has AIDS, the nurse said.

Lletre ferit: AIDS.

The nurse brought back the flowers stuck in a clear plastic vase. She moved a vase of lilacs on the bedside table, set the flowers down, left the room.

Fiona plugged in Brian Eno.

One of Harry's hands jumped.

Thank God you didn't buy carnations! Fiona said.

ON THE STREET, a young man with a shaved head and big sideburns was sitting between two cars, in the gutter, his head lying on his arms. When I first heard him, I thought he was laughing.

The WALK / DON'T WALK on Seventh Avenue flashed to WALK, and the heels of Fiona's Doc Martens hit the asphalt crossing Seventh Avenue the way shoes sound on women who know where they are going.

Fiona was another black hole in the gray day. I caught up with her, and we crossed Greenwich Avenue, walked down Seventh past a grocery store, past a place you could buy old books, then a porn shop.

Fiona stopped in front of the Art Family in the window, at the one in the leather head mask, hanging from a chain hooked to a leather harness.

Fiona reached into her red leather purse, pulled out a compact, a lottery ticket, a Seven-Up can, a Trojan, and then the joint. She put the joint in her mouth. I lit it. Fiona sucked in hard, let the smoke come out, French inhaled.

Fiona held the joint to me.

Kiss? Fiona said.

I looked up the avenue, down, took the joint, toked, gave the joint back to her.

My mother called, Fiona said.

Fiona's red lips under the black veil were rubber around the joint.

Mother says, Fiona said, To tell you thanks.

For what? I said.

For getting her ass out of that crack! Fiona said. Dog Shit Park—you know!—the night I turned into a total asshole in front of my very eyes.

Smoke from out of Fiona's red lips, from out of the curl, through the veil.

Not to mention my whole family, Fiona said. Kiss? Fiona said.

I took the joint, toked, gave the joint back to her.

We were all scared, Fiona said. Scared the shit out of me!

Me too, I said.

In the plate glass of the porn-shop window, an ambulance drove by slow, behind us on Seventh Avenue, no siren, just the amber light flashing.

The Art Family mannequin had both her legs helium heels in the air.

Loud disco music when some guy opened the door of the porn shop.

Seems like such a long time ago, Fiona said. My God.

It was a great opening night, I said. Magical.

Fiona's black hat and veil, the orange marijuana fire, were reflected in the window exactly between the Art Family mannequin's helium-heel legs.

And how's *your* friend? Fiona said. The homeless guy who pulled the knife on us.

Ruby Prestigiacomo, I said.

The junkie, Fiona said.

He's fine now, I said.

In rehab? Fiona said. Or dead? Kiss? Fiona said.

I took the joint, toked.

Dead, I said, holding in my breath like you do.

Fiona leaned against me, the veil of her hat tickling my nose. She put her arm around my waist, looped a finger in a back belt loop.

I thought so, she said.

Why's that?

Death, Fiona said. You can feel it around people.

Like Harry? I said.

Fiona quick pulled away. Put her arm on the window glass, leaned her head against her arm.

I put my hand onto Fiona's shoulder.

Never touch me.

Kiss? I said.

Fiona took the joint and flipped it into the gutter.

Before he died, I said, Ruby told me your name was Fiona. He also told me not to fall in love with you.

Fiona lifted her face up off her arm, stared into her reflection.

Fiona? Fiona said. Fiona what?

Fiona, I said to Fiona's reflection in the glass, Or Phaedra, or Persephone, or Daphne, or the fair Ophelia— one of those fucking *f*'s.

Fiona lifted the veil and pulled it back over the black hat. Her red lip a life all its own.

Her skin, white cake batter with vanilla.

Fiona! Fiona said.

Beautiful according to Dracula.

In my forearms, up to my shoulders, down through my heart.

Fiona stepped closer to the porn-shop window. She touched her face and her reflection touched its face.

My name is Fiona! Fiona said.

Fiona stared into the window. Her index across her forehead, down her cheek, to her chin, around her chin, up to the corner of her mouth, to her lip, the scar, the red red scar.

Death is only a door, Fiona said.

Fiona's index across her upper lip, up the side of her nose, down her Roman nose.

Hunter and Gus are in the hospital, Fiona said.

Your brothers? I said. The YUFAs?

Fiona's index across her eyebrows, down under her eyes.

The Hyannisport Homos, Fiona said. They do everything together.

Is it . . . ?

Fiona closed her left eye, touched the eye.

Fiona closed her right eye, touched the eye.

All of us silent, all of us all one thing.

Dehydration, Fiona said. Exhaustion. Mother says they've been working and playing much too hard.

Fiona raised her head, put her index to her chin.

They just need some rest, Fiona said.

CHAPTER
TWENTY-THREE

The end of October, Bobbie and Charlie and I hitchhiked into Pocatello in the back of some guy's pickup. He dropped us off at Idaho State College, which was pretty close to the house where Bobbie had her appointment.

The house was narrow, with that gray siding that's supposed to look like bricks, on Fifth Street next to the Fanci-Freez across from the cemetery.

Bobbie opened the screen and knocked on the door. Charlie and I stood behind her. The guy who opened the door was maybe forty, gray at the temples, a mustache, and horn-rimmed glasses. He wasn't wearing any doctor clothes, just a mustard-colored shirt with a white T-shirt under it and brown slacks.

Barbara Parker? he said.

Bobbie, Bobbie said.

I thought they told you to come alone, he said.

These are my brothers, Bobbie said. They come with me.

Very well then, the guy said, like a Holy Cross nun. He opened the door and we walked into a small room with white clapboard walls and a copper and yellow linoleum floor.

Have a seat, he said. Do you have the money?

The only place to sit was on an old orange couch that was in front of a window with a yellow sheet hanging over the window.

Bobbie took the hundred and fifty dollars out of her front Levi's pocket—a big wad of dollar bills and fives and tens and twenties—and the twelve rolls of quarters we'd rolled up, and put the bills in the guy's one hand and the quarters in his other hand.

The guy looked at the wad of money and at the rolls of quarters in his hands. All at once, his face looked like he was going to cry and I felt sorry for him.

How far you along? the guy said.

Bobbie shrugged her shoulders. Two months, she said, maybe three.

Did your bring your Kotex? the guy said. You're going to bleed.

I've got it in my backpack, I said.

Give it to me, the guy said.

I took the box of Kotex out of my backpack and gave it to him.

The guy told Bobbie to come in the other room, which was the kitchen, and Bobbie walked in after him, and Charlie and I stayed sitting on the orange couch and could hear his footsteps and hers on the linoleum floor, and then we heard a door close.

I moved closer to Charlie on the couch. The light in the room was ugly because of the yellow sheet, and there were dust balls on the floor in the corners. No pictures on the walls, no coffee table or magazines or floor lamps, just a square white room with the orange couch and the yellow sheet over the window. The room smelled closed up, and there was an awful smell of something like in hospitals.

Bobbie yelled, more of a shout—angry, like Fuck you—and Charlie and I looked at each other. Then we heard something that sounded like a vacuum cleaner and that's all we heard for several minutes and then we heard Bobbie really yell.

Charlie and I ran into the kitchen and went to open the door but the door was locked. Bobbie was crying and moaning and sighing low sighs and every once in a while would go, Oh! Oh! Oh! My God!

Charlie and I were banging on the door, saying Bobbie Bobbie you all right in there? Then Charlie: You motherfucker better open this door, or we'll break the fucker down!

The guy yelled at us to keep it down, that Bobbie was fine, that it was sometimes painful, he was almost finished, and not to worry because everything was going fine and Bobbie was going to be all right.

It's OK, Bobbie said. It's OK.

Charlie went to the kitchen cupboards and opened the doors. There were no dishes or anything in the cupboards. He turned all the burners of the stove on but none of them got red. There was no refrigerator. A yellow sheet over the window in there too.

Charlie and I stayed standing in the kitchen. After about twenty minutes or a half hour, the guy unlocked the door.

Bobbie looked like hell. Real sweaty and her face all scrunched up, her eyes were puffy, and she was holding her stomach. She looked yellow. I thought it was the sheet over the window, but when we got outside, Bobbie was still yellow.

Drink lots of liquids, the guy said. You'll bleed for a couple days, and there'll be discharge, but that will end. You'll probably feel sick for a while. Get some rest.

Charlie and I helped Bobbie across the street and into Mount Moriah cemetery and went to the Chinese section under a huge cottonwood tree and Bobbie lay down in a pile of leaves. Charlie lay down too, and so did I.

Bobbie curled up in the leaves and held her stomach and didn't say anything at all, even though Charlie and I kept asking questions.

Just shut the fuck up, Bobbie finally said, and laid her head so her face was in the sun. Charlie was on one side of her and I was on the other, but neither one of us touched her. She just lay there with her arms between her legs.

After about an hour, Bobbie pulled her hands from her crotch and there was blood all over her fists.

Fuck! Bobbie said, and got up and walked slow to behind a Chinese marble pillar that had Chinese writing on it. I could see her take off her pants and take off the bloody Kotex; then she wiped herself with another Kotex and put a third Kotex on. Threw the bloody pads in the ditch just beyond the cottonwood tree.

BOBBIE TIED THE sweatshirt I was wearing around her waist like an apron in front of her. At Idaho State College, we stuck our thumbs out, and a '58 Mercury stopped and it was a priest, for chrissakes, Monsignor Verhooven. We told him we'd come into town to make confession at Saint Anthony's and went to visit relatives in the cemetery, but you could tell he didn't believe us.

Young lady, are you feeling all right? Monsignor Verhooven said.

I'm fine, Monsignor, Bobbie said, Just fine.

While the monsignor drove, he was preaching at us that we were too young to be out on the road, and he was going to call our parents, and what were we going to amount to, living like we were living, and he made us say the Act of Contrition.

I made the sign of the cross and Charlie made the sign of the cross after he watched me do it. Then I started the Act of Contrition. Charlie mumbled along. Bobbie was holding her stomach and saying it too, but she didn't make the sign of the cross, just held her stomach, and there were big tears in her eyes and she stared out the window.

*Oh my God I am heartily sorry for having offended thee. I detest all my
sins because of thy just punishments.*

Charlie told the monsignor that Mother was going to pick us up in
front of the Green Triangle Café, so he should drop us off there.

That's a bar, the Monsignor said.

It's also a café, Charlie said. We got money for hamburgers, Charlie
said.

WE WEREN'T STANDING on the Yellowstone Highway ten minutes before we got a ride with Father's Indian friend, Lou Racing, who'd just
been elected reservation sheriff, in his white '60 Chevrolet Apache
with RESERVATION POLICE on the side.

I didn't want to ride in front with Lou Racing, so Bobbie and Charlie
rode in front, Charlie in the middle even though the girl is supposed to
sit there.

Bobbie said, I need the air and that's all there's to it, so I'm sitting by
the fucking window.

Bobbie hung her head out the window all the way home, her short
brown hair every which way in the wind. Lou drove us right up to the
front door of the Residency. Mother was out in the yard in her violet
dress with the orchid all the way down the front, pinning an American
flag on the clothesline upside down, like it was a bedsheet.

Lou yelled out his window, Afternoon, Mrs. Parker! Lovely day,
isn't it?

Yes, Mr. Racing, Mother said, It is a lovely day.

I got down out of the back of the truck and stood between Bobbie
and Mother. Charlie was standing on the other side of Bobbie. I looked
on the seat and there was a smear of blood, so I jumped in and sat on
the blood and when I got out again pulled my butt hard against the seat
and took the blood smear with me.

You know, Lou Racing said, I think this whole family of yours is plumb
crazy.

Fuck you very much, Lou Racing, Bobbie said, smiling with her
mouth, and slammed the pickup door.

Charlie and I got Bobbie past Mother and to her room no problem.
Mother didn't even ask where we'd been.

Charlie said, What's with the flag?

Who knows? I said.

Maybe it's Flag Day, Bobbie said.

Bobbie went into her bathroom and Charlie and I heard the shower. When Bobbie came out, she was yellow as ever, sweating. She had a towel wrapped around her head and she was wearing her flannel night-gown and there were stains of blood on the back.

Bobbie dried her hair and then laid the towel on the bedsheet. Made sure that each corner of the towel was equidistant side to side, top to bottom, then lay down on the bed, straight, facing the map of the Known Universe, folded another towel over her crotch and then pulled the sheet over her.

I put my hand on her forehead. It was so hot.

Bobbie, I said, Are you sure about this? I mean, we could call Doc Hayden at the Fort Hall Clinic.

No fucking way, Bobbie said. Now get out of here, she said. I need some sleep.

Charlie and I kept a glass of water at her bed and cool washrags to wipe her face with. I made her some Campbell's tomato soup, her favorite, but Bobbie wouldn't eat it. We stayed by her all night, Charlie sleeping on one side of the bed, me on the other. In the middle of the night, I felt something dripping on my arm. I turned Bobbie's Marilyn Monroe light on, and there was blood all down the side of the bed and onto the floor.

When Charlie and I pulled the covers back, it was awful, all the blood and stuff there was coming out of Bobbie.

I thought for sure she was dead; then just like that Bobbie sat up quick and opened her eyes and looked down at the bed. She didn't even flinch.

He said I would hemorrhage, Bobbie said. He said there'd be discharge. Jesus, you guys, Bobbie said. This is hemorrhaging and discharging, OK?

Bobbie held her stomach as she got out of bed. She stood up, going back and forth, back and forth, for a moment, like she was going to faint, and Charlie and I jumped quick to help, but Bobbie said: I'm all right, I'm all right. Just got to clean this mess up.

The towels were soaked and so were the sheets. We put the towels and sheets in the bathtub. Bobbie showered again, and when she came out she said, Things look a lot better, Bobbie said.

I think the worst is over, Bobbie said.

We flipped the mattress over and put clean sheets on and a clean pillowcase and a clean towel equidistant up and down, side to side, corner to corner, and Bobbie lay down again, arms and legs straight like she was pointing her body at the Known Universe.

You guys are so sweet, Bobbie said. I love you guys.

My two brothers, Bobbie said. Thanks for all the help.

THE NEXT DAY, Charlie and I thought Bobbie was sleeping, and we checked and there was only a little blood, so we had our cereal and then got on ayaHuaska and Chub, played Going Slack fancy riding to Spring Creek. Charlie did the Free Lazy Back and the Lazy Back Rollback. I did the Backward Crouch Stand from the Withers.

We were back home by noon, in time for Bobbie's lunch.

I took up the tray of milk and Wonder bread and bologna with mustard and mayonnaise and lettuce and Clover Club potato chips.

Bobbie wasn't in her bed.

We followed the drops of blood down the stairs, through the hallway, across the cement playground, past the rusted swing set and teeter-totter, past Grandmother Cottonwood, into the barn, up the stairs of the barn, to the hayloft. Bobbie had slung the lariat around the ridgepole and made a hangman's noose, exactly in the middle of the barn, then crawled up the old stepladder.

The stepladder was lying flat on the floor, and Bobbie was hanging, the noose around her throat, her soft brown hair hanging down into her face, eyes rolled up Saint Theresa Gone to Heaven, not on the premises, her lips blue, her face yellow, her feet dangling in the air, blood all over the back of her nightgown, blood dripping down onto the barn floor, onto the floorboards and dust and straw and pigeon shit.

The moment that, after, you're different.

The wind through the barn, the wind all around Bobbie, Bobbie swinging slowly, slowly, side to side, back and forth, back and forth. The sound of the rope.

Charlie and I stood, my arm around Charlie's waist, Charlie's arm over my shoulder. Beneath us, around us, the toothpick barn, dry kindling, just one step out of place and the barn would snap.

CHARLIE SET THE ladder up straight. I went in the house, up the stairs to Bobbie's room, turned on the Marilyn Monroe light, got her red Swiss army knife out of where she always kept it in the top drawer. I got the black dress with the straps that Father gave her, her nylons with no seams, and her black high heels. Her black brassiere and black panties.

Charlie cut the rope and Bobbie fell into my arms.

We washed her, Charlie and I. The steaming hot water in the porcelain pan. Washed the blood off her legs and her vagina. Washed her face. Washed her hair with her Prell shampoo. Combed her hair back off her face. I put Bobbie's lipstick on her mouth, the red red lipstick she liked, staying exactly inside the curve of her lips. Charlie put on her blue eye shadow, and the eyeliner, and the mascara.

Then Charlie went to the house to get Bobbie's Marilyn Monroe light and her purple flowered bedspread, and the map of the Known Universe.

While Charlie was gone, I lay down right next to Bobbie, exactly straight, perfect, just like her, my hands folded over my breast like her. Pigeon flutter and wind through the shingles. Then silence, perfect silence.

I put my ear to Bobbie's mouth.

Dead silent. No more secrets.

Charlie and I pinned the map of the Known Universe to the barn wall, exactly above the old Zenith. The old Zenith exactly in the middle under the map.

We laid Bobbie on her purple flowered bedspread. Exactly centered in the middle. Plugged in her lamp with the white grapes and grape leaves bumps on it, turned on her Marilyn Monroe light.

It had to be a certain way.

Bobbie in her makeup, her red lips, her black dress, nylons, and black high heels on the purple flowers of her bedspread, in the Marilyn Monroe light.

Charlie turned on KSEI on the old Zenith. Perry Como was singing "Faraway Places."

Bobbie had such a good look on her face. I'd never seen her look so good.

Charlie rolled cigarettes with one hand.

We harmonized "The Idaho State Song," then "America the Beautiful."

WHEN THE AMBULANCE drove up the lane, red and white and yellow lights were all over the cottonwood trees.

Mother thought they were coming for her and hid in the kitchen closet.

CHAPTER
TWENTY-FOUR

iona was cold. She just couldn't get warm that night, so Fiona and
I were under a quilt in Stranded Beings Searching for God on the
Conran couch listening to Leonard Cohen and watching *Autumn
Sonata* at the same time. Fiona had made popcorn and I was drinking a
St. Pauli Girl and she was drinking Southern Comfort two rocks. We'd
had several tokes on the erect pink penis. I was sitting, and Fiona's head
was in my lap.

Harry was in the hospital again. KS. The doctors were doing tests to
see if the KS was in him as well as on him.

Fiona's brothers were still in the hospital. When the doctor told her
mother that Hunter and Gus had AIDS, Margo MacIlvane fell over
backward, hit her head on the edge of a waiting-room chair, and had to
have five stitches. Dave, Fiona's father, was taking antidepressants.

John the Bartender didn't have tuberculosis, he had a brain fever
nobody knew what to do about. Toxic-something-or-other.

The place inside me the Custer kid had told me to open up, I'd opened
up, but True Shot still hadn't showed up.

Neither had Rose.

So there we were, me and my thongs and cutoffs and T-shirt next
to Fiona on her Conran couch, in the television light, Fiona under
the quilt, on a hot September night, Fiona in a purple wool stocking
cap, wearing three layers of sweatshirts, thermal underwear with two
pairs of sweatpants, those kind of gloves with holes for the fingers,
Fiona shivering shivering, and me in my black T-shirt rolling cigarettes, watching Ingmar and Ingrid Bergman.

We should be watching *Duck Soup*, I said, or *It's a Mad Mad Mad
Mad World*.

Fiona pulled herself closer to me. She was a child in my arms, she
was so curled up and close.

When the movie was over, Fiona took the quilt in with her to pee, and when she came back she said, Did you see the black Mercedes limo out in front about four o'clock today?

In front of where? I said.

In front of here, Fiona said. A woman with a scarf tied around her head and dark glasses got out and walked into this building. I could have sworn it was Elizabeth Taylor.

Language my second language.

I lit my cigarette, lit Fiona's.

Maybe, I said, It was.

What do you mean? Fiona said.

I pulled the smoke inside to where it hurt.

Promise not to tell a soul? I said.

Fiona's lips were puckered around the cigarette and her cheeks were all sucked in.

I promise, Fiona said. Blew the smoke out.

No, I said, Really. You got to promise!

So I promise! Fiona said. Jeez, I promise!

Only silence for a moment, in all the world, all of New York City, only silence.

Fiona's hair poking out under the purple wool cap, her red lips. Her upper lip trying to smile.

E-li-za-beth Tay-lor, I said, emphasizing every syllable of her name, Is Rose's best friend.

Oh . . . My . . . God! Fiona said, and put her white white hand in front of her red red mouth. Cool, Fiona said.

Fiona threw part of the quilt over onto my legs. She sat down next to me on the couch. Pretty soon Fiona's fingers were in my hair just above the back of my neck, curling my hair in her fingers.

Trouble in my forearms.

What? I said.

Right out my back door, Fiona said, pointing her partly gloved finger, The fire-escape section that's supposed to be cranked up to the second floor, Fiona said, Has been at ground level since I moved in here.

You mean you want to crawl up the fire escape and look in Rose's windows? I said.

No! Fiona said. How could you possibly think that?

Fiona's open palm against my open palm.

I want *us* to crawl up the fire escape and look in Rose's windows, Fiona said.

More power in a pair of tits than any chariot.

Somebody will see us, I said.

Nobody's going to fucking see us! Fiona said.

What about the dog? I said.

What dog?

The pit bull in the chain-link fence, I said.

Oh, Chauncey! Fiona said. He's such a pussycat! There's dog biscuits next to the toaster. Get him one.

We can't invade somebody's privacy like that, I said.

You invade the E.T.-phone-home guy's privacy every chance you get, Fiona said.

That's different, I said. All I have to do is stand in my kitchen, I said.

With the lights off! Fiona said.

But Rose is not home, I said. He hasn't been home for days.

I think you might be surprised, Fiona said. Come on! Fiona said. It won't be *spying*, it will be *adoring*!

CHAUNCEY WAGGED HIS tail when he saw Fiona, sniffed at my hand first, then, through the chain links, took the dog biscuit.

Fiona climbed up the fire-escape steps first. She was wearing her grandmother's black Persian lamb coat. The iron of the fire escape rattled, and I looked around at all the windows above us, around us.

When Fiona got to the first landing, she said, Come on, Will!

I had my hands around the ladder but I couldn't make my foot make the step. Spineless ass.

So I told my foot to just go ahead, and pretty soon just like that I was standing on an iron grating one story up.

The second story was wobblier. I could feel each one of Fiona's steps up the stairs all through my body. Then Fiona was crouched down on the second-story landing. Rose's red velvet drapes were open, and his venetian blinds were strips of light across Fiona's face and purple wool cap.

William of Heaven, Fiona whispered loud, Get your ass up here!

Wobbly wobbly iron grating, all that was between me and mid-air. My steps onto the stairs so loud, banging off all the walls of the courtyard. When I got to the second landing, my knees cracked when I crouched down next to Fiona.

The sky was a philosopher's sky, lapis-lazuli blue. The moon was bright and kind of pink-yellow, and you could even see some stars.

Through the cracks of Rose's venetian blinds, Fiona put her eyes. I put my eyes into a strip of light.

The room was full of red roses. Red roses on the brass coffee table next to the gallon jug of gasoline, red roses on the kitchen table and on top of the stereo, roses on the windowsill we had to look around. Roses in Rose's Italian chandelabra. Rose's silver ice bucket was on the brass table, and the top of the bottle sticking out of the ice was the widow Veuve Clicquot.

Rose had the lighting just perfect so everything looked soft and made you feel warm.

Rose was sitting on the velvet blonde-fainting couch, a tulip glass of bubbly in one hand, a Gauloise in the other. His head was shaved and shined with rosemary oil. He was wearing a big white African gown embroidered at the top, one big gold loop in his queer ear.

The woman was sitting with her back to us in the velvet overstuffed chair. We could see her hair was black bouffant ratted up. She was wearing white also, a gown just like Rose's. On her left hand, lying on the arm of the purple-velvet overstuffed chair, was a huge diamond ring. In her other hand was a tulip glass of bubbly.

Rose's index went back and forth, back and forth.

No no Yoko Ono, Rose's lips said.

I'd never seen Rose laugh like that, a cats-fucking laugh, the veins in his forehead sticking out, his mouth wide open, his white teeth, rosy lips stretched wide, the inside color. The woman had to set her glass down on the brass table because she was laughing so hard, and she put her head down and covered her face with her hands for a moment. The light on the diamond. Then she sat back up.

It's some guy in drag! Fiona whispered.

It's all drag, I whispered.

The music was Brazilian, I guess, or salsa—something with a lot of drums that, even outside, Fiona and I were moving our shoulders to.

Then a ballad came on, slow, in Spanish or Portuguese. A woman singing. Rose set his tulip glass on the brass table, stood up, and bowed; then the woman set her tulip glass on the brass table, extended her hand to Rose, and stood up. Rose escorted the woman to the kitchen, to the place where Rose's Persian rug goes from the front room, and onto the linoleum of the kitchen floor.

Rose took the woman in his arms, and they danced, slow, graceful, Rose looking down, so happy to be looking into the eyes he was looking into. Her head was up, her arm on his shoulder, the dogs running around their feet barking.

When Rose turned and the woman twirled, the woman's face turned toward the window, turned toward me and Fiona on the other side of the venetian blind.

Holy Fucking Jesus Harold Christ! Fiona whispered. It's Elizabeth Fucking Taylor!

Cool, I whispered.

WHEN THE SONG was over, in the silence after the song, and only the sound of the needle on the record, Rose and Elizabeth stood close, holding each other, holding on to the moment. Then Elizabeth sat down. Rose poured more Veuve Clicquot, the whole time the two of them talking, talking, the way friends do and then laughing and talking some more.

Rose was standing just fine, talking talking, then all of a sudden, just like that, his knees went and he hit the floor.

Elizabeth jumped, and I jumped, and so did Fiona.

Elizabeth knelt down, she kissed his shaved head, touched his throat, his ears, put her hand into his Sahara Desert palm.

My hand was back, just ready to rap on the window, when Fiona grabbed my wrist.

What, Fiona said, Are you crazy?

He's sick! I said.

You can't invade their privacy, Fiona said. If he wants you he'll call you.

AFTER A WHILE, Rose stood up. Elizabeth held his arm. The black and the white of them in the chandelabra light in their white flowing robes.

Rose sat on the blonde-fainting couch, lay back, fainting.

Elizabeth brought him a glass of water, then went to the stereo, picked out a cassette, put the cassette in, pushed the buttons, sat down, clinked her champagne glass to Rose's water glass: *Salud, Na zdarovya, L'chayim,* Here's Looking at You.

Bellini. Maria Callas, "Norma."

Elizabeth stood up and raised her arms above her head and touched her hands together. She went up on her tiptoes.

Liz is so fucking beautiful, Fiona whispered.

Elizabeth, I said. Never call her Liz, I whispered.

Rule number five, I whispered.

Then Elizabeth did a turn, a ballerina, and she started singing with Maria Callas. Elizabeth moved her lips exactly to the words. She was looking at Rose exactly the way she looked at Montgomery Clift in *A Place in the Sun*.

Elizabeth walked over to Rose, her arms out to him, still moving her lips just right. She sat next to Rose, and Rose put his extra-lovely arms around her, and she put her head on Rose's chest. Her shoulders were shaking and you could hear she was really crying. Then Rose was crying.

Who knows how long Rose and Elizabeth cried?

Outside, on the fire escape, Fiona laid her head on my chest. I put my arms around her.

Inside crying.

Outside crying too.

ELIZABETH AND I took a little vacation, Rose said. To Miami Beach.

Behind Rose, Buddha was floating on a sea of plastic medicine bottles. You couldn't see the votive candles anymore, just the flame of them through the plastic.

Rose was lying on his belly. The votive candles flickered across Rose's naked legs and butt and back. He had lost more weight.

My breath in. My breath out.

I was lying on my back, naked too.

Inside my chest where I smoke was sore. I put my hands on my chest. Rose. Beloved Rose. My eyes on his face felt good, felt finally open.

Rose put his hand on my butt cheek.

Miami? I said.

Rose rolled over onto his back, put his arms up, hands under his head.

Miami Beach, Rose said.

Why didn't you ask me? I said.

I was smiling. Stopped smiling.

Elizabeth and I always go alone, Rose said.

Why didn't you tell me you were going? I said.

Spur of the moment, Rose said.

That was the moment, right then, when just like that, spur of the moment, I jumped up, threw my leg over Rose, sat down hard on his thighs, put my hands in his armpits, pushed Rose's arms back.

Rose karate-chopped me in the neck, and threw me off the bed. I was a smashed bug on the wall.

But it's not the truth.

Christ, Rose, I said, I was worried about you. Why didn't you call? I had no idea where you were. I didn't know what to think. You could be dead in a ditch. Or in the hospital. Did you take your meds? Did you eat well? Did you drink a lot? Did you kennel the dogs? Hell, I would have taken care of the dogs.

Rose, I said, Are you ashamed of me?

Rose's hands were on my face, his thumbs across my cheeks. He lifted up, kissed me on the sore bone between my eyes.

Then: The scared stallion, Rose said. Is that how you're feeling?

My belly, my chest, went down on Rose, my face in his armpit.

Yeah, I said.

My dear William of Heaven, Rose said.

Rose's arms, his legs, all around me. Rose's inside color of his lips full open onto mine.

Who knows how long we kissed.

JUPITER WAS RED-yellow, and Saturn too with its rings. Pluto was purple. Mars, Venus, all those planets of the Known Universe up on Rose's ceiling, all the stars.

The raw smell of Rose, his armpit hair against my mustache, my mouth. Up my nostrils down to my balls.

Only a body can know another body.

I kissed Rose's rosy lips, kissed his eyes, the purple bags under his eyes, his nose, down his neck, his chest, my tongue around his nipples. Pushed my body up next to his body, next to his heart, his big arms around me. My hand into the crack of his ass. His legs spreading. I licked down his belly, around his heavy balls, up the shaft of his extra-lovely cock. Rose's body and my body a maze of black and white, rose-colored in the flicker.

My dear William of Heaven, Rose said, bracelets clack-clack, This white horse is definitely a stallion.

Now you say it, Rose said.

This white horse is a stallion, I said, And he ain't no ordinary horse.

Rose and I kissed again. I couldn't get close enough to him.

The rubbers and the KY are in the top drawer, Rose said. Just be careful.

* * *

MY HANDS WITHIN Rose's hands. Rose's still-huge legs draped over my shoulders. The mass of muscle of his thighs. His thighs together at the crack, at the spot, to the soft warm hole beneath his sagging balls. The entrance to the underworld. My lovely erect pink penis at the cave, inside slowly slowly, inside dark loam, inside Rose. Fucking Buddha, fucking dark earth.

The meteor inside me, getting bigger, closer and closer.

My hands were under Rose's shoulders, my feet curled around Rose's feet, my lips at his ear. I pulled on his shoulders as I pushed myself in. On every backstroke, the sweet pull against the crown of my cock.

Rose was pushing his cock up and down against my belly. Up and down, up and down. Under the stars of the Milky Way, I was a tiny pink boat on a black raging sea.

So much like crying, cumming.

Who knows how long we lay there, just the candles, our breath.

My body was still, my mind was still, and only Rose was holding me up.

I wiped my mouth and nose, pushed up, rolled over, and lay on my side.

Between me and Rose, one big love strand.

I reached down, touched the end of Rose's cock.

No! Rose yelled, grabbed his cock.

Stop that!

The cum on my index in the votive candle light shined tiny illuminations in the dark.

I rubbed the cum between my thumb and index, then opened both my hands, palm up, drew a line of cum on my left palm, along the lifeline.

How did this start?

I flushed the rubber, washed my hands, took a leak in Rose's fuchsia twalette, got the Dwight D. Eisenhower ashtray, and brought it to the bed. Rose was propped up on his elbow. I sat cross-legged on the bed and rolled a cigarette, one for Rose, one for me. Lit Rose's, mine.

Rose lifted his leg up like the Sistine Chapel God, laid his hand on his knee, pointed his cigarette at Buddha.

There was this one time, Rose said, In the third ward in Houston. My family moved close to a white neighborhood and there was this big grocery store we sometimes shopped at: Weingarten's. One Christmas, Weingarten's was raffling off a bicycle. It was the coolest bike. A Pee-Wee Herman bicycle, green with a yellow star on the ridge skirt.

The bicycle was on display above the cash registers. Sometimes, I'd go into Weingarten's and just stand there and look up at the bicycle—not for too long, mind you. You got to put your name in the raffle box when you bought twenty dollars' worth of groceries. I must have had my name in that box ten times. But I didn't use my real name. I didn't write down Roosevelt Washington King. What I wrote down on the raffle slips was R. W. King. So one day, the phone rings and it's Weingarten's. The guy says, R. W. King, you just won yourself a bicycle. I hung up the phone—didn't stop to tell my mother or my brothers and sisters—I just ran to Weingarten's, ran to the green bicycle with the yellow star on the ridge skirt.

When Mr. Weingarten saw R. W. King was Roosevelt Washington King, when Mr. Weingarten saw I was black, instead of the bicycle, I got a three-dollar gift certificate for candy.

How'd you get here, Rose, I said, All the way from Houston?

How'd you get here from Idaho? Rose said.

Instinct for survival, I said.

But tell me the story, I said. You know just about everything about me. After the cops beat up your father, after the blood stain on the whitewall tire of your father's Buick, after you got three dollars' worth of candy instead of a bicycle, what did you do? Where did you go?

Rose put his cigarette out, crawled over me, went into the bathroom, closed the door. When he came out, his extra-lovely naked body made me take a deep breath. Rose walked long strides to his stereo. Ronald Reagan and Nancy were standing next to the speakers. Pretty soon it was Maria Callas, "Norma."

When Rose got back into bed, he lay on his side and pulled me into him, my back to his front, his extra-lovely arms around me, his massive thigh and leg draped over my butt.

My father wasn't a preacher, Rose said, He was a janitor. We were raised Catholics, Rose said.

So you're reupholstering too? I said.

Tuck and roll, Rose said.

Mother died of breast cancer, my father a heart attack. My brother Calvin joined the army, lost his legs, and got a purple heart in Vietnam. L'Irah makes computer chips in Kentucky and has two children, a boy and a girl, Jason and Michelle. Magnolia married a cop, and moved to Dallas. They had one daughter who's going to art school in Minneapolis. Elnora, she's a bigger drag queen than me. Big as me too. She lives in San Francisco. Run through the wringer with drugs and rehab. Last I heard she was on methadone.

I got a scholarship to Brown in '64. Got my B.A. in English literature. Got my doctorate in Theater Arts. Then, Rose said, Merriweather College, a small college in Portland, Oregon, hired me. Everything went lily-white fine for two years till I came up for tenure. The committee said my teaching was excellent, my faculty participation was excellent, but the students didn't like me. I kept trying to tell them the students didn't like me because the students were spoiled dope-smoking rich white kids who'd never even met a black man, let alone called him Doctor. My tenure application was refused. I got an outside evaluator to come in, a professor from Cornell, and this guy couldn't find one speck of dust on any of my records. He even sat in on a week of classes. His recommendation was that I be granted tenure. The tenure committee revoted and they were tied three to three, so it went to the Dean—a white woman, co-chairman of the Democratic party. She voted against me.

I swear I was born to be insulted, Rose said, I figured fuck it. It was best to get out of academia, go somewhere safe.

So I moved to New York, Rose said, And became a drag queen.

LATER IN THE night, Rose's cock was hard and up and down against my crack.

I jumped out of bed, both hands over my butt hole, threw my clothes on, ran down the stairs, and locked my door behind me.

But it's not the truth.

The KY, the rubber.

I pushed my ass into Rose's cock. Prayed for the space in between to get big enough. Put my hands on the bedposts, tying my fingers around them.

Then it was white light, unrelenting, and pain so deep it was everywhere.

Who knows how long the unrelenting, the pain.

When I opened my eyes, there were stars, the planets, red Jupiter, purple Pluto, Saturn's rings, the moon, and Rose inside me, way deep inside me rubbing against everything, my soul, the Known Universe.

I was riding high, bucking bronco. Fucked up the ass gorgeous. The Hippodrome Stand. Why birds like to fly so much.

The cry inside we have all our lives.

The scream we all live for.
Rose's scream.
Mine.

I LEFT MESSAGES on Fiona's phone for days, knocked on her door every morning, knocked on her door before I went to work. Then one night, after work, late, almost three o'clock, I knocked on the door of Stranded Beings Searching for God. Knocked again. Then I pushed on the door and the door opened.

The Conran chairs were all stacked up against the wall. Fiona was sitting on the couch, smoking, with the stand-up lamp on low.

Fiona's hair was a bushel of black in the shadow the light cast against the wall. The way she moved was the first clue, how she moved forward and flicked the ash off her cigarette.

But like all first clues, you don't pay attention to them.

Slow, she moved slow, but slow isn't the word. It was like the world for her was thick and she was floating through it.

A black cat jumped up on Fiona's lap. Slow, Fiona's hand rubbed the cat's back.

Is that Green Date? I asked.

Fiona didn't say anything. The way she was staring ahead, I wondered if she'd just shot heroin.

Then: Madonna, Fiona said, and inhaled on the cigarette. Harry named her Madonna, Fiona said.

Fiona blew out the smoke.

The other morning, Fiona said, The cat was scratching on the door so Harry let her in.

The way the light was hitting the side of Fiona's face, the shadow was the scar on Fiona's lip. She sat stiff, propped up.

Slow, Fiona put the cigarette to her lips, inhaled, exhaled.

Next to the couch and stand-up lamp was a suitcase and a duffel bag and Fiona's red leather purse, all standing next to each other.

Going somewhere? I said.

I walked to the couch, sat down on the couch, slow like you'd sit down next to a murderer.

How's Harry? I asked.

Fiona didn't turn her head. She was looking at something just in front of her—at a flame in front of her just out of her reach.

He's dead, Fiona said.

The silence. So much silence and then in the silence in the rooms, Fiona's rooms, in Stranded Beings Searching for God, I heard my words.

Harry's dead? I said.

He was in a lot of pain, Fiona said. Yesterday morning I gave him the whole bottle of morphine.

I put my hand on Fiona's hand. Fiona's whole body an electric shock. The cat yelled and jumped off her lap.

Never touch me.

It's all an . . . illusion, I said, Death is a door, I said, Harry just stepped through the door.

Fiona sucked on the cigarette, and as she sucked she blew smoke out her nose.

The scar of her lip was a swollen wound.

Death, Fiona said, Is a motherfucker.

I pulled the filter from between Fiona's fingers, put it in the ashtray.

I called you, Fiona said.

Fiona reached for the pack of Camel straights on the coffee table and pulled another cigarette out, lit the cigarette with a Bic, and threw the Bic on the coffee table.

I got the machine, Fiona said. I didn't want to leave the message on your machine.

Fiona still stared at the flame.

I was on the couch, Fiona said. I woke up and went in and Harry was sitting up in bed. Madonna was sitting by Harry's pump that pumped medicine into Harry's heart. Madonna was sitting by the pump. The blind was drawn. The only light in the room was the amber night-light, the Christmas-tree kind you plug in the socket.

Harry said this, Fiona said, her lips rubber around the words. I'm the luckiest man. Life is absolutely, mysteriously beautiful. Life has always been here all around me, in me, of me, has always been this fascinating mystery, but it wasn't until now that I have been present, completely present, been aware enough to witness. I am here now in this room in this light with the sound of the pump and Madonna watching the pump and listening to the pump, and just now, Fiona, you were in the other room snoring and I realized I was alive and I was aware.

Harry said, When you're thirsty, water is so beautiful.

I got up from the bed, Fiona said, went to the kitchen and poured Harry a glass of water, took the glass of water to Harry. I sat on the bed and helped Harry hold his head up. One by one, Harry ate the whole bottle of pills I fed him. When he finished the water Harry said, Beautiful, just beautiful. All at once, Harry was staring at me. And then his eyes rolled up and Harry wasn't present, wasn't with me anymore.

SO STILL IN the room. I got up and knelt at Fiona's feet, parted her legs, and laid my head in her lap. Fiona's heartbeat. My heartbeat. Lost, stranded.

I was getting snot all over Fiona's T-shirt, so I sat up and snuffed up, but when I looked at Fiona, into her eyes, her eyes looked through me to the fire in front of her she couldn't reach. My chin started quivering and I started in all over again.

Fiona handed me her handkerchief.

Thanks, I said.

Where is he? I said. Is he still in your bed?

Fiona listened to my words like they were French.

Yesterday, Fiona said, I sent Harry's body to Connecticut. He's probably being cremated right now. I called and told his father. His father hung up on me.

Fucking asshole, I said. His own father.

Fiona bent down, put her arms around my head. Her arms were heavy.

We'll bury Harry in the family plot, Fiona said. Next to my mother and my brothers, Fiona said.

With her heart beating and her arms close around my ears, I waited a moment so I could know for sure what she said.

Fiona? I said, and lifted my head up. My face, my eyes, my nose, my lips right up against Fiona's eyes, nose, lips.

Gus and Hunter always did things together, Fiona said. They even died together.

Fiona's lips, the snarl, the quivering lower lip, her mouth the first time speaking the words.

When? I said.

Today, Fiona said.

Shit themselves to death, Fiona said.

The stillness. My God, the dead quiet. I thought times like this would be loud and bright and full.

But you said your mother? I said.

Fiona lifted the cigarette between us. Her red lips inhaled hard and mean on the cigarette, exhaled into my eyes, my nose, my mouth.

A bottle of diazepam, Fiona said, And a bottle of sixteen-year-old Macallan single malt.

I put my arms around Fiona, my hands on her back.

My God, Your poor father, I said.

My God, I said. Fiona, What is happening to us?

I PUSHED MY face deep into Fiona's crotch. Just like that, the words were out of my mouth.

Don't ever leave me, I said.

I'm going to four funerals, Fiona said.

Don't leave me, Fiona, I said.

I raised my head up. Fiona and me: wet faces, tears, snot. And we kissed, a sweet long dark kiss. I pulled up her T-shirt, put her nipple in my mouth, then went to the other. Fiona slumped down on the couch, the stiffness out of her and into me. I thought the cat was on my back the way Fiona was scratching. I got her pants and panties down and was face deep in her wet poon. Fiona pulled my white shirt up over my head. Something ripped. I stood up, Fiona stood up. Then clothes went flying every which way, the whole time I was apart from her it hurt, everything hurt, and when I lay down on top of Fiona, she was so soft, so alive, so completely real. I watched her eyes, her lip, as I pushed into her, slow. My God, I wanted to eat her up. Then it was the slap-slap of fucking hard and fast and mean that hurt the way you wanted it to hurt. Fiona was slapping my face and crying and kicking her feet against my back. I slapped her back once and she grabbed my face and squeezed my face and bit my lip till it bled. And when her body started the deep come I was coming too and Fiona and I, face to face, nose to nose, eyes to eyes, lips to lips, screaming screaming screaming.

THE NEXT DAY, when Fiona left from Penn Station, before she got on her train, she kissed me like in war movies.

Both of us were the soldier.

No steam and whistles, just an electric hum.

Standing on the platform waving waving, I knew I would never see Fiona again.

But it's not the truth.

CHAPTER
TWENTY-FIVE

There was an inquest. Lou Racing informed the Pocatello police, and Charlie and I had to go into the police station and tell the cops where we had gone with Bobbie on Fifth Street in the narrow house with gray siding that was supposed to look like bricks, but when the cops went to the house, no one was there, not even the orange couch or the yellow sheets on the windows. The cops took fingerprints and stuff in the house, and Charlie and I had to look through a bunch of photographs, but neither one of us could find the guy who did Bobbie's abortion.

The Sergeant of the Pocatello police, Robert Thompson on his badge, told me and Charlie we were going to be charged with accessory to murder in the first degree.

It wasn't no murder, Charlie said, It was suicide.

What about the murdered baby? Sergeant Robert Thompson said.

But it's not the truth.

We didn't have to go to jail. They just sent Charlie home to Viv's double-wide and me home with Mother and Father.

IT RAINED AT Bobbie's funeral. They let her get buried in the church because Monsignor Verhooven was there driving his '58 Mercury when Bobbie made the Act of Contrition. Plus Father was a member of the Elks Club and so was Monsignor Verhooven, plus Father gave the Monsignor some money, a hundred dollars, I think.

Father refused to allow Charlie 2Moons to come to the funeral, so Viv didn't come to the funeral either or any of her friends from Viv's Double-Wide Beauty Salon.

Lou Racing and his wife came, and two girls from Pocatello High School I didn't know, and then there was Father and Mother and Monsignor Verhooven and the two altar boys and me.

Bobbie wore the black dress.

Father didn't want Bobbie to wear the black dress, said it made his little girl look too old.

Mother said, Why'd you buy it for her then?

I didn't buy it for her! Father said, It was just a dress that got mixed up with my costume stuff at some dang rodeo.

Lying bastard! Mother said.

Crazy bitch! Father said.

AT MOUNT MORIAH cemetery, not far from the Chinese part where Bobbie had thrown her bloody panties and Kotex into the bushes, not far from where the three of us lay that day in the leaves, they put Bobbie in a hole.

Father drove his swimming-pool-blue Dodge pickup the fifteen miles back home, the seat I'd wiped down with soap and water so our good clothes wouldn't get soiled; Mother in the middle, me shotgun by the window.

Father driving, in his blue tweed suit and white shirt and blue tie with leaves on it and black shoes and Old Spice, Mother between us in her violet dress, sequined orchid all the way down the front, her nylons seams a mess of swoops, her high heels with the holes in the toes, Evening in Paris, her Orange Exotica lipstick, her knees pointed my way away from the gearshift, me in clean Levi's and white shirt and clip-on bow tie, and the green corduroy jacket Viv sent over with Charlie to give me when Father wasn't there.

Father, Mother, and I, driving home, driving and driving and driving.

I went straight up to my room. All I wanted was to see Charlie, but I knelt right down and prayed my rosary to God that Charlie wouldn't come over with Father in the house, but I knew Charlie would, so after the rosary, all I could do was lie down on the bed, straight, my arms close by my sides, and wait for what was going to happen.

When it got dark, I crawled out my bedroom window and slid down the cottonwood. The moon was so bright, the night had shadows.

In the hayloft, the Marilyn Monroe light was on. The Marilyn Monroe light on the map of the Known Universe made the planets glow, especially Jupiter and Saturn and Pluto. KSEI on the old Zenith, playing Your Dancing Hits.

If we could freeze moments in time.

That night, the Idaho wind was high in the cottonwoods and the sky was a perfect deep navy blue behind the yellow leaves, yellow leaves sigh and scratch. Big gusts of wind through the hayloft, rattling shingles.

I stood at the window, rolling cigarettes for Charlie and for me. The moon was full, the blue mountains far off an even darker blue than the sky. Along the foothills, tumbleweeds rolled and rolled up to the fences. *Together Again* was on the big brown Zenith in the corner, Bobbie's map of the Known Universe hanging above the white-trash couch. The old black-and-white quilt, wedding-ring pattern, draped over the couch, ends tucked into the cushions, just so.

Perfect, just perfect.

That night—wind through the shingles, pigeon flutter, barn spirits—Charlie walked up the stairs.

Sexually haunted.

Want to dance, stranger? Charlie said.

On KSEI, *I've got you under my skin/I've got you deep in the heart of me*. Charlie's Michelangelo bare feet, my new shoes stiff, Shinola. Cheek to cheek—this is how it started, remember Charlie?—where it ended—sliding a two-step on the barn floor through straw and cottonwood leaves.

Heaven, I'm in heaven.

Raven-black wavy hair, big shoulders, beautiful according to Crazy Horse.

Little brother, Charlie said.

I hadn't cried yet but was waiting to, waiting to let loose on a big wail. But then Charlie 2Moons was crying—and hearing him cry made me stop right off.

Charlie 2Moons up against me, crying crying, his body shaking, holding on so tight to me, so tight, tears rolling down his cheeks, onto his chin, onto my neck, down inside my shirt, down my back.

Charlie climbed under the old black-and-white wedding-ring quilt with me, lay down next to me, him a vision smelling of sagebrush, Grandfather's medicine pipe, nothing but blue skies, Old Spice, sperm.

Charlie's visitation was his hand in my crotch. Charlie said he was just warming his hand, warming my crotch, his sure hand unbuttoning me, his sure hand around my medicine pipe, revealing the wound, our secret wound that he know about: the beginning of, the middle, how it ends.

Hard, ancient, roadkill erotic.

When all else has failed, in a hell of a fix, up Shit Creek, things gone haywire, when your sister is dead and there's no hope and you can still hear the rope swaying in the barn, the sexually haunted barn, my breath into Charlie's ear was the only place left.

THE FLUORESCENT TUBES on the ceiling of the barn, the unrelenting light from above, flashed down on Father, casting hard shadows close around him on the floor, Father standing in the hayloft, his black bullwhip wrapped around his arm.

Mother walked in behind him, barefoot, wearing her yellow terry-cloth bathrobe. She was smoking a Herbert Tareyton. Her hair was sticking up. Mother lost, not on the premises.

Please remember me.

Don't ever betray me.

Don't ever leave me.

That look. At me.

I sat up quick on the white-trash couch, pulled the old black-and-white wedding-ring quilt over Charlie.

Between Charlie and them, me.

Charlie, I was in between. Can you understand that?

Will, mother said.

Mother handed the Herbert Tareyton to Father, slid her bare feet across the pigeon shit and straw on the dusty barn floor toward the couch, hands out, palms up.

Only silence, in all the world, the whole Known Universe, only silence.

Halfway to me and Charlie, she stopped and knelt down, her bare white knees on the dusty barn floor, put her hands over her face, big sobs, snot running out her nose, her chest up and down, her yellow terry-cloth bathrobe falling open, just her bare chest, Charlie, open.

Lost soul, lost the way, lost the world, lost for words. No lost and found.

Then Mother wiped her eyes with the back of her wrists, snuffed up, swallowed and knelt up straight, put her arms out again, palms up toward me.

Will! Mother said.

My son! Mother said. You must tell me the truth!

Father's long hard shadow unwinding the black bullwhip.

Bobbie had no boyfriends, Mother said. She hardly left her room. The high school girls at the funeral said Bobbie didn't have a boyfriend,

Mother said. They said she was a good girl. She didn't go with boys in the backseats of their cars.

Mother's eye makeup from the funeral was a mess of black-and-blue smears, dark holes on either side of her nose.

Will, Mother said, My son, promise me you'll tell me the truth!

I know you love Charlie, Mother said, And we'll protect him, but, please, I beg you, do not protect him by lying to me.

I must know the truth, Mother said.

Father's shadow growing growing, a storm cloud, a thunderhead between Charlie and me and the light.

Charlie was the only boy around Bobbie, Mother said. It couldn't be anyone else. Charlie is the only one. Charlie had to be the father of Bobbie's child.

That's when Charlie grabbed my shoulder.

Remember, Charlie?

Father spread-legged John Wayne, the black shadow of him pouring out onto the floor. Father's eyes straight into my eyes, unwinding the black bullwhip, laughing, his chest up, down, then up again.

Will! Mother said. My only son, my child, please!

The horrific whisper.

I beg you please, please! Mother said. Tell me the truth!

Your husband has been fucking your daughter for five years now, I said, And you know it. You buried Bobbie in the black dress, bitch. You've always known and you've never had the strength to stand up to Father, not really, not even when it came to saving your daughter's life. You betrayed Bobbie as you have betrayed me as you have betrayed yourself. So don't give me any of this Oh-my-only-son-tell-me-the-truth shit, I said. And, oh yeah, here's something else too. The truth you want to hear so badly.

Yes, Charlie fucked her. And I fucked her too, I said.

But it's not the truth.

Charlie's the father, I said.

Charlie jumped. You jumped up, Charlie.

The first lash of Father's bullwhip caught you around the waist, stopped you in your tracks. The second crack of the whip was vertical, a flip of his wrist down and then up and the leather snapped against your face and the cut went deep from under your eye through your upper lip.

You didn't flinch, Charlie. Not a tear, not a sound.

You never looked me in the eyes again.

Father's shadow and your blood on the straw and pigeon shit on the dusty barn floor.

This is what you said, Charlie. The words that hurt.

You Parkers, all of you, you said, Are haunted.

And just like that you were gone, into the night, down the back stairs, Charlie 2Moons out of my life, forever.

Forgive me, Charlie.

The moment that, after, you're different.

You, Charlie 2Moons.

Gone.

CHAPTER
TWENTY-SIX

The message on my red answering machine was street noise and somebody breathing. True Shot? Rose? Fiona?

All at once a deep sexy voice.

William of Heaven! What a sweet name, honey! Can I borrow it? Just called to tell you I got a hard-on I'm saving just for you! Remember me? Crystal? We met one night in the meat-packing district. I'll bet you thought little Crystal forgot all about you, but she didn't.

Listen, honey, I never did find your friend 2Moons. I didn't find the Ruby guy either. But I did find a very large, very drunk 'skin named True Shot.

When he's awake, he insists his name is Peter Morales. But I tell you something. I never forget a face, especially his. And yours.

Anyway, he won't stop talking about you, and he's driving us fucking *mad*. Come pick him up, will you? Meet me on the corner of Eighth Avenue and Forty-third, this afternoon around four.

Love ya.

Mean it.

OUTSIDE, POURING RAIN, whirling whirling big wind like to knock you over. I turned my ball cap back around so the bill could keep the rain off my face, turned the collar of the pea coat up, hunched my shoulders, head down, tried to bury my ears, but it was no use. Stuck my hands in my big pea coat pockets. My red Converse tennis shoes were wet in no time.

A Checker taxi pulled out from the corner of 42nd and Broadway, the back tires spinning, making a sound I thought at first was the wind, then some kind of Asian music, then the sound was somebody screaming, then I looked and it was the tires.

I walked to Eighth Avenue, my head down, just looking at my wet shoes. On Eighth Avenue, the gust of wind made me stop.

On 43rd Street, people were three deep on the avenue waving and screaming at the headlights coming at them, thousands of headlights coming at them, taxis splashing on by.

I stood under the next green awning I could find, at the deli on 43rd and Eighth, just for a moment. Took my ball cap off, beat my ball cap against my leg, put my ball cap back on. An Asian guy carrying a crate of oranges inside screamed at me, his language high-pitched and sour and spinning tires, and used the crate of oranges as a battering ram to push me back out into the street. Right then this truck goes by and throws a wave of New York City gutter water all over me, like some huge dragon piss, soaked.

On the neon-bright marquee were the red words CHICKS WITH DICKS. PRIVATE BOOTHS. XXX.

Four-ten.

Four-twenty.

Even my nuts were soaked.

Then a young man in a black stocking cap and a shiny pink parka walked up to me, stood too close.

Spare some change? he asked.

He was wearing black tights. On his feet, fuzzy gray slippers.

I was New York drop-dead fuck-you.

Love ya, he said. Mean it.

I turned quick, looked hard into his eyes, and inside in there was Crystal.

Crystal's lips were a boy's lips, no red life all their own. A bruise under his eye. When he smiled, his front two teeth were missing.

William of Heaven, Crystal said, You'd never make it on the street. It's all right to forget the dick, he said, But don't forget the face.

What happened to your face? I said.

Follow me, Crystal said.

Halfway down the block, on the right, I followed Crystal up the stoop. He shoved a plastic card between the doorjambs, and the door swung open hard. Narrow hallway, painted lemon yellow, unrelenting light. Seventeen steps to the second floor.

No lightbulbs on the second floor.

A smell of propane and something else.

Crystal pushed open a door without a lock.

The cold dark room was stripped down to the two-by-fours. No chairs, no table, no beds. The only light was a blowtorch burning blue in one of the double kitchen sinks. The other sink was full of needles, plastic things, a Roy Rogers bag of french fries. People everywhere on the floor, twenty or thirty of them. People up close to each other wrapped in blankets, coats, plastic bags, newspaper.

Somebody coughing hard the way Ruby used to.

Two candles. Hands, palms open, reaching for the flame.

He's over here, Crystal said.

The purple bumps on Crystal's wrist were big black raspberries in the blue blowtorch light.

True Shot was lying on the floor. He looked like a tree root or a half-frozen length of mud. Stringy long black hair and no shoes and dirty white socks. An empty bottle of Night Train lying next to his extra-lovely Wrangler jeans with the boot flare. No boots. His red corduroy shirt stained with something dark. Wine? Blood?

I was kneeling over him before I even knew it.

True Shot? I said.

I put my hand under his neck, lifted his head, put his head in my lap. Pulled the hair from his face. His skin was gray to green and he smelled something awful and I thought for sure he was dead, and then he coughed and threw up all over his shirt and down my leg.

We got to get you to a hospital, I said.

True Shot jabbed me with his elbow, jumped his huge dead bulk up, his bunched-up dirty white socks on the wood floor, fell over again, got back up on his knees, walked on his knees, fell flat.

No hospital! True Shot said. No hospital!

People yelling, running in the dark room through the arched door-way into the blowtorch blue of the kitchen. Big grotesque shadows on the walls.

Someone knocked a candle over. I quick picked the candle up.

True Shot was standing with his arms out like a man who couldn't see. I stepped one step toward True Shot and I felt a hand on my shoulder.

Easy, Crystal said. Take it easy, Papi.

The archway of blowtorch blue was a halo around Crystal's head. Crystal stepped up close. His lips at my ear.

You got any money?

A little, I said.

True Shot was a buckled-knee vertical crawl. His head hit the floor hard.

How much? Crystal said.

Thirty dollars, I said. Maybe forty.

Give me twenty, Crystal said. You got two tens?

My hands were like Catholic statues in the light. The inside of my wallet, shadows of bills.

Crystal reached in my wallet, took two bills. He held one in each hand and held the bills like Dumbo ears next to his head.

Ten, Crystal said, And ten.

Let me look at those, I said.

Crystal dropped his hands, crumpled the bills into his fists.

Do you want your friend, Crystal said, Or not?

Crystal paid two big guys, a black guy and a brown guy, ten bucks each to carry True Shot down to the street.

Ten bucks in the house. Ten bucks on the street.

The black guy grabbed True Shot's arms. The brown guy grabbed True Shot's legs.

Into the arch of blowtorch blue light, through the dark door, down the narrow dark hallway, down the seventeen steps, into the unrelenting lemon yellow, out the front door, down seven steps of the stoop.

The black man and the brown man leaned True Shot against a lamppost, and when they let go, True Shot's hair stuck to the lamppost, but True Shot started to slide.

Hold on a little longer! Crystal yelled.

The two men quick put their arms behind True Shot.

Just help us get him into a fucking cab! William of Heaven, Crystal said, Hail us a cab!

Crystal pulled a joint out of his pocket, lit it with a silver lighter, inhaled big.

Can I have some of that? I said.

Crystal kept sucking, and as he sucked he shook his head.

Then, in the gray exhale: This shit will kill you, he said. Now get us a cab, Crystal said.

I'll hold True Shot, I said. You hail the cab.

In your dreams, Crystal said. Get your white ass out there and get us a cab!

A CAB FINALLY stopped, I opened the door, and when the cabdriver saw the extra-lovely dead-drunk True Shot, he threw the car in gear and started off.

But Crystal was standing in front of the cab screaming, his arms in the air: Evita.

The headlights on Crystal were spotlights. Crystal was the host of the cabaret.

The black guy stepped around to the driver's door.

The brown guy and I got our shoulders underneath True Shot's arms, lifted, and when we got to the cab door, we looked at each other and just let True Shot fall, like a large bag of potatoes, into the backseat of the cab. We folded his legs up and closed the door.

I got in next to the cabbie. He looked Armenian, and there was sweat running down his forehead.

I rolled down the window. In the mercury-vapor light, Crystal was brown-gray-purple.

Now, Crystal said, Give us a kiss.

I leaned up and out and kissed Crystal on the cheek, just below the purple bump.

Crystal, I said, Thank you. What can I do for you?

The wind blew hard just then, and a *New York Post* scraped along the sidewalk.

Crystal was sucking on the joint again, a Lakota Sioux James Dean.

Just come back and see us sometime, Crystal said.

As he spoke the smoke in him came out his nose, and he laughed a quick up-and-down of the chest, and then he coughed, and coughed, and coughed.

THE CABDRIVER wasn't Armenian. He was part Greek and part Moroccan and his friends called him Jusef. He lived in Queens with his grandmother, his mother, his wife, his sisters, and a granddaughter.

When I tipped him ten dollars, Jusef offered to help me get True Shot out of his cab.

It wasn't pretty. True Shot had gone shit spray. And it was just Jusef and me, pulling and shoving True Shot out of the back door, the same way True Shot and I had pulled and shoved Ruby out of the basement.

The eleven steps up the stoop were the hardest. Just me and True Shot and the cold wind. One step. One step. One step.

Inside my apartment, I laid True Shot on the floor next to the futon.

My Art Family were all dressed in Halloween costumes: a clown, a queen, a sailor, a cowboy, and an Indian.

True Shot stank even worse inside, so I got his red corduroy shirt off and his Wranglers, his socks, and his stretched-out shit-stained gray-brown Fruit of the Looms. I tried to undo the knot on the buckskin strand the beaded-blue horizontal and the red-beaded vertical buckskin bag hung from, but the knot was tied too tight.

I opened all the windows.

In a garbage can outside, I dumped his clothes.

I filled a pan with hot water and got a washrag and a bar of Ivory soap and started scrubbing. True Shot's skin was turning back to cinnamon brown inside in the heat. I washed his face, the big brow hanging over his eyes, his delicate eyelids, down the sides of his long nose, his cheekbones, above the curve of his lips; washed his lips, his chin. Held his head up and washed underneath the buckskin bag with the blue-beaded horizontal and the beaded red vertical. Washed his arms, under his arms, his big hands, and long fingers. The fingernails so beautifully oval. All his silver rings were gone.

I washed down his chest, his extra-lovely nipples. Washed his extra-lovely belly and down to his privates. Washed everything extra-lovely down there too. A grower, not a shower. Anteater. Washed down his legs, his feet, his toes.

I got him rolled over. Washed his shoulders, his back, his butt, down inside the nasty shit-spray butt crack, down his legs.

I turned him over again and lifted True Shot up from his waist, put my legs under him, scooted the pan of water closer, and put the pan under his head.

When I put the Herbal Essence shampoo on his head and started scrubbing, True Shot opened his eyes. I'd never been that close to him before, looking into the jade-green Saint Vitus' dance of his eyes.

I smiled. Stopped smiling.

True Shot hit me with his open palm, hard in the chest, stood up, weaved around, knocked the pan of water over, and crashed into my Art Family, knocking them every which way.

Apartment Cauchemar.

True Shot! I yelled. Lie down! You're sick!

True Shot kept stumbling around, shampoo dripping into his face and eyes. He fell against the east wall, then against the west wall. True Shot bouncing off the walls.

When he found the bathroom, he dropped to his knees and barfed like Bobbie, real loud, into the toilet, for what seemed like an hour. I sat with him, the washcloth on his forehead, almost barfed myself a couple times.

When True Shot was just sitting there on the floor holding onto the rim of the toilet, when he was deep inhaling and exhaling, I said, True Shot, I said, You're sick, real sick. We need to get you to a hospital.

No hospital! True Shot yelled. Hospital is where you go to die! I'm not dead yet! True Shot said.

Can you stand up? I said. Let's get you into the shower.

True Shot used the wall. He put his one arm over my shoulder, I put my arm around his waist, and we got him in the shower. The water was cold at first, and he yelled so loud I thought my heart had stopped beating. Then the water got warmer and True Shot leaned against the shower stall and put his head under the water. I got the Herbal Essence from the front room and handed it into him. True Shot looked at the bottle, tipped the bottle up, and started to drink.

Jesus Christ! I yelled, and yanked the bottle away. For your hair! I yelled, the way you yell at people who can't hear. Shampoo! Shampoo!

I need a drink, True Shot said, and leaned back into the water.

I took my shirt off, stepped partway into the shower, squeezed Herbal Essence into my hand, scrubbed True Shot's long black hair.

With the clean towel, the blue one, I rubbed his back, down his back, his legs. Dried the water from his face, his chest, his arms, under his arms. Brought the towel down over his cock but didn't stop there—kept going straight down to his legs. Then I stood on the toilet, True Shot leaning against the shower, and I rubbed his hair dry.

True Shot put his arm over my shoulder. I put my arm around his waist, and we walked that way to the futon. True Shot lay down on the futon and I pulled the covers over him.

I need a drink, True Shot said. Get me a drink.

There's nothing to drink here, I said.

But it wasn't the truth.

How many beers, how much wine was in the refrigerator? The bottle of tequila above the refrigerator.

True Shot kicked the covers off him, starting yelling something, then rolled back and forth on the futon. I tried to hold him, hold on to him, saying, True Shot! True Shot! This is William of Heaven, True Shot! You're safe here!

Who knows how long True Shot thrashed around.

Finally, about 4 A.M., he crawled to the corner and lay down among my Art Family. He put his head to his knees, curled into a ball, and fell asleep.

Slow, like a flower blooms, my Art Family each placed an open palm onto his body.

Quietly, quietly, I got the bottle of Laforet, the bottle of Domaine Chandon, the six-pack of Budweiser, the half-gallon jug of Gallo red, and the tequila into a big brown paper bag, the erect pink penis and the bag of rabbit-turd Sho-ko-lat, tiptoed to the door, unlocked the locks on my door, opened the door, then pulled the door closed. Locked the door.

Upstairs, Maria Callas was real loud singing "Norma." Rose opened his door. He had his Dolly Parton wig on and a red bustier and a red slip, fishnet stockings, and black stiletto heels. Mascara was streaming down from his eyes. In one hand, he was holding a snifter half full of VSOP, in the other a Gauloise.

Bonjour, Rose said.

It's *soir,* I said.

Details, details, Rose said.

The dogs were running around, barking barking.

You feeling OK? I said.

Fine, Rose said, Just fine.

But it wasn't the truth.

The black snake coiled up in Rose was spitting.

Rose, I said, I wondered, I said, If you could keep this stuff for me. For a couple days.

Rose looked at the bottles in the bag.

Are they empty? Rose said.

No, I said.

Then come right in! Rose said.

I put the bag on Rose's fuchsia kitchen counter. There were still Elizabeth Taylor rose petals everywhere in the room. The kitchen table a mound of pills, pill bottles. Dirty dishes in the sink, cockroaches.

Maria Callas was so loud, I had to shout. *You got anything for the DT's?*

You got the DT's? Rose said.

No, I said. It's for a friend.

I do *not* have the DT's, Rose said, bracelets clack-clack. I am merely having cocktails.

Not you, I said, My friend True Shot. He's downstairs in my apartment. He's in a bad way.

Rose walked like you do when you're wearing skyscraper heels, over to the stereo, and turned down Maria Callas, then walked into the bathroom, pulled open a drawer, and took out a Mason jar full of pills.

Your jar of Valium? I said.

And other things, Rose said.

Rose poured out a handful of pills into the Sahara Desert palm of his hand, and picked out the round yellow ones.

These are Valium, Rose said and counted out twenty into my open palm.

How many should I give him? I said.

As many as he needs, Rose said.

Not all twenty? I said.

Not at once, Rose said. Unless, Rose said, That's the way he wants it. In that case I probably should give you twenty more.

These should be enough, I said.

This your Indian buddy? Rose said.

He's not Indian, I said.

I'll light a candle for him, Rose said.

And some clothes, I said. He'll need some clothes.

Is he a winter or a summer? Rose said. Couture or Camp?

Sweatpants would be fine, I said. Maybe some underwear and socks and a shirt, a winter coat if you got an extra one, and some shoes.

Rose walked like you do when you wear skyscraper heels into the bedroom. He came out with a pair of pink bikini briefs, black sweatpants, a gray sweatshirt that said FUCK THE NATIONAL ENDOWMENT FOR THE ARTS on it, a pair of white socks, and his combat boots.

What size shoe does he wear? Rose asked.

Extra lovely, I said. I'm sure they'll fit.

The coat was a faux leopardskin, collar and cuffs faux mink.

It's not too much, is it? Rose said.

Nothing's too much, I said. Then: Rose, I said, What did you have for breakfast this morning?

Wheaties, Rose said, The Breakfast of Champions.

And lunch? I said.

Braised breast of duck veronique, Rose said.

And your AZT? I said.

American Zero Tolerance? Rose said, bracelets clack-clack. No thank you.

I was just closing Rose's door, when Rose said, Yoo-hoo!

In Rose's Sahara Desert palm was a pair of sunglasses. The cat's-eyes kind, with a rhinestone swoop above each eye. Mirrored sunglasses.

I think he'll be needing these, Rose said.

* * *

THREE DAYS IN a row, I called in sick to Café Cauchemar. The third day it was Daniel on the phone.

John was cremated yesterday, Daniel said. They sent his ashes home to Cincinnati.

Silence on the phone, all across, in between us, inside the phone wire: silence.

And Joanie? I said.

She's lost thirty pounds, Daniel said.

Then: Spud, Daniel said, You aren't going to die on us too, are you?

No, I said. I just got a personal problem here I got to take care of.

Now listen up, Daniel said. You fucking listen up, Spud! Are you going to come back to work at all?

I'll be back, I said. Just give me a week.

You're a good man, Daniel said. Rare to come by. And I think of you as a friend. But I can't let you have too many more days off, Daniel said. My brother the boss says he won't allow it.

OK, I said.

Then: Daniel, I said, How are *you* feeling?

Like hell, Daniel said.

I BOUGHT A foam rubber pad, laid the pad down just across the room from the futon. In the night, in the mercury-vapor light, True Shot rolled back and forth, back and forth, his arms fighting the air.

After the first week, he didn't scream out or yell. He cried softly to himself, the way a baby cries when he's cried so hard there's nothing left.

UPSTAIRS, ROSE WAS into his second week of heavy drinking. Mary, Mona, and Jack Flash were all lying on Rose's bed. They didn't bark when I came in.

Rose's breakfast table was covered with medicine bottles and boxes of pills, and piles of pills, and saucers and cups of pills, and black Magic Markers, and a thermos of coffee so thick it poured like syrup.

Lamu coffee, Rose said. The real stuff.

The roses from Elizabeth's visit were dead and wilted, and the vase water was stinking. There were stains on Rose's Hawaiian muumuu, the pink and red one.

Rose, I said, When's the last time you slept?

Rose had invited me up for coffee and bagels, but there were no bagels. Only Lamu coffee, and the pills, and the black Magic Markers.

No time for sleep now, Rose said, The battle lines are drawn. He uncapped a black Magic Marker that smelled of poppers.

Rose had taken down a photograph of Elizabeth Taylor in *Jane Eyre* that used to hang in the kitchen. Rose stood next to the sink, pointing at the bare fuchsia wall, like the wall was a blackboard and he was the teacher and I was the student.

With each word Rose wrote on his kitchen fuchsia wall, the black Magic Marker against the plaster sounded like a tiny animal screaming.

My reasons for killing Ronald Reagan, Rose said.

Rose, I said, Have you been taking your Xanax? I said.

Fuck the meds! Rose said. I didn't ask you up here to talk drugs, Rose said, bracelets clack-clack. I have something very important to outline here for you, and I'd hoped you'd be considerate enough to listen.

Rose stopped. His black black eyes looked hard at me. At first I thought he was going to attack me, the black coiled-up snake, but then his eyes got soft, got the love for me back in them.

I'm going to kill Ronald Reagan, Rose said. I mean soon, Rose said. Time is running out.

But Rose, I said. I thought you were going to infect the cardinal?

Only silence. Rose's red velvet curtains were closed and the Italian chandelabra above us was on bright, unrelenting. Rose sat down hard in his purple-velvet overstuffed chair, lit a Gauloise, crossed his legs.

There's this film, Rose said, Called *Autumn Sonata*. It's about a mother and her two daughters. One daughter is mentally ill and bedridden. The mother, Ingrid Bergman, is a famous pianist, and her daughter—the one who is caring for the mentally ill daughter—is Liv Ullman. At the climactic point in the story, Liv Ullman goes ghetto on Ingrid and reads her beads. And then Ingrid Bergman says this wonderful thing.

A talent for reality, I said.

How did you know? Rose said.

I saw the movie, I said. Bergman, I said.

Ingrid, Rose said.

* * *

THIS MAY HAVE been a dream.

One night, when I woke up on the foam pad, True Shot's ear was on my chest and the rest of his extra-lovely body snuggled up against me. His hand was around my cock and balls.

True Shot? I said.

Uh-huh? True Shot said.

What are you doing?

Proving that Ruby was wrong, True Shot said.

What? I said.

That the only cock I'd ever have in my hand would be my own.

True Shot! I said. Are you back?

I'm back, True Shot said, But I'm not True Shot, I'm Peter Morales.

Peter, I said, Morales.

It's nice, True Shot said. You got a nice cock.

THE NEXT MORNING, somebody was poking me in the shoulder. I opened my eyes to a cup of coffee and a chocolate doughnut on my white dish.

Wake up, buttercup, True Shot said. It's ten o'clock.

When my eyes came back to this world, what my eyes saw I couldn't believe.

True Shot with a crew cut.

He looked like a Catholic school kid, or a drill sergeant.

Then there was his New Age rhinestone-swooped mirrors. The black sweatpants with the pink bikini briefs under them, the gray sweatshirt that said FUCK THE NATIONAL ENDOWMENT FOR THE ARTS, the combat boots. The buckskin bag with the beaded blue horizontal and the beaded red vertical hanging down his neck. The red bandanna tied around his head.

Geronimo on acid.

True Shot sat down on an orange vinyl chair I'd found in the garbage. I put my blue terry-cloth bathrobe on and sat on the second rung of the ladder. Our cups and spoons and the doughnuts all together on the *Father Knows Best* table.

True Shot wasn't drunk, and he was in my house.

The bright gray sky came in through the window, onto the shiny table-top, on our hands, the cups, the doughnuts, the spoons, onto the wood floor, onto my red to pink walls.

My Art Family was in the corner, acting as if we weren't there, like at a party when a famous person has just arrived and everybody pretends they're not interested.

True Shot was treating them the same way.

Then, after the second doughnut: Who's the crowd? True Shot said.

True Shot—I mean Peter, I said. What the fuck is going on?

Bright gray daylight on the bright gray table. True Shot rubbed his hands where his silver rings used to be. Put his hands all the way around the backs of his arms, held himself in a hug.

It is this way, True Shot said.

Bullshit, I said. It ain't no fucking way, Peter Morales. Just tell me the truth.

True Shot's extra-lovely chest up and down. FUCK THE NATIONAL ENDOWMENT FOR THE ARTS up and down.

True Shot's hand came over the bright gray shiny table, past his cup, past his spoon, across the bright gray air, the hand shadow across the bright gray table. His hand past my cup, my spoon, into my open hand palm up.

My face on the New Age rhinestoned-swooped mirrors was circus wide and flat.

Will, True Shot said, I've got something to do first. Then I'll tell you the whole story. The truth, True Shot said. I promise.

My Art Family had stopped not-listening. They were all ears.

I reached up, took True Shot's New Age rhinestone-swooped mirrors between my thumb and forefinger, pulled them down to the end of his nose. Put the end of my nose to his nose. Looked inside deep right into the dance of his eyes.

Get the fuck out of here, I said. That was Charlie's pipe.

It was, True Shot said. That was Charlie's pipe.

How did *you* get it? I said.

I need your help, Will, True Shot said.

Who are you? I said.

We've got something to steal, True Shot said, As soon as we've got it in our hands, I'll tell you all about me, True Shot said. And Ruby, and Sebastian Cooke.

And Charlie, True Shot said. I promise.

AT THE CORNER of Central Park West was the Sabrett guy selling hot dogs. I saw True Shot's face when he smelled the hot dogs, and I knew underneath True Shot's mirrors his eyes were quivering like light through sycamores for a hot dog, but I didn't buy him one.

True Shot—red bandanna, New Age mirrors, crew cut, sweatshirt, black sweatpants over pink bikini underwear, combat boots—never seen him look so beautiful.

Up the stairs of the Museum of Unnatural History, past the statue of Theodore Roosevelt, past the bronze horse testicles, past the terrible things done to the world by the father, into the big hall with dinosaurs, past ALL DARING AND COURAGE, ALL IRON ENDURANCE OF MISFORTUNE, MAKE FOR A FINER, NOBLER TYPE OF MANHOOD.

True Shot walked by where you had to pay and I walked by too, and this time the woman didn't stop me.

Once more I followed True Shot through Eastern Woodlands and Plains, Asian Peoples, past Mecca upstairs, to the Primates of the Eastern Woodlands, and then to the tipi.

The image of a tipi.

Behind the thick glass was the tipi scene, Native American Art Family: two women and two men, all wearing buckskin and beadwork on their buckskins.

In the museum, to the right of us, there was a man and a woman with a child in a blue stroller, a tall African American woman with her hair in a French twist, wearing a long black leather coat and carrying a leather purse, and a white guy with a mustache wearing green coveralls. That was all. I didn't see any other people. No guards.

True Shot was standing in front of the glass in front of the Native American Art Family. He spread his arms out wide and looked at the ceiling, then he looked straight into the glass.

It is this way, True Shot said, real loud and wavy, like Martin Luther King, Jr.'s *I've Got a Dream* speech.

I don't think you know me, True Shot said. My name is Peter Morales. I was born in Puerto Rico and came here to the United States with my mother and father. My mother was a Mexican woman. She loved me very much. She called me Gordito because I eat too much. My father was from the upper classes, and he wanted me to get a good education and become a dentist like him, but that path was not for me.

True Shot still stood, arms stretched out, his gray FUCK THE NATIONAL ENDOWMENT FOR THE ARTS sweatshirt hanging over the black sweatpants. The man and woman pushing the blue baby stroller walked into the next room. The woman with the French twist hair was walking closer and closer to us. I tried to get True Shot's attention so he'd see her, but True Shot was too busy standing with his arms out wide, talking talking.

It is this way, True Shot said. In my time, I have lied about many things, even lied about who I am. I have stolen. For many years I was a professional pickpocket. I've sold drugs, taken drugs, been a stupid drunk, been a pimp, whored myself my whole life. I've never been in love. I killed a man once—a white man on the subway. And I have to say there's a man out there in this city right now, a cop, who given the chance I'd drive a wooden stake through his heart.

The African American woman with the French twist was walking closer and closer to us. She bent closer to a window, shielding her eyes from the glare.

I am not especially generous, True Shot said, Or kind, or smart. I think the best thing about me is that I found Ruby Prestigiacomo, found Fred, and found this one here next to me, my true friend William of Heaven.

Forgive me, True Shot said. I don't know a lot about spiritual matters. Only from books, the real True Shot, and Fred. Only recently did I get sober and find out about my own sacred Taino and Aztec roots.

The woman with the French twist walked right up to the Native American Art Family, stood almost right in front of True Shot, and looked in, looking especially hard at the woman braiding the other woman's hair.

I have done a terrible thing, True Shot said. I was given a medicine bag, a pipe, from a very wise old man named Fred, who told me to always use the pipe in a good way. Fred told me that when I held the pipe I was taking part in the universe and was, in fact, the universe myself. Fred told me always to follow the red road and live in a good way. But I have lied. In front of the pipe, I claimed to be someone I am not. Consequently the pipe was taken from me, a pipe much cherished by me and also, as it turns out, by William of Heaven.

The woman with the French twist knelt down; leather sounds when she knelt. She reached out and touched the glass.

Three or four years ago, True Shot said, I pissed on this glass and marked this spot for my own. And now I have come to take this medicine bundle—this pipe held by an image of an Indian man inside this glass in this Museum of Unnatural History. I have not come to do harm or be disrespectful in any way. I have come to take the pipe back home to its people. I feel this is my task. This is why I was born, to take this prodigal pipe back to its people.

Here is the truth, True Shot said. I don't know the red road, I don't know if I'm traveling it or not. I don't know the rituals of the pipe, even though I was shown once by Fred.

I know about Crossover, and about fools and pharisees. I know the story of Wolf Swamp. I know the Jewish story. And I know about the iron horse.

So I figure this is enough, True Shot said, This truth that I speak. And that this path my heart has chosen is the correct path.

True Shot stood there, his arms out wide. You could hear people in other rooms walking. Still no guards. I figured True Shot had a skeleton key or a pry bar or something to get one of the doors open, but he just stood there, arms sticking out.

The African American woman stood up.

The moment that after you're different.

Everything is there all along and you just don't realize it. Just like that, I was the still point in the turning world, inside me and outside me was the mystery.

The one Art Family guy inside the window—not the one holding the pipe and the pipe bag, the other guy—just like that, all at once—abracadabra!—this guy walked behind the guy holding the pipe and opened the door on our right.

Ho! he said. Welcome! *O mitakuye oyasin.* Come on in. Make yourself comfortable.

True Shot walked past the woman with the French twist and I followed. She looked at me when I passed her. I smiled. Stopped smiling.

Shit happens.

She turned her face away real quick.

True Shot stepped inside the door and I stepped inside and the Native American guy closed the door behind us.

Just us injuns relaxing here in our tipi, the Native American guy said. Just me and my family. The women are playing dice and my name's Gray Wolf and I'm just standing here and my friend Yellow Wolf here is holding a medicine pipe and a pipe bag and a stone bowl.

What took you guys so long? Gray Wolf said. We been waiting here forever.

When Gray Wolf said *We've been waiting here forever*, everybody started laughing big and hard—even the baby in the cradle. The women and Gray Wolf and Yellow Wolf were laughing so hard, tears were rolling down over their high cheekbones.

That kind of laughing is like puking. Once somebody starts it, you can't help but get in on it too.

Then True Shot was talking in Indian to Gray Wolf and Yellow Wolf and the women. True Shot was saying a lot more than *Où est la bibliothèque*. It was pretty cold in the tipi—too much air-conditioning, I figured—but the fire was warm, and it was smoky in there and the smoke smelled wood-fire good. Other smells too: buckskin and horse shit.

A gust of wind hit the tipi and the hides moved in and out. I looked down at the fire and the fire was a real fire, and the smoke was real smoke. Then I took a good look at the Indian people and they were as real as True Shot or me. I looked out to where the glass was and there was no glass—no African American woman with French-twist hair staring in on us.

My body felt like the first day I did the Hippodrome Stand on Chub. Like it was natural to be flying, except I was standing in one place, on the earth. I bent down and picked up some dirt and felt the dirt between my fingers, smelled the dirt—it was the kind that was dust when it's dry and sticky mud when it rains, Kind of like the dirt we buried Ruby in, the dirt like in the rectangle of earth where I'd plant the cherry tree, and the more I looked at the dirt, the more it was Idaho dirt, sandy.

The baby in the cradle board started fussing a bit, and his mother—the woman whose hair was being braided—crawled to him and said some words in her language.

All of a sudden I had to pee something fierce.

I walked clockwise, like you're supposed to in a tipi, toward the tipi flap. When I opened the tipi flap, I had the thought that the glass window used to be where the flap was, but I told myself not to think about it.

Nothing could have prepared me for what was outside. The sun was setting and the land was rolling rolling green and gold with touches of burnt red to the horizon. There was one big tree, a big old grandmother cottonwood tree, and there were tipis all around, smoke coming out of them.

All around me, everywhere, I was surrounded by Indians, most of the people in buckskin, some men wearing cowboy hats and wool coats with buttons. I wanted to look real close at them and see how they were dressed, but you don't do that sort of thing in New York City.

I walked away from the tipi, over to some brush by a slough where a bunch of mustangs were standing in the water. Even pissing was fun. The yellow of the sunset made my pee look fancy. And my pink penis in the yellow-orange setting-sun light, so lovely.

There were horses and wagons. Kids running around like a bunch of wild Indians. There was a little hill—not even a hill, really, just a big mound of rolling earth.

After I buttoned up, I walked up on the mound just as the top of the sun went down and all at once everything glowed gold. I looked down at my body, at my hands and legs, at my feet. My feet on the earth.

Home sweet home was my feet on dirt, the June grass fancy with wind, the smell of horse shit, wet slough, charcoal, my hair blowing in the wind. Sky above me blue-blue and orange, big white fluffy clouds going on and on forever.

For a moment, I knew I was dead.

What I'd died of was love.

When I pulled the tipi flap aside to walk back in, it wasn't just a tipi anymore. It was a huge lodge and there were hundreds of Indians sitting around, some of them dancing, four men on a drum singing a *Heya-heya-heya* song.

True Shot was sitting between Gray Wolf and Yellow Wolf, and Yellow Wolf was passing the pipe to True Shot. Then, just like that, I was sitting next to True Shot, and when True Shot handed the pipe to me, True Shot's face was the face of Charlie 2Moons.

I felt a whole big goodness inside me, a feeling like heaven itself, a finger drawing a circle around my heart, and I smiled at Charlie and Charlie shook the pipe a little so I'd take it.

Then the pipe was in my hands, the whole universe in my hands, and I was the universe too. The only way out is in. I puffed on the pipe, blew smoke to the four directions, blew smoke to the sky, then to the earth, and when I went to pass the pipe on, the pipe was my lovely erect pink penis.

And I turned to Charlie to show Charlie my lovely erect pink penis, but Charlie wasn't Charlie. Charlie was True Shot, and True Shot and I were standing in the Museum of Unnatural History.

THE AFRICAN AMERICAN woman with the French twist and the long leather coat and leather purse was just getting to her feet in front of the glass.

For a moment I thought True Shot was on fire, there was so much smoke coming off him. Then I looked down and I was smoking too.

Charcoal.

There was a snake, a diamondback rattler, right there in front of us, curled up, shaking its tail.

True Shot said some Indian words and the snake unwound its long body, rolled off on the shiny floor, and slipped around the corner.

I went to say some words but it wasn't any use. It was like the one time after work when I smoked heroin with John the Bartender—I thought I was talking but I was only thinking I was talking.

The Native American Art Family were back in their places, the two women on the left and the two men on the right, baby on the cradle board. The women were sitting by the game of sticks on the floor and the one woman was braiding the other's hair. But Yellow Wolf was just staring down at a green plastic Star Wars sword in his hands, as phony as the fire.

True Shot? I said, Did you get it?

True Shot lifted up the medicine bundle.

I got it, he said.

I could smell the wet slough and the earth and the horses and the fire and the sunset in the buckskin and beads and porcupine quills of the bag.

The pipe is inside? I said.

It is this way, True Shot said.

WE BOUGHT COFFEE and doughnuts at a Dunkin Donuts, and True Shot and I drove down to lower Manhattan, Door of the Dead van winding around stone outcroppings, True Shot shifting down to second through the narrow streets of Wall Street. Every once in a while a single black Mercedes would pass, but there was no other traffic. On the corners, huge unrelenting lights from above; then, beyond, only dark, asphalt, steam rolling out of holes, monoliths. Not a soul in sight.

True Shot parked Door of the Dead van in a place you weren't supposed to park. DO NOT ENTER, the sign said. But the big chain across was unhooked, so True Shot drove in over it and parked next to the water. Out in the harbor, Our Lady of the Paintbrush was the same color as my father's old Dodge pickup.

I was new-shoe stiff at first, afraid about cops and DO NOT ENTER and the medicine bundle on a blanket in the back of Door of the Dead van. But then True Shot started talking, and I wasn't afraid anymore.

True Shot had a rag under his seat, and he pulled out the rag and blew his nose. He sat for a while like you do when you're trying to get it together. The plastic statue of the Virgin Mary on the dashboard, the green sequin-framed Brigitte Bardot glued next to the jockey box, Our Lady of the Paintbrush out the windshield.

True Shot pushed in the Sioux tape, and the song was all wavy for a while; then the Sioux tape was a drum, a heartbeat drum inside Door of the Dead van.

I didn't say anything because of the heartbeat drum. I just stared out onto the water.

As I lit the cigarette, the World Trade Center was in the rearview mirror, and I turned around to look. The World Trade Center buildings were so beyond human they'd disappeared.

I was born in Jackson Heights, True Shot said. My father was Puerto Rican, a dentist. He considered himself Spanish, not Puerto Rican. He claimed there was no Taino blood in him, but he was a liar. His mother was half Taino. My mother was a Mexican woman, a housewife, and my father considered her lower class.

There was never a sweeter person to live on God's green earth than my mother.

I was the only child, True Shot said. Distant father, overindulgent mother, same old story. In the early sixties, I started reading the beat poets: Ferlinghetti, Allen Ginsberg, Jack Kerouac. In 1964, I bought a Dodge van—not Door of the Dead van, it was a '58—and after reading *Dharma Bums* decided I'd make the all-American trek across the country. Taos, New Mexico, is where I was headed. I was going to find me an Indian chief and we were going to go on a vision quest and I'd find the meaning of life.

I did meet an Indian chief, True Shot said. His name was Hanford Littlejohn. But instead of a vision quest, Hanford and I started dealing marijuana. Lived pretty high for a couple years, till I got busted in Phoenix. Spent six years in prison for selling a controlled substance.

Prison was one of the best things that ever happened to me, True Shot said. My cell mate was this Sioux guy. His name was True Shot.

The cigarette papers were in my shirt pocket. I reached for them, started rolling cigarettes. True Shot just sat there, the sound of the Sioux drums, the ocean hitting the rampart, seagulls, and one of those bells you hear way out on a buoy in the dark.

True Shot took a sip of coffee, wiped his lips.

The real True Shot and I got as close as two men can get without fucking, True Shot said. The real True Shot was at Wounded Knee, True Shot said, But not me.

For four years, night after night, True Shot and I talked. He taught me Lakota, told me Lakota stories about the sun dance, the sweat lodge, the ghost dance. He told me of the Lakotas' final humiliation at Wounded Knee.

My friend True Shot was in for life, True Shot said. He killed a cop, shot him in the forehead because the cop called him a dirty heathen savage son of a bitch.

One morning I woke up, True Shot said—I slept on the bottom bunk—and my friend True Shot's legs were hanging right next to my eyeballs. At first I thought he was just sitting on his bed with his legs dangling over. But then I stood up and saw the rope around his neck.

I think I cried the whole next year, True Shot said.

Fog drifted in over Our Lady of the Paintbrush, first around the light, then around her head. The lights of the boats on the water below her shone green and red and amber in the fog. The slow monotonous bell. The water against the ramparts.

I grew my hair long, True Shot said, Wore it braided Indian style, and read every book I could get my hands on about Native American culture—mostly Plains Indians, mostly Sioux, the Indians of the Northwest, and the Hopi and the Navajo.

When I got out of the pen, True Shot said, I didn't know what to do. I just thought I didn't want to be no *pendejo* Puerto Rican anymore. I hitchhiked back to New York City. My mother was dead and my father had remarried. He was a golfer and lived in Washington Heights. He gave me a hundred bucks and wished me well.

True Shot zipped up the faux leopardskin coat. His breath was white exhaust coming out his mouth. The light from Our Lady of the Paintbrush made True Shot look like Rose's Buddha.

I reached for my tobacco, started rolling a cigarette.

Roll me one of those too, True Shot said. I'm going to need some tobacco to get through this.

I rolled True Shot a cigarette, lit his cigarette, lit mine.

I went back to selling drugs in Dog Shit Park, True Shot said. That's where I met Ruby. That smile of his could charm a rattlesnake. Ruby and I dealt drugs and stayed stoned for years. Somewhere in there, Ruby started calling me True Shot, and in bars sometimes I'd pose as this wise old Indian from Taos who could barely speak English, and Ruby was one of my followers who was showing me around the town. It's amazing how many people believed us. People say New Yorkers are hard mean souls, but down deep each one of us wants to believe.

Eventually, me and Ruby started going different ways, True Shot said. Ruby started shooting heroin with Fred, and I quit drinking, quit smoking, quit picking pockets, started up my company, Spirit Schleppers.

Fred? I said.

I didn't know Fred then, True Shot said. Fred was supposed to be some poet or something, but he was just a junkie.

Then one night, True Shot said, Ruby and Fred crashed at my house. They were way stoned and slept on the couch. When I woke up, Fred was giving me a gum job.

A gum job? I said.

I hit Fred with my fist and knocked him down, True Shot said. I was going to kick him, but he looked so pitiful lying there all skinny and old with strands of hair sticking up in patches here and there on top of his head and blood coming out his nose.

Even more than that, True Shot said, He looked like Gandhi lying there in a pair of orange coveralls that said FRED on the pocket. I felt like a raving redneck lunatic asshole for committing violence on such a holy old gentleman.

So I gave him my handkerchief instead, True Shot said.

Fred said, Thank you. You're very kind.

Then I realized I was standing there with my cock poking straight out, and that scared me even more than Fred, True Shot said, So I quick tried to put my boner back in my pocket and that got the old guy to laughing and the way he was laughing, I saw how ridiculous I looked and I couldn't help but laugh too.

True Shot's breath in. His breath out. Big chest heave. True Shot took off the swooped rhinestone mirrors. Wiped his eyes. Blew his nose in the rag again.

It didn't take me long to figure out Fred was about to croak, True Shot said. Ruby took off early the next morning, so I let Fred stay there with me, four days, just me and Fred. Stay with me till he died.

A HELICOPTER BUZZED around the head of Our Lady of the Paintbrush, yellow lights like a yellow jacket on a picnic you swat away. The ocean sound against the ramparts was breathing in, breathing out.

My breath in. My breath out.

In all my life, True Shot said, I never heard one man tell so many stories. Fred was a skeleton with an oracle inside him. We'd wake up in the morning and he'd have instant coffee with Cremora and two teaspoons of sugar waiting for me and his toothless mouth would just start talking talking, puffing on his More menthol cigarettes, one after the other, talking about all kinds of shit. Indian stories, Buddhist stories, Greek stories, Bible stories, the rabbi story, O'Henry stories, Scheherazade.

On the fourth day, Fred wasn't eating at all, True Shot said. He just lay there on his sleeping bag, a skeleton possessed by More Menthol cigarettes, telling everything he knew and had learned, chattering away all the shit that was inside him.

I lay close to him at night, True Shot said, Like you and me last night. Fred was mostly babbling. I couldn't make a lot of sense out of what he was saying. Fred wasn't *not* making sense. It was me who couldn't comprehend.

That last night, I leaned against the wall and held him in my arms on my lap. He was nothing but a bag of bones. He recited some poem, True Shot said, By some Turkish guy. The poem was about a horse called the Stallion of Love. But I've forgotten the poem and the name of the Turkish guy.

Late in the night, True Shot said, When I woke up, Fred was sitting cross-legged at the bottom of the bed from me, and he was talking talking smoking smoking again.

Then Fred pulled out his old suitcase from under my bed, True Shot said. He opened it and took out all the herbs, sage, cedar. He drew a circle around us on the floor with his foot. He unrolled the pipe from the ocelot skin. Put the pipe stem into the pipe bowl.

At sunrise, True Shot said, We smoked the pipe and prayed in a good way. After we prayed, Fred rolled the pipe back into the ocelot skin, put the pipe and the herbs back into the suitcase, closed the suitcase, and gave the suitcase to me.

I am dying, Fred said. My grandfather gave this pipe to me many years ago. My intention has always been to give this pipe to another man, but the Great Mystery has not intended it so. So now, my friend, it seems you are the one I am to give it to. Treat it always with great respect. Honor the pipe, for it is the universe. Follow the good road, the red road, Fred said. I did not. Perhaps you will.

Fred died in my arms, True Shot said.

A long time ago, True Shot said, The night we went to the meat-packing district, you told me Charlie had a scar across his face. That freaked me out. Fred had that same scar. But he was old, I told myself, He had no teeth. How could this possibly be Charlie? And then I knew, True Shot said. Fred had AIDS. You get old fast with AIDS. You lose your hair, your teeth.

Then the pipe, True Shot said. The pipe I had at Ruby's pipe ceremony was Fred's pipe, and you recognized it. You had heard the rabbi story and the locomotive story. Only then, really, did I let myself know.

The light from Our Lady of the Paintbrush was one long line of illumination toward Door of the Dead van. The line came up the hood, through the windshield, onto True Shot's chin, his lips.

True Shot laid his head on my shoulder, his right hand, palm up, into my hand, lips at my ear.

You got to know that when Ruby and I first saw you at the airport, True Shot said, Ruby fell in love with you. I never saw anything like it. The man looked over, saw you, and was smitten. He thought if he got you in the van, he could get into your pants.

You looked so . . . so raw, so vulnerable. But Ruby could tell you were cautious because you *knew* you were too raw, too vulnerable, too delicious.

To trick you, True Shot said, Ruby and I made this plan: If he got you in the van, I'd play a wise old Indian chief. We figured you'd go for a wise old Indian chief your first night in Manhattan because you had all that Wild West wind-and-big-sky wilderness in you.

But as we went on, True Shot said, The act got too real. Ruby was more and more in love with you.

In my forearms, up to my shoulders, splash down through my heart to my stomach. Cattle prod to cock.

So it was all a scam, I said.

I rolled down the window of Door of the Dead van.

My breath in. My breath out.

You got to understand, Will, True Shot said. It started out a lie, but the lie brought us all to the truth. By pretending to be a wise old Indian chief, I have become one, True Shot said.

LATER ON THAT night, True Shot on the foam mattress right up next to me on the futon. We were holding on tight to each other, to the someone else there, like Bernadette would do.

Was the story of Wolf Swamp part of the scam? I said.

No, True Shot said.

Fred told you the story of Wolf Swamp, didn't he? I said.

How did you know? True Shot said.

There weren't any horses I said, In America until after the white man. Charlie could always tell a good story, I said, But he didn't always get his facts right.

True Shot leaned up on his elbows. Only silence for a moment, in all the world, all of New York City, only silence.

Then: What happened to Fred's body? I said.

We took up a collection, True Shot said, And had him cremated.

What did you do with his ashes? I asked.

The wind took most of them, True Shot said. A big dust-devil wind came up and took the ashes with it. But I got some of them ashes, True Shot said.

Where are they? I said.

True Shot touched the buckskin bag with the beaded blue horizontal and the beaded red vertical. He put his thumbs and fingers on each side of his neck, pinched the buckskin strand, lifted it over his head.

I bowed my head. My ears tingled as the buckskin necklace passed them and settled on my neck.

The buckskin bag touched my throat: the beaded blue horizontal and the intersecting beaded red vertical. The surprising weight of it.

With my hand, my right hand, palm up, I held the buckskin bag, held the ashes of Charlie 2Moons.

To be brothers. To always respect and love each other and always tell each other the truth and to keep each other's secrets and to never forget.

BOOK FOUR

CHAPTER
TWENTY-SEVEN

F ifth Street Videoland went into Stranded Beings Searching for God. They tore off the whole front of the place and made it all windows. Tore off the sign with the Sacred Heart of Jesus and the three Polaroids.

The light was real bright in Fifth Street Videoland, unrelenting. The light came out onto the sidewalk at night and pushed garbage and garbage-can shadows into the street. And Videoland played the same music: one big loop of Top Hits round and around and around again.

The light from below me came up to my windows, in through my windows. At night, lying on my futon, the fluorescence glowed all around me.

At midnight the lights went off and the music stopped. Weekends one o'clock.

It ruined the stoop. You can't sit on a stoop with light like that and pop hits over and over.

So the summer of '88 I didn't do much stoop sitting. Because of the light and because Rose started chemotherapy. Karposi's sarcoma.

I don't know which was worse, the purple berry bumps on Rose's legs or the brain fry he came home with after a chemo session.

One night as I turned the corner from the Bowery onto East Fifth, there was Rose. There in the mercury-vapor dust-storm light, Rose was sweeping. Three o'clock in the morning.

Rose was all in black with a black stocking cap. The closer I got to him the more he didn't look like my Rose, but Rose as some character of the night: the Hunchback of Notre Dame, the Old Lamplighter, a chimney sweep, Frankenstein.

My open palm on beaded blue horizontal, beaded red vertical. My open palm on Charlie.

Evening, Rose, I said.

Rose didn't look up, kept on sweeping.

The whole problem, Rose said, With this garbage, Rose said, Is there are people out there who are hungry and have no home and no place to take a shit. And to these people, a garbage can means food and clothing and salable items.

Lined up on the sidewalk were five silver garbage cans, plastic garbage liners a ruffle of black under the silver lids. On each silver lid was a piece of duct tape; written on the duct tape, black Magic Marker words.

On the first garbage can were the black words EDIBLE FOOD.

On the second garbage can, the black word CLOTHING.

The third garbage can, HOUSEHOLD ITEMS.

On the next, the black words REFUND: BOTTLES AND CANS.

On the last garbage can: NOTHING OF VALUE. KEEP THE FUCK OUT. TRUST ME ON THIS ONE.

Rose's prizefighter nose, his clitoris-bump forehead, his eightball cheeks, his keep-your-chin-up chin were covered with purple bumps. In the mercury-vapor light, the bumps looked like Ruby's cockroaches.

Trickle down, Ronald Reagan likes to call it, Rose said. You know what trickle down is, don't you? Rose said. That's what goes down your leg if you don't shake it.

What trickle down means, Rose said, Is feeding the horse, so when the horse takes a shit the rats get something to eat too.

Rose's black T-shirt said FUCK THE UNITED NEGRO COLLEGE FUND.

Pollution is everywhere, Rose said. Right now did you know that there are a hundred tons of New York garbage circling the island on a barge nobody wants to take?

We are so busy filling up the void, Rose said, We are filling our world with the garbage it takes to fill the void.

I took the broom handle away from Rose. He did not resist.

Come on, Rose, I said, Let's go smoke some Sho-ko-lat.

Tea, Rose said, Herbal tea.

I've got peppermint, I said.

I took Rose's arm, and we were one step, two. On the third step, Rose stopped.

In Rose's eyes, no coiled-up black serpent.

I unlocked the front door, pushed the door open. The unrelenting light on Rose's purple bumps.

You did a great job on the garbage, I said. I've never seen the place look so clean.

We live in our throwaway, Rose said. When there's no place to shit you can't walk for shit.

ANOTHER NIGHT, I found Rose up on the roof. He was standing where the roof slopes up, on the cornice, on the edge, his toes dangling over East Fifth Street. He was wearing his gold lamé pajamas and holding a martini-up cocktail glass in his right hand, a Gauloise in his left.

My open palm on the beaded blue, the beaded red. My open palm on Charlie.

Rose?

A gust of wind found Rose and fluttered his pajamas. Rose leaned forward a little against the wind, then leaned back, spilling some of his martini. Rose leaning back and forth, back and forth, side to side; I thought for sure he was going over, thought for sure Rose's blood was on East Fifth Street, all over the garbage cans, so red on the sidewalk in the fluorescent Videoland light.

I started singing:

> On the roof's the only place I know
> Where you just have to wish to make it so.

Rose didn't turn around. He started singing too:

> When this old world starts getting you down
> And people are just too much for me to take.

Then we were singing together, and when Rose turned around he almost fell over into chaos, into unrelenting light, but he steadied himself and walked down the slope of cornice, walked up to me, and we started dancing, me the girl, me Elizabeth Taylor, and we sang "Up on the Roof," all the choruses, and when we finished that song, we sang Peggy Lee's "Is That All There Is," and when we finished that song we sang Nina Simone's "Wild Is the Wind," and after that Rose was tired.

I helped Rose down the stairs, Rose not so extra-lovely anymore, not even lovely.

When I unlocked his door, Mary, Mona, and Jack Flash were barking barking and running around our feet and jumping up on us.

I got Rose to put on his Moroccan caftan, got him to sit in his purple-velvet overstuffed chair. I made tea.

Rose didn't drink the tea, just sat and stared, so I went down to Fifth Street Videoland, into the unrelenting bright and Top Hits tape loop, and rented *Sunset Boulevard*.

Rose knew every one of Gloria Swanson's lines and said each line right along with her.

When I rewound the video, the TV came on, and it was an old Barbara Walters interview with Ronald and Nancy Reagan before the Oscars.

When Barbara Walters said to President Reagan that he was the most popular president since John F. Kennedy, Rose stood up, walked into the kitchen, came back with his silver revolver, and shot the television.

It's the truth.

The dogs ran yelping under the bed, and there was smoke that smelled of electric wiring and a gassy smell. I was sitting on the blonde-fainting couch holding onto my teacup for dear life. Shards of glass on everything. My hands, my shirt, my black waiter pants, my legs, tiny pieces of glass like sequins stuck to me.

Rose yelled at the black hole where the television used to be, Barbara Walters, you are such a *dumb* bitch.

Bracelets clack-clack.

Don't you know Ronald Reagan wasn't the most popular president since John Kennedy until *you* fucking said it? You have completely overstepped the bounds of accountability, Rose yelled, And have forgotten that the medium is the message!

So Noam Chomsky.

By that time, the dogs were all sitting on the blonde-fainting couch next to me. Rose was pointing the gun at us, like Sister Barbara Ann's pointer stick.

Don't let anybody tell you different, Rose yelled. The media are fully aware of their power.

Across the room, on top of everything in the room, exploded opaque glass. Under the light of Rose's Italian chandelabra, the room was glitter, tiny illuminations.

My open palm on the beaded blue, the beaded red. My open palm on Charlie.

Rose, I said, I think you should lie down.

*   *   *

IN DOG SHIT Park, I sat down on the green bench by Ruby's Home Sweet Home. I was drinking my morning coffee and eating a corn muffin. It was already a hot day. Dog shit stinking real bad. I was telling Ruby again about the medicine bundle and the Museum of Unnatural History. In all the world, there I was, just another crazy New Yorker sitting on a park bench talking to himself.

That same morning, a figure walked past me on the sidewalk. I say *figure* because I don't know what else to call it. It was a walking umbrella with a red plastic shower curtain hanging down all around off the spokes of the umbrella. The bare feet were coated with tar. There was also a humming. The person inside the red shower curtain was humming a song. The tune was familiar but I couldn't place it.

A week later, I saw Umbrella Red Shower Curtain in the meatpacking district. I'd gone over there just walking walking, maybe to see if I could find Crystal again, but there was no Crystal and not one dragon on the street.

No Charlie 2Moons to look for anymore. Charlie was a buckskin bag, the blue and the red, against my throat.

I was standing on the corner of 14th in front of the pink triangular building whose basement door had been the entrance to Hell. It was maybe seven, twilight, *entre chien et loup,* when all of a sudden, just like that— abracadabra!— Umbrella Red Shower Curtain walked by. It made a sound when it walked that was the same as the first time I saw it in Dog Shit Park. It was the sound of plastic sliding along the sidewalk, and the sound of the knees of the person inside against the plastic as it walked. Plus the humming. From inside came the humming of the song I knew but couldn't place.

THE THIRD TIME I saw Umbrella Red Shower Curtain was in Tribeca. I'd walked down to a greenhouse and nursery down there to check out their cherry trees. I was looking at a Kwanzan cherry, looking at its beautiful peeling purple-red bark, when I heard the plastic against the sidewalk and looked up to see Umbrella Red Shower Curtain and the tarred feet. Humming the same song.

Then, a couple of weeks later, in Dog Shit Park again, on the green bench, morning coffee and corn muffin again, talking to Ruby again, just like that, Umbrella Red Shower Curtain came walking and plastic-sliding and humming by. I stopped mid-slurp of morning coffee and listened hard. Then I said it. "Famous Blue Raincoat!" I said.

Umbrella Red Shower Curtain said, William of Heaven! So nice to see you again.

Susan Strong? I said.

Fiona, Fiona said. Ruby Prestigiacomo gave me my name, remember? My whole name is Fiona Yet. When you knew me I wasn't quite Fiona Yet.

Fiona's laugh just like her mother's.

Fiona opened the shower curtain and said, the way you'd say come into my apartment, she said, Come in! Come in!

My open palm against the red; I stepped inside under the umbrella.

Bad breath. Sweat. Fiona put her arms around me, her big red leather purse in one of her hands. I thought she was embracing me, but she was just closing the curtain.

Mustn't let them see! Fiona said.

See what? I said. Fiona, what are you doing?

What was two inches from my face was a face I barely recognized. No red lips, no eye makeup. Her blue eyes were bloodshot and puffy, the scar above her lip a blue-scarred bruise. I didn't recognize the body either.

Shit happens. Fiona was pregnant.

Fiona smiled. One of her front teeth was missing.

What happened to your tooth? I said.

Tooth? Fiona said.

You've lost a tooth, I said.

Tooth fairy! Fiona said.

Then: I've seen you all over the place, I said, The past month or so. When did you get back from Connecticut? How's your father? Where are you living? Why are you dressed like this?

Fiona was wearing a wife-beater and men's boxer shorts with I ❤ NEW YORK on them.

I touched her hair, all matted together, and said, What? Are you going Rasta on me?

Fiona reached up to my neck, the buckskin bag in the palm of her hand. I like your medicine bag, Fiona said. Cool!

Then: You're going to need all the medicine you can get your hands on! Fiona said. There's going to be a war!

Fiona's arms were so thin, her legs.

War? I said.

Here! Fiona said.

In America? I said.

Here! Fiona said, and pointed her finger down to the sidewalk.

You mean in New York? I said.

In Dog Shit Park, Fiona said. Here! Soon!

When the horse shit hits the fan, Fiona said, You'll know where to find me. I'll be right fucking here.

Fiona stamped her bare foot on cement.

Fiona's face was dirty, her eyes not on the premises; her breath stunk, and her hands and arms and legs and feet were almost black with dirt and grease.

There was no stepping away.

Where are you staying? I said.

In here, Fiona said. In the Famous Blue Raincoat. You know in the song when Leonard sings, *Did you ever go clear?* Well, one night, I'd bought a bottle of Everclear. I was in Connecticut then. I'd just got out of Silver Lake. How long ago was that? God, what a dreary place that is! Makes Betty Ford look like Betty Crocker! I was on the ramp for the train heading back to the city, Fiona said, And I had my Walkman on, and I was drinking my Everclear and just as I took a swig, Leonard Cohen sang *Did you ever go clear?*

And I went clear, Fiona said. Completely clear. It isn't *present* so much that you want to be completely in. It's *clear* where you want to be completely in, Fiona said.

Fiona turned just her eyes up at the umbrella and how it was attached to her head. It looked like a crown of coat-hanger wires. Fiona dragged her long fingers against her red plastic shower curtain. I looked at it. In all the world, under Fiona's umbrella, a pack of white wolves on the shower curtain. Some of the white wolves howling, some of them lying in the snow, wolf puppies wrestling with each other.

My home's a trip, Fiona said, don't you think?

The wolves, I said.

Cool, huh? Fiona said.

Way cool, I said.

What's the rent? I said.

You can't imagine people's reactions, Fiona said. Those who are brave enough to talk to me, after they step in and I close the curtain behind them—these brave souls tell me the most incredible things. I'm like a walking confessional, Fiona said. One guy told me he raises chickens in his backyard, and when he wants a chicken dinner he fucks it and he kills it and eats it, Fiona said. This one woman told me she was the in-carnation of Cleopatra. She was a stunning black woman, and she said it was her karma in this incarnation to be the most beautiful woman in the world and be black because Western civilization won't cop to the fact that Cleopatra was a black woman. Another guy told me he was afraid of falling asleep. That his little brother died in his sleep and as a kid he got it in his head that if he falls asleep, he'll die. He asked me what he could do, Fiona said, So I told him to just go ahead and die.

Fiona's lips at my ear.

The horrific whisper: Everybody dies.

How about a Sabrett? I said. Or Shrimp Fried Rice and barbecue ribs from the Bamboo House? I said. Or maybe some Chicken Tandoori at Panna?

No, Fiona said.

Then: Fiona, I said, Where's your father? Do you have your father's phone number? I said, Why don't you come home with me now?

Who knows? Fiona said. These days who can tell? Did you know they were changing the name of the *Village Voice* to the *Inner Voice?* Or is it the *Village Idiot?* Fiona said. Or maybe the *Inner Idiot?* Anyway, who cares what a bunch of assholes think.

Where in Connecticut does your father live? I said. Is it Greenwich?

Green Witch, Fiona said.

Green Witch? I said.

Then Fiona's smile, big smile. The gap between her teeth. The bruised blue scarred lip. Fiona put her arms around me and hugged me.

Oh, Will! Fiona said. I'm Diogenes and you're my honest man. It's so good to see you, Will, Fiona said. We must get together soon sometime. Maybe next week?

Sure, I said. How about tomorrow, Monday? I said. I'm off. Dinner at my place?

I'd love to see your Art Family again, Fiona said. I'd appreciate them so much more now. But I'll have to check my schedule. I'm so fucking busy with the cure and all.

The cure, I said.

Oh, fuck, Will, Fiona said, I didn't tell you? Oh! Jesus Christ! What, am I losing my mind? It's only the total basis of my very existence right now!

I had to step back some so Fiona could dig through her huge red leather purse. She pulled just about everything out of it—matches, Chinese takeout, a bra, candy wrappers, dominoes.

In all the world, under an umbrella, surrounded by a Conran's red plastic shower curtain with a pack of white wolves on it, pressed up against a skanky Fiona Yet in Dog Shit Park.

Here it is! Fiona said, and held a dirty Extra Strength Tylenol bottle up to my eyes.

The cure! Fiona said. I've found the cure for AIDS!

Only silence. Dead silence.

Cool, huh? Fiona said. I worked with the doctors while I was in Silver Lake and our studies are conclusive.

Extra Strength Tylenol? I said.

No, silly, Fiona said, That's just the bottle. We put the cure in this bottle so nobody can see. If it gets into the hands of corporate America we're all fucked!

What is it, I said, The cure?

Don't tell anybody, Fiona said. Quiet is kept. Loose lips sink ships. I'm taking the cure to the exactly right most perfect person. I was just on my way, Fiona said, When I saw you.

Fiona kissed me on the cheek.

My lovely lovely Will, Fiona said, Oh, I miss you so much! Got a cigarette?

Pouring out the tobacco. The papers. Tough rolling in the cramped space.

Fiona put the cigarette right where the scar lifts her lip. I lit the cigarette. She inhaled hard, blew smoke out through her nose.

I also took a course in belly dancing, Fiona said. Silver Lake had all the comforts of home. Can you imagine a course in belly dancing in an insane asylum? Wealth and privilege! Cool. I'll have to belly dance for you sometime, but now I've got to run.

Maybe I could walk along with you, I said. I'd love to meet this exactly right most perfect person you're going to give the Extra Strength Tylenol to.

Fiona grabbed my earlobe, pulled hard, hung on.

Ouch! I said, Fiona! Shit!

Get this straight! Fiona said. It is *not* fucking Tylenol, OK? It's the cure for AIDS!

Fiona's blue eyes, cloudy blue into my eyes. A deep breath of bad breath into my face.

Don't fucking patronize me, Will! Fiona said. This is serious shit! You fuck with me and I'll kick your ass!

OK! OK! I said. Let go my ear!

Fiona pulled down harder, then let go.

You need an earring! Fiona said. Right ear or left ear? Queer Ear or Beer Ear? Ah-hah! Fiona said. Both ears!

My earlobe was hanging down around my chin.

Where is this exactly right most perfect person? I said. Who is he?

What makes you think it's a he? Fiona said.

Who is *she*? I said.

She is Auden, Fiona said. And Argwings Khodek and Rumi and Chief Joseph and Princess Diana and Leonard Cohen and Julie Christie and Joni Mitchell and Ethyl Eichelberger and Martin Luther King, Jr. and John Kelly and Malcolm X and Harvey Milk and the Dalai Lama!

He is the Virgin Mary, Fiona said, And Rosa Parks and Gandhi and Tarkovsky and Vanessa Redgrave and Marilyn Monroe and Mathilde Krim and Cavafy and Leonard Peltier and Larry Kramer and Meher Baba and Baba Ram Das!

And where is this person? I said.

I'm not sure, Fiona said. I keep ending up back here in Dog Shit Park, but everybody's not doing the belly dance all together yet, and dancing and dancing yet, and singing "The Song of Bernadette."

Fiona, I said.

I know it sounds crazy, Fiona said, But actually it's very similar to something you once told me about Charlie 2Moons and the game you played on your horses.

Going Slack? I said.

That was it! Fiona said.

Well, Fiona said, Here in Wolf Swamp, we call it Walk/Don't Walk.

Wolf Swamp, I said.

You're the one who told me about Wolf Swamp, Fiona said. And Walk/Don't Walk started as soon as I got back to Manhattan, Fiona said. As soon as I got safe in my new home.

Fiona touched the red plastic shower curtain, the howling wolf's head.

Here's how you do it, Fiona said. When you come up to a corner, the direction you go is the direction the sign says WALK. The direction you *don't* go is the direction the sign says DON'T WALK. When one sign says DON'T WALK and the other sign is *flashing* DON'T WALK, you can exercise your own free will to don't walk, or to dash for it, or to go back the way you came, or to take the wild card and go in the Fourth Direction.

Amor fati, love of one's fate, Fiona said. Walk/Don't Walk leads those who will; who won't, they drag.

They keep dragging me here, Fiona said. Dog Shit Park. So I got to trust it, that's all. Even though some of the time I feel like I'm lost in a labyrinth. But I just got to honor my practice!

Your practice? I said.

Complete acceptance of whatever the Divine sets in my path, Fiona said.

What if there isn't a Divine? I said.

Fiona's bruised blue lip curled up.

You stupid asshole! Fiona said. Believe that it hath been given, Fiona said, And it shall be given unto you.

Fiona looked up at me like I was a camera she was pointing at herself. Her blue eyes cloudy blue, too close to the fire blue.

So, Fiona said, it looks so far like the right place is Dog Shit Park. Now I just have to wait.

Wait for what? I said.

It has to be a certain way before it can start, Fiona said, The belly dancing and the singing. I'll know when the extra right most perfect person is here, Fiona said. When in all of Wolf Swamp—or at least in all of Dog Shit Park—when every person in the park will all at once make the same movement. That movement is the first movement of the belly dance. They'll be singing, and what they'll be singing is "The Song of Bernadette," Fiona said. And that's when the exactly right perfect person will show up and that's when my inner voice—not the *Village Voice* inner voice but my own inner voice—will tell me and I'll know.

Did you know the belly dance is really a dance for men and is called the Dance of the Wounded Male? Fiona said.

Fiona put her bottom lip over her top lip, stretched the blue scar, then opened her mouth.

My inner voice, Fiona said, Says the war is coming any day now.

Fiona, I said, Come with me to my apartment. You can take a shower and we'll listen to music. Order Chinese.

My inner voice, Fiona said, Says to remain situated.

Does your inner voice, I said, Say it's OK to give me your father's phone number in Connecticut?

Fiona dug through her red leather purse and on the inside flap of a White Horse Tavern matchbook she wrote her father's phone number.

Fiona, I said, Promise me you'll stay here on the green bench. I said, I'll only be a half hour.

I'll remain situated, Fiona said.

I opened the shower curtain, stood for a moment, and looked at Fiona. Her face was greasy white, marble white, her blue eyes painted onto marble, the scar.

Promise? I said.

Promise, Fiona said.

I closed the shower curtain and ran to the pay phone. The receiver hung down like my limp dick, out of order. I didn't have change anyway, so I ran to my apartment and made the call on my red telephone. A pleasant computer voice said the phone had been disconnected. I tried again and the pleasant computer voice said the same thing. Again.

Then I called information to see if I had the area code wrong, and I didn't have it wrong, so I called for directory assistance.

David MacIlvane, I said.

That number has been disconnected, sir, the operator said.

Is there a new number? I said.

No new number, the operator said.

I ran the whole way back to Dog Shit Park, ran to the green bench. Fiona was gone. Not on the premises. Nowhere. Lost the way. Lost the world. Lost for words. Lost on the blue road. No Lost and Found. No no Yoko Ono.

TWO DAYS STRAIGHT, True Shot and I drove Door of the Dead van around not-looking for Fiona Yet. We stayed mostly in the Lower East Side, but didn't see her, so we drove to Tribeca and didn't see her, then drove to the Phoenix on 14th and didn't see her.

The second day, a hot muggy industrial-gray day, Door of the Dead van's heater was melting the rubber on my red Converse tennis shoes.

Did you use a rubber? True Shot said.

I jumped so high off the seat I hit my head on the headliner.

No! I said. It was this overwhelming thing that came over the both of us.

It is this way, True Shot said. Yadda yadda yadda! Next time use a rubber.

Fuck you! I said.

Rubbers are in the glove box, Papi! True Shot said. So's the cigars!

WHEN TRUE SHOT dropped me off at 205 East Fifth Street, he shut off the engine. I went to grab for the door handle, but True Shot put his extra-lovely arm out, touched my shoulder with his open palm.

Wait a minute, True Shot said. I got something to say.

I sat back, pushed my back against the seat.

My breath in. My breath out.

How long ago has it been, True Shot said, Since Ruby and I let you off here that first night?

Almost five years to the day, I said.

True Shot took off his swooped rhinestone mirrors, folded them, put them in his shirt pocket.

You and me, True Shot said, We've had us quite the times together, haven't we?

True Shot, I said, What's going on?

One tear right under True Shot's swooped rhinestone mirror, slow rolling down his cheek.

What you're thinking, True Shot said, Is making me very very sad.

True Shot? I said.

I must take the medicine bundle back to the Blackfeet nation, True Shot said, And I must do it soon. I was planning on taking the trip with you. Going back to Idaho with you.

True Shot's open palm in mine. A crooked rectangle of sun coming in hot through the windshield.

True Shot lifted my hand up with his and shook our hands back and forth, back and forth, the way you do if you're the champions.

It would be fun, True Shot said, You and me on the road in Door of the Dead van, finally out of this fucking Wolf Swamp, wouldn't it?

Flies all over the garbage cans. A smell like something dead and over-ripe bananas.

True Shot, I said, I—

It is this way, True Shot said, I know you can't go. You've got Rose and Fiona, True Shot said, And now maybe a kid. It's no time for you to leave.

But, I said, You'll be back in a couple weeks?

True Shot let our hands down slow, let go of my hand, put his thumb and index on his nose, in between his swooped rhinestone mirrors. He shook his head.

Months? I said.

No, True Shot said. I'm not ever coming back to Wolf Swamp.

My open palm to the blue-beaded horizontal, the red-beaded vertical.

Maybe you can come see me, True Shot said, When your task is over?

Mrs. Lupino and the yellow New York drop-dead fuck-you cat were looking out her window at us.

Task? I said.

It is this way, True Shot said. You've still got to kill the monster and save the maiden.

I wiped the snot off onto my wrist, snuffed up, pulled my head back, looked into True Shot's swooped rhinestone mirrors.

True Shot's red bandanna. Short black hair getting longer. True Shot's cinnamon-brown skin.

How do you know? I said.

You told me, True Shot said. You've been telling me that for about five years now.

What monster? I said. What maiden?

I'm leaving tonight, True Shot said. I'll send postcards.

TWILIGHT, *entre chien et loup*, the last time ever I sat in Door of the Dead van. The plastic blue and white Virgin Mary. Brigitte Bardot and her frame of shiny green sequins. The steering wheel. The dashboard. The hole in the floorboard. My red tennis shoes on the floor. The brown vinyl seat cover. The jockey box button. True Shot's hand. His extra-lovely hand. My open palm in his.

Who knows how long we sat there.

I opened the door of Door of the Dead van, put my red tennis shoes onto the pavement, stepped out, closed the door.

The gap between True Shot's two front teeth.

Remember, True Shot said. It's the responsibility of the survivor to tell the story.

Door of the Dead van was hot when I leaned my elbows up against the door.

True Shot, I said, You'll always be a wise old Indian chief. Either that, I said, Or full of horse shit in his pocket.

True Shot reached and pulled out his swooped rhinestone mirrors, handed the mirrors to me.

Here, he said, You'll be needing these.

True Shot's swooped rhinestone mirrors in my open palm.

Won't you want them, I said, On the open road?

Them's Wolf Swamp glasses, True Shot said. I won't be needing Wolf Swamp glasses anymore.

The steady even gaze of True Shot's jade-green eyes.

True Shot! I said. Your eyes!

Only silence for a moment. In all the world, all of East Fifth Street, only silence.

I put True Shot's swooped rhinestone glasses on.

True Shot reached over, touched my throat, touched Charlie.

All Dodges sound the same when you start them up.

Happy trails to you, True Shot said.

Good-bye, Gordito, I said. Until we meet again! I said.

The sun was just setting when True Shot shifted into first, let out the clutch. I stepped back and Door of the Dead was driving west down East Fifth Street. The van was just three doors away when the brake lights went red.

True Shot stuck his head out the window and let loose on a loud *Geronimo!*

In all the world, this distracted globe, I stood on the rectangle of earth where I'd plant the cherry tree, in the light from another incarnation, one hand waving waving at True Shot, the other open palm to buckskin bag. True Shot turned on Third Avenue, waving as he drove up Third. Then he shifted into second, and just then, just like that—abracadabra!— True Shot and Door of the Dead van disappeared behind the dark six-story vertical wall, and the wall was in between, and True Shot and Door of the Dead van were gone.

IN MY APARTMENT, twilight.

All around me, roses.

All my rooms were filled with roses. In the front room red roses, pink roses, white roses, yellow roses, peach-colored roses. In the middle room, roses. In the kitchen, roses. In the bathroom, roses.

Floribunda, multiflora, tea.

Thousands of roses. You couldn't even smell the cat piss for the roses.

Roses on the floor, on the windowsills, on the kitchen sink, on the bathroom sink, in the shower. On top of my ladder, roses. Vases of roses among my Art Family. My Art Family with roses in their hair, in their hands, on their lapels, pinned to their clothes. A dozen long-stemmed red roses on the futon.

And something written on the wall. In black Magic Marker. Above my *Father Knows Best* table, between two vases of roses, written on the red wall.

Ah, my friend, if I were king
Beneath your feet what treasures I would fling.
The stars should be your pearls upon a string,
The world a ruby for your finger ring.
And you should have the Sun and Moon to wear.
If I were king.

The *kings* were crossed out, *queens* written above them.

Then the envelope on the table, *William of Heaven* written on it in Rose's round curly handwriting. I opened the envelope, and the card was van Gogh's self-portait with his ear cut off.

I read the note out loud to my Art Family.

The time has come for all good men to come to the AIDS of their country. All daring and courage, all iron endurance of misfortune, make for a finer, nobler type of manhood. Don't worry about the puppies. Elizabeth has taken them.

Love, Rose
XXXOOO

I ran up the stairs to Rose's room, unlocked the door. No Mona, Mary, and Jack Flash barking barking jumping up onto me. The silver revolver in the kitchen drawer was gone. The two-gallon jar of gasoline was gone. A tourist pamphlet of Saint Patrick's Cathedral was stuck to the kitchen wall with a butcher knife.

A butcher knife in Ronald Reagan's heart.

A butcher knife in Nancy's heart.

Rose was gone.

True Shot was gone.

Ruby dead.

Charlie dead.

Fiona nuts.

SAINT PATRICK'S CATHEDRAL, I said to the cabbie. It's an emergency.

The cabbie was a woman with long blond hair and pumped-up arms, a tattoo of a butterfly on the back of her hand. She pulled the meter down and put the gas pedal to the floor, squealing tires, throwing me back against the seat.

Fourteenth Street was a mess. A Mercedes had back-ended a Volkswagen. Steam and car alarm coming out of the Mercedes and two New Yorkers in the middle of the street yelling at each other. Everybody going to hell.

At 23rd Street, the light turned yellow and I thought the cabbie was going to try and make it, but she stopped. Cars passed in front of us, bumper to bumper, real slow. Some old guy in a Cadillac blocked the box. When the light turned green, the blond cabbie stepped on the gas, then put on the brakes, stopping only inches from the Cadillac.

The cabbie stuck her head out the window.

Fuck you, you greedy Jew dirtbag! she yelled. Get the fuck out of my way!

At 42nd, rush-hour cars jammed up, horns honking. Everywhere you looked, cars cars.

I gave the cabbie a ten-dollar bill, didn't wait for change.

RUNNING. I WAS running up Third Avenue, dodging in and out of people, my red tennis shoes on sidewalk and, when there was no room on the sidewalk, my red tennis shoes on asphalt. When I turned the corner on 50th, I ran smack into a big man, gray at the temples, starched white shirt, dark gray suit, striped red tie, attaché case. Knocked him on his ass.

Avenues are so much longer than streets.

At Park Avenue, the WALK/DON'T WALK was DON'T WALK.

I didn't stop, didn't even look, just made my intention across that damned avenue to the median, brakes and squealing tires, jumped clean over the hood of an Austin Healy convertible, got to the median, didn't stop, didn't even look, ran back into traffic, horns honking, yelling, some old lady pulling her poodle up by the chain—almost choked the fucker— before she jumped aside. I landed safe on the sidewalk.

Cussed cigarettes, kept running. At Madison Avenue, the WALK/ DON'T WALK was WALK, but I kept running running. The sound of my red tennis shoes on the pavement. The evening air hot from a long day of hot. Things beginning to glow with heat from the inside. The sun low. Running through shadows.

The door to Saint Patrick's on Fiftieth Street was locked, so I ran around the corner. In the window of Saks Fifth Avenue, the Art Family was two skinny white women in little black dresses. I ran up the front steps of Saint Patrick's Cathedral, up to the big bronze doors.

My breath in. My breath out.

My open palm on Charlie 2Moons.

My hand on the bronze handle, I pulled.

Locked.

In all the world, this distracted globe, there was no doubt in my mind: Rose was inside that fucking cathedral.

And I was out, locked out of church.

My knees went to hard granite. I was kneeling, breathing hard, in and out. Then I fucking let go, let my body sprawl out like a car wreck. The granite was hot through my khaki shorts, my T-shirt, hot and hard on the back of my arms, the back of my head. Behind my closed eyes, blood pumping red.

WHEN I OPENED my eyes, the front of the cathedral, up the juts and spires and things poking up, up above, the sky was a dark navy blue circus tent hanging from the spires. Two stars on the circus tent.

My body. My aching fucking body.

I rolled over, thought I'd lie that way, but the granite stunk of pigeon shit.

Slid my ass over to the steps. Two steps down, my feet. Took off my red Converse tennis shoes, spread my feet.

Below, Fifth Avenue speeding light, darkness, speeding light. The stoplights green yellow red, green yellow red. WALK/DON'T WALK, WALK/DON'T WALK.

And beyond, out there, past Rockefeller's globe of gold, far enough ahead west it was east, and in someplace not Wolf Swamp, the sun was rising on a new day.

I did what I always do when I don't know what to do: started rolling cigarettes. One for me, one for Saint Pat, one for every sorry mother's son.

The yellow-stained palm of my hand, my yellow-stained index, my yellow-stained thumb, its bitten cuticle, on the match.

The orange snap, the flame crisp at the paper, and the smoke in my mouth, smoke around my teeth and tongue, down my throat, down deep inside.

My breath in.

Each cigarette, every inhale deep to the top of my lung, on the left, the place where I needed to suck smoke in, where I needed it to hurt, the burn. Down in there faraway inside, already dead.

From around my neck, I took the buckskin strand, held the bag, the blue-beaded horizontal, the red-beaded vertical. Touched the beads. Prayed Charlie's buckskin bag like the rosary.

Sorrowful mysteries, I prayed for all that was lost, locked up, taken away.

I prayed for when my body knew hope. When I'd live a whole day just on Charlie's smile. When sunlight on June grass was enough.

I prayed to come back into my body again. Make it a place where I could stay.

THERE WAS ONE day, Charlie on ayaHuaska, Bobbie and I on Chub, we played Going Slack down to Spring Creek. But this day instead of going to the swimming hole, where the water was deep and the creek made a turn, ayaHuaska and Chub headed upstream, to the source of Spring Creek, a little waterfall coming out of the plateau.

It was green all around where the spring came out, and watercress was growing on the water. We tied the horses up where there was some grass, and Bobbie and Charlie and I took off our shoes and rolled up our pant legs and waded through the water, on the rocks the clear water was running over. The sound of the water rolling over the rocks was nice in our ears. There was a wind, too, Idaho gusts that whipped around. The water was so cold I had to keep getting out to stand on the side of the creek in a sunny spot.

The waters of the spring ran into two other springs at this one place, and the three springs, especially in springtime, coming together, made enough water to look like a river. The rocks there just underwater were red with white stripes in them, and the sun shining into the water onto the red rocks made the water look like there was blood in the water.

Bobbie and Charlie and I sat down in the sun, right next to the river, in a place where the earth goes down and the water goes down with it and the water makes a wonderful sound and you almost have to shout.

Charlie lay down on the grass, picked up a stem of grass, put the stem of grass in his mouth.

Bobbie went off to sit alone. Charlie and I didn't think much about it. She was older and bored with us a lot. But for some reason that day, I went over and sat down next to Bobbie. She was looking out at the water, the sun shining low into those sad eyes she had. I tried to say some things to her—about the day or the water or something.

The day was one of those perfect days in spring in Idaho, a green not even green yet, too lime for green. Everything too lime green and the bloody river catching the sunlight. From where Bobbie and I were sitting, all we could see was sunlight, shrub trees, rolling earth, and river.

Why are you always so sad? I asked.

Bobbie spit grass juice, pulled out another stem of grass, chewed. She looked like she was thinking. She scratched a mosquito bite on her leg, and made it bleed.

Bobbie said, The river is going by and the river is beautiful and the day is quiet and warm and green and everything is going by. I can't make the river stop or the day stop and I can't make myself stop. And I am here by the river and I could jump in, but the river would still flow on and I wouldn't be the river, I would still be me.

WHO KNOWS HOW long I sat on the steps of Saint Patrick's?

I'm still sitting there.

But it's not the truth.

I sat there praying on Charlie's bag, waiting for sunrise. Until the big bronze doors of Saint Patrick's Cathedral opened at sunrise.

But I didn't have to wait that long.

First it was the sound of the doors, the heavy high-pitched sound of the hinges. My elbows were on my knees, my head was down, and my eyes came open quick. But I didn't move.

My eyes on my hands, then my eyes through the space under my right armpit.

In all the world, through the triangle my elbow made to my knee, just past my T-shirt sleeve, across granite, in the doorway of the cathedral stood Rose and some bishop guy.

Cardinal O'Henry.

It's the truth.

Rose in drag as a priest.

Just as my eyes saw, a wind came up to them, their cassocks the sound of sails.

The cardinal was a big man, extra-lovely, but short next to Rose. He was wearing a black cassock with red buttons down the front, and a black cape that came down to his elbows. Around his big belly was a tied red sash hanging down one side. A gold cross on a gold chain around his neck.

Duct tape over his mouth.

Rose's silver revolver at his ear.

My body did all those things people describe when shit happens, and before I knew it I was rolling through somersaults and cartwheels, and when I jumped to my feet, just like that, I was standing right in front of Rose, up close.

Rose was gray under black, his lips chapped, the whites of his eyes yellow and red. Sweat rolled off Rose's head over the purple bumps. He smelled of wet wool, and his white Roman collar was brown and yellow.

Backpack straps cut into his shoulders.

The gap between his two front teeth, Rose's smile.

Rose? I said. Rose, are you all right?

Rose's free hand wiped the sweat from his forehead, wiped his face. No clack-clack of bracelets.

Oh, blessed, blessed night, Rose said, *I am afeared being in night, all this is but a dream, too flattering-sweet to be substantial.*

Rose, I said, Please don't do this.

Rose's laugh was a hard cough, the mucus inside him. Rose bumped his hip against the cardinal's, laughed again so hard his chest sunk in.

Too late, Rose said. We're getting married in the morning.

The cardinal's face was so red his whole head was glowing. His twenty-seven years in the navy was in his eyes, James Bond, searching around for escape. His hair was messed up. He'd lost his little hat. Only one lens in his plastic glasses. A little throat hair just above where the red-covered buttons of his cassock were undone. The red satin sash tied at the hip into a big red bow.

Cardinal O'Henry? I said. Are you him?

The cardinal's wide-eyed steel blue into my eyes.

In the flesh, Rose said.

Sucking snorting sounds through the cardinal's nose. His eyes open wider. Deep inside his eyes, fear.

Rose, I said, The cardinal can't breathe very well, I said, With that duct tape over his mouth.

He can breathe all right, Rose said. The cardinal has a bit of a temper, Rose said. A real holy terror.

He's turning purple, I said.

Wait till he has AIDS, Rose said, And he's in a respirator, he won't be able to breathe at all.

Rose, I said, Let's go home and you and me can lie down in the Joey Heatherton bed, what do you say?

Rose ran his tongue along his chapped lips, let his head drop down and at the same time took a long deep breath. Rose raised his chin up as he spoke.

If the tides were turned, Rose said, This asshole would have you be-headed by noon. I'm dying here, Rose said. This is the end of my life. And you're not going to fuck it up, Rose said.

Rose pulled the silver revolver away from the cardinal's ear, turned the barrel, pointed the silver revolver straight between my eyes, then kept the barrel going around to the side of his own head, pushed the barrel hard against his skin, squeezed on the trigger.

Now get the fuck out of here! Rose said.

Only silence, in all the world, at Saint Patrick's Cathedral's open doors, only silence.

Dead silence.

Don't fight me on this one, Rose said.

Behind Rose, through the open brass doors, the dark vaulted hall of the nave, the Gothic pillars, the stained-glass windows.

My God, Rose, I said. No, I won't fight you. As long as we get to go home.

Promise! Rose said.

I promise, I said.

Then get me the handcuffs, Rose said. They're in the backpack.

My mother's nerves.

The handcuffs were in the side pocket of Rose's backpack. I gave them to Rose. Just like that, Rose handcuffed one cuff around the cardinal's wrist, the other cuff to the bronze door handle.

The cardinal pulled his hand against the swinging door.

The cardinal's wide-eyed steel blue into my eyes.

Rose was right. Another time, another place, this man would have me burned at the stake.

Rose bowed deeply to the cardinal.

Thank you, My Eminent Opponent, Rose said, For giving me this great opportunity.

Rose slung his backpack over his shoulder.

We're going to leave you now, Rose said, But we're not going far—just down the steps for a bit. And don't forget, Rose said, I still have the revolver and you don't. And I still want to shoot your ass.

The WALK changed to DON'T WALK on Fifth Avenue.

Behind us, the cardinal was a darkness inside a shadow.

Rose was a lump that sat down heavy onto the steps just where I'd been sitting. His combat boot kicked at the pile of cigarette butts.

Looks like somebody's been smoking here, Rose said. How long you been waiting?

Shouldn't we get out of here? I said.

Nah! Rose said, We're as safe as Bette Midler in the baths.

Somebody's bound to see him, Rose, I said. The cardinal could start waving with his free hand.

Rose's head was hanging between his knees.

Who? Rose said.

There was no dawn in the dark sky yet. The night was a cool summer night. You could see a few stars.

In all the world Rose and I sat there on the stoop of Saint Patrick's, staring way up past the top of Rockefeller Center, to the stars in the sky.

No traffic. Silence. The silence just before the sun rises. *Entre loup et chien.*

Rose reached in his backpack, pulled out a bottle of Courvoisier VSOP and a plastic snifter.

I left the Baccarat at home, Rose said.

Rose handed me the plastic snifter, pulled the cork on the VSOP, poured two fingers into the snifter.

A toast, Rose said, To Shy Hunters! Rose said. And to the unrelenting darkness of their city!

Rose's hand in mine, together we raised the plastic glass to the darkness that was New York on the other side of Fifth Avenue.

Here's to the City of Shy Hunters! Rose said.

To the City of Shy Hunters! I said.

Rose drank first.

Then me.

Rose's shaky hand poured two more fingers of VSOP.

I rolled cigarettes, one for Rose, one for me.

Rose was dripping sweat, so I put both cigarettes in my mouth, lit one for Rose, one for me. Put Rose's cigarette between his lips.

Rose inhaled deep, exhaled. Rose's cats-fucking laugh bouncing off Saint Patrick's, off Rockefeller Center, off Saks Fifth Avenue, bouncing off horizontals and verticals all around the city.

Why wish for the stars when we have the moon? Rose said.

What? I said.

Rose coughed and coughed.

Oh, never mind, Rose said. That's why I love you so much!

I love you too, Rose, I said. I hope I haven't betrayed you.

Rose's beautiful black eyes yellow and red and full of tears.

Was it as good for you, Rose said, As it was for me?

Rose's cats-fucking laugh bouncing off the buildings, louder and louder. Wasn't long and the whole city was just Rose's cats-fucking laugh.

Rose put his hand open palm on my open palm, lifted my hand up with his. He shook our hands back and forth, back and forth, the way you do when you're the champions.

Only in New York City, Rose said, Would I meet the likes of you, dear William of Heaven. To Manhattan! Rose said.

To Wolf Swamp! I said.

To the city, Rose said, Who daily sells its soul for an image of itself!

To Harlequin, I said, And the city of fools!

Rose reached in his backpack, pulled out a bottle of pills, emptied the blue pills into his Sahara Desert palm.

Valium? I said.

Morphine, Rose said.

Where'd you get morphine? I said.

Never you mind! Rose said. A girl has to have some secrets.

You going to share? I said.

No no Yoko Ono, Rose said.

Rose lifted his Sahara Desert palm, poured all the pills into his mouth.

Jesus, Rose, I said, Isn't that too much?

Nothing's too much, Rose said.

Why you doing morphine? I said.

Because I'm a chicken-shit asshole, Rose said.

What? I said.

Just shut up and pour me some more brandy, Rose said.

I emptied the VSOP into Rose's glass.

L'amour de la bouteille! Rose said. The last drop, Rose said.

Rose tried to stand but couldn't, so I stood up and Rose took my hand.

Get me my backpack, would you? Rose said. Be careful!

The backpack was heavy.

I got to piss, Rose said. Help me back to the doors.

Rose put his arm over my shoulder. I put my arm around his waist, and we walked that way, back to the bronze doors.

Rose's hand was shaking so much he couldn't undo the cassock buttons, so I undid them. Had to pull up all the cotton robes. Rose pissed on the opposite side of the cardinal, into the corner where the bronze door met granite and cement. A long line of piss, a little yellow river just south of the Courvoisier bottle and the snifters, flowing down the steps.

Ocean is big because ocean is lower than rivers.

The darkness across the doorway was purple, silent.

YOU'RE GOING THIS way and then shit happens and then you're going that way.

There was a handcuff click sound and then Rose took my hand. His hand was so hot.

Rose's other hand was handcuffed to the other bronze door.

Rose? I said.

Rose put the handcuff key in his mouth, swallowed the key.

More handcuffs? I said. Rose? You said we were going home.

Rose pulled his top lip under his bottom lip. His chin and his lips were moving in a way I'd never seen. Rose's jaw was up and down, up and down, teeth against teeth.

Look who's stuttering now, Rose said.

This, Rose said, Is our final chapter. Now listen to me!

I pulled Rose away from the door, shook him by the shoulders.

Fuck final chapter! I said. Unlock that shit! Come on! Let's go home!

Rose took my chin in his hand, held my chin up, kissed me hot and wet and full and fast. He leaned heavy against the bronze doors, then bent over slow, pulled the jug of gasoline out of his backpack.

Only silence. In all the world, in all of Manhattan, only silence.

Dead silence.

I couldn't feel my arms, my legs. God in heaven! I said.

Exactly, Rose said. I've strut and fret my fifteen minutes. Now it's time to exit stage left, Rose said. Something dramatic, with a bang, a big fucking bang! No whimpers here!

Time to say good-bye, Rose said.

I grabbed for the bottle of gasoline.

No! I said. You can't do this!

Rose's black eyes, ebony stones rolled smooth, went deep into my eyes. His Sahara Desert palm grasped the bottle.

The lucid compulsion to act polemically.

This is my death, Will, Rose said. Capisce?

My breath in. My breath out.

My open palm onto the beaded blue road, the beaded red.

My feet walked backward to where the steps started.

Thank you, Rose said.

I put my arms out, hands palms up at Rose.

Rose, I said, If you're going to do what I think you're going to do with that gasoline, you're just another black queer scapegoat!

You said, I said, That on TV black people never make it to the next episode. Rose! I said. What about the next episode?

Read up on the Cambodian monks who self-immolated, Rose said. There's no victim here! This is my final act as a Shy Hunter, Rose said. A Shy Hunter always chooses life until he chooses death.

Rose unscrewed the lid to the gallon of gasoline.

Then: Rose, I said, Who will anoint your body?

So strange just then, Rose's laugh coming out of him.

Ah! My dear dear William of Heaven, Rose said, Thou hast already anointed me. But to make sure, Rose said, Bring your body back over here for a minute.

Eleven steps back, over the yellow river of piss, back to Rose. I put my palm out and touched Rose's face. His prizefighter bump, his eight-ball cheeks, the clitoris bump between his eyes, his lips, the lines from his nose wings to the corner of his mouth, his keep-your-chin-up chin, his shiny bald head.

We'll perform a sacrament, Rose said. Extreme Unction, the Last Rites. We'll anoint the body *before* it dies, Rose said.

Reach down inside your pants, Rose said. Touch your cock, Rose said.

Rose, I said.

Reach! Rose said.

I reached down in my pants, touched my cock.

The end of it, Rose said. Touch the end, the piss slit.

I touched the end of my cock, the piss slit.

It's wet, isn't it? Rose said.

Yes, I said.

Now draw your hand across your asshole, Rose said, and anoint me, Rose said.

I pulled my two fingers across my piss slit, gathered the moisture there, then up through my crack, across my butt hole. I brought my fingers out, brought my fingers to Rose's forehead, made a vertical and a horizontal on Rose's forehead, on his lips, on his heart.

The top of the head too, Rose said.

A vertical and a horizontal on top of Rose's head.

And at the navel, Rose said.

I reached in, lifted the white cotton robes, made a vertical and a horizontal on Rose's belly button.

And the cock, Rose said.

Rose's cock, the 2001 monolith hard.

Wow! I said. What a piece of work is man!

And *that's* after a pound of morphine, Rose said. Death be not proud! There's so much hope in a hard-on.

A vertical and a horizontal on Rose's extra-lovely cock.

Now my glistening perineum, Rose said.

Your glistening what? I said.

Between my asshole and my balls, Rose said. The root chakra.

A vertical and a horizontal on Rose's glistening perineum.

Rose's silver revolver was in Rose's Sahara Desert palm.

Here, Rose said. You're going to need this.

I am? I said.

You are, Rose said.

Rose's silver revolver in my hand again, so heavy, slick, shiny.

Then Rose's lips at my ear:

> *Doubt thou the stars are fire;*
> *Doubt that the sun doth move;*
> *Doubt truth to be a liar;*
> *But never doubt I love.*

Rose placed his palm against my heart, a steady push away. My feet walked back to where the steps began. My foot hit the Courvoisier bottle, and the bottle rolled down the steps of Saint Patrick's. Broke on the third step.

Turn around now, Rose said, And keep going. And put the revolver in your pocket.

I stared at the silver revolver, put the silver revolver in my front pocket.

That a forty-five you holding, Rose said, Or are you just glad to see me?

Rose, I said.

Turn around! Rose said. Get your ass out of Dodge!

I was just over the yellow river of piss, just about to the steps when Rose said, Will?

I turned around.

Got a match? Rose said.

Language my second language.

In my back pocket, Fish Bar matches.

I pitched the blue pack of matches, an arch through the night air, into Rose's free hand, palm up.

Thank you, Rose said.

Now whatever you do, don't look back! Rose said. Or you'll turn into a pillar of salt.

Rose's chin up up, his eyes rolled back in his head, Saint Theresa Gone to Heaven.

My feet were soldiers, new-shoe stiff, about-face.

The splash of gas.

Left, right, left, right, my red Converse tennis shoes walked down Saint Patrick's steps.

The unmistakable sound: the match.

The cardinal a raven's scream, high-pitched, off, wrong, horrible, ripping the duct tape.

My breath in. My breath out.

Just like that, I turned slow, like an old snake in the sun. In my ears, the air imploded. In front of my eyes, a brilliance.

The touch of the match covered Rose's cassock and roman collar like a blue flame ghost.

A big bang, a big fucking bang.

The scream from Rose from another incarnation. Wild, finally home. Finally free.

The scream we all live for.

Rose's lips, the inside color of his lips on fire, his shiny head, his ears, Rose's extra-lovely Sahara Desert palms on fire. His eight-ball cheeks, the prizefighter bump of his nose, the black serpents in Rose's eyes on fire.

Rose's free hand went up. Perhaps it was his final good-bye, but to me it looked like a fist.

Inside Rose, there was a crumbling down and back, like he'd leaned up against the fire, and a far greater fuchsia flame burst up, high sparks into the great Manhattan, into the greater dark sky.

Tiny illuminations in the dark.

The cardinal had the bronze door pulled open all the way. He was standing behind the door. The silver cuff hooked to the handle was all you could see.

Another crumbling and Rose was on his knees.

Rose was only fire now.

And smoke. Billows of fuchsia smoke.

The only sound was flames—and something else.

The muffled whimper from the tiny Catholic heart in the darkness behind the bronze door.

AT 50TH STREET, the WALK/DON'T WALK was WALK. I didn't look back, just walked. In Saks Fifth Avenue, the two skinny Art Family women in the little black dresses held their hands over their eyes.

In all the world, this distracted globe, policing my body, new-shoe stiff, my heart, the broken pieces scratching against my chest, my red Converse tennis shoes step by step, all the way down Fifth Avenue, along the windows of Saks, in each window, each of the Art Family people inside there, the men in tuxedos, the men in sports clothes, the women in navy blue suits and hats with veils, the woman in the long shiny red evening gown, every one of them, weeping.

Weeping.

The gnashing of teeth.

Weeping.

CHAPTER
TWENTY-EIGHT

A nything can happen, now that everything has.

Who knows how long everything happened after Rose died: three weeks, three years, three days.

On the evening news, Channel 7 had a special about a bum who'd been set afire by a gang of punks on the steps of Saint Patrick's Cathedral.

The black woman newscaster, holding the microphone with TV-7 on it, said, So if you're going to Saint Patrick's Cathedral you must use the side entrances.

Behind her was Saint Patrick's Cathedral. There was a big white tent in front of the bronze doors.

The headline in the *Daily News* was BUM BURNED.

The headline in the *New York Post* was ST. PAT'S INFERNO.

I shaved my head and mustache. Got a heart tattooed over my heart, a red heart, with a black circle around the heart. Across the top of the heart, an arc of black Magic Marker words, *William of Heaven*. I got my queer ear and my beer ear pierced. Gold loops.

Sleep was something I forgot how to do. Eating something I forgot too.

My Art Family and I stayed up all night, most nights, talking talking, drinking coffee, smoking cigarettes, drinking beers, tequila, Courvoisier VSOP, toking Rose's rabbit turds in the lovely erect pink penis, listening to WBLS at the end of the dial.

One night, I stood in the middle of my Art Family, and my Art Family held hands around me like in the hippie days trust-falling, and we sang "Slow Poke" or "My Buddy," or harmonized on the "Idaho State Song" or "Song of Bernadette" or "Famous Blue Raincoat" or "America the Beautiful."

We started writing on the red walls with Rose's black Magic Marker: *Amor fati. Asobase kotoba. Complete presence. Wolf Swamp. Crossover. Shy Hunters. Vertical incest. Horizontal incest. Hero. Monster. Savage* beast. A fuck-you kind of motherfucker joy. Tiny Catholic heart. Antigone. Polynices. The putrefaction of the flesh. The joke was on the white man. New York's only Irish Catholic homosexual. James Joyce's idiot savant daughter fucked a truck driver. Vin et Vous. Fuck hope. Sexy Totale. YUFAs. Even myself, I am just here, isn't it? Green Date. Fools and pharisees. To admit ignorance is the highest knowledge. Shit happens. The red road. The blue road. Noam Chomsky. Tony and Tina. Savoir faire. Postured disregard. Now here. Nowhere. Autumn Sonata. Stranded Beings Searching for God. The three Polaroids. Self-immolated Cambodian monks. The map of the Known Universe. Divide and conquer. Travel mode's the key. All daring and courage, all iron endurance of misfortune, make for a finer, nobler type of manhood. In this distracted globe. Hell of a fix. Up Shit Creek. In a world of hurt. Complete acceptance of whatever the Divine sets in your path. The lucid compulsion to act polemically. The space in between. Gordito. Lletre ferit. Policing my body. New-shoe stiff. The hope of theater to lay bare the human heart. The rule is to have some rules. The Badland Boys. Perfect, just perfect. Chaos is unrelenting brightness. If wishes were horses then beggars would ride. The only way out is in. Harlequin is the fool who knows he is hiding. Performance art is a man dancing alone in his room. Make it aware, make art out of it. Trickle down. Ronald Reagan and Nancy. No no Yoko Ono. Solitary illuminations in the night. Horrific whisper. Lips at my ear. Responsibility of the survivor to tell the story. Swooped rhinestone mirrors. With every gift there is a sacrifice. Never touch me. It's all drag. Never call Elizabeth Taylor Liz. Law of the jungle. Vicious Totalitarian Assholes 'R' Us. A talent for reality. Not on the premises. Revelation the result of covering up. I can fuck you blind and keep it simple. Try me. Scared stallion. Exactly right perfect person. WALK/DON'T WALK. Wounded Male belly dance. The Song of Bernadette. Extra Strength Tylenol. The cure.

THE NEXT DAY, the headline in *The New York Times* was:

CARDINAL O'HENRY TAKES LEAVE OF ABSENCE.
WILL WORK IN UNDISCLOSED HOMELESS CHARITY.

The first two weeks, I was able to go to work, but not much more than that. I started getting afraid of the ironing board and the iron, so for those two weeks I bought myself a new white shirt every day I worked, and finally had to buy two more pairs of black pants. I was afraid of the '53 DeSoto too. I would stand in front of the '53 DeSoto, shaking shaking, my hand too afraid to reach out and take the handle, and at the same time I was crying because I knew it was stupid to be afraid of a refrigerator. I had to start drinking my beer warm.

The shower too, I was afraid of the shower. Washed my face and hair, sponged off my pits and butt crack and crotch at the kitchen sink. But I couldn't step into the shower.

Forget about elevators.

The full-length mirror in the bathroom screwed to the door that whanged out my body in bulges, I hung my blue towel over.

The only other place, besides my apartment, where I felt safe at all was on the green bench near Ruby's Home Sweet Home in Dog Shit Park.

Not enough air. My breath in, my breath out could not bring in enough air. A high ringing of bees in my right ear. The strange sense of an otherness about me. Even myself, there was some other self of me hanging on my bones. Something about myself I'd never recognized before that was with me, that was on the objects of my world, on my body, the way after a hot shower fog gets on the mirror.

Rose's apartment was too too too much. But sometimes I'd go up there and turn on Maria Callas's *Norma* real loud and touch his brass coffee table from Kenya, the purple-velvet overstuffed chair, the blonde-fainting couch, the Randolph Scott lunch box, the Dwight D. Eisenhower ashtray, his red lava lamp, Joey Heatherton bed; touch Buddha; touch the fuchsia bathtub and sink, the fuchsia walls; touch the photographs of Elizabeth Taylor. Elizabeth Taylor as Cleopatra in the deco frame I gave Rose. The Italian crystal chandelabra.

The E.T.-phone-home guy got married. Across the courtyard, one night there was a party, and I stood in the dark and watched the E.T.-phone-home guy in a tux and a woman in a white dress and veil and a bunch of white guys and white chicks drink and dance all night. Just before it got light, E.T.-phone-home guy lay down on the couch. In the rose-colored light, with just his starched white tuxedo shirt on, he spread his legs and, still in her veil, his bride put his cock in her mouth. The up and down, up and down, of the white veil, his hand milky white against the white of the veil, the black hairs on the back of his hand, his gold watch. His argyle socks, the garters on his calves, his calves around his bride, his scream, the scream we all live for, a tiny sound in the big Manhattan dawn.

Mrs. Lupino died of heart failure. She was in her apartment with her cats for four days before they found her. I smelled her death but thought

I just needed a bath. The morning they hauled the dishonored putrefaction of her flesh out of 205 East Fifth Street, there was a knock on my door. I opened my door and it was Ellen's Uncle David's secretary in a blue outfit with matching espadrilles, red frizzy hair, and half-glasses that hung around her neck by a strand of pearls. All I was wearing was my underwear. She didn't even blink. She asked me why I had never reported to the office that Mrs. Lupino had twenty-seven cats.

I started at her blue-espadrilled feet and looked up, looked back down again, both times stopping my eyes just below her middle.

New York drop-dead fuck-you.

Speak up, honey! I said. Can't hear you!

I *said*, she said, Why did you not report to the management office that Mrs. Lupino had twenty-seven cats?

I pulled the front of my underwear down.

She looked at my cock, then back up at me.

It's a cowboy dick, I said. Suck on it.

Slammed the door.

MY LAST DAYS at Café Cauchemar just about everybody was new. Daniel, the boss's brother, was on vacation, and Davey Dearest was in the hospital, and Walter was in the hospital, and Mack Dickson was in Florida on some sort of shoot. Nobody knew anything about Joanie.

I kept my head down, did my job. Hardly spoke to anybody but my customers. I walked home after work, never took the subway, couldn't bear it. I was afraid of cabs, so I walked. Didn't care if it was WALK or DON'T WALK; I just put one foot in front of the other. Everybody else had to move.

I was dead and everybody else was too.

THE FIRST POSTCARD from True Shot was from somewhere in Pennsylvania. A photo of the Lazy Dutchman Motel on the card, the big neon sign LAZY DUTCHMAN red-white-and-blue, the kind of one-story white wood-framed U-shaped motel where you park your car in front of your room.

True Shot's handwriting was shaky like his eyes had been and all the sentences sloped down:

Me and Plastic Virgin Mary and Brigitte Bardot are moving forward into the unknown disgracefully. Door of the Dead van is eating a little

oil but otherwise doing fine. Had to disconnect the heater altogether.
My feet were melting. Travel mode's the key!

Love, Peter Morales

The second postcard was from Peoria, Illinois. A photo of a bunch of high-rises alongside a dirty river. WELCOME TO PEORIA in red letters. True Shot wrote:

It'll never play here. Travel mode's the key!

Love, Peter Morales

The third postcard was from Wall Drug in South Dakota. A big green dinosaur.

It is this way. Had me a Green Date with this here Green Dinosaur.
Travel mode's the key!

Love, Peter Morales

THE SECOND MONDAY, when I went to work, Chef Som Chai asked me back into the kitchen. With his chef's hat on, he was as tall as me. He was cutting lamb shanks with a meat cleaver. Blood all over on his apron.

The chef slammed the meat cleaver into the butcher table. He wiped his hands off on his apron. The kitchen was loud and bright and full as ever, but when I looked around, no one was working, everyone in the kitchen was looking at the chef and me.

Chef Som Chai's breath in. His breath out.

So sorry to tell you, Chef Som Chai said, But I must tell you. Walter the waiter has died. AIDS, Chef Som Chai said.

The next Wednesday, in the employees' dressing room, when I was taking off my Levi's, the Kung Fu salad guy came in the door, walked up to me, took off his white cap, and put his hand on my shoulder.

So sorry to tell you, Kung Fu salad guy said, But I must tell you. Davey Dearest died last night.

The next Monday, the chef waited until after work. I was sitting with my Heineken, where Fiona'd always sat with her Southern Comfort two rocks, on the banquette right under the Sistine Chapel God, when Chef Som Chai set the Flower Bottle into the ice bucket and set the ice bucket next to me. He sat down and Darin, one of the new waiters, opened the bottle for us.

Such hard times, Chef Som Chai said, So much death. We learn many things in hard times.

The chef and I clinked glasses to learning new things in hard times.

So sorry to tell you, Chef Som Chai said, But I must tell you. Daniel, the boss's brother, was not on vacation, and Mack Dickson was not in Florida on a shoot. Unfortunately, the chef said, Both of them died yesterday. Same day, different hospitals.

Where's Joanie? I asked.

Dead, the chef said, She shot herself.

Mack Dickson's memorial service was on Staten Island in a white house with a wide porch. The porch roof was painted swimming-pool-blue. A wisteria growing on the porch.

His mother and father were old, old-country old, all in black. Big old black shoes. They sat on folding chairs, holding hands.

On the Dicksons' mantel, next to Christ hanging on a horizontal vertical, surrounded with carnations and roses, was a photo of the three of them: Mack Dickson, Walter, Davey Dearest. Three young men in soccer drag, their arms about each other, male friends, mates, healthy young Americans.

Such a small photograph. Such a large room.

A HOT AND humid day in August, sitting on my safe green bench next to Ruby's Home Sweet Home.

When I closed my eyes what I saw was red. In the red was another pair of eyes looking at me, my own eyes looking at me that I was looking back into. I was holding one hand tight around the buckskin bag around my neck, my other hand, palm cool against Dr. Brown's Celery Soda, in all the world August in New York, only criminals left in New York City in August. In Dog Shit Park, next to my green bench, just looking back at the other me looking at me.

Heat rash. I reached down and scratched my balls.

The sound of her knees against the plastic as she walked, the plastic sliding against the sidewalk. I opened my eyes.

Standing in front of me was Umbrella Red Shower Curtain.

Green Date on the green bench? Fiona said.

Fiona? I said. Where have you been? I said.

William of Heaven, Fiona said, I knew I'd run into you.

You did? I said.

My inner voice, Fiona said.

I jumped up, ran over to Umbrella Red Shower Curtain, ripped open the shower curtain.

Jesus! Fiona yelled.

The Sacred Heart himself! I yelled. Where the fuck have you been? I've been looking all over for you! Why did you fucking leave last time? You promised you'd stay and wait for me!

I tossed what was left in my can of Dr. Brown's Celery Soda into Fiona's face. Fiona's dirty face slick with sweat and Celery Soda.

Just like that, Fiona kneed me big time in my heat-rash balls.

My knees immediately down onto hot cement.

You fucking fool! Fiona yelled. I had to go! It wasn't safe here! The police, you know, and the war and all.

Bent over, kneeling, holding on to my balls.

And the FBI and the CIA, I said.

Go fuck yourself! Fiona yelled.

No, fuck you! I yelled. You and your fucking Famous Blue Raincoat!

No, fuck you! Fiona yelled.

Jesus! I yelled. A woman will never know how it feels to get kicked in the balls!

True friends, Fiona yelled, Stick by one another through thick and thin!

True friends, I yelled, Tell fucking true friends when they're acting like complete fucking idiots!

I'm not a fucking idiot! Fiona yelled. You're the idiot! Can't you see what's going on here?

Fort Detrick, Maryland, Fiona yelled, The Center for Biological Warfare—as far back as 1968, the CBW has been studying Vervet Monkey Disease, the disease that caused seven deaths in Germany. Infected material was sent to four laboratories in the USA and one each in Germany, Panama, South Africa, Uganda, and the USSR.

You're nothing but a fucking hick, Fiona yelled, And too fucking gullible to fucking comprehend this whole disease has been manufactured. Can't you see? Fiona said. I *know* I'm walking around under an umbrella surrounded by a shower curtain. I *know* I'm lost in a game called Walk/Don't Walk. Believe me, I'd much rather be watching this on TV. But I'm not! It's here! It's now! And it's me!

And how dare you not trust me? Fiona yelled. You want mediocrity go back to fucking Poontang, Idaho, man! Goddammit, I know I'm fucking crazy. But the grief and the rage are real! And the disease is real and the war is real! You just mark my fucking words!

Fiona's fist doubled up straight and hit me hard as any man.

On the cement, I wasn't kneeling anymore, I was sprawled, bleeding.

Fiona knelt down beside me, reached into her huge red leather purse. The shower curtain bent up funny. She brought out a roll of toilet paper, wound some around her hand, touched my bleeding lip.

Who knows how long she touched my lip.

Jeez, Fiona, I said, When you going to brush your teeth?

You ain't exactly Mr. Irish Spring, Fiona said.

Fiona smelled her armpit. It's like I want to go back and shower, Fiona said, And put on clean clothes and take the subway to a movie, go shopping, but just as much I'd like to slit my wrists and find the tallest building and jump off.

The piece of toilet paper was blood-soaked, so I reached for the toilet paper roll, ripped off another wad, put the wad of toilet paper to my lip. More blood.

But I stay dirty, Fiona said, And I don't slit my wrists. Showering and suicide are both such impossible acts. I'd like to be Madonna too, Fiona said, But I'm not. Never will be.

Fiona sat up—crinkle plastic sound—leaned her body weight against her hand, her hand on the hot sidewalk. Her dirty cuticles and fingernails.

My open palm on the top of her hand.

And the cure? I said. Are you any closer to finding the exactly right perfect person to give the cure to?

Fiona turned her hand up, open palm into mine.

No, Fiona said, I'm just wandering around and around. The Walk/Don't Walk circle is getting tighter and tighter, though. I always end up back here in Dog Shit Park by late afternoon.

I put my arm around Fiona's shoulder, she put her arm around my waist, and we walked that way, both of us all one thing, umbrella poking me in the head, sliding red plastic along the sidewalk, the plastic sticking to my skin. I sat down on my green bench. Fiona sat down on red plastic and white wolves on my green bench.

Isn't that thing uncomfortable? I said. Doesn't it hurt your head?

It's cool, Fiona said.

She pulled the edges of the plastic away from her legs.

Your neck must be killing you! I said.

Fiona moved her neck side to side.

It's cool, Fiona said.

You're awfully skinny, I said.

New diet, Fiona said.

Daddy's Visa still works, Fiona said, Although Daddy doesn't.

Then: The war, Fiona said. It's close, Fiona said. Any fucking day now.

My arm on the back of my green bench, I pulled my leg up, turned my face to Fiona. We buried Ruby Prestigiacomo under that arborvitae, I said. I nodded at it with my head.

Fiona had to stand up so she could turn around and look.

I always felt something special about that arborvitae, Fiona said. And the elms, the graceful English elms. Aren't they beautiful?

I love those trees, I said. I love you, Fiona, I said. I just want to help, but I don't know how.

Fiona put her hand on my neck, then her open palm on my chin.

Her blue eyes, her filthy white skin.

I know, Fiona said, But I don't know what to tell you what to do.

Fiona, I said, How pregnant are you?

Did I tell you how to dance the Dance of the Wounded Male? Fiona said.

Fiona, I said, How pregnant are you?

Stand up and I'll show you, Fiona said.

Goddammit, I said, Fucking New Yorkers! Listen to me! Read my lips! *How. . . fucking. . . pregnant. . . are. . . you?*

Then: Is the child mine?

Fiona folded her arms in front of her. Her lip curled up into a big blue scar.

It's a maybe, Fiona said. A maybe not. I'm not sure.

What are you going to do? I said. You should see a doctor.

I'm waiting, Fiona said.

For what? I said.

My inner voice, Fiona said.

Oh, shit!

Fiona reached over, grabbed me by the T-shirt at my neck. If she hit me again I was going to hit her back.

Listen up, Fiona said, And listen good! Because this is the last time I'm saying it. This is *my* body. Do you understand?

I understand, I said.

Now, Fiona said. We were talking about the Dance of the Wounded Male.

You were talking about the Dance of the Wounded Male, I said.

Fiona doubled her fist, right hook. I ducked.

You can't hit a pregnant woman.

I held my hands up in front of me, palms out.

The Wounded Male, I said. What's that?

Fiona was standing on the sidewalk the way those Asian kick boxers stand.

You know! Fiona said. At the end, when the exactly right most perfect person appears.

The exactly right most perfect person, I said, Who you give the Extra Strength Tylenol to.

Fiona raised her leg, kicked her kung fu foot out, barely missed my ribs.

Don't fuck with me, Will! Fiona said. I told you. It's not Extra Strength Tylenol, it's only the bottle. The cure is *in* the bottle.

Gamma something or other, I said. A neurotransmitter.

Right, Fiona said.

That you discovered with the doctors at Silver Lake, I said. And Silver Lake is an insane asylum.

Believe me or don't believe me, Fiona said, I could give a flying fuck! In my heart I know it's true.

Do you want to see the movements or don't you? Fiona said.

Can you do the movements with that thing on your head? I said.

Fiona's New York drop-dead fuck-you was back.

So I stood next to Fiona, on the sidewalk in front of my green bench.

The belly dance always tells a story, Fiona said, Revealing truths through discreet gestures.

How was the Wounded Male wounded? I said.

Fiona pushed the red curtains as wide open as they could get.

The Wounded Male entered the underworld, Fiona said. Dionysus was a Wounded Male. He had to fuck himself with a fig bough before the gods would let him enter the underworld. That's his wound.

You learned all this in a belly dance class? I said.

My teacher was queer, Fiona said. A beautiful Greek man named Ajapo. Ajapo was the absolute authority on the belly dance.

And crazy? I said.

Very cool guy, Fiona said. Few who enter the underworld return, and those who return walk with a limp. The limp, Fiona said, Is the first step of the dance we call the belly dance.

Fiona stepped out with her left leg. The leg collapsed under her and she fell a bit. Fiona caught herself, then leaned her body forward, swaying out her hip, swaying and straightening her back with the power of her shoulders, then stepped with her right leg, raising herself to her full height, swaying her hip out, then dragged her right leg next to her left.

Now, Fiona said. Do it with me.

So I stood next to Fiona, on the sidewalk in front of my green bench.

I stepped with my left leg as she stepped out with hers. I let my leg collapse and I fell a bit. Then, as Fiona leaned her body forward, I leaned my body forward, swaying out my hips with hers, swaying and straightening my back with the power of my shoulders; then Fiona stepped with her right leg, and I followed, and we raised ourselves to full height, swaying hips out, then dragged our right legs next to our left.

What do you do with your hands? I said.

Pretend they are swans, Fiona said, Or serpents. Whatever. Just let the arms move because the waist has moved and because you've stepped out and your leg has collapsed.

Fiona and I together swayed our hips, stepped out, moved our arms like swans or serpents.

This is the point, Fiona said, This point here! Fiona nodded her head down at her position.

When everybody starts singing, I said.

Yes, Fiona said. "The Song of Bernadette."

There was a child named Bernadette. Fiona sang. Do you remember the night I sang the song?

Only silence.

That's when the exact right most perfect person will appear, I said.

Yes, Fiona said.

How will you know, I said, This exact right most perfect person?

All I know is it will be dramatic. It will be just so fucking dramatic that I will know, Fiona said.

Fiona, I said, Why don't we go to my apartment and take a shower? I said. I'll fix us some pasta.

Fiona bit her lip. Her breath in. Her breath out.

I can't go in showers, Fiona said. And toasters terrify me, and refigerators. I'm even afraid of my vibrator, for chrissakes, Fiona said.

Only silence.

I'm afraid of my '53 DeSoto, I said, And I'm afraid of the shower too, and elevators, and subways, and cabs, anyplace confining, and people can't get too close to me.

Really? Fiona said. The only place I feel safe is in my shower curtain. I'm going to get over it, Fiona said, In time.

Just come home with me, I said, Lie down on the futon. Or we could go to Fish Bar, I said. There's a great new song on the jukebox. Mercedes Sosa, "Gracias a la Vida."

Will, Fiona said, I can't go inside.

How do you feel about irons and ironing boards? I said.

Not yet, Fiona said. It's just not right, Fiona said. I know it's unbelievable.

The war, Fiona said. Any day now. The Dog Shit Park War.

FIONA'S INNER VOICE wouldn't let her leave the green bench. I bought her a knish and some scalloped-looking potatoes from Odessa and took the knish and potatoes back to the green bench. Fiona was still sitting there. She ate like a farmhand.

She ate like she was eating for two.

We sat there on my green bench holding hands, watching the light *entre chien et loup*. On the corner of Eighth Street and Avenue B, the streetlamp came on, the color from another incarnation. Ruby Prestigiacomo's arborvitae was right behind us.

Then Fiona's inner voice called her back to Walk/Don't Walk.

I went home without her. Took my clothes off, washed my face in the kitchen sink, sponged off my pits, my crack, my balls. I was standing among my naked Art Family.

I hadn't checked my mail for about a week, so I got my keys, walked out into the narrow blue hallway, and under the unrelenting light of the fluorescent halo, I opened up my mailbox. Inside was my Con Ed bill, the rent bill, and a big manila envelope from Peter Morales.

I turned on my reading lamp, set my reading lamp on my *Father Knows Best* table, Rose's poem on the red wall in black Magic Marker just above me. Swiped the dry rose petals off the table. Put down True Shot's manila envelope. Threw the Con Ed and the rent bill in the garbage can.

I pulled up the ladder, sat on the second rung.

Across the courtyard, the E.T.-phone-home guy was phoning home again. Newspapers spread around him on the floor, the phone receiver cradled in his neck, his other hand pumping on his cock.

I rolled another cigarette, lit it, and opened the envelope from True Shot. A photograph fell out of the folded paper.

True Shot was standing in front of a tipi. He was smiling extra lovely with his arm around an old man, an old Indian man, smiling with his arm around Grandfather Alessandro. In front of them—Alessandro's old hand and True Shot's extra-lovely hand—in their hands, the ocelot medicine bundle, Charlie 2Moons's pipe.

True Shot's handwriting was shaky like his eyes had been, and all the sentences sloped down.

I read True Shot's letter out loud to my Art Family.

> *Dear William of Heaven:*
> *So much has happened since I arrived here in Fort Hall. So much it would take a novel to tell you all of it. First off, there ain't no Blackfeet in Blackfoot, Idaho. The Blackfeet are all up in Browning, Montana. Alessandro says we'll take medicine pipe up there next spring on Mother's Day. Then there's Charlie's pipe, which as you can see is safe here with Alessandro. Alessandro says to tell you to come get it anytime you want. And something else, Will. You were Charlie's brother, Will. Your father had an affair with Viv. Charlie's father is your father, Will.*
>
> > *All my love,*
> > *Peter Morales*

> *P.S. Doublewide Viv wants me to tell you a story. It's a Shoshone story and it goes like this: When a woman gives birth, first she births a rabbit. The rabbit runs from the womb, runs here and there, to the river, to the mountain, to the forest. Then when the child is born, the child must follow the path of the rabbit.*
> *Wherever the rabbit goes, we have to go too.*
> *So on your journey, Will, Viv says to watch out for rabbit turds!*

Only silence. My apartment, all of the whole Known Universe, silent. I turned off the light, rolled a cigarette, stood with my Art Family, smoked. Rolled another cigarette, smoked. The mercury-vapor light was dust-storm light from another incarnation and the unrelenting light from Fifth Street Videoland was coming in my windows onto the floor. The cigarette an orange jewel.

The photos:

Mother in her red housedress and Bobbie in pedal pushers and white short-sleeve blouse and me in jeans and a striped T-shirt with suspenders, standing in front of the Residency squinting into the sun.

Father standing in front of his swimming-pool-blue pickup, Levi's leg up, his cowboy boot on the running board, his Stetson cocked back.

Father in his clown suit in front of his swimming-pool-blue horse trailer with his German shepherd Heap Big Chief and Ricky the monkey and Sea Bass the mean goose.

Photos of cowboys steer-wrestling, bulldogging, bronc-riding, bull-riding.

A photo of Father with his buddy Lou Racing in front of the old Tribal Council building.

A photo of Bobbie standing in front of the sexually haunted barn, wearing the black dress.

A photo of Mother—the one of her from her magenta album with the gold edges on the pages—where she was lifting up her skirt and dancing in Saskatchewan when she visited her cousins. She was smiling so much her gums showed.

A photo of Father as a young man. In front of Saint Veronica's Church in Blackfoot, wearing a suit with pleated pants and shined shoes, white shirt and a tie with the pattern of butterflies and dice.

His black hair, his smile.

THAT NIGHT AT Café Cauchemar there was some big to-do with *Les Misérables*, and we were all in the weeds. I had Section Five, which is right in the middle of the restaurant, right under the Sistine Chapel God. It was about eleven o'clock and Andrew, the new maître d'hôtel seated three people at table 33: a heavyset tall man, an American, with wild graying blond hair in a white turtleneck and double-breasted blue blazer with gold buttons; a dark-haired, dark-eyed small-boned woman who looked Italian; and a thin beautifully skinned silver-haired man, maybe Swedish.

The big American man ordered a bottle of Chablis Grand Cru and appetizers for the table—escargots and a dozen bluepoint oysters.

The silver-haired Swedish man was wearing a cornflower-blue suit and a blue silk shirt, the same blue as his eyes. His wife—I guessed—was wearing a sleeveless scoop-neck long black gown. Her voice was deep; she smoked one Marlboro after the other.

I poured the '84 Mugo.

All three of them were laughing laughing as I served the American man his steak frites rare with ketchup and a steak knife, the Italian woman her cassoulet, the Swedish man his steak tartare.

Dessert was fresh fruit compote for the woman, *tarte tartin* for the silver-haired man, deep-fried ice cream for the American. Espresso all around, decaf for the American.

The American guy was talking.

Paris is so clean and beautiful, he said. And Barcelona, so clean and beautiful. And Madrid. But here in New York, garbage strewn across our streets—rats, vermin. We live in fear and filth. Homeless people, beggars are everywhere. You'd think they'd have the courtesy to stay in their own parts of the city.

The moment that after, you're different.

My fist hit the table. The water, the wine in the glasses rippled.

Quiet as only New York can get that fast.

Abracadabra! My fist was a John Wayne punch, a big bang, a big fucking bang, right into the American guy's big mouth.

I don't remember much about this next part.

Big crashes, people yelling. The American guy—chair and all—went flying onto the black and white tiles of Café Cauchemar. Someone, some people, pulled me off the American, ripped my shirt. In no time at all, I was through the swinging red doors and in the kitchen.

I made my way to Chef Som Chai. The chef was sautéeing sole *meunière*. I kissed Chef Som Chai on the cheek, then the other cheek. The chef looked down at the sauce pan. He didn't say anything. He just knew. Kung Fu salad guy gave me the high five. I changed my clothes in the locker room. Put my ball cap on, my Levi's jacket on. Walked out through the dining room, through the front door, the same way I came in.

So long ago.

AT PARADISE GARAGE, the beautiful man behind the red velvet rope winked at me when he lifted the rope and let me in. I winked back, walked up the cement incline you could drive a truck up—blue emergency lights on each side of the ramp, blue light back and forth around and around—I turned right, and walked up some more.

In the crowd, my eyes went right to a woman in a yellow dress. She looked like the cover of a Marvin Gaye album. She was at the bar, dancing with the brass bar pole, pulling against the pole, stretching, pushing her butt out, dancing with herself.

Just her in her body in a moment in her life, such a brave and lovely act it is to let the body celebrate.

Then I was not just kind of dancing off to the side by the speaker like usual. Just like that, my skinny arms, my big butt, nipples poking out my T-shirt too much, my big bare frog-belly-white Idaho legs, my wish my dick was bigger, my mother's nerves—I was walking out alone into the middle of dancing humanity.

Who cares what a bunch of assholes think. I was invited to this party.

Dancing. Not locals kicking up closing time. No ranchburger home sweet home.

In all the world. America's dark basement. Charcoal. Wolf Swamp. Down here in the jungle. In drag as me. Where the heart is. Where you fuck hope. Where you never touch me. Where you be one and get one.

Where the hunter is the prey and paradise is out in the garage.

Horizontal, I am vertical, hula-hula walking like an Egyptian, shoulder bone connected to arm bone, folding in on myself, crossed over, polemical fool, lucid, slow-water circles down the corner drain, dervish, whirling labyrinth, William of Heaven in heaven, another New Yorker gone to hell, broken open, a puddle of blood, cum in the palm of my hand, vasty deep, spilled open, head bone connected to butt bone, round and round, up and down, side to side, back and forth, strong yellow piss, spit. Finally totally too too too out of my fucking mind.

CHAPTER
TWENTY-NINE

The people of Dog Shit Park had built a barricade around the park. Those who lived in Dog Shit Park were inside; everybody else, the rest of New York, especially the police—the Riders—were outside.

Anything you could imagine was set in front of the gates and against the old wrought-iron fences: cardboard, car parts, wood scraps—two-by-fours, two-by-sixes, four-by-fours—plastic tarps, canvas, blankets, shopping carts, old couches, armoires, dressing tables, chests of drawers, kitchen tables, chairs, old wood doors, destruction rubble, an old Dodge Dart, pieces of plywood, sheets of corrugated metal, Sheetrock, pressboard, a huge cornice from a building, bicycle frames, tree limbs.

A barricade seven to ten feet tall all the way around Dog Shit Park. A banner across the front gate facing Avenue A, HOMES FOR THE HOMELESS: FUCK PIGS. FUCK THE RIDERS. FUCK SERGEANT WHITE SUPREMACY.

The first night there was one hell of a party going on inside the barricade. A big bonfire and people yelling and waving banners and chanting, *We want a home! We want a home!*

And there was music—guitars and flutes and saxophones and tambourines and drums—and people singing and dancing. Inside the barricade, Dog Shit Park bacchanalia. Outside, the puritan undertow.

Divide and conquer.

When the horse shit hits the fan, you'll know where to find me.

Fiona Yet was inside the barricade, dancing and singing, twirling. The flames of the bonfire on her red shower curtain made of her a reflected fire, a dancing twirling dervish of fire.

Me outside the church.

All around Dog Shit Park was crawling with cops. Hundreds of cops, maybe a thousand. As many cops outside as homeless people inside.

The first night of the Dog Shit Park War, Fish Bar got held up. Two guys wearing ski masks walked in, held everyone at gunpoint, took the money from the cash register, took money and valuables from all the customers. Precinct Nine half a block away, but not a cop in sight.

The next day, Mayor Ed Koch gave the order.

I was sitting in Life Café, dipping french fries into my coffee, when the Riders came around the corner, four abreast, line after line of big horses galloping galloping—horse sweat, horse hooves on the pavement—from the east on Tenth Street, from the west on Tenth Street, on the sidewalks of Tenth Street, cops on horses, clubs in their hands, clubs raised in the air. Charging ahead of the legions of four, a white stallion. On the white stallion, Sergeant White Supremacy.

Just then a man crossing the avenue dropped his grocery bag and ran across Tenth Street in front of the horses. Sergeant White Supremacy caught up, leaned into the blow, and hit the man in the back of the head. The man screamed and fell, horse hooves all around him, graceful English elms inside the pool of blood on the pavement.

From the south on Avenue C, more horses, more cops.

Riders swinging clubs from the north on Avenue C.

You could hear the horses' hot breath in and out, in and out. People running everywhere. At the sidewalk table next to me, a young black woman with long braids, copper bracelets, copper necklace, and long green jeweled earrings catching light, had been sitting, reading a book, drinking her cappuccino. When she saw the Riders, the woman let her book drop. She stood up and raised her fist.

You motherfuckers! she screamed. You can't do this!

Sergeant White Supremacy reined in his steed, choking the stallion back. The white stallion reared up, and when the horse came back down on all fours, his eyes were somewhere else. Sergeant White Supremacy's left shoulder leaned forward. He clasped the gun at his waist. The woman's crotch was just over from his boot.

There was tape over the name on Sergeant White Supremacy's badge.

Then his boot kicked hard into the woman's crotch. I heard the sound of steel-toed boot to soft flesh. The woman doubled over, her braids hanging down, jewelry clink, sunset light onto the drooping green jewels.

People screaming and shouting. Horses horses everywhere. People running every which way.

Sergeant White Supremacy locked his eyes on me. Smiled.

Some people know it's a horse race and some people don't. I knew it, have always known. Just never thought I'd have a chance.

I smiled back. Gave Sergeant White Supremacy a big wink. Grabbed my crotch, puckered up my lips together, made sucking sounds with my lips.

Sergeant White Supremacy kicked the flanks of the white stallion, and the white stallion started through the tables after me. I dived into the open doors of Life Café, hit the floor, rolled, got up, ran behind the counter, through the screaming people in the kitchen, out the back door, jumped up onto a garbage Dumpster, grabbed the bottom rung of the fire escape, pulled myself up.

On top of the building, I was running west, climbing up, jumping down, on and off buildings. Below me, all along my left side, was Dog Shit Park, the mercury-vapor light, the bonfire light, and the humanity battling the Riders. Through the graceful branching limbs of the English elms, cops banging heads left and right, people screaming, the incredible sound of all those people screaming, the horses, the sound of hardwood blow to bone, knife into flesh, fist to mouth. Gunfire.

Up on the roof, halfway to Avenue A, staring at a brick wall too high to climb, I stopped.

Sergeant White Supremacy was not behind me.

I leaned against the brick wall. My breath in. My breath out. In and out, my heart beating beating.

To the south, just over the cornice, below me, the Dog Shit Park War.

Kick over an old rotten log, and underneath the log, partially submerged, the ground is a thick mass of insects, slugs, crawling things, a living swarm of dishonoring putrescence.

Just over the cornice, below me in Dog Shit Park, in all the world, this distracted globe, the helmeted bugs in blue, the armored shiny beetles on horses, were getting the better of the welfare queens, the humanity.

Just over the cornice below me, framed by the north-east-south-west of Dog Shit Park, framed by the streetlamps, solitary illuminations in the night. Streaks of brown-shit sobs, purple lost lives, black despair, yellow hope, red rage. Humiliation.

Unrelenting light scattering the shadow swarm.

Dividing.

Conquering.

No matter how hard I looked, into speeding light, darkness, speeding light, into the brown-shit purple black yellow red ocher dust-storm rage, no red plastic shower curtain.

No Fiona.

* * *

MY ART FAMILY was huddled together, a Greek chorus of weeping and gnashing of teeth. I held each one of them, kissed them all good-bye, stuck Rose's silver revolver in my pants. The silver revolver was hard and cold next to my cock. Charlie 2Moon's ashes around my neck, my lovely erect pink penis in my pocket.

Entre chien et loup. Between dog and wolf. Twilight.

Lamplight ocher dust-storm light from another incarnation clicking on.

Down from Dog Shit Park, below Houston, the Saint Jude phone booth, receiver hanging down like my limp dick, inside the phone booth painted all over with words.

When all else failed, hell of a fix, things gone haywire, when there was no place left to go, when I was up Shit Creek, in a world of hurt, I walked straight to Ruby Prestigiacomo's Saint Jude phone booth. The direct line to God.

I picked up the receiver. Silence on the other end of the line. The receiver was not attached to the rest of the phone.

Last call.

YOU'RE GOING THIS way and then shit happens and then you're going that way.

In all the world. The moment that after you're different.

One cold round eye, metal against the back of my head. When I turned around, Sergeant White Supremacy was a big pink smiley face. The barrel of his gun now between my eyes.

The horrific whisper: You Italian? Sergeant White Supremacy said.

Hi, Dick, I said.

His smile, his little white teeth.

I'm the survivor, I said.

Little teeth set hard against little teeth, a bigger smile, piggy gums. You're the faggot, he said.

Whiskey and marijuana breath, the smell of his sweat something flinty. Handguns and testosterone.

Put the gun down, Dick, I said. You don't have to use a gun.

Faggot? Sergeant White Supremacy said.

His thin lips, his pink skin, red freckles, his Cardinal O'Henry steel-blue eyes behind those big, almost square, rimless, thick plastic glasses.

Inside his blue eyes, his tiny Catholic heart.

Sergeant White Supremacy pushed the gun barrel hard between my eyes. There was something quick with his arm, like it had a life all its own.

Dogs were barking, lots of dogs, wolves howling, monster roar.

It is this way. You may tell of power, and how power is received only when war happens, only when you are on the battlefield, only when you're ready to fight for your life. Only then are things told—what power has been given, what power you must use.

It is at such a time that power previously hidden enters you. When you stop being who you are and become a warrior.

Pull your pants down, bitch! Sergeant White Supremacy said. And then grab your fucking ankles!

The moment that, after, you're different.

My intention was to do that very thing, to reach down and unbutton the five buttons, let my cutoffs drop, pull down my shorts, but just like that—abracadabra!—something got into my arm, and my arm knocked his weapon away, and my arm reached out and my open palm slapped Sergeant White Supremacy, knocked the square ugly plastic glasses off his face—his poor squinty blue eyes. Then I slapped him again. Then my arm reached down and my hand grasped Rose's silver revolver and pulled the silver revolver out of my pants next to my cock, and then I shot him—the lucid compulsion to act polemically—I shot him, shot Sergeant White Supremacy, shot him between the eyes.

Bracelets clack-clack.

Light from another incarnation.

All at once, just like that—abracadabra!—drops and drops of rain.

Sergeant White Supremacy lay in a bunch of dry weeds and rocks and shiny bits of glass and garbage, and his blue eyes were open and his red hair was thin on top of his head. The bullet hole in his head was a red emergency button, blood was coming out his nose and onto his blue shirt, and when I pulled the tape off his NYPD badge there was his name: White, Sergeant Richard White.

Rain beating down hard on things, beating down the dry weeds, pinging against a garbage can lid, turning the light-brown earth dark.

After some time, who knows how long, I undid my pants and pulled my cock out, policing my body, new-shoe stiff. From the top of the head chakra to bullet hole between the eyes chakra, to Adam's apple throat chakra, to tiny Catholic heart chakra, to big belly chakra, to little dick chakra, to glistening peritoneum, I anointed Sergeant White Supremacy with my strong flow of yellow piss.

The terrible things done to the world by the father.

I paid the devil his due.

The telephone receiver was lying on the ground. I picked up the receiver, cradled the receiver into my shoulder, walked stepping stepping slow toward the stallion. The stallion could smell Chub and ayaHuaska all over me. Talking nice talk to the beautiful white stallion, I took him by the reins and swung my leg over the saddle.

Back in the saddle again.

A western saddle, worn smooth. Leather sounds as my ass settled in.

The stallion's ears were up. My open palm against horse mane.

The white stallion's big live body under me, raring to go.

I tied the reins together, let the reins drop.

Lifted Charlie 2Moons up from my chest. Kissed the blue-beaded horizontals and the red verticals. Held Charlie in my open palm.

Charlie 2Moons and his stories.

My lips against the stallion's ear: Quiet is kept, I whispered. Do not fear. The maiden has shape-shifted into wolf!

Darkness is in its place, I whispered. Order is restored and the universe is safe!

THINGS START WHERE you don't know and end up where you know. When you know is when you ask, How did this start?

How did this start?

With Wolf Swamp, with this city—that's how this started. When I crossed over to New York City, the fuck-you city.

Now everything's different. Now it's been told.

I fucked my sister. I betrayed my brother. Murdered a cop. Killed the monster.

My task was nothing compared to True Shot's, or Rose's, or Fiona's.

True Shot's task was to restore order to the universe.

Rose's task was to make the ultimate sacrifice.

Fiona's task was to find the meaning of life.

Ruby's task to give us all a name.

And now, at sunrise, sitting on a white stallion, my task is easy: Get on the horse and ride out of town.

But it's not the truth.

Fiona would say: Riding out of town was a typical guy thing to do. True Shot would say: It is this way—the cavalry rode out after Wounded Knee. Rose would say: You honkies are all alike, you think the movie's over when the white guy rides off. And Harry: I'm ready for my close-up, Mr. DeMille! Ruby'd be laughing his ass off; I can hear Ruby right now: William of Heaven, what am I going to do with you?

Standing next to Saint Jude phone booth, when all else has failed, up Shit Creek, in a world of hurt, when I've killed a cop, my bad breath into a dead line of NYT&T is the only place left.

Sitting on a stallion, looking for a stallion.

In all the world, even myself I am just here, isn't it?

Everything about the world is brighter, clearer, like the kind of painting that when you first look at it you think it's a photograph the photographer took when the light made the edges of things hard and more real, or the photographer took acid and took a photograph of how he was seeing, but then you step closer and you see the brush strokes, you see how the guy painted a painting to look like a photograph that looks just like the world, only brighter.

I am the Will of Heaven. Why else do we live except to love and remember those we love?

You could call this a prayer. Going Slack is what Charlie and I called it.

If you ride fast enough, let the reins go slack, if you shut your eyes and dream, you can make the warrior's stallion your own and live forever that way, riding free.

RIDING FREE, HORSE hooves against the pavement, the hard heartbeat against the asphalt chest. This city, a grid of the horizontal and the vertical, buildings up to the clouds, buildings down to bedrock, north and south and east and west in between.

Horse hooves bouncing off the six-story red-brick tenements, rain dripping off the cornices from above, the stoops, the long narrow windows, the sidewalks and curbs, past the garbage cans, I am riding free through the ocher dust-storm light from another incarnation. Rain on my face. My breath in, my breath out, in and out, in and out, riding free on a white stallion.

No longer scared.

I go straight into the Hippodrome Stand. My feet are on the saddle, and I say, I'm going to stand up now, so just hang in there with me, please.

My knees push up and then I'm standing up, in the air. I put my arms out horizontal. I feel the way I've always wanted to feel and never knew it. What we live for. It's the way the ocean feels, rolling rolling, or why birds like to fly so much.

I let out a big whoop! and look over at two old men in T-shirts that barely cover their bellies. They're standing in a doorway, passing a brown bag back and forth, talking. Their arms, their hands, every which way, never still. They look up and out at the rain and when I whoop they look at me, at me letting go.

Across Houston—horns honking, cars sliding sideways—from both directions, just like in the movies, brakes squealing, tires screeching, banging crashing yelling, a New York drop-dead fuck-you lot of fuss.

Me and the white stallion are in a flat-out gallop.

A car alarm goes off.

Yet another New Yorker.

At the corner of Second and Avenue C, under the mercury vapor, is a figure all in black with a shopping cart: Black Plastic Woman. There is a smile inside the black plastic shiny dark of her from another incarnation. She is waving.

I do the Crupper Jump for Black Plastic Woman, go into a Double Vault.

Why do we have to stay in the fucking corral? I yell.

There is no corral! she yells.

At the corner of Third Street and Avenue C, the white stallion turns left. Evens east; me and the white stallion are headed west. The rain in the lamplight, onto the pavement and sidewalks—it's raining cats and dogs, lions and wolves. The white stallion gallops past the after-hours club Fiona found that first night, gallops to the corner of Avenue B, into the streetlamp light where Fiona stood so long ago in her little black dress, and sang "Song of Bernadette."

On the side of a building on the corner of Avenue A is a photo of Andy Warhol repeated a hundred times. Across the photos, the black Magic Marker words: *I'm Andy Warhol and I'm dead and you're not.*

Under the Neck; I come around, do an Indian Squat around the horn, lay back, then slide down the side of the white stallion, keeping my feet off the pavement by hanging off my right elbow. With my left hand, I wave at the Hell's Angels standing in front of their bar—elbow elbow, wrist wrist wrist. I'm taking very long, slow steps in the air, so as if to appear to be walking beside the white stallion.

The Hell's Angels are laughing and clapping, hollering to me.

*   *   *

ON THE CORNER of First Avenue, I am back up Hippodrome Standing.
People on their stoops, on the sidewalk, are shouting at me and waving. A cabbie puts on his brakes, skids to a stop. The white stallion
does not shy away. He gallops faster and faster. My arms out horizontal, I am vertical. I go into a Single Vault; my red Converse tennis
shoes splash onto pavement; then I flip myself back up and over into
a Double Vault.

At Second Avenue, the light is flashing yellow, but the white stallion knows, and we go through. Horns honking everywhere.

Just as the light turns red, all at once—abracadabra!—the white stallion leaps totally over a Checker cab, and I reach up and count coup
on the traffic light.

Complete acceptance of whatever the Divine sets in your path.

God is anything that stands in your way.

The lucid compulsion to move him the fuck out of the way.

Fatum.

Whether you fight it, cop an attitude, fuck it, or fall in love with it,
you're still going to die.

We're all just in our bodies for a moment in our life. Such a brave
and lovely act it is to let the body celebrate.

Past the men's shelter, under the garage on the corner of Third and
Bowery, hundreds of black men, brown men, some white men, the trick-
led-down welfare queens in designer jeans, Ronald Reagan's faceless mass
waiting for handouts, are standing, waiting for a chance, for a break, for
a hand up, for a fix, a cigarette, just to be seen, for redemption. Praying
for truth.

When you throw out darkness, I yell, And there is no place for darkness, I yell, The light is unrelenting and darkness is everywhere.

You've got to deliver yourself from your concept of God, I yell.

Those who would hunt a man, I yell, Need to remember that a jungle
also contains those who hunt the hunters.

But it's not the truth.

I ride past the men's shelter, only silence; on all of East Third Street,
only silence.

The men stare up at me: Teddy Roosevelt, white man on a white horse.

One guy—in a red T-shirt with white letters that say YOU CAN'T IMAG-
INE HOW BIG IT IS—steps out into the street and raises his hand,
Sahara Desert palm up and out. Flying by, I slap the open palm of my
hand to his hand, and he yells, Go, girl!

On Bowery, the white stallion knows, and we lean right, almost all the way over, and the white stallion heads upstream.

I do a Reverse Crupper to Backward Stand in the Saddle.

The white stallion turns east on East Fifth Street and this street is odd. Against the traffic.

You get to know the cracks in the sidewalk, the star on the manhole cover, the smell of certain doorjambs, the fountains, the curbs, the WALK/DON'T WALKS, the stoops and garbage cans; you get to know the puddles, the pothole where the city repaired the sewer line.

Past the old service station and the Senior Citizen Housing built in '86, past Mother's Sound Stages and the slobbering Doberman in the window. Past 205 East Fifth Street. On the street where I lived.

Horse hooves clack-clack, I'm riding the Stallion of Love, past the garbage cans, past my windows, my Art Family dressed to the nines, hanging out my windows, all waving cocktails and cigarettes, elbow elbow, wrist wrist wrist. Past Fifth Street Videoland, past the stoop, past the rectangle of earth and the beautiful blooming cherry tree. In all the world, bursts of fuchsia blooms in August.

Past Fish Bar, past our table in the corner by the window. The light on First Avenue is green, and we charge right through the Village View housing project with its windy sidewalks all cul-de-sacs like in suburbs, right on Avenue A, gallop past the Pyramid.

Two blue shiny beetle cops on brown horses right behind me.

Weapons drawn. In hot pursuit. Speeding light, darkness, speeding light. Sirens. Flashing cop-car lights.

At the corner of Fourth Street and Avenue A, there are people everywhere, sitting and lying on the sidewalks holding their bruised and bloody heads, their broken arms, their busted ribs. Cop cars' red and white flash. On the telephone wires sits a line of black crows. People are handcuffed together around the lampposts. You can smell the blood, the guns, the testosterone. A man on his belly is lying in a bloody puddle, his hands handcuffed behind his back.

Some cop is yelling at me over a loudspeaker.

Hippodrome Stand, I'm doing the Twist, the Jerk, the Mashed Potatoes, the Boogaloo, the Surf, the Swim, the Dance of the Wounded Male.

The power of the dance is to dance with God. The only way out is in.

I kick my red Converse tennis shoes off, pull down my cutoff jeans.

In all the world, this distracted globe, I'm buck naked, cock and balls bouncing up and down, original, pure, red-blooded American boy, high enough to think I am New York, out there in the spotlight.

Nowhere. Now here.

Something from nothing.

How this started—I don't know how all this started.

The stallion's mane is parted in the middle. I'm holding on to the saddle horn for dear life.

I've got a maiden to save.

Arms out like a bird, I'm flying past the corner of Sixth Street and Avenue B.

The whole world is applauding. A fucking standing ovation.

But it's not the truth.

The Pentagon is not applauding, the Vatican is not applauding, Cardinal O'Henry is not applauding, Ronald Reagan and Nancy are not applauding.

The cops are not applauding. In their steel-blue eyes, in their tiny Catholic hearts, I am the enemy.

It is this way. They are correct.

At the corner of Seventh Street and Avenue B, it's Dog Shit Park. It's police cars and ambulances. It's paddywagons and SWAT teams. It's flashing lights and sirens. It's an arsenal.

Every weapon, every gun, pointed at me.

All daring and courage, all iron resistance of misfortune, make for a finer, nobler type of manhood.

Then the moment.

All at once, just like that, before I know it, the Stallion of Love is over the barricaded wrought-iron fence of Dog Shit Park. One solid silent leap.

Frozen moments in time.

Only silence, in all of New York City, all of Dog Shot Park, in all of the known universe, only silence, only mystery.

See you in Life Café! I yell.

The open palm of my hand is against the beaded blue horizontal and the beaded red vertical of the buckskin bag. I am holding on for dear life.

The road is red. I am headed south.

I am why birds like to fly so much.

Geronimo!

ONLY THE WIND in the English elms: sigh and sway and scratch. The sky going blue. The soft warm wind of sunrise.

The space in between is the Dance of the Wounded Male.

In all the world, as far as I can see, all of Manhattan, all of the known universe, even the cops step out with their left leg, and the leg collapses under them and every person falls a bit, catches themselves, then leans their bodies forward, swaying out their hips, swaying and straightening their backs with the power of their shoulders, then step with their right legs, raising themselves to their full height, swaying their hips out. They drag their left leg next to their right.

We are all wounded. Sexually haunted.

So silent. The morning light is pink and orange in the blue. The wind is all around us, lips at our ears. The elm leaves shake back and forth, back and forth, catching light.

The Stallion of Love jumps through the gold loop.

In all the world, as far as I can see, all of the known universe, even the cops, waving their arms like swans or serpents.

Silence, only silence. This is the point. Right here, at sunrise, the still point in the turning world, when even the cops are dancing the Dance of the Wounded Male.

Then it happens, just the way Fiona said.

All at once, just like that—abracadabra!—as far as I can see, the whole world, every person in the whole world, even the cops, starts to sing how their hearts are inside them, the way my heart is inside me too, on fire the way the morning is, longing for things that probably won't come, and sad because we know they probably won't.

Yet still foolish enough to wish.

But most of all clear and smooth and beautiful.

> *I just want to hold you,*
> *Won't you let me hold you*
> *Like Bernadette would do?*

FIONA THROWS OFF her red plastic shower curtain. She is glowing white marble. Her bushel of black hair. Fiona's red lips have a life all their own. The gap between her front teeth.

Never seen so much leather on one chick in all my life.

In her hand, in her open palm, Fiona is holding the bottle of Extra Strength Tylenol. She is walking Spanish.

Perfect, just perfect.

The Stallion of Love, Going Slack flat out, I lean forward in the saddle, reach down, scoop Fiona up.

Fiona's in the saddle. I'm riding double, behind, holding on to her, my arms around her waist.

All of us all male and female, all of us all one thing.

My hands on Fiona's shoulders, I push myself to standing, let go, put my arms out wide. Fiona stands up too, my arms are around her waist until she has her balance.

Fiona puts her arms out, both hands, her index and her fuck-you fingers sticking up.

I put my arms out too.

Double Hippodrome Stand, heading north, away from Dog Shit Park.

At the tunnel, Fiona and I crouch down. The Stallion of Love gallops into the dark hole. Fiona's breath in, her breath out. My breath. The stallion's breath. The stallion's horseshoes against the railroad ties, the gravel, the iron rails, are all that we can hear.

The stallion knows the way exactly.

A whistle blows. A car alarm. Up ahead, there's a bright light. The bright light is a locomotive iron horse, a one-eyed monster blowing steam, headed right for us.

But it's not the truth.

The bright light is not a monster. It's the end of the tunnel.

Ahead of us is the road is red. Ahead of us Crummy Dog is trying to outrace two rabbits.

Fiona's smile is so big her scar is bleeding. She puts the Extra Strength Tylenol in my open palm.

Complete acceptance of whatever the Divine puts in your path, Fiona says. A neurotransmitter, Gamma something or other, Fiona says. Opens up the part of the brain that is directly connected to the Divine.

I'll tell you something, so you'll know.

My eyes look down at the substance of myself.

Charlie's buckskin bag around my neck, the beaded blue horizontals, the red verticals.

In my hands, my open palms, the cure:

My lovely erect pink penis.

Ocelot skin and a cherry blossom.

It is this way.

A kind of fuck-you-motherfucker joy.

It's the truth.

I promise.